TWILIGHT IMPERIUM™

The SHATTERED GALAXY

A Twilight Imperium Omnibus

The FRACTURED VOID

The NECROPOLIS EMPIRE

The VEILED MASTERS

by TIM PRATT

ACONYTE

First published by Aconyte Books in 2025
ISBN 978 1 83908 322 8
Ebook ISBN 978 1 83908 323 5

The Fractured Void first published by Aconyte Books in 2020
The Necropolis Empire first published by Aconyte Books in 2021
The Veiled Masters first published by Aconyte Books in 2022

Cover art by Scott Schomburg.

Printed in the United States of America and elsewhere.

9 8 7 6 5 4 3 2 1

ACONYTE BOOKS

An imprint of Asmodee North America
Mercury House, North Gate,
Nottingham NG7 7FN, UK
aconytebooks.com

TWILIGHT IMPERIUM

Intergalactic empires fall, but one faction will rise from the ashes to conquer the galaxy.

Once the mighty Lazax Empire ruled all the known galaxy from its capital planet of Mecatol Rex, before treachery and war erased the Lazax from history, plunging a thousand star systems into conflict and uncertainty.

Now the Great Civilizations who span the galaxy look upon their former capital hungrily – the power and secrets of the Lazax await a new emperor…

To lay claim to the throne is a destiny sought by many, yet the shadows of the past serve as a grim warning to those who would follow in their footsteps.

THE SHATTERED GALAXY

THE FRACTURED VOID

For Effie, a player of games.

CHAPTER 1

Felix waited in the darkness on the lower deck of the *Temerarious*. The only illumination came from faint guide lights running along the floor, pulsing in the direction of designated exits. Carefully, silently, he began to move, confident that he wasn't being watched, at least for the moment. He crept along a corridor and moved past unoccupied crew cabins, converted to storage for emergency relief supplies. He moved slowly, looking into each crowded room for a moment before moving on, listening for the faintest whisper of sound, and feeling for minute disturbances in the stale air.

Felix was *hunting*.

He considered taunting his prey, trying to provoke an error he could exploit, but it was a risky move, and better tried when he was in a more defensible position. He paused at the end of the corridor, with open doors on his left and his right. In a more demanding posting, the cabins on either side would provide housing for two crew members; instead, the cabin on the left held pallets of potable water, while the one on the right, for some reason, held crate after crate of signal flares. The mysteries of military procurement were doubtless baffling in all societies, but in the Mentak Coalition they were even stranger – the various supplies the raider fleets pillaged had to end up somewhere, and an over-stocked quartermaster had taken the opportunity to cram the *Temerarious*, with its whole deck of unused space, full of odds and ends of no great use to anyone.

He ducked into a side room and crouched behind a pallet of shrink-wrapped air purifiers, listening hard, but the only sound was his own breath. He jostled the pallet and gasped, short and swiftly cut off, as if he'd injured himself and made an involuntary sound. He immediately, silently, moved to the far side of the room, waiting to see if his bait would be taken. There was no movement, no sound, nothing. He might have been alone down here, in the dark, but he knew better.

Felix crept back out into the corridor, carefully scanning for the most minute shift in the shadows, the slightest disturbance in the air. Nothing. His quarry was elsewhere. He considered the T-intersection before him: if he went left, he'd reach the deserted lower galley, and if he went right, he'd reach a workout room full of unused training machinery. There were more hiding places in the galley, but–

Something clattered in the cabin on his left. It sounded like a water bottle jostled by mistake, bouncing off the frame of a bunk, and skittering across the floor. Felix immediately spun and faced right instead. There was no way his subtle and deadly prey would make a sound like that by accident. The little monster was trying to distract him, which meant the ambush would be coming from the *other* side – In fact, the attack came from above: a weight crashed down on Felix's neck and shoulders, driving him to his knees, and a slick smooth limb he couldn't see snaked around his throat. Felix was bigger and heavier than his opponent, though, and he threw his weight back, hoping to crush the attacker between his own body and the wall, or, failing that, at least dislodge her. Instead, she slithered around his body, shifting from his back to his front, so all he did was rattle his *own* spine on impact.

"Die, scum!" a voice hissed, hot breath on his face, but there was no *face* there, just a sort of shimmer that made his eyes water if he focused too hard, and strong thin fingers wrapped around his throat–

The overhead lights came on brightly, and the voice of the ship's security officer, Calred, purred laconically from hidden speakers all over the deck: "Captain, if you and Tib are finished playing hide-and-seek, we have an urgent message from one of the colonies."

The shimmer stopped shimmering and resolved into the round green face of Captain Felix Duval's first officer Tib Pelta, her yellow lamp-like eyes shining as she smiled, showing all her teeth. The rest of her body, dressed in the uniform of the Mentak Coalition navy, came into focus a moment later. The Yssaril ability to hide from sight – "fading" – wasn't technically invisibility, but functionally there wasn't a big difference. As an infiltration specialist, her uniforms and spacesuits were woven with rare fabrics that could bend light and augmented with devices that stymied detection of heat signatures and other life signs.

Tib let go of her captain's throat, straightened his collar, and patted him gently on the cheek, before hopping off him and heading for the elevator.

"Acknowledged, on our way up," Felix said. Then: "We weren't playing hide-and-seek. We were conducting tactical training exercises to keep ourselves sharp. That's really something you should be organizing, as security officer."

"My job is to keep you from getting killed, and to prevent this moderately valuable ship from getting blown up," Calred said. "Not to keep you entertained."

"I won," Tib said as Felix fell into step beside her, though she had to take two steps for every one of his. "Current score is seven hundred and five to me, one hundred and twelve to you."

"It's one-thirteen to me, Tib," Felix said. "You always leave out that time when I was fourteen, and I tracked you through the ventilation system to the station administrator's secret wine store–"

"That doesn't count, and it will never count. I wasn't trying to hide from you, so the fact that you found me is not a win – it's just you being nosy."

"You were going there in secret, hoping to sell the wine for yourself, so you were hiding from everyone, and by extension, therefore, you were hiding from me."

They continued the old argument – which was less a real disagreement after all these years, and more a pleasant exercise in call-and-response – as they took the lift up to the command deck. Not that it was much of a command, Felix thought; he was in charge of himself, Tib Pelta, Calred, and a bunch of drones. The drones obeyed instantly without arguing, which was nice, but they were otherwise terrible company. It was hard to radiate the effortless aura of mastery Felix wanted to project when your crew consisted of your best friend since childhood and an unflappably competent and unimpressed Hacan soldier. The ship was nice enough, if nothing special: the *Temerarious* was a Freebooter-class cruiser, a lightly armed ship built for speed, meant to strike fast and disappear – the sort of vessel that played a crucial support role in the Mentak Coalition's military fleet, and made up the bulk of its unofficial raider forces.

Of course, in this remote posting, there was little need for speed or armaments, light or otherwise. The *Temerarious* was stationed here to "defend and lend material support" to the three coalition colony worlds (two planets, and one moon orbiting a gas giant) in this system. Felix and Tib had grown up on a shipyard space station near the core of the Coalition, and being way out here on the fringes was teeth-grindingly dull. This posting was both a punishment *and* a promotion. Felix had been first officer on a ship in the raider fleet, and had acted with great daring and courage in a raid, winning glory (and also riches) for the Coalition… but he'd also ignored orders from his captain in order to commit said daring act. The fleet commander had been impressed and pleased with the results, but Felix's captain had been understandably furious about the method, and after some consultation a compromise was reached: in recognition of his service, Felix would be promoted to captain of his own ship and as punishment for his insubordination, he would be assigned to the backwater Lycian system, home to a scant million inhabitants scattered over three worlds, who produced a minimal quantity of resources that nobody back home much wanted anyway.

The unstated but clear message for Felix was: show that you can obey orders by being a good boy out on the edge of everything for a few years, and you'll be welcomed back to do something that matters. The arrangement had seemed reasonable to Felix at first, but after eight months of making a slow and pointless circuit of three colony worlds, he was bored. The colonies were small, scattered, and rural, and none of them had much of a nightlife, so even R and R was in short supply – though there was a cute medic with great legs on one of the planets, and an enjoyably burly gas-extraction engineer on the moon, so Felix wasn't entirely without entertainment, even discounting the running game of hide-and-seek – no, damn it, *tactical exercises* – with Tib.

Mostly Felix fantasized about something *happening*, some occasion he could rise to, some world-shaking challenge he could overcome or disaster he could avert, thus shortening his penance and returning to the fast track. He wanted to sit at the Table of Captains one day, and help guide his polity to ever more greatness. The beautiful thing about the Coalition, this pan-species nation founded by prisoners of the old Lazax Empire's most brutal penal colony, was that *anyone* could rise to the greatest heights, no matter how humble their origins, if they demonstrated the wit, the speed, the daring, the ingenuity – all qualities that Felix, unburdened by false modesty, knew himself to possess in ample supply.

There were no opportunities to demonstrate those qualities, though, because nothing ever happened out here. Sometimes there was a storm or a flood, and in those cases Felix delivered food and blankets. He was also responsible for picking up and delivering cargo from the colony worlds to supply ships, and bringing back medical supplies and trade goods. Not exactly the intended use for a fast warship, but the Coalition had lots of cruisers, and this one had plenty of empty room for crates.

Felix and Tib stepped from the lift onto the bridge, a semicircular room dominated by a large viewscreen that currently showed nothing but the empty star field before them, the brighter glow of Alope standing out in the lower left. Alope was the next planet on their circuit, a world rich in timber, ore, mildew, mutton, and bristly predators called wolferines, who were still delighted by the sheep and goats the colonists had introduced to the ecosystem decades earlier.

Tib went to the comms and navigation station, not that there was much navigating to do, since they more or less just went around in circles. Felix dropped into his command chair: best seat in the house, even if the house wasn't all he might wish. "What's the problem? Did a sheep wander off? Are we urgently needed to help with a barn-raising?"

Calred, an immense Hacan with braids in his mane, shook his leonine head. He stood at the tactical board, which was even less use here than the navigation controls. "Something stranger than that, and my requests for clarification have gone unanswered."

"Show me."

"The message is audio-only." Calred manipulated the board, and a crackling voice blared out from the blank viewscreen: – *unknown* – *landed outside settlement* – *jammed* – *boosting as best we can* – *immediate assistance* – *armed*

The message ended abruptly. "Where's it from?" Felix said. There were scores of communities on Alope, from small timber camps and mining towns to the relatively booming trading city and sole spaceport Solymi, home to a whole fifty thousand souls (and that cute medic Felix liked to visit).

"A small farming settlement on the northern continent," Calred said. "Doesn't even have a name on the surveys, though I gather the locals call it Cobbler's Knob."

"Do they really?"

"So I'm told," Calred said. "The message came from their emergency distress system, which is probably the only communications apparatus within a hundred kilometers powerful enough to get a message this far."

Could this be it? Felix thought. Could something finally be *happening*? Probably not. It was probably a prank. Felix thought about how bored he was, and extrapolated out to how bored a teenager living in a place called Cobbler's Knob must be. But then, if it were a hoax, you'd think they'd say something more dramatic: "We're being attacked by alien invaders," maybe, or at least, "Help, a wolverine ate my mother."

"Let's get down there," Felix said. "It's probably nothing, but it's not like we were doing anything else."

Calred nodded. "With my amazing tactical prescience, I anticipated your order. We're already heading there at speed. Does that count as insubordination? I hope not. I'd hate to be assigned to some remote posting as punishment."

"We'll call it the sort of initiative that befits an officer of your stature." Felix had no idea why Calred had ended up on this ship, but he must have annoyed *someone*. The Hacan would only say, "I go where I'm assigned." He was competent, gave the impression of being effortlessly deadly, and was completely unflappable, not that they encountered many things worthy of getting into a flap about out here. In a storm last year, though, Felix had seen Calred wade into a surging river that had burst its banks, rescuing a young boy who would have been swept away, and returning him to his tearful family. Calred had done it as matter-of-factly as Felix might take a bottle down from a shelf. He hadn't known Calred anywhere near as long as Tib, but he'd already come to depend on him.

The planet grew, a greenish disc in the corner of the screen. "Something's moving," Calred said. "Looks like a shuttle, coming from the vicinity of Cobbler's Knob, heading into orbit."

"That doesn't make any sense," Felix said. "Where's it *going*?" A shuttle didn't have the range to make it to one of the other colony worlds, and there was no space station. "Is there anything in orbit for the shuttle to rendezvous with?"

"There isn't," Calred said. "Maybe they're just sightseeing."

"Or," Tib said.

"Or what?" Felix said.

"Or there is something in orbit, and we just can't see it. Let me see." She bowed her head to the terminal, and the screen shifted through various false color arrays, visualizing discrete pulses of sensor data. "*There* it is," Tib said, voice a throaty murmur. "A ship, orbiting Alope."

Felix leaned forward. The screen was back to true color, and there was no orbiting ship to be seen, though the shuttle was highlighted, a silver lozenge rising from the planet's surface. "Show me."

"I can't show you. The ship is using some sort of stealth technology – I think it's a variant of light-wave deflection."

"Then how do you know it's even there?"

Tib rolled her eyes, and given the size of her eyes, that was very dramatic. "Felix. I have a particular interest in stealth, and no system is perfect. It can hide from sensors, and even bend light to avoid visual detection, and against a big expanse of empty black, that's almost always enough. Against the backdrop of a planet, though, there are visual distortions, little shimmers and glimmers, and you can see them if you know where to look, kind of like we detect black holes by seeing the light from stars bend around them."

Felix took her word for it. Yssaril were famed throughout the galaxy for their skill as spies – they'd taken their natural ability to fade, augmented it with technology and training, and spent centuries building their networks. The Tribes of Yssaril sold their skills throughout the galaxy, and doubtless used what they learned to pursue their own interests and imperial ambitions. Tib had never been within a billion kilometers of the Yssaril homeworld, but she had all the natural abilities of her species combined with the legacy of the Mentak Coalition, the descendants of thieves, renegades, smugglers, and *survivors*. The Yssaril members of the Coalition were the backbone of their clandestine forces, and Tib had vanished for a year once for "special training" that Felix assumed included plenty of spooky spy techniques. She'd certainly gotten even better at playing hide-and-seek afterward. "Who could it be?" he asked. "Why would anyone come out here in the first place, let alone in a stealth ship?"

"It's not a dreadnought or something," Tib said. "Not that those are really built for stealth anyway. The distortions indicate something cruiser-sized."

"Don't give them any indication that we've seen them," Felix said. What *was* this unfamiliar feeling, like his blood was fizzing? Oh, yes: excitement. The thrill of the hunt. He'd missed it. Stalking Tib in the basement was a poor substitute for the real thing.

"My communications array just lit up." Tib put the incoming message up on half the screen, the other half still tracking the slow ascent of the shuttle as it inexorably approached the big red question mark Tib had generated to indicate the location of the stealthed ship.

A dirty-faced woman hunched over a console in a small dark room appeared, her eyes wide and wild. "They took Mr Thales!"

"This is Captain Duval of the *Temerarious*." Felix leaned forward. "Who took who?"

She ran a hand through her messy hair. "These soldiers, five or six of them, they wore armor and had these guns, they broke into his house and dragged him out! They took him and a bunch of his stuff – we asked what was happening, who they were, and they told us to shut up or they'd *shoot* us! I tried to call before but they did something, they jammed the signal or something."

"I guess now we know who's on the shuttle," Tib said. "I've pinged the vessel, but there's no transponder, and they don't reply. No indication where it's from or where it's going."

"Should I blow up the shuttle?" Calred said.

"There's probably a kidnapped civilian on board, so no," Felix said. "Can we move to intercept the shuttle, disable it, scoop it up?"

"Sure. Assuming we're faster than the invisible ship, which we might be. Also assuming the invisible ship isn't better armed than we are, which is more doubtful."

"Start moving that way. Weapons hot. Hail the shuttle again, Tib. Tell them if they don't respond we'll be forced to disable them." Felix returned his attention to the woman on the screen. As far as he knew there was nobody worth abducting in this system, at least not for conventional reasons like ransom. Felix had been furnished with a list of notable citizens when he came here, mayors and heads of local business concerns, and none of them seemed like targets for a heavily armed strike team with stealth tech and jamming equipment. Thales hadn't been on it anyway. "Why did they come for this Thales? Who is he?"

"I don't know," the woman said. "He moved here not quite a year ago. He mostly keeps to himself, and when he doesn't, you wish he had." She paused. "I mean, everyone here hates him – he's terrible, really – but I don't know why anyone would bother to *kidnap* him."

"Huh. Thanks for notifying us. We'll take care of things from here." He ended the call and watched the shuttle get bigger in the viewscreen as their courses converged.

"The shuttle just answered us," Tib said.

"What did they say?"

"'Stand down, or die.'"

"Oh," Felix said. "I don't much like either of those options. Cal, you know that ship we can't see?"

"I am familiar with it."

"The shuttle is still pretty far away from said invisible ship, right?"

"It's outside the maximum blast radius, if that's what you're asking."

"That is what I'm asking. There you go, showing initiative again." Goodbye boredom, Felix thought. "Let's turn that invisible ship into a cloud of radioactive dust, shall we?"

CHAPTER 2

The missiles Calred launched did not, in fact, turn the invisible ship into radioactive dust. Felix hadn't really expected them to. He had, however, hoped the mysterious ship would be forced to drop out of stealth in order to deploy countermeasures, and that's what happened: the empty space on the screen was suddenly full of spaceship, its countermeasures dazzling the incoming missiles with guidance-disrupting lasers, sending them spinning off on harmless courses to burn up in the atmosphere of the planet below.

"Looks like the Federation," Calred said. "A cruiser, built for speed, not violence."

The Federation of Sol, Felix thought with reflexive irritation. Sure, he was human himself, but he was from the Coalition, and he knew being human didn't make him particularly special – something his ambitious, expansionist cousins-by-ancestry didn't seem to grasp. The Coalition had decent relations with the Federation, insofar as their interests ever overlapped, so what were they doing sneaking around and kidnapping people out here? This Thales must be pretty important to risk an act of war over. Unless… "Are we sure it's from the Federation?"

"Not necessarily," Calred said. "We've even got a few Federation ships in our raider fleet, and they sell their old military cruisers sometimes."

"There's no transponder indicating that they're an accredited diplomatic or trading vessel," Tib said. "They're running dark. It could be anybody. Anybody with the resources to field a snatch team and operate cutting-edge stealth tech, anyway."

"Target lock the shuttle, and tell the big ship to stand down," Felix said. "If we can see them, I assume we can yell at them."

"Are we going to actually shoot down the shuttle?" Tib asked. "That would prevent them from abducting one of our colonists, the same way cutting off my head would stop me from sneezing."

"I'm still thinking about it," Felix said. "How long do I have to think about it, Cal?"

"In about five minutes, the shuttle will be close enough to the ship that firing on one will mean firing on the other."

Felix considered. "If the shooting starts, would we win?"

Cal shrugged. "They might die of heatstroke before we die of thirst."

Felix had served with Calred long enough to know that was a Hacan phrase that either meant it was a no-win situation or, more generously, that the fight could go either way. He almost asked for clarification, but both interpretations were bad, so he didn't bother.

"There's an incoming transmission from the ship of mystery," Tib said.

Half the screen filled with a visibly irritated human woman's head and shoulders. She wasn't wearing a uniform, but she was wearing the sort of armor favored by the better class of mercenaries – and she wasn't even part of the ground force that did the snatch, so who knew how they were outfitted? What Felix could glimpse of the enemy bridge (they had an enemy now – how exciting) was bare of insignia, flags, or other identifiers. She glared, but didn't say anything.

"Hello," Felix said. "Return the person you abducted, and we won't kill you."

"We're capturing an escaped prisoner," the woman said. "He's not a citizen of the Coalition. He's a fugitive from justice."

"Assuming that's true, we have diplomatic relations with the Federation, and there are channels for this sort of thing. You're not allowed to drop in and kidnap people without turning in the appropriate paperwork first."

"We never said we were from the Federation."

Felix smiled. "I apologize for the assumption. Maybe you're from Jol-Nar? Or are you from a faction we don't have diplomatic relations with? In that case, I'm pretty sure this is definitely an act of war, instead of just probably. Do you want to reconsider this…" he waved his hand in the air. "… whole thing?"

She gritted her teeth. "We are independent bounty hunters."

"Interesting. What crimes did Thales commit, and in what jurisdiction?"

She winced. She was clearly unhappy that Felix knew that name. Felix was just sad he couldn't play cards with someone who wore her emotions so clearly on her face. He quite liked taking money from strangers. "Phillip Thales is guilty of theft, murder, and destruction of property."

"Where did he do this thieving, murder, and vandalism?"

"That's classified."

Calred laughed out loud. "By whom? Let me guess. Also classified?"

Felix cupped his chin in his hand and looked at her. "Thales must have stolen something pretty big if you mentioned the theft part before the murder part. Cobbler's Knob is an unusual choice for spending ill-gotten gains, but to each their own, I suppose. I'm sure we can clear all this up. If you're bounty hunters, just send the credentials proving you're authorized to operate in Coalition space."

She worked her mouth like she'd taken a bite of something sour and couldn't decide whether to swallow it or spit it out. "Perhaps we could come to some other arrangement."

"Are you offering me a bribe?" Felix said.

She shrugged. "Where I'm from, we have a saying: every Coalition ship is a pirate ship. The man we took is not one of your citizens, and none of your citizens were harmed in the course of taking him. We'd be happy to send you a substantial quantity of Federation credits if you'd agree to let us leave in peace, and refrain from filing any sort of official report. Everyone goes away happy."

"How substantial?" She named a sum. Felix went hmm. "What's the exchange rate right now, Tib?"

"One-point-five Federation credits to one Coalition credit."

So, not that substantial, but still. "Sure. Tib, send them the account info."

The woman blinked at him. "Really?"

Felix shrugged. "Why not? I like money." He almost said, "I'm Coalition. What do you expect? I'd sell my mother's teeth if I could get a credit for them, right?" but decided that might tip his hand.

After a few moments, Tib said, "Transmission complete. From an untraceable account – very slick."

"Thank you for your generous contribution to the Bereaved and Orphaned Benevolent Fund," Felix said. "The Coalition will be eternally grateful. Now, release your prisoner, or we will fire on your ship."

"We had a deal!" she shouted.

Now Felix shrugged. "I gather my people are famously untrustworthy. Shall I count to, let's see, five? One, two–"

He didn't get to finish, because the other ship fired on them, and the *Temerarious* had to deploy their own countermeasures. Felix was surprised. The *Temerarious* had the shuttle target locked, and surely the enemy ship knew they were well matched tactically, but they still chose to fight? Bounty hunters were all about balancing risk against reward: these weren't bounty hunters. (Well, obviously. The amount they'd paid Felix was more than any bounty he'd ever heard of.)

"Do we return fire?" Cal said. The shuttle was so close to the ship now, it would inevitably be destroyed if the *Temerarious* fired back.

Damn it. Maybe Thales was a citizen – Felix wasn't about to take the word of the people shooting at him on that – but even if he wasn't, someone was willing to go to a lot of trouble and expense to abduct him, and that meant he was valuable. The Coalition really liked taking valuable things, and didn't like having them taken away. "No, pull back. Can we keep up with that ship when they run?"

"Unless their stealth technology is better than anything I've ever heard of before, yes," Cal said.

"Good. Then let them go, follow at a safe distance, extrapolate their likely course, and see if any of the raider fleets are in a position to intercept." There was no regular military way out here, but they weren't far from a shipping route, and there were often a few of the Coalition's irregular troops lurking in the dark between the stars, keeping an eye out for easy targets.

The *Temerarious* withdrew as the shuttle disappeared into the belly of the enemy cruiser, which rose out of orbit and accelerated away.

"They must know we're going to call for help," Felix said. "What's their plan?"

"I think their plan was 'don't get caught,'" Tib said. "It's a reasonable plan, way out here, where we're the only possible threat in the system. It's just their bad luck we happened to be passing this way. Otherwise, they would have been long gone by the time we heard about the abduction. Their new plan is probably 'run fast and hope for the best.'"

Felix nodded. That wasn't a good plan, but he didn't judge the humans too harshly: after all, they didn't have any other plans available. "See what we can find out about this Thales, would you, Cal?"

"I'm already compiling a dossier. It's going to be short, though, I can tell."

"Good news," Tib said. "I've got Commander Meehves and a small fleet that should be able to intercept our new friends in half a day or so."

"Good old Meehves," Felix said.

"Oh, we can catch them." Meehves slouched in a chair in her quarters, a drink in her hand, her grayish skin and blank eyes revealing her Letnev ancestry. Those eyes made her damnably hard to gamble against, as Felix had learned during officer training. Meehves taught tactics occasionally, with a special emphasis on surprise and misdirection, and had cheerfully explained that taking money from her students constituted teaching them a valuable lesson in her areas of expertise. "Do you want to lead the boarding party?"

"It would make a nice change from flying around in circles, if you don't mind."

Meehves waved her free hand lazily. "We've just been lurking out here waiting for a fat, lonely cargo ship to drift by. Thanks for bringing us something to do. I'm a bit baffled by the whole thing, though. Who is this Thales, anyway? Why would the Federation, or someone hiring a bunch of mercenaries, go to so much trouble to kidnap him?"

"We don't know much." Felix flicked his fingertip and scrolled through the information Calred had scrounged up in the past several hours. "We don't have any record of him on Alope until about ten standard months ago, when he showed up in Cobbler's Knob—"

"*Whose* knob?" Meehves said.

"I had the same question. It's just what the locals call their little patch of grazing land, a river, some fields, and a few housing modules. Maybe it was founded by someone named Cobbler, or there's a mountain nearby that looks like a shoe or something. Anyway, this Thales immigrated, perfectly legally. Claimed he was from the Federation of Sol and, I regret to say, the security officials didn't poke too hard at his identity, or they would have realized all his documentation was fake."

"Doing deep background checks on colonists to remote worlds isn't a good use of resources," she said. "It's not like Alope is a prime target for terrorism. Most of the people who immigrate to places like this have shady backgrounds and no other options."

"Fair enough," Felix said. "He showed up in Cobbler's Knob looking for a place to live, and for some reason the good country people didn't just steal his money and throw his body down a well. Instead they fixed up an abandoned cottage for him, one with a big root cellar, which he was particularly pleased about – he said he could use the space for his work, without saying what that work was. He shut himself away and only came out to buy supplies, and to complain about the food, the weather, the hygiene of his fellow colonists, and every other subject imaginable. No one had any idea what he was doing there, and he didn't volunteer information. The locals thought he might be an artist or a writer, a reclusive genius devoting himself to his work, or else that he was hiding out from the law. There was some disagreement on that score, but everyone *does* agree that he's rude, unpleasant, and a total bastard."

Meehves sipped her drink, a perfectly clear liquid that Felix suspected was highly flammable. "People don't usually send stealth ships full of mercenaries to kidnap artists, and whoever came for him wasn't the law."

"The locals took the opportunity to snoop around his house after he was taken, and there's no sign of any artwork anyway. They're not exactly trained investigators down there, but they say it looks like the kidnappers took everything but the furniture with them. No documents, no personal effects, nothing."

Meehves swirled her drink. "Maybe he was a fugitive, but if so, why not reach out to us through normal channels? Why risk a fight with the Coalition?"

"I was thinking about that. Maybe he's a special kind of fugitive – the kind with a head full of state secrets the Federation, or whoever, is afraid he'll give away. Or maybe he stole something they were really keen to recover?"

"Why not just kill him, then?" Meehves said. "They had the firepower. Honestly, they could have paid someone in Cobbler's Knob two sheep to kill him, the way it sounds."

"They need him alive, then, for whatever reason," Felix said. "Maybe it's not something he has, but something he knows."

Meehves nodded. "So he's not a brilliant artist, but he could be some other kind of brilliant – some useful variety. You hear about people kidnapping Hylar scientists sometimes, trying to get a jump on weapons research."

"Or he could be a spy with intel that's not recorded anywhere, or he was witness to something and they need his testimony, or, or, or. Suddenly I can come up with all sorts of scenarios."

Meehves shrugged. "We'll find out soon enough. Unless they kill him when we try to board their ship, in the spirit of, 'if we can't have him, no one can.' Unless they all choose death before dishonor, though, one of them will tell us what's going on, anyway. We just have to ask them the right way."

"Mercenaries don't tend to sacrifice their lives for honor."

"They do not," Meehves agreed. "So let's hope they're mercenaries, and not some flavor of true believer. We should intercept their vessel soon." She pushed herself out of the chair. "I'm going to make sure the guns are loaded and the boarding pods are prepped. Or, rather, tell other people to make sure of those things – the burden of command, you know." She leaned down and looked into her screen, and through it, into Felix's mind. "The money you scammed out of them for the Benevolent Fund. How much did you skim?"

"Only two per cent," Felix said. "I'll split it with my crew, of course." No one expected an officer of the Mentak Coalition to be scrupulously honest – it would have been suspicious if they had been – but you didn't want a reputation for being too greedy, either, or you'd lose out on crucial opportunities to profit in the future.

"Fair enough. Not many opportunities for plunder out in the territories, are there?"

"There's plenty to steal, as long as you want to steal dirt or sheep," Felix said. "Unfortunately, it all belongs to people I'm supposed to protect instead of profit from. I call first pick on any personal weapons we recover on the enemy ship. Carrying a regulation sidearm is so basic."

"Spoils of war, eh?" Meehves switched off.

CHAPTER 3

The kidnappers had the good sense to stop running when a destroyer and its attendant fighters appeared before them (and beside, above, and below them). The *Temerarious*, which had lagged behind at a distance where they could counteract any attacks lobbed at them, rapidly closed the gap to cut off the last avenue of retreat.

"They're trying to send out some kind of encrypted communication," Calred said over Felix's helmet radio. "It's adorable, really."

Felix grinned. Meehves had jammed outgoing signals, of course. He clambered into the *Temerarious*'s shuttle and let the computer chart the course. The little hemispherical boarding pods were already spinning off from Meehves's ship, *The Bad Cat*, and would soon attach to the hull of the enemy vessel like leeches on a swimmer. They weren't quite sure what they'd find inside – the enemy ship was shielded against deep sensor scans, like most vessels with military specs, so they had to guess at the interior layout and the crew complement. The boarding pods were full of electronic countermeasures and security circumvention tools meant to convince ships to pop open their airlocks, and, if those failed, they also had lasers, cutting blades, and acid nozzles to make their own openings through the hull.

Usually, the pods weren't necessary. The unofficial raider fleet of the Coalition wasn't in the murder business, nor did they wish to discourage interstellar trade; they were basically just a toll you had to pay if you strayed too close to Coalition space without making proper prior arrangements. The merchant vessels knew to bring along a little extra so they could satisfy the raider captains and still make an appropriate profit, and worked that expense into their projections of the cost of doing business. Every once in a while, you encountered a ship with a crew that didn't understand the rules and needed them explained, in person, at the end of a gun. Even then, there was usually no reason to kill anyone. After all, if you murder someone, you only get to steal from them once.

This ship wasn't like the others, though, and would not be extended such courtesies. Once you fire on a Coalition vessel, especially an official one like the *Temerarious*, negotiations are pretty much over. By the time Felix's shuttle was close enough to dock, the boarding pods had taken control of the aft airlock, and Meehves's first officer, an Xxcha named Qqmel, was on board waiting for Felix. Being confronted by hulking reptilian bipeds was inherently disconcerting for humans who hadn't grown up around Xxcha, so who better to lead the party?

Qqmel was patient and thoughtful, but those qualities tended to come across to strangers as emotionless menace, an impression compounded by the elaborate shouldermounted cannon he wore. The cannon moved independently, with audible whirs and clicks, to remain pointed steadfastly at the face (or equivalent) of anyone he target-locked. "How would you like to handle this?" Qqmel said.

"Oh, right. I'm the ranking officer here." Felix straightened his shoulders.

Qqmel made the weird little cough that Xxcha used for laughing. "I'm in charge of the boarding party, reporting to Commander Meehves. You're tagging along. But Meehves said I should ask you how you'd go about it, to see if you learned anything in tactic class."

Felix slumped, but he thought about it. "They'll have Thales in some remote part of the ship, where he's safe, with a guard or two, while the bulk of their forces try to keep us from reaching him. Except they must know we have overwhelming force, so they'll also have some plan to escape this ship, maybe an escape pod they'll try to slip away in unnoticed with Thales, to reach some predetermined rendezvous point. So, why don't you and your large violent comrades do the big noisy seizing-the-bridge thing, and I'll creep along the service corridors and see if I can find the actual prisoner? They'll either be hiding in the tunnels, or using them to reach their means of escape, I bet."

"Acceptable," Qqmel said. "If you lose Thales, though, you'll be the one who gets the blame, not me or the commander."

"Yes, I realize that. Good tactics on your part."

"Want to take a marine with you?"

Felix shook his head. He had a secret weapon, and didn't need a big obvious one too. "I'll be faster and quieter on my own. I'd better go silent, too, so don't contact me; I'll contact you. I'd welcome any schematics we have for the ship, though."

After briefly scanning the layout in his heads-up display (the diagrams were for the generic model of this ship, so any modifications would be an unwelcome surprise, but it was the best they could do), he moved left down a passageway to a service access hatch.

Felix had grown up on a shipyard space station near the center of Coalition space, and was comfortable clambering through the innards of vessels, though he'd moved a lot more easily as a ten year-old than he did nearly twenty years later. He moved quietly, ducking under bundles of cable, turning sideways to slip past pipes, occasionally consulting his display to make sure he hadn't become lost. The only light came from thin strips along the floor, turning the tunnels into a shadowland, but Felix had no trouble negotiating such environments. He had all that practice hunting Tib, and being hunted. This was the same thing, except at the end of this exercise, his prey might really try to kill him.

He heard occasional booms, shouts, and thumps that told him battle had been joined elsewhere on board. The raider fleet was expert at boarding hostile craft, and came armed for that specific purpose with anti-personnel weapons, lethal and non-, so he didn't worry much about whether his people were winning. He *was* beginning to feel silly, though, because he'd gone through a whole lot of tunnels without seeing anyone. Maybe he was giving his opponents too much credit, and they weren't that clever after all – what if Qqmel was waiting impatiently with Thales already in custody up on the bridge? Felix considered risking the use of his comms to ask – *Ah ha, what's this?* He reached a narrow, downward-slanting passageway that wasn't marked on his schematics, which meant it was an after-market alteration to the ship's design, which meant it was potentially interesting. He started to make his way down, toward the belly of the ship – home to the shuttle, and cargo, and maybe other things too. A secret hidey-hole, maybe, for a small escape pod.

He slithered down a vertical shaft barely large enough to accommodate him. That gave him more doubts: it would be hard to manhandle a prisoner through a space that cramped, though he supposed if someone pointed a gun at him and told him to start crawling, he would. No way to tell where he was going until he got there, so on he went. *If I end up in a trash compactor or something, Tib will never let me live it down…*

Felix crawled through a duct on his hands and knees, toward a vent, the grille that should have been covering the opening dangling askew. So, either this ship was maintained in a slovenly fashion, or someone had come this way before him. He eased forward on his belly and peered through the opening.

The vent led to a small cylindrical room, about the size of an airlock, with no visible points of entry. An escape pod shaped like the closed bud of a flower filled most of the space, leaving a thin strip to walk on all the way around. A woman in black mercenary armor – but no helmet; that was lucky – crouched by the pod's entry hatch, tapping away on a handheld terminal. There was no sign of Thales, but he might be inside the pod already.

Felix unclipped a noisemaker, set it for a five-second delay, then slung it toward the woman. The small object bounced off her head, making her curse and lift her eyes to him. She was the one he'd talked to earlier, the one who couldn't hide her emotions and who'd tried to bribe him. How nice to see her again.

Noisemakers were little blue spheres, sized to fit comfortably in the hand, and when you set them off they released sonic waves of such intensity that they obliterated thought and left their victims dazed, blinking, and bleeding from the ears and nose. Felix, of course, had his noise-canceling earpieces in, so the onslaught was just an unpleasant whine for him, and a rumble that made his skeleton tingle. He scrambled out of the vent, dropped to the floor, and dashed to the woman. She was on her back, staring up blankly – but, wait, her ears weren't bleeding, and neither was her nose, so – Felix flung himself to one side just as she raised her sidearm and fired. The energy blast melted a section of the wall behind him. Damn. She must have protective gear on too. He scrambled toward her, getting too close for her to shoot easily, and tried to pin her gun arm down. Even using both hands, he could barely manage – her armor was powered, making her easily twice as strong as he was. His own suit was made for infiltration rather than brute force, which had seemed like a good idea at the time.

She started punching him in the side with her free hand, and if he didn't make her stop soon he was going to end up with broken ribs, as his armor was not as comprehensive as hers. She snarled and yelled things, calling him a traitor to humanity and so on, but he ignored that, flicking his eyes across his helmet display, selecting the countermeasure he really should have queued up earlier, and blinking to activate it.

His suit used most of its remaining battery life to discharge an electromagnetic pulse, and her eyes bulged as her armor locked in place. Felix's suit systems went down too, of course – EMPs didn't discriminate – but *he* had a secondary, shielded, temporary power source that kicked on immediately to compensate. He took her gun away and threw it aside, then peeked into the escape pod.

It was empty.

He sighed and looked down at her. She still had one arm raised, armor locked in position, fingers twisted into a claw. "Where's Thales?"

"Gone." She grinned savagely. "Long gone. You're too late. My team leader escaped with him."

"You mean you aren't the team leader? Wait, never mind – of course not. They left you on the ship, after all, while the competent people went down to do the actual job. Oh well. At least tell me why you wanted him. What's so special about Thales, anyway?"

"I'll never tell you anything, pirate scum."

"That's hurtful." He leaned against the rounded side of the escape pod, crossed his arms, and gazed down at her. "I don't have much experience with Coalition interrogation methods – that was never my area of training – but I gather they're quite effective. We'll find out what you know eventually, so you might as well spare yourself some trouble and tell me now."

"Never." She clenched her jaw, grinding her teeth, then spasmed, foamed spit through her lips, and went limp.

"Great Edwin's ghost," Felix murmured. He hadn't expected *that*. Had she bitten down on a suicide pill or something? He hadn't realized people actually did that, outside spy adventure serials. He prodded her with his foot, in case she was faking, then checked for a pulse in her neck. Apparently, people did.

Felix considered himself a patriot, but really, there were limits. Did this mean Thales was so important it was better to die than to risk the Coalition even finding out why?

He activated his comms. "Qqmel, I found one crew member trying to escape, but no sign of Thales. She killed herself before I could ask too many questions. Tell me you had better luck?"

"We took some very nice guns off some corpses. The armor is mostly ruined though. No survivors among the enemy up here – they fought to the last. We offered nicely to take them prisoner, but they preferred certain death. Where's the percentage in that? Your cousins are strange, Felix."

"Tell me you just forgot to mention recovering their hostage."

"Sorry, Felix. No sign of the mysterious Thales. We're still searching, so don't give up hope yet. We found a bunch of documents and equipment, the former encrypted, the latter mysterious. My techs are digging through the ship's computers, but there's nothing yet to indicate who hired these people or the purpose of their mission. If I had to guess, I'd say it's a classic black ops setup, verbal orders only, highly compartmentalized, all need-to-know. Clearly no one thinks *we* need to know."

"Did you lose anyone?" Felix asked.

"No, we came in heavy, since your reports indicated they were pretty geared up. We sacrificed mobility for armor. Lieutenant Roarge will be out of commission for a while – they got lucky and shot his arm off at the elbow, so the medics will need to grow him a new one – but otherwise it's just bruises and dents."

"Glad to hear it. I'll come up and help with the search." He looked around, but there really weren't any doors, so it was back through the ventilation hatch again. That was an unnecessary addition of insult to injury.

Hours later, Felix sat slumped in the captain's chair on the enemy ship, where the woman he'd watched die had snarled at him not long ago. "Where did they *go?*" he said, not for the first time.

"I don't know, but *I'm* going back to my ship." Qqmel's shoulder-mounted cannon drooped like a wilted flower, pointing at the floor. "We've searched every inch of this vessel, found two more of those hidden escape pod bays – both with their pods still in place. Maybe they jumped out an airlock with a personal propulsion device, something too small to show up on our sensors, and met up with another stealth ship. Wherever they went, they're gone." Qqmel patted Felix on the shoulder. "This was some kind of well-funded clandestine operation, so take heart – you didn't accidentally declare war against anyone, since the assets were obviously deniable. The raider fleet gained a nice new cruiser and a bunch of guns, and you'll get a share of plunder deposited in your account, which you official military types don't usually get to enjoy. The analysts back home will keep researching this Thales, and maybe we'll figure out who wanted him, and what for."

"Maybe." Felix wasn't cheered up. He'd really believed this was it: his ticket out of backwater patrol and back to the fast track, where he belonged. He'd spent enough time gambling over the years to know this feeling well: seeing the big score vanish from sight with one bad turn of the cards or roll of the dice. "Guess I'll head back to the *Temerarious*. Give Meehves my best."

"She said to tell you she'll send you a bottle of something nice. Said you'd have sorrows that need drowning?"

"She knows me better than she has any right to," Felix grumbled.

Felix returned to the airlock where his shuttle was docked. The lockers on either side of the corridor were hanging open, environment suits and supplies scattered on the floor in the aftermath of the search. At least cleaning up the mess was someone else's job. He punched the button to open the inner doors, entered the airlock, waited for it to seal shut, then unlocked the doors leading to the shuttle. He ducked as he stepped into the long, low-ceilinged space. The shuttle was simple, a box of air attached to engines and a guidance system, the interior just a row of seats and walls made up entirely of storage compartments, without so much as a window.

Once on board, he strapped into one of the front seats and ordered the computer to begin the detachment sequence and return to the *Temerarious*. The shuttle's mechanical voice droned a countdown, and when it reached zero the shuttle kicked away from the captured vessel and began its journey back home.

Something off to the right went *thump* and *crack*, and Felix turned to look. A woman in black mercenary armor stepped out of the largest storage locker, the one where the spare environment suits should have been. She pointed her sidearm at him, and for a moment they regarded one another silently. He'd never seen her before, and he would have remembered: she had a face made of diamond-sharp edges, with dark and merry eyes, topped by a crown of spikily short dark hair. Her grin was as self-satisfied as any Felix had ever seen in the mirror.

There was someone else in the locker, slumped over to one side, unmoving: a man with thinning gray hair, a string of drool hanging from his thin lips, eyes closed.

Felix inclined his head toward the man, without taking his eyes from the gun. "Mister Thales, I presume?"

"Doctor, actually," she said.

That was interesting. "What kind of doctor?"

"Based on our brief interactions," she said, "he's a doctor of being a huge asshole."

CHAPTER 4

"So, not the medical kind," Felix said.

"Nope," she replied. "He won't be any help at all after I shoot you in the knee."

"Ah. Could I persuade you *not* to shoot me in the knee?"

"The knee is already my compromise. My first impulse was to shoot you in the face."

"But I'm too pretty?"

"Not from where I'm looking, no," she said. "You are a giant pain in the ass, captain Duval. You very nearly ruined everything, but fortunately I'm a professional, so it can still be salvaged. You took my ship, so I'm going to take yours. I won't need it for long, and then you can have it back. You can captain with one knee, I'm sure."

"I'm grateful, understand, but why did you decide on maiming me rather than killing me?"

"After your people killed all of mine, you mean?"

"That is the question that arose in my mind," Felix admitted.

"My people were all willing to die for this mission. So am I, technically, but I'd rather keep it a hypothetical willingness. They were doing their job, and you were doing yours. Even if I didn't need you alive to give your crew orders, I don't operate based on revenge." She rolled her head around on her shoulders. Probably had a cramp from being jammed in a locker that, while big enough for spacesuits, was not really made to hold spacesuits with the people still inside them. "If I did, I'd be more likely to go after the analyst who told us your patrol ship would be on the other side of the system yesterday."

"Ah, that. We had to leave the system to pick up an emergency delivery of antivirals for one of the mining outposts a few days ago – they picked up some nasty bug in a mineshaft, makes the eyes swell shut and get all crusty, disgusting business. That altered the patrol schedule a bit, but it didn't matter, because nothing ever happens out here."

"I guess I'll spare the analyst's life after all then. Sorry to shatter your bucolic peace."

"Oh, no, it's been a welcome distraction. Until this part, anyway. You mentioned orders. What orders am I meant to be giving? Where are we taking the old man?"

"I'll tell you when you need to know–"

The woman's jaws snapped together, she twitched and spasmed, and then fell over.

"You took your time about it," Felix said mildly.

Tib Pelta shimmered into view, putting her stun gun back in its holster. "I wanted to see if she'd say anything useful, but you are very bad at interrogating people."

"I'm excellent at flirting, though."

"You think so? She certainly wasn't flirting back."

"I was still getting warmed up." He sighed. "You could have *told* us they'd stowed away on the shuttle, Tib, and saved us all a lot of time." He untethered himself and tried to figure out how to remove the enemy's armor.

"Don't be stupid. She would have heard me if I called you on the comms. It's not like there's a quiet corner in this shuttle where I could go to make a call, and opening the doors to go out would have drawn attention. I'm sneaky – I don't teleport."

"You're extremely insubordinate today."

"Ah. I meant to say, 'Don't be stupid, captain'. Better?"

"Much. Forgive me. I'm just annoyed." He thumped the armor. "How are we supposed to crack this shell?"

Tib crouched beside him, pressed a spot on the armor that looked like any other spot, and the plates separated with a hiss of escaping air. The enemy was wearing a plain white jumpsuit underneath. Still no identifying marks, not even a ship name. They wrestled her out of the armor and propped her in a corner. Felix put her weapons in a locked compartment while Tib opened a supply panel and brought out a roll of gray industrial tape. Perfect for binding wrists and ankles. "How'd all this happen, anyway?" he said. "I wondered where you'd gotten off to. I almost called you."

"Don't worry. I turned off my comms in case you tried." She bound the prisoner's wrists while Felix did the ankles. "I was creeping around the ship, being as invisible as possible, like you ordered." She paused in her work long enough to give a little salute. "I followed along behind the boarding party, to see if anyone tried to slip away behind them. No luck. I did the same thing during the search, in case someone was moving around to hide in places they'd already checked, but still nothing. So I wandered back here. Just luck that I happened to be faded out, still. I was planning on jumping out at you later and making you wet yourself."

"I would not have wet myself."

"No? You know you're supposed to stay hydrated, captain. Instead, I found her, tossing our spare environment suits into the corridor with the rest of the search detritus, and hiding in the locker. I spent a long time staring at the closed door, wondering if I could wrench it open and knock her out before she killed me, but I could just picture her, holding her gun in front of her, ready to fire at the slightest movement of the door."

Felix could picture it too. "So you figured you'd wait for her to come out."

"I knew she would eventually. A suit locker isn't much of a long-term residence. If she'd stayed sealed in until we got back to the ship, I could have slipped out after you and then we could have cut the oxygen to the shuttle and knocked her out or something."

Felix nodded. "You did well, Tib. On balance. With extra points for style."

"Feel free to reward me with bonus money in addition to praise." She inclined her head toward the woman. "What do we do with her? And with *him*?"

"Ask them various pointed questions, I would imagine."

"Sounds important," Tib said. "Very much captain-level work. You can do that part."

The prisoner stalked back and forth in the brig – which was halfway filled with cases of emergency rations, of course, so at least she wouldn't go hungry – while Felix watched her on the screen from the bridge. Half the screen, anyway: the other half was filled with the dossier Calred had compiled on their prisoner, based on DNA and facial recognition results.

"Amina Azad," Cal rumbled. "Citizen of the Federation of Sol. Ten years in their navy, the last three as a training officer specializing in close combat and incursion tactics. Most of her service record is redacted, even in the Federation databases our analysts aren't supposed to be able to access. She was discharged two years ago, and set up shop as a freelance security consultant, with a confidential client list. So confidential I'd be willing to bet none of the clients actually exist."

"You think she's still working for the Federation of Sol as a deniable asset?" Felix was neither shocked nor appalled by the possibility. The Coalition had its share of unofficial state actors, after all – a whole raider fleet of them.

"Seems likely. The Federation doesn't like to let valuable people go any more than we do."

"She's some kind of black ops super soldier, and we were still able to find out more about her than we were about Doctor Thales?"

"I know," Cal said. "Makes you curious about what *he* does for a living, doesn't it?"

"Is he awake yet?" Felix asked.

"In and out," Tib said over the comms. She was in their infirmary, watching over Thales. His status was a bit fuzzy: he wasn't a Coalition citizen, as far as they knew, but the Coalition was certainly interested in him, so he was somewhere between a guest and a prisoner. "Azad hit him with a massive dose of sedatives, and the safest approach is just to let them work their way out of his system. I could counteract the effects with *more* drugs, but he's on the far side of middle age, has high blood pressure and some arterial clogging, and I don't want to shock his system."

"Let me know when he's lucid. I suppose I'll go chat with Azad in the meantime."

"Captain. Neat trick back on the shuttle. Our analysts said you had an Yssaril on your crew, but I didn't realize she came to my ship with you. You fooled me once, which is one more than most people get."

Felix sat outside the brig, on a crate full of cloned eel-meat canned in red jelly – the drones had moved several crates into the corridor to make room for Azad. He thumped the side of the box. "Cloned eels. Ever had them? I guess I'd eat them, if it was the aftermath of a disaster and the choice was cloned eels or nothing at all."

"They're better in yellow jelly," Azad said. "Why are we talking about eels?"

"I'm attempting to establish a conversational rapport with my prisoner for purposes of interrogation."

"Try harder," she said. "How's *my* prisoner?"

"You mean Thales? He's not yours any more. He'll be all right, though no thanks to you. That level of sedation? Pretty dangerous for someone his age."

"One of my people is an expert at judging that sort of thing. Or was, before you killed him. I guess Thales hasn't started talking yet, or you'd see why I wanted him unconscious and quiet." She leaned against the bars, gazing at Felix with disconcerting directness. "What are you going to do with me?"

"Hand you over to the Table of Captains. Or, rather, their general staff. They'll ask you various difficult questions, and then decide if keeping you alive has any strategic value. Or you could cooperate with me, tell me everything right now, and I'll use my influence with the Table to intercede on your behalf."

She snorted. "Ha. I'll pass. My analyst said you're competent, but reckless even by Coalition standards, which is why you're stuck running a glorified transport ship in one of the most remote systems in Coalition space. Thales came way out here precisely because it's the middle of nowhere. Scratch that – the deep dusty back corner of nowhere. I think I can live without your influence."

"You can live for a little while, anyway, though it might not be very pleasant."

"Going to make me walk the space-plank?" she said. "Keelhaul me?"

"Nobody ever really walked planks, and keelhauling someone on a spaceship isn't very effective. It's just not the same unless you're being dragged underwater across a hull covered with barnacles."

"There's a sad shortage of barnacles in space, I've noticed. Just the usual interrogation techniques and methods of execution, then? That's too bad. I was hoping for exposure to the local culture."

"I'm sure you'll find our little customs fascinating. We're meeting up with Commander Meehves in a few hours and transferring you to her custody."

"Is this commander taking custody of Thales too?" She tried to make the question sound casual, and didn't do a very good job.

"I'm afraid not. The general consensus is that you and Thales shouldn't be on the same ship, if that can be avoided, in case you're tempted to do something reckless."

"Aren't you afraid I'll do something reckless *here*?" She smiled. With a smile like that, she would have made a pretty good pirate.

"Desperately." Felix took out his hand terminal, pushed an icon on the screen, and a clear sheet of unbreakable plexi slid out of the ceiling to cover the bars of the brig. "That's what this gas is for."

"You absolute piece of–" Azad crumpled to the floor before Felix could learn any new Federation of Sol insults.

Qqmel came over to escort Azad back to *The Bad Cat*. She was unconscious and restrained on a floating stretcher. "Be careful with her," Felix said. "Nobody's that arrogant without at least a little to back it up."

"Oh, I don't know about that," Qqmel said, eyeing him with reptilian amusement, but his cannon clicked and whirred and shifted to fix on her face.

"When do I get rid of Thales?" Felix said.

They strolled from the brig toward the airlock, with one of Qqmel's marines pushing the stretcher along. "Ah, the good doctor of nobody knows what. The commander says you should return to your usual patrol route and babysit him for the time being. You'll receive further orders after a while."

Felix frowned. "I'm not sensing a lot of urgency."

"The Table hasn't decided what to do with the man yet, Felix. We could return him to Cobbler's Knob, deport him to wherever he's originally from, make him disappear – all options are on the table, because we don't know why he was abducted. We're not sure any of this is Coalition business, honestly."

"None of our business!" Felix pointed at Azad.

"Obviously, Azad fired on you, so *she's* our business. She may have some useful intelligence from her time in the service, so we'll get what we can from her before we lock her up, or shove her out an airlock, or someone in the clandestine branch tries to turn her. Thales, though, isn't nearly as interesting to our superiors. We don't know why she came for him. Maybe he's just a wealthy recluse Azad wanted to ransom. Who knows? He's the victim here, anyway."

"Come on. He must be important. If the Federation sent a black ops team–"

"That's just Calred's theory," Qqmel interrupted. "He's a security officer, which means he's professionally paranoid. We checked out the dead, and they're all freelancers, just like Azad. Our working theory is that they were hired to do a snatch-and-grab that went disastrously wrong, and the Federation doesn't have anything to do with this mess at all."

Of course. "The Table doesn't *want* to believe the Federation was involved," he said. "Or at least they don't want to admit to the possibility officially. Because that would mean the Federation of Sol sent an armed vessel secretly into Mentak

Coalition space, which then proceeded to fire on one of our ships. That's the kind of thing that endangers diplomatic relations and trade deals and all sorts of other things."

"That kind of speculation is for higher ranks than me," Qqmel said cheerfully. "I just break open ships and steal stuff. But I may have overheard the commander musing along similar lines. She always said you were smarter than you look. Look, we're going to interrogate Azad, but she's going to be tough. Why don't you see if you can get Thales to talk, and if he says something interesting, pass it on? You can handle one old guy, right, Felix?"

"Right." Felix saw his hope of glory receding. Even if he found out Thales had some big secret, and he told the Table, they might choose not to hear him, because of politics. He watched Qqmel load Azad onto his shuttle, and once they were away from his ship, took a nice deep breath. At least that woman was someone else's problem now. Maybe he had time to grab a bite or a nap or both before – "Captain." Tib spoke in his comms, voice sharp. "Thales is awake. You'd better get down here."

"I'm on my way." Someone shouted in the background. "Are you all right? What's going on down there?"

"He's throwing things at me and calling me names," Tib said. "I've heard worse, but I'd rather have you here than me."

"Get that slimy sneaking frog away from me," Thales snarled, crouching behind the exam table in the infirmary. His gray hair stuck up in wild whorls, and he held his fists up like he was about to get into a brawl.

"OK, monkey." Tib glanced at Felix. "May I be excused?"

"I think I can take it from here," Felix said. "Doctor Thales, I'm Captain Felix Duval, of the *Temerarious*. I'd appreciate it if you'd stop hurling abuse at my first officer."

"You know what those creatures are like," Thales said. "They're spies, you know, all of them, they sneak and steal and sell your secrets. I can't believe you have one on your ship! Are you some uncommon variety of idiot?"

Tib shook her head and left, the door sliding shut behind her. Felix perched on the edge of a counter. "She's a valuable member of the crew and my oldest friend, so I'm not the right audience for this little show. Let's move on. How are you feeling? Do you have everything you need?"

"I don't have *anything* I need. Where are my files? My equipment?"

"Everything we recovered is here in storage." Meehves didn't want Azad and the files on the same ship either, just to be safe, so Felix was babysitting those, too. "Could you answer a few questions for me, Doctor Thales?"

He scoffed, but lowered his fists and stood up. "Why should I?"

"Courtesy, since you're a guest on my ship? No? Gratitude, because we saved you from a team of mercenaries who attempted to abduct you? No, not that, either? How about pragmatism, because I can make your life easy, or I can make your life difficult?"

"Hmph." He sat on the exam table. "Go ahead. Ask. I can't promise you'll understand any of the answers."

"Where are you from?"

"Oh, all over." He waved his hand vaguely.

Right. "Why did you choose to settle on Cobbler's Knob?"

"I like peace and quiet and privacy. It's good for my work. People are always trying to steal my work."

"What is your work, exactly?"

Thales blinked. "You mean you don't *know*? Ha. I'm a scientist, boy. My research is going to transform the galaxy."

"Oh, is that all. What kind of research?"

Thales stuck his little finger in his ear, wiggled it around, looked at the tip for a moment, then wiped whatever he'd found off on the edge of the table. "The kind that's going to make me very rich." He looked down at the floor and spoke more quietly, as if to himself. "There's no going back to Alope – they found me once, and they will again. I used the last of my funds getting settled out here, establishing a fresh identity, covering my tracks… I can't afford to do all that over again. Hrmph. I need resources." He looked up and met Felix's eyes with his own bloodshot ones. "I suppose the Coalition is as good a partner as any. All right. If your government will help me complete my work, I'll give them the privilege of buying the results." He waved his hand. "Convey my offer to your superiors at the Table."

"I'm going to need a lot more information before I bother the captains."

He glared. "It's not enough for you to know the Federation of Sol wants me? I thought you people were *pirates*."

Felix pinched the bridge of his nose. "Just tell me why the Federation wanted you."

"Because whoever controls my invention will rule the galaxy."

Felix waited for a moment. Nothing more seemed to be forthcoming. "That was a good line, really, and well delivered, but, again, I'm going to need more context."

Thales sniffed. "I'm not sure your clearances are high enough to hear this."

"You're not going to talk to anyone higher ranking anytime soon, Thales, and you don't *work* for us, so nothing you have to say is classified in the Coalition."

"Fine. What do you know about wormholes?"

Felix frowned. "As much as anyone does."

"And what's *that*? I may travel in more informed circles than you do, and I don't want to leave out any *context* you might need to understand."

Felix was beginning to see Azad's point about keeping the man sedated. "Wormholes are naturally occurring portals, scattered randomly throughout the galaxy. They link distant points in space, so they're one of the main reasons interstellar nations and trade are even possible. They're vitally important strategically – control a wormhole, and you control vast swathes of space. A trade dispute over the Quann wormhole a few thousand years ago turned into a shooting war that brought down the old Lazax Empire."

"Solid grade-school-level overview," Thales said. "Except for the bit about them being naturally occurring. Some of them might be, but they can also be *made*. The Creuss do it."

Felix shuddered. The Ghosts of Creuss. He didn't know much about the aliens – nobody did – but they were bogeymen, beings composed of energy instead of matter, difficult or impossible to kill or even fight, with a mastery of technology beyond anything the other races of the galaxy possessed. If Thales said the Creuss could make wormholes, he believed him. "If you say so."

"My personal area of expertise is wormhole physics," Thales said. "When we found out the Creuss could create wormholes, replicating their technology became my personal mission. Creating wormholes isn't easy for them, apparently – they do so rarely, at great cost, and mostly use FTL ships like everyone else. Still, if the Creuss can do it, that means it's possible, and I refuse to believe there's anything they can do that I can't, given sufficient time and resources. I turned my mind toward the problem, and quickly began to make progress. Just knowing it *could* be done removed the greatest psychological block." He leaned forward. "Tell your superiors I've found a way to open wormholes anywhere I want, anytime I want. Tell them, if they can afford me, I'll give them the keys to the galaxy."

CHAPTER 5

"You're saying you can make wormholes. You can actually, really, physically make wormholes." Felix was staggered by the implications. Thales might as well have said he could eat a planet.

Thales showed all his teeth in what must have been intended as a smile. "Imagine what a bunch of pirates like the Coalition could do with my technology. You could open a wormhole, without warning, anywhere you wanted. You could drop a fleet into orbit around any planet or station in the galaxy, strike your target, and then vanish. I can *close* my wormholes, too, so no one will be able to follow you back. Ha. What do you think of that?"

I think it sounds too good to be true. "I think extraordinary claims require extraordinary evidence."

"I always knew I'd have to give a demonstration to potential buyers. I'm prepared to do that, if the Coalition will help me complete my prototype. The theoretical basis is essentially complete – at this point, I just have to solve a few small engineering problems."

"What exactly are you asking for?" Felix asked.

"I'll require the Coalition's full support in gathering the resources and materials I need, and protection from the forces arrayed against me. I was hoping that security through obscurity would prove sufficient, but the Federation found me, so I'll concede that security through being surrounded by armed people with guns also has its advantages." He waved his hand. "Go on and tell the people who pull your strings my terms."

Ordered around by a civilian on my own ship. Felix snapped off a salute so formal and stiff it could only be read as mockery, turned smartly on his heel, and marched out of the infirmary. Then he initiated quarantine procedures so nothing short of a catastrophic hull breach would allow the door to open. At least he could keep Thales from wandering loose on his ship.

Felix didn't get to talk to a representative of the Table of Captains, of course. They were far too busy and important. He invoked the name of the well-respected Commander Meehves, opening contact with a higher echelon of officials, and after a circuitous route of transfers, his screen connected to the office of the assistant undersecretary of special projects, a Hylar named Fololire Jhuri. Jhuri was a member of a sub-species that didn't require any special breathing apparatus to live out of the water, and he spoke through an artificial voicebox in tones clearly based on the human star of a popular adventure romance serial– a mellow, deep voice Felix found a bit incongruous coming from a bulbous green head trailing fronds of tentacles, with a face glistening with cybernetic implants.

"It all sounds a bit implausible," Jhuri said. "We've heard stories of what the Creuss can do to space-time, but there are so many outrageous tales about them it's hard to know what's true and what's nonsense. Wormhole physics isn't my area, but I reached out to a few of the local experts, and they haven't heard of anyone making the kind of progress Thales claims. Since he refuses to give his real name, I can't vet his qualifications, but on the whole, I'm inclined to think he's overstating the level of his research at best, and outright lying at worst."

Felix felt a little disappointment, but it was mingled with relief. An exciting mission would have been nice, but having Thales on board the *Temerarious* was like having a splinter under a fingernail. "So, should I drop him back at Cobbler's Knob?"

The Hylar's tentacles undulated. "I didn't say that. Commander Meehves assures me that significant resources were expended trying to capture Thales, so we can't discount his story utterly – someone wants the man for *something*. Once we properly interrogate the mercenary you captured, we may find out more. In the meantime, we are willing to provide Thales with limited support, at least until it becomes evident that he's a fraud. It's a gamble, but we're the Coalition. We try things. Honestly, I don't believe his claims, but if he *can* do what he says it's worth exploring just on the off-chance. We don't want to be the fools who threw away a winning lottery ticket."

"What are you giving him?"

"I'm authorizing the reassignment of some Coalition personnel to provide protection for Thales, and to assist him with logistics, and the acquisition of any necessary materiel."

At least Thales wouldn't be Felix's problem any more, though his sympathies went out to whatever crew had to deal with the man. "Understood. Where am I taking him?"

"Anywhere he wants to go, I suppose," the Hylar said.

"Wait," Felix said. "What? Oh."

"Quite. You, your ship, and your crew have been seconded to my office, temporarily reassigned from your patrol duties. Officially, you and your crew are not operating as military assets, but as contractors and consultants hired out to a civilian scientist." The Coalition sometimes rented out personnel for money, so the explanation wasn't implausible. "In reality, you're working for Operation Chicane, and reporting to me."

Felix had various questions, but for some reason the one that popped out was, "Why is it called Operation Chicane?"

"We have a long list of code names generated by computer. That was the next one."

How unsatisfying. "What about my, ah, regular duties?"

"Patrolling the Lycian system? Your work helping the colonists is vital, of course, in its way, but we can move things around to cover your territory. It's one of the quietest systems we control, after all."

"Historically," Felix said. "I'd like to point out that there was an armed attack on this system by violent outsiders rather recently."

"The first such incident since that system was settled, in fact. You dealt with the attack well, which is why you're being given a better assignment. I'm surprised you aren't more enthusiastic – Meehves told me you were eager to serve the Coalition in a more active capacity. Was I misinformed?"

Felix scrubbed a hand through his hair and let himself look as sheepish as he suddenly felt. "No, of course not, I am eager, it's just… Thales. He's awful. I don't like the idea of working for him."

"Then console yourself with the fact that you're actually working for *me*. Get Thales whatever he needs. Prevent anyone else from abducting him. See if he can build the thing he claims he can build."

"When you say get him whatever he needs…"

"Within reason. He doesn't need a platinum statue of himself, or his own personal warship – but if he asks for something that seems plausibly necessary for his research, accommodate him. Don't start any wars. If you break any laws outside Coalition territory, try not to get caught. Otherwise… use your judgment. If your judgment proves inadequate, well, you're a deniable asset now, captain. If you get into serious trouble, we'll just say you went rogue and cut all ties with you."

"Oh good," Felix said. "That's comforting."

"Come now, captain. Don't be worried. If you do well, you'll be rewarded. Even if Thales doesn't accomplish anything, I'll remember your service, and if he *does* produce a miracle… you'll play an instrumental role in helping the Coalition rule the galaxy. Look at the potential advantages. Anyway, I'm sure it won't be too strenuous an assignment. The man is a researcher. I can't imagine he'll require anything too difficult from you."

"What, all I get is *you*?" Thales said. "Ugh."

Thales was wearing his own clothes again, and sitting in Felix's office, leaning back in a chair and scowling. Felix sat behind his desk, partly to lend himself an air of authority, and partly because it put Thales farther away from him. The authority part wasn't really working; Thales didn't seem impressed by any authority outside himself. "I'm happy to tell undersecretary Jhuri that you don't require our services, if you're unhappy."

"Jhuri, eh? Sounds like a Hylar name. My life is infested with those creatures."

He sighed. "Don't be stupid. You're better than nothing, if only barely. Once I give that wriggling squid you report to a demonstration of my technology, he'll start treating me with the proper respect. My whole life, I've had to prove myself to my inferiors. I'm used to it by now. In the meantime… well, you're enough to be getting on with."

"I'm so delighted we meet your immediate needs. We can set you up with lab space on the lower decks. I'll have the files and equipment we recovered from the mercenary ship taken down. We're going to take the *Temerarious* out of this system, since people might come looking for you here, though we're still deciding where to go. It depends on the supplies you need, but we can find a place near a trading route, with a raider fleet nearby in case we need backup. Just give me a list of materials and–"

"All that's fine," Thales interrupted, "but the *first* thing I need, the very first thing, before we do anything else, is Shelma."

"What's Shelma?" It sounded like some kind of chemical reagent, or, possibly, a drug.

"Not what. *Who.* Meletl Shelma. My research partner. I've reached a point in my work where I require her expertise – she's the best engineer I've ever known, and she's absolutely crucial to transition from theoretical underpinnings to practical applications."

Felix sighed. He was going to be a taxi service, then. "All right. Where is she?"

"The last I heard," Thales said, "she was in a prison camp in the Barony of Letnev."

"But you specifically said, don't start any wars," Felix said.

Jhuri was unmoved. "You won't start a war, because you aren't a military operative right now. You're a civilian contractor, and we don't have any treaties or diplomatic ties with the Barony. If Thales really needs this engineer, see if you can get her. At least look over the situation and decide if a breakout is feasible. Try not to get captured yourself – we won't be able to do much for you if the Barony locks you up."

"I thought Azad was contemptible for doing basically what you're asking me to do," Felix said.

"Perspective is so important," Jhuri said. "Anyway, there's a difference between abducting someone from a planet where he's chosen to settle, and rescuing someone from a Barony prison. Their habit of jailing political dissidents is shameful. Tell yourself you're striking a blow for freedom if it helps."

Felix thought about it. Plotting a prison break was, in the abstract, an appealing idea – his whole nation was founded on a prison uprising, after all, and the work certainly wouldn't be boring. "I may need extra resources. Mercenaries of my own, or equipment, or money bribes."

"I realize. I'm providing you with access to one of my department's discretionary funds. There's not enough to retire in luxury – I'd hate to tempt you so – but you should be able to fund a small operation like this. It's amazing the sort of things you can classify as 'research and development' in a budget report. Technically true in this case, even."

Resources, and a mission – this was exactly what Felix had been hoping for. Of course, he was stuck working with Thales, but no situation was perfect. "I assume you'll want regular mission updates?"

"Is that what you assume?" Jhuri said. "The whole deniability thing works better when we don't talk constantly, you know. You needn't tell me about every little prison break. The less I know about what you're doing the better, in some ways. I am interested in results. When Thales has a working prototype, get in touch. Or when it becomes clear he's a complete fraud. Or, I suppose, if you run out of money – though that won't make me happy. Otherwise, do your best to muddle along, and if I want updates, I'll reach out to you." The connection went dark.

"I suppose I've got my orders, then," Felix said aloud. He checked the ship's operating account – the funds held in common to buy supplies and repairs if needed – and saw it was much healthier than it had been a few minutes ago. Time to have a family meeting, then.

Tib was present in the galley, but not visible, since she wasn't in the mood to have abuse hurled at her. Cal sat across the table from Thales, looking at him with those large predator's eyes, taking him in calmly. Thales was smiling at the Hacan in a way that made Felix queasy. He sat at the head of the table, slouching in what he hoped looked like easy and effortless command, not that anyone was admiring the pose. "So," he began, but Thales interrupted him.

"What did your ancestors do to get exiled to the penal colony?" Thales asked Calred. "Currency manipulation, was it? Loan sharking? You Hacan do love your money, don't you?"

"Family tradition holds that my many-times-great grandmother had a disagreement with a representative of the Lazax emperor who behaved rudely in her presence," Calred rumbled. "She ate him." Cal showed all his teeth, which usually tended to render people speechless.

"Devoured a tax collector, eh? Sounds like Hacan."

"Can you *please* be less racist toward my crew?" Felix said. "We have to work together, you know."

"This again." Thales shook his head. "I'm not racist. I hold all the species of the galaxy in equal contempt."

"I don't doubt it, but you're expressing your contempt through horrible stereotypes and–"

"Humans are also garbage," Thales interrupted. He interrupted a lot. "For one thing, they talk endlessly and never get to the *point*. Are we going to break Shelma out of the prison camp or not?"

Felix took a deep breath. "I have been authorized to assist you in creating a prototype of your wormhole device, whatever it takes. I have been given complete discretion and autonomy–"

"You're not a total waste of my time, then. Good. First–"

Felix leaned across the table and flicked Thales on the tip of the nose, hard, making the scientist rear back and blink furiously. "What? How dare you–"

"The Table of Captains think you're full of shit." Felix spoke quietly, so Thales would have to stop sputtering to hear him. "If they believed you, they would have assigned more than three people and one ship to this operation, don't you think? Since there's a small chance you're telling the truth, though, they're willing to waste my time and a small quantity of money to hedge their bets. They see it as a small risk with a potentially large reward." He leaned over the table. "But here's the thing, Thales. You don't have any direct line of communication to my superiors. Everything goes through me. If I tell them you're a con artist trying to bilk the Coalition for money, they'll believe me."

"*You* people are the thieves and swindlers and pirates!" Thales cried.

"True enough," Felix said. "We take pride in being clever and sneaky and getting the upper hand by any means necessary. Which is why we don't trust people who tell us they just need a *little* help to make all our dreams come true. You seem to be under the impression that I have to keep you happy, Thales. I don't. You have to keep *me* happy, because as soon as you annoy me too much, I make a call, declare this mission a waste, and drop you off on the nearest rock to starve to death. Do you understand your situation?"

Thales glared at Felix furiously for a moment, then leaned back, and then began to chuckle. The chuckle built into a belly-rumbling laugh as the scientist smacked the table. "You showed a little backbone there, captain! I can't work with someone I can't respect, as much as I can respect anyone. I thought you were a pudding-hearted sort of man. Of course, if I *could* push you around, I would, but if you say you have limits, I can accept that. I'll keep my opinions to myself unless they're relevant to the mission at hand, then, all right? The lion and the toad won't hear another harsh word from me."

"He's so much better already," Cal murmured.

"That would be marvelous. I'd like you to apologize to my crew first, though. So we can move forward with a clean slate in a spirit of collaboration." Felix thought that was probably pushing it, but he couldn't help himself.

Thales nodded, and turned to Calred. "I apologize for insulting your ancestors."

Calred inclined his great head graciously.

Thales went on. "If you're lurking around in here, First Officer Pelta, I'm sorry for all the shouting earlier. I had a bad experience with a spy from your tribe, but I'll try to judge you on your personal merits, and leave old associations out of it."

Tib shimmered into visibility. "Fine." She sat next to Felix. "Now that we're all happy and functional, what's the first step toward our glorious shared future?"

Felix said, "Thales tells us everything he knows about his partner Shelma and the place she's being held, and we make a plan to reunite them."

Hours later, Felix lay in his bunk, alone in his cabin, staring up at the ceiling, trying to get some sleep. They were making their way to the nearest Coalition-controlled wormhole gate, which would get them closer to the part of Letnev space where Thales believed his fellow scientist was being held. Life was likely to get very eventful soon, but, for now, things were quiet, and he needed to get some sleep while he could. Of course, his mind was spinning and uncooperative, with better things to do than dream.

His comm channel buzzed, and Felix groaned, rolled over, and squinted at the terminal on his bedside table. Then he sat upright. He had an encrypted message, highest urgency, from a command-level officer. He smoothed his hair down and answered.

Meehves appeared on the screen, face puffy from her own interrupted sleep. "We lost her," Meehves said.

CHAPTER 6

"You lost who?" Felix said, and then realized. "The mercenary, Amina Azad? What do you mean you lost her?"

"I mean the guards in the brig didn't check in as scheduled, so someone went down to see why not, and found both guards dead, and her cell empty. The security footage was erased, which I would have sworn wasn't even possible. Our best guess is, Azad had hidden implants that didn't show up on our scans, super-soldier black-ops enhancements that enabled her to escape and hack into our systems. There was no indication of any ships or pods leaving, no evidence of an airlock opening, so we scoured the ship for her, searching for hours. I finally sent the deck master to do a visual check of the launch bay, and that's when we realized one of our fighters was missing – according to the computers, the fighter is still sitting in its launch tube. She manipulated the security footage, so there's no record of the departure, or which way it went. Those fighters aren't meant for long-range travel, but they're fast, and there are inhabited systems in range on multiple trajectories, so we can't mount a meaningful search."

Felix whistled. "She's just gone, then?"

"We sent out her name and description system-wide, claiming she's wanted for murder, but if she can escape my brig, she can hide. It's a big galaxy."

"She'll go back to her handlers in the Federation of Sol and tell them we have Thales," Felix said.

Meehves shrugged. "If she was working for the Federation at all. We didn't prove that. We didn't prove anything. She just stared at us during our initial interview, didn't say a word, and we were planning a more intense interrogation for tomorrow."

"So, you *don't* think I should worry about the full force and power of the Federation of Sol bearing down on me?"

"The Federation doesn't want a war any more than we do. Even if Azad is an operative, and reports back, she doesn't know where Thales is now. We could have put him in a bunker somewhere. The Federation won't be able to do much about *that*." Meehves sighed. "I'm sorry, Felix. I was hoping to get confirmation that Thales was telling the truth – or that he's full of shit. I hear Jhuri made you his babysitter?"

"I thought that was super secret?"

"This is the best encryption we've got," she said. "Anyway, Jhuri was pretty interested in what Azad might have to say, so we've been liaising. I'm sure now that I'm not helpful any more I'll be left in the dark."

"Do you know the undersecretary well?"

"A little by acquaintance, a lot by reputation."

"Am I in good hands? Or, tentacles?"

"If you prove useful to Jhuri, the undersecretary will take very good care of you. If you prove less than useful, he'll throw you away like a broken tool and reach for a new one."

"I do not find that reassuring, commander."

"Oh, cheer up. For someone in the murky upper echelons of the clandestine services, Jhuri is a pretty straight shooter. Didn't he tell you basically the same thing himself?"

"He said if I succeed, I'll be rewarded, and if I get caught committing crimes outside Coalition space, he'll pretend he never heard of me."

"See? You know exactly where you stand. I'll let you know if we hear anything about our escapee. Good luck with your mission, captain."

"I hate the idea of Azad running around loose out there."

"It's a big galaxy," Meehves repeated. "I doubt you'll ever run into her again."

Amina Azad sat in the deepest darkest corner of a cantina in Misna, the most cosmopolitan city on the planet Ryma, which was primarily a world of temperate oceans inhabited by immense but only marginally intelligent cetaceans. The areas of habitable land included a scattering of archipelagos and one island large enough call a continent, at least by local standards. The city of Misna hugged a bay on the western coast, and most of the nicer restaurants featured views of the water. The place where Azad waited didn't have any windows at all.

She wore a wide-brimmed hat she'd stolen from a booth in the bazaar. Misna was big enough to have cameras capable of facial recognition, and she had to assume she was a wanted fugitive in Coalition space, so it was better to keep her features in shadow. She didn't have any contacts here, but cities were cities, and a couple of discreet inquiries had brought her to this portside bar, and the Xxcha bartender had agreed to make the right introductions. He'd get a finder's fee for his trouble if it worked out, and a knife in the neck from Azad if it didn't. He only knew about the first option.

The woman who slid into the chair across from Azad was Letnev. The wild variety of species present in Coalition space always delighted Azad – back home in the Federation, nonhumans were rare, and most of the times Azad had interacted with other races she'd been shooting at them or getting shot at or both. Having other sorts of interactions was always interesting. A lot of her compatriots in the navy were xenophobic, but Azad had decided early on that she wanted to see the galaxy, and she reveled in the vastness of the universe.

"You have a ship to sell." The stranger was young, wearing dark glasses; the Letnev were sensitive to bright light, but the bar was dim, so Azad figured she was probably just an asshole.

"I don't have the title on me," Azad said. "The ship is salvage. Did you take a look?" She'd passed along the coordinates for the ship to the prospective buyer earlier. That was a risk, but a calculated one. The fighter was locked up tight, the engine wouldn't turn on without her permission, and as a military-grade vessel, it had countermeasures that would make it dangerous for anyone to scrap it for parts. The fighter was more valuable in one piece, anyway.

"We sent someone to take a look," she said. "We don't see a lot of Coalition fighters for sale, certainly not tucked away in the glass flats outside the city."

"Couldn't dock legally," Azad said. "See above regarding the lack of title. Besides, the fighters are made to evade detection. Why not spare myself the port fees?"

"That's just good financial planning," the woman said. "We're interested. You have the access fob?"

"If you have the money."

The woman slid across a card, and Azad passed her hand over it, the implant in her palm reading the data. More than she'd expected, but less than she'd hoped. Enough to finance the next part of her mission, though. "Acceptable." She slid a teardrop-shaped access fob across the table in return. The woman did her own authentication check, nodded, and left without a look back.

Azad wondered who she'd just sold the fighter to, or who would end up with it in the end. Gangsters, terrorists, revolutionaries? Oh well. It was unlikely to end up shooting at Federation ships, so she didn't really care. Now she had sufficient funds to get off this ball of mud and whales and resume her mission. She paid her tab, left a tip, and went looking for a ship to hire.

As she walked through the narrow, winding streets of Misna, she did her best to focus on the future. Pondering past mistakes could be a valuable exercise, if it prompted you to avoid similar mistakes in the future, but there was no point in dwelling on misfortune. She'd done everything properly, but you couldn't account for bad luck, and Duval and the *Temerarious* being in the wrong place at the wrong time was nothing else.

Azad *could* apportion some blame to her second-in-command for blowing their entire emergency fund on a pointless attempt to bribe Captain Duval, but she'd used her selfdestruct button – as the squad called their poison-filled hollow teeth – to avoid capture, so there was no point. The dead couldn't learn from their mistakes.

Azad had a poison capsule too, but she couldn't imagine using it. There was no scenario where she was more valuable dead than alive, and she preferred redemption over sacrifice. Better to stay alive and look for an opportunity to escape, and the sloppy discipline in the raider fleet and her own hidden enhancements had provided one. Now she could complete her mission: bring home the runaway Thales and put him back to work for the Federation of Sol. Thales wasn't a Federation citizen – he'd grown up among the talking squid on a Hylar world – but he'd made certain commitments and then abandoned them. His only loyalty was to himself. Azad was going to show him the error of his ways.

Azad strolled through the spaceport, a series of landing areas and support buildings arrayed on the edge of the island, not far from the bristling cranes and docks of the deep-water port. If she only looked at the sky and the glittering reflections of sunlight on the sparkling water, or closed her eyes and smelled the salt and exhaust, she could imagine she was back home on Jord, in the fishing village where she'd grown up before joining the navy. The illusion broke when she looked around and saw the Xxcha dockworkers carrying heavy loads alongside humans in exo-suits, the Hacan ship owners supervising, and the occasional head of a Hylar popping out of the water as they went about their business.

Misna was refreshing, and a nice change from cramped ship life, but she'd been here too long already. The pirates would be looking for her. She needed a vessel built for speed, something that could be piloted solo if need be, and, fortunately, the Coalition was full of smuggler's ships.

She settled on a newly arrived light cruiser, low-slung and shaped like a sleek aquatic predator, and approached the obvious captain, a dark-skinned human woman standing on top of a crate and yelling at people while wearing an alluring quantity of leather. (*Stop that*, Azad told herself. She was on a mission. There was time enough for pleasure later, if she lived.)

"I need a ride to Thibah." Thibah was an arid place, almost the opposite of Misna, with small oceans that looked like mud puddles from orbit. Its only virtue was its location, making it an ideal staging point for deep-space exploration – it was the last place to get fuel and supplies before venturing out into contested and unknown lands. It was also the first stop for people returning from those depths with items for sale, usually ore or other plundered resources, but sometimes alien artifacts and stranger things.

Azad didn't have any interest in going there, but it was a plausible destination from here.

The captain looked Azad up and down. "Nice hat. I'm not available for hire. I've got a load of mixed liquor I'm planning to unload on a mining planet."

"Take it to Thibah instead. Explorers like to drink."

"Yes, and I like to fill my cargo hold. I sell liquor, I get ore, I sell ore, I get liquor, and around and around I go. It's a virtuous circle."

Azad leaned back against a crate and gave her a lazy smile. "Sounds boring. You're too young to be that boring. Besides, there are plenty of things to pick up on Thibah. Even if you don't get a decent load there, that's where me paying you comes in handy."

The captain hopped down from the crate. "I'm sure you can find a ship going that way without bothering me."

"I like the look of *your* boat. I want something small, fast, and private. Maybe we could crack open a bottle or two of your supply and enjoy the journey."

She grunted. "What's the offer?"

Amina plucked the card from her pocket and held it up. The captain scanned it, and she *was* young, because she couldn't stop her eyes from widening. "You could almost buy a ship for that much."

"Not one as fast as yours, and anyway, then I wouldn't have any company. What do you say?"

"I say, are you on the run from anybody I should be worried about?"

Azad laughed, deep and throaty. "I never run *from* anything. I run toward things." She held out her hand. "I'm Carmen Goodwin." It wasn't an alias she'd ever used before, and it wasn't the name of her dead aunt or her hometown or any of the other stupid false identity choices amateurs made. She had a list in her head of the names of human women approximately her age who'd emigrated as children to remote parts of the galaxy and never shown up in public records since, and when she needed a new name, she picked one, after a cursory check to make sure they hadn't reentered civilization. As she recalled, Carmen had grown up on a space station until her family went to seek their fortune on a colony world, where they'd probably been eaten by local predators or something. Azad had always possessed a good memory, and the navy had provided technological augmentation to make it even better.

"I'm Zayne ad Itroc," the captain said. "I'll need half up front, half on your safe delivery to Thibah."

"I find your terms acceptable, captain. How soon can we leave?"

"I'm almost done with loading. I'll tell the cargo handlers they aren't needed, and pay the docking fees – no, wait, it's cheaper to bribe the dockmaster here, I forgot – and then we can be on our way. Say two hours?"

"I can't wait."

Azad got something to eat from a kiosk nearby – hot spiced meat wrapped in broad leaves, nowhere near as good as the seafood she could get back home; she had the sinking suspicion it was whale meat – and then hunkered down to wait. She had a tactical engine in her head, and she ran it through various scenarios, but the immediate problems were trivially easy to solve. The bigger issue – tracking down Thales – was harder. They'd planned to put a tracking device on him in case he tried to escape, but with all the chaos and pursuit, they hadn't got round to it. She'd have to find him the old-fashioned way: deduction, investigation, and intelligence gathering. First, she considered what she knew about him: he was a genius, an egomaniac, a bigot, and a holder of grudges. He now probably had the resources of the pirate nation at his disposal. What would he do with those resources? Or rather, what would he do *first*?

Ah. She thought she had an idea. When their mission was being put together, there'd been two potential targets: Thales and the Hylar scientist he'd collaborated with before the whole thing fell apart and they both disappeared into the depths of the galaxy. Her superiors had settled on recovering Thales first because he was the softer target. But Thales would be interested in their other possibility, too – their research showed she was the builder, while he was the theoretician, and he probably needed her to continue his work. Now that he had the resources of the Coalition at his back, Thales might try to get her.

If Azad could get there before he did, and lay in wait, she could recapture Thales. And if she was totally wrong, and he didn't go there, she could break in and take the secondary target for herself. Going back to her superiors empty-handed wasn't an option. If she came back with Thales, all her past transgressions would be wiped away. If she came back with Meletl Shelma, she'd at least get to keep breathing and drawing a paycheck. If she came back with *both* targets… ahh. Her handler would shout at her for excessive improvisation, but, in the end, she'd be covered in glory.

Azad always felt better when her mission parameters were clear. Now she could enjoy the trip with the intriguing captain ad Itroc. At least until the regrettable, inevitable, unenjoyable part.

Once the course was laid in, they settled back in the captain's small lounge with glasses of firewine. Azad made a point of keeping her glass full, trusting that the captain's piratical pride would make her match her, sip for sip. Of course, the captain probably didn't have metabolic enhancements like those Azad used to keep herself from getting tipsy, let alone drunk.

They talked for hours as they drank, swapping life stories – most of Azad's were fictitious, and most of ad Itroc's were hilarious – and flirting. The flirting grew ever more outrageous as ad Itroc got drunker, and soon she was sitting next to Azad on the bunk, nuzzling her neck, one hand sliding from her knee up her thigh.

Azad's control of her own body was greater than normal, but not total, and it was impossible not to react. Her heartbeat sped up, her breath shortened, her face flushed. Azad had been through a long and lonely few months, and the captain was pretty and witty and willing.

Azad took ad Itroc's face in both hands and gazed into her eyes, centimeters away. "You're lovely," she said, and ad Itroc smiled.

Azad twisted the captain's head around savagely, snapping her neck, her augmented muscles turning the head nearly a hundred-and-eighty degrees around. Ad Itroc didn't even have time to be surprised before she died and slithered off the bunk to sprawl on the floor.

Azad knew from past experience that she usually regretted sleeping with someone she'd have to kill later. Looking at someone in the throes of passion and imagining their corpse was a downer. She gazed at the captain's body and sighed. Such a shame – she'd liked the woman – but the mission came first, always.

After Azad used the captain's glazing-over eyes and cooling fingertips to unlock the biometric controls and take over the ship, she kissed ad Itroc on the forehead, then dragged her down to the airlock to jettison her into space. "The Federation of Sol thanks you for your assistance," she said as she watched the body spin away. As good a prayer as any. Most people were no service to anyone but themselves, and even that was hit-or-miss.

Azad went to the cockpit and adjusted the trajectory to take her to Letnev space.

CHAPTER 7

"Have you ever been to the Barony?" Felix asked.

Thales made a face. "I went to one of their colonies, once, for a scientific conference. Beautiful place, full of lush jungles, towering trees, clear skies. Naturally, the Letnev had burrowed their settlements into the planet's crust, living in subterranean tunnels that never saw the sun. They could have grown anything there – it was a classic garden world – but they brought their mushroom farms and cloned meat vats with them."

"Ah, well, everyone enjoys a little taste of home." Felix leaned back in his chair at the galley table. He had to admit, Thales had become less objectionable since they had their little talk. Most of the scientist's conversation still consisted of insulting people (and entire peoples), but he was mostly insulting people Felix didn't like much either, which was more tolerable.

"I don't think the Letnev are allowed to enjoy things. Fascists and bureaucrats. One of them approached me at that conference, offered me a position at one of their scientific academies. From the look on his face, he learned some new Hylar swear words that day, ha."

"Is that why they imprisoned your colleague?"

Thales waved his hand. "No, that was years ago, when I was just a promising young academic at the Universities of Jol-Nar."

"I didn't think there were humans at the Universities," Felix said. Admittedly, most of his knowledge about the Hylar research worlds was based on their appearance in technothriller serials, where they were inevitably home to mad scientists crafting doomsday weapons.

"The Universities accept applications based on merit." Thales grinned. "They mostly see merit in other Hylar, but there are exceptions."

Felix would pass that tidbit of information on to Calred, and see if it helped him discover anything more about Thales. There couldn't be that many humans of his age, description, and purported area of expertise who'd studied or been employed at the Universities, and it might help to figure out his real name and background. Assuming he wasn't lying about any of those details, of course.

"Have you figured out how to break into the prison yet?" Thales asked.

"About that. Calred did some research, and the place you told us about isn't one of the Barony's penal facilities at all. Officially, it's an orbital weather monitoring station above a colony planet. Mentak Coalition intelligence suspects it's a secured research facility."

Thales waved that away. "They can call it whatever they like – it's still a prison. The Barony kidnapped Shelma, just like the Federation tried to kidnap *me*. She's being held there against her will. We have to help her. Especially since I can't easily complete my work without her – or vice versa, so be careful not to let the Barony get their hands on me, or they'll be ruling the galaxy. Besides, this is good news, isn't it? Surely it's easier to break into a research facility than it is to break into a prison."

"You might think so," Felix said. But he did have the inklings of an idea.

"Listen," Thales said. "When you rescue her, don't tell her you're working with me. I want to surprise her when she gets on board. She'll be delighted."

Felix tried to imagine someone being delighted to see Thales, especially when they weren't *expecting* to see him, and he failed, but perhaps he simply lacked sufficient imagination.

"You think all Hacan know one other?" Calred growled. He was lounging in the good chair in Felix's quarters, sipping a glass of clear liquid that could have doubled as engine degreaser and would have probably killed a human. The liquor was distilled from a desert plant native to the Emirates, and Felix kept a bottle on hand for those occasions when he needed a favor from a Hacan. "You're a human – you must know Juan Salvador Tao, right? Are you related?"

Felix sighed. "Don't act so offended. I know your mother did that genealogy project a few years back, and connected up with a bunch of your fifteenth cousins or whatever back in the Emirates. Don't you all share some glorious common ancestor?"

"We're distantly related to the third Quieron, yes. My branch of the family tree is on the disreputable side of the trunk, though. My oldest known direct ancestor once sold a map of the legendary Temple of the Burning Sands to the Mowshir Emirate."

"What's disreputable about that?"

Calred took a sip of his murder fluid. "She also sold it to the Creena clan, and then the governor of Eilaran." Another sip. "Also, the Temple of the Burning Sands doesn't actually exist."

"I begin to see the family resemblance."

Calred snorted. "Yes, fine, it's true. I talk to some of my cousins back in the ancestral homeland occasionally. They like to hear my tales of derring-do."

"No one ever wants to hear the tales of derring-don't," Felix said. "Do you think any of your relatives might have useful contacts for this mission?" The Emirates of Hacan had tentacles – well, claws – in every aspect of galactic trade, including business in the Barony, and Felix was hoping for a crack he could exploit.

Calred stroked his tawny chin. "Hmm. I do have a cousin who works for a consortium in the specialty agricultural sector. She was telling me about something that might prove useful."

"Agriculture? We're trying to break into a space station, not a farm."

"*Specialty* agriculture, I said."

"Ohhhh," Felix said. "You mean drugs."

"In most cases, yes," Calred admitted. "In this case, not quite. Let's just say high-ranking Letnev officials stationed far from the center of the Barony will pay dearly for a taste of home. I'll make some discreet calls, and I should be able to get some information, if you can pay for it."

"Pay? Does family count for nothing?"

"Of course it does," Calred said. "My cousin wouldn't even take *your* call."

Once the *Temerarious* was stripped of its Coalition markings and transponder, and temporarily renamed the *Swift Emergence*, they cruised into Barony space and sent a message to the research station. The response came back immediately: "You're a day early."

"We made up time on Rigel III," Calred said from the captain's chair. Felix was in the first officer's position, Thales was in his new lab, and Tib was... elsewhere. "We won't even charge you extra for expedited delivery."

The Letnev sneer was audible in the reply. "How considerate of you. Approach the cargo bay, and have your manifests ready for examination."

"Don't worry, we know how much you love proper documentation." The channel closed, and Calred raised an eyebrow at Felix. "I'm a natural. I should be captain full-time."

"Good. Then you can deal with Thales."

"I withdraw my request for a promotion."

The cruiser approached the station, an angular collection of dull metal modules connected by gantries and corridors and tethers, which resembled a child's mobile if it were conceived by one of the twisted horrors of the L1Z1X. One of the larger modules was the cargo bay, and Calred guided the ship in to dock.

Once they were settled inside the belly of the station, Cal and Felix trooped down to the cargo bay. They'd rearranged some of the countless crates of supplies that filled the ship for maximum camouflage effect, complete with fake bills of lading and inventory lists. Felix stood beside a stack of crates with a hand terminal and tried to look busy while Calred continued his merchant captain cosplay.

The ship's ramp opened and slid down, revealing the "weather station's" cargo bay. Felix took in the layout in a glance: a cavernous space big enough for five of his ship, with neat stacks of crates and barrels, mostly along the walls. A few robots trundled to and fro, moving cargo around, and there were several cranes, both small mobile ones and larger ones in fixed positions. Stairs on either side of the space led up to a series of catwalks with a guard holding a long rifle stationed where he could see everything below. There were two more guards with sidearms loitering near the doors that led deeper into the station. All three wore shiny black uniforms and full-face masks that resembled stylized skulls with bulging silver eyes. The lower halves of the masks were probably full of filter systems to protect against gas attacks, and those shining eyes would include fancy optics and maybe even automated threat assessment and targeting programs. *That* was a lucky break.

The doors opened, the guards snapped off salutes, and three Barony officials tromped into the bay, one greater bureaucrat and two lesser, all wearing black uniforms with silver accents, all stiff and pale and formal. They mounted the ramp, and the one in the lead looked around at the *Swift Emergence's* hold and sniffed in disgust, at who knows what; just general disgust, probably. "Manifest." He snapped his fingers, but, since he was wearing thick dark gloves, they didn't actually make a snapping sound.

Calred tapped his tablet, sending information to the officer's terminal, then turned and gestured to a stack of crates on a pallet. "Here they are. Do you want our help unloading? There's a modest stevedore fee–"

"Wait." The officer frowned, and the two other officers frowned too, though they couldn't possibly know what they were frowning about. "This is wrong."

"Oh?" Calred said.

"It says here you have ten crates of… sunscreen?"

"Yes, that's right."

"Sunscreen," the official repeated.

"Protects you from the sun, as I understand it," Calred said.

"We're Letnev!" The homeworld of the Barony of Letnev, Arc Prime, famously drifted through the void without orbiting a star. It was a lightless place, and the natives lived in vast underground cities oxygenated by fungal growths and heated by the planet's core.

Calred nodded agreeably. "I thought so. The Letnev are a rather pale people. Very prudent to order sunscreen in bulk."

The lead bureaucrat grimaced. "The station is shielded from the light of the local star. We didn't order any sunscreen. We're expecting a shipment of fungal growth matrix." According to Calred's cousin, the botanist for an agricultural cartel, one of the most treasured delicacies in the Barony was a particular mushroom that grew in the caverns of their dank homeworld. Whenever a sufficient number of Letnev congregated in outer space, they brought that delicacy with them, if they could afford it. The mushrooms were difficult to grow, and thus rare and valuable, in their original environment, but when cultivated artificially in hydroponic gardens, using a proprietary growth medium created in the Hacan Emirates, the mushrooms thrived. (Of course, connoisseurs claimed they could smell and taste the difference between *true* cave mushrooms and those grown elsewhere, but that was connoisseurs for you; the results were certainly close enough to satisfy most Letnev, though.) There was indeed a shipment of the matrix headed to the station on the real cargo ship *Swift Emergence*, which would arrive right on schedule sometime tomorrow. The *Temerarious* didn't have any such thing in its stores, so they'd had to improvise.

Calred peered at his tablet, peered at the officer, looked back at his tablet, looked back at the officer, and then brightened. "Perhaps it's both! Sunscreen *and* fungal growth matrix. Think about it: sunscreen protects things from sunlight. Mushrooms hate sunlight. Go on, give it a try. I bet mushrooms grow all over the stuff."

The Letnev took an aggressive step forward, but stopped at that, since he was, after all, being aggressive at a two-and-a-half-meter-tall bipedal lion. "This is unacceptable. We will not pay for this."

"Listen," Calred said. "Your procurement officer checked the box that says if your actual order is out of stock, we should substitute the closest available product. Looks like that's what we did. It's not my fault. If you weren't willing to accept a substitution, you should have said so."

The argument went on, around and around, with various appeals to various authorities. More bureaucrats appeared with more documentation, and Calred remained unfazed, meeting every outrage with a shrug. Eventually, as planned, he agreed to soften the blow of the lost matrix by providing them with a few extra items drawn from their store of emergency supplies, including food and medication; that mollified the outrage somewhat, but not completely, because Letnev were culturally resistant to being mollified. The crowd dwindled once the pallets were offloaded and moved into the Letnev cargo bay, and the officer in charge said, "All right. Be on your way."

Calred put a huge hand to his broad chest. "Regretfully, I cannot leave yet. My trading company has strict regulations regarding rest for the crew, in order to avoid accidents, as stipulated in our contract."

"What crew?" the office sputtered. "It's just you, that useless human loitering by the crates, and a bunch of semi-autonomous machinery!"

"We are the ones who *operate* said machinery, and it's imperative that we get our rest – especially my human. You know how disagreeable they can be when they don't get enough sleep."

"This is preposterous. First you bring us the wrong cargo, and now you want to take up space in our–"

"Peace, peace," Calred said soothingly. "Understand, these regulations are as much for your protection as our own. Last year a cousin of mine – well, a cousin of a nephew, to be precise, for I know how the Letnev value precision – decided to ignore the safety regulations and leave in his ship without first taking his prescribed period of rest. He hoped to earn a bonus for swift delivery of his remaining cargo, you see. Well, he entered the wrong commands in his navigation system, and – because he'd also skimped on proper safety checks – his ship's protective measures failed. His navigation system thought he was departing from orbit, not from within a space station, and do you know what happened?" Calred brought his hands together and said "boom" very softly. "His ship struck the edge of the launch bay while accelerating at unsafe speeds. The containment field on his engine breached, and the resulting explosion took out half the station. The devastation made the station's orbit unstable, and it promptly decayed and began to plummet into the atmosphere. I heard they got almost half the survivors off the station before–"

"Enough." The officer held up a hand, wincing. He had his terminal in his other hand, and scanned through it. "I understand, and yes, there's a provision in the contract that requires us to honor any mandatory rest breaks, on page one-thousand-seventeen, in a footnote."

"You find the most wonderful things in footnotes, don't you?" Calred's good cheer was as relentless as a desert sun. "Might my first mate and I avail ourselves of your shower facilities, perhaps enjoy your doubtless lavish guest quarters–"

"You are confined to your ship," the officer snapped before turning on his polished black heel and storming away. "Your eight hours start *now*!"

Calred crossed his arms and looked benignly on his departure as the ship's cargo ramp slowly closed. Then he turned and grinned at Felix. "Eight hours. That should be plenty of time, even for you."

"Do you think Tib made it out OK?" Felix said.

Calred made a great show of looking around the cargo hold. "I don't see her here anywhere."

"Ha, ha," Felix said.

CHAPTER 8

"My *human* is resting," Calred said, voice relayed to the comm in Felix's ear. "He's the one who needs the sleep. I, however, grow bored. I happen to have a set of void dice here, though, which could help pass the time." Playing void dice was a Letnev national obsession.

"We're supposed to keep an eye on you, not fraternize," a menacing, machine-altered voice said.

"You could keep a closer eye on me if you were sitting in my cargo hold, at this table, playing void dice. I've never played against Letnev, and I'm curious to see how my abilities stand up against those who invented the game."

"Well…" one of the guards said, but the other snapped, "Stop talking to the trader. Mind your duty."

They'd never expected the guards to let their, well, their guard, down far enough to actually play a game, but the back-and-forth distracted them long enough for Felix to slip out undetected through an emergency access hatch. He began to make his way carefully across the cargo bay. They'd deliberately taken the landing spot closest to the interior wall, but Felix still had an intimidatingly large distance of bare floor to cover, especially with the sniper up above. The ship's tactical systems had carefully plotted out a route that should keep Felix hidden from the overwatch guard's view, but the back of Felix's neck itched anyway; he fully expected a blob of molten metal or charged plasma to obliterate the back of his head as he hurried from one pile of crates to another. A normal guard back home, especially this far into a long and boring shift, would have hacked his helmet display to show entertainment vids or scroll the text of a book to pass the time, and could be relied upon to be distracted and inattentive, but the discipline of the Letnev was as legendary as their lack of humor.

The shimmering overlay in Felix's contact lenses showed him the proper route in blue, a narrow path leading from a pile of crates to the shadow of a crane and so on, and would flash red if he so much as stepped one toe off the path. He went carefully, methodically, knowing sudden movement was more visible than slow. Not for the first time, he envied Tib's ability to fade. He supposed humans had their own unique advantages, too, though just at this moment he couldn't remember what any of them were.

To make up for his lack of natural resources, he had a variety of small and useful items in his pockets, the sort of things favored by Coalition raiders, very few of them legal in the galaxy's more civilized jurisdictions.

He finally ducked behind a stack of barrels marked "protein slurry, grade three," slipping into the narrow space between the supplies and the wall. There was a ventilation grille there, and as he crouched toward it, the screen slid aside. Eyes like lanterns shone from within, and Tib's hand emerged and beckoned before vanishing from sight.

Felix had to slither into the duct on his belly. There were maintenance tunnels in the station meant for people his size, but none with access hatches in the cargo bay, and *these* were never meant for anything bigger than a drone repair unit to enter. Tib fit easily, of course, but Felix had to push himself along mostly with his toes, wriggling more than crawling, following Tib's whispered directions in his comms. After a couple of sharply angled turns, and a distressing head-first slide down at about a thirty-degree angle, they finally emerged into a dim room full of thrumming machinery, furnaces, and air filtration systems.

Felix gasped and wiped sweat from his forehead. He wasn't claustrophobic – he'd grown up slithering through tunnels on a shipyard station, though he'd been smaller then – but it was still a relief to stand up and stretch his limbs. A nearly naked Letnev was propped unconscious in the corner, wrists bound to ankles with zip ties. "You've been busy," Felix said.

"I hope the uniform fits."

Felix put on the guard's clothes. The Letnev ran slightly smaller than humans as a species, but Felix was slim. The shirt was tight across the chest, but not enough so that anyone would notice, and the long black gloves would hide the shortness of the sleeves, just as the tall black boots concealed the shortness of the pants. The full-face mask was the best part, though – Felix couldn't pass for Letnev at a glance, but with his face hidden, he could move anonymously through the station.

"What's the lay of the land?" he asked. Tib had spent the past hour doing reconnaissance and acquiring Felix's disguise.

"I think I know where Shelma is being held," Tib said. "Unless there's more than one Hylar on board. She's not in a cell, though – she's in a laboratory or something."

"Or something?"

"All I know is, there are a lot of screens, a lot of terminals, and bits of disassembled machinery all around. She went to get something to eat and she was escorted by a guard, and later she had to return to what I assume are her quarters, and a guard took her there, too."

"She must be a dangerous character."

"She also summoned guards on three occasions to fetch her equipment from other rooms and, once, to remove a spider from a corner of the ceiling. The poor man had to stand on a wobbly table, and she told him not to kill it, just to take it to the gardens, so it could eat pests. She treated the guards more like servants than jailers."

"Maybe she's just valuable rather than dangerous, then," Felix said. "The Letnev must be forcing her to continue the research she did with Thales. Can we get her out?"

"No one seemed to pay attention to her at all, so long as there was a guard walking beside her. You look like a guard. I think we can work out a cunning plan based on those conditions."

"Getting her to the ship and off the station is the tricky part," Felix said. "That's not something a guard would do, and the Letnev ask questions with lethal force. I'd rather get out of here without being murdered. Can we bring her back through the tunnels?"

Tib shook her head. "She's one of the fully aquatic sub-species of Hylar – her tank is set in an exo-suit, and she scurries around on a lot of little legs and manipulator arms. Her rig isn't huge – she can fit through ordinary doors – but she's not crawling through any tunnels."

"Damn," Felix said. "We need to leave here quietly."

"Not a problem for me," Tib said. "I just don't know what to do about you and the squid."

"Maybe," Felix said, "we don't need to be quiet. Maybe we just need to be *less* noisy than something else."

They had to peel open the guard's eyelid and put his head half in the mask to unlock the biometric locks on the operating system, but once they did that Felix had access to a wealth of information about the station. Maps, a navigation system, and even a personnel roster – which notably didn't mention Shelma, but did include a distressing number of guards, a dizzying array of bureaucrats, a few scientists, assistant under-directors, assistant directors, and just the one director. He took particular note of the security provisions, which were extensive, but mainly focused on preventing outside threats – once he was inside, assuming he wasn't challenged, he should be able to move fairly freely.

Tib faded out of sight and went off to handle her part of the operation, while Felix stepped out of the machine room and followed the glowing path to the lab where Shelma was working. He passed a couple of other masked guards, who ignored him completely, and he did the same in return, though he fine-tuned his own stiff walk and ramrod posture to better match theirs. The station was a joyless sort of place, all gray metal and white tile and dim recessed lighting. He turned a corner, entering the corridor that should have led him to the research wing, and almost collided with a dark-haired woman, dressed in the requisite amount of gleaming black, who stood talking to a pair of masked guards. She stopped mid-sentence, looked at him, and frowned.

Felix's heads-up display helpfully identified her: this was Severyne Joelle

Dampierre, technically an assistant director, functionally the head of security. Felix automatically noted that she was pretty, in a severe, hair-pulled-back-too-tightly way – not that it mattered. It wouldn't have mattered even if they'd met in some difficult-to-imagine social setting, instead of during a jailbreak. He'd dated Letnev who'd grown up in the Coalition, but the ones from the Barony were by all accounts immune to charm, fun, or entertainment. The old joke was, "Why don't Letnev have sex standing up? Because someone might think they're dancing."

"Where are you going?" she asked, sharp and peremptory.

Well, why not? Unnecessary lies only got you in trouble. "To the Hylar's lab, Director Dampierre."

"That's AD Dampierre," she snapped. "You're on her detail, are you? What does Shelma want *now*?"

"She says one of the tables is wobbly, AD Dampierre. She wants me to level it."

"Someone should level *her*." Dampierre scowled again. "Well? Carry on, don't dawdle in the corridors."

Felix snapped off a salute and went on his way. That had gone better than it could have. As he walked, he scrolled up the available information on AD Dampierre. She'd only served the mandatory minimum of Letnev military service, so she wasn't a professional soldier – maybe her job running station security had been bestowed for political rather than practical reasons, or maybe she was a terrifying clandestine operative whose training was so secret it didn't show up in her public-facing files. Ideally, he'd never have to find out.

Felix's helmet had the necessary authentications to make the next four sealed doors unlock for him, and to open the elevator that led to Shelma's floor. He exited the elevator and approached the blinking icon in his display that marked the door to the lab. A guard stood stiffly before it, arms at his sides. "Is the Hylar in there?" Felix asked, the suit modulating his voice to an amusingly menacing degree.

"Where else would she be during working hours?" the guard replied.

"Good point," Felix said, and punched her in the throat. He had on a pair of rings beneath his gloves that discharged a single-burst electric shock sufficient to paralyze the body and scramble the brain, and the guard slid down the door. Felix's HUD obligingly showed him the location of a storage closet, so he dragged the guard inside, found a roll of tape, and wrapped it around and around the masked head, to serve as a blindfold and to make it hard to remove said mask, which he thought was rather funny. Then he bound the guard's ankles to her wrists and turned to the door.

He stopped, turned back, looked down at the guard, sighed, knelt, and laboriously unpicked and unwound all the tape from the mask. He undid the clasps and removed her mask, then put it on a high shelf, because otherwise when the guard woke up, she would have called for help on the mask's integrated comms. "There's such a thing as being *too* clever, Felix," he muttered.

His display assured him there were no other guards in the immediate vicinity, so he went into the lab, the door sliding silently shut behind him. "Shelma?" he said.

The Hylar was enclosed in a transparent globe full of pale fluid, the sphere set into an exoskeletal body with scores of many-jointed limbs, some for walking, others for manipulating objects, still others for specialized purposes he couldn't imagine. Shelma herself was small, head shaped a bit like a lemon, trailing fronds of tentacles and feelers that wriggled into the controls of the exo-suit. Her large, dark eyes gazed at him. Her skin, a pale green at first, flushed through oranges and reds. Felix knew the Hylar communicated among themselves with color changes, but he didn't understand what these meant.

Apparently, the colors didn't indicate a warm welcome. "What is it? You're interrupting my work." Her voice was querulous and sounded like a human with nasal congestion. Despite her assertion, her manipulator arms continued to solder components into the guts of a torpedo-shaped object resting on the work table.

"I've come to rescue you," he said.

"Oh, by the bubbling crevice," she said, becoming an even deeper red. "Are you from the Federation of Sol? The last time you reached out, I told you, I have no interest in going back. As far as I'm concerned, our relationship ended when our lab was destroyed." She waved a cluster of manipulators at him. "Shoo."

Felix blinked behind his mask. "Ah, no. I'm not from the Federation. I represent other parties interested in your research. I was under the impression that you were a prisoner here?" A red light began to blink in his peripheral vision.

"Prisoner or employee? I suppose it's a fine distinction." She turned away from him, back to her apparatus. "If I'd refused to help the Barony, they probably would have imprisoned me, and if I said tomorrow that I'd grown weary of my project and wanted to retire to the hot springs of Wun-Escha, I doubt they'd be supportive. But I agreed to work for the Barony, and they have honored the terms of my agreement. Who told you I was a prisoner?"

Don't tell her you're working with me, Thales said. *I want to surprise her*, Thales said.

"Phillip Thales did," Felix said.

She didn't turn around, but the color drained out of her. "He's still alive, then. And still a liar."

"A liar," Felix repeated. "Do you mean he can't do what he claims?" If Thales was lying about his invention, the Table wouldn't mind if Felix stranded him on an asteroid somewhere. It would be the end of glory, but it would also be the end of being sent to infiltrate Barony research stations on false pretenses.

"Did he claim he can share credit, display empathy, or listen to anyone else's ideas without shouting at them? In that case, no, he can't." Sparks cascaded up from the device, but apparently that was supposed to happen, because she kept working. "If he claimed he can create wormholes, though, that part's true. He's the only person in the galaxy who's come close to creating that technology – except for the Creuss, if you believe the rumors, and myself, of course. Thales has a brilliant scientific mind. It's a shame the rest of his mind is a burning pile of garbage."

"Ah. I haven't known him long, but I don't disagree."

"Why did he send you here? Our partnership ended… dramatically."

"He says you're essential to completing his prototype."

"Does he? That's actually flattering. Last time I saw him, he said I wasn't qualified to clean fish tanks. He may have reached the limits of his abilities, though. He was always better at theory than application, and I'm making great progress on a working prototype. It's–" She abruptly went silent. Felix almost felt bad for her. She was a scientist, not a spy, but she was doubtless feeling bad about spilling so much to the representative of some unknown force.

"Is *that* the working prototype?" Felix pointed at the cylinder.

The pause was just a moment too long. "No. No, that's just, ah… an air purifier. The air here, I'm told, is very impure. Smells of mushrooms. I'm helping."

"My ship has a terrible odor. We think something died in the vents. I'd better take the purifier with me." He drew his sidearm, but didn't point it. "You should probably come with me, too, and show me how to work it."

"And see Thales again? I'd really rather not. We didn't part on good terms."

"I'm afraid I must insist."

"Insist all you like. I hit my panic button four minutes ago. Guards should be descending here en masse any moment."

"I noticed. I'm hooked into the station's security system." He tapped his mask. "'En masse' might be overstating things. There are two guards coming, and they're having some trouble with the elevator. That's fine. We're going out another way anyway. I hope you like service tunnels." Tib couldn't compromise the station security systems from the maintenance area she'd secretly accessed, but she could break a few things, which was why those guards were currently pushing buttons futilely in an elevator stopped between floors.

"I won't go anywhere with you."

Shelma was faced with an armed man, professed agent of an unknown organization sent to rescue – make that "abduct" her – and she was still stubbornly acting like she was in charge. Felix began to see why she and Thales had worked together.

"I'm still insisting. Things are going to get very loud and chaotic on this station, and even though you don't want to be rescued, I've gone too far to stop now." He stepped toward her, and her manipulator arms stretched out defensively. They probably could have soldered, laser-etched, or sliced him up, but they didn't stop him from lobbing one of the objects from his pocket at her – a little thing, the size and shape of a plum – where it struck her glass dome with a splat, sticking to the side.

"That's a very small, inward-pointing explosive, coated in epoxy resin. It's now firmly attached to your helmet. If you attempt to remove the device, it will explode. If I don't disarm it in half an hour, it will explode. The solvent I need to remove it…" He made a show of patting his pockets. "I seem to have left it on my ship. We should go there, don't you think?" He hadn't planned to use the little bomb for *this*, and in fact it wouldn't explode at all unless he triggered it deliberately, but he was a Mentak Coalition officer: they were expected to improvise.

"Severyne won't let you take me," she said. "I'm very valuable."

"Severyne is going to be busy soon," Felix said, and his tactical display lit up with emergency alerts as the first of the bombs Tib had set up in the station went off.

CHAPTER 9

At first, Severyne didn't take Shelma's latest push of the panic button serious-ly. In the ten months since Severyne had taken over security for this station, she'd learned that the Hylar scientist didn't share the same definition of the word "emergency" the rest of the universe did. The first time the panic button went off, Severyne responded personally, charging into her quarters followed by six elite soldiers. Shelma had looked up from a tablet and said, mildly, "The lights in this room are too dim. Please get me brighter ones."

Severyne had dismissed the soldiers and given Shelma a stern talking-to about the proper channels for maintenance requests. "I tried those channels," Shelma replied. "They said they would add my request to the non-essential queue. That is not acceptable. I thought perhaps this button might bring a more rapid response, and I was correct."

"That button is for moments when your life is in danger, or when you have reason to believe this station is under attack, or that our security has been compromised."

"I believe that's what *you* intended the button for," Shelma said. "But I'm an engineer first and foremost. I'm interested in what things actually do, not merely what they were designed for."

After that, the Hylar used the panic button indiscriminately, for the most triv-ial things, until, in desperation, Severyne finally gave her a dedicated comms channel and a small rotating group of guards who could take care of her endless insignificant needs – the lights too dim, the liquid in her tank an imperfect pH, her tools not calibrated perfectly to her liking, her quarters not the right tem-perature (even though she could control the temperature of her tank!), and a thousand other trivial details. After that, her use of the panic button trailed off, but didn't stop entirely, especially when she was in a bad mood or frustrated by setbacks in her work. She enjoyed spreading the annoyance around.

So when the panic button went off this time, Severyne sighed and dispatched a pair of guards to look in on the scientist, then went back to working on the duty rosters. Lestrande had shown up for his last shift with a tiny blot of protein slurry on his elbow, and such slovenliness must be punished, so she decided to assign him to be one of Shelma's babysitters for the week, and put a note about conduct unbecoming in his file. He'd probably never be promoted again with a mark like that against him, but he should have thought of that before he ate like a slough-beast.

One of the guards she'd dispatched reached out over comms to say there was a malfunction in the elevator. A tingle of foreboding started up at the back of Severyne's mind. She was a creature of order who loved routine, and disruptions gave her an almost visceral twinge of disgust. The panic button was one disruption, albeit a common one. The elevator breaking down was a second. And there was a third – the merchant ship, the *Swift Emergence*, was still idling in their cargo bay. There'd been some fuss about the manifests, the ship carrying the wrong cargo, that she'd picked up on the assistant director-level comms channel – Melisante Couray, the AD in charge of procurement, had been complaining about the mix-up. *Was* it a mix-up?

Officially, this was just a research facility studying weather patterns, but Severyne knew anyone who looked at them closely would realize there was something more serious going on. Their delivery schedule, for example, would reveal they seemed to be feeding and supplying more staff than such a station would normally require. Had someone gotten curious, and sent spies to see what they were doing here? Or, had someone already *figured out* what they were doing here, and come to stop them, or steal their research – and their star researcher? They were only in this station at all because the Federation of Sol had discovered Shelma's previous lab and sent her a message trying to tempt her back to their service. Had they tracked her down again, and decided to take a more direct approach?

The deck beneath Severyne's feet vibrated. That didn't set off another tingle of foreboding. That set off an *earthquake*. The screens hovering before her eyes, projected from her contact lenses, blared red: there was hull damage in one of the hydroponic gardens, though apparently no injuries. She called the assistant director of resource management and barked "Report!"

"There was an explosion – that's all I know so far. It could have been caused by a build-up of static electricity, discharging and igniting a hydrogen tank–"

Another boom rocked the room, this one much closer, and another section of the station diagram hovering before Severyne's eyes turned red and started flashing. This time, an explosion had torn apart the lab at the top of the station's central hub, where the weather monitoring equipment was located. There were no injuries there, either, because no one actually *worked* in that section; the lab and all the equipment were purely for show, to make their cover story plausible.

"My new theory is enemy action," the voice on Severyne's comms said. She cut the contact without a word and called the leaders of all her guard divisions, on-duty and otherwise: "Scan the ship for more explosives, and report anything unusual immediately." An array of affirmatives cascaded into her ears. "Second squad, go check on Shelma. I *know* the elevator is out – go through the maintenance tunnels!"

She gritted her teeth as she watched the blinking dots of her guards spread out through the ship diagram. Could this be internal sabotage? The Barony was full of competing political currents, and some factions thought this station – dedicated to the work of a Hylar who was somewhere between a defector and a prisoner – was a misallocation of resources, either because they had a natural distrust of other species, and/or because they thought the idea of generating wormholes on demand was a ridiculous fantasy. Usually attacks from within the Barony were rather more subtle than this. You didn't bomb a station to shut it down; you snarled the station in red tape and did your best to encourage small, deniable problems that added up into cumulative disasters. When the heating or plumbing broke, you made sure the work orders got lost, or that the repair crew showed up with incompatible parts, and contrived to make it look like incompetence on the part of the station head. Or you introduced errors into the supply chain, to deny the crew their necessities and their comforts – That thought reminded her of the cargo ship – the one that had shown up a day early, and with the wrong supplies. Severyne had ascribed that error to either a genuine mistake, or petty political maneuvering… but what if the ship was more than that? What if the enemy had come from *outside?*

She pulled up her security override panel and began to lock down portions of the station, simultaneously calling her guards in the cargo bay. "Don't let that ship go anywhere–" she began, and then the hangar bay where *her* fighters and support ships were docked exploded.

Felix crouched beside Shelma's exo-suit as boots pounded in the corridor around the corner. The guards were headed to the Hylar's lab, and if they'd been a little faster, they would have run head-on into Felix. Fortunately, he was beyond their entry point, but adding some distance was a good idea.

"Come on," he muttered, adjusting the straps of the duffel over his shoulder. The bag contained various data-sticks, which didn't weigh much, and Shelma's torpedo-shaped device, which weighed so much he assumed it was made of lead-wrapped osmium. He hurried along the narrow tunnel, past bundled cables and humming pipes, with Shelma clattering along ahead of him.

They reached a corridor that led to the cargo bay doors – the ones with guards on the other side – and he paused to call his ship on their private comm channel. "Calred, I'm on my way back with our guest."

"Are we being noisy or quiet?" Calred said.

"I'm hoping for the latter, but let's be prepared for the former." He glanced at Shelma, who waited with poor grace, her many-jointed legs delicately bent. Her skin was bright red; she looked like a walking danger indicator. "Don't say anything during this next part." She glared at him, which he supposed counted as agreement.

The doors to the cargo bay slid open as they approached. He could see his ship, barely fifty meters away, but you could die a lot of times in a lot of ways in the course of fifty meters. The guards on the door turned to face him, guns held up.

Plan A was just to brazen things out. "The bomber took out our hangar!" he said, voice modulated with menace. "AD Dampierre sent me to commandeer that civilian vessel and get the Hylar to safety." Felix thought it was a plausible cover story – he was pretty proud of it – so he was disappointed when they kept pointing their guns at him. He promptly stepped behind the Hylar, hoping they wouldn't risk shooting through her to get to him.

"Drop your weapon!" the first guard said.

"You drop yours!" Felix said.

"Right now!" the second guard shouted.

"Guess we're going loud, then," Felix said.

The guards dropped, with barely a second between the falls. Felix looked past them to Calred, who stood on the ramp of the *Temerarious*, holding his favorite precision plasma rifle. He'd placed second in the all-Coalition long-range target shooting competition the year before, and wore the silver pin he'd earned on the collar of his uniform with pride. Taking out two men from fifty meters was nothing to him; Felix was surprised he hadn't worn a blindfold or something to make it more interesting.

Seeing Calred poised with his weapon reminded Felix of the sniper, up there on overwatch. Calred was shielded from fire by the roof of his own ship, and Felix and Shelma were partially protected because they were still in the corridor, and hadn't yet passed into the cargo bay. A sufficiently eager sniper could hit the legs of her exo-suit. If her suit was disabled, that was it – Felix couldn't manhandle hundreds of kilograms of metal and liquid and Hylar five meters, let alone fifty.

Felix crouched down, imagining the long barrel pointed right at him, attempting to calculate the angles, creeping forward to get a glimpse of the sniper, knowing if he could *see*, he could *be* seen – The sniper was poised, pointing his gun right at Felix, and he flung himself back, trying to hide behind Shelma again. No shot rang out, no plasma seared the deck plates or sheared off Shelma's legs – nothing happened at all.

Felix edged forward again in time to see the sniper's rifle fall from the catwalk, bounce off the top of the *Temerarious*, and fall onto the deck with a clatter. The sniper appeared to be choking himself, hands clasped to his throat as he stumbled jerkily to and fro, bouncing off the railings of the catwalk. The sniper's mask came loose and went flying and falling to the deck, flung by an unseen hand.

"Let's get on the ship, shall we?" Felix prodded the back of Shelma's tank, making the liquid inside slosh.

"Is that guard having some sort of seizure?" Shelma scuttled toward the ship's ramp. "Did you disperse a nerve agent in here? Their masks can filter most of the common ones." Her voice held nothing but professional interest. Scientists were so strange.

"Oh, no, he's just being strangled by an invisible woman. It's a disconcerting sensation, as I know from experience." The sniper finally stopped struggling and slumped to the catwalk floor, as if gently lowered.

Felix had instructed Tib to set bombs with the aim of crippling pursuit capabilities with minimal casualties, and he'd hoped to get off the station without killing anyone, but that was hopes for you. Sometimes he thought they existed just to be dashed.

Shelma went up the ramp, delicate legs spidering her along, and paused in front of Calred.

"Greetings," Calred said. "Welcome to my humble merchant vessel."

"Get this bomb off me, captain," Shelma demanded.

"Hey, *I'm* the captain," Felix said, turning to look back at the cargo bay doors. Trouble could come bursting through them at any moment.

"He seems much more commanding than you do," Shelma said.

"You are keen and perceptive," Calred said. "Once we're underway, we'll get that bomb off you." He handed Felix the precision rifle, a device of exquisite craftsmanship that was largely wasted on the captain. Felix had placed in the bottom hundred in the long gun competition – he was more adept with sidearms, at least – but even he could hit a personsized target at this distance. Calred escorted Shelma deeper into the ship, while Felix watched the doors and waited for Tib to shimmer into visibility. Once she got on board, they could close the ramp and get out of here – "You aren't where you're supposed to be," said a voice in his ear. Felix flinched – he'd muted the station's internal comm channels, since all the yelling and blaring of alarms was too distracting – but, of course, certain people would have override codes. "Which means you aren't *who* you're supposed to be – you're an outside agitator in a stolen helmet. Did the Federation send you?"

"Assistant Director Dampierre," Felix said. "I'm sorry for all the fuss we caused." He paused. "The guard I took this helmet from is fine, if you were wondering."

"He won't be once I get my hands on him," she snapped. "Neither will you."

"I'm afraid our meeting will have to wait for another time. We're about to be on our way, and we won't bother you again."

"You won't bother *anyone* ever again."

Felix had a sudden stab of insight, dropped the rifle, and undid the clasps on his helmet. He flung the mask away just as it sparked with electricity and thumped, smoking, on the deck. He picked up the rifle with trembling arms, heart pounding in his chest. Of *course* the Letnev would have corrective and coercive measures built into their standard-issue equipment. He wondered if that electrical discharge would have killed him, or merely incapacitated him. He kicked the helmet as hard as he could, sending it spinning off the ship and into the cargo bay. For all he knew, it was packed with explosives too.

Tib materialized, dancing out of the way before the helmet could hit her. "Good idea. They could track you with that thing."

Among other things. "My thought exactly." The ramp receded as she raced up it. The ship's cargo door started to lower just as a crowd of guards poured through the hangar doors, taking up an attack formation with drilled precision, the ones in front kneeling to clear the field of fire for the back rank. Tib and Felix flung themselves behind piles of crates as blobs of superheated metal and streaks of energy struck around them. When the cargo bay was sealed, Felix shouted, "Calred, get us out of here!"

"I'd be happy to," he drawled. "Once someone opens the door."

"Oh, right," Tib said, and pressed a button on the chunky bracelet on her right wrist.

Tib's bombs blew open the station's closed bay doors with a dull *whump*, and she and Felix were pressed against the stack of crates as the ship accelerated out through the hole she'd made. They rose, shakily, and Felix went around to the other side of their makeshift barricade. The fire from the guards had shattered the crates and their contents, and bits of jellied eel oozed out onto the floor. "It's going to smell like fish in here forever," he lamented.

"Better than smelling like our dead corpses," Tib said.

"Oh, the day is young," Felix said. "What kind of pursuit are we looking at?"

"I blew up their cruisers and shuttles and fighters, but I couldn't shut down their comms," Tib said. "They won't be chasing us from the station, but they'll call people who *can* chase us, soon enough."

"Do we have enough of a head start to lose them?" Felix said.

"I'm good at disappearing," Tib said. "I think we'll be OK, but we probably shouldn't come back this way anytime soon."

Felix grinned. "What a shame. It was such a nice place to visit. You did excellent work back there, Tib."

She grinned back. "This is why I went to raider school. Breaching charges work just as well when planted on the inside of a vessel as they do from the outside. Of course, we used up all our heavy explosives back there, so you'll have to come up with more subtle plans next time."

Felix picked up the duffel and gave it a pat. "I think we're out of the black ops business. We got the expert, and we got her data and her prototype, so Thales should be good to go. Let's organize the happy reunion."

CHAPTER 10

Severyne was having a bad day. Her superiors were not pleased – the station director had shouted at her until she went hoarse, then paused to take a throat lozenge, then screamed some more. "I won't let your disaster bring me down, Dampierre," she concluded. "I can contain this situation, and blame the damage and casualties on accidents and executions for insubordination, but we have to get Shelma *back* before my superiors get suspicious."

"Of course, director." Severyne stood stiffly at attention, as she had been doing for the past hour. Her calves ached, and her feet hurt, but she would never let her discomfort show.

The director was in her chair, perfectly at ease, frowning at something parsecs away. "Do you think the Federation is behind this attack?"

"Perhaps, director." Severyne had reviewed the security footage from Shelma's lab. The kidnapper was masked, of course, and he hadn't confirmed he was from Sol, but he appeared human, and he'd claimed he was working with Thales. The Federation had attempted to co-opt Shelma before, and it made sense that if they were after her, they'd gone after her old partner, too. The Barony had been interested in Thales too, of course, but they hadn't been able to track down his location. "We aren't sure."

"What *are* we sure of?" The director's voice was soft, and that seemed more dangerous, after all the shouting.

"Their ship, the *Swift Emergence,* was ostensibly a Hacan merchant vessel, but the real *Swift Emergence* is a day away. The attackers spoofed their transponder. The captain of the *real Swift Emergence* insists he has no knowledge of an imposter, and that someone must have stolen their schedule and data, but we can't rule out collaboration–"

"I've already canceled their contracts," the director snapped. "Don't worry about any of that. Worry about finding Shelma and getting her back. What do you know that can help with *that*?"

Precious little, but Severyne wasn't about to admit it. "If they're going to Federation space, they're doubtless on their way to the Kellkillian wormhole. We can send interceptors to–" An alert filled her vision – something serious, if it overrode director-level privacy settings; the boss didn't like being interrupted when she was dressing someone down. Severyne scanned the message and suppressed a gasp. "Forgive me, director, there's a visitor to the station.

She claims… director, she says she has information about the people who took Shelma."

"Then go and talk to her," the director said. "Find out what she knows, even if you have to squeeze it out of her with a vise. *Get me my squid back*, Severyne. If I go down for this, you'll go down with me, but it will be *so* much worse for you. I have friends, influence, connections, and all *you'll* have is me for an enemy. I still might end up assistant head of operations on some horrible tropical island somewhere in the sun, but I'll use those same connections to make sure you rot in a Barony cell."

"I understand," Severyne said.

The director flicked her hand. "Dismissed. Don't come back until you have good news."

Severyne turned and walked calmly out of the director's office.

Once the door shut behind her, she broke into a sprint.

"Amina Azad." The Barony head of security was a little younger than Azad, her hair pulled back in a severe bun, her uniform perfect even though portions of her station were still literally on fire. "An unemployed Federation navy veteran. What possible use can you be to me?"

"I was part of a small team sent to capture Phillip Thales," Azad said. "He was hiding out on some backwater in Mentak Coalition space. Unfortunately, we ran afoul of a raider fleet, and now the Coalition has Thales." The Letnev's expression didn't change, and Azad felt a grudging respect for her self-control – the news of Coalition involvement had to be a surprise, but the woman didn't show it. "It occurred to me that the Coalition might want to complete the set and get their hands on Shelma, too. We knew where she was being held – my employers looked at liberating her ourselves, actually, but we decided Thales was a better target."

"Your employers. The Federation of Sol?"

"Sorry, I couldn't say. Confidentiality, you know. Let's just say, interested parties. Tell me about the attack. I might know who your enemies are."

The woman grudgingly gave an account of what she knew. It was a decently slick operation, Amina thought, heavy on the pirate shit, but it wouldn't have worked if *she'd* been running security. "Play me a recording of the guy's voice?" she asked. "Let me confirm a hunch."

The speakers crackled, and a male voice said, "I'm afraid our meeting will have to wait for another time. We're about to be on our way, and we won't bother you again."

Azad nodded. "That's captain Felix Duval, of the Mentak Coalition, though I'm sure they'd claim he's on vacation or he's been discharged or whatever. He's got a pet Yssaril, she's probably the one who snuck around and planted the bombs. Don't feel too bad – she even got the drop on *me*. Natural advantages, sure, but the Coalition must have trained her to be sneaky too, and I bet her suit has countermeasures to make her even harder to detect."

"Never mind the Yssaril," she said. "Duval." The word was a curse in her mouth. "He will pay for what he's done."

"I've got a bill to present to him, too." Azad considered. The Letnev was smart, but she was also desperate, the right lie, deployed at the right moment, could work wonders. "Anyway, I have a tracking device on Thales–"

That got the Letnev's attention. "You can track them?"

The hook was set. "Not with any precision from this distance, but if I can get even a weak ping, that will give us a direction, and once we're in the same system as their ship, I can narrow things down."

The woman frowned, though her default expression was *already* a frown, so really it just deepened. "We had trackers on Shelma, too, in her containment suit, but they were deactivated."

"The tracker I put on Thales is hidden rather deeper. What I'm saying is, we put it in his body. Implanted while he was sedated, so he doesn't know he's on a leash." That had been the plan, anyway. "The device should be undetectable to their bug sweepers, too – it's the latest tech."

The woman looked at Azad for a long moment. "You will give me the device you use to track him." She extended her hand.

"Please. I *am* the tracking device." Azad tapped her temple. "It's integrated technology, connected to all my other tactical systems, left over from my days doing special jobs in the navy. If you try to break open my head to get the tracking system out, all the tech will fuse itself into slag. No good for my brain, but no good for you, either. It's a standard countermeasure, prevents enemies from extracting Federation technology."

"Sol technology?" She turned up her nose. "Your species just crawled out of the gravity well yesterday. You're still basically drawing on cave walls and poking each other with pointy sticks."

Ha, she was livelier than she looked. Azad smiled. "I seem to recall we kicked your pale Barony asses a few times."

The Letnev sniffed. "You had superior numbers, not superior technology. No one denies your people can field a large force. I blame your prolific and unrestrained breeding."

"It's a big galaxy, lady. Somebody's gotta fill it up. Might as well be us. What do you have against unrestrained breeding, anyway? You have to pass the time somehow."

"You sicken me," the woman said. "You humans career around the galaxy, disrupting the balance of power, causing chaos, and demonstrating a reckless disregard for the traditions and values of the elder species of the galactic community."

"When you put it that way," Azad said, "you make us sound pretty badass."

The woman pressed her fingertips to her temples as if massaging away a headache, and for a moment she looked younger, less severe, and almost vulnerable. Then she looked up, and that glimpse of the woman underneath the uniform was gone – her eyes were once again ice floes adrift in a frozen sea. "I am not opposed to a temporary strategic alliance in order to further our mutual interests."

Azad cackled. "You mean, we can use each other, as long as we both get something out of it?"

"That is *literally* what I said. My name is Severyne Joelle Dampierre. I am the head of security for this facility."

"Were you head of security yesterday, too, or are you replacing the person who oversaw this monumental fuck-up?"

Severyne bared her teeth. "Officially, there hasn't *been* a fuck-up. Not yet. If I can get Shelma back soon, no one ever has to know what happened here."

Azad nodded. "I can do that dance too. I won't be welcome back home if I arrive empty-handed, but if I can recover Thales, all will be forgiven, hearts and flowers, big parade, backslaps all around. Except none of that actually, because officially I don't exist, but there are other rewards, not least of all my continuing status as an alive person. I have a tracking device, and I've studied Thales like you studied for the boot-polishing final, so I can make some educated guesses about where he's headed next. What do *you* have to offer this partnership?"

"The key to this cell, for one thing," Severyne said.

Azad shrugged. "I escaped from a Mentak Coalition pirate flagship. I can usually get out of cells on my own. You haven't impressed me with your ability to stop jailbreaks so far."

"We'd be more careful with you than we were with Shelma. She was more of a highstatus guest, with various privileges. You will be denied those privileges."

"Yes, fine, you showed me the stick, and it's a big scary stick, I'm very impressed. Let's move on to the carrot."

Severyne wrinkled her nose. "I can offer more tangible benefits. Access to a fast gunship, and weapons, and the assistance of my own personal security force."

"The security force likewise hasn't impressed me, but I do like gunships. I came here on a freighter, and it only has enough firepower to nudge the odd asteroid out of the way. So let's say we set out together, and chase down our fugitives, and I get Thales, and you get Shelma, and then we dissolve our partnership?"

"Those terms are acceptable to me," Severyne said.

Azad shook her chains. "Take these off?"

"I have a sidearm," the Letnev said.

"How nice for you. Guns are a great comfort when you're in a room with me, I'm told."

Severyne looked off into space, interacting with some heads-up display Azad couldn't see, and a moment later her shackles unlocked themselves and slithered back into recesses in the table. "There. Partner, not prisoner."

Azad spat into her palm and reached across the table. "Shake on it to seal the deal?"

Severyne stared at her hand with undisguised horror. "Is this some horrible human custom? I will never touch your hand, let alone your hand when it is covered in – in *saliva*."

Azad shrugged, wiping her hand off on the table. "Oh well. I can settle for a verbal agreement." She could tell that needling Severyne was going to be fun. The Letnev was cute when she got horrified. You had to find entertainment where you could.

Severyne cleared her plan with the director, which wasn't very difficult, as the director snapped, "Don't tell me what you're doing, just do it, and you'd better succeed or I'll see you rot forever in your own filth." Severyne tuned her out after that, turning her mind toward logistics. She was good at logistics.

Severyne's own authorizations were sufficient to requisition a gunship, though it took a bit of creative paperwork to account for why she needed to bring a ship from the planet instead of using one from the station hangar, since said hangar was officially still intact. The station director would eventually fake some equipment malfunction, ideally blamed on a mistake by an outside contractor, to account for the damaged and destroyed parts of the station, but, for now, Severyne had to work within the constraints of their cover. You didn't rise this high in the Letnev service without learning how to convince the system to do what needed doing, though, so she got her ship.

Officially, Severyne's mission was to investigate reports of pirate activity in the system, and to neutralize any threat they discovered. Under that aegis, she could stay out for several days, or even a week, without triggering an oversight check from the accountability office. Such flexibility was rare in the Barony, but their station was a high-security covert facility, and their rules were consequently relaxed, at least by Letnev standards.

Her ship arrived: the *Grim Countenance*, a heavily armed cruiser previously assigned to protect the thoroughly unremarkable and unthreatened planet below, and the best ship available in the system. The displaced captain had taken over the next-best ship, and that displaced captain the next after that, and so on; somewhere at the bottom would be a captain left with no ship at all, but that was life in a hierarchy. If you didn't like it at the bottom, you should have worked harder to get to the top.

The *Grim Countenance* had a small crew, now under Severyne's command, consisting of engineering and pilot and navigation personnel, but the rest of the complement that tromped aboard when the ship docked was composed of her personal, hand-picked guards, the best security people on the station, or at least the best ones that weren't dead after Duval's cowardly sneak attack. Casualties has been surprisingly low – that would help with the cover-up – but she had lost her best sniper.

"I'm good with a rifle," Azad said beside her, and Severyne realized, to her horror, that she'd muttered some portion of her thoughts aloud. That was a shocking break in her customary discipline.

She covered it with hauteur. "Good by human standards, or Letnev ones?"

"The Barony was banned from the last round of pan-galactic games on account of being fascists, so it's not like I have a lot of data about your peak marksmanship, but the human who won the bronze in target shooting? I broke her record at the last interservice rifle competition, so it's kinda like I took the silver, at least."

Severyne grunted and refused to be impressed. They walked along the ship's corridors, toward the bridge. "If you're so good with a rifle, why didn't you compete in the games yourself?"

"You've heard of the L1Z1X? Sometimes they take a break from fighting with the Nekro to cause trouble for actual people, so I was busy shooting cyborgs on a colony world way out in the eastern spiral arm. Sadly, there were no impartial judges on hand to score my shooting, and they weren't ideal competition conditions, since some of the targets were shooting back. There were twelve hostiles, though, and I took out eleven with headshots. I think that gives you points for style."

"Eleven of twelve?" Severyne said. "Imperfect. My sniper would have hit the whole dozen." The doors to the bridge slid open before them, and they passed through side-by-side.

"Oh, I hit the last one," Azad said. "I just shot him in the stomach. He killed one of my squad-mates, so he didn't deserve a clean and easy death. I wasn't even sure if those cybernetic types could feel pain, but then he started hollering and wailing and carrying on when I perforated his guts, so I guess they do."

How distasteful. One's enemies should be crushed, of course, and it was sometimes useful to cause gruesome injuries as an example to others, but as the last killed, that victim had provided no such instructional value. "Do you enjoy inflicting pain?"

"Huh." Azad appeared to take the question seriously. She followed Severyne, standing beside the captain's chair when Severyne seated herself and surveyed the bridge, glaring at the crew going about their preparations. "Nobody's asked me that since my psych evaluation when I first joined the navy. I don't enjoy hurting people on its own merits, no – not like some people do. The thrill of combat, for me, is about pushing yourself to new heights of excellence. Plus, you never feel more alive than you do when death is right there beside you. But, I will admit, I'm sort of a grudge-holder. I find spite and vengeance highly motivating, and yeah, I do like to hurt people who've hurt me. Does that make me a terrible person?"

"I am sure you are a terrible person for many other reasons as well."

Azad grinned. She had a scar on her cheek that made her look quite rakish when she smiled, and it annoyed Severyne, because the mark could have easily been removed with a simple cosmetic surgery, which meant Azad *wanted* to look that way, that she knew it made her look dangerous and, and a bit *alluring* – She shook herself. Despite superficial physical similarities, the woman wasn't even the same *species* as her.

"What about you?" Azad said. "Do you have a sadistic streak? I'd like to know, since I'm likely to annoy you occasionally, just being who I am."

"Pain is a tool. If it is the proper tool, necessary to achieve the desired outcome, then I wield it as readily as any other."

"We're going to get along really well, Severyne."

"We are not."

"See, you say that, but I sense this spark between us. Talking to you is thrilling the same way being in combat is. We're going to push each other toward new heights of excellence. Is there a shooting range on this ship?"

"That was an abrupt transition," Severyne said. "There is a holographic training simulator, yes."

"Eh, a virtual range can't compete with the feel of real rounds hitting real targets, but it's good enough. I'll teach you to shoot."

"I am fully qualified for my rank," she said frostily.

"Sure, but fundamentally, you're a supervisor, yeah? An *officer*."

"You say that like it's a bad thing."

Azad seesawed her hand in the air. "It's a different thing. I don't deny being an officer requires a certain set of skills. But this Duval is a pirate. Sometimes you have to shoot pirates, and being good enough to get a passing score in officer training might not be good enough for *that*. What do you say? I'm a resource, Severyne. Exploit me."

"We'll see," Severyne conceded. "If we have time. Speaking of time – I think it's time you told me where we're going, don't you?" She gestured to the crew, all at their stations, awaiting orders.

"How about I just give you a heading first. I'll tell you the destination once we've got some distance between us and my cell. I don't want you tempted to leave without me."

"I'm already tempted to do *that*."

"Maybe I can tempt you to do other things too, Sev."

CHAPTER 11

Felix sat down in the corner of the cabin they'd assigned Shelma. The quarters had been full of pallets of sunscreen earlier; their ruse on the Letnev station had also conveniently cleared out some space for the Hylar to move in. "How are you settling in?"

The front of her exo-suit was turned away from him, and she didn't bother to move so she could look at him when she answered. "I no longer have an explosive connected to my tank, so circumstances are improving."

"I was never going to blow a hole your suit, Doctor Shelma. I just needed to motivate you. I'd like to apologize for the, ah, whole situation. Thales gave us the impression you were a prisoner, and that we were on a rescue mission."

"You must not have known Phillip for very long if you believed something he said."

"Our relationship has been brief, but eventful. If you don't mind, I was hoping you could fill me in a little bit about him. We're usually pretty good at digging up background on people, but we haven't found much about him in our database, even with his genetic profile in hand."

"You're probably looking in the wrong places," Shelma said. "I can't imagine why I'd want to help my kidnappers, though."

Felix nodded, not that she could see it. "The thing is, you're here now. We can't call up the Barony and say, 'Oops, sorry, we thought it was a jailbreak, not an abduction – you can have your scientist back.'"

"I suppose not." The exo-suit turned, and she floated in the tank, gazing at him. "The Letnev are not famously forgiving."

"That's my understanding," Felix said. "I want you to know, my employers are willing to provide you and Thales with whatever resources you need to complete your work." That was close enough to the truth, anyway.

"From the Federation to the Barony to your mysterious employers. I'm quite popular these days. You're with the Mentak Coalition, aren't you? I'm assuming, based on the unusual makeup of your crew."

"I should probably deny it, but I'm sure Thales will tell you soon enough. Yes, we're Coalition. Can I ask how you ended up working for the Letnev?"

"They were the least bad option available to me at the time."

"Who were your *other* options? The doomsday cult on Tendil Two? That swarm of homicidal machines out in Nekro space? Some kind of large, angry, carnivorous monster?"

Her tank bubbled as she moved her tentacles in what Felix interpreted as a shrug. "The Letnev aren't that bad. They're a bit unimaginative, but they respect science and technology, and they take research and development seriously. The Coalition is prejudiced against the Letnev because the Barony is such a disciplined culture, while your lot enjoys playing the rogue."

"Who's playing?"

The Hylar burbled a laugh. "You really don't know much about Thales at all, do you?"

"Almost nothing. We only want him because the Federation of Sol was willing to send a black ops team to snatch him, so that means he's probably worth having. Do you agree?"

"Mmm. I hate to say it, because his arrogance is so vast, but Phillip's breakthroughs are legitimately galaxy-changing. With him – and me – in hand, the Coalition has now cornered the market on cutting-edge wormhole technology. You will soon have capabilities completely unheard of. The universe is a chaotic and strange place, isn't it? Your faction could become the most powerful in the galaxy, entirely because your ship happened to be in the right place at the right time. Though you could lose that advantage just as easily, when the Barony comes for me. Or the Federation of Sol comes for Thales. Or the Creuss come for us all."

Felix blinked. "Why would the Creuss come for us?" Thales had mentioned the Creuss had wormhole tech already, but Shelma's concern sounded more immediate.

"You have no *idea* what you've gotten into, do you?" Shelma said.

"Tell me," Felix said.

"Thales isn't showing up in your database searches because he was originally a citizen of Jol-Nar, and Hylar systems are not as easy to infiltrate and penetrate as those of other factions. The twin planets are populated mainly by Hylar, of course, but there are a smattering of other species present – the Universities aren't as cosmopolitan as the Coalition, but we value knowledge and learning above all else, and Phillip is the last son of a long line of scholars and researchers. He was still called Phillip back then, but he went by his real surname, Caruthers, not Thales."

Ah, the man's real last name – that would have been more helpful before, since they were getting the dirty details about the man's life now, but still, Felix made a mental note.

"Phillip lived with his parents in a house grown of coral, partially above the surface, partially submerged. Never quite in or out – that's the story of his life. Phillip demonstrated brilliance from an early age. We play a strategy game called Tides, one of the most sophisticated games in the galaxy, and Phillip is the only human who has ever attained master rank – which he did when he was only thirteen. On the strength of that showing, and his test scores, he earned a place in the physics department in our great city, Wun-Escha. He spent four years there, never breaking the surface, and the entire time he wore protective gear that allowed him to dwell at those depths underwater – he refused physical adaptations that would have allowed him to live beneath the waves more comfortably. Some considered that refusal eccentric. Others thought he was a bigot, a human supremacist in the midst of the Hylar, but those who got to know him well realized he had contempt for humans, too. He had contempt for everyone who wasn't him."

Felix nodded. "That much hasn't changed."

"I was the one exception to that contempt, for a while. We met in an advanced lab, working on improvements to starship engines. He watched me work for a while, and then said, 'You're not a complete idiot like the rest of them.'

"'You charmer,' I said. 'No wonder you're the most popular boy in school.' He laughed and said he didn't need to be popular: 'I'm smart, and that means I'll be rich, and once I'm rich, I'll be as popular as I want.' I asked him how he expected to get rich in academia, which seemed to be the path we were both on.

"He said 'Bah'– actually said the word, like a human in a historical sim. He told me he was *human*, in case I hadn't noticed: 'I'll never become Headmaster, and if you aren't the one running the Universities, someone *else* will always tell you what to do.' He said he'd had enough of taking orders from inferiors when he was a child. His parents weren't as smart as he was, but somehow they got to decide what was best for him? That outraged Phillip. He fled their house as soon as he could, only to find he'd traded one bunch of authorities for another. Now he had to answer to professors, advisors, committee heads, all of them standing in his way."

"They were also the ones teaching him, supporting him, giving him opportunities, weren't they?" Felix said.

Shelma's skin tinged softly blue; was that amusement? "Phillip has a tendency to discount the importance of advantages that don't come wholly from within himself. He certainly discounted the value of my help often enough. He told me he didn't intend to suffer under the yoke of oppression and so forth forever. His plan was to do his own research, invent something the galaxy would clamor for, sell it for an emperor's ransom, and then, finally, take charge of his own fate. I told him that sounded good, but until he became master of the galaxy, maybe he could help me with the energy-flow problem we were working on? Back in the early days you could still poke fun at him, a little, if you were careful."

Felix smirked. "Oh, I don't know, I poke fun at him pretty often now."

"Yes, but he probably wants to murder you for it, captain." Shelma undulated in her tank, her large eyes looking beyond Felix, perhaps into the past. "We got along, strangely enough. I could keep up with him intellectually, which he appreciated, and when he began to rant and rave, I tuned him out – he was my own personal white noise generator. We also complemented one another as research partners. He was always better at the theoretical side of things, while I'm an engineer at heart – oh, I've made conceptual breakthroughs too, but I'm happiest when I'm tinkering, adjusting, and making the practical applications actually work, a process that is seldom smooth or easy. Those kinds of challenges thrill me. For Phillip, the only reason to move beyond the theoretical is because it's easier to sell a product than the conceptual outline for one." That blue tinge again. "Maybe that's why he needs me now. He might have hit the limit of what he can build alone."

Maybe we can do without Thales entirely, Felix thought.

Shelma gestured aft. "I'm fairly sure the engine powering this vessel is based on one Phillip and I created during our partnership. Our improvements are still the state of the art. We both received offers to work for the state shipyard, running their propulsion department as co-heads, but Phillip refused, because anything we created there would be property of the Universities, just like the design for this engine is. We received a generous bonus for the engine's development, but Phillip railed about the injustice of having his work 'stolen' – if he'd received even one tenth of one percent of the price of every unit sold, after all, he'd be wealthy enough to buy a small moon. He wanted to do *independent* work, he said."

"What would he even do with a moon?" Felix said. "He's barely emerged from the lab we gave him. He lived in a shack on Cobbler's Knob. He seems to spend most of his time inside his head. Vast wealth would be wasted on him."

Shelma said, "It's true, he's a scientific ascetic in his way. You need to understand, the money is just insulation. A way to put himself above caring about the needs or opinions of anyone else. With enough money, he'll never again have to put himself in someone else's power. I was happy enough with the career advancement our work offered me, so I went to work for the shipyards, while Phillip took his bonus and set up his own lab. He found investors, too, though I'm sure it galled him to have even that much accountability, and he continued to work on propulsion systems, this time with the promise of a share in the profits... but he didn't manage as well on his own. He made little incremental improvements, enough to keep his investors from dropping him, but nothing seafloor-shaking. The gossip among my colleagues was that Phillip was one of those prodigies who peaks early and then burns out. Such people often become fringe figures, railing against an unfair system and espousing horrible political views, which everyone agreed would be a natural fit for Phillip. I wasn't so sure – I thought he was just *bored*. Small improvements didn't interest him. He was always about revolutionary change. Phillip abruptly shut his lab a few years after it opened, having failed to become rich, and he largely withdrew from society."

"If only he'd stayed withdrawn," Felix murmured.

Shelma ignored him. "After about a decade – during which I thrived at the propulsion lab, I might add, and *did* make significant improvements – he suddenly published a slew of papers, a few in respectable venues, but others just released onto the net, presumably because they couldn't pass peer review. He was attempting to achieve the ultimate aim of conceptual physics, a theory of everything that could reconcile the contradictions between general relativity and quantum theory, and he was publishing his intermediate steps. Some of the papers *were* promising, but others were either flawed, or inadequately explained. Phillip never had much patience for making things clear to those he considered his intellectual inferiors, which, as you might have gathered, is everyone. He would occasionally show up at a conference, usually to stand up in the audience and decry some other scientist he considered ill-informed or misguided."

"He really does make friends wherever he goes, doesn't he?"

"We had a drink once at one of those conferences. I asked a couple of clarifying questions about his latest paper. He told me being a cog in the University machine had made my mind 'smaller than ever.' I didn't see him again for a while. After that flurry of activity, he went dark again for several more years. His parents died, he locked himself away in their coral house, and no one knew what he was doing, besides spending his meager inheritance on living expenses. I kept an ear out for news of him, because of our old relationship, and I heard he'd sold the house and used the proceeds to buy a second-hand spaceship capable of long-range travel. No one knew where he was going. No one was especially sorry to see him go. Years passed, and we all assumed he'd settled somewhere, or met with misadventure."

Thales was a cause of misadventures, not the victim of them, Felix thought. "He came back, though."

"Two years ago," Shelma said. "He just showed up at my office. I was running the whole engineering department at the shipyard by then. It was a good position, plenty of perks, but it had been ages since I'd so much as laid a pseudopod on a wrench, and I often looked around and wondered how it was I'd come to *manage* engineers instead of being one. That's why I was amenable to his offer. That, and the fact that he was almost humble. He said, 'Shelma, I need your help.'

"He *needed* my help! During our collaborations, he'd only grudgingly accepted my presence, calling me 'an adequate sounding board' and 'more socially acceptable than talking to myself' and 'a competent grease-monkey.' He found the latter endearment quite funny, since he was the primate, not me. I found it less amusing, but, as I said, I was good at tuning out his more objectionable qualities. I was flattered despite myself at his approach, and asked him what he needed. 'I've been studying wormholes,' he told me.

"I wasn't surprised. He'd always been interested in those. He thought understanding their nature was essential to understanding the universe. We can use wormholes to traverse vast distances in space, but we don't really understand how they function. There are various competing and mutually incompatible theories, none of which Phillip found satisfactory. If he could figure out how wormholes worked, he always said, *really* worked, that would provide a key insight and maybe even unlock the theory of everything. I asked how a theory of everything was going to make him rich – or had he changed his mind about the value of academic accolades these days? Formulating such a theory would be good for a permanently endowed reefdom in the theoretical physics division, even for a human."

The thought of Thales shaping young minds made Felix shudder.

"Phillip said I was being ridiculous. Didn't I see it? A natural side effect of a total understanding of wormholes would be the ability to *create* them. I did my best not to laugh at him. I just said, 'That's impossible.' Back then, I thought the rumors that the Creuss could create wormholes were just stories – part of the legend of the galaxy's greatest bogeymen. The Creuss are energy beings, after all, with a strange relationship to matter, so I thought there were other explanations for their ability to show up in places where you wouldn't expect them. But Phillip told me he'd gone out and studied the Creuss, met some of them, observed others, and that he'd seen them do it – open a wormhole where no wormhole existed before. Once he knew for sure it could be done, he devoted himself to figuring out *how*. He told me he'd nearly cracked it. He was just… having trouble with the practical side. 'You need your old grease-monkey back,' I said. He actually looked ashamed! He told me he'd always meant it as a term of endearment – "'I was a lot cruder and crasser in the old days', he explained. More sure of himself and his own importance. He'd come to realize he couldn't do it all on his own. He flattered me, too – said, 'I've tried to work with other engineers, but they lack your vision and your understanding of the deeper science.' He told me he'd secured funding and had a top-notch lab. He looked around my office, and I saw a flash of that old contempt. 'Could I really be happy here?' he asked, 'overseeing new strategic initiatives, when I could be tentacles-deep in the guts of a machine that would alter our fundamental understanding of space-time and make us rich'?"

"It's a pretty good pitch," Felix admitted.

"And I was tempted, captain! But I didn't trust an apologetic Phillip. I asked who was funding him. He told me it was a wealthy human in the Federation of Sol. I asked what his patron planned to do with the technology, if we managed to create it, and Phillip said, 'He's in shipping. I imagine he's going to demolish his competition.'"

"Oh, sure," Felix said. "And the inventor of the plasma rifle was just interested in using it to kill flies. No obvious military applications at all."

Shelma went bluish again. "I wasn't an academic, captain, not really. I worked in the shipyards, which means I worked with the military, which means I fully grasped the implications of the work Phillip proposed. Even if he *was* funded by some civilian businessperson, I knew the tech would eventually end up in the hands of the military, and then it could be used against *my* people. I told Phillip I was interested. It took a bit of organizing, but I took a leave of absence from the shipyard and went with him to his lab, on a remote moon, and we got to work. I mostly went to… assess him. I thought maybe Phillip's reach was exceeding his grasp again. It wouldn't be the first time. But if he *was* close to perfecting practical wormhole technology, I wanted to be there when he did it. Not because I was intrigued by the technical challenges and the opportunity to work on truly transformative science, though that didn't hurt – but because if anyone had that kind of tech, I wanted to make sure my people had it too… or had it first. I could watch his work, contribute enough to keep him happy, but hold him back from creating a working prototype. When the time came, I could give the technology to my people, who have a long track record of using new technology responsibly. Phillip doesn't understand patriotism, or loyalty, to individuals, or governments, or species. He doesn't comprehend any bond that isn't based on self-interest, which is disturbing, but it also makes him predictable. He wouldn't expect me to join his team in order to slow down or limit his research, because he assumed I wanted wealth and glory too."

"An impressive declaration of patriotism and loyalty to your homeworld," Felix said. "Which makes me wonder how the hell you ended up on a Barony of Letnev station?"

Shelma was quiet for a long moment. "Because of what happened after the Creuss found us, captain."

CHAPTER 12

Felix, Calred, and Tib sat together on the bridge, all deep in their own thoughts. The viewscreens displayed darkness and a smattering of distant stars. They were hurtling through space on a trajectory generated by the ship's computer specifically to stymie any extrapolations the Letnev might have made about their route or destination. Evasive maneuvers were easier because they didn't know their actual destination yet. Thales said he had to consult with Shelma before he explained their next steps, and Shelma said she'd been through a traumatic experience and needed to rest before she talked to Thales about anything.

"The Ghosts of Creuss," Calred said, breaking the silence. "I have a cousin who saw one, once – the Ghost was just strolling through a bazaar out in the Ilanan system, dressed in that weirdly ornamental armor they wear. All the vendors and customers ran away, because even the ones who didn't know it was Creuss knew it was dangerous… or wrong, somehow. The Creuss didn't seem to notice everyone flee. A street kid watched it through a crack in a wall, and he said the Creuss went to a stall and touched a bunch of the rugs. How can they feel anything when they don't have bodies, and their hands are armored? He said the Creuss picked up one of the rugs and threw it over its shoulder. It left something sparkly on the counter of the stall – a jewel that glowed with its own inner light. Some idea of payment, everyone figured. The merchant had the jewel mounted under glass and proudly displayed it, called himself 'rug-merchant to the Creuss.'"

"Was that good for business, or bad?" Tib asked.

"My cousin didn't say. She was more fixated on the fact that two weeks later, the rug merchant was dead from a previously unknown form of cancer, and half the customers who'd visited the stall needed extreme oncological treatments. The gem didn't trigger any radiation sensors, but there was *something* wrong with it – something that caused the flesh to corrupt itself. The rug merchant's family buried the gem in a hole deep in the desert, in a casket lined with lead. I imagine it's still there. The opposite of a buried treasure."

"Ghost stories," Felix said. "Lots of people have them. Usually second- or third-hand, though. You can't take them too seriously."

Tib said, "I heard one that was first-hand, supposedly. Felix, do you remember that ambassador from the Yin Brotherhood, Errin, the one we met at academy graduation?"

Felix nodded. The Yin always disturbed him. They were clones, genetically identical, and religious zealots – everything about them was antithetical to the individualism at the core of the Mentak Coalition. "I do."

"I was talking to him at the reception that night, and he claimed he'd been part of a delegation the Yin sent to the Shaleri Passage. They were hoping to found an embassy there, if you can believe it, and open some kind of formal trade relations with the Creuss. The Yin are masters of the biological sciences – what could they possibly offer a species that doesn't even have bodies?"

"Forget that," Felix said. "What could they hope to get in return?"

"A cure for Greyfire," Calred said. "They're always in the market for *that*. They've exposed embryos to every known form of radiation, hoping the consequences would modify the genes in some useful way. Maybe they thought bathing their unborn in the light of an inside-out star in the Passage was worth a try."

"Errin didn't get into all that," Tib said. "He just told me the Creuss welcomed them and met them on a space station – a replica of a station from Yin space, apparently, probably identical down to the last rivet, but completely new, like it had just been built the day before, specifically for that meeting. Errin said it still smelled of fresh welds and hot polymers. The Yin were disconcerted, understandably, but the Creuss were polite, very formal, spoke their language perfectly, and offered them food that could have been served on any Yin outpost – but Errin did say the food was all exactly the same temperature, just this side of cold, like it had been fabricated or extruded instead of cooked. The Yin tried to talk business, and the Creuss asked questions and made statements, but the stuff the Ghosts said didn't seem to have any connection to what the Brotherhood said – just random utterances. The ambassador remembered a few of the questions the Creuss asked – they said, 'Why is a frog?' and, 'What is the strategic importance of the color you call blue?' and 'Your armor is soft. Should we make soft armor too?' Pretty baffling, but the Yin attempted to answer as best they could. As far as the ambassador could tell, their answers didn't make any impression at all – there were never any follow-ups, never any sense of understanding."

"Sounds a lot like talking to Thales," Felix muttered.

Tib went on. "The ambassador's theory was that the Creuss weren't communicating at all – he thought they just had random phrase generators built into their armor, to create the illusion of conversation. After a while, the Creuss all turned and left, right in the middle of their nonsense dialogue. The ambassador and the rest of the delegation sat there for a while, waiting for the Ghosts to come back, but then the station started to disintegrate around them – the artificial gravity failed, rivets started to pop out, plates started to separate on the interior walls. No alarms went off, and there were no warnings, nothing you'd get on a normal station when the infrastructure started to fail. The Brotherhood delegation rushed back to their ship and managed to get on board before the whole station turned into a debris cloud."

"The station exploded?" Felix said.

"No, it just came apart, the ambassador said. Not violently. More like all its joins and welds failed at once. They thought maybe it was a threat, but the Creuss didn't make any further contact at all, friendly or hostile or otherwise, so the Yin withdrew beyond the Passage. That was the last time the Brotherhood sent a delegation to the Ghosts, as far as Errin knew. He said they counted themselves lucky to get out alive."

"We're drifting away from the current disaster," Calred said. "Why don't you tell us Shelma's ghost story, captain? What did *she* see?"

Felix stared at the darkness between the stars. "She didn't see the Ghost personally. Only Thales did. She got to the lab after the Ghost was gone, but she saw the consequences. Their whole lab was destroyed. Everything, from equipment to furniture, was reduced to fragments so fine they might as well have been sand. She said you couldn't tell what had been glass and what had been metal without examining the debris with a mass spectrometer. The lab building was totally unscathed, the walls unmarked, the floor not even scuffed, but everything else was just multicolored sand. The data they'd stored offsite drove computers insane when they tried to access it – that's the word she used, 'insane.' Their terminals wouldn't respond to commands in the expected ways, and after a few minutes the data just overwrote itself with nonsense."

"Why is a frog?" Calred said softly.

"Thales didn't give her a lot of details about the Creuss he met," Felix said. "He told Shelma a Ghost appeared in the lab, looked around, and said, 'You must not fracture the void.' Before Thales could reply, he blacked out. When he woke up, everything was demolished, and the Ghost was gone. Shelma showed up moments later."

"What did they do?" Tib asked.

"This is Thales we're talking about," Felix said. "They had a big fight. Shelma said the visit from the Ghost should be considered a stern cease-and-desist notification from a patent holder concerned about infringement on proprietary technology."

"Ha," Calred said. "I like the way she thinks."

"Thales said their lab getting destroyed was just a temporary setback, and that they'd just have to be more careful about security next time. They hadn't hidden their research, really – they sent updates to the people funding them, occasionally spoke to other experts about thorny problems. They never came out and said 'we're building wormholes,' but someone paying attention might have pieced it together. Thales told Shelma they should just implement new security measures and carry on with their work under assumed names – that's when he stopped being Caruthers and became Thales."

"What work, though?" Tib said. "I thought all their research was turned into sand?"

"It will shock you to learn Thales is eccentric," Felix said. "He likes hard copies. He printed things out, because he liked to spread his files around him on the floor or pin the papers on the walls. Having the data arrayed around him in physical space allows him to better comprehend the whole and visualize new connections. That was one of the reasons he left the Universities of Jol-Nar, apparently– it's hard to sort piles of paper underwater."

"What a strange man," Calred said. "That explains the file boxes we recovered from the human ship. I wondered why he had pounds of dead trees when a couple of data sticks would do."

"Thales still had copies of their research, then?" Tib said.

"Most of it, yeah, tucked away under his bed. Their first model prototype for what Shelma calls the 'activation engine,' was reduced to sand, but they still had schematics."

"Did Shelma go along with his plan?" Tib asked.

"She did not," Felix said. "She told him to go to hell, gave her regrets to their Federation investors, and went back home to run the shipyard. Except when she got to work, her office was just like the lab. Everything was reduced to sand, drifting in the currents. She went to her house, and it was the same. That's when she got scared. She thought the Creuss were following her, making sure she knew she'd crossed a line. She moved, but things in her life kept glitching. The University would lose her records – she said at one point the system insisted she was deceased, and another time it listed her as a minor in need of state guardianship. She did her best to clear up the errors, but so much of life in an advanced society is mediated by technology." Felix shook his head. "She went to the Headmaster and told him about everything that happened, and asked for help and protection. The Headmaster refused and told her that, as far as he could tell from looking up her records, she was not a citizen of the Universities of Jol-Nar, and she should remove herself from Hylar space."

Tib whistled. "That's shitty."

"Huh," Calred said. "I ran a search when you gave me the Caruthers name, and still didn't turn up much beyond the bare facts of his birth and citizenship. Maybe the Ghosts manipulated his records too."

"There were people who knew Shelma personally, though," Tib pointed out. "She ran the shipyard for years. Does she think the Creuss erased memories or something?"

"She didn't go that far," Felix said. "She thought the Headmaster knew more about the Creuss than she did – that all the higher-ups do – and decided it was better to cut Shelma off than risk annoying the Ghosts."

"Maybe the people who run things have a better understanding of how terrified they should be of the Creuss," Cal said.

Felix nodded. "Shelma said when she told the Headmaster the Creuss had taken action against her right there, on Nar, the Headmaster basically banished her."

"But the Letnev gave her a new home," Tib said. "*They* aren't afraid of Ghosts, are they?"

"They won't admit they are, anyway," Felix said. "The Letnev think they're better than everyone else, including the Ghosts, who don't even have *bodies*. Shelma didn't particularly want to work for the Barony, but they reached out and offered her a place, and protection, and security."

"How did Thales know where to find Shelma, anyway?" Calred said. "He indicated he'd heard about her imprisonment through some kind of scientist whisper network, but now we know nobody talks to him, and if there's one thing the Barony is good at, it's secrecy."

"That's where Shelma made a tactical error," Felix said. "She reached out to Thales through a back channel he'd set up in case she changed her mind about joining him. She told him about the offer of protection she'd gotten from the Barony, to see if he'd join her. He told her he was confident in his ability to protect himself, thanks. But he learned enough from the communication to track her down."

"Intelligent and unscrupulous is a terrible combination," Calred said. "I know they're founding virtues of the Coalition, but still."

"Shelma told me one other thing," Felix went on "She said she was stringing the Letnev along, pretending to make progress on the activation engine, but secretly ensuring they'd never have a working prototype. She didn't want to risk another visit from the Creuss."

"Do you think we have the Ghosts on our ass?" Calred asked.

"It's been more than a year since Shelma joined the Barony," Felix said. "Longer than that since their lab was destroyed. Maybe the Ghosts lost track of them in the meantime. Maybe they got distracted. Maybe it was only ever one Ghost, with some weird obsession, and they've moved on to a different form of entertainment. They're Ghosts. We don't understand why they do anything, so how can I predict what they'll do now?"

"Felix," Tib said. "*Do you think we have the Ghosts on our ass?*"

Felix sighed. "I'm definitely afraid we do."

"I had an interesting conversation with Shelma today." Felix perched on the edge of a work table in the rooms Thales had taken over for his lab.

"That squid does love to hear herself bubble on. Did she tell you all my deep dark secrets?" Thales poked at a tangle of wires with a screwdriver. He hadn't shaved or showered in some time, and his company was unpleasant even when he wasn't smelly and disheveled. Felix wondered if Thales was merely oblivious to matters of hygiene, or if he was trying to create a personal forcefield of foulness.

"More pathetic than deep and dark, really," Felix said. "She made you sound like a sad outcast who never lived up to his early promise."

"I'm still upright and breathing, captain. I have plenty of time to live up to plenty of things. And at least I *showed* early promise."

"She told me about the Creuss, Thales."

He stopped poking at the device, slowly lowered the screwdriver, then turned to face Felix, his face blank. "Did she?" His voice was carefully neutral.

"Is it true? Did you actually see one of the Ghosts, face to face?"

Thales scowled. "Ghosts! What an idiotic name. The Creuss are energy beings – sapient entities composed of coherent light. They don't *have* faces. No biological creature has ever seen a Creuss in its true form. Their bodies aren't stable outside the twisted physics that exist within the Shaleri Passage anomaly. The Creuss I met was wearing armor, like they always do when they interact with meat-creatures like us. The armor is usually humanoid in shape, but there's no reason it should be. Maybe they're mocking us. The one I met had a helmet like a mantis head, decorated with ornamental knotwork. It wasn't as big or imposing as you might think – it was slim, lithe, and the armor moved as smoothly as flesh. The Creuss have done amazing things with materials science, which is interesting, since as energy beings–"

"Thales, I'm more interested in the fact that the Ghosts of Creuss *destroyed your lab.*"

"Yes!" He balled his hands into fists and shook them in the air. "That's the proof, captain! I was *close*! I never told Shelma this, but before the Creuss came, I was beginning to worry – what if their wormhole technology could *only* be replicated in the Shaleri Passage? There are bizarre space-time anomalies there, the same sort of anomalies that allow stable wormholes to exist, but on both a grander and more intricate scale. In the Shaleri Passage there are dark places, folds, dips, pinpricks, funnels, corners you can see around – corners that can see around *you*. Places where light misbehaves and entropy spontaneously reverses itself. I visited the Passage in my travels, and came out alive, which makes me part of a small and select group. *That's* where the Creuss do their science, under those bizarre conditions, and I thought – perhaps something about that Shaleri Passage allows their tech to work. Maybe you can only open wormholes from there, or with a machine *constructed* there, or with energies drawn from that place?" He grinned. "But then the Creuss came, threatened me, and destroyed my lab. There's no reason they'd do that, unless I was on the verge of a breakthrough. Their intervention was proof I was on the right track!"

"Shelma says the Ghosts might be coming after us, Thales."

"Oh, nonsense." Thales waved his hand like he was shooing away flies. "Shelma just frets. The Creuss think they scared us off. If they were still worried about us, they wouldn't have stopped at one act of vandalism."

"The Creuss did pursue Shelma, Thales. They followed her all the way back home and ruined her life."

"Paranoid ravings. If anything happened to her at all, the Barony probably did it, to scare her into joining them. The Creuss never bothered me in Cobbler's Knob."

Maybe that's because Shelma was the one making the real breakthroughs, Felix thought.

"If you're scared of the Creuss," Thales went on, "I have a simple solution: we just have to build a working prototype. Once we have wormhole technology, the Creuss won't have any reason to hurt us – it'll be too late to stop us then. The genie, as they say, will be out of the bottle."

"You're assuming the Ghosts will respond logically–"

"Go tell your boss you're afraid of Ghosts, then," Thales snapped. "Well? No? Then stop this pointless whingeing. I need to talk to Shelma. Surely she's rested by now?"

Felix wanted to say a lot of things, but as much as he hated to admit it, Thales was right: there was no point. The Coalition wasn't going to rescind Felix's orders because of rumors about the Creuss. The sooner he finished this mission, the sooner he could stop worrying about Ghosts. "I'll check on her," Felix said.

CHAPTER 13

Felix didn't sit when he visited Shelma's quarters this time. He stood with his back against her closed door, looking up at the ceiling, as if lost in thought. "It occurs to me, and I'm just thinking out loud here, but, if you're willing to bring your skills to the Coalition… could we do without Thales? My superiors are only interested in him because he claims he can generate wormholes for us. If you can do the same thing…"

Shelma changed color, her body flushing to a deep orange. Felix had picked up that red coloration meant "angry" or at least "annoyed," but the fine points of Hylar body language were still outside his skillset. "In the realm of engineering, I can do anything Phillip can do, better. I admit he's brilliant, and I never would have created his conceptual and theoretical framework, but that framework has been built. I know how to implement his theory. At this point, he needs me to continue – I don't need him."

"My only concern is, you'll do to us what you did to the Barony. String us along without making real progress."

"I understand your worry, but don't see what I could do to assuage it, even if I were motivated to do so. I've been honest with you, which is more than Phillip ever was. At this point, I think it's inevitable that wormhole technology will be developed. Phillip was right – once people know it *can* be done, they'll figure out how to do it. At least, this way, I can try to guide the process and protect my people. I'll need a promise, in writing, from your highest authority, that this technology won't be used for acts of aggression against Jol-Nar or its allies."

The idea that such a document would hold up if the political situation shifted the wrong way was touchingly naive, or maybe she was just trying to make herself feel better and tell herself she'd done her best. "That sort of thing is rather above my pay grade, but I can contact my superiors."

"Do that. If you can agree to my terms, then, yes. You can lock Phillip in a cell while I get on with the work. Just don't set him free. His mind is a weapon, and he holds grudges."

"His mind is a sewer I'm sick of swimming around in." Felix left her quarters and went to call his boss.

"Thales is banging on Shelma's door," Calred said over the comms.

Felix swore. He was still bouncing his signal through the numerous layers of encryption and obfuscation necessary to safely contact Jhuri. "Can you send a drone to drag him off?"

"She opened the door. They're talking. Should I intervene?"

As long as Shelma didn't say, "Ha ha, they're firing you and hiring me," what was the harm in letting them talk, really? Surely Shelma knew him well enough to avoid antagonizing him unnecessarily. Just then the connection clicked in, and Jhuri's face filled the air over Felix's desk.

"Just keep watch, and if they start to argue, break them up," Felix said.

"I assume you aren't talking to me," Jhuri said.

"Sorry, sir." Felix closed the ship channel. "I have an issue I can't resolve without exceeding my authority." He explained, without getting into specifics that needed to stay deniable, that they'd "rescued" the "prisoner" – and that she was requesting certain assurances before she'd consent to work with the Coalition. He told Jhuri about the Ghosts, too – both the visit to the wormhole lab, and the stories Tib and Calred had shared.

"Tell this Shelma whatever she needs to hear," Jhuri said. "Tib Pelta can forge whatever documents are necessary."

Felix winced. "We can't work with her in good faith?"

"She's an unwilling defector from the Barony, and by joining the Barony she already betrayed her homeworld. So, no. I'd say good faith seems rather inadvisable. If it's any consolation, we're on friendly terms with the Hylar, so it's possible you'll inadvertently tell her the truth."

"Ah. Right." Felix didn't like it, but he understood it. "But what about the Ghosts?"

"Oh, what's that thing you humans do, when you go spend the night in the woods for recreation?"

"Er, have outdoor sex, sir?"

"No, captain. I was thinking of campfire stories. I've heard variations of that disassembled space station story half a dozen times – sometimes the ambassadors are Yin, but sometimes they're Naalu, and sometimes they're *us*. As for the merchant and his deadly jewel, if you question Calred, I think you'll find he heard it from a cousin's cousin's friend, and that curiously there's no actual planet, let alone city or quarter, specified in the story. They're legends, Felix, and I suspect Thales is just taking advantage of those legends for his own purposes. He probably screwed up an experiment and destroyed his own lab and blamed it on the Ghosts. He hasn't been a paragon of honesty so far."

"That's true, sir, but–"

"But what?"

But I am afraid of Ghosts, Felix thought. Which wasn't something he could say to his superior. "Nothing, sir. How do you feel about us sidelining Thales in favor of Shelma?"

"Get us working wormhole tech, captain, and no one will care how you did it. Assign your personnel however you see fit. But keep Thales around. Ideally, don't let him *know* he's been sidelined. You may still need him. Shelma wouldn't be the first defector to overstate her own value."

"Yes, sir." Felix had known, deep down, that getting rid of Thales completely was unlikely, but without hope, what did you have?

He shut down the communication and answered a pulsing priority call from Calred. "What is it?"

"It's Shelma," Calred said. "She's having a seizure or something."

They didn't have a ship's doctor – the ship *was* the doctor, with an automated medical suite and a database filled with the data necessary to treat a variety of injuries and illnesses for all the species that lived in the Mentak Coalition, even the rare ones like the odd Ember of Muaat, male Naalu, unhived Sardak N'orr, or renegade Yin.

By the time they wrestled Shelma's clearly malfunctioning exo-suit tank into the sick bay, though, it was too late – she floated lifeless in her sustaining fluid like a specimen in a jar in a medical museum.

Felix punched a wall, hurting his knuckle, then turned and pointed his finger at Calred. "What did Thales do to her?"

Calred frowned, then pulled up security footage and sent it to the nearest screen. "Thales went to her door," he said, narrating what Felix could see for himself. "She opened the door. He stood there talking to her for a while. She didn't invite him in. After a couple of minutes, he left."

"What did they say?"

Calred fiddled with his gauntlet, and the video started over again, this time with audio. "Are you excited to work together again?" Thales said.

"You know I find the work interesting. I still have the same reservations I did last time, but the work itself seems inevitable, and the Coalition is no more objectionable than the Barony was."

"Just remember, Shelma, you're working for *me*. I'm still the lead on this project."

"Ha." Her tank bubbled. "I always let you think that, didn't I?"

They didn't have a clear angle on Thales's face, but Felix could sense his scowl. "Shelma–"

"I'm tired, Phillip. Can we do this later?"

"You know what has to happen next, Shelma. You know what we need. I saw your files. I saw the *absence* in your files. You came to the same conclusion I did."

"I don't know what you mean."

Thales reached out, touching her above one of her suit's manipulator arms – like a friendly hand on the shoulder, except nothing like that at all. "Yes, you do. You tried to obscure the problem, to hide it from the Letnev, but it's a glaring hole in your otherwise thorough breakdown of the engineering problems. I'm talking about the *power source*, Shelma. There's only one reason you'd omit mentioning the power source. You know there's only one place we can get it. One place we can *steal* it."

"I don't know what you're talking about, but if you have to steal something, it's good you have a pirate crew on your side," Shelma said.

"It's a shame you made such a mess of your job at the shipyard, or we could use your connections to get the source more easily."

"I was targeted by the Creuss–"

"That's your story, yes." Felix could hear the man's smirk. "I know the truth. You went back home and found they'd given your job away. You made a scene. They asked you to leave. Ghosts. Ha. The only ghost is your dead career–"

"You have no idea what you're talking about." Shelma shut the door in his face, and Thales shrugged and walked away.

Ugh. Had Shelma lied to Felix, too, or was this just more mind games from Thales? "Play it again," Felix said. "No sound this time." He watched, then said, "There. When Thales touches her. Did he do something? Put something on her armor? Insert something? Manipulate something?"

"The resolution isn't good enough to tell," Calred said. "But if he did… A suit malfunction could have killed her, absolutely. The suit certainly isn't working now – it doesn't even turn on. Maybe her filtration system failed, or there was an electrical fault. I saw her spasming on the feed. We'll have to see what the ship says after the autopsy."

"Thales killed her." Felix was suddenly, absolutely, sure.

"I don't like the man any more than you do," Tib said, "but why go to all that trouble to break Shelma out of the Barony station just to murder her?"

"He's got her files. He's got her prototype. Maybe that's all he needed."

Tib considered, then shrugged. "It's possible, but it still seems like going the long way around. Stealing her files would have been *much* easier than stealing her, too."

"So let's find out," Felix said. "Take her body to the infirmary. Can the ship's computer examine her and determine cause of death?"

Calred said *hmm*. "Ships with bigger crews usually have a medical officer on board to handle such things, but I imagine the automated systems can do it, if I can figure out how to configure the tests. The results might take a while if the cause was something unusual, though."

"We've got time," Felix said. "I'm going to talk to Thales."

"Just talk, though, right?" Calred said. "We're down to just the one wormhole scientist, and I think undersecretary Jhuri would be upset if someone gave him brain damage."

"I can control myself," Felix said.

•••

"She's dead," Felix shouted. "We went to all that trouble to rescue her, when she didn't even want rescuing, and now she's dead!"

"How regrettable." Thales didn't look up from tinkering with the prototype they'd taken from Shelma's lab. "She was a capable engineer. Still, her death isn't entirely tragic – it has certain clear advantages."

Felix had a bit of a temper as a teenager. He'd worked hard to get it under control and to channel his flashes of rage into energy to fuel his ambitions. This time, though, that energy was too much to contain. He flashed across the room, spun Thales around, and slammed him into the bulkhead, pinning the man against the wall by his throat. "You're *happy* she's dead?"

Thales gurgled, and Felix eased his grip enough to let him talk. "I didn't say I was happy, captain. I said there were advantages." He tried to shove Felix away, but the captain didn't budge. Thales exhaled heavily into Felix's face, then said, "I realize the state of economic theory in the Mentak Coalition is primitive – that's because you steal instead of actually producing anything of value – but in the rest of the galaxy, there's a concept called 'supply and demand.' With Shelma gone, the supply of scientists capable of creating working wormhole technology has been reduced by half, while the demand remains constant. That means *my* value has doubled. I was already worth ten of you, Duval. Now I'm worth twenty."

Thales was remarkable, in his way. He'd insult you to your face while your hands were literally around his throat. Felix let him go and took a long step back, to reduce the temptation to strangle him some more. "With Shelma dead, you have a monopoly on wormhole technology? That's your advantage?"

Thales rubbed his throat and scowled. "It's not a true monopoly, since the Creuss can do it too. But since they won't sell their technology, they don't matter much in practical terms. Otherwise, yes, of course. I couldn't leave Shelma in the hands of the Letnev. She might have duplicated my work – with their resources, she might have gotten there first! Then where would we be? Being second to market just drives prices down. New technology is most advantageous when it's asymmetric. If *one* faction can open wormholes, they can dominate the galaxy. If two can... there's an old term for enemies who possess equally powerful technology: 'mutually assured destruction.' That kind of situation leads to gridlock, no progress, no *winning*. My technology is valuable *because* it's unique."

"You didn't need or want Shelma's help. You just wanted to make sure she couldn't help anyone else. You used me."

"You *exist* for me to use. That's your purpose." Thales went back to his work bench, apparently content that Felix was no longer a threat. "That's why you were assigned to this mission. It's true, I didn't *need* Shelma, but she might have been helpful. I'd hoped to collaborate. She was hardly amenable, though. I'm sure you saw our conversation. Her death is a setback, and a shame, but it's not insurmountable."

"I know you killed her, Thales. You murdered your own friend, maybe your *only* friend, just to make another few credits."

"Three untruths in one sentence! That's impressive error density, even for someone as consistently dense as yourself, captain. Shelma and I weren't friends. We were colleagues. We had a certain amount of respect for one another's capabilities, I suppose. I didn't murder her, either. Her death was probably caused by a fault in her exo-suit – you probably damaged the mechanism during your messy rescue attempt. Either way, it's a pity. As for the third error… it's not about *money*, captain. It's about changing the galaxy. About being the *man* who changed the galaxy."

"After my ship performs an autopsy, do you think it will confirm accidental death?"

"I'm only making an informed guess," Thales said pleasantly. "But I imagine I'm correct in the broad outlines." He didn't seem worried, which meant he knew the autopsy would show no wrongdoing, or else he was so convinced of his importance that he thought it wouldn't *matter* if they could prove he'd murdered the Hylar.

The problem was, if Thales was the only person in the galaxy who could create wormholes on demand, he really *was* that important.

"When this is all over…" Felix began, and then stopped. He couldn't think of any threat he'd be allowed to follow through on, and he hated to make empty ones.

"When this is all over," Thales finished, "I'll be rich, and you'll be promoted, and we'll never have to see each other again. Now, if you'll excuse me, I should look over the rest of Shelma's files. I doubt they'll be any use, but you never know. Meanwhile, *you* should call your masters and tell them you crippled the Barony of Letnev's wormhole technology program and pillaged its resources for yourself. You people love pillaging. I'm sure you'll get a pat on the head." Thales waved a dismissive hand, and Felix left, because another wave of rage was building within him, and this time he might not stop at pushing the man against a wall.

We should have shoved Thales out an airlock when we had the chance, he thought.

CHAPTER 14

"Where are we going?" Severyne demanded.

"I love it when you get that tone." Azad lounged in her quarters – pretty cushy by Letnev standards, as they'd belonged to the commandeered ship's first officer, but they could pass for a solitary confinement prison cell anywhere else – and looked up at Severyne, who stood in the doorway, doing her best to be imposing and severe. Azad could be respectful when the chain of command made it necessary, but Severyne wasn't part of that chain of command, was she? And being insolent with her was much more fun. "Come sit beside me. Craning my head back to look up at you is giving me a cramp. I don't want to end up all stiff-necked like you." Azad sat up and scooted over on the bunk, patting the thin mattress.

Severyne entered, turned, and sat down. She kept her eyes front as Azad slouched against the bulkhead and looked at the Letnev woman sidelong. "We have limited time, Azad." Severyne clipped off her words. "I've followed your course settings so far, but I demand to know our ultimate destination."

"What will you give me for it?"

"You have your life, the promise of freedom, and my agreement to give you the Hylar scientist when we capture her. What more could you possibly want?"

"A little kiss?"

A muscle in Severyne's jaw twitched.

Azad grinned. "I'm just kidding. I'll take lives, and I'll take the spoils of war, and I'll coerce confessions, and I'll blackmail assets to turn them to my cause… but I only enjoy kisses when they're given freely."

"How nice to learn there are limits to your depravity."

"I thought you'd find it comforting. All right, I'll tell you where we're going, and as a bonus, I'll even throw in why. When we captured Thales and scooped up his files, I had my squad's analyst do a quick look through his data. She had cognitive implants that enhanced her pattern-recognition, that kind of nerd stuff, so she was able to collate a large amount of information quickly. She found something interesting in the reports he sent to his old investor."

"You mean the human businessperson who funded their original lab?"

"That's the one." The funding for Thales and Shelma's lab had actually come from the Federation of Sol's black ops military budget. The affable "investor" they'd taken meetings with was just a useful idiot the covert branch employed when they needed a plausible front, and Azad had read all the reports before she even started this mission. "Going over those reports, I noticed a weird omission – Thales never once talked about a power source. It seems like ripping holes in space-time would take a lot of juice, doesn't it? But he never even sketched a drawing of a fusion reactor. That got me curious." It had actually gotten the analysts curious, and they'd asked Azad to help them satisfy that curiosity. "I flipped through the rest of his files, looking for anything pertaining to power, and there it was – a notebook with page after page, full of exclamation points and circles and underlines. Turns out, yeah, their design needs a lot of power – more than you could get from a reactor of conventional size, even the ones that power warships. You'd drain a war sun just warming up their activation engine. Using conventional energy sources, you'd have to turn a whole planet into a power plant, and something like that's not exactly practical or portable."

"I assume Thales found a solution?"

"Sort of, but it's one of those solutions that generates a whole new set of problems. Thales had a power source in mind, something experimental and well-guarded, and he was pulling his hair out because there was no way he could get his hands on it, and couldn't think of a plausible alternative. Apparently, your friend Shelma told him about it – an experimental energy source, very portable, that taps into so-called 'dark energy.' You know what that is?"

"It's the theoretical energy source that causes the universe to expand," Severyne said.

"I knew you were smart. Dark energy is limitless, or damn near, but it's also theoretical – nobody's figured out how to plug a starship into the engine that moves the stars. Back when she was running the shipyards, though, Shelma had connections in the blue-sky R&D division–"

"The what?" Severyne interrupted.

"Blue sky – oh, right. Where you're from, you never see the sky. I don't know what the equivalent idiom is in the Barony. It means no limits, wide open."

"Ah. We say 'endless dark.'"

"Who says it's not a beautiful language? So, anyway, Shelma knew people in the endless-dark research and development division, and they told her they were working on a device that taps into the dark energy field that's present all around us. Thales was excited about that, and his notebook was full of attempts to figure out how such a thing would work – he figured if he couldn't get his hands on the power source, maybe he could reproduce it. He didn't have much luck, though. Too far outside his area of expertise, I guess. When he gave up on cracking the problem himself, he started trying to figure out how to steal the one the Hylar were working on. He scrawled the names of various powerful people and factions – even the Nomad, can you believe that? – who might have the resources to break into the Universities of Jol-Nar. One of those names was the leader of the Mentak Coalition, so Thales ended up with partners he was thinking of joining up with anyway. Funny, huh?"

"You think they are headed to Jol-Nar, to steal this power source?" Severyne said.

Azad slouched deeper. "They must be. The Coalition won't let them ride around in circles in space forever. Those pirates are going to want results, and that means they need the power source. So let's go to Jol-Nar and wait for Duval and his crew to show up." She tapped the side of her head. "Then I'll get a ping off Phil's tracker, we'll swoop in, kill the pirates, recover our scientists, and go our separate ways. I can even use their ship to go home, once I hose off the bloodstains."

"You make it all sound so simple and straightforward."

"I always try to keep my plans simple. Do you know why?"

"I'm sure you'll tell me." Severyne sniffed.

"Because plans almost always fall apart, and if you keep them simple, at least you didn't waste too much time on something that doesn't work anyway. That's OK though. The part where the plan fails – that's where things get interesting."

"My life has been entirely too interesting of late," Severyne said. "I'll set a course for Jol-Nar."

"You might want to hold off on that." Azad looked around at the cheerless bare bulkheads and low ceiling, designed to make subterranean control freaks feel slightly more comfortable in the vastness of outer space. "Before we go to squid city, we need to switch ships."

"Switch. Ships. This is the *Grim Countenance,* a state-of-the-art Barony warship, the finest vessel in our system–"

"About that," Azad interrupted. "Don't you know it's lousy operational security to have a ship this nice patrolling some strategically insignificant mining planet? A ship this nice makes people wonder what's down there that's worth protecting – or what's on the supposed weather station in orbit. My analysts figured out where you were keeping Shelma because they got curious about this ship."

"I raised the same objections!" Severyne said. "I was overridden by the station director."

"Smart and tactically sound too. Be still my heart. So, yes, the *Grim Countenance* is a great ship, and I'm sure it could blow Duval's *Temerarious* into radioactive dust, but that's not our goal, so this ship is more gun than we need."

"You want us to proceed with *fewer* armaments?"

"I'm just saying, something with fewer guns would still get the job done. The problem isn't the armament, though. The problem is, this is a Letnev ship. It's covered in spikes and shit, Severyne."

"Our distinctive ship design strikes terror into the hearts of all our foes, and inspires respect in our allies–"

"You don't need to read me the brochure, Severyne. I'm not insulting your culture's aesthetics. I like big spikes as much as anybody. I'm saying, what happens if the Hylar see this ship slide into their system? They're going to get curious, and when we don't have a good explanation for our presence besides 'We're here to kidnap a human and a Hylar,' the squids are going to get annoyed. If this were a less distinctive ship, the kind you see sold secondhand all over from the Federation or the Coalition, we could fake a transponder, maybe do a little creative welding to change the silhouette, dirty the place up a little, and no one would be able to tell the warship *Grim Countenance* from the long-range merchant freighter *Sunny Smile* or whatever. But… spikes and shit."

Severyne groaned. "I requisitioned the best ship. My only thought was pursuing and destroying Duval's vessel, not infiltration. If I'd realized–"

"It's not your fault. You don't do covert ops. Prison guards aren't spies. Different skill set." Azad scooted a little closer to Severyne on the bunk. "I can teach you some of what I know, if you like."

Severyne scooted an exactly equivalent distance away. "First of all, I don't intend to make a habit of activities like this, so your tutoring won't be necessary. Second, why would you want to teach me anything?"

"For the time being, on this op, you're my partner. I go out in the field and do dangerous things with dangerous people for a living. I often have to team up with people who might betray me at any moment – local assets with divided loyalties, or opportunists who don't stay bought. You and I, amazingly, have a unified purpose: we both want the same thing, and we need each other's help to get it. That provides us with a rare opportunity to build trust. Also, I'd like you to be good at 'activities like this,' since my survival could depend on you at some point."

"I will consider what you say. What do we do about acquiring another ship? I cannot return home without the *Grim Countenance*, so selling it or trading it is out of the question."

"I know a guy," Azad said. "I think I can work something out."

Severyne's grim expression brightened infinitesimally.

Azad suppressed a sigh. She was almost certainly going to have to kill Severyne at some point. Her superiors wouldn't like it if she missed the opportunity to take the Barony out of the wormhole competition. Conversely, there was no way an agent of the Barony would let a Federation operative take Thales, for the same reasons – Severyne would, inevitably, try to betray her, too. In a way, killing Severyne when the time came would be self-defense. Azad had already murdered one woman she liked this week, and she didn't look forward to doing it again.

She was cute, though. Azad had never even kissed a Letnev. Not a good idea, with the whole having-to-kill-her thing, but there was no harm in looking and appreciating, right?

Severyne was entirely too aware of the heat of Azad's body, so close to hers on the bunk. Did humans have higher body temperatures than Letnev? Severyne had never spent much time around humans – certainly not this close to one who was wearing so little clothing. Azad seemed to think a thin tank top and loose pants were appropriate attire for everything. Severyne could see Azad's *shoulders,* and her collarbone, and her biceps, and… Their species weren't *that* different, physically, and Azad's skin was dark and seemed somehow burnished, not like the bland paleness Severyne had observed in the other humans she'd met. Azad had a smell, too, a sharp mixture of sweat and something else, something uniquely *her,* that Severyne found strangely appealing.

Nothing mattered but the mission. Severyne focused her mind like the beam of a welding laser on the issue at hand. "You have 'a guy.' Is that meant to reassure me?"

"He's Hacan. Runs a scrapyard out near Vega Major. Lots of ships pass through there, mining vessels and freighters and so on. He buys used ships, fixes them up, and sells them on. Now, I don't want to shock your sensibilities, but he's been known to make deals that aren't strictly legal. Sometimes people bring him a ship for sale, and he doesn't always check the provenance as carefully as he should."

"He is a thief," Severyne said. Thieves were despised in Letnev culture. Life in the caverns of their homeworld was hard, death just one bad harvest away, and those who chose selfishness and personal gain over the good of their society were shunned. Of course, stealing from other species didn't count; if you weren't Letnev, you weren't exactly people, anyway.

"I don't know, he drives a hard bargain, but by and large I've found him – oh. I see what you mean. In most places, *receiving* stolen goods is a different offense than stealing them in the first place, but sure, basically, say he's a thief. More importantly, he has a great inventory of ships and he owes me a favor. He can get us a less distinctive vessel and hold onto the *Grim Countenance* without a lot of pesky hangar fees, or any records that we docked with him."

"How expensive are these ships of his? I have to submit my expenditures for approval–"

"Don't worry about that." Azad waved it away breezily, as she waved away so many things. Severyne hated that she found Azad's confidence appealing. The human wasn't *that* much older, but Azad had spent her years acquiring practical experience, while Severyne had spent most of hers in classrooms and lecture halls. Severyne's grasp of textbook tactics was excellent, and in theory she knew how to suppress prison riots, secure a station, and protect VIPs, but the first time she'd needed to put any of that knowledge into practice, she'd lost her prisoner. Maybe she *could* learn something from Azad. There were many areas where Severyne had largely theoretical knowledge – areas that could benefit from further practical experience…

She realized her eyes were lingering on the hollow at the base of Azad's throat, and slowly, deliberately, she turned her gaze away. Was it the transgression of finding a human attractive that made Azad so alluring? Severyne had long feared she had a streak of contrariness hidden inside herself, and Azad brought it out. "I hope this doesn't take too long. Duval has a head start already."

"Oh, I think we'll be all right. Duval has to steal something from the starship propulsion laboratory of the Universities of Jol-Nar. That's not something you just stroll in and *do*. He'll have to do research, make plans, figure out some angles. He'll probably have to source materiel, maybe even recruit more confederates – even if he's a criminal genius and does most of his thinking on the way to the Hylar system, we've got a couple of days."

"I desire a swift conclusion to this mission."

"Aw, Sev. Here I was thinking how much I enjoy spending time with you."

Severyne stood and stepped away. "Send me the coordinates for your guy."

Azad sketched a lazy salute, lounging across the bunk and grinning.

As the door closed behind her, Severyne felt a pang of regret. Azad was an interesting person. Infuriating, but interesting. It was a shame she'd have to kill the woman. She couldn't let the Federation of Sol get their hands on wormhole technology. If she did, her superiors would have her executed, so, in a sense, killing Azad would be self-defense. That didn't make her any happier about it. Severyne decided, as a gesture of respect, to pull the trigger herself, rather than ordering one of her guards to do it.

Then again, with Azad dead and gone, Severyne wouldn't be plagued by these increasingly intrusive *thoughts*…

CHAPTER 15

"Apparently we need to break into an experimental research and development laboratory in the Universities of Jol-Nar, steal a prototype power source, and get away without being arrested or killed. Does anyone have any suggestions for how we can accomplish that?" Felix looked from Tib to Calred. To think, he'd once found sitting on this bridge with his crew relaxing. Of course, back then his biggest problem had been fielding calls from colonists who wanted him to use the ship's impressive sensor array to find a lost sheep. (He'd done so once, naturally, because he'd had nothing else particularly pressing to do.)

His crew was silent. Felix said, "I'm sorry. That wasn't a rhetorical question. I am asking how we do the thing that I just said we need to do."

"If Shelma hadn't died, I'm sure she'd have useful information," Tib said. "She used to run the shipyard, so she had connections in the experimental labs. She could have sketched us floor plans, maybe even told us about security measures. I wish Thales had brought up stage two of his plan before her unfortunate 'accident.'"

"No use weeping over broken eggs," Felix said. "Can we do the same thing we did on the Letnev station? Fake our credentials, pretend to be a delivery ship, get close, sneak in?"

Calred shook his head. "My cousin is very angry with me, so she won't be offering us any more assistance along those lines. Her company lost their contract with the Barony, and it was a *big* contract. Speaking of which, I promised I'd make it up to her by securing them an equally lucrative arrangement with the Coalition. Didn't you sleep with the chief supply clerk for the Lucanis system once, Felix?"

"There's a reason it was only once," he said.

"Ah, well. Until I make things right with her, we won't be able to borrow any schedules, authorizations, or manifests, so we wouldn't pass inspection. Sorry."

Felix sighed. "It's not your fault. Once we're covered in glory and flush with success and the Table is handing out rewards for our exemplary accomplishments, we'll see about setting up your cousin with a good contract."

"What if we fail?"

"Oh. Failure would probably mean incarceration or execution by the Hylar, and in that case, you'll be well beyond your cousin's wrath."

"I am comforted," Calred rumbled.

Felix drummed his fingers on the arm of his captain's chair. "I noticed one interesting thing in the dossier you compiled about the head of the research and development lab," he said. "There was that little fluff piece that mentioned his collection of alien artifacts. He likes mysterious objects of mysterious provenance from mysterious places, so if we had such an artifact, and made an appointment, maybe we could get into his office, which is in his lab, so he could take a look?"

"It's a shame we don't have any mysterious artifacts handy," Calred said.

"I bet we could come up with something," Tib said. "Or at least a convincing facsimile."

"We'd need to be convincing facsimiles ourselves," Felix said. "The kind of adrenaline junkie deep-space explorers who stumble on unknown alien tech don't travel in ships as respectable as the *Temerarious*. We'd need to show up for the meeting in a smaller long-range craft, something beat-up and pitted with micrometeoroid impacts, scarred by weird energy weapons wielded by uncontacted alien cultures, that sort of thing. Where can we get a plausible ship?"

"I know a guy," Calred said.

"A cousin?" Felix said.

Calred shook his head. "He's Hacan, but we're not *all* related. I know him from some work I did for the Coalition. You know I spent time in the asset distribution arm of the pirate service?"

"You sold stolen goods to fences, you mean," Felix said.

"I did. And our favorite fence when it came to converting stolen ships to currency was a gentleman named Sagasa the Disciplinarian."

"That is not a very welcoming name."

Calred grinned. "'Disciplinarian' is a title used by members of a certain Hacan religious order – specifically the monks in charge of making sure none of the initiates stumble into heresy, or shirk their duties. Sagasa is an apostate these days, though he was devout when he lived in the desert. The way I heard it, he was so devout and incorruptible that when an acolyte ran away from the order, they sent Sagasa to track the cub down, even though their order eschews exposure to worldly things. Once Sagasa got on his first starship, though, he realized he liked worldly things. The order sent a couple of people to bring *him* back, but that didn't go well, and the order decided to let him go. Sagasa kept using the title in his new life, because it sounds scary – but it also sounds like he'll only punish you if you give him a reason. That pretty much fits the way he does business. Sagasa and I are on good terms. He can get us a plausible ship, probably one some genuine adventurers died in, and he'll let us dock the *Temerarious* in his shipyard until we're back."

"Perfect," Felix said. "We can figure out the details of our plan on the way. Where's Sagasa based?"

"Not too far out of our way," Calred said. "His scrapyard is out by Vega Major."

• • •

"I have already given you a crucial element necessary to complete your plan," Thales said. "Now you ask more of me? I am not a crafter of trumperies. Would you have me sew a monkey's torso to a fish's tail and claim it's a mermaid? Glue antlers to a jackrabbit's head and call it a jackalope? Put wings on a snake and display it as the mythical Aaalu? You are distracting me from my work, captain."

The rooms Thales had taken for a lab no longer reflected even the relaxed military order that characterized Coalition ships. Now the walls were covered in printed pages and sketches from Shelma's files and Thales's own, and he'd gone even further, drawing on the actual bulkheads in places. The floor was dotted with cairns of stacked papers, and there were coils of wire, clumps of crystal, and assorted machine components on every surface. Felix recognized one of the ship's repair drones, upside-down, its carapace open and half its parts removed. There was a pile of blankets and cushions in one corner – according to Calred, who monitored the security cameras, the scientist slept there, taking short naps every few hours in lieu of longer cycles before snapping awake and continuing to tinker with Shelma's torpedoshaped device: the activation engine.

Felix felt a headache coming on. Talking to this man was bad for his mental and physical health. "Your *work* is opening wormholes, and you need this power source to do it. We can't buy it, because it's not for sale – officially, it doesn't even exist – and if we're going to steal it, we need your help."

"I already helped."

"We need *more* of your help," Felix said.

"You're pirates. I'm a scientist. I don't need your help to calibrate a neutrino detection array. Why do you need my help to steal something?"

"This isn't piracy. This is burglary, if we're lucky, and robbery if we're not."

Thales looked up briefly. "There's a distinction?"

"Piracy is going out on a ship and stealing something from *another* ship. Sometimes, you steal the other ship while you're there. Burglary is entering a place illegally with the intent of removing something that doesn't belong to you. Robbery is stealing something from another person directly, usually with threats of violence, or *actual* violence."

"I suppose every field of study has its own terminology. Burglary and robbery are outside your skillset, then?"

"I didn't say that, but part of doing a job like this is making use of expert assistance." Flattering Thales couldn't hurt. "You're an expert on alien technology, aren't you? So help us fake something that looks plausible enough to catch the director's interest."

Thales put down his tools and scowled. "You need something that will pass for an alien artifact of unknown provenance. Something that has properties, or purports to have properties, that the head of experimental research and development at the University will find interesting, and want to see in person. I'm sure I can come up with something, though I may need some source material to create it. There's nothing on *this* ship that would pass for a component of an alien device."

"Fortunately, we're headed for a huge junkyard," Felix said. "It should have all the weird trash you could ever want."

"No doubt you'll feel very at home there," Thales said.

"Because I'm trash, you mean?"

"That was my implication, yes."

"Do you remember our conversation about how you need to be less terrible all the time?"

Thales chuckled, and it was a low, nasty, oily sound. "I thought we understood each other, captain. You've proven you'll do whatever I ask, if it's necessary for my project. That even if you suspect me of murder, you'll obey your superiors and give me what I want. In light of those facts, I think we can dispense with all that nonsense about courtesy."

"Do you really want to see how far you can push me, Thales?"

"I'm a theorist first and foremost, captain, but I'm also an engineer, and it's useful for engineers to know the tolerances of their equipment."

Felix stared at him. "I'm your equipment, am I?"

"You are one small component in a machine I am creating – a machine that will transform the galaxy and shift the balance of power, and in favor of your nation. You're a *vital* component, captain, rest assured. I couldn't do this without you. There's no shame in serving your role properly. Let me know when we've reached this junkyard of yours, and I'll solve your problem." He turned his back. Felix was dismissed.

Felix looked at a heavy wrench on a nearby table. He could pick it up, swing it hard, cave in the man's skull, and ruin all that remarkable gray matter. Of course, he wouldn't do that, but it gave him a warm feeling to know he *could*.

I never used to daydream about murdering anyone, Felix thought. Thales was such a terrible person, he was making Felix into a worse one, like his terribleness was contagious. Or even radioactive.

Vega Major wasn't a particularly nice place to visit. The planet had beautiful rings, but those rings were infested by mining ships and surrounded by orbital habitats to support the miners – which meant, at least, that there were plenty of bars and other entertainments available, though they were a bit grease-stained and grimy. The surface of the planet was habitable, technically, but its seas were inhabited by vast numbers of unintelligent giant squid. There were colonies down there, but the colonists required a high tolerance for eating squid and, potentially, being eaten by squid, if they strayed too close to the water.

The sister planet, Vega Minor, was a nicer place, and home to a respected company, the Vega Propulsion Corporation. (Felix asked if there was maybe an experimental power source *there* they could steal instead, but Thales said they didn't have anything suitable, and then went off on a long rant about how the corporation had cheated him on some engine component he'd devised.) The stilt-cities that dotted the shallow seas there were home to thriving populations drawn from all over the galaxy, and the one time Felix had visited, he'd thought the place would fit right in as part of the Coalition.

Alas, they weren't going to Vega Minor. They were on the far side of Vega Major instead, approaching what looked like the aftermath of a horrific space battle. A vast cloud of floating wreckage filled their viewscreen, with hundreds of ships of all descriptions floating in various states of destruction or disrepair. There were Mentak cruisers, Federation pickets, Letnev thorn ships, even – "Is that a Muaat *war sun*?" Felix stared.

"It's almost half of a Muaat war sun," Calred said. "Last time I was here, Sagasa was bragging about winning the contract to scrap it. Someone else won the other half – the Embers didn't want to give anyone the whole thing, lest they try to get it up and running again. All the armaments were removed, of course, but still. It's an impressive hunk of metal, isn't it?"

Felix whistled. The Coalition had big terrifying weapons platforms too, of course – all the major factions did – but the Muaat war suns set the gold standard for horrifying military overkill. He'd never seen one of them this close up, and had always assumed that if he ever did, it would mean he was about to die.

When they got closer to the debris cloud, it became more obvious this wasn't a graveyard, but a recycling center. Drones floated everywhere among the wrecks, blowtorches sparking, saws spinning, articulated arms plucking and sorting components into carts that looked small in comparison to the ships around them but were actually the size of houses.

A bored voice spoke over the comms. "Welcome to Sagasa Scrap and Salvage, we make old things new again, how can we help you today?"

"I'd like a meeting with Sagasa," Felix replied.

"The Disciplinarian is very busy today, I'm afraid–"

"Tell him I have a large black ops budget I'd like to spend on him," Felix said.

A moment's pause. "The Disciplinarian doesn't take new clients of that sort without a referral."

"Tell him Calred the Hacan is part of the crew," Felix said.

A long pause. "From Moll Primus?"

"That's the one," Calred rumbled.

"One moment please." A longer pause. "Proceed to dock B and follow instructions."

Their ship interfaced with the Sagasa Scrap and Salvage docking system, the Disciplinarian's computers guiding them on a safe path through the field of wreckage. From a military perspective, this place was incredibly defensible – any force that tried to get to the station at the center of this mess would have to navigate the debris field, and a lot of those ships still had working fuel and propulsion systems, which meant a lot of them could be easily turned into *bombs*. Calred said once you got deeper into the debris field, some of the ships weren't wrecks at all, but fully functional warships, disguised as junk. Attack could come from any or all directions, in there. "I'm glad Sagasa is on our side," he muttered.

"Ha!" Calred laughed from his security station. "Sagasa is on his own side. He'll make deals with anybody and everybody. He says we're all equal in the eyes of the divine, so who is he to discriminate?"

"I can't wait to meet him," Felix said.

CHAPTER 16

"I hate ocean planets." Severyne gazed through the viewport at the looming shape of Vega Major, and the gentle curve of Vega Minor beyond. "All that water, none of it fit to drink. Wasteful and inefficient. There is darkness and depth and pressure, yes, if you go down far enough, but then, those depths are so often full of teeming monsters."

Azad stood beside her. "On the other hand, there's lounging on the beach, maybe someone attractive rubbing lotion on your back, you swim in the warm water, it's got upsides."

"There are species who consider such activities pleasant, I know, but the relentless sun is my own vision of horror."

"So you sit under an umbrella, or wear a big hat. You'd look good in a big hat, Sev. Much better than you do in that flat cap with the little brim and the silver stars on it you were wearing when we first met. You can sip fruity boozy drinks out of hollowed-out examples of the very same fruit that's blended up in the drink. Surely you can appreciate *that* – it's efficient, right?"

Severyne's lips twitched. She very nearly smiled. "You must think the Letnev a joyless people. It isn't true. We simply take pleasure in things that your species, as a whole, does not. I find joy in competence, and order, and important work done well."

"Sure, all that stuff is great," Azad said. "But have you tried getting drunk and sleeping with a stranger?"

Severyne resolutely ignored that. "I assume this cloud of wreckage is our destination?" The screen lit up with hundreds of targets, ships all ringed in green to show the system didn't consider them current threats.

"Welcome to the scrapyard of Sagasa the Disciplinarian. Biggest and best junkyard in the sector."

Severyne narrowed her eyes. "I see Letnev ships among his inventory. How did he come by *those*? We decommission our own vessels in the Barony."

"You're looking at the far end point of battlefield economics, Sev. The Barony gets into the occasional fight, doesn't it? And, contrary to what your national propaganda says, you don't win *every* engagement. After a battle, the winning side recovers what they can, but usually they have to rush off to kill some other people someplace else, or they need to resupply, or they're chasing down survivors, or they got beat up badly enough themselves that they need to limp home for repairs both medical and mechanical. There are teams of freelance scrappers who pay closer attention to politics than most politicians do, so they know where battles are likely to break out, and they hang around. After the surviving forces withdraw, the scavengers go in, and they gather what's worth selling."

Severyne had never really thought about what happened in the aftermath of a space battle. Logistics wasn't her area, and neither was military engagement; she worked in what was sometimes called "inward-facing" security. "They loot battlefields and sell the spoils to people like Sagasa?"

"Only the junk." Azad leaned on the curving black rail in front of Severyne's chair, a posture that thrust out her rear end in Severyne's direction in a rather distracting way. "Salvage that still works gets sold to mercenaries, or local forces, or sometimes they sell it back to the military that lost it in the first place, at a price that's *slightly* cheaper than sourcing new stuff from a factory would be. The scavengers also perform other, ah, crucial functions. Delivering mercy, and the like."

"That sounds like a euphemism. We don't like euphemisms in the Barony, Azad. We prefer to view the world as it is."

"They kill the dying, Sev. Space battles are different from terrestrial ones – they tend to be a lot more all-or-nothing, because if your ship gets destroyed, *you* get destroyed, so there are fewer wounded, overall. Fewer doesn't mean zero, though, and there are always people lingering with significant bits of their anatomy missing in the aftermath, and no help on the way."

"The scavengers *murder* battlefield survivors?" Why had Severyne's required courses on military engagements not covered this material? Probably because the Barony didn't like admitting to losses of any kind.

Azad said, "Oh, not always. Only the ones who are too far gone. They patch up people who can be patched up without too much trouble, and get them back home, for a price. Most factions will pay for the safe return of officers, and for grunts… well, ideally their return gets lumped into a purchase of weapons and supplies. If you're an outside contractor or a mercenary though? Forget it. Nobody's paying to get you back."

That was disturbing, but Severyne knew the military had to make difficult decisions. "Freelancers are summarily executed?"

"No, you're not thinking like a scavenger," Azad said. "Try again."

A test, then. An intellectual exercise. Severyne had always excelled at those. It was translating them to practical application that was proving harder than she'd ever anticipated. "If the point is to extract maximum value, turning what others view as waste into profit, and there are survivors who cannot be converted into money, they must instead be converted into… labor? The scavengers enslave them?"

Azad turned and gave her a smile. "Very good. Really it's more like indenture, because that's almost as good as slavery, and you get fewer rebellions from within and sapient rights complaints from without. If the scavengers save your life, and nobody pays them for the trouble they took to save you, you can always work off your debt. The pay is reasonable, and they treat their employees well, overall. Plenty of people choose to stay on even after their debt is paid, and some of them settle into scavenging for life. It's dangerous work, salvaging battlefields – there's always lots of unexploded ordnance that might explode when you touch it, flying debris that can puncture your suit or your lungs, things like that. There's a lot of, let's say, turnover, so new recruits are always welcome. Honestly, though, after you've barely survived a battle, being a salvager seems pretty safe in comparison."

There was something about Azad's voice. "You speak as if from experience."

"I've spent a good chunk of my career as a deniable asset – nobody pays for *my* safe return. Either I make my own way home, or I don't go home at all. I spent six months working for a salvage outfit that found me stuck in a crumpled escape pod tube in a wrecked ship after an engagement went bad. That's when I met Sagasa, actually."

"You have had a rich and varied life, haven't you, Azad?"

"I like going new places and meeting new people." She winked. "Just think, if my mission had gone more smoothly, and I'd snatched up Thales without getting all tangled with Duval and those pirates, you and I would never have met. Wouldn't *that* be a tragedy?"

"If you hadn't failed in your mission, Duval would never have attacked my station and put my life in danger, and I would be in my quarters right now, sleeping, instead of going to meet a criminal Hacan in a junkyard."

"Life does take some unexpected turns, doesn't it?" Azad said.

A voice over the comms said, "Welcome to Sagasa Scrap and Salvage, we make old things new again, how can we help you today?"

"Tell the old crook his favorite scrapper Amina just brought him a top-of-the-line Letnev warship," Azad said.

"*What?*" Severyne gasped.

The station at the center of the debris cloud was a tangle of metal bolted together from castoff habitat modules, with entire scrapped ships welded into the middle of corridor rings. "It looks like a work of very bad art," Felix said.

"The station started out as a standard modular system, but over the years Sagasa has embellished the place," Calred said. "I know it *looks* like a haphazard garbage heap, but it's built solid, and the placement of those ships isn't random – they're placed at set intervals, and their weapons systems are still intact, and pointed outward."

"This is like a warlord's fortress," Felix said. "Does Sagasa really expect to be attacked?"

"Scrap and salvage is a cut-throat, low-margin business, and when you add in the Disciplinarian's not-strictly-legal activities… a man like him can make a lot of enemies. The Vega Corporation doesn't love having a hub of slime and criminality so close to their headquarters, either. Sagasa has repelled an assault or two over the years. He repelled them robustly enough that not many people have tried him since."

"I'm glad we don't have to steal anything from *here*," Felix said.

"Indeed. Stealing from Sagasa would doubtless result in disciplinary action."

They docked with the station and headed down to the airlock, Felix in the lead, Cal a step behind on his left, Tib in the back, clearly wishing she was invisible. (Calred said sneaking around Sagasa's station wasn't advisable. The Disciplinarian would be annoyed if he found out.) The interior of the ship did away with the scrap-heap motif, the corridor walls and floor made of smoothly polished metal, with discreet cameras dotted everywhere – but not so discreet you'd fail to notice them if you looked, which was presumably the point. Sagasa wanted you to know you were being watched, and watched by a professional.

A Winnaran in an elaborate jeweled headdress waited for them in the corridor beyond the airlock, hands clasped behind him. "Do you have any weapons to declare?"

"Not on us," Felix said.

The Winnaran seemed unconvinced, and pointed a handheld scanner at them each in turn before nodding. "This way." He turned smartly and led them down a twisting maze of corridors, and as they made it closer to the heart of the station, they encountered several reinforced doors with recessed gunports. Those doors didn't open right away, and the Winnaran waited patiently at each one, clearly used to this level of security. Eventually their little group reached a cavernous waiting room that Felix recognized as the repurposed bridge of a Coalition dreadnought; that gave him a weird sense of pride. The stations and seats had been stripped out, replaced by large pots of lush green climbing plants that wound around the stripped frames of tactical panels and navigation screens. The overall aesthetic was like being in a spaceship that had crash-landed in a jungle some years before.

The door that would have led to the captain's ready room on a functioning ship was flanked by a pair of guards wearing armored exo-suits so elaborate that Felix couldn't guess the species of the beings inside. In addition to the plasma and kinetic weapons built into their suits, the door guards also held more primitive weapons – wooden poles with elaborately curved and recurved spikes of bronze on the heads.

"The Disciplinarian has a sense of theater, doesn't he?" Felix murmured.

"Oh, just you wait," Calred replied.

The Winnaran gestured for them to sit on a metal bench that was only partially covered in vines. Felix expected to be offered refreshment, but instead the secretary (or whatever he was) just said, "You will be called," and left the bridge.

Felix looked at the guards. "Hi there," he said. "Having a good day?"

The guards might as well have been statues.

"They don't do small talk," Calred said. "It would ruin their whole sense of menace. You might as well try to strike up a conversation with a particle cannon."

"I bet he would," Tib said.

"I just try to make meaningful connections wherever I go. It's called networking. It's the key to diplomacy. You could both learn–"

The doors to the ready room slid open, and a burly, hairy humanoid bustled out, muttering to itself and adjusting a brown cloak. He was a Saar! Felix didn't think he'd ever met one of that species. The Saar kept to themselves so thoroughly that you could forget they were part of the galactic community at all. Didn't most of them live out in an asteroid field somewhere, among the rubble of their exploded home planet? They probably had a pretty vast and ongoing need for ships, in that case, so they must be a great market for Sagasa. The Saar took no notice of Felix and the others as he stomped by and away.

Felix half rose, but the guards lowered their pikes, crossing them over the open doorway, and then the doors slid shut again. Felix sat back down, and the guards moved their weapons to vertical.

"The Disciplinarian likes to take a breath between meetings," Calred said. "He centers his mindfulness or whatever. I'm pretty sure it's just a show-of-power thing. Make it clear to us we're penitents, and he's the one granting an audience."

Moments later, the doors slid open, and a voice beyond barked, "Come."

They went in, Felix in the lead, only hesitating a moment as he passed the imposing armored guards, but they didn't even twitch. The ready room was as lush and green as the waiting area, but dominated by a large desk made from artfully welded-together starship parts, surfaces polished like the rest of the station.

The Disciplinarian sat behind the desk in a chair that was really more of a gleaming metal throne, high-backed and elaborately decorated with vines made of twisted wire stems and gold-foil leaves. Strange choice of décor, overall, for someone from a monastic order in a desert… or maybe Sagasa's arid background explained why he liked growing things here in the different desert of space.

Sagasa was flanked by a pair of unlikely guards, or attendants, or recording secretaries, or who knows what. On his left stood a Naalu, though "stood" probably wasn't the right term for what a man-sized serpent with arms did. Rested on its huge scaly tail? He… it had to be male, since the Naalu were a matriarchal culture, and you'd never see a female working for a Hacan or anyone else. Naalu could read minds, or sense intentions, or detect lies, depending on who you asked, though some people said it was just the females who had that power. There were a few Naalu in the Coalition, but Felix hadn't met any. He decided to be scrupulously honest, just to be safe.

A N'orr crouched on the Disciplinarian's right: a looming nightmare of chitinous claws, a head made of hideous triangles, a mouth surrounded by dripping mandibles, the whole thing balanced on entirely too many spiky legs. Felix wasn't bothered by spiders, but spiders weren't usually taller than him, with mouths big enough to engulf his head. There were a few unhived N'orr in the Coalition, Felix knew, descended from prisoners on the original penal colony, but he wondered how this one had ended up here. The N'orr didn't have a hive mind, despite popular misconceptions, but they didn't prize individuality either, and so their species didn't produce many outcasts or rogues or wanderers.

"Just you wait," Calred had said. The Hacan definitely knew how to make an impression.

There was one chair, suitable for humans, on the other side of the Disciplinarian's desk. It was made of wood-textured plas, had one leg visibly shorter than the others, and the back support was held together with wire and industrial tape. As if the power imbalance wasn't stark enough already, but any edge you could get in a negotiation was worthwhile. Felix decided he'd stand.

The Disciplinarian gazed at them. He was older than Calred by at least a few decades, his mane nearly white, his eyes steady and dark, his muzzle marked with scars. He wore an elegant buff-colored robe worked around the neckline and sleeves with a vine motif, and even seated, he gave off a sense of strength and mass and gravitas. His eyes settled on the security officer. "Calred. May the sun warm your back, brother."

"May blood redden your claws," Calred said with equal formality.

The Disciplinarian smiled broadly. "It's nice to talk to someone with manners. I had a Saar in here a minute ago, and he actually spat on the floor!" He inclined his head toward the N'orr. "Counselor An'Truk here wanted to spear him through the thorax but I said, 'Maybe spitting is a compliment in their culture.' It's important that we all get along, eh? Look at you three, all working together on a starship. The *Temerarious*. You're supposed to be patrolling a colony system, Captain Duval, yet you arrive at my humble scrapyard boasting of a covert operations budget. Have you been under *very* deep cover, or is this a recent promotion? Given the presence of Calred, who I know to be a steady sort, I will omit the third possibility – that you're lying or delusional."

Felix inclined his head in an acknowledging nod. "We are on a mission. I can't tell you much about it."

"That's fine. I deal in tangible things, not information. Information gets too close to politics, and I value my reputation as a neutral party who plays no favorites. How can I help you with this mission I don't want to know any details about?"

"We need to borrow a ship," Felix said. "I'd also appreciate it if you'd let a scientist we're traveling with paw through some of the more exotic wrecks out there."

"All things are possible," Sagasa said, "if the price is right."

CHAPTER 17

The *Grim Countenance* was assigned to docking port YB-2. Azad stood next to Severyne on the bridge, watching the station grow in the viewscreen as they approached. "That docking port can't be sequential," Severyne said. "How many airlocks does this misbegotten scrapheap of a station have?"

"Oh, lots," Azad said airily. "The Disciplinarian tries to park everyone where they can have a bit of privacy. Sometimes people don't want to be seen visiting. And there's always the risk that he'll have visitors from both sides of some conflict dropping by at the same time. Sagasa is steadfastly neutral, and doesn't like fuss or conflict." She paused. "What I mean to say is, he doesn't like conflict *here*. He loves conflict elsewhere. I suspect he even funds the occasional rebel alliance or splinter political faction, knowing his small investment will reap big returns in salvage later. But maybe not – he always claims he stays out of politics, and it could be true. Not *everyone* lies constantly, but Hacan can be tough to read, even for other Hacan, let alone a humble swabbie like me."

"You shouldn't have told him he could buy our ship," Severyne said, not for the first time. "We are *not* selling him this ship."

"I know, I know," Azad soothed. "We're going to work all the details out when we get in to see him. I just had to snag the guy's attention. We're going to *borrow* another ship, for a nominal fee, and leave him the *Grim Countenance* as collateral. He'll take the deal, because if we come back, he makes a little money, and if we don't come back, he gets a Letnev warship, and that's worth a *lot* of money. Alternatively, we can offer him a lot of money in the first place, no collateral necessary, but I'm trying to help out your expense report situation."

"Your plan is acceptable. I dislike the suggestion that we won't return, however. We will come back, and we will be triumphant."

"Ah, right. The Letnev spirit. Never admit even the possibility of defeat, right?"

"What benefit can there possibly be in imagining one's failure?"

Azad shrugged. "Overconfidence has brought down a lot of generals, Sev."

"Better to be overconfident than to doubt one's capabilities."

"Now, there I agree with you." She slung her arm over Severyne's shoulder, and the Letnev squirmed away with a deftness and grace that surprised Azad. Had Severyne trained as a dancer? No, ridiculous, Letnev didn't dance. What, then? That movement had been more than merely natural. Azad kept talking as if nothing had happened. "Some people think I'm overconfident – do you believe that? When really I just have clear-eyed self-regard and a complete understanding of my own abilities." Azad knew that was a little pompous, and was hoping to needle Severyne a little.

Instead, the other woman said, "The presence of excellence often disturbs the inferior."

Oh, I like you, Azad thought. She hated her a little, too, but that just made things more fun. If Azad had wanted a simple life, she wouldn't have joined covert ops.

They went to the airlock, and into the station. A Winnaran with a gaudy jeweled thing on his head looked at them all snooty and said, "Any weapons?"

"A Letnev military officer is never without her sidearm," Severyne said.

The Winnaran pushed a button, and a drawer slid out of the wall. "Place your weapons in this locker. You may retrieve them on your way back."

"It's OK," Azad said when Severyne stiffened. "This isn't a shooting place. It's a money place."

Severyne glared at the Winnaran, then put her sidearm in the drawer. Azad did a little twirl to show she was unarmed – she was wearing a close-fitting top and shorts, so she couldn't hide much of a weapon, and hadn't bothered with the ones she could – but the Winnaran scanned them both with a handheld device anyway before saying, "This way."

"Let me do the talking when we get in there," Azad said.

"That is acceptable, as long as you say the right things," Severyne replied.

"OK!" Felix held up his hands. "I give in. You are the better negotiator. It's not my money, anyway. I just have to fight hard enough to keep my supervisor from yelling at me afterward. We have a deal."

"Fine," the Disciplinarian rumbled. "You don't care if I starve. And why should you? I am only a Hacan, and you – you are a human, most favored race of the galaxy. Though it grieves me to take such a loss, we have an agreement."

Felix cleared his throat. "Do you think you could, ah, invoice us for two percent more than we actually agreed? Just as a favor?"

"A favor?" The Disciplinarian looked at the N'orr, then looked at the Naalu, then looked back at Felix. "I don't know this word."

"He is describing a transaction where only *one* person gets something," Calred said.

"That doesn't sound right," the Disciplinarian said. He was clearly enjoying himself. "I will invoice you at two percent more, in exchange for one percent more. Calculated after the addition of the two percent, of course."

"But – that's – never mind. It's fine. It's good. Excellent." A Coalition officer who didn't skim a *little* was suspicious, so Felix had to get something, but the Disciplinarian was better at this sort of thing than he was.

"The exchange rate is really not in your favor today, unfortunately," Sagasa said. "Speak to my secretary on your way out – he's in the waiting room now, escorting my next appointment. He'll take your payment. Then you can pick up your new ship and let your scientist scrounge around in an unidentified vessel we bought years back from some long-range scrappers. My experts say it's millennia old and doesn't match anything in any known historical database. I bought the thing because I was intrigued, but as I said, there's nothing of any value there – what isn't fused into glass is completely inert, and I couldn't even sell the parts, since they aren't compatible with any known propulsion system."

"As long as there's weird stuff in there that looks really weird," Felix said.

"I am sure there is a good reason you need something like that. I am pleased that I have neither the need nor desire to know that reason. Good day, my friends."

Felix gave a little salute and turned away. That could have gone worse, he thought. This might even work. The doors slid open before him, and he led the way out of the office.

There were two people sitting on the bench they'd recently vacated, a human and a Letnev, and the Winnaran secretary loitered nearby. Felix nodded his head in a friendly greeting and smiled one of his default charming smiles – which froze on his face just as Calred said "Huh," and Tib said "Uh-oh."

She was wearing workout clothes instead of terrifying mercenary armor, which explained why he hadn't recognized her right away, but the human was Amina Azad, the operative who'd gotten the drop on him (before Tib got the drop on *her*), who'd subsequently escaped the custody of a raider fleet flagship, and who had apparently somehow tracked them *here*. But why ambush them in the waiting room? Why not hide in the debris field and – Wait. The Letnev woman with her. *She* looked familiar too. She was the head of security from the Barony research facility. What was her name – Several? Severus? Severyne.

"That is an odd couple," Calred said, and then Severyne lost her shit.

She leapt from the bench with a roar, slapping her hand against her hip. For a moment she looked utterly bewildered, as she realized whatever weapon she'd reached for wasn't there. Felix was suddenly very grateful for the Disciplinarian's security measures.

Severyne was undaunted. She decided to take the direct approach, rushing at Felix and shouting what were presumably insults in her native tongue. Felix was OK not knowing exactly what she meant; he got the general idea. The Winnaran tried to restrain Severyne, but she did some fancy hand-to-hand combat thing, and the man was suddenly on his ass, looking around in a daze.

Felix tried to dodge out of her path, but he bounced off one of the guards, who was yelling too, and waving his halberd or whatever that thing was around. The other guard stepped forward to block the Letnev's attack – and she jumped, grabbed the polearm shaft in both hands, twirled around it, and kicked the guard in the knee.

The kick had absolutely no effect – the "knee" was an armored hydraulic mechanical joint, so it probably hurt the kicker more than the kickee, even through Severyne's shiny black boots – but the Letnev kept moving. Somehow her angle and momentum (and, possibly, the guard's shock at being attacked by an unarmed person half his size) allowed her to yank the polearm smoothly out of the guard's hand.

Now she was armed. With a bit of wood that had a pointy thing on the end, true – it was hardly a pulsed-energy rifle – but she was highly motivated. Felix could understand that. He'd blown up her house and probably gotten her in a lot of trouble.

Felix jumped out of the way when she jabbed at him, only dimly aware of the rest of the fuss going on around him: the guards were trying to aim their weapons, but the secretary was stumbling around, dazed, in their field of fire. Severyne wasn't an easy target, dancing and spinning and whirling her polearm, progressing gradually toward Felix. She would have sliced him up, except she had to keep dodging the guards. Then the Naalu came slithering into the room, and the N'orr scuttled through, and the place was plunged into even deeper pandemonium. The Disciplinarian came out of his office, bellowing, "Stop this! Everyone stop *now*!" to no particular effect.

Felix did a diving roll to avoid a slash from Severyne's polearm, and ended up next to the other guard, who still had his ceremonial weapon. "Little help?" he said, and grabbed the weapon from a surprisingly unresisting hand. He swung the pole up and blocked one of Severyne's blows.

"So," he began, then stepped back as she jabbed at his face. She wasn't much for small talk either, apparently. Felix had done some fencing at the academy. This was not very much like fencing really, but there were a couple of commonalities: it was all about timing and distance. She was pressing the attack, and he couldn't change the tempo – she was coming at him furiously, and he was constantly on the defensive, barely blocking her blows, which fell hard enough to make his hands numb. She was backing him into an ivy-covered wall, so distance was going to be in short supply soon, too.

Beyond Severyne, Felix saw Azad sneak up behind Tib, and tried to shout a warning, but his cry was lost in the general shouting. Azad punched Tib in the back of the head and shouted, "How do *you* like it?" and then the N'orr snatched them both up in complex unfolding limbs. Calred was waving his arms around in front of the guards, who were trying to get a clear shot at Severyne, probably, but were, in the process, also taking aim in Felix's direction.

Felix tripped on a vine, lost his footing, and fell backward. Severyne stepped up to him and raised the polearm in both arms, spinning it so she could drive it down point-first into his body like a spear. Oh, this was going to *hurt* – A huge paw plucked the weapon from her hands like it was a toothpick from a cocktail glass. The Disciplinarian grabbed Severyne by the back of her neck and lifted her bodily off the ground. She kicked and writhed and hissed furiously, and he gave her a little shake, at which point she stopped, hanging limply in his grasp, breathing hard.

"You have been very bad," the Disciplinarian said.

"That was some impressive hand-to-hand action," Azad said to Severyne. The N'orr crouched behind her, its front limbs on her shoulders, their serrated edges just brushing the sides of her neck. The Naalu stood behind Severyne, his own hands pressing down on her shoulders firmly. Felix thought they looked like interspecies couples posing for pictures at a Coalition formal military ball, except they all looked miserable.

As if she'd read his mind, Azad went on, saying, "We should go dancing sometime, Sev. I can only quibble with your choice of time and place to *deploy* your hidden skills–"

"Shut up," Severyne said. "You, Sagasa. I will give you my Letnev warship and all the money in my discretionary account if you turn these criminals over to me."

"Oh, babe," Azad said.

"You mean us criminals?" Felix was sitting in a chair – a decent one, brought into the office for the occasion – beside Calred. Tib was also seated, pressing a medpack to the back of her head where Azad had punched her. "*Us*? Criminals? You – you criminals!"

The Disciplinarian slammed his hands down on the desk. "I will negotiate almost anything, but I will not negotiate that. Can you imagine what would happen to my business if word got out that I sold visitors to my yard to their enemies? No one would come here any more. That means you'd have to offer me more money than I would make in the rest of my career before I'd even *consider* it." He paused, then lifted an eyebrow. "Are you? Offering me that much? Probably a few percent of the annual gross domestic product of the Barony would cover it, I think. I'd have to do some calculations."

"That is beyond my current resources. But if you hand them over, we can reach an accommodation–"

Sagasa sat back down. "I don't offer credit without collateral under the best of circumstances, and these aren't those." He swiveled his gaze. "You are in my bad books now, Amina. Why did you bring such a rude person to my place of business?"

"Call it a crime of passion, Sagasa. Duval's Devils are the deadliest bunch of renegade pirates and slavers in the sector – they kidnapped Severyne's mother and husband and baby and sold them to the Embers of Muaat as a discount fuel source–"

"Oh, come *on*," Felix cried.

The Disciplinarian sighed. "Amina. You amuse me, as always. But I am not currently in a state in which I crave amusement. I abhor violence in my office, and my waiting room is next to my office. My secretary sees two fingers when I hold up one. Your associate cut down one of my plants. There will be consequences." He turned to Felix and his crew. "I apologize for the inconvenience. As recompense, I will give you that extra two percent on the invoice at no charge."

"That's very generous," Felix said.

Sagasa shrugged. "It's fine. They're going to pay for it." He gestured to Azad and Severyne. "I think our business is concluded, or nearly so. You can be on your way."

Felix cleared his throat. "The thing is, they're going to immediately chase us and try to kill us again, so…"

Sagasa chuckled. "Not *immediately*. Believe it or not, this Letnev isn't the first person to behave recklessly upon encountering someone they dislike on my station. We have a policy: we hold the aggressor in a secure room for a minimum of three hours. That gives those transgressed against time to get *out of my system*. If you want to fight after that, I don't mind, because you'll be doing it elsewhere. I suggest you make haste."

"We, ah, have to do that thing, though, with the stuff, before we go–"

The Disciplinarian nodded. "Of course. An hour for that should be sufficient? I'll hold these naughty sapients for four hours, then."

"What thing with what stuff?" Azad said. "What are you even doing here, Duval?"

"We're just leaving." Felix sketched a salute to Severyne. "That was good spear-work. I hope we never meet again. And I am sorry about your people back on the station. We meant to leave more quietly than that."

"Human scum." Severyne looked like she wanted to spit, but she was better at containing herself now, with the Naalu's hands pressing down on her shoulders.

Calred and Tib said their farewells to Sagasa, and they all filed out.

"Duval's Devils," Felix said as they passed through the waiting room. "Kind of has a nice ring to it."

"I don't know," Tib said. "'Human scum' suits you pretty well too, don't you think?"

CHAPTER 18

The Disciplinarian escorted them to his brig personally, with one of the heavily armored guards along, just in case they got squirrely. Azad was a little worried Severyne *would* do something rash – again – but the Letnev woman seemed lost in her own thoughts.

Azad had to try. "Sagasa. Be reasonable. Just give us an hour. We barely even broke anything."

"You were the aggressors, Amina. We have rules here. You can leave in four hours. If you hurry, you can catch up with them… if you can figure out where they're going."

"Two hours. I'll bring back their ship for you as a gift after we capture them. It's a Mentak Coalition cruiser! Top of the line!"

"Maybe ten years ago it was."

"Still. It's a good trade, huh, for a couple of hours? You'll have to give me another ship in exchange, I can't *walk* out of here, but I'll take one of those junkers you can't offload."

"Would you like to stay for eight hours?"

"You jump from four to eight? That's a bit much. I thought you were a master negotiator."

"When one negotiates from a position of strength, one can be a bit unreasonable."

They reached the brig – not that it was really a brig, because this was a privately owned scrapyard, not a military ship or a local jail; those were the kind of places where Azad usually got locked up. There were just two cells here, the low-tech kind with metal bars, but the locks were too complicated to pick, especially with no tools except her teeth and fingernails. Low-tech was better than high-tech, in some cases. None of Azad's implants would do her any good here.

The guard opened the first cell door, and Azad stepped inside. He had to shove Severyne, who didn't stumble, but almost danced in as she caught her balance. That grace again. The cage door clanged shut, and the Hacan and his guard turned to leave.

Azad reached through the bars and snapped her fingers. "Hey, Sagasa, before you lock us up, can we at least talk *business*? We came here for a reason, and it wasn't getting into a fight with Duval's Devils."

The Hacan turned. "Ah. In all the disarray, I forgot you had a proposal. I am willing to hear it, if you still wish to proceed, because business comes first, but I hope you're prepared to be charged a penalty for making me get up from my chair."

"Severyne is really sorry about that. You know how the Letnev are. Hot-blooded and impetuous." Azad thought she could *hear* Sev grind her teeth behind her.

"That is indeed their reputation throughout the galaxy," the Disciplinarian said solemnly, and then chuckled. "You *do* amuse me, Amina. What did you want to sell, and more importantly, what do you want in return?"

They haggled and argued, and the Hacan pointed out more than once that Azad was in no *position* to argue, given that she was locked in a cell on a space station that might as well be his own sovereign nation… but Azad would never let a little thing like having no leverage stop her from advocating for her own interests. Eventually they reached an agreement: they'd get a fast and unobtrusive ship, in exchange for a not-that-modest financial consideration, and the *Grim Countenance* as collateral.

Once he was gone, Azad turned to Severyne. Her feelings had grown rather more complicated. She'd enjoyed teasing Severyne, liked her company, and found her attractive, but all that was just mental amusement. Seeing Severyne fight like that, her grace, her absolute conviction in the face of impossible odds… now Azad liked her, thought she was attractive, and *admired* her. She began to reconsider her stance against sleeping with people she might have to kill. Maybe there was a way to keep Severyne alive, and, if not, she could at least die with a happy memory, right? She put her hand on the Letnev's shoulder. "I know this seems bad, but really, we're not any worse off than we were before."

Severyne said nothing, staring at the wall beyond the bars, her forehead creased. Azad had seen that little line there before; it could be annoyance, hate, or deep thought, but it was definitely cute.

Azad put her back against the rear wall of the cell and settled in. It wasn't too disgusting a cell, as far as private dungeons went. She'd seen worse. "We made contact with the enemy and it didn't go our way, but that's just the way it is sometimes, and we're both alive. We didn't get eaten by Counselor An'Truk, we didn't get our arms ripped off by the guys in the exo-suits, and in a couple of hours we'll be on the trail again–"

"Your tracker didn't beep." Severyne's voice was even more devoid of emotion than usual.

"What's that?"

"This tracker in your head, that tells you when Thales is close. It *didn't beep.*" Severyne stood up from the bench, her hands balled into fists. "We were docked on the other side of a space station from him, he was *right there,* and you didn't know it!"

"They must have found the tracker and disabled it," Azad said. "I didn't think they would, but it wouldn't be the first time I underestimated Duval and his crew."

Severyne shook her head. "There was never any tracker at all, was there?"

"That is also a possible interpretation of the available information. Listen, Sev, don't be mad. I couldn't tell you the truth, because back then you didn't know me, but now you can see the truth: I don't need a tracking device, because I know Thales. I researched him thoroughly before my mission. Haven't I anticipated where he'd be *twice* now?"

"Once!" she shouted. "You predicted he'd come to *my* facility, and then you predicted he'd go to the Universities of Jol-Nar, but you did *not* predict that he would come *here!*"

"I must have known it *subconsciously* though." She tapped her forehead. "There's a lot going on in here, all the time. I do wonder why they came here. Must be part of their plan to infiltrate the Universities."

"I am leaving you here." Severyne turned and stormed away, as far as you *could* storm in a cell that was only three meters square.

Azad cleared her throat. "Are you sure? The thing is, if you leave without the *Grim Countenance,* I'm going to have to take your ship for myself. I'll *have* to, because I have a mission here too. If you leave *with* the *Grim Countenance,* you have the same problem you had before: sailing a heavily armed Letnev ship to the Universities, and getting all the wrong kinds of attention in the process."

Severyne scowled. Oh, that line on her forehead. "I will simply warn the Hylar that they are the target of a gang of thieves."

"OK, let's game that out." Azad crossed her legs and leaned back. "Let's say they believe you. Let's say they believe you so much they agree to arrest Duval and company before they even commit a crime, with no proof apart from your word. Then the Hylar will have Duval in custody, along with Thales and Shelma. The Hylar aren't huge fans of the Barony. They aren't going to hand their prisoners over to you. They're big believers in due process, and their trials take forever, so even if you work out some kind of extradition agreement, which would be an impressive feat, it'll take ages. Or do you see it differently?"

Severyne didn't answer.

Azad made her voice softer. "Haven't I been helpful, Sev? Let me continue to help."

She could see the Letnev's practical side warring with her anger. In a human, the balance could have shifted either way, but Letnev culture was about suppressing the emotional in favor of the practical. "No more lies," Severyne said finally. She turned to look down at Azad. "Do not mislead me. Do not omit things. Be honest. I cannot make plans unless I am aware of all the factors."

"No lies at all? That's a pretty big tool you're taking out of my toolbox, Sev, but all right. For you. I am sorry I wasn't straight with you before. That thing about the tracker, it's the same way I had to tell the Disciplinarian some bullshit to get him to meet with us. I had to tell *you* some bullshit to get you to take me with you."

Severyne sat back down. "I understand your reasoning. We need speak of it no further."

Apology accepted, then. Azad managed not to grin. "Hey, I was really impressed by your moves back there." Severyne looked at her sharply, and Azad held up her hands. "Honestly! If Sagasa hadn't stepped in, you would've had Duval's heart on a stick."

"I trained for more than *just* sitting behind a desk," Severyne said. "I excelled at hand-to-hand combat training, and was invited to take advanced study. I noticed that you struck a blow of your own, against the hideous little creature who killed my sniper."

"I really hate her. I hate Duval more, because his face is so smug, but yeah, Tib Pelta is up there on the hate list."

Severyne seemed to struggle with something. Finally she said, "I must apologize. I behaved impetuously. If I had remained calm, we might have turned that chance meeting to our advantage. Or, at least, not suffered this delay. This is my fault."

"You did fine," Azad said. "In most circumstances, when you encounter your enemy at a moment when neither one of you expects contact, you *absolutely* move just the way you did – hit first and fast and hard. You can settle the whole situation right then, most of the time."

"At first I wanted to capture him," Severyne said. "To force him to give me Shelma. Then I thought, I could kill him and force his *crew* to give me Shelma. Insofar as I thought at all."

"I admit, when we first met, I thought you were a basic bureaucrat, and that if your workstation so much as got messy, you'd melt down. But you showed real badass instincts back there, Sev. It just happened to be a situation where a good offense *wasn't* the best idea, but that's not your fault."

"You have said this word, badass. I do not know it."

"It's the highest compliment I can offer, Sev. It means you're a lot like me."

"I am not at all like you," Severyne replied, but Azad noted there was no little hateline on her forehead that time.

Felix was babysitting Thales as he scrounged through the mysterious alien vessel, because Tib and Calred refused to spend any time with the man. When Felix tried to pull rank, Tib said, "I was *injured* in the line of *duty*," and Calred just pretended he couldn't hear Felix, making obviously fake static noises into his comms. That was gross insubordination, even by Mentak Coalition standards, but they'd all had a trying few days, so Felix let it go.

This ancient wrecked vessel didn't have any life support, and it had probably never supported their kind of life anyway, so Felix and Thales were in environment suits. The ship was an unsettling place, full of twisting dark corridors with walls that must have been some kind of metal or plastic, but that had an organic, swirled texture, like fingerprints. The corridors changed size gradually, sometimes contracting so small they had to go on hands and knees, other times dilating to nine or ten meters high. What kind of creatures would be comfortable in such a vessel? "This place is creepy," Felix said, shining his light into yet another empty corner of yet another empty and oddly proportioned room.

"*Still* afraid of ghosts?" Thales said in his comms. "I thought we went over that. Ah, here we are. An engine room. I bet there's something suitable here."

The new chamber was the biggest yet, and it was, at least, less bare – there were dangling cables and wires; things like gearwheels, except they were triangular; a huge crankshaft that floated, unconnected in the lack of gravity; and various smaller bits of machinery, variously sprouting blackened crystals, surrounded by transparent globes, or with overlapping loops of material that made Felix's head hurt when he tried to trace all their intersections. "A completely unknown species built this thing, so long ago your ancestors weren't even in jail yet," Thales said. "Those creatures made this ship, they traveled in it, they abandoned it or wrecked it, and some wandering idiots found it millennia later and towed it back here because they thought it might be worth a credit or two. It all makes you feel insignificant, doesn't it?"

"I guess we are pretty small, measured against the vastness of everything," Felix agreed.

"What?" Thales said. "No. I mean, it must make *you* feel insignificant. Which you are. *I'm* not insignificant. I'm the man who invented wormhole technology. No one in the galaxy will ever forget *my* name, unlike the pathetic fools who built this thing. I was musing on my own immortal greatness, captain. Do try to keep up."

"Right. How foolish of me."

"Even a fool has his uses." Thales picked up one of the crystal-encrusted things, a device or component about the size of two fists put together. "This should do. It doesn't look like anything I've seen before, and a matching scan through the available databases doesn't turn up anything similar."

"The Disciplinarian said it's worthless, though."

"Oh, probably – it certainly seems inert. But it *is* genuinely alien, and it's unlike any other artifact that's been publicly logged. Mere novelty is not enough, on its own, to interest Director Woryela, but that's where the fakery comes in. I'll use this as the basis to create something truly enigmatic and alluring."

"Woryela?"

"The person you're going to *scam*, captain. Head of the experimental research and development division, propulsion section. You should really read those dossiers Calred compiles for you."

"I know his name," Felix said. "I didn't realize *you* did."

"Oh, I used to work at the Universities. I'm not up on all the latest gossip, but I know the major players." He turned toward Felix. "We should go. It's disturbing to have this Azad woman so nearby, even if she is in a cell. She has a tendency to escape those, as I recall?"

"She probably could escape. I don't think she will, though. She doesn't want to piss off the Disciplinarian."

"How did Azad find us? You assured me there were no tracking devices on Shelma or myself."

"There was one on Shelma, but we neutralized it. We didn't detect any on you, and we did a pretty deep scan. The thing is, I don't think they *did* find us. They seemed as surprised as we were."

"It's a big galaxy, captain. To suggest that our meeting is coincidence rather strains credulity."

"It *is* a big galaxy, yes, but it's not that big a sector. In this particular region of space, there's only one person you go to if you need an untraceable ship, and that's Sagasa. They're after us, and clearly needed something from Sagasa to help catch us. I wish I knew what."

"I'm sure your brilliant military mind will unravel the puzzle," Thales said. "Or, more likely, there was a tracking device, and you just missed it."

"Your confidence means everything to me, Thales."

CHAPTER 19

Felix and Tib floated in space in the cloud of wrecked ships, inspecting the exterior of the vessel Sagasa had loaned them. Calred was on the *Temerarious*, helping Thales pack his notes and equipment, which he understandably refused to leave behind.

The *Endless Dark* was a far smaller vessel than the *Temerarious*, meant for longrange travel and exploration, not battle. This little ship had gone a long way and come back whole, though the same couldn't be said about its original crew.

"I think it looks like a bird wearing a tiara," Felix said.

"That tiara is all its sensors. You want a lot of sensors in a ship meant for exploring, captain."

"I know what it is. I just think it looks stupid."

"The *Temerarious* looks like a fat fish with tusks." Tib put her hands on either side of her mouth and hooked fingers into fangs.

Felix snorted. The *Temerarious* had a big belly of a cargo hold, and its fore cannons *were* a bit tusk-like. "I always say our ship reminds me of a shark, but that's just me being poetic. Now that you mention it, I can see the similarity to a walrus. While I'm complaining, what about this *name*? 'Endless Dark' is a little bit ominous for a ship meant to go out into deep space and come back with riches, don't you think?"

"You're just uncultured, captain," Tib said. "'Endless Dark' is a Letnev idiom. It means the same thing my people mean when we say 'unbroken canopy.'"

"Oh. Well. That clears it up."

"I think you'd say 'the sky's the limit?' If you're Letnev, endless dark is a *good* thing, just like for my people, an unbroken canopy means you're safely under cover of the trees as far as you can see, and free to go where you like without fear."

"Oh. Thanks, Tib. That makes me feel better."

"That's the most important part of my job as first officer. Do you want to check the interior, and I'll finish looking over the exterior?"

Felix concurred and went into the ship. They had to look the vessel over quickly, just keeping an eye out for major, likely-to-kill-them-all-in-transit-level problems, because they were on a ticking clock. Severyne and Azad would be coming after them in just a couple of hours. He didn't think the Disciplinarian would tell the duo which way Felix and his crew had gone, or in what kind of vessel, but Azad had somehow tracked his crew here, and they might pursue them to the Universities, too. *Just what you want in a heist: extra time pressure.*

The interior of the ship was cramped by the standards of the *Temerarious*, but they'd manage, and the life support, engine, and other functions all checked out green. There wasn't much in the way of weaponry on board, but where they were going, weapons wouldn't help much anyway.

"It looks good in here." Felix sat in the cockpit. There was a little plastic figurine of a Xxcha in war armor glued over the control panel, which he recognized as a character from an adventure sim popular a decade before. A stab of melancholy went through Felix as he looked at that little personal object, put there by a crew that had set out for adventure and riches and had come back, diminished, to sell the remnants of their dream to a scrapper. He looked out the bulbous viewport at the dead ships hanging all around him and suppressed a shudder. A lot of broken dreams ended up here. "How do things look on your end, Tib?"

"I don't see any great big cracks in the hull," Tib said. "I'd like to check things over more thoroughly, but I don't think we'll die as soon as we turn the engines on or anything."

"This ship went all the way to the fringes of the galaxy and made it back," Felix said. "That gives me comfort."

"That's completely irrational, but I'm glad it makes you feel better, captain."

"I just mean, if the ship has worked this long, it's probably fine, right?"

"Everything works, right up until the moment it stops working," Tib said.

"I'm trying to remain optimistic here. Go get Thales and Cal, would you?"

"Aye aye."

Felix powered up the ship. Once he was confident the systems were humming properly, he stripped off his environment suit and sat down in the cockpit again to lay in a course.

Sagasa had assured him the ship had been thoroughly cleaned and bathed in sanitizing light, but there was a small, dark smear on the side of the navigation console. It looked distressingly like blood. Another little personal touch left behind by the former crew.

Optimism, Felix thought.

The *Endless Dark* didn't really have a bridge, so once they were underway the crew met in the galley, which was just about big enough for the four of them, if they didn't mind their elbows touching; this ship had originally held a crew of three.

Calred dished out bowls of nutritious protein glop, and Felix dutifully ate. Mostly what he wanted was sleep and a shower. Those would come next. He slurped the last bit of slurry off his spoon and said, "This is an official mission briefing. Sagasa was kind enough to provide us with fake identities, belonging to real explorers who, in reality, are still out there somewhere exploring." *Or dead.* "I'm Heuvelt Angriff, swashbuckling outcast scion of a wealthy family, spendthrifting my inheritance on expeditions to uncharted regions of space. Tib, you're Dob Ell, my loyal family retainer and all-purpose adjunct and helpmeet."

"I'm your what now?" Tib said flatly.

"I know, I know, but it was tough to find ID that made sense for a crew made up of a couple of humans, an Yssaril, and a Hacan, OK?"

"Who am I, then?" Calred said.

"You're Ferocious Naadin, deep-space guide for hire, Hacan of a thousand talents."

"I like it."

"I hate mine even more now," Tib said.

"Swashbuckling. Loyal. Talented. Ha," Thales said. "Who am I, then? An applecheeked maiden you rescued from space pirates?"

"You're nobody. Sagasa got you a flimsy ID, but it doesn't have to stand up to scrutiny – you're just a passenger we picked up on Vega Minor, and we're transporting you to your next destination for money. We don't know you, or anything much about you. You'll be staying on the ship, so the Universities won't take as close a look at your ID anyway."

"Calred is staying on the ship too," Thales pointed out. "And *he* got a fancy bespoke identity."

"Yes, but Calred would have felt left out if I didn't include him," Felix said.

"You don't care if *I* feel left out?"

"We would all prefer to leave you out, Thales," Tib said.

"I'd like to leave you out in the desert," Calred said. "Perhaps tied to wooden stakes."

Thales showed his teeth in what could not accurately be called a smile. "The contempt of simpletons is as good as the praise of geniuses." He stood up. "I'm going to go finish faking your wondrous mysterious artifact, unless you need me to sit and listen to further prattle?"

"Go on," Felix said.

The whole crew relaxed when he left. "Is he *really* going to walk free and be wealthy when this is all done?" Tib said.

Felix sighed. "If he delivers wormhole tech to the Coalition, they'll probably put up a statue to him in the Plaza of Heroes on Moll Primus."

"He's a murderer," Calred said. "We know it, and we might even be able to prove it."

"Several of our most illustrious ancestors in the Coalition were murderers."

"That was then, and this is now," Tib said. "Thales had us kidnap Shelma just so he could kill her and steal her stuff."

"The Coalition has a whole raider fleet devoted to killing people and stealing their stuff."

"That's not fair," Calred said. "The raider fleets only kill people who make trouble or can't follow instructions. Thales is something else entirely."

"I don't disagree with you," Felix said. "I'm just saying what the Table of Captains will say to justify shrugging off any allegations we bring them."

"He only wins if he succeeds," Tib said.

"I know. I've thought of sabotaging things too, for the pleasure of seeing Thales fail. But what he can offer is too important to the Coalition."

"His success would be good for us, too," Calred said. "We'll have more promotions and bonuses than we know what to do with if we bring this thing home."

"That's why I haven't stabbed him in the neck yet, personally," Tib said. "My selfinterest is stronger than my him-hate."

"That's the Mentak Coalition way," Felix said.

"I'll be glad when we're done with the part where we earn our rewards," Calred said, "and get to the part where we can start enjoying them instead."

Felix sent a message to the Universities, knowing it would probably take a while to navigate the necessary layers of bureaucracy to reach director Woryela. He used all the key phrases that Thales fed him: "previously unknown technology," "unidentifiable chemical signature," and, "produces energy without a discernible source," the last to appeal to the director's professional as well as personal interests.

He included some pictures and video of the crystal-studded machinery; the crystals glowed pale blue now, thanks to something Thales had done, but insisted wasn't poisonous or radioactive. Felix also sent a bunch of graphs and charts of diagnostic data that meant nothing to him but that Thales assured him would make any Hylar scientist drool, or whatever the squid equivalent was. "We have a paying passenger at the moment, so we don't have time for endless meetings," Felix's message concluded, "but if we can have an initial meeting with someone high up – the head of the propulsion lab seems like the obvious choice – who can determine whether what we have is valuable, we can make a deal. If you're too busy, we have a contact in the Barony who's willing to see us next week. We're in your neighborhood, though, and we're eager to recoup the costs of our expedition as soon as possible." He hoped that last bit added the right note of desperation to make Woryela think he could snag a bargain.

Then Felix went to sleep, for the first time in what felt like days, as the *Endless Dark* cruised through its namesake.

The ship roused him a couple of hours out from the Jol-Nar system. He'd missed their passage through the wormhole on their route – Calred had handled the transition – which struck him as funny, considering the overall nature of their mission. He yawned and checked the system, where he found a reply from Woryela himself: "We're very interested in appraising your find. I can spare a little time tomorrow morning if you can make it to Wun-Escha," with an invitation to digitally accept the appointment.

Tomorrow morning. Felix checked the local time and groaned. He had to wait another fifteen hours before they could meet. That was probably considered swift by academic standards, but right now it felt like eternity. He accepted the appointment, then met with Calred and Tib. "I don't like it. Azad and Severyne will have plenty of time to catch up with us. Are you *sure* there isn't a tracking device on Thales?"

Calred sighed. "I did everything short of a cavity search, and I only skipped that because it's not necessary with my scanning equipment. There's nothing inside that man he wasn't born with, except gallstones. Azad and Sagasa clearly knew each other from some past business. She was probably just there to buy a ship to chase us with, or weapons to kill us with."

"They *had* a ship, though – Severyne said she'd trade the Disciplinarian a Letnev warship in exchange for us. Why trade down?"

"Why did *we*?" Tib said. "Those thorny Letnev ships are distinctive. Maybe they wanted to be more subtle."

Felix pondered, then opened comms. "Thales, is there any way Amina Azad could know we're heading to the Universities of Jol-Nar?"

"Of course there's a way," Thales said. "She didn't strike me as much of an intellectual, but she had some time with my files, and she may have looked over them."

Felix closed his eyes. "You're saying your files mentioned the need for this power source?"

"I did say that, and see no need to say it again. I'm *working*." The channel closed.

The crew sat in silence for a moment, then Tib said, "There are only two of them. Three of us. We've got the numbers."

"Severyne will have others with her," Felix said. "She's a supervisor, so she's going to be supervising people. Guards from her station, who will be eager to see us again, since we left a few of their colleagues dead back there."

"I'm worth two of any of her guards in a fight," Calred said.

"Let's hope she only brought two, then," Felix said. "We might be OK. They don't know what ship we're in. We're under assumed names. The Hylar system is bustling. We'll be tough to find."

"Unless they go straight to the experimental propulsion lab," Tib pointed out. "Which is exactly where they will go, if they read the files, which we have to assume they did."

"We'll just have to be extra vigilant," Felix said.

"Oh, well. *That* will make a nice change from our current atmosphere of total relaxation," Calred drawled.

"Give me some good news," Felix said. "Tell me the ship found proof that Thales murdered Shelma."

Calred tapped his fingertip on a tablet. "The ship is running screens, and has ruled out one-hundred-and-sixty-two known toxins, poisons, and chemicals so far. There are lots to go."

•••

"You're free to go." The Disciplinarian's Winnaran secretary opened the cell door. His headdress sat askew because of the lumpy bandage fastened to the back of his skull.

"Your head injury was regrettable," Severyne said. "You should not have attempted to restrain me."

"That was not an apology," he said.

"It sure wasn't." Azad stood from the bench and stretched. "But she's from the Barony. It's about the best you're going to get."

They followed the Winnaran along the station's corridors. "We have to hurry," Severyne said. "We need to get my sidearm, gather my guards, board whatever heap the Disciplinarian has seen fit to saddle us with, and burn as fast as we can for the Jol-Nar system. With luck Duval and his devils will still be there, and if not, we can try to pick up their trail–"

"I was thinking about that, while you were napping," Azad said. "I know you're all hot to chase after them, and I get it, but how about if instead, we don't?"

"What are you talking about? Our very lives and futures depend on recovering Shelma and Thales!"

"I don't know about 'lives.' I'd have to go rogue, and never return home, but the Federation navy invested a lot of effort teaching me how to disappear completely, and I have marketable skills, so I'd survive. I'd prefer not to live that way, though, and at this point, it's gotten personal – I *do* want to settle my score with Duval and his sucker-punching sidekick. I'm not saying give up. I'm suggesting we approach the problem in a different way."

"What did you have in mind?" Severyne asked.

"I'm still working out the details. Let me work out some more of them." She trotted ahead to walk beside the secretary. "Hey! Let me talk to you for a minute. Remember me from last time I was here, when we made that little side arrangement? Maybe we can help each other again…"

CHAPTER 20

The twin planets Jol and Nar hung in the viewscreen, blue spheres against the black, shining in the light of their local star. "I've never been here," Felix said. "But it's your home. Are you sad you won't be landing?"

Thales sat in the co-pilot's chair. He grunted. "Not really." He gazed quite fixedly at the planets in the viewscreen, though, Felix noted. The man wasn't totally incapable of human feeling; he'd just buried whatever good impulses he had beneath meters of resentment and grievance and grudge. "I grew up on Nar. The waters are warm enough to swim in without freezing your testicles off, which is more than can be said about Jol. There's even an archipelago – off-worlders call it the Reef; you couldn't pronounce the Hylar name for it. My family spent a lot of time there, since it's one of the only places hospitable to air-breathers. Some of my only good memories are from those days."

Felix tried to imagine Thales having a happy day at the seaside with his family. It was like trying to imagine a moray eel reciting poetry. Still, this side of the man was interesting, and might even yield useful information, so Felix kept listening.

"I began my studies in Nuun-Dascha – that's where I met Shelma. The greatest city on Nar, and the whole place is a school, really, surrounded by businesses and workers who support or provide for the scholars."

"What's the city like?"

"It's ancient. Not made for human comfort. There are great coral towers, though, dating from the days when the Hylar had to hide from predators, before they mastered the seas, and because humans like having roofs, the off-worlder dormitories were in those towers. I counted as an off-worlder, though I'd spent my life in the Jol-Nar system. The halls were cramped, with corridors designed for creatures who don't have bones. The locals never made much of an effort to provide for the comfort of other species. The idea was, we were lucky to be allowed to study at the greatest institution of higher learning in the galaxy, and if we didn't like it, we were welcome to go elsewhere. The hell of it is, they were right – the Universities are unmatched, at least in the sciences, which are the only fields of study that actually matter. Oh, there are embassies and businesses with domes and such that hold atmosphere, but those are meant for dignitaries and tourists, not students." Thales seemed to realize he'd been talking for a while, because he scowled. "None of that matters. You aren't going to Nar, anyway. You're going to Jol. A world of frigid seas, with a few islands no one would want to live on. The city *you're* going to is Wun-Escha, and it is admittedly more welcoming for off-worlders, since it's the seat of government, where the Hylar leader the Headmaster lives, and they get so many diplomatic and trade delegations from elsewhere. There's a whole section of the city with an atmosphere hospitable to humans and several other species of airbreathers. You won't even get a momentary sense of what my life down there was like."

No one can possibly understand my suffering – the cry of every aggrieved adolescent, even Felix himself, once upon a time... But like most people, he'd grown out of it. "Why doesn't Woryela work in the other city, if that's where the schools are?"

"Plenty of scientists work for the experimental propulsion lab, captain. I did myself, once upon a time. But it's not an academic setting in the way you're thinking – it's better to think of it more as a military installation than the sort of training academies or scholastic institutions you're familiar with."

"I was a lot happier about stealing something from a university than a military base, Thales."

"I'm sure you were. I've given you everything you need, though. More than you need. Woryela's office is near the labs, and there are only a few places the power source could be. Once you're with him in the office and you deploy my surprise, you'll have all the time you need for your slippery friend to search for the power source."

Felix nodded. Thales had come up with a good idea, he had to admit. Woryela was one of the Hylar who could breathe air for weeks at a time, and he was meeting them in his office, where the atmosphere was conducive to their biology as well – visiting researchers came there from all over, after all. The mysterious alien artifact now had a small reservoir inside, and when Woryela handled it, it would disperse a sedative and dissociative gas designed to work on the Hylar – he'd pass out, and wake up an hour later with no memory, or at best a confused one, and by then, Felix and Tib would be long gone.

Felix had found the idea of using gas absurd – "Won't we be underwater?" But Thales had called him an idiot and said Woryela would doubtless meet them in a room with air: "He won't risk examining a potentially delicate alien artifact in a submerged zone. Water can be too damaging. Woryela is the sort of Hylar who can breathe the same air you do, too, so he won't be in a tank or anything – those are cumbersome and avoided when possible. I *have* thought this through."

Felix had other concerns, though. "Are you sure the gas won't affect us?"

"Did you steal a Hylar's nervous system at some point?"

"Not the last time I checked."

"Then you'll be fine. The gas may not smell very nice, but it won't hurt you."

"OK. How do I look?" Felix was wearing adventurer garb: black tactical pants and a vest covered in pouches, his head topped by a battered broad-brimmed hat he thought looked rather dashing.

"Like an idiot, but like the kind of idiot you *should* look like."

"Good enough."

Director Woryela sent a shuttle to pick them up, and Tib and Felix sat together, strapped into their respective seats, as they plummeted bouncily through the atmosphere. Felix hadn't felt planetary gravity in a while, and it was more intense than the artificial kind. His lower back ached. When had *that* happened? That seemed like something that should happen to people older than he was.

Felix felt the splash when they hit the water, and heard a hum as the engines kicked in. From orbit to the bottom of the sea. Quite a journey. "It's exciting, visiting the Hylar homeworld. One of the great cities of the galaxy, down there below us somewhere."

"If you say so," Tib muttered. "Who am I to disagree? I'm just a humble loyal retainer." She wore a version of Felix's outfit, with a rucksack strapped to her chest. The bag contained the fake artifact and the other thing Thales had made for them.

"I haven't even asked you to polish the silverware or pour me some tea. You're getting off easy. Honestly, I think of our staff like *family*, don't you know. Let's take a look at the view. Shuttle, let's have some windows, please."

Rectangles all around them went transparent, or rather, created a convincing illusion of transparency; they were screens connected to external cameras. Felix had expected to see schools of brightly colored fish, vast coral structures, or maybe a kelp forest; instead there was just dim, murky water, and as they descended, their surroundings became indistinguishable from darkest night. "Oh," he said. "No light down here."

"Space is brighter than this," Tib said. "Ugh."

"Shuttle, what's underneath us?"

This time the whole interior of the shuttle went transparent, like they were in a glass bowl. Darkness surrounded them. "Wow. Shouldn't we have some kind of safety gear? Life vests or air tanks or something?"

"At this depth, if we got out of this shuttle, our lungs wouldn't be able to expand against the crushing pressure, and we'd promptly die, so no, there's not much point in safety gear."

"You are very bad for morale, Tib."

"We loyal retainers do what we can."

After a while, lights glimmered beneath them, dim and far away, like distant stars. "That must be Wun-Escha."

"Or else the bioluminescent bulbs of deep-sea predators trying to lure prey into their nightmare maws."

"Or that," Felix said.

The lights gradually brightened, revealing domed structures and organic coral towers, and soon they passed other vehicles, smooth and streamlined and aerodynamic – or, Felix wondered, was it aquadynamic? Their shuttle zipped along, and Felix was surprised at how fast it moved, now that he could gauge their progress by the city whipping past beneath them. They sailed between two towers, and through windows (he hoped very thick ones), Felix could see off-worlders, living and working in their pockets of air so far below the world above. How strange it would be, to live in a place like this … but then, was it any stranger than living in space, like he did? Space and the sea were both vast and inhospitable and rather chilly environments that would kill you if you didn't have the right equipment. At least down here there weren't micrometeoroid impacts or radiation. Though in space there weren't toothy underwater predators, and you might suffocate, but you wouldn't drown. There were always trade-offs.

The shuttle docked at a sprawling but low facility, a series of cylinders and domes hugging the seafloor. "I thought the lab would be bigger," Felix said.

"I think it's mostly underground."

"Oh, good. I was thinking we weren't far enough down yet. We'd better get suited up." They fastened on their helmets and checked their air supplies.

The doors hissed open, revealing a – well, not an *airlock*. A water-lock? Some system to equalize the pressure with the submerged areas beyond, anyway. They stepped into the cylindrical chamber, and once the ship was closed behind them, water slowly filled the space. The heaters in their environment suits clicked on to compensate.

Once the lock was filled with water, the outer door opened, revealing a clean white room. A Hylar, slightly smaller than Tib, waited for them, floating in the faintly green-tinged water and holding a glowing tablet in one thin pseudopod. Felix had gotten so used to Shelma in her exo-suit that it was strange to see a Hylar unencumbered. "Mx Angriff?" she said on their open comms channel. "And Mx Ell. Let me help you." She offered them each mobility packs that strapped onto their suits, and showed them how to use the controls to adjust their buoyancy and propel themselves forward and back with jets of water. Felix spun himself around in a circle at first, but got the idea fairly quickly. She attached visitor passes, little round badges in bright orange, to their chests with some adhesive. "Keep these visible at all times. They'll allow you to leave the facility once the meeting is over."

"You won't be escorting us out?" Felix said.

"It's a busy day," she called. "Don't worry, the badges will only open the doors necessary to lead you back to the shuttle, which is programmed to return you to your ship after you board. The badges also track your location, of course, so there's no danger of you getting lost in here."

Felix glanced at Tib, who shrugged infinitesimally. They had restricted access and this was a place full of security doors, but they'd expected that. Tib would figure out a way to work around the problem. Felix hoped.

"Come along. The director carved out an hour for you, and that hour has already started." The Hylar approached a round door, which opened to reveal a textured tunnel with walls of white coral. Branching corridors appeared at irregular intervals, some open, others sealed with formidable-looking metal doors. There were no windows, and Felix was grateful he didn't have claustrophobia, as the tunnels were made for Hylar physiology, and fairly tight for someone his size.

They reached a security checkpoint with a guard – a Hylar bristling with needle-like extensions that must have been weapons – and floated through into a sea cave lit by bioluminescent orbs stuck to the walls. Their guide turned and left them without a word, and a Hylar at the center of the room glanced up at them and said, "Wait." She was operating three terminals at once with six pseudopods.

Why does no one ever offer me refreshments? Felix wasn't sure how that would work underwater, but still, it would have been a nice gesture. *And I thought we were already late for our very brief appointment?*

After a few moments, the receptionist paused in her work, in response to no stimulus that Felix could detect, and said, "Director Woryela is waiting for you. Go on up."

"Up?"

Tib nudged Felix and pointed up. The ceiling was a shimmering circle. They adjusted their buoyancy and rose, breaking through the top of the pool into air. They clambered out into a sort of conference room, though one where the floor was dotted with other pools, presumably giving access to other parts of the facility.

A Hylar perched on a stool behind a long table, wearing a sort of headband that held a complex array of lenses on adjustable arms. "Welcome! You can take off your helmets. The air in here can sustain you."

Felix removed his helmet and set it on the table, sniffing cautiously at the briny but breathable atmosphere. "Thank you, ah, Director Woryela?"

"Indeed! And you are Heuvelt Angriff and Dob Ell!" His artificial voice was booming and hearty. "Back from the depths of space with bountiful mystery! How I envy you, dauntlessly exploring the vast unknown!"

Felix had expected a calm and measured academic, or a humorless bureaucrat, but Woryela was positively jolly, and he wasn't sure how to respond.

The Hylar could tell. "Not what you were expecting, eh?" he said. "I always get that – too much energy, too much verve, for someone in a position like mine. But I got here because I'm good at my job, not because I'm good at playing politics. What was my job, do you know?" *That look must be Hylar for "expectant."*

"Ah, propulsion?" Felix said.

"That's right, Heuvelt, may I call you Heuvelt? I always get mixed up on human honorifics. I come from *propulsion*! Before I moved into the technical side, I was a test pilot. I used to spend more time in the void than I did in the ocean, strapping untested technology to a seat and launching myself as far and fast as I could. Experimental propulsion is the most exciting discipline we've got, as far as I'm concerned – anything that can propel a starship faster than any other starship has ever gone before also has a good chance of exploding or turning your body inside out. There's no substitute for that kind of thrill. That's half of why I met with you, and cleared a whole hour – the artifact is interesting, of course, and if it does half what you say, we'll pay well for it – but it's really for the chance to spend time with other people who *understand*. That's a real treat. The people who work for me, they're good at what they do, the best in the galaxy, but I never get to talk to the rocket jockeys any more. That life never get old, does it? I miss those days."

"We, ah, appreciate you having us," Felix said. "It's true, there's nothing like feeling the hum of a starship accelerating as you blast into the uncharted. That's what Dob and I live for." A sudden impulse seized him. "I heard rumors you were working on harnessing wormhole technology here, though – that would make most forms of propulsion pretty redundant, wouldn't it?"

The Hylar shook his head. "Wormhole tech, perpetual motion machines, mind uploading and digital immortality – there are always rumors that we're about to achieve those, but we're not. All that stuff is impossible, and, I for one, am glad, because overcoming engineering challenges is a lot more fun than waving a magic wand and poof, every difficulty is overcome."

"They say the Creuss can open wormholes, though," Tib said.

"They say the Creuss can kill you in your dreams, too. They say the Creuss can turn into mist, and if you breathe that mist they can possess your body and use you like a puppet. They say lots of things." He swiveled on his stool. "I won't say making wormholes is impossible. Once upon a time, there were Hylar in these seas who didn't even know there *was* a surface, let alone anything beyond – the ocean was their whole universe. They didn't know we had a sister planet, or that there was such a thing as outer space, or a whole community of intelligent alien species. Now, there are Hylar all over the galaxy. But I will say, I think we're as far from having wormhole technology right now as those ancient Hylar were from building their first starship. We've had a couple of researchers over the years who thought they'd cracked the wormhole problem, but they never convinced me, and they don't seem to have accomplished much without me. In the meantime, I'm happy enough with what we *can* do. But maybe you brought me something impossible today! Shall we take a look?"

CHAPTER 21

Felix nodded to Tib, who opened the airtight carrying case she wore across her chest, removed their "artifact," and placed it in on the table.

The Hylar picked up the crystal assemblage with delicate pseudopods, and some of the lenses on his face rearranged themselves. "Interesting. These crystals could be part of the original specification, but they're more likely caused by chemical leakage, or the side effect of some process gone wrong. This glow looks like... huh. It appears to be a simple luminescent gloss, of the sort that fades over time. This paint isn't nearly as old as the rest of this object appears to be – in fact, I recognize it as a variety produced here on Hylar. People paint it on their windows during the Festival of Luminous Depths." He looked up at them, his eyes magnified by the lenses. "Gentlepersons, I hope you haven't wasted my time with some amateurish attempt at a hoax–"

The device abruptly cracked open, breaking into two unequal halves, and a tightly rolled piece of paper slipped out. "What's this? A message from the ancient aliens, written conveniently in a language I can read? Really, Heuvelt and Dob, this is disappointing." He unrolled the paper and stared at it, lenses telescoping.

Felix looked at Tib. What the hell was going on?

"'Courtesy of Phillip Caruthers,'" Woryela read. "What, that man who published those absurd papers about a theory of everything? What is the meaning of this –"

Gas began to hiss from the sundered device, and Felix instinctively held his breath. Thales had claimed the artifact wouldn't hurt them, but he also hadn't mentioned his plan to include a personal note for the director. Felix waited for Woryela to slump over and pass out, but instead the Hylar gasped and writhed, limbs spasming wildly, knocking the artifact off the table. Woryela fell off the stool and looked up at them, lenses askew, eyes somehow pleading. He tried to crawl to the door, then shuddered all over again, and slumped.

Tib knelt and looked the Hylar over. "He's not unconscious, Felix. He's dead."

Of course he was. Felix clutched his helmet. "Thales. He *used* us, and we – Tib, we just assassinated a high-ranking official! We committed murder!"

"We were used as murder weapons, anyway." Tib scooped up the artifact and put it away in the case. "Wrestle with the implications later, captain. We need to finish the mission and get out of here."

Of course. Bad as this was, getting caught wouldn't make it any better. Felix found the note from Thales and shoved it in a pouch on his suit. No reason to leave any evidence behind.

"You stay here," Tib said. "I'll go look for the power cell. We've come this far." She opened the bag and removed a small spherical device, half matte black, half crystal. It was, Thales claimed, a perfect replica of the power source they were stealing – not functional, of course, but with a mess of fused wire inside that might fool the engineers into thinking the device had merely malfunctioned, at least for a while. The original plan was, Tib would take the real cell and replace it with the fake one, and when Woryela woke up in a confused daze, no one would even know a robbery had taken place.

Tib searched the director's body until she found a badge and held it up. "Our key to victory. Let's hope the plans Thales drew up are accurate. I don't want to get lost down here." She peered into different pools, finally settling on one in the far corner that should lead to the deeper labs, then put on her helmet and dropped out of sight.

That left Felix, sitting there with a cooling body, desperately hoping the receptionist wouldn't decide *now* was the time to offer him a drink, that no emergency would occur that required the director's urgent assistance, and that no Hylar heads would pop out of any of the pools of water all around him. He put on his helmet and listened to his own heavy breath in his ears.

Felix wondered what slight, real or imagined, the director had committed against Thales. Woryela had called the man a lunatic – an assessment that seemed more accurate the longer Felix knew him. That comment Woryela had made, about people who'd come to him over the years talking about wormhole technology – was that about Thales? Had he tried to get Woryela's support and failed, been laughed out of the office, and nursed a grudge for all these years?

How long before Thales tried to kill Felix? Maybe never. Maybe he didn't think Felix was important enough to kill. That thought should have been more comforting than it was.

Tib reappeared, from a different pool this time, and spoke on a private comm channel. "We're all set. The layout was just like Thales described, and the power cell was in one of the first places he suggested I look."

Felix was impressed. "That didn't take you long."

"I only saw one Hylar, and they didn't see me. There were security doors to deal with, but this got me through all of them." She held up Woryela's badge.

"Maybe we should hold on to that, in case we have trouble getting out," Felix said. He tried to focus on the logistics of getting safely away, so he wouldn't focus instead on the coil of rage and hate he felt for Phillip Thales. Thales may have killed Shelma himself, albeit with Felix's unwitting help, but this time, like Tib said, he'd actually used Felix as a murder weapon.

Felix and Tib stepped into the pool, adjusted their mobility units, and submerged. The receptionist glanced up, surprised, as they floated down. "Done already?"

Felix realized they hadn't used up their hour. This had been both easier and far more horrifying than he'd anticipated. "Our ancient alien artifact is a hunk of useless junk," Felix said. "At least the director broke the news to us gently. He said at least now he had a free half hour to catch up on his reading."

"Oh, that's too bad," she said. "He was so excited to meet you. Better luck next time."

"We appreciate it." Felix and Tib exited the room into the tunnel beyond, giving a little wave to the spiny guard, who ignored them. Their visitor badges gave them brief audible directions, leading them through the rounded tunnels back to their shuttle. The trip back seemed to take much longer than the trip in. If the receptionist popped her head into the conference room and found the director unresponsive, would the facility get locked down? Would Felix and Tib be tried for murder in the slow-but-inexorable court system of Jol-Nar? Would anyone believe them if they named Phillip Thales as the mastermind and claimed to be unwitting pawns? *We're not guilty, Headmaster, we're just gullible fools?*

They reached the shuttle without incident. Once they boarded and strapped in, Felix said, "I just realized: if the real Heuvelt and Dob ever come back from their trip, they'll be wanted for murder."

"Maybe Sagasa can sell them new identities," Tib said. "I'm more troubled by the fact that we're *actual* accessories to the crime. This can't go on, Felix. We can't just keep helping Thales fulfill his various vendettas. He's going to send us to kill some editor who rejected one of his papers next at this rate, claiming he needs his kidneys to build a filtration system or something."

"I'm going to… I don't know what, Tib. Speak sharply to him, I guess. What can I do? Jhuri won't let me summarily execute the man. I can't even hit him in the head without risking damage to his valuable brain."

"I'm just registering my displeasure, captain."

"It's noted. And shared."

They were near the surface of the ocean – light beginning to faintly shine from above – when the shuttle stopped, paused, and began to descend again. "Crap," Felix said. "Shuttle, why are we descending?"

"Destination changed," the shuttle said blandly.

"Change it *back*," Felix said.

"Authorization required."

"I'm authorizing it!"

"Proper authorization required," the shuttle clarified.

"They found his body," Felix said.

"Yes. Let's hope they haven't canceled his privileges yet." Tib pressed Woryela's badge against one of the shuttle's sensors. "Director-level override. Resume original course, and disable all exterior communications and tracking."

"Complying with route request. Engaging confidential mode."

"That's all it takes?" Felix said.

Tib shrugged. "The person we killed is a director-level member of the Universities of Jol-Nar, captain. He reported directly to the Headmaster. Until someone down there remembers to disable his access, which isn't something just anybody can do anyway, this shuttle thinks we're him. Since we shut down the shuttle's comms, they can't seize control of the shuttle again anyway."

"So once we get to orbit, we're free and clear?"

"No. Once we get to orbit, we get chased by Jol-Nar forces."

"Oh."

"We'd better call Calred and have him pick us up someplace else."

Felix opened his encrypted channel to the ship and explained the situation.

"I'm going to break his legs," Calred said. "Thales can science without his legs."

"We're going to discuss that option, and others, but first we need to avoid getting captured by the proper authorities."

"I'll turn off the ship's transponder and pick you up at these new coordinates, at an earlier point on the original intercept course. I'll have to skim down into the atmosphere, but the *Endless Dark* can handle that. Then we'll run away as fast as we can. And *then*, the legbreaking."

Once their shuttle rendezvoused with the *Endless Dark,* they set a thermal bomb on a timer inside the shuttle, so it would explode while still en route to its original destination in orbit. Maybe the people on the ground would think "Heuvelt" and "Dob" had exploded, too, and even if no one was fooled by that, at least the devastation would remove any skin flakes or other trace evidence they'd left behind – Felix didn't want the Hylar sequencing his DNA and rifling through databases to find him.

Back on board the *Endless Dark,* Felix peeled off the thin laminate he'd worn over his fingers, which bore Heuvelt's prints, and removed the skullcap and wig that had prevented him from dropping hair follicles that could be traced back to him – all part of the false identity package they'd paid so well for.

Overall, Felix felt good about their chances of getting away with murder, assuming no one caught them on their way out. That only made him angrier at Thales. Woryela had clearly been a nice, conscientious professional, and Thales had killed him just to salve his own ego.

"The shuttle just went boom," Calred said. "Looks like there are security ships converging on that location, scanning the debris field. They haven't noticed us. Our transponder is spoofing a fake name and identity" – that much was standard Mentak Coalition military protocol, often useful on piratical missions – "and

I'm going to mingle with some of the trade route traffic, where at least no one will try to shoot us with *large* guns, for fear of hurting profitable innocents. From there, we're off to the big empty, and maybe we can get away clean. Not that I feel very clean."

"You've got the helm, then. I'm going to talk to Thales." Felix stomped through the cramped corridors and found Thales taking one of his naps. He kicked the scientist in the side, and Thales rolled off his bunk onto the floor, then looked up, blinking.

"I take it something went wrong," Thales said, "and you've decided, once again, to take out your own failings on me?"

"Woryela is dead!"

Thales made a face that Felix supposed was meant to be indicative of surprise. "What, since you made the appointment? You didn't meet with him?"

"No, we met. We gave him your artifact, and he read your note, and then it gassed him, and then he *died*."

Thales stood and ostentatiously brushed himself off. "The note, I confess, was a bit cheeky, but I knew you'd have the good sense to pick it up on the way out, and he wouldn't remember it when he woke up anyway–"

"He isn't going to wake up! He's dead!"

"That is regrettable. I take full responsibility."

"Is that a murder confession?"

Thales gave that exaggerated look of surprise again. "Murder? It was an accident, at worst. My degrees are in physics, captain. I consider myself a capable chemist, but xenobiology is hardly my area of expertise. I based the gas I created on a certain recreational drug that Hylar youth enjoy – I used to manufacture it and sell it during graduate school, to help fund my studies – and while I *did* intend to make it more powerful and fast-acting… oh, dear. I must have miscalculated, and made it too strong." His expression and voice were both perfectly level. "Or else the director had some underlying health problems, unknown to me, that proved fatal in combination with the drug. Or perhaps he was on other medication that interacted badly with–"

"You killed him, Thales. I know it. You know it. Why are you pretending otherwise?"

"You insult me, captain. My work is meant to *improve* life in the galaxy, to usher in a new age, where even the most distant stars can be as close as our nearest neighbors. Think of the new sense of community and galactic harmony my invention will foster. I am a *benefactor*, not a killer."

Felix couldn't believe what he was hearing. "A while ago your big selling point was the way the Coalition could drop raider fleets on our enemies from anywhere without warning!"

Thales nodded. "I adjusted my sales pitch to suit my audience, but I assure you, my ultimate goals are altruistic. I will be remembered as a hero to the galaxy, captain. Murder accusations would only muddle my legacy. So even if I had deliberately engineered a Hylar-specific neurotoxin, one that would kill and then exit the victim's system without leaving a trace, I'd hardly admit to it, would I? I have my reputation to consider. My legacy. They'll name buildings after me in the Universities when this is done – they'll clamor to claim *they* were the ones who recognized my genius and nurtured my mind." He looked Felix up and down, like he was a machine too broken to bother fixing. "Why would you want to accuse me of such crimes, anyway? Any confession I made would implicate you alongside me." To Felix's absolute shock, Thales patted him on the cheek. "Now be a good boy and run along until I need you again."

Felix punched Thales in the face, knocking him back into his bunk. It felt so good, he punched Thales again when he tried to stand up. Thales stayed down that time, holding his bleeding nose, squinting through an eye that would start to swell shut soon. Felix shook his hand, wincing – punching someone straight on like that was hell on your knuckles.

"You will regret that, captain." Thales's voice was low – even mild. "If you really think I'm a cunning and remorseless murderer, was it wise to strike me?"

"Who said I was wise? I'm just a useful idiot, aren't I? But you're on my ship, in my custody, and the bullshit is done, Thales. You will not use me any more. You can build your machine, and test it, and if it works, we'll deliver it to my superiors, and I'll never see you again. That's it. If you do anything else, I will execute you."

"Your superiors–"

"My superiors think you *might* be useful. You haven't proven it yet. Until you do, you are vulnerable. If I tell them you choked to death on a protein nugget, do you really think Tib or Calred will contradict me? Do you think we can't create footage to match the story, in the unlikely event there's an official investigation into this very *un*official mission?" Felix grinned at him savagely. "If there's one thing I've learned from you, it's how easy it is to get away with murder if you just plan a little. I have been pushed as far as I will be. Don't push me any farther. Just be glad I'm the one who came in here to talk to you, or you'd have worse than a bloody nose and a black eye. Calred wanted to break both your legs, and I was tempted to let him."

"*Finally*," Thales said. "I thought you were as spineless as a Hylar – that the Coalition had saddled me with a jellyfish for a minder. It took you long enough, but you showed a little mettle in the end. I'm moderately impressed."

"I hate you, Thales. You repulse me."

"I'm sorry to hear that. I'm just starting to like you, captain."

The contempt of simpletons is as good as the praise of geniuses. So what did receiving the praise of monsters mean? "What's the next step, Thales? You have your power source. Where do we go from here?"

Thales kept smiling at him in a dishearteningly friendly way. "I'll need a few days to complete the assembly, and then I have a few good test sites picked out–"

"Captain!" Calred called over Felix's comms. "We're being pursued by a ship!"

Felix cursed. "From Jol-Nar? How many?"

"Not from Jol-Nar," Calred said. "I evaded *those*. I evaded us right into sensor range of another ship. It's the Barony, captain."

CHAPTER 22

"This is Severyne Joelle Dampierre of the… I don't even know what this stupid ship is named. Call it the *Garbage Scow*." The face on the *Endless Dark's* viewscreen was grim, with a line of concentration vertically centered on her forehead. Azad was sitting behind her, and she waved at the screen. The rest of the crew consisted of masked guards, like those on the Barony station, all holding energy weapons and looking distressingly competent. "Stand down and prepare to be boarded, Duval. You will hand over Phillip Thales and Shelma, and submit yourselves to my authority for trial and punishment in the Barony."

"Severyne–" Felix began.

"This is not a negotiation," she continued. "We will not contact you again. Comply, or we will board your vessel and summarily execute you for resisting." The screen winked out.

"She's still a charmer." Felix was seated in the cockpit, though at the moment the ship was flying itself, executing a series of evasive maneuvers that Calred assured him were doomed to fail. "You have a better sense of this ship's specs than I do, Calred. Think we can outrun them?"

Calred's voice crackled over the shipwide comms. This was a conversation everyone could contribute to, even Thales, if he had anything worth saying. "In this thing? No. Their ship is a cruiser, secondhand, looks like Federation make, but much faster than ours. The *Endless Dark* is built for distance, not speed. We'd beat them in a marathon, but this is a sprint."

"I assume we're outgunned too?"

"An *actual* garbage scow could outgun us. Their ship has three cannons fore and two aft, looks like."

"How long until we're in range of said cannons?"

"They could turn us into very small hot pieces of metal and meat right now, captain. They just haven't."

"They won't shoot us while we have Thales and, as far as they know, Shelma. So that's something. How long before they're in range to board us?"

Cal *hmm'd*. "If they were Coalition raiders, I'd say we had fifteen or twenty minutes. Since they don't have the specialized equipment or training our fleets do, they'll have to get close enough to disable our engines without risking blowing us up. That means… maybe forty minutes?"

"Great. How do we set up an impregnable defense in forty minutes?"

The silence was long.

"Well," Felix said finally. "Do we surrender, or go down fighting?"

"They're from the Barony," Tib said. "Letting them capture us would be worse than dying. Their prison camps are infamous."

"We could offer to trade Thales," Calred said. "In exchange for our freedom. If Dampierre would take our calls and negotiate. Which she won't."

"I think Severyne has something personal against me, anyway," Felix said. What a depressing way to die. The prospect of going down fighting for the Coalition, sure, that was always a possibility, but fighting for *Thales*? Dying to protect a murderous egomaniac? It was hard to take any comfort in that.

"Aren't you lot supposed to be soldiers?" Thales said. "As you've pointed out, the Letnev won't destroy us. History is filled with stories of small bands of warriors defending against superior forces! Put me in the center of the ship. Rig some booby traps in the airlocks. Find narrow apertures you can defend. This Severyne woman can't have *that* many soldiers with her. Fight back! Protect me, protect yourselves, protect our future–"

"Shut up," Felix said. "They're not going to swing over here on ropes and kick the airlocks in. In forty minutes–"

"Thirty-eight," Calred said.

"– thirty-eight minutes, they're going to get close enough to disable our engines with sufficient precision to avoid accidentally killing us. At that point, our ship starts to coast. They'll overtake us. They'll open up their huge cargo bay doors and swallow us up, like a big fish swallowing a little one. *Then* they'll board us."

"So we defend ourselves then!"

"They'll pump the ship full of gas to knock us out before they board," Felix said. "Or poke a hole to let our air *out*, and come in for us after hypoxia makes us lose consciousness."

"We'll put on our environment suits–"

"Those have limited air, and after they've caught us, they're in no hurry any more. They'll just wait us out. This is field manual stuff, Thales. We *are* soldiers. There are times you fight, even when the manual tells you the fight is hopeless, because where there's life, there's hope, but in this case… not much hope. So." Felix cracked his neck. He was captain, and he was going down with his ship, even though this wasn't even really his ship. He was going to miss the *Temerarious*. Or, well, he wouldn't – the dead had no regrets – but he missed his ship preemptively. Sagasa would sell her back to the Coalition for a reasonable price, at least. "We'll swing around, open fire on them with our piddly little guns, and give them no choice but to shoot back and try to disable our engines. Which, at this distance, there's a good chance they can't do safely – they might hit the core and kill us, which I'm assured is the quickest of all possible deaths. If by some chance they *do* manage a disabling shot, and leave us dead in the lack of water–"

"We scuttle?" Calred said.

"That's the idea."

"I'll prepare to overcharge the reactor," Calred said. "If they swallow us up, they'll get indigestion."

"Wait, are you saying you're going to blow up our ship?" Thales cried.

"And I don't see a reason to say it a second time," Felix said.

"Wait. *Wait.* I can't die here, on the cusp of my greatest triumph!"

"I bet no one in history has ever said *that* before," Tib muttered.

"You said 'piddly guns,'" Thales said. "Why are the guns piddly?"

Felix sighed. "Because this isn't a warship, Thales. If we were in the *Temerarious*, we'd have a fighting chance. But the *Endless Dark* is an exploration vessel. It has weapons, because every adventurer fantasizes about fending off space pirates, or *being* a space pirate, or making first contact with a new species and blowing them up, but they're just small energy weapons. They aren't powerful enough to hurt something like the *Garbage Scow*, at least, not in the time we have – if their ship sat still and let us shoot them for an hour or two, sure, we could put enough holes in them to make a difference, but I doubt they'll be that cooperative."

Thales went *hmm*. "Energy weapons… so the limiting factor is the power supply. Our cannons are powered off the ship's reactor?"

"Big warships have separate power sources for their weapons," Calred said. "This one doesn't. So, yes, I know what you're thinking. We can divert *all* the ship's power to the weapons battery, to make the cannons stronger. It won't help much, though. This ship's reactor is built for long-distance efficiency, not bursts of output. Even if we juiced the weapons up, we'd get double their usual power for a few short bursts, but it wouldn't make any real difference–"

"We do have a separate power source for our weapons, you idiots," Thales said. "You just *stole* one."

Felix looked at Tib, who looked back at him. "Wait. That power cell thing. That's powerful enough to run the guns?"

"It's powerful enough to *rip holes in the fabric of space-time*, you dolts," Thales said. "Yes, it can power your lasers."

Felix's heart sped up. Hope was a powerful thing. "Calred, can you configure the guns to run off an external power source?"

"The lasers are aftermarket additions wired into the reactor here anyway, so yeah, it should be easy, but do you think this will really work?"

"No, but since our other plan is a pointless last stand, it can't hurt to try."

"They'll have us in ten minutes, Cal," Felix said from the cockpit.

"I'm the one who told *you* how long we had, captain, I *know* – there! It's connected! Power is flowing, board is green, available energy is… I don't know, because my diagnostic tool only reads up to nine-hundred-and-ninety-nine petawatts. So, more than that."

"That's… wait… that's…"

"More powerful than a gamma ray burst," Thales said. "More energy output than a star. Yes. That's the whole *point*. This power cell draws on the energy that drives *galaxies* out into the greater dark."

Felix whistled. "You said it was powerful, but I didn't realize."

"The question, of course, is how much power these cannons of yours can actually use," Thales said. "Without melting in the process."

"Cal?" Felix said.

"I'm looking up the tolerances!" Calred said. "Huh. OK. These things are ridiculously overengineered. Whoever equipped the *Endless Night* bought very expensive cannons, way more than they needed. Some salesperson got a good commission that day."

"Probably somebody like Heuvelt, spendthrifting the family fortune," Felix said. "You're saying we can put up a fight now?"

"We can start and finish a fight, captain. Especially since the *Garbage Scow* will not expect us to punch this hard."

"All right then. Let's take out their weapons and their engines."

"Why not life support?" Thales said. "That seems simpler."

"Engines and weapons are on the *outside* of the ship," Tib said. "That's so they can propel the ship through space, and blow up things they encounter in space. Life support systems are buried deep inside the ship, where the alive things are."

"Fine," Thales grumbled. "I assumed the order was due to a combination of weakness and sentimentality. Carry on."

"I wasn't waiting for your permission, Thales," Calred said. "Ready to flip and shoot on your mark, captain."

"Mark." Felix braced himself as the ship stopped short and spun around to face the *Garbage Scow*. Thales squawked over the comms, and Felix muted him. His crew had known to brace for the maneuver, of course. Thales hadn't. Oops.

The enemy ship was hurtling toward them – an immense bulbous vessel, with the black dots of cannons pointing their way.

"Weapons hot," Calred said. "*Extremely* hot. Felix. Can I push the button?"

Felix's fingers twitched, but he put them in his lap. Sometimes being captain and taking care of your crew required sacrifices, and though he desperately wanted to do the shooting himself, it was Calred's job. "Please. Do the honors."

The viewscreen darkened to near opacity, but even so, the flash of the firing cannons was blinding. For just a moment, their ship was almost certainly the brightest thing in the universe. The cannons pulsed twice more, in quick succession. "That's all three of their fore weapon arrays," Calred said. "If they get anything like the same combat training *we* did, they'll wheel around to aim their aft guns – there they go."

The *Garbage Scow* was invisible through the darkened screen, but their ship's sensors showed its actions on Felix's tactical board. The Barony ship did its own hard spin, and when is engines were in sight, the *Endless Night* fired again, several times in succession, and the glow of the enemy engines went dark.

"That's it!" Cal shouted. "Engines and cannons gone. Good thing, too. Our cannons weren't well maintained and, ah, it turns out, maybe I shouldn't have pushed them to the absolute maximum of their specifications."

"We don't have guns any more?" Thales said.

"We don't have anyone to shoot at any more, either," Felix said. The *Garbage Scow* could still maneuver with its reaction wheels, but those were meant for minute adjustments – it wouldn't be going very far without extensive repairs. "Did you take out their comms, too?" Felix said. "I'd expect Severyne to start yelling at us right about now, vowing revenge and promising doom and all that."

"Maybe she's too embarrassed," Tib said. "She seems like the kind of person who gets embarrassed easily."

"The Letnev aren't very good at failure," Thales said. "Perhaps they just need more practice." He paused. "Well? Don't you people have anything to say to me?"

"Shut up?" Calred said.

"Shut up, you murderer?" Tib said.

"They pretty much covered it," Felix agreed.

Thales huffed. "I'd expect a little gratitude. I just saved your useless lives."

"You did," Felix said. "But only as a side effect of saving yourself. If throwing us into the ship's reactor would have saved you instead, you'd have done that just as readily."

"You're becoming quite curmudgeonly, Duval. You remind me of myself at your age."

"Gross," Tib said. "What's next, captain?"

Before Felix could answer, Thales did. "Next, you take me back to my lab on the *Temerarious*. I'll connect the power source to my prototype. We'll travel to one of the test sites I've identified. I'll switch on my activation engine and change the course of galactic civilization. I'll be rich and famous, and you'll receive largely undeserved promotions and accolades."

"Works for me." Felix switched to a crew-only channel, cutting Thales out. "What do you think?" he said. "Could the end really be in sight?"

"Thales doesn't want us to assassinate anyone else, apparently," Tib said.

Calred said, "Severyne and Azad are floating in a disabled ship, and getting farther behind us all the time. Thales hasn't decided where we're going next, so it's hard to imagine they'll beat us there."

"Maybe this awful mission could actually succeed," Felix said.

"As long as the Creuss don't show up and reduce us to our individual atoms for meddling in their business," Tib said.

"Thank you for that, Tib."

"My pleasure, Felix. A captain with nothing to worry about is barely a captain at all."

They returned to the Disciplinarian's scrapyard, and Felix hailed him on their comms, surprised when the Hacan answered personally. "We brought back the *Endless Night*, undamaged," Felix said. "Well, we broke the guns. But they weren't very good guns anyway."

"I'll bill you for them," Sagasa said. "Did you run into your friends out there?"

"We did."

"Are they dead? Did you destroy the cruiser I sold them?"

"The ship is disabled and adrift, but they're probably alive."

Sagasa sighed. "I wish you'd blown them up. They might still bring my cruiser back, and I won't get to keep the far superior ship they left behind as collateral."

"Were you rooting for *us* to lose, too, so you could keep my ship?" Felix said.

"I never pray for the death of a customer, Captain Duval. I thrive on repeat business. But taking ownership of the *Temerarious* would have eased my grief. Dock at port AZ-5. I'll send someone to do a walkthrough of the *Endless Dark*."

"A walkthrough? Seriously?"

"I'm always serious about business. I need to make sure the vessel is as undamaged as you claim."

"I need to get to work, captain," Thales groused. "I don't want to sit here while some fool examines the paint on this bucket."

"None of us want to spend an extra moment with you, Thales," Felix said. "Cal, take him back to the *Temerarious*. Keep an eye on him while he gets to work. We'll join you after Sagasa finishes looking for dings and scratches to overcharge us for."

"Excellent," Thales said. "Just fetch the power supply–"

"I'm going to hold on to that part," Felix said. "I'm sure you have other things to do first. You can plug it in later, when we're on the way to your test site."

"Why?" Thales demanded.

"Because I don't trust you," Felix said. "There are three crucial components to your success: your brain, Shelma's prototype, and this power supply. I'm not going to let all three of them be in one place at one time unless I'm there too."

"Outrageous. What are you afraid I'll do with it?"

"Shoot Calred in the back of the head and steal my ship," Felix said.

"Like I'd turn my back on him," Cal said.

"Or you might contact Sagasa and offer *him* the deal of a lifetime," Felix said. "Partnering with an independently wealthy businessman would be better for you than working with the Coalition, since Sagasa is motivated purely by profit, just like you."

"You're paranoid, Duval," Thales said. "More and more you remind me of myself–"

"Just go," Felix said.

Amazingly, the walkthrough was just slow, not slow and expensive. Sagasa's Winnaran secretary noted the damaged cannons, but after a thorough inspection of the ship inside and out, declared there was no other damage that would require repayment. "I'm surprised you didn't charge us for wear-and-tear on the engine," Felix said.

"Oh, that's included in the original price," he explained, entirely straight-faced. He presented a hand terminal for Felix's approval, and he authorized the charges. Jhuri was the one paying, anyway. "Thank you for visiting Sagasa Scrap and Salvage," the secretary said. "We–"

"We know," Felix said. "Point me to my ship, please?"

Felix and Tib set off through the station, toward the airlock where the *Temerarious* waited. "A couple more days, Tib, and we're free. This whole mess will be over."

"It has been an ordeal," Tib said. "Do you wish we'd stayed on patrol duty?"

Felix considered. "I don't, really. This is the kind of work I've always wanted to do. We organized a jailbreak, pulled off a heist, prevailed in ship-to-ship combat – it hasn't been boring, and the crew really pulled together."

"I've always trusted you, and I had a good feeling about Cal," Tib said. "But that feeling wasn't ever tested before. Now I *know*. If it wasn't for Thales, and the murders – especially the murders – I'd be happy with this mission. Even with all that, I don't want to go back to flying around in circles any more, using my skills for hide-and-seek."

"We will get promotions after this, if Thales gets his engine working," Felix said. "We'll have our choice of postings. Jhuri will take care of us."

"Maybe we can start thinking about where we want to land after this is all over."

"Shouldn't we focus on the immediate future, Tib?"

"Why would we want to do that?" Tib grimaced. "The immediate future has Thales in it."

"That is an excellent point. I've been on this officer track, working my way up to a command bigger than my best friend and an endearingly insubordinate Hacan, but maybe the covert ops life is more appealing. What do you think?"

"I had to work hard to keep *out* of covert ops, Felix. They always want Yssaril to work as spies. As if that's the only thing we're good for – sneaking around and listening through doors. But what we've been doing out here isn't exactly espionage. We haven't been gathering much in the way of intelligence."

"If anything," Felix said, "we've been rushing around with a regrettable lack of intelligence."

"We're essentially the personal get-shit-done-squad for undersecretary Jhuri, at the moment," Tib said. "That gives us connections, support – of a sort, anyway – and a lot of novelty. We could do worse than to continue in this capacity, if Jhuri wants us."

"I don't know if Calred would want that kind of gig," Felix said. "*His* dream is to run the weapons board on a dreadnought."

"I'm sure Jhuri would ask us to steal a dreadnought at some point, if this mission is any sort of indication."

"Don't say that. This mission isn't over yet, and I don't need any more challenges today."

His comms opened, and Calred's voice shouted, "Felix! We have a problem!"

"Don't we always?" Felix said.

"Not like this!" There was something strange about Cal's voice, and it took Felix a moment to recognize the tone, because he hadn't heard it from Cal before.

The Hacan security officer was afraid.

CHAPTER 23

Severyne was nervous about how nervous she *wasn't*. She should have been more worried. She was, after all, in the midst of violating all Barony best practices, on a deniable mission that could very well end up with her execution, and she was currently trusting her fate to the criminal skills of the most annoying human in the galaxy – a human who also inexplicably made Severyne's palms sweat and her heart beat faster when she stood too close, which she did *all the time*.

Instead of cold fear, though, Severyne felt exhilaration. Why? She'd sent her entire complement of guards – without any supervising officer! – off to the Jol-Nar system in a cruiser she'd purchased from a Hacan crime lord. Her guards were in pursuit of the fugitive *she* was meant to be pursuing. By all rules and regulations, Severyne should have been there too, running the operation. But after they reached the *Grim Countenance*, Azad had said, "Let's be real. We're not going to catch Duval's Devils out there."

"Why do you say that?" Severyne demanded.

"We don't know what kind of ship they're in. We don't know how they're planning to steal the power source – strongarm robbery, some sort of confidence game, bribing a technician to smuggle it out to them, or something I haven't even thought of yet. I'm not a fan of the Coalition, but when it comes to parting people from their property, the Mentak have *skills*. Without knowing their plan, we don't know their timeline, where they'll strike, or when they'll leave. Jol-Nar is one of the hubs of galactic civilization, so it's not like Duval and company will stand out against the usual traffic. We'll be looking for one specific grain of sand on the beach."

"Don't mention beaches," Severyne muttered.

"Now, when chasing them was our only option, going to Jol-Nar and hoping to catch them coming or going was our best bet," Azad said. "I'm lucky almost as much as I'm good, after all. But now we don't have to chase them: we can sit here and wait for them, because we know they're coming back."

"You're sure the information you received from the secretary was reliable?" Severyne said. "I don't understand why he would help you. Surely Sagasa places a premium on discretion in his employees?"

"Oh, totally, but that Winnaran *hates* Sagasa's ass. One time he overhead Sagasa tell a client he liked to hire Winnarans because they're a 'naturally servile race' that's 'only happy when they have boots to lick' and that they've been 'looking for a new emperor to serve for centuries, and who's more imperial than me?'

He could still quote that years later. So now, for a price, the secretary is willing to slip people info about Sagasa's clients, as a way of proving his own independence. We did some business last time I was here, and we just did a little more business today, though you paid for it."

"How did you discover this Winnaran's tendency toward duplicity?"

"In my line of work, Sev, it pays to talk to people. That's the first step toward developing an asset."

"Am *I* an asset, Azad?"

"You certainly have many notable ones," Azad said.

"You will not deflect me with your innuendos," Severyne said.

"Here I thought I was flirting."

"Are you manipulating me?" Severyne said, more quietly.

Azad put her hand on Severyne's shoulder, briefly. "Only insofar as I'm always manipulating everybody. You and I have goals that align, so there's no need for a bunch of bullshit. The only problem we have is figuring out how to achieve those goals. I have strong opinions, and I will make every effort to bring you around to my way of seeing things. Fortunately, you have a bright analytical mind, so as long as my ideas are good, I have confidence you'll agree with them – and if they aren't good, you'll make them better."

Severyne was flattered by the compliment, though she didn't want to feel flattered. "We know, if your source is to be trusted, that Duval left his ship here for safekeeping, and that he intends to return for it. Your plan is to lie in wait on his ship and ambush them."

"That's it exactly. Why rush around to Jol-Nar when we can just sit here and get our scientists *and* the power cell delivered into our hands?"

"I can see one reason why not," Severyne said. "What if they fail? What if their daring heist is a disaster, and Duval and his crew are captured by the Hylar, along with *our* scientists?"

"That would be unfortunate," Azad said. "I'm not sure us being in orbit around Jol or Nar would make it any less unfortunate."

"Nevertheless. We will dispatch my guards to Jol-Nar in the ship Sagasa has loaned us, where they will wait on the outskirts of the system, close enough to monitor comms traffic. If there *is* a disastrous crime, there will be news reports, yes? The Hylar have very poor information control, as I recall."

"If you mean they have a mostly free press and that their news doesn't consist entirely of government propaganda, then yes, their information control is poor as piss."

"Excellent. I will put my squad leader in charge, with strict and specific orders. If there is any suggestion that Duval and company have been arrested, he will send a message to us, and we will formulate a plan to liberate Shelma and Thales. I will have my guard station whatever garbage vessel Sagasa has for us along the most direct return route for Duval's ship, so even if our enemies do succeed in their mission, my people will have an opportunity to disable and capture Duval's vessel on their way back. It is *always* wise to have contingency plans in place."

"I like it. Don't send them on the most direct route, though. Have the computer compute the best route from Jol-Nar to evade and mislead pursuers, and station your people somewhere along that trajectory. Even if Duval isn't literally running from the cops when they leave Jol-Nar, they'll be careful when they depart."

"You think like a criminal, Azad." Severyne did not mean it as a compliment, but the human grinned.

"See, you've improved our plan already. Belt and suspenders is a good idea, when you have the resources to deploy both. I have to admit, I hope your crew *doesn't* catch Duval, though. I want to snag him personally."

"All that matters is the outcome," Severyne said, though secretly she agreed.

"I have one little refinement to suggest. On the off-chance that Duval encounters your guards but manages to evade them, we can make sure they're *really* taken by surprise when they get back. All we need to do is record a little video of you being threatening and imperious, and I *know* you're good at that."

Now they were sneaking through an airlock to break into Duval's ship, preparing to lay an ambush. There were so many variables in play that Severyne could not possibly account for them all. But instead of terror, she felt only exhilaration. Perhaps a life in station bureaucracy *wasn't* the most fulfilling possible future for her. "I may have misjudged myself for my entire life," Severyne said out loud.

Azad glanced at her. "It's never too late to figure out who you really are, Severyne."

She scowled, annoyed at herself for revealing her inner state. "How are you going to gain access?"

"Oh, the external controls for the airlock can be operated in a couple of ways. There are transponders in the ship's environment suits, of course, to allow re-entry from spacewalks and whatnot. But there's also a backup system that's keyed to biometrics, to allow people to enter from stations. This door should open for any member of Duval's crew."

"We are not Duval's crew."

"True, but we've been up close and personal with them. These doors are pretty forgiving, since people might be trying to board in a hurry while getting shot at and stuff, so you don't have to get your retina scanned while singing three verses of 'The Sun Shines over Jord' and having your blood drawn – you just gotta show the ship real quick that you're you. When I smashed that little Yssaril bitch over the back of the head, I made sure some blood and hair stuck to my fingers." She dipped into her pocket, and then smeared her fingertip over a sensor. The airlock door unsealed. "Ta da."

"You couldn't have known you were going to need Tib Pelta's genetic material to open a door," Severyne said.

"Hey, I like planning for contingencies too."

"Do you have *my* hair in your pockets?"

"No, Sev, I have not collected any of your genetic material. We're partners, not adversaries. I don't need to use you. I work with you."

"You are a very convincing liar. I can see why you are moderately successful in your chosen career."

"I'm the best there is at whatever it is I feel like doing. Shall we explore our new ship?" They stepped into the airlock and on into the vessel itself. "I was wondering, why didn't you send the *Grim Countenance* out on your contingency mission?"

"And risk losing a ship of the Barony? The garbage scow Sagasa foisted on us is more than a match for the small vessel Duval took, if your treacherous Winnaran is to be believed. The superior firepower of the *Grim Countenance* is hardly necessary."

"Ha, fair enough. Better hope that garbage scow comes back, though, or Sagasa is going to claim the *Grim Countenance* as his collateral."

"We will solve that problem if it arises." Severyne wrinkled her nose at the state of the Coalition vessel as they inspected it. There were dirty dishes in the galley, personal items at workstations on the bridge, and wrapped pallets of emergency supplies in almost every bit of unused space. "Is this a ship of the Coalition fleet or a cargo vessel?"

"I think they did relief missions back in the colonies. Look, in here, it's some kind of lab."

"Is there anything of value here?"

Azad poked through the bits of wire and sheared pieces of metal scattered on the bench and shook her head. "Looks like they took everything with them when they left. Makes sense. You don't want to leave that kind of tech lying around unattended. Let's keep looking around, though."

They found Duval's cabin – Severyne was tempted to urinate on his bed, but decided that would qualify as conduct unbecoming a Barony officer – but she did pick up a bottle of liquor and was about to smash it on the wall when Azad plucked it from her hand. "Hey, that's Coalition gin. There's this botanical on Moll Primus, sort of like a citrusy version of a juniper, I can't really describe it, and they use its needles to infuse the booze – we're going to keep this and celebrate our success later."

"Fine. But I wish to desecrate this space somehow."

"I'll wipe my butt on his sheets later or something. Let's move on."

They found Shelma's body not long after.

CHAPTER 24

First, Azad noticed the exo-suit tank, tucked into the corner of a storage space. She didn't know what it was, but Severyne's reaction told her it was something important, and bad: the Letnev stiffened, and then emitted a sort of keening wail. "Where is the medical bay?" she snapped.

Azad, who had the basic schematics for a whole bunch of different ship models filed away in her head, didn't ask questions; she just led the way. The medical bay was gleaming and sterile – there were automated systems in place to keep it that way, even on a Coalition ship – and Severyne was clearly familiar enough with the basic layout to pull up the information she needed. She consulted a terminal, then went to a wall full of rectangular panels of various sizes and pressed the smallest one.

The panel hissed, then slid open with a gout of icy vapor, a drawer extending into the room. There was a Hylar body on the rack, pseudopods curled up, body shriveled in the cold, various sensors connected to her. Was the ship conducting some sort of diagnostic, perhaps to determine cause of death? There was no obvious sign of injury.

"Shelma is dead." Severyne's voice, always icy, was now absolute zero.

"I'm so sorry, Severyne," Azad said.

"I will be executed for this."

Azad winced. Sev was probably not wrong. "You don't know that. There are still ways you can turn this around."

"*What* ways?" She spun, fists clenched, and glared at Azad. "My sole mission was to recover Shelma! As long as I brought her back, we could cover up everything else, and life would go on. My director would have *hated* me, and I would have had to transfer to another posting at some point if I hoped to advance, but my life would have continued. Now I will be on record as overseeing a catastrophic security breach, and failing to redress that breach. I am dead. I am walking, and talking, and dead."

Azad took a step toward her. "We still have Thales. *He's* not in a drawer here, and if he was gone, Duval wouldn't be rushing around making moves. Your lot tried to recruit Thales, too, so…" She trailed off.

Severyne laughed. "So what? Do we cut him in half? Or do you propose to share custody of the man? A joint project between the Barony and the Federation? We'll make wormholes and explore the universe together? You were going to betray me and try to take both of the scientists and all their files *anyway*. Now that there's only one scientist, you want to share?"

"You were going to betray me, too," Azad said quietly. "It's the business. We work together until we don't. But now I don't have to betray anybody, and neither do you." Relief flooded through her. There was a way through this. "Sev, why don't you come with me?"

The Letnev blinked at her. "What are you talking about?"

"You said it yourself. If you return to the Barony empty-handed, you're dead. So stay with me instead. Help me complete my mission. Don't go back."

"The director will send people to find me. They have ways of tracking down rogue officers."

"If you defect to the Federation, we can protect you."

Severyne shuddered. "You want me to join the *humans*?"

"Is that worse than joining your ancestors?"

"You will have to give me a moment to think about that."

Azad laughed.

Severyne took a deep breath, then closed the morgue drawer. "I will consider your offer. In the meantime, my personal mission has changed. It is no longer possible to recover Shelma. Instead, my new objective is to destroy Felix Duval. To ruin his life as thoroughly as he has ruined mine."

"Well, hey," Azad said. "We're standing on his ship. That's a pretty good start–"

"You have made overtures toward me," Severyne said abruptly. "Were they sincere, or were you merely mocking me?"

Whoa. Having your life destroyed could do a number on anyone's sense of self and priorities, but that was a pretty abrupt turn, even by catastrophe standards. Unless Severyne had been interested all along, and now that her old life was over, she was willing to loosen up certain strictures…

Oh. Or it could be for another reason. "They were sincere, but I didn't think you'd take me up on them. Listen, you're under a lot of strain. I don't want you to do anything you'll regret later–"

"Letnev do not allow themselves regrets," Severyne said. "We only move forward. Let us go." She turned and stalked back toward Duval's cabin.

Azad watched Severyne go and ran a complex mental calculation. She had no particular need to kill Severyne now, that was true, which opened up the way for a different kind of relationship… but Severyne had even *more* incentive to kill Azad. That was the only way she could lay claim to Thales, after all, and halfway redeem herself with her superiors. Azad figured this sudden desire for carnal connection was about thirty percent terror-induced arousal (that was absolutely a real thing, as many eve-of-battle assignations over the years had proven to Azad's satisfaction). The other seventy percent was an attempt to get Azad to let her guard down – to make her think Severyne had feelings and affection for her, so she wouldn't see the gunshot to the back of the head coming.

Azad made her decision. Sure, it violated her rule, but transgression made it more exciting in a way, didn't it?

She was used to people trying to kill her. At least this way, they'd both get some enjoyment out of being alive first.

Afterward, Azad stretched like a cat and turned over in Duval's bed – the captain's quarters had the best bunk, which was nice – and looked at Severyne's face. The Letnev woman had the slightly stunned expression of someone who'd just tried, for the first time, something that would become their new avocation, passion, or addiction. "Nice, huh?" Azad said.

Severyne turned her head, looked at Azad for a moment, then looked back at the ceiling. "I am not inexperienced. At the academy, sometimes… well. The nights in the dormitory were cold, and there were few ways to warm up. But humans *do* run hotter than Letnev, it seems."

"Could be that's just me."

Severyne's expression shifted to seriousness. "We should prepare ourselves for Duval's return."

"Oh, even if they went to Jol-Nar, committed the theft in five minutes, and came straight back, we'd still have hours."

"Nevertheless, I desire no further surprises. We need to fully seize control of the ship's systems."

"Look at you, going from all pleasure to all business. Fine, I'll put my pants on." Azad kissed Severyne's cheek and rolled out of the bunk. It was still safe, to a high degree of certainty, to turn her back on Severyne; the Letnev still needed her. But once they subdued Duval and had Thales in hand, then Azad would have to get properly vigilant.

That was fine. Vigilant was pretty much her default state.

Severyne sat in the captain's chair on the bridge while Azad hacked the ship's systems. "What's funny is, the intrusion tools I'm using are *made* by the Mentak Coalition. It's no good being a pirate captain if you can't take control of captured vessels, so they've got a whole suite of techniques for spoofing authorizations and cracking encryption. But because the Coalition is full of people with rather flexible moral systems, those tools didn't stay proprietary for long – they got sold on the black market, and Sol got their hands on one, reverse engineered it, made some tweaks so the tools could attack Coalition safeguards too, and here we are. A nearly universal spaceship key. And… there. Welcome, Captain Severyne, to the good ship *Temerarious*, now yours to command."

"Wait. You're giving me the priority authorizations?"

"You're the one sitting in the big chair. I'm much better at running weapons anyway. The ship is ours. Now we just wait, for word from your people on the garbage scow, or for Duval to stroll through the door."

So they waited. They ate in the galley, ran diagnostic checks on the weapons, and took turns showering in the captain's bathroom. Severyne considered showing open affection to further distract Azad and keep her off balance, but was afraid it would be seen as manipulation; better to carry on as she had been.

Sleeping with Azad had been enjoyable, she had to admit, if only to herself. Severyne didn't have much time for pleasure for pleasure's sake in her usual life, let alone with someone of a different species, but that sense of the forbidden had ultimately made it exciting instead of disgusting. *Maybe I really* have *misjudged myself my whole life.* She thought, briefly, of what would happen if she took Azad up on her offer, but "Come with me" didn't mean "Travel through the stars committing various interesting crimes and having sex" – not really. It meant "Defect, and sit in a Federation of Sol military interview room for one million hours describing Barony security protocols." That was not appealing. It was even less appealing than going home a failure and being executed; at least that would be over relatively quickly, and cause her less shame.

Severyne's comms buzzed with a message from the squad leader on the garbage scow. "We engaged the enemy, assistant director," he said, and his tone was so stiff she couldn't tell whether he'd succeeded or failed. "They disabled our ship and escaped."

"How did they disable your ship?" she demanded. "They were in a long-distance exploration vessel, not a gunship!"

"They utilized a weapon of unknown provenance."

"What? Did they steal some kind experimental weapon while they were on Jol-Nar too?"

"I lack necessary data to draw a conclusion–"

"Never mind. Can you repair the ship?"

"We are attempting repairs, and expect to have partial function restored to the engines within seventy-two hours, which should allow us to return to the scrapyard. Unless you would prefer to rendezvous with us in the *Grim Countenance* – if you can bring repair parts, we would not have to fabricate them here, and that would greatly reduce our–"

"You'll have to make your own way. I'm going to be busy succeeding at the mission where you *failed*."

"Yes, assistant director. I will send status updates–"

She cut the connection, squeezing the armrests of the captain's chair tight. "Duval apparently has some kind of super-weapon now."

Azad, standing at the tactical board, shook her head. "I bet they just plugged the ship's shitty little cannons into the power source they stole. That's what I would have done."

Severyne blinked. "That would work?"

"Your basic energy cannon is just a conduit for and focuser of power. How strong the cannons are depends on the energy source. That thing they went to steal is supposed to be like a hundred fusion reactors, only so small you can carry it around in a backpack."

"Then the power source, in itself, has great value," Severyne mused.

"If you brought that back to the Barony, you might not get executed, it's true," Azad said. "Unfortunately, I can't let you have it, since Thales needs it to power his prototype. Sorry about that. Maybe we can get you the schematics or something, and your people can reverse engineer the thing, if you want to give that a shot."

"How very generous."

Azad shrugged but didn't look up from the panel. "I like you, Severyne. I'll help you as much as I can without hurting myself. But that's as far as I can go. Would you respect me if I did anything else?"

"This is a miserable situation," Severyne said. "I am miserable."

"Ah, but there's an upside. Duval is on his way back here. And if your crew played your video like they were supposed to–"

"Of course they did. They follow orders to the letter, without deviation. The Letnev are not as prone to improvisation as humans are." Though Severyne herself had done some improvising lately, hadn't she? Azad was corrupting her.

"Then Duval thinks *we're* floating in a dead ship in the void," Azad said. "He's going to walk in here with supreme and misplaced confidence. Even more than usual."

"And then I can kill him?" Severyne said.

"And then you can kill him."

"I feel slightly less miserable now."

"Aw, hell," Azad said.

Severyne hurried over to the security station. "What is it?"

"Two people just stepped into the airlock. *Only* two." She pulled up the camera feed and saw Thales carrying a rucksack, and the Hacan security officer, Calred, holding a file box. He was awkwardly juggling the box in an attempt to hold it one-handed while unlocking the ship with his fingertip.

"Where is Duval?" Severyne demanded.

"Maybe he had to take a piss."

"Then where is the Yssaril?"

"Could be lurking invisibly, I guess, though it's bad etiquette to sneak around on Sagasa's station, and they've got no reason to expect an attack, so she's probably with Duval. Yssaril have to piss sometimes too."

"They'll be on board any moment!"

"They'll *try* to get on board any moment. They'll be unconscious a moment after that. Let's get down there and collect them."

Sev grabbed her arm. "We have to wait for Duval."

"Sev, it's Thales, and his stuff. What I need is Thales, and his stuff. I'd like to see Duval dead, too, but that part isn't mission critical."

She tightened her grip, nails digging in. "It is critical for *my* mission. My only mission is revenge."

Your only mission is killing me and taking Thales for yourself, Azad thought. But… Sev really did want to kill Duval, and waiting for him would put off her inevitable betrayal for a while longer. Azad did enjoy having the Letnev woman alive. She calculated risk and came up with an acceptable number. "All right. But only because you're so cute when you're homicidal. Let's secure the owl and the pussycat, and then we'll wait for the others to show up."

They went down to the airlock, weapons ready.

CHAPTER 25

Azad was listening to the feed from the airlock on her comms, so she heard the Hacan swearing about how the inner door wasn't working. She learned a few new Hacan blasphemies in the process. She took up her position in the corridor, facing the airlock doors, and checked that Severyne was in her spot. "Ready?"

"I wish I was about to shoot Duval, but yes."

"Keep it non-lethal," Azad reminded her. "We can't risk a stray shot hitting Thales."

"I know." Severyne's voice was even more grim than usual.

Azad triggered the inner door to open. As soon as the doors slid apart enough to give her a sliver of a sightline on the people on the other side, she aimed at Thales and hit him with a shock-pulse, carefully calibrated to lock up his nervous system without doing any permanent damage.

She was aware of the Hacan, and of Severyne firing at him, but she was focused on her own target, and when she shifted her attention, it was too late.

Calred's right arm hung loose at the shoulder where Severyne's pulse had hit him, off-center and thus ineffective. Maybe Azad should have taken point on disabling the Hacan, but Thales was the more important target, and she'd made a judgment call. Now a few hundred pounds of enraged humanoid lion came barreling toward them, bellowing. If Calred had stopped to fight them, she could have subdued him, but instead he just straight-armed Severyne out of the way and rushed deeper into the ship.

Azad fired after him, but he was around a corner and gone. Azad heard him shout, "Felix! We have a problem!"

"That could have gone better." Azad put the ship into lockdown, then checked on Severyne, who was leaning against a wall, rubbing her chest where the Hacan had struck her, face stoic. "But it's not a total disaster."

"There is an angry Hacan weapons expert loose on this vessel."

"Sure, but I just locked everything down – he's stuck in a corridor, banging on a door. He's no danger to us. I shielded comms too."

"Not before he warned Duval," Severyne said. "We can't surprise him now."

"That's true. I'm sorry, Severyne. Revenge will have to wait. I promise, we'll get Duval, OK? I want him too. But for now, we've got Thales, and we've got his data, his prototype, the power source–"

A dry laugh crackled from the floor of the airlock. They both turned to look at the scientist, who was still mostly paralyzed, but conscious. "You've got three out of four. Which isn't enough. This is an all-or-nothing situation. Duval still has the power cell. Idiots. I'm surrounded by idiots."

"That is a complication," Azad said.

"Hello, Duval," Azad said. She was calling him from the *Temerarious*, which made him vibrate with rage.

"Get the fuck off my ship." He paced up and down in the corridor as he spoke, while Tib stood against the wall, seemingly lost in thought. Felix hoped she was figuring out some angle. He was too angry to figure out anything other than a direct attack, personally.

"Your people are pirates, Duval. You know how this works. I'm in control of the ship. That makes it my ship. That's not the only thing of yours I've taken, either. I've got your lion in a cage here."

"If you hurt Calred–"

"Then Calred will be hurt very badly indeed. Stop blustering, Duval. It's unbecoming. I don't want to hurt anyone, oddly enough. I'm a pragmatist, not a sadist. I just have a problem you can help me solve. You have a power source. I need a power source. I have one of your crew. You need one of your crew. That means we can make a deal. Straight trade. The battery for your boy. Oh, and I'm going to need your ship, too. Fortunately, you can pick up another one at the scrapyard."

"You can't be serious."

"It's not only serious, it's a limited-time offer. Think it over. Don't make me wait too long, or I'll start cutting off non-essential parts of your security officer. Then you'll have to pay the same amount to get less and less in return. It's a brutal negotiating tactic, I know. I learned it from the Disciplinarian. I'll give you a few minutes. I know it takes time for that 'I'm totally fucked' feeling to really sink in."

She clicked off. Felix stared at Tib. "What can we do?"

"Lots of things."

"What can we do that will get Thales back and won't kill Calred in the process?"

"Many fewer things. I can think of… zero things."

"Maybe there's nothing we can do on our own, but…" Felix opened another channel. A bored voice said, "Sagasa Scrap and–"

"Let me talk to Sagasa!"

"Captain Duval. Perhaps I can be of–"

"I don't *want* to talk to you!" Felix bellowed. "Get me Sagasa, now!"

It wasn't "now," but after a long interval, Sagasa rumbled into Felix's comms. "How may I be of further service, captain?"

"You let those assholes get on my ship!"

"Which assholes are those?"

"Severyne and Azad!"

"Ah. Those assholes. I thought they were adrift in a disabled ship many parsecs away?"

"Yeah, well, so did I. But it turns out they sent their crew to harass us while they stayed here, in *your* scrapyard, and broke into my ship. What are you going to do about that?"

"You paid me to dock the ship here, captain." The Hacan's voice was mild and untroubled. "If you wanted me to guard it, you should have said so. I offer very reasonable rates for security services. What's the problem? I won't let them leave with your property – that much is covered by our agreement. Would you like to employ some of my personnel to help you take the ship back?"

"I can't go in hot. They have Calred."

"Ah ha. A hostage situation. I see. What do they want in return for his freedom?"

Felix hesitated. Sagasa was honorable, in very specific ways, but the power cell would be a morality-warping temptation for even a less shady businessperson. "They're demanding a certain item in my possession."

"Then you should decide whether to give it to them, or not. I'm still not clear about why you're calling me. Did you want to secure my services as a negotiator on your behalf?"

"Doesn't breaking into my ship and kidnapping my security officer count as an act of aggression on your station?" Felix said. "Shouldn't you discipline them?"

"Arguably. But such things bother me less when they don't happen right outside my office. If someone starts shooting in the corridors, I will be moved to intervene, but it sounds, at this point, more like an aggressive business negotiation than anything else. I don't meddle in such affairs. Besides, you said you don't want to go in hot. It's not as if I have options for retaking the ship other than the use of force, captain."

Felix was getting desperate. "What if they kill Calred?"

"I would mourn the loss of a brother Hacan. Then I would offer my security forces for hire again, since the impediment against violent intervention would be removed. I might even carry a weapon myself."

"None of this is very helpful, Sagasa."

"Alas, being helpful to Duval's Devils is not one of my duties. I wish you luck." He paused. "I will remind you, though, that if *you* start shooting in my corridors, I'll consider you the aggressor instead, and subject to my discipline."

"Unless I hire you to help."

"Of course. In that situation, *you* wouldn't be the one shooting – I would."

"Right. I guess that's all, then."

"Until next time. Thank you for using Sagasa's Scrap and Salvage. We tear down the past to build a better future." The comms went dead.

Felix slumped against the wall. The clock was counting down, and he didn't doubt that Azad would carry through on her threat. He glanced at his first officer. "You look like you're thinking, Tib. What are you thinking?"

Tib shrugged. "I was just thinking back to the propulsion laboratory. I took the real power cell and switched it with the fake Thales made. I don't know why I bothered. The whole point of swapping it was to make it look like no crime had even occurred, and at that point, there was already a murder victim in the next room. But that was the plan, and I executed the plan. If I hadn't, we'd still have the fake power cell, and we could trade *that* for Calred. Azad and Severyne would still have Thales, but they wouldn't be able to use his device. We'd still have *some* hope of winning."

Felix nodded. "That would have been nice. Elegant. Roguish." He sighed. "But we don't have a fake power cell, and I don't have the skills to build a new one. You?"

"I skipped constructing-fake-technology class at the academy."

"So."

"So."

"I guess we lose."

"It's the second time today we thought we'd lost," Tib said. "Last time, we thought we'd lost, and were about to *die*."

"True. But last time we didn't think anyone else was going to win, either. I am really not happy letting Azad win."

"I'd say there's a good chance that she and the Dampierre woman will end up murdering each other," Tib said. "They have mutually incompatible goals, when it comes down to it."

"That's a comfort," Felix said. "How mad do you think Jhuri will be that we lost Thales?"

"He hasn't invented anything yet," Tib said. "So only roughly the same amount of mad as he will be about you losing the *Temerarious*."

Felix groaned.

There was no way the parties involved were going to trust one another to make the exchange without some attempts at murderous treachery, so they enlisted Sagasa's help after all. He, his Naalu, his N'orr, and two armored guards went with Felix and Tib to their dock. The airlock doors opened, and Azad stood there with Calred, who was clearly sedated and shackled.

"Where's Severyne?" Felix called across the airlock. "Did you kill her already?"

"Nah, she's watching our pet scientist," Azad said. "Hey, Sagasa. Thanks for stepping in to facilitate matters."

"It is sad when two parties cannot trust one another to deal fairly," the Hacan said. "But such mistrust enriches me, so I cannot bring myself to hate it entirely." He gestured. "Captain Duval? The object in question?"

Felix opened his bag and handed over the sphere. Sagasa could hold it in one huge paw. "This little bauble is the cause of so much strife?"

"Only about a quarter of the cause," Azad said. "But we've got the other three quarters already."

"Intrigues buzz about me like flies around a carcass," Sagasa said. "It is fortunate that I am fundamentally an incurious man." He strode into the airlock. "Release Calred, please."

Azad gave him a nudge, and Cal stumbled forward. Tib hissed in frustration at Felix's side. "I know," Felix murmured.

Sagasa snapped his fingers, and the Naalu slithered forward, undulating across the deck, and helped Calred out of the airlock. Sagasa handed the power cell to Azad. "Does this conclude your business?"

"Once Captain Duval gives you permission to release the docking clamps and let us go on our way."

Sagasa turned to him. "You'll allow her to take your ship, captain?"

"That's… the deal." Hard to speak, through gritted teeth.

"I assume we'll be discussing the purchase of a new vessel, then? Or another rental?"

"Probably," Felix said.

"Just don't use your new ship to chase after us, OK?" Azad said.

"If you were me, would you give up?" Felix said.

"Of course not. There's no fun in giving up. But I figured I'd give you fair warning. I've got a ship with *big* guns, and a power source that will make them even bigger."

Felix winced. They'd talked to their goons on the other ship, then, and deduced the nature of the secret weapon. "Your advice is noted."

"All right, then. See you in the void."

"Not if I target lock you first."

The airlock slid closed. Calred slumped against the wall, blinking. "Sorry, captain." His voice was slurred. "They sealed me in a corridor and gassed me. I couldn't do anything about it."

"We're just glad you're OK, Cal." Felix turned to Sagasa. "Hey. You sold them that cruiser we disabled."

"I don't comment on my business affairs. Confidentiality is key."

"I already *know* you sold it to them – Severyne said so. What I want to ask is, where's the ship they *came* here in? They didn't swim to your station."

"Why do you ask?"

"Because they took my ship," Felix said. "I'm interested in taking theirs."

"It just so happens that I'm in a position to sell it," Sagasa said.

•••

"The *Grim Countenance*." Sagasa stood in the middle of the Letnev ship's black-metal bridge and spread his arms. "A top-of-the-line Letnev battle cruiser, one of their famed thorn ships, sure to strike terror into the hearts of et cetera. A fine choice for the unaffiliated privateer, because you can sow terror throughout the stars, and since the ship is so distinctive, the Barony will be blamed – their reputation for dark deeds providing cover for your own."

"Are all the original data banks intact?"

"I haven't even had the vessel cleaned," Sagasa said. "I didn't know I owned this ship until those two flew away without returning the ship they traded this one for. They left the *Grim Countenance* as collateral. I have now collected it. It is new inventory, ready to move."

"Name your price."

Sagasa named one. Calred, who was nearly recovered from his sedation, roared. "That's more than it cost the Barony to build it!"

"Try buying one from the Barony, then," Sagasa said.

Felix sighed. "You two negotiate, and come to an agreement that won't bank-rupt us, OK, Cal?"

He went to the command station, considering the unfamiliar controls. The Mentak Coalition studied how to operate all sorts of different vessels – that was the raider's life – and though it had been a while since he'd done his Letnev tutorials, he thought he could muddle along.

Tib joined him. "Apart from the symmetry of taking their ship when they took yours, is there a reason you wanted this boat in particular?"

"It's fast," he said. "It's got guns. It's a match for the *Temerarious* in a fight."

"Except that they have umpty-petawatt-laser cannons, and we don't."

"It's as close as we're going to get to a match for the *Temerarious* in a fight, then," Felix said.

"Fair enough, but we don't know where they *went*. They'll shut down the transponder and run dark. They might go back to Jord. They might go to the Barony. Thales said he had various test sites in mind, so maybe they'll go to one of those, but we don't know what those sites are. We're good at hide-and-seek, but we're not *that* good."

"We can find them." Felix figured out how to pull up the ship's personnel roster. The information he wanted was locked, but he had his fob full of Mentak Coalition pirate tools to break that security. He put them to work. "Once we own this system, we can track them down, if we hurry."

"How?" Tib said.

"The Letnev are a paranoid, suspicious, distrustful culture. Their culture heroes are all snitches and informants. They sell out their own grandmothers for promotions."

"The version of the Letnev that appears in sims as villains is all that, absolute-ly, but it's an exaggeration–"

"They're paranoid enough to track their officers, though." He pulled up Severyne's file, her frozen face on the screen. "Anyone who might defect or sell secrets or who poses a danger to the motherland is fitted with a tracking device, the kind you can't get out without a bomb disposal unit that's also capable of thoracic surgery. If we get moving before that device is out of range, we can track them."

"Calred!" Tib shouted. "Hurry up and close that deal. We're going to cheat at hide-and-seek!"

CHAPTER 26

"I can't believe we left the *Grim Countenance* behind." Severyne sat with her head in her hands. "I delivered one of the Barony's finest ships into the hands of a Hacan crime lord."

"It's a shame," Azad said. They were in Felix's cabin, Azad lounging on the bed, Severyne seated at the small desk. "If I'd seen a way to keep both, I would have."

"Loss of a Barony warship is an offense punishable by death."

"You've committed a couple of those. The nice thing about death sentences is, they aren't really cumulative. It's not like the Barony can execute you twice."

"They *can*," Severyne said. "They kill you, then restart your heart, then kill you again. It's fairly common."

"Wow. I stand corrected. So, have you considered my offer?"

Severyne sighed. "My people are taught to choose death before dishonor, Azad."

"But are you really expected to choose *double* death before dishonor? That's a lot of death." Azad rose and stood behind the desk, where she began to massage Severyne's tense shoulders. Severyne willed herself to relax into the touch. Azad had skillful hands. She should have killed the human by now, but it was nice having her to talk to. Without Azad, Severyne would be stuck here alone with Thales, who had not proven pleasant based on their brief acquaintance. Shelma had been annoying, but Thales was vile.

"Maybe I can make you feel better, or, at least, make you feel *good*," Azad purred.

Then the comms blared. "This is Thales!" the scientist yelled, as if there were anyone else it could be. "We need to talk about my experiment, ladies, right now."

"He does not seem to realize he's a prisoner," Azad said. "He appears to believe he is our boss."

"I have noticed that," Severyne said.

"We'll meet you in half an hour in the galley," Azad replied, shipwide.

"Half an *hour*? I demand we meet–"

Azad turned off the comms. "So. What do we do with half an hour?"

They only got ten minutes, because at that point, Thales started pounding on their door and screaming, which rather ruined the mood.

• • •

"You two are disgusting," Thales said. "You aren't even the same species."

"You grew up on Nar." Azad leaned way back in one of the galley chairs, her boots up on the table. "You never kissed a squid? No sense of adventure."

"When I think of you two–" Thales began.

"We aren't here to listen to your fantasies, Doc," Azad interrupted. "You insisted we meet. What's the ruckus?"

Thales composed himself. "I assume you plan to deliver me to your superiors in the Federation of Sol?"

"That's the idea," Azad said. "We sure took the long way around, but the end is in sight."

"You shouldn't take me back there yet."

"Oh? Why not? You have some more errands you need to run? More old rivals to gas or poison?" Azad and Severyne had both read Duval's private log entries, including his speculation about what Thales had done. Azad had checked, and the ship was still running diagnostics on Shelma's corpse. She was curious to see what it turned up.

"It is a long trip back to the heart of Federation space," Thales said. "There is only one nearby wormhole you could plausibly use to get there. We're in a stolen Coalition warship. Their raider fleets will be on alert, looking for this vessel. Don't you think they'll be waiting for you at the gate?"

"Oh, probably," Azad said. "You forget I'm a covert operative by training, Doc. There are ways around that problem."

"Are those ways entirely without risk?"

Azad shrugged. "Taking a *shower* isn't entirely without risk. You could slip and fall. There could be a fault in the heating system, and you could get electrocuted. I guess, if you were particularly stupid, you might even manage to drown."

"I think avoiding Coalition forces is riskier than taking a shower, woman."

"Call me Amina, Doc. We're all pals here."

I don't even call her Amina, Severyne though. *It would feel far too familiar.* Considering some of the things they'd done together, that should have been a ridiculous thought, but it wasn't.

"Damn it, admit I'm right," Thales said.

"Yes, fine, there's danger." Azad yawned in his face. "So what? It's the only path. I was sent to fetch you, and here I am, fetching you. I know you don't want to work with the Federation any more–"

"I don't care who I work with," Thales said. "These idiots, those idiots, you idiots. I only left the Coalition because it seemed wise to put some distance between myself and the ruins of my lab. All I care about now is the work. Duval and his crew acquired the last pieces I needed – the prototype trigger and the power source. I've been working on them in my lab, and the activation engine is ready. We don't *need* to go through a heavily guarded wormhole, risking our lives in the process. We can open our *own* wormhole, and return to the Sol system directly."

Azad whistled. "Really. Your magic button is done?"

"It isn't *magic*."

"Shelma was that close to completion?" Severyne said. "She told us it would be years before she had a device ready for testing!"

"Shelma was toying with you," Thales said. "By the time I got her prototype, it was practically done, except for the power supply – which she didn't even mention to you. She didn't want the Barony to have this power. I don't think she wanted anyone to have it, frankly. She was afraid of harnessing such power. Coward. I would like to note, her design was based entirely on *my* research–"

"You'll get full credit, Doc, don't worry," Azad said. "The dead can't demand a byline. So the thing really works. In that case why shouldn't I just kill you and take it home? We don't actually care about Phillip Thales. Just about what Phillip Thales can build – or, in this case, steal from a Hylar and plug into a battery."

Thales sniffed. "Such threats are so predictable. Only I know how to operate the device, and, moreover, most of my additions to Shelma's design were instituted to make the whole thing tamper-proof. Anyone who tries to open the case to examine the interior, or do a more than purely passive scan, will fuse all the components into melted slag. I will share my designs only when I have proper assurances from the Federation authorities that I'll be compensated to my liking."

Azad nodded. "I thought you'd have something slippery in mind. Your brain is powered by grievance and paranoia."

"How do you know it really works?" Severyne said. "You haven't even turned it on yet."

"When the theory is sound, the practice is mere formality, young lady."

"That is not even a little bit true," Azad said.

"It is easier to sell a finished product than just the plans for one," Thales admitted. "That's the only reason I stooped to doing actual engineering."

Azad said, "I admit, I'm curious to see if it works. It's not like my bosses are expecting me back anytime soon – they probably assume I'm dead, since I've been gone this long. Being presumed dead offers some operational flexibility. What do you say, Sev? Should we see if this guy's as smart as he thinks he is?"

"It would be advantageous to verify the functionality of the device," Severyne said.

"You are so hot right now," Azad said. "I'd like to verify the functionality of your–"

"Stop!" Thales roared. "You repulse me. I never thought I'd miss Duval and his cretinous crew." He put his hands flat on the tabletop. "We need to travel to an appropriate test site."

"I thought the whole point of your wonder-device was that it can open a wormhole from anywhere to anywhere?" Azad said. "Fire it up right here and now."

"I would rather not. It's possible there could be ripple effects in space-time after I open the wormhole. Or the wormhole might not open precisely where

I intend. We're within a few thousand kilometers of an inhabited asteroid belt right now. I don't expect any problems, but I want to open the first wormhole in an uninhabited area, to *another* uninhabited area, until I can verify all the readings fall within expected parameters."

"So we're headed to the big empty. I can see how opening a wormhole in the middle of a civilization would be a big problem."

"Or a huge opportunity," Severyne said.

"What do you mean?" Azad said.

"I mean, if you opened a wormhole directly above, say, Jol or Nar, the resulting warping of space-time would destroy the planets." That was why the Barony really wanted the device – for the remote planet-killing capabilities. The ability to move a fleet from anywhere to anywhere was of secondary importance.

"Now, 'destroy' is an overstatement," Thales said. "But opening a wormhole near a planet would have powerful gravitational effects, and would likely cause mass casualties. There are safeguards in place that won't permit the wormhole to open if–"

"Huh. So could you open a wormhole inside an enemy ship?" Azad said. "Just tear them to bits?"

"Again, there are safeguards against such accidents, but if those safeguards were disabled, then in theory–"

"Theory is just practice that hasn't happened yet, isn't that what you were saying?" Azad interrupted. "Oh, I like this. I like this a lot. You should have led with the whole 'I can destroy planets' thing, Thales – you would have gotten way more funding."

"That is not the purpose of this device. My activation engine is meant to facilitate exploration, and trade, and to help galactic civilization flourish. I don't want my legacy to be that of a war criminal."

"Nobody gets to choose their legacy. One side's war criminal is the other side's war hero, usually, anyway. Besides, the Federation researched you thoroughly, Thales. The purpose of this device is to make you so rich and powerful you never have to do what anybody else tells you to ever again. That's all you really care about."

"I also want respect, Amina." His eyes blazed. "I have been belittled, dismissed, laughed at, for my entire life – that stops. The moment I turn on this device, I will prove my brilliance. Even *you* will be forced to admit that I'm the man who transformed the galaxy."

"Fine by me," Azad said. "Let's find a place to turn it on. Someplace where we *won't* kill a bunch of asteroid miners by accident."

"I have considered the nearest options." Thales called up a star chart on his tablet and showed it to them, zooming in on a marked point in space. There was nothing there, which, Severyne supposed, was part of the point. "I say we go here."

"Does that work for you, Sev?"

Severyne looked at the scientist. "Do you have anything else you'd like to share about your device, Thales?"

"Nothing that people with your lack of education would understand–"

"I worked with Shelma," Severyne said.

"Yes, I'd assumed you were sent to fetch her back. Why else would a Letnev and a human be working together? Do you expect me to express some sympathy for the loss of our mutual colleague? Fine. Her death was a tragedy. She simply couldn't handle the strain of–"

"I don't care about sympathy," Severyne snapped, and was pleased to see his face shut down. "I wasn't friends with Shelma. She was infuriating – though having met you, I must say, I miss her. But she told me about her work, and her worries. She was concerned about that ripple effect through space-time, too, Thales. But she wasn't *just* worried about harming nearby inhabitants. She said there was a chance the ripple effect would propagate. That the wormhole would become unstable, and spread, corroding the fabric of space-time, in all directions… forever."

Thales sniffed. "I obviously don't think that's a serious concern. Shelma was always too cautious. There are legends about the first humans to discover the power of atomic energy. When they built an atom bomb, they were afraid to test it, because some of their scientists theorized that setting off an atomic weapon might create a chain reaction that would ignite the hydrogen and nitrogen in the oceans and the atmosphere and kill everything on the planet in a cataclysm of endless flame."

"I assume that didn't happen," Azad said. "Since there are still a few humans around."

"It did not happen. Shelma's worry is even *less* likely. She didn't want the Barony to have this technology, as I told you, so she over-emphasized the risks."

"And yet, I am not reassured," Severyne said. "You are a megalomaniac with a device that might burn down the galaxy."

"When you put it that way, even I get a little shiver," Azad said. "But, hell, he built the thing already. One thing you should know about humans, Sev, is that once we've built something, we're gonna turn it on."

CHAPTER 27

"We've got them." Calred loomed over the security station on the *Grim Countenance* – or the *Incontinence*, as Felix had taken to calling it. "We're gaining on them, even. They don't seem to be in any particular hurry."

"Are they heading toward the wormhole to Sol, or to Barony space?" Felix asked. "Tib bet me that Azad would kill Severyne and head back to Jord, but my money's on Severyne killing Azad and heading to the Barony – people underestimate her."

"I could go either way," Calred said. "But *they* didn't. Go either way, I mean. They're headed, as far as I can tell, for a big old stretch of nowhere."

"They're going to test the device, then," Felix said. "They must be."

"It's a working hypothesis," Tib said. "What do we do about it? Hang back and see if the activation engine even works? If it doesn't work, we can just slink away and let *them* kill Thales."

"If it does work, though…" Felix shook his head. "If they open a wormhole, they might go through it, and then they could end up anywhere. I say we take back our ship."

"You want to fight them hand-to-hand in the corridors, huh?" Calred said. "All right. As long as Severyne doesn't have a halberd this time."

"I think it was a glaive guisarme," Tib said.

"Weapons nerds," Felix said. "How long before we intercept?"

"A couple of hours if I push it," Calred said. "Longer if I try to creep up on them, hiding in the sensor-shadows of asteroids along the way. The problem is, they're headed for wide-open nothingness, so if we go in slow, they're definitely going to see us coming at the end, and they have horrible super lasers they can use to blow us up."

"Fortunately, we don't really care if they shoot holes in this ship. And we have our secret weapon."

"Secret weapon nerd," Tib said.

"Set the fastest intercept course you can," Felix said. "We'll– hold on." A priority message lit up in his comms. It had been sent some hours ago, but to the *Temerarious*. Felix had only now gotten close enough for his ship to recognize his personal comm system and forward the message.

Undersecretary Jhuri gazed at him in his heads-up display. "I know I said you should act with autonomy, Felix, but you need to call me, right now, and explain why you just bought a Barony warship from the most notorious criminal in the vicinity of Vega Major."

Connecting a call all the way back to Moll Primus from said Barony warship was tricky, but eventually Felix got through, using the right call signs and passwords to reach the undersecretary's desk, since he lacked the proper encryption protocols on the *Grim Countenance*. The Barony ship's ready room was all black metal and dim light, and Felix worried he'd get tetanus from sitting in the ornamentally spiky captain's chair, but he settled himself as comfortably as he could.

Jhuri appeared, a figure drawn in light above the desk. "I refuse to believe you've defected to the Barony, Felix. They make their alcohol out of fungus."

"I can explain. But only if you *want* me to explain. Explaining will involve telling you things that officially you should not know about."

"I'm good at compartmentalization, Felix."

"This is a secure channel?"

Jhuri barked a laugh. "It's so secure we can barely talk to *each other* through the layers of encryption. You're on a Barony ship, and I'm communicating with you like you're a deep-cover double agent. Tell me your tale of woe."

Felix filled him in on everything: the jailbreak, Shelma's death, their run-in with Severyne and Azad at Sagasa's station, the heist on Jol, the propulsion lab director's death, their *additional* run-in with Severyne and Azad, and their current situation.

Jhuri blinked at him when it was done. "Have you had time to eat or sleep?"

"Not enough, sir."

"Duval's Devils, eh? So. What's your plan?"

"Overtake, board, and recover the *Temerarious*, and bring back Thales–"

"I thought it would be something like that," Jhuri said. "No. The chance of successfully reclaiming Thales and the device is minimal. Destroy them instead."

Felix leaned back, and one of the spikes on the chair poked him in the side of the neck, so he leaned forward again. "Sir, this isn't a lost cause – we can get Thales and his device back – I know we can. Boarding ships and taking their stuff is what we *do*."

"This whole situation has become very messy, Felix. They don't know you're behind them. You can target them, all weapons hot, and annihilate them. We won't get the wormhole tech, but neither will anybody else. Tipping the balance in our favor would be wonderful, but maintaining the status quo is a decent second option. If you try to board them and fail, and they get away… I don't like to imagine the consequences, especially since Sol *and* the Barony have reasons to be annoyed with us after all this. If either or both of their governments gain the power to open a wormhole over the skies of Moll Primus…"

"If you order me to destroy them, sir, I will. But I'm asking you to have faith in me. What's the motto written on the seal of the Table of Captains?"

Jhuri sighed. "It says, 'Who Dares, Wins.' It's a nice sentiment, Felix, but the truth is: who *wins*, wins."

"If we do it your way, sir, the best outcome is: we don't lose. At least let me *try* to win."

The undersecretary gazed at Felix – or, perhaps, off into space – for a long moment. "I'll offer you a compromise," Jhuri said.

"That's great, sir."

"The terms of the compromise might require you to die."

"That is less great, sir," Felix said, "but I'm still listening."

"I don't get to board the ship and shoot people?" Calred said. "The only thing that's been keeping me going is the thought of boarding the ship and shooting people! Specifically, Severyne. She shot me in the arm. It's still tingly."

Felix shook his head. "Someone has to stay here. It's Jhuri's compromise. Tib and I can try to board, and fight, and recover Thales, and seize control of the ship, but if we fail, you have to blow up the *Temerarious*."

"With you two on board?"

"If we fail, we'll probably be dead anyway," Felix said.

"That is a terrible compromise," Tib said. "Why aren't we going with option one, and just blowing them up? That's also the only plan where Thales dies, so that's a plus."

"Not you, too?" Felix said. "They stole Thales from a colony we were supposed to be protecting. They stole my ship, Tib. They stole Shelma's research. They stole the power cell. They stole all that stuff that we stole in the first place! We're the Coalition. We don't get robbed. We *rob*."

"I am very excited to blow up a spaceship," Calred said. "I am significantly less excited to blow up a spaceship with my friends on board."

"Consider it avenging our deaths," Felix said. "You have your orders, Calred. Come on, Tib. Let's go get in our secret weapon."

Azad woke up with a yawn, looked around, and saw Severyne was gone.

She checked in with the ship while she got dressed. There was nothing showing on their sensors except some distant asteroids. Nobody had messed around with the life-support functions or security controls. Everything seemed in order. Ostensibly, Azad had given Severyne full control of the ship, but of course, she'd kept her own backdoor access. She scanned through the ship's cameras. Thales was still bustling around in his lab. There were some cleaning and repair drones doing their thing. No sign of Severyne at all.

The ship had a lower deck. That space was usually meant as crew cabins and support spaces, but on this ship it was all just cargo storage for relief supplies. There were, for reasons Azad had been unable to determine, no working security cameras down there. Maybe the Coalition hadn't bothered to install any, figuring nobody would ever go down there anyway, or maybe Felix had disabled the cameras so he could have discreet sex with prostitutes, or he ran an illegal knife-fighting ring back in the colonies. Who knew? That deck was a surveillance dead zone, though. "Sev," she said over the loudspeakers. "Where are you?"

"I'm on the lower deck," she called back promptly. "There's something down here I think you'll want to see."

Here we go, Azad thought. Time to play hide-and-seek.

"I'll be right there," she said, and went to the galley to pick out a knife.

Severyne waited in the darkness. She'd shut off all the lights, even the emergency ones, and she wore a helmet with gas filters and a heads-up display featuring thermal imaging and night-vision overlays. She'd raided the armory and supplied herself with small arms, then disabled the armory door controls, locking the other weaponry inside. Even if Azad was suspicious, she would be relatively defenseless… though someone like Azad was never entirely so.

The lack of cameras down here left her as much in the dark as anyone, but she could monitor the rest of the ship and see Azad coming – until suddenly her feeds went dark. "What?" she said aloud. She tried to reboot, but her system said, "Authorization revoked."

"Oh you're clever," she muttered. Azad had access to the ship's core controls after all. "'You're the one sitting in the big chair' indeed." Her attempts to distract the human had failed, then. Azad knew exactly what was happening here.

"You know, it doesn't have to be this way, Sev." Azad's voice over her personal comms was low and insinuating and right in Severyne's ear, just like it had been earlier, but it was saying much less pleasant things now. "I really do like you. There's zero incentive for me to kill you. Your death gains me nothing. Keeping you alive is good for me, even – my superiors will be excited to have a Barony defector. Let me keep you safe and happy."

Severyne crouched behind a pallet of shrink-wrapped air purifiers. She wasn't going to chat. She wasn't going to roam around. She was going to wait for Azad to creep close, and then shoot her in the back of the head. Severyne wasn't Azad's equal as a hunter, but she could be a very capable spider, lying in wait for prey to stumble into her web.

"You have choices here, Sev. I know they're shitty choices! I get that. But you're betting you can beat me in a fight in the dark, and that's just… Look. You know I think the world of you. You've got talent, and you've got potential. The dance you did with Duval back on Sagasa's station, that was a thing of beauty, and you've got some real steel in you. I've seen that. I respect it. But, babe. You can't win in a fight against me. Especially not a dirty fight. Come out, drop your weapons, and we'll forget this ever happened. If Thales comes through, my superiors are going to be delighted, and I can negotiate a great deal for you. I'll visit you. Conjugals, even. What do you say?"

Briefly, Severyne considered. She decided to speak. "Azad. If we could go on like this, you and I, traveling and fighting and winning, that would be a temptation. But you offer me a future locked in a secure Federation facility. I used to *run* a facility like that. I would be in the same position Shelma was in: something between a pet and a prisoner. I can't take that. Could you endure such a thing, if our positions were reversed?"

"I guess not," Azad said. "But now you're tempting me. We could do it, huh? Just go our own way. Take this activation engine Thales made and sell it to some third party – the Naalu would love it, and I know people over there. We could get rich, buy a ship, do crimes, make out. Is that your proposal?"

"Amina," Severyne said. "That sounds wonderful." It really did. Severyne didn't have to lie.

"Yeah, it does. It's a shame you'd never actually do it. I'm not saying I would either – I'm fifty-fifty on the idea, I see pluses and minuses – but I know you wouldn't. You're Letnev, Sev. All the way through. Death before dishonor, and being with me, as much as it might turn you on, it's still dishonor."

"Then we do what we must," Severyne said.

"That we do."

There was a sound, a sort of *thump*, and Severyne's heads-up display went dark. She cursed, tried to reboot it, but found the system entirely unresponsive. The faint glow of the charge gauge on her sidearm was dark, too, and that meant – It had to be an electromagnetic pulse. Azad must have used an EMP grenade, and just having one of those on hand meant she'd planned for this scenario, or something like it.

Severyne no longer had the advantages she'd so carefully created. In fact, she had *disadvantages*, because when it came to fighting with nothing but your bare hands, Azad was much better.

"Hey, Sev!" The voice was not on comms, but echoing through the air. "I'm down here in the dark, and you're down here in the dark. We used to have so much fun together in the dark, huh? I bet you have some guns that don't work any more. I don't have guns either, if that makes you feel better. I do have a knife. I'm guessing you probably don't, though. Just remember, even a gun that won't shoot is a pretty good club. I'm the sharp edge, and you're the blunt object. So, let's see who's going to be dead, and who's just going to be heartbroken."

Carefully, silently, Severyne began to move.

CHAPTER 28

Down in the belly of the *Grim Countenance* rested the *Endless Dark*, burnt-out laser cannons and all. "This is not a boarding craft, Felix," Tib said. "It is barely even a craft at this point."

"Secret weapon," Felix said stubbornly. "It's so small, they might not even notice our approach, and if they do, we'll be harder to hit, because we're small and maneuverable. We're going to creep up on them and cut our way in." Sagasa had loaned them (for, of course, a price) a set of "salvage tools" – which were really the sort of drones raiders used to breach ships that didn't want to open their doors voluntarily. The drones squatted in the *Endless Dark*, filling much of the limited space inside the small craft, their bodies round and matte black, their wicked little manipulator arms and cutting torches all tucked away.

"We are going to die," Tib said.

"You always think that. If we do, Calred will make sure *they* die too."

"That will be no comfort to me, because I will be dead."

"Don't the Yssaril have the concept of an afterlife?" Felix said. "I read about it once. Your heaven is some kind of jungle, full of endless game, prey too slow to run away, and there are miniature versions of the predators that used to eat your people, and instead, you eat *them–*"

"That is what one tribe, out of a very large number of tribes, believes, yes. It's not the tribe my ancestors come from, but that doesn't matter. I'm from the Coalition, Felix. All I believe in is drinking, pillaging, and having a good time before you die."

"Are you telling me we haven't been having a good time?"

"I'd like to have a good time for a *longer* time."

Felix bowed his head. "Tib, if you want, you can stay here with Calred. I know I'm asking a lot of you, that it's dangerous, that–"

"Oh, shut up, you stupid human," Tib said. "I'm not going to let you die by yourself." She clambered into the ship. "Let's go. Time to put all that hide-and-seek training to use."

Felix strapped into the cockpit and called up to Calred. "Ready when you are."

The bay doors opened, and the *Endless Dark* dropped into space and began to accelerate toward the distant *Temerarious*. "Be safe, you two," Calred said.

"I think we'll be dangerous instead," Felix said. "Hang back at the very edge of effective weapons range. You know what to do if we don't call you from the bridge before time's up."

"Boom boom," Calred said. "The most depressing boom boom in the history of all boom booms. I will never forgive you if you ruin boom boom for me, captain."

Felix sat in the pilot's chair, with Tib right beside him. "I like having you in that chair much more than Thales."

"I can't believe we're going to all this trouble to get that asshole back."

"Mostly I want my ship. Thales is a side project."

"They're going to see us coming," Tib said. "I know we're small, I know we're flying manual, but if they bother to look, they'll see us. You know it."

"Maybe Thales is keeping them busy." The *Temerarious* grew in the viewport as they crept closer. "He is very distracting."

"I should have given more thought to my last words," Tib said.

"I heard a story once about Erwin Mentak's last words."

"The glorious founder of our glorious Coalition? What did he say?"

"According to this guy I met in a bar," Felix said, "Erwin Mentak's final words were, 'Don't let it end like this. Tell them I said something.'"

Tib snorted laughter. "Thanks for amusing me as I wait to die."

But they didn't die – at least not yet. The *Endless Dark* reached the *Temerarious*, and sailed beneath its belly. "We're here," Felix said. "They can't hurt us now unless they open up a window and lean out to shoot us with a sidearm. Their sensors can't pick us up, either – we just look like part of the ship. See, Tib? Optimism."

"I can't understand how they didn't notice us," Tib said. "Is nobody monitoring their sensors? What are they *doing* in there?"

"Maybe they all killed each other." Felix spun their ship upside down and activated the magnetic clamps, so the *Endless Dark* could cling, parasitically, to the belly of the *Temerarious*. He unstrapped and went to the back of the ship, activating the boarding drones. They scuttled out of the small airlock, crouched on the hull of the *Temerarious*, and started cutting.

Once the hull was breached, Felix and Tib planned to enter a service tunnel, then slip through an access panel onto the lower deck, where there were no security cameras, because that's where they liked to play hide-and-seek. From down there, unseen, they should be able to sneak up and retake the ship.

Waiting was hard, and Felix checked and re-checked his weapons while the drones did their work. They finally beeped a completion tone to their comms, and Tib and Felix made their way out of the *Endless Dark* into the endless dark.

Felix took a moment, clinging to the skin of his ship, to look around. There was nothing out here. He couldn't even see many stars. Which, he supposed, was the point: Thales wanted a big stretch of empty to punch a hole in, out where no one would see the triumph of the human mind over the physics of the cold and uncaring universe.

"Felix, we have pirating to do," Tib said. "Stop striking a noble and thoughtful pose. There's nobody here to appreciate it."

The drones had deployed a temporary airlock, a sort of rounded tent made of "densely woven polymer" – which was to say, a plastic tarp. Felix unsealed the opening, and Tib slipped in. Felix clambered after and resealed the airlock. The hole the drones had cut in the hull was big enough for his body to fit through, but only just. He followed Tib up – or down – or through – the layers of armor and radiation shielding, on into the ship. The walls vibrated around him as the drones placed a more permanent seal over the hole they'd cut. They wouldn't be getting out the way they got in.

Felix wasn't particularly claustrophobic, but tight spaces *and* darkness *and* a mission to retake a stolen ship *and* the low-level discomfort of wearing an environment suit all combined to make him sweaty and tense. He waited, vibrating himself with tension, while Tib unsealed the access hatch to the service tunnel. They moved on into that objectively cramped but relatively generous space. They were still in the dark, though. Hmm. That wasn't right.

Once the hatch was closed behind them, they took off their helmets and shrugged out of their suits. "Why are the lights off?" Felix said. "There should at least be safety strips on in here. Did those assholes break my ship?"

"There's still air and artificial gravity," Tib said. "Maybe they just wanted mood lighting."

"It is very romantic," Felix said.

"Do you think everyone makes jokes before they walk into possible death, or is that just a Mentak Coalition thing?" Tib said.

"I'm not convinced the L1Z1X or the Nekro do it, being partly or wholly mechanical, but otherwise, I'd guess it's a pretty universal urge."

"I know a Nekro joke," Tib said. "Want to hear it?"

"I might not be alive to hear it later."

"Knock knock."

"Who's there?"

"Zero."

"Zero who?"

"Zero one one zero zero one zero zero, zero one one zero one zero zero one, zero one one zero zero one zero one–"

"OK, I get it. We've had the laughter. Let's move on to the tears. Stay quiet on comms until there's something to report. I'll get the bridge, and you secure the armory."

Tib went dim, just a shimmer in the corner of Felix's eye, and the access hatch opened seemingly by itself. Felix crawled out after he was sure she'd had time to get clear.

He was in a corridor, not far from the ladder that led up to the crew quarters, but he only knew that because he'd spent so much time down here playing hide-and-seek with Tib, and could navigate the space blindfolded if need be. The lower deck was totally dark. Had there been some electrical fault?

"Last chance, Sev!" a voice called. Felix went still. Was that Azad? "If I find you down here, I'm going to stab you, and that's way down on the list of things I want to do with you."

Oh, no. Or… oh, yes? Severyne and Azad were trying to kill each other *now*? That explained why they hadn't noticed the approach of the *Endless Dark*. Felix considered. He could just climb up to the next deck, lock the hatches, and leave them trapped down here to kill each other in peace. He opened his comms to suggest that idea to Tib.

Then light glimmered – someone had opened a hatch on the deck above, letting illumination in. "Are you idiots down there?" Thales bellowed. "There are alarms going off up here, it's *distracting*."

"What alarms?" That was Severyne – and she was very close to Felix, it sounded like, right around the corner.

"Something about a hull breach, though it stopped saying that a minute ago, and now there's a call to repel boarders – not that I've seen any boarders. I think your sensors are malfunctioning. This is not my *job*, ladies. I'm trying to work up here. You'd better not be having sex down there. Duval's bed isn't enough for you?"

"Sev!" Azad called. "Truce? Just while we make sure we aren't being attacked? By someone other than each other, I mean?"

A long, long pause, and then, "Truce," Severyne called. She walked right past Felix and into the shaft of light. Azad joined her. "It's always something, isn't it?" the human said.

Severyne ignored her and clambered up the ladder, bickering with Thales as she vanished from sight.

Azad started up the ladder, then paused and looked around in the dark. "I know you're there," she said. "You may as well come out."

Felix twitched, but didn't move.

Azad waited a moment longer, then snorted. "Worth a try." She climbed up the ladder.

Tib let her get almost all the way to the top before shooting her with a stun charge, so Azad had farther to fall. Tib shimmered into sight next to her supine form, peering up the ladder. Severyne and Thales were gone, and hadn't noticed Azad's tumble.

Felix hurried out of concealment and began binding Azad's arms and ankles with tape while Tib kept lookout. Azad groaned but didn't wake up. "I got the drop on her twice," Tib whispered. "She only got me once. I win." Tib plucked a kitchen knife from Azad's belt, frisked her, then held up the blade. "This is the only weapon she has on her. What were they *doing* down here?"

"Playing hide-and-seek," Felix said. "Just like we used to. But for somewhat higher stakes."

They dragged Azad to one of the store rooms and propped her between a pallet of chemical toilets and stacks of shelf-stable mayonnaise. "Did Thales say they were having sex?" Tib asked. "In your bed?"

"I haven't even had sex in that bed. Now I have to set the whole thing on fire. I'll be moving into your cabin. You can have Cal's. Cal can sleep in the gym."

Tib looked at Azad's limp form. "I guess it wasn't true love, if they were still trying to kill each other."

"They were trying to kill each other over who got the privilege of keeping Thales," Felix said. "Can you imagine?"

The electrical locks weren't working down here for some reason, so they blocked the cabin door with about fifty bags of mulch, piling them up nearly to the ceiling. It probably wouldn't hold Azad back for long, but for now, it was the best they could do.

"Now we go for Severyne," Felix said.

"Leave me alone, Thales, I'm trying to read this. I thought you had work to do." Severyne stood at the security station in the bridge, though she hated having her back to the door. Where was Azad? Shouldn't she be doing this? Was her "truce" just a trick to make Severyne let her guard down? The ship had detected a hull breach, but now it didn't – which either meant it was a glitch in the system, or someone had breached the hull and covered their tracks. "Shipwide scan," she said. "I want to know everyone who's on board."

"Two sapients onboard," the ship replied.

"Just two?" That didn't make any sense. "Does that include the lower deck?"

"Lower deck systems offline. System rebooting."

So Azad was still down there. But why? Severyne was sure she'd been right behind her – Something cold struck her back, and then her vision went white, and then dark. Some unknowable moment later she returned to herself, her face pressed into the smooth floor, her arms bound behind her. She wriggled and rolled over – and saw Duval sitting in the captain's chair, his horrible Yssaril second-in-command leading Thales off the bridge. "Ambush," she spat. "A cowardly strike from behind. The Coalition has no *honor–*"

"Probably true," Duval said. "But I still won. You know the old saying, Severyne: Who wins, wins."

"That is not an old saying. You are a very stupid person who is also annoying," Severyne said. "And unattractive. And you need to shave. Your haircut is a disgrace. You–"

"The Letnev," Felix said. "Magnanimous in victory, gracious in defeat."

CHAPTER 29

Severyne and Azad were in the ship's brig, secure behind a set of bars and an energy field. Severyne sat on a bench, dressed in hideous soft pants and a plain gray shirt. Azad was similarly garbed, but she was shackled by wrists, ankles, and waist to the wall, and wore a metal collar with an ominous blinking red light on the front. Severyne was annoyed that she wasn't considered enough of a threat to bother restraining so thoroughly.

"I'm glad I didn't have to kill you," Azad said.

That was the first time either of them had spoken since being locked up here. Severyne considered ignoring her, but what was the point now? "I am glad I did not have to kill you, too. What is your plan to escape and retake the ship?"

"Oh. Babe. I have no such plan."

"You escaped a Coalition dreadnought, did you not?"

"They didn't have me in shackles and a collar that explodes if I leave a ten-meter radius. Sometimes, Sev, you're just beat."

"A Letnev never admits defeat."

"That's a funny thing about defeat. It's still defeat, whether you admit it or not."

Sev considered. "If I can neither escape nor fulfill my mission, I would like to accept your offer to defect to the Federation now."

Azad chuckled. "My ability to follow through on that deal depends on various factors, like us not being Mentak Coalition prisoners forever, but I'll see what I can do."

"I might have bested you, on the lower deck. I found a screwdriver down there. I was not unarmed."

"Lovers turned deadly enemies, armed with screwdriver and knife, fighting for their mutually exclusive futures in the dark. It's kinda romantic, in a way."

"You are a ridiculous person, Amina Azad. If we had not let our personal rivalry distract us, we might have stopped Duval from retaking the ship."

"You're not wrong."

"Perhaps there is a valuable lesson there."

Amina belched. "Probably. Let me know when you figure out what it is."

"You disgust me."

"I love you too, Sev."

Severyne blushed.

•••

"I mean, I guess, since we're already here, we might as well let him do his test." Felix was back in his ready room, because he wasn't ready to face his defiled cabin.

"You've gone this far," Jhuri said. "No reason to stop here. At least if his device malfunctions horribly, no one is likely to get hurt."

"Except us."

"Except you."

"What if the Creuss show up and declare war on all the biological entities in the galaxy when we switch this thing on?"

"What if the kelp fairy appears and wraps you all in ropes of kelp?"

"Is the kelp fairy even a real thing?" Felix said. "Like from Jol-Nar folklore or something?"

"How should I know?" Jhuri said. "I've never been to Jol-Nar. I hate long space voyages. Maybe if you can open a wormhole from my office to Wun-Escha I'll finally take the trip. I'll let you get to work."

"Wait! I wanted to know… What do I do with the prisoners?"

"What prisoners?"

"What do you mean, what prisoners?"

"I mean, I wish the human and the Letnev had died in a dramatic firefight. This whole situation is a potential diplomatic nightmare. A probable Federation operative, and a *definite* Barony security officer, knowing all the things they know about our own covert activities? I don't want a whisper of either one on the official record."

"Then what should I do with them?"

"What should you do with *who*? Let me know how the test goes." Jhuri flickered and vanished.

OK. Severyne and Azad were a problem for later. Other problems came first.

"I'm ready," Thales said simply. Thales, Felix, Tib, and Calred – who'd shuttled over from the *Grim Countenance* – stood together on the bridge. The huge viewscreen showed the expanse of empty space before them.

Thales had his torpedo-shaped device resting on top of a workstation, attached to the stolen power supply, and wired into the ship's weapons systems – he'd be using some of the focused energy weapons to direct the force he was about to unleash. "We'll open the wormhole, and then launch a probe into it," he said. "I have programmed the other end of the wormhole to open a safe distance from the wasteland world Xanhact – the probe should be able to confirm that location from the configuration of stars, and return to us with data on the journey."

"Oh, good," Calred said. "I was afraid you'd want us to drive into the wormhole to test it."

"I'd love to jettison all of you into space," Thales said. "All this pointless to-ing and fro-ing and fighting and stealing you've dragged me through. I understand

I'm valuable, but this inter-faction squabbling has been a grievous distraction." Thales gazed at the empty screen. "Would you transmit an image of this screen to the brig, captain?"

"What? Why?"

"So Dampierre and Azad can witness my triumph."

Felix scratched his chin. "Huh. I'm not opposed to a little gloating, I guess, but why do you care?"

"I want more witnesses, captain," Thales said. "More eyes on the moment I transformed the galaxy. More voices to tell the tale of this achievement."

Felix sighed. "Cal, go ahead and give the brig a screen. I don't need them on comms, though. I've heard enough out of both of them."

Thales cleared his throat. "I've prepared a few words for this occasion–"

"I've heard enough out of *you*, too," Felix said. "Just push the button, Thales."

The scientist glared at him. "This is history happening, right now, you ignorant thug. The occasion must be marked–"

"I promise we'll make sure the official records reflect whatever long speech you wanted to give, Thales. Let's just get this over with."

"We're not getting anything over with. This is a glorious *beginning*–"

"Shut up, or *I'll* push the button," Tib said.

"It's not a button," Thales muttered, but he turned his attention to his terminal. The power cell began to emit a faint hum. They all looked at the screen expectantly.

"Shouldn't beams of coruscating light be shooting from the cannons?" Calred asked.

"The energies involved aren't visible." Thales spoke through gritted teeth. "Don't ruin my enjoyment of this moment."

They watched, and nothing happened… until something started to happen.

At first, Felix thought it was just his eyes inventing things, an optical illusion caused by staring too long at emptiness, but there was a flicker, like a snake slithering through the grass, only the snake was space-time and the grass was more space-time. Thales made more adjustments to his terminal, and a sinuous bright line appeared, gleaming yellow like a thread of gold. "Pretty, isn't it? That's the sort of visual the idiot masses will appreciate when they watch this recording in their classrooms for all time going forward."

"I'm sure they'll appreciate being called idiots, too."

"You already said you're going to manipulate the record. I can say what I please."

"That doesn't look much like a wormhole," Calred pointed out. The golden thread rippled. "I've been through a few wormholes in my time. They're big, bulgy, and round. Not a wavy line, golden or otherwise."

"I'm still adjusting the calibration," Thales complained. "Give me a moment. Altering the fundamental physics of the universe doesn't happen in an instant."

"I always thought going through a wormhole was like passing through a giant water droplet," Tib said. "You know, the way it shimmers a little, and you can faintly see what's on the other side."

"I never understood why they call them 'holes' at all," Felix said. "They're more like… crystal balls."

"Because 'wormballs' sounds disgusting," Tib said.

"Fools," Thales muttered, still adjusting his controls. "If space were two-dimensional, then yes, wormholes would appear as circles punched in the surface of space. Passing through those circles would lead to a *three-dimensional* shape, a cylinder, and you would emerge from another flat circle on the other side. But space isn't two-dimensional, so instead we perceive wormholes as three-dimensional spheres, and they lead to a *four-dimensional* space that your minds can't visualize, until you emerge from another sphere."

"That is not a sphere," Calred said. "It's more like a rip. A tear in a piece of cloth." The gold thread widened, becoming a ribbon of uneven width, and the light became less yellow and more white.

Thales grunted. "I would expect it to start coalescing into a sphere by now."

"Do we need to abort the experiment?" Felix said.

"Of course not," Thales barked. "I think I see the problem. The other end of my wormhole isn't where it should be. Damn it. These readings about the far end of the wormhole are just gibberish. The other side must have opened in the Shaleri Passage – that's the only place I know of where normal physics are twisted, and it's where the Creuss live, so they must be meddling, trying to ruin my triumph!"

"You think the *Ghosts* are doing this?" Felix demanded.

"They must be. There's no other explanation. It's called deductive reasoning, captain."

"So, what, the Creuss are going to come out of that hole?"

"That tear," Calred said.

"I am trying to *determine–*" Thales said.

The light brightened, and suddenly the ribbon became a yawning chasm, a ragged tear big enough to swallow their ship.

Felix scrabbled for the device, but Thales hunched over it, blocking him with his body. "Turn this thing off, Thales!" Felix shouted.

"No, I can get control back, I just need to boost the power." Thales twisted the controls, glaring out the viewport at the shimmer in space. "This is *my* moment – I won't let some aliens who don't even have *bodies* spoil it."

"We're going to get murdered by the Ghosts of Creuss," Tib said. "You find such interesting ways for us to die, Felix."

The power source started humming much more loudly, and – was the spherical case *vibrating*? "There!" Thales said. "The connection is stable! It – no, that *still* doesn't make any sense. Why isn't the wormhole opening where I told it to?"

"Why is it a *gash*?" Felix said. "What the hell did you do, Thales?"

The tear in space widened before them, and beyond it, something moved. Colors flickered in there, like aurora, but there were other things, too. Writhing things. Felix thought of maggots in rotting meat. Of baby spiders bursting out of a wound. Of worms wriggling up out of a wet hole.

"Send the probe," Thales said.

"*Why?*" Felix said. "That's not Xanhact through there! It's not even a wormhole!"

"Maybe artificial wormholes present themselves differently!" Thales said. "Send the probe!"

Felix caught Calred's eye, shrugged, and nodded. Calred operated the panel at the security station, and a small gleaming sphere studded with sensors burst out of the ship and sailed toward the rift.

They watched the probe get closer and closer to the chasm – and then tendrils of coruscating darkness lashed out of the rift, grabbed the probe, and pulled it in.

"What," Thales said flatly. "What are you getting from the probe?"

"It's just throwing error codes," Cal said.

"Is that the Shaleri Passage on the other side?" Felix said. "Damn it, Thales, did we just shoot a Coalition probe at the Creuss?"

"I… I don't think…"

"Look," Tib said. "There's something in the crack. A shape, a structure, I can't quite make it out, it's–"

Felix heard a whimper. He realized a second later it had come from his own throat.

There was something inside the crack. Felix had no sense of scale, so he couldn't tell how big the thing was – the size of a starship, the size of a star, bigger. He just knew, whatever size it was, it was impossible.

The thing beyond the crack in space was a burning wheel, facing them side-on, slowly rotating, flickering with a corona of white fire. The spokes of the wheel seemed to be made of yellowed, splintered bone. The rim of the wheel was an immense red serpent, devouring its own tail. The hub of the wheel was an open, bleeding eye.

The eye stared at them. The eye *saw* them. More tendrils began to reach out of the rift, this time, toward the *Temerarious*.

CHAPTER 30

Felix reached for the power source, but Thales hugged the battery and the trigger to his chest. "No! I can fix this!"

Calred tackled him, and the sphere fell from his hand, clattering to the deck, the case cracking loudly on impact. The power cell whined louder, and thin, acrid smoke started to rise from the crack in its side. "Look out!" Felix shouted, diving for Tib and throwing himself on top of her.

The power cell overloaded with a loud *pop* and filled the bridge with a flash of white light and a buzz that made Felix's teeth ache. He staggered upright and looked, through blinking eyes, at the viewscreen. The rift was already shrinking, like a sped-up recording of a wound healing, and the dark tendrils receded into the dark just before it closed. The afterimage of that brightness – and that burning wheel – floated in Felix's vision, though.

Felix leaned against the nearest station, breathing hard. "Tib, Cal, are you OK?"

"I'm a little bruised from you jumping on me," Tib complained.

"I thought it might explode like a grenade," Felix said. "I was being selfless."

"Be selfless on top of someone else next time, captain."

Calred was all right too, but Thales was picking over the remnants of his device, sobbing. The power cell had ruptured into several pieces, and the trigger was cracked too. "You broke it open when you knocked me down!" he shouted. "The interior is fused, it's a melted mess, I'll have to start from scratch–"

Cal stomped down on the device and ground his heel. "That was not a wormhole," Cal said. "That was something else. That was something bad." He was breathing hard, like he'd just run an obstacle course. "Sagasa the Disciplinarian comes from a sect that believes that in the afterlife evildoers are punished forever by demons of blood and fire. I have never believed in that place. But now... now I've seen it, and you, Thales, *you* opened that door. You nearly let that hell into our world."

"It... the device just needs refinement, is all, I'll look at the math–"

Felix grabbed Thales by the back of the neck and dragged him to his feet. "It's over, Thales. Your machine didn't work. That thing, that place, whatever we saw... no one should ever see that again. There are some rocks you shouldn't turn over."

"I- I don't know what went wrong," Thales said.

Felix frowned, remembering. "The Ghost. The one that destroyed your lab. What did it say to you again?"

"What? Why are you talking about that? It's ancient history, and anyway, this wasn't the Creuss, I don't know what it was, but–"

"The Ghost said, 'you must not fracture the void,' right?"

Thales stared at the empty screen. "Something like that."

"The Ghost wasn't trying to scare you off," Felix said. "It was trying to warn you. The Creuss weren't upset because you'd figured out their technology. They were upset because you *hadn't*, not correctly, and they knew if you kept going, you were going to… to do *that*. To open a passage to that place. To the things that live there."

"I… you…" Thales was never slow with a vicious comeback. Until now. "You can't know that. Not really."

"I know enough. Watch Thales for a few minutes, you two. I need to call our boss."

"Then what are you going to do with him?" Calred said.

"Then I'm going to escort him down to the brig," Felix said. "That's where we keep our murderers."

Felix shoved Thales into the cell beside Azad and Severyne. "Hello," he said. "Did you two see the show?"

"That was real?" Severyne said. "It wasn't a trick, to make us think the experiment failed?"

Felix pointed at Thales, who sat on a bench, weeping. "Would he be doing that if he'd succeeded?"

"No, he'd be doing a little dance," Azad said. "Huh. I have seen some messed-up things in my day, captain, but that hole he tore in space was beyond the beyond."

"I devoted years of my life, and ruined my career, for a project that would have failed anyway," Severyne said. "That is disheartening. What will you do with Thales now?"

"Oh, I'm offering this fine specimen of human theoretical physicist to the highest bidder," Felix said. "What will you give me for him?"

Azad frowned. "Even if I had access to funds, why would I pay for something like that? I'm not saying *nobody* wants a weapon that rips open holes in space and lets nightmare monsters out, but I'm not going to give my superiors the option. Can you imagine, Severyne, if the humans could do *that* on demand?"

"The humans might actually use such a thing," the Letnev said.

"Exactly. So, no, captain. You can keep him."

"What do you think, Severyne?" Felix said. "Would the Barony be interested in Thales?"

"I… Why do you ask? Are you sending me back to the Barony?"

Felix shrugged. "I just assumed that's where you'd head after I let you go."

"Ha," Azad said. "The Coalition doesn't want us, huh? We're a big old can full of way too many worms, and some of those worms might bite."

"I don't understand," Severyne said.

"You don't bring prisoners back from a covert operation," Azad said. "Not prisoners like us, anyhow, from an operation like this. Now, if it was me in the captain's place, I'd shove us out an airlock without suits and let nature take its course. But Felix is sentimental, isn't he?"

"I've killed enough people because of Thales. I don't want to kill any more, if I can avoid it. I never want to see either one of you ever again. Can we arrange that? None of us want to talk about anything that went on here, I bet. As far as I can tell, there's no reason for us to try to shoot or strangle each other any more. No reason beyond personal vengeance, anyway."

"Don't discount the power of personal vengeance," Azad said. "But, nah, I'm good. Live to fight another fight."

"Will you give me back the *Grim Countenance*?" Severyne said.

"The *Incontinence* is yours. I don't have any use for it."

"Ha," Azad said. "*Incontinence*. Nice one."

"My people disabled all the weapons," Felix went on, "just in case you *do* feel a twinge of vengeance. Take your ugly spiky ship and fly far away. But back to Thales. He kidnapped and then murdered a Barony scientist. Don't you want to haul him back to your superiors and put on one of those show trials your people like so much?"

Thales finally seemed to realize what they were talking about. "You can't *sell* me, Duval! You have no right!"

Severyne ignored him. "I seem to recall you were involved in those crimes as well."

"Yeah, but I have a warship, and the key to your cell, and Thales doesn't, so he's easier to apprehend."

Severyne shook her head. "I see no advantage in taking him. Officially, no crime was committed. The research facility was secret, and Shelma's research was, too. As for myself, I am not even sure I can return to the Barony–"

"Sad story, hate to hear it," Felix interrupted. "I'll take that as a no. There's no profit in you at all, is there, Thales?"

"I was thinking, Sev," Azad said. "I can make a report to my superiors that only massages the truth a little, tell them I recaptured Thales and decided to test his prototype, and it was a disaster. I can cover my own ass–"

"Why would they believe you?"

"Oh, I got footage of the eldritch horror show on my eyeball cams." She tapped her temple with a forefinger.

"Wait. Your eyes are recording devices? Does that mean…"

"I don't record everything. Though if you wanted…"

"Stop!" Severyne shouted.

"Listen. What I'm saying is, *I'm* going to be all right. I don't need to bring in a Barony defector to appease my bosses – I'll just show them Thales was a dead end and no great loss."

"So. You deny me my only chance at survival." Severyne slumped.

Azad rolled her eyes. "Will you listen to me? Try this: go home after all, and give them a gently massaged report too. Tell your superiors Thales murdered Shelma, so you took him instead, tested the device, all hell tried to break loose, and you left him stranded in space. We can stitch together some footage to support that narrative. We can even include you kicking Felix's ass in the scrapyard."

"She did *not* kick my ass," Felix said.

"Only because Sagasa stopped her," Azad said. "But it doesn't matter, because Duval's Devils are covert. There won't be any kind of official report to contradict Severyne's story." She grinned at the Letnev. "We're going to give you a total hero cut, Sev. I mean, I'll have to escape your custody at the end of the story, but I'm Amina Azad. I escape stuff. No one will be too mad."

Severyne frowned thoughtfully. "It could work, especially if I shift blame to the director of the research facility. After all, ultimately, Shelma's kidnapping was *her* responsibility. If you look at events in a certain way, I just went into the field to correct her failure—"

"I have some friends in the Barony who might be able to weigh in on your behalf, too, and support your version of events," Azad said. "I didn't mention that before, because I wanted you to defect."

Severyne's head snapped around. "Friends? In the Barony? Do you mean *assets*? You have spies in my government?"

"I told you, Sev, I make friends wherever I go."

"Speaking of going," Felix said. "Can you two get your story straight *elsewhere*?" Azad shook her chains.

"Don't try to kill me when I let you loose," Felix said.

"I don't kill people for fun. What kind of sicko do you think I am? I only kill for the mission, and the mission is over."

Felix released Azad from her bonds with the push of a button. Azad tore the collar off, flung it into a corner of the cell, and then went to Severyne, putting an arm around her. "You know, Sev, I could get one of my friends in the Barony to recommend a new career path for you. You're wasted on a space station. You should be out in the field, like me, kicking ass. Just think – we might get to try and kill each other again someday."

Severyne looked at Azad, a speculative glint in her eyes, then stood up straight and fixed her gaze on Felix. "Farewell, Captain Duval. You were an intermittently capable adversary."

"Thanks?" He opened the cell door and stepped aside.

Azad and Severyne walked past him, still arm in arm. "When we get back to the *Grim Countenance*," Azad said, "we can celebrate our mutual survival. I'll do that thing. The thing you like. With the thing."

Felix watched the play of expressions that flitted across Severyne's face. He could only identify a couple of them – disgust was in there, and lust – but that was enough to get the general idea. Everyone was having more fun in space than he was, even the joyless Letnev.

Well, almost everyone. Thales was still crying.

"Calred will escort you to your ship," Felix said. "I look forward to never seeing either of you ever again."

"Bye, captain. Good luck with Doctor Bullshit there." Azad gave a little finger-fluttering wave and sauntered out of the brig with Severyne.

Thales looked up, his eyes rimmed with red. "What happens now?"

"There's no profit in you," Felix said. "In the absence of profit, I have no choice but to pursue justice."

"You're going to kill me, then."

"It would be an execution, but no. I've been thinking about it, and I want you to live a long time, marinating in your own failure." Felix grinned. "I hope you enjoy our fine Mentak Coalition prison facilities."

"Prison. On what charge? You can't prove any crimes. I was working for your Coalition–"

"The *Temerarious* finally finished the tox screen we ran on Shelma. It turns out she was killed by a synthetic neurotoxin introduced into her tank. Something pretty unusual, which is why it took so long for the computer to isolate the cause. We have video of you touching her armor, right next to a valve where we found traces of the toxin. We have records of you synthesizing that chemical in your lab the day she died – you deleted the chem-jet printer's local history, but the ship keeps a backup. Not just murder, but premeditated murder, and an attempt to cover it up. That, along with testimony from me and my crew, should be sufficient to put you away."

"This whole operation was covert," Thales said. "You can't have a trial."

"Not a public one, it's true. But my boss, undersecretary Jhuri, says he's happy to lead a secret tribunal. He's Coalition through and through, but he's also Hylar, Thales. He takes you murdering two of his species personally." Felix closed the door and rapped his knuckles against the bars of the cell. "That's about it. Enjoy your ride back to Moll Primus. Get used to confinement."

"At least you won't get *your* promotion," Thales said. "This failure sticks to you too."

"You'd think so, wouldn't you? But it turns out, Jhuri sees potential in my little group, and wants to keep us on in our new capacity. The *Temerarious* is being re-assigned, and I'm now special attaché to the undersecretary of special projects." Jhuri had actually said "because I want to keep an eye on you," but Felix decided to gloss over that part. "Don't worry about us, Thales. Duval's Devils will ride again."

EPILOGUE

Phillip Thales – that was as good a name as any, and how he usually thought of himself these days – woke in the cell where he'd spent more time than he cared to remember, and gazed up at the dark.

Mentak Coalition prisons weren't the overcrowded hellholes he'd first expected based on the culture's bloodthirsty reputation – indeed, the Coalition's history, rooted in a horrific penal colony, had led them to create more benign conditions for their inmates. Thales was better off than he would have been if he'd failed the Barony or the Federation. Still, the irony of being imprisoned in a small space – him, the man who was supposed to open up the whole of the galaxy – was not lost on him.

There was sufficient food and water, and if the meals were repetitive and bland, that didn't matter. Food was just fuel, and his body was only a vessel for what truly mattered: his mind. He'd often thought he was born to the wrong species, first as a human in a world full of Hylar, and later, as a creature of matter at all – he should have been Creuss, composed of light and intellect.

The worst thing about being here was the boredom. There was a prison library, but it was limited and contained almost no technical material – certainly none on his level. When he complained about the lack of mental stimulation, one of the warders – in what she considered an act of kindness! – brought him a thousand-piece puzzle depicting some artist's conception of the Lazax imperial palace. Bah. Thales should have *lived* in a palace. Thales still had the puzzle, unopened, under his bunk. Perhaps someday things would get so bad he'd start putting it together.

His powerful mind had nowhere to go but in circles, retracing old grievances and plotting elaborate revenge fantasies – including revenge against the *universe*.

Why was he awake? His wing of the prison was quiet – the inmates who screamed all night were kept together elsewhere so they could only annoy each other. The dark was deep, no glimmer through the small high window, so morning must be a long way off. He didn't have to urinate, which was *usually* what woke him in the night, as he got older. So then…

"Thales. Thales. Thales."

The voice was whispery, like crumpling paper, and Thales moaned. He'd heard that voice before – and its difficulty with, or amusement at, his assumed name.

That voice belonged to the Ghost of Creuss who'd destroyed his lab, so long ago.

Thales started to sit up in bed, then glimpsed the shape of the armored figure sitting on the cell's one uncomfortable chair, and decided he was fine where he was – on his back, looking up at the ceiling, not at the creature. "Why are you here? I'm not meddling in your affairs any more. I'm in a box. Me, the man who was going to–"

"See." The Creuss gestured, and light appeared on the ceiling, a vision in the darkness. Thales saw a star system, and nearby, a wormhole – not the misbegotten thing he'd made, but a real one: a bulging convex bubble in space-time.

"Acheron," the Ghost whispered.

"Eh?" Thales said. "Never heard of it."

The wormhole bulged, and burst out red light, like a popping blister. The planet below was torn apart by a cataclysmic twist in space-time, a piece of pottery smashed with a hammer, shards and fragments flying everywhere.

"Did you do this?" Thales said. "*Your* mistake this time, so much worse than mine?"

"Mahact," the Ghost said.

"This is something that happened in the age of Mahact kings, then? Why are you showing me this? Why–"

"No. Now. This is now. See."

Thales looked back at the – recording? Dramatization? Where the wormhole had been, there was something new, now – a long tear in the fabric of space, a ragged rift, very much like a wound. Beyond the wound there were writhings, and glimmerings, and light in an alien spectrum.

Thales whimpered. "There. Yes. That. It's – what I saw, when I turned on my device. But, no… ours was smaller. That one, with the scale of the planet and the star… that rift is *huge*."

"It grows," the Ghost said.

Thales squinted. Yes, the rift did appear to be growing, both widening and lengthening, like someone pulling at a rip in a piece of cloth. The star began to distort and twist in the strange gravity, and other planets in the system started to crumble as well. "Why are you showing me this?" Thales said.

"See."

The wound in reality began to spill out new forms. They were too small for Thales to make out at first, but the perspective moved closer, until the rift filled his whole field of vision. There were ships emerging from the tear, but not like any he'd seen before – these vessels were broken, twisted, organic things. There were creatures too, crawling and slithering and flying through the void, which should have been impossible – they were creatures with too many eyes or none at all, teeth and mouths in the wrong places, spines and fur and spikes and scales and feathers, sometimes all on one beast. But… were they ships, too? They couldn't be individual creatures, the scale was all wrong, or else his perception was. None of this made sense, in terms of biology or physics or anything else, so – "This is an entertainment? Fiction? Some sort of horror vid–"

"Truth." The Ghost shifted, and when Thales turned his head, the armored creature was kneeling beside his bed. One of its gauntleted hands touched his leg, and the metal was terribly cold. "Truth. Now."

"What is it? What are they?"

"Vuil-raith," the Creuss whispered.

"I don't know what that means."

"From outside."

"Outside *what*?"

"Outside everything. Outside the universe."

"That's nonsense," Thales said. "There's *nothing* outside the universe."

"Monsters are outside."

Monsters. This coming from the Creuss, who *were* monsters, by most accounts. Thales glanced at the helmeted creature, so strange and blank… but the armor was broadly humanoid, wasn't it? The Creuss made an attempt to take on a form that would be comprehensible to other beings in the galaxy, even though as energy creatures, any shape they took was optional. The things pouring through that rift – insofar as they resembled anything known in the galaxy – were the nightmares of a score of different species.

Something tumbled through the rift. A great burning wheel, with spokes of ragged bone. The hub a single bleeding eye. He'd seen that eye before.

"No," Thales said. "My device. I got something wrong, and I didn't open a wormhole at all. I opened a rift, to another place. One teeming with monsters. That's what happened."

"A crack. A glimpse. Yes. See."

"And now you want my *help*." Thales smiled in the dark. The Ghosts had come to him, because, expert as they were in wormhole technology, *Thales* was the first person to open an interdimensional rift – he was a pioneer in a whole new branch of physics. "Absolutely. Just get me out of here, and–"

"Fault." The Creuss pointed at the rift – how was it still pouring out monsters, how could there be so many, and – and were they far away? Please, let that hole in space be far, far away from here.

"Yes? I suppose it is a bit like a fault line."

"No. This is *your* fault."

"How can it be my fault?"

"You opened the way."

Thales shuddered. "Yes, I opened a crack, but not a great horrible gash like this–"

"You looked. The Vuil'raith looked back. They are still looking. They can *see*."

"You're saying those things only noticed us in the first place because of my invention?" His guts turned to ice. "And they've been, what? Waiting, ever since, all these years? Waiting for a chance to come through? A chance they have now, for some reason you haven't bothered to explain?"

"Yes," the Creuss said. "You see now. Your fault."

Thales groaned. "But what do they want?"

The Ghost held up its armored hands about half a meter apart. "They are here." It waved one hand. "We are here." It waved the other. "They want this." The Ghost slowly pushed its hands together, palm to palm, and then interlaced its fingers.

"They want to… bring our worlds together? But from what little I can see, their universe, or whatever it is, it's incompatible with ours, the rules are different... That would destroy everything. That would turn this universe into hell."

"Yes. You see. You were warned. You ignored our warning."

"All right. I made a mistake. I know that. But I don't know what you want me to do *now*."

"You can do nothing. We can do something. We will do this."

The Ghost stood up, turned its back to him, and stepped into the darkness.

"Do what?" Thales shouted. "What are you doing?"

He tried to get out of bed, but he couldn't. He couldn't, he realized, because his legs were gone. He threw the sheet back, and grains of something like sand sprayed across the cell. He watched his thighs come apart, painlessly, swiftly, reduced to individual inert components, just like the contents of his lab, the first time the Creuss warned him, so long ago.

Soon, his body would be nothing but a thin layer of sand, scattered across the bunk and the cell floor.

No, he thought. No no no.

But then, at least he wouldn't be around to see what this universe would become when the Vuil'raith were done with it. What hope did the galaxy have, against a threat like that?

Last words. He only had a moment to make his final statement, to sum up a life of potential greatness, viciously denied. But there was no one to hear what he said, no one to record it, no one to ponder a final wise exhalation, no one to appreciate him, no one had *ever appreciated him*–

"Idiots," Thales said, and then his heart dissolved.

ACKNOWLEDGMENTS

Thanks to Marc Gascoigne, who bought my first attempts at space opera, the Axiom trilogy, when he was at Angry Robot, and kindly thought of me for this gig too. Further thanks to the Aconyte team, especially Lottie Llewelyn-Wells and my editor Paul Simpson. My gratitude to the *Twilight Imperium* creative team, too; they created a wonderful world for me to play in and answered all my weird questions patiently. How about that artwork by Scott Schomburg, huh?

My agent, Ginger Clark, continues to offer invaluable professional support. My wife, Heather Shaw, and son, River, deliver top-notch personal support. River is twelve now, and great at games, though I haven't gotten him into anything as long and involved as *Twilight Imperium* yet; we've done *Fury of Dracula* and *Dead of Winter*, though, so it's only a matter of time.

My near and dear ones are always there for me, so thanks as always to Ais, Amanda, Emily, Katrina, and Sarah. My community of fellow writers is vast, but I'd like to especially thank Daryl Gregory, Jenn Reese and Chris East, Effie Seiberg (look, I dedicated this to you!), and Molly Tanzer for providing support and advice on matters of art and craft.

Finally, thanks to you readers. I hope this book is at least half as fun as the games you play.

THE NECROPOLIS EMPIRE

For Aleister, off to make his own way in the universe.

PROLOGUE

On a scientific outpost clinging to an icy moon, orbiting a world of mud, jungle, and abominable light, Doctor Archambelle worked to change the galaxy.

She gazed at her screen, at an array of images found in scores of archaeological sites – including the most recent, in a crumbling metal temple on the planet below. Isolated glyphs and symbols lit up on the screen as her system collated, cross-referenced, and attempted translations. They'd found these same ideograms and symbols over and over, in samples taken from planets, moons, and technological ruins scattered throughout the galaxy. None of these symbols belonged to any known culture, but they clearly belonged to *one* culture – something ancient, that had spread throughout all of inhabited space, and perhaps beyond, an incalculably long time ago.

Over and over in these fragments, Archambelle had found references to a secret world, a hidden place, a paradise, a promised land: Ixth.

That was a place she *had* heard of before, in the prophecies of her own people, the Letnev, who imagined that paradise as a hollow world full of caverns crammed with weapons and treasure. But Ixth appeared in the legends of most of the other species in the galaxy, too. For the Muaat, Ixth was a place of volcanic forges and endless geological riches. To the Hylar, it was a teeming temperate sea, with dormant alien factories waiting in the depths. To the humans, Ixth was all cities of gold and fountains of liquor. Every culture had their own idea about the nature of that paradise, but all agreed that anyone who found it would be granted immeasurable wealth and power. If *everyone* had stories about that place, however varied, those stories had to be rooted in some fundamental truth, didn't they?

If Archambelle's theory was right, Ixth was *much* more than a story. It was the homeworld of an ancient race, almost totally forgotten, but once rulers of the galaxy. Those people were gone, but she believed their treasures remained, and that even the memory of those treasures was great enough to inspire songs, stories, and prophecies all these millennia later.

There had to be a way to find Ixth. Archambelle would be the one to–

Her computer purred, and several items on the screen rushed to the forefront and fitted themselves together into a whole, though their source materials came from millions of kilometers apart. There were small sections missing, yes, but there was enough for her to discern a star map, and a spot marked, a *world*, could this be Ixth? Surely it couldn't be that simple?

She ran the image against the astronomical database and found the coordinates. To her surprise, the fragments depicted a known system, though not a very interesting one, and the planet was definitely not Ixth. That world was nobody's promised land. It was, if anything, a planet that anyone with sense would try to get *away* from.

It was something, though. A clue. A stepping stone.

The computer hummed again, translating another reference to this unimpressive little world: *"the key to the key"*.

That was promising. "I'll step on you soon, little world," Archambelle said, and went to call in the necessary favors.

CHAPTER 1

The night before the aliens came, Bianca Xing stood in the south meadow and gazed up at the dark. As always, her eyes were drawn to one particular part of the night sky: a blank space at the center of an irregular triangle formed by three stars. That seemingly arbitrary point drifted around the sky as the seasons progressed – dipping low, rising high, sometimes hidden behind the horizon – but since she'd been old enough to look up, something about those three stars and the dark they surrounded had fascinated her. After nearly twenty years here on Darit, her whole life defined by cliffs and meadows and forests (and the flock of caprids, horns and dirty wool and all), she was no closer to understanding why that spot in the sky drew her attention.

"Maybe because it's the most faraway place I can imagine," she said aloud. "A place so far away even the stars they have there aren't visible from here." The wind blew her long white-blonde hair back from her brow in a way she hoped looked romantic and tragic, even though no one was watching. Bianca had a dramatic streak, to the bemusement of her parents, and was known to wear a flowing nightgown and walk the fields at night while lamenting the state of her life. She was too self-aware to do so entirely seriously, but it helped to pass the time.

There was no real danger in her nightly wanders. Predators were kept out by the scramble-fence – meant to protect the caprid flock, but equally good at protecting her – and the nearest human was kilometers away. Even that was just Torvald at the mech farm, and he didn't mean her any harm. He was so old he couldn't chase her across the fields anyway, with ill intent or otherwise.

Nobody ever chased her across the fields, with murder *or* romance on their minds. She was very put out by it. On her family's rare visits to town, to trade or attend the monthly Halemeetings, she sometimes saw other village youths making eyes at her, but there weren't any she wanted to make eyes *back* at, except maybe Mallory Zeen (her biceps!) or Compton Sadler (his eyelashes!), but they were already dating each other, and rich besides, not a farm girl on the outskirts like her. Bianca steadfastly ignored the occasional flirtations from the sons and daughters and androgynes of the outskirters who visited the farm; she'd given her neighbor Grandly a little too much encouragement one summer when she was bored, and he'd clung to her like a tick for ages. Grandly was nice enough, and both sets of parents thought they'd make a good match, but Grandly's life was just like Bianca's, give or take a biteweed patch or a bigger root cellar. She wanted *more* out of life, not more of the same.

Her mother, Willen, said she set her sights too high: "You're always looking at the stars, Bianca, but there are wonderful things down here all around your feet." Her father, Keon, would just puff his pipe and say, "Mmmm, ayuh." Parents.

Bianca was about to turn twenty, though, and the hints had become more explicit lately. She needed to figure out what she was doing with her life, because mooning around in the fields every night wasn't sustainable, even if she did always make sure to do her chores first. Her options were just all horrible. Pair-bond with Grandly? No, thank you. Go work for Torvald at the scrapyard? Better, but still too small. Steal a sack full of food and set off to seek her fortune? Much better, but she could walk the circumference of Darit and never get any closer to the stars, where she *really* wanted to be. She'd read stories about space travel, but no one on Darit could do it.

A new light appeared in the sky. At first, Bianca thought it was a stray reflection from one of the orbital mirrors. Darit was a rocky, frigid, inhospitable place, but the long-dead original colonists had taken steps to make regions of the planet habitable, chiefly orbital mirrors that focused light to raise the surface temperature in dozens of zones. There were also the perpetually floating rainmakers, bulbous pale-gray shapes that drifted high above, collected water, and stimulated the clouds to make rain. Old Torvald speculated that there were other ancient technologies at work – atmospheric engines disguised as mountains, carbon sequestration devices in the guise of trees, buried soil-enriching technology – but who knew for sure? The ancients had possessed great power, but no one knew the extents or the limits, or why they'd bothered to make parts of an iceball like Darit habitable in the first place.

She squinted and decided the light couldn't be a mirror-glint, because it was moving too fast. Just a shooting star, then? No, because its streak slowed and stopped, and it became a fixed point, not twinkling. It looked like a star now, but Bianca knew every star in her part of the sky, and she wasn't fooled.

She stared at the light for a long time, but it didn't do anything interesting. Maybe it was a ship? A real, actual starship? Torvald had pieces of what he *claimed* were ships at the mech farm, but those were broken, rusting, and cracked. This starship would be sleek, shimmering, and powerful, like those in the stories.

Maybe it was an envoy from the emperor of the galaxy! She'd read about the empire in books scavenged from the vault under the Halemeeting hall, and old Torvald had a lot of stories about wars and battles and intrigue, though they didn't add up to a consistent history, as he was the first to admit. What could the emperor want with a place like this anyway? Maybe Darit had some rare resource the empire needed – there were empty mines everywhere, so perhaps there was an ore you couldn't obtain anywhere else? Or maybe a rare plant, or perhaps the caprids were the source of some miracle drug that granted immortality, and the emperor was going to build a spaceport here, and bring in new people from all over the galaxy.

Or, maybe they'd come for *her*. That was the start of an old fantasy, one she'd refined carefully over the years: she was secretly a princess, hidden away on a backwater planet for her own safety, but, when the time came, she'd be rescued and restored to the glory of her birthright.

It wasn't *that* farfetched. Bianca was adopted, and her real parents were unknown: that much was true. Her father had found her in the forest when she was a baby, squalling and helpless, and her parents had raised her as their own ever since. The truth of her origins was the mystery at the center of her life – in a small community like hers, the appearance of an unknown child was genuinely baffling. What if she was secretly the emperor's daughter, born of a mistress, and the emperor's wife would have killed her, so her father sent her away to this remote planet where she'd be safe, because no one would ever look for her *here*? Maybe that new light in the sky belonged to a ship full of assassins, come to murder her before she could take the throne?

Bianca frowned. No, too dark. Better: the emperor's mean wife was dead, and the emperor was sick, and since there were no other heirs, they needed her, because without her presence on the throne, the empire would crumble! They were here to whisk her away on an imperial pleasure ship, to dress her in shimmering gowns, to crown her with rare jewels, and to teach her proper manners and comportment. When she landed on the imperial homeworld – she forgot what Torvald called it, Mehibatel Rocks or something? – her loyal subjects would shout her name and scatter flowers at her feet. She'd get to meet her *real* parents then, her mother promoted from mistress to queen (or empress, or whatever), the emperor recovered from his illness but ready to embrace his long-lost daughter, and teach her the ways of battle and diplomacy and culture and–

A caprid, shaggy and blunt-horned, head-butted Bianca in the rump and bleated at her.

Bianca sighed, patted the caprid on the head, and trudged back to the farmhouse, the new light in the sky already forgotten as thoughts of tomorrow morning's chores filled her mind.

The next day Bianca rolled out of her small bed at dawn and lit the house fires. Her mother had done that for most of Bianca's life, but Willen was getting older and didn't move as well as she used to, and Bianca was keenly aware that she herself was aging out of being a responsibility and into being a burden, so helping out was more important than ever.

Her father emerged while she was heating the water, and kissed her on top of her head, bending down to do it. Bianca was the shortest person in her family by nearly half a meter. That was just one of the things that marked her out as a child of fortune rather than blood: she also had hair so pale it was nearly white, compared to her mother's bushy red exuberance and her father's curly black; her skin was golden and unlike either her mother's paleness or her father's deep brown; and while Willen and Keon were both broad and thick-limbed, Bianca was more petite, though you couldn't spend your life working on a farm without putting on muscle. Her mother had blue eyes, and her father's were a hypnotic green, while hers were so dark they were nearly black, and – well, she could go on.

The sense that she didn't fit in with her family was just the start of her outsider feelings. The people on this part of Darit were a varied bunch, but almost all of them were taller than her, and heartier-looking, and she'd often heard people say she looked "sickly" , though she'd never been sick a day in her life. In the books she read, people with unusual qualities were objects of speculation and attention, but around here, people just frowned and looked at her like she was a problem someone else should work on solving. That was when they looked at all, which wasn't often.

"Could you go over to Torvald's and get a new power cell for us today?" her father said.

"He doesn't have anything *new*," Bianca muttered, warming up a pot of grain mush for family breakfast.

"New to us is good enough," Keon said affably. "The well pump is drawing water real sluggish, and the lights in the barn are getting dim. We can limp along a few more days on the cell we have, I reckon, but I'd like a new one on hand when the lights go out."

Bianca sighed and said, "The journey will be long, and perilous, but if my family needs me, I'll brave the–"

"Much appreciated."

Her father was impossible to annoy. That didn't stop Bianca from trying. She didn't mind going to the mech farm, honestly. It would be a nice break from the routine farm work. But it was the principle of the thing: all chores were abhorrent, all errands were wastes of her time, and her whole life on the farm just an obstacle standing in the way of… well. That was the problem. Her parents would have supported most anything she wanted to do. But what was there *to* do? She just couldn't bear to settle down with Grandly and have some kids and spend her life feeding babies and caprids. Not yet. There had to be more to life than this, or she wouldn't feel like she'd lived a life at all.

She put on a short yellow dress – her mother grumbled that those were for Halemeetings, and weren't practical for farm work, but Bianca could at least have style, couldn't she? She put on trousers and boots underneath the dress, and added a dark brown canvas jacket because it was a little crisp today, which sort of spoiled the light effect she was going for, but again: it was the principle of the thing.

Bianca had a bicycle with nice fat tires for getting around the property, and there were trails that would take her all the way to town if she wanted, but the mech farm was on the other side of a few kilometers of uneven uphill ground, perched on a bluff overlooking the bay, and since she didn't have mechanized transport, the easiest way to get there was on foot.

She set out, a walking stick in one hand, good for fending off bandits, she liked to imagine. Not that there were any bandits hereabouts. In books, cut-throat marauders lived in the forest, but anything that tried to live in the forest here would be lucky to survive a week. After dark, the nightclimbers came out, and they'd carry off a person just as promptly as any other prey. Even during the day, there were dangers in those woods. Old things were buried in the forest, ancient machines from Darit's mysterious past, and some of them weren't buried very deep. Bianca had grown up hearing stories of glowing stones, shining pillars, and buzzing wires twined around trees like ivy, all remnants of an older age. Some of those remnants would kill you faster than a nightclimber would… or much slower, which was worse.

The sky was mostly blue that day, with a few fat clouds and one rainmaker drifting aimlessly along. The sun was sending out light but not much in the way of real heat, and of Darit's three moons, only a pale crescent of Child was visible, Father and Mother hidden by the horizon. Torvald said he'd once visited a distant valley where the people called the moons Mum and Pop and Babe. How silly was that?

She followed the trail over a ridge and paused at the top to take in the view. Off to the south, she could just see the jeweled sparkle of the sea, its true vastness hidden in distant haze. To the west, the spire of the Halemeeting hall was the only visible sign of her village, though the road to the next nearest settlement was that way too. To the east and north, there was only the forest. From here it was a brown blur, but up close it was a dense world of towering trees and twining vines (and the delicious mushrooms the brave, the foolish, or the well-armed went in to harvest). The northern part of the forest was less menacing, since the foresters picked away at the edges there, but the eastern expanse was purely wild.

Bianca turned and looked back the way she'd come. Her house was there, surrounded by fields and pasture. Smoke rose from the fire she'd lit. In the nearest meadow, the tiny speck of her father walked around their caprid flock. The animals made milk and they made wool and, every once in a while, they made meat, but mainly what they made was dung and noise and mud.

Bianca wanted so desperately to get out of the mud. There was no mud among the stars.

She continued along the ridgeline until she reached the dry streambed that led her at last to the proper trail, almost a road, that meandered from Torvald's gates down to the town. The last part of the road was steep, though, and in poor repair. She'd asked Torvald once, "Why don't you fix it? Surely you could cobble together a road-building mech."

"Ah," he'd said, "but since the road is bad, and people can't get carts or wagons up here, that means they usually rent one of my cargo mechs to carry things to and from their transport, and that's good for old Torvald, innit?"

She'd snorted, knowing he was full of it – half the people he dealt with bought on credit that Torvald wasn't too zealous about collecting, and many of the others paid him with a portion of the harvests his mechs made so much easier. He just liked pretending to be a canny trader sitting on a hoard of treasure. In a way, he was as prone to fancy as Bianca was. That was probably why they got along so well.

She stood before the tall gates of the mech farm, made of welded-together scrap, and pounded on the metal with her walking stick.

"State your name and business," the gate said, its mechanical voice harsh and grating.

"My name is Empress Bianca, and I'm here to kill the old man."

"Enter," the gate said. The small door set into the left gate clicked unlocked for her. The big gates only opened when something *really* large had to come in or out.

"I mean it," she said. "I am here on a mission of murder."

"Enter," the gate said again, this time buzzing afterward, as if for emphasis. During business hours, the gate opened and closed for visitors, but that voice didn't actually understand or care what you said. Torvald said he'd read about intelligent machines, but there weren't any of those on Darit, and he didn't know if those stories were any more real than the tales of forest demons or alien sorcerers or sea monsters he'd collected over the years.

Once inside, Bianca gazed around the chaos of the mech farm to see if there was anything new. Mostly she just saw piles of scrap junk, some merely as tall as her, others three times as high, all waiting to be repaired or repurposed or melted down. Some of those piles had been waiting for decades. There were wheels, and rods, and sheets of metal; mysterious cylinders, and spheres, and cubes; and messy coils of wire, cable, and conduit. The predominant colors were gray and dull silver, but there were flashes of bright paint or peculiar iridescence. There were bits of things that *might* have been automated transports or even spacecraft, once upon a time, but they were all jumbled in with iron bedframes and rusty farm implements, metal drums and busted appliances. Grandly's family had a working icebox, courtesy of Torvald; that had halfway tempted Bianca to accept Grandly's last proposal, during the hottest part of the summer.

There were also countless busted-up mechs, ranging from ones half her size to behemoths as big as her house. Once upon a time, Torvald said, Darit had been a mining planet, a colony of the empire, and there'd been legions of mechs to work the seams and serve the inhabitants. Of course, that was so long ago nobody even knew if the empire still existed, and most people didn't know it had ever existed in the first place. There were still remnants aplenty buried all over, though, and Torvald's family had been experts at salvage and repair for generations. People found things in their fields sometimes, and more often in the forest (when they dared to venture in), and brought those curiosities to Torvald for trade. Bianca had earned enough money for a few dresses over the years with her own lucky finds while stone-picking in the fields – just bits of colored glass and mud-packed springs and fist-sized bolts, but Torvald could get them shiny and useful again.

Torvald emerged from his shack, wiping his greasy hands on his perpetually stained overalls. He grinned, his wrinkled face lighting up. "Bee! Did you bring me something nice?"

"I brought myself. What's nicer than that?"

"I'd trade you for a broken rheostat, but I suppose you'll do, if that's all you've got." Torvald had never pair-bonded or had children of his own – rumors were that exposure to some of the more exotic items in the depths of the mech farm had made him infertile, but Bianca was pretty sure he'd just never bothered – and she wondered, sometimes, what would happen to this place when he eventually died. He'd pretty much told her she could sign on as his apprentice if she wanted, and that was currently at the top of a mental list titled "The Least Terrible of All the Terrible Options I Hate," just above "Run Away from Home" and "Pair-Bond with Grandly And At Least Have Ice All Summer." (Running away from home would have been higher up, but this habitable zone was only so big, and the places she could reach without transport and cold-weather gear to navigate the tundra in between weren't much different from her own.)

"What can I do for you, if you didn't come bearing gifts?" he asked.

"Pa says our power cell is running down. I came to see how bad you'd cheat us for a new one."

He rolled a toothpick around in his mouth. "Oh, only medium bad. One of the foresters tripped over a rock that turned out to be the corner of an autonomous cargo container buried in a dry streambed. I don't even care to guess how long it's been there. He used a stump-puller mech to clear the ground around it until he found a hatch, and do you know what he found inside?"

"Certain death?" Bianca was seething with jealousy. She'd never found anything bigger than she could pick up in both hands.

"He mostly found a bunch of crates that used to hold rations, probably, before they got filled with mold instead. He *did* recover fully half a dozen power cells, hardly even drained. They were slow to wake up, of course, but I got them refreshed. I can let you have one if you'll butcher down a caprid for me before the year turns."

That was a good deal. She sighed heavily and shook her head. "You're a bandit, Torvald. If I take that offer back to Pa, he'll butcher *me*."

"You have to invite me over for Turnsday dinner, too," he said placidly. "I've been missing your ma's root mash."

They always invited him to that anyway. "I'm just a humble farm girl, and no match for your cruel and avaricious big city wiles," Bianca said. "It's a–"

Something came howling across the sky from the direction of the sea. Bianca screamed and clapped her hands over her ears as the horrible roar vibrated her from skullbones to toes. The – ship? – passed over them in a moment, the wind of its passage so ferocious that it kicked up a huge cloud of dust and sent a pile of sheet metal falling over with a crash.

"What *was* that?" Bianca shouted, her ears still ringing from the din.

"Aliens, I reckon," Torvald shouted back. "And they're headed for the forest."

CHAPTER 2

"Why would they go to the forest?" Bianca said. "Why not land in town?"

"Where they go depends on what they came for, I suppose," Torvald said. "Come on into the shack with me. I need to look at something."

She stared at him. "What are you talking about? There're aliens here! From *space*!"

"Probably not from space, Bee. People – even alien people – don't usually live in space. Not too hospitable up there. Cold, nothing to breathe, lots of radiation. They're aliens from a planet or a moon, more likely, or a space station, or just possibly an asteroid."

"What do you know about it?" She spun to face him, fists clenched, unsure why she was suddenly so furious. "You always talk like you know the secrets of the galaxy, but you were born on this dirt ball just like I was, and you don't *know* anything!"

"I don't know much about anything *currently*, that's true." Torvald wasn't unflappable like her pa, but he tended to react to her outbursts with a sort of distant amusement. He led her toward his little shack. "I couldn't tell you who sits on the throne on Mecatol Rex these days, if anyone even does. But I know a lot about how things *used* to be. I have a… family heirloom, you could say, in my shack. Or under it. A keeper of secrets, except mostly they're secrets nobody on this planet would care about even if I got up in the middle of a Halemeeting and gave them all away. I think *you* might care, and if you'd accepted my offer to sign on as an apprentice, I was going to show you. But today…" He paused a moment and looked at the sky. "Today might be the beginning of a whole new world. Suddenly the idea of hoarding my secrets seems silly, especially since ancient history might just have some bearing on current events. Now will you come on, so I can expand your understanding of the universe and our little place in it?"

She nodded, her fury draining out of her. Secrets? She did like those. Or she thought she would. She'd never really known any worthy of the name.

Torvald opened the flimsy door and gestured her inside. She'd been into his home a few times, but there wasn't much to see: it was one big room with a bed, a couple of chairs and a table, a desk, a screen that mostly just flickered, and shelves of books. There was a kitchen with all the appliances she'd ever heard of (most of them even worked, though a couple were purely decorative, like the one that was supposed to make toast). There was a little dome-headed serving mech that did a bad job of cleaning up when it even worked, currently switched off in the corner. The shack only had one door, and that led to a small tidy bathroom with a toilet and a shower.

This time, though, Torvald lifted up the faded old rug, revealing... more stone floor. She'd been hoping for a secret hatch or a trapdoor or something. "Stand beside me," he said. She obeyed, and he cleared his throat. "Two friendlies, coming down."

The floor lurched, and she stumbled against Torvald as the ceiling receded above them. A square section of the floor, two meters to a side, was dropping down a smooth-walled shaft, and it was dropping fast. "What *is* this?"

"An elevator," he said.

She let go of him, straightened up, and refused to be impressed. "Stupid name. We're going down. It should be called a descender."

"It goes back up too, Bianca."

She looked up at the growing distance above her head. "That's good. It would be a long climb otherwise."

After a few moments, they thumped to a stop. "Good job," Bianca said. "We're at the bottom of a dry well–"

The wall in front of her split in two, one side sliding to the left, the other to the right. She grabbed Torvald again. She'd seen automatic doors before – in Torvald's gate, of course, and the Halemeeting hall had one – but those just swung in and out! They didn't disappear into the walls!

"Come on." Torvald stepped into darkness, and recessed white lights switched on, revealing a space roughly the size of the living quarters above, though there was a metal door on the far wall, suggesting deeper recesses beyond. The walls, floor, and ceiling were all gray metal, and there were only a few pieces of furniture – a simple bunk, a chair on a swivel, a table.

One of the walls held a huge blank screen. The burgher in town had a working screen, one that showed a ten-minute loop of bizarre birds like no one had ever seen in real life flying over a purple ocean, but this screen was easily twice as big. Bianca could have walked right up to it and stretched her arms out and not quite touched the edges. "What *is* this place?"

"We call it the bunker," Torvald said. "It's been in the family so long nobody remembers who originally found it. My parents told me there are probably chambers like this scattered across Darit, but I've never found one, or met anybody else who has. I sure wish I could, because if they held treasures like *this* one does, I'd be a rich man. Of course, I don't know what I'd do if I was a rich man. Buy more junk, probably. It's all I know."

"Go back. You said treasure. What kind of treasure?" There were no chests full of gold coins, no racks of alien weapons, no shining crowns or bolts of rare cloth or works of art.

"Information, Bee. Knowledge." He approached the screen. "Access local surveillance." The screen lit up and showed a view of the mech farm, and his shack, seen from a strange angle – what you'd see if you stood on top of one of the vertical posts on one side of the gate, she thought. "Roll back to, hmm, ten minutes ago."

The screen flickered, and now showed Bianca and Torvald standing among the scrap heaps, talking. "That's us!" she said.

"There are cameras up there, recording. Here it comes." The ship streaked across the screen, and Torvald said, "Freeze."

The ship hung frozen on the screen, just barely in the top of the frame. The vessel was bigger than Bianca's house, and made of dark metal, with spikes and spines all over it, like some sort of airborne cactus. "Analyze ship to determine origin," Torvald said. The wall began to hum.

"Who are you talking to?" Bianca said. "You said there weren't any smart machines on this planet."

"Oh, well. The bunker isn't smart, exactly. It doesn't actually know things – it just contains knowledge. Sort of like a book. The bunker can't think, any more than a book can, but imagine if you had a book where you could say, 'Turn to the page with that kissing scene I like,' and it would flip right to it? Or where you could say, 'What's the name of the character who killed the hero's daughter,' and the book could answer you? It's like that."

"Sounds pretty smart to me," Bianca said.

"Could be the lines between smart and not-smart get a little blurry with some machines," Torvald conceded. "The bunker isn't much of a conversationalist, let's say that much at least. But what it does have is a long memory, full of the history of this planet from the days when it was an imperial mining colony, mostly in the form of records kept by a woman called the 'interim provincial governor.' I couldn't tell you what's happened outside Darit for the past three thousand years, but if you want to know what was going on in the galaxy before that, I know at least part of it."

"Ship unknown," the wall said, in a warm, womanly voice.

Torvald sighed. "I was afraid of that. I didn't figure the aliens would be flying a ship so old my bunker would recognize it, but it was worth a try. Hmm. Bunker, what's the closest known vessel to the ship we just saw?"

"The closest comparable vessel is a Barony of Letnev light cruiser." A drawing appeared on the screen, and it did share a lot in common with the ship they'd seen, especially the way the hull bristled with hostile-looking protuberances. "There are multiple points of structural and design overlap, but the ship most recently recorded is far smaller."

"That's because it's some kind of shuttle," Torvald muttered. "But if the design and the aesthetics and such are that similar, then maybe it's a Barony vessel."

"What are all those spikes for?"

"Maybe they're sensors," Torvald said. "Or weapons. Maybe the Letnev just like how they look, the way Milt Karnecki painted flames on the side of his auto-cart. I couldn't tell you."

"You're the one with the secret database of hidden knowledge!" Bianca was so frustrated. Torvald had been sitting on a talking encyclopedia of the outside world all this time. "You knew about everything outside Darit, *real* things, instead of just hints and forgotten stories! You could have… have…" She slumped. "You could have done… something for me."

"The bunker doesn't have directions to the nearest spaceport, Bee." He said it kindly, and that was worse. "Nor does it know any special radio frequency to hail a passing ship to take you out into the stars. I know you've always set your sights higher than the next shearing or harvest, Bianca, and I admire that. My own interest in what lies beyond our atmosphere is more about the knowledge than the experience. But if I could have cobbled a working spacecraft together from the junk on my mech farm, you would have flown out of here three years ago on your sixteenth birthday, and you can believe that."

"Sixteenth birthday observed," she muttered. Her birthday was a guess, since she was a forest foundling, but based on how new she was when her pa found her, it was probably right to within a day or two. "But thank you. I still wish you'd told me."

Torvald nodded, perfunctory. "Maybe I should have. What's done is done. The reason I brought you down here now is because aliens have come to Darit. Even if they're human, they're aliens to *us*. They might be your ticket off this planet, or they could be trouble for all of us. My database is thousands of years out of date, but it's all we've got to go on, unless the aliens start talking. If those visitors really are from the Barony of Letnev, and the Barony still bears any resemblance to the one that was part of the empire way back when… Well. It could be worse, but it could be better, too."

"What do you mean?"

"I mean, the Letnev aren't human, but they're enough like us that we can talk to them. They aren't giant murderous spiders, or hungry slime mold, or a burning cloud that's mad at you for some reason and you don't know why. They aren't here to literally *eat* us, at least, though I suppose they might have come for the caprids. Seems a long way to go for stringy meat, though. The Barony was – let me see, it's been a while since I read about them – a militaristic, bureaucratic society, big on rules and shiny boots. They spent a lot of time in caverns and tunnels underground. They were involved in some unpleasantness that kicked off a big war, according to the journal the interim governor kept. Something about blockading a wormhole and making a whole lot of people mad."

"A wormhole." The very word was magical to Bianca. When she was little, before she'd read enough to understand what wormholes were exactly, she'd poked her arm (and sometimes head) into every hole she found, thinking one might lead her to another world. All they ever led to was dirty faces and the occasional insect bite.

"The Letnev enjoyed their rules, but didn't worry much about following anyone else's, because theirs were the only ones that mattered. They were also the type to invent new rules to punish people if the old rules weren't doing a good enough job." Torvald sighed. "The Barony is fairly high on the list of alien cultures I would hesitate to invite over for a slice of cake and a cup of tea. You might be able to use them as your stepping stone to the stars, but it won't be as easy as politely asking them for a ride."

"It's worth a try," she said. "If they even land. Maybe they're just here to see if there's anything interesting on the planet, and when they see there's *not*, they'll fly away again."

"That might be the best thing for all of us," Torvald said. "I–"

The screen flickered to a view of the junkyard again. "New environmental stimulus detected," the bodiless voice said. A loud, high-pitched keening filled the room, until Torvald said, "Lower volume eighty percent!" and it became a distant whine again.

"What *is* that?" Bianca cried.

"Emergency siren. The one in the burgher's house. I haven't heard it since the big fire, and that was, what, five years before you were born? The village elders don't like using it because they don't know how many charges the thing has left, and they're afraid one of these days there will be a *real* emergency and they'll hit the button and it won't make a sound at all. I guess this must be a real emergency. Everyone within the sound of that siren is supposed to go to the village immediately."

"We have to go!"

Torvald nodded. "We should. But I'll tell you what. I want to do a little more research here. You go down and see what's going on, and you can fill me in later. There's a power cell on the table upstairs. Take that with you. Aliens or not, your parents will still want what they sent you for."

Bianca nodded, then scowled. "It will take me forever to get to town, I'll have to run home and get my bicycle–"

"Take the trailrunner," Torvald said. "Just be careful and don't break your head. It's not a very good head, but I've gotten used to it."

Bianca grinned, threw her arms around his neck, and kissed his whiskery cheek.

"Thank you! I'll bring it back and tell you everything. I bet they're calling us to talk about the aliens."

"I doubt it's about traders come in from Upper Creek, or somebody who needs a new barn put up," Torvald said.

He led her to the elevator and sent her back up to the surface. When she arrived in his shack, alone, she allowed herself a whoop of excitement. Alien spaceships! Emergency sirens! Things were *happening*! She grabbed up the power cell – about the size of a book, but much denser – and shoved it into her pack. Probably a waste of time. The aliens would probably offer them limitless power and spaceships and all the other wonders of the galaxy soon anyhow.

Bianca went out into the mech farm. The trailrunner was parked behind the shack, as usual. Torvald had allowed her to ride it around his property, but never beyond the walls. "That thing will be my legs when my legs don't work anymore," he said. "I can't risk you running it off a cliff just because you want to feel the wind in your hair as you fall." He used the trailrunner when he came to town, or went on scavenging expeditions himself, which he didn't do nearly as often as he had in his younger days. "You can ride the trailrunner to my funeral, Bee, but I won't risk you taking it off the mech farm before that," he'd said once, and no amount of pleading would change his mind.

This was an unprecedented day in a lot of ways, though.

The trailrunner was a mech of Torvald's own design, cobbled together from pieces of mining robots, broken-down transports, and miscellaneous junk. The machine consisted of a padded metal chair surrounded by a set of multi-jointed legs, each as long as Bianca was tall, with a little control panel you could reach while seated. The controls were just used for inputting directions and preferred speed, though; the trailrunner mostly drove itself, thanks to the computer brain and cluster of sensors underneath the seat. Torvald had taught her to use it, and she'd even helped him tinker with it a bit over the years to improve its performance.

Bianca got her pack situated in the little cargo crate behind the seat and made sure it was secure and well padded. Power cells could crack if they took a fall, and sometimes when that happened there was a flash of light, and sometimes they leaked goo that smoked and ate holes in the ground … but at least once a dropped power cell had caused an explosion that blew off both a roof and a local boy's head.

She climbed into the chair, fitted on the straps, and punched in the eighteen-digit code required to unlock the controls, a level of security she thought was a bit much, but it made Torvald happy. He'd been surprised she could remember the code after he rattled it off just once, but Bianca had always been good at remembering important things. It was just boring things she forgot.

The trailrunner hummed to life and stood up tall on its six legs. She punched in a course to the center of the village and set speed to "maximum." The vehicle *jumped*, leaping over the shack in a single bound, but Bianca stayed steady in her seat; there were things called "gimbals" and "shock absorbers" and "gyroscopic balancing mechanisms" to ensure that even if the trailrunner tilted sharply or landed with a hard thump, she'd still keep her head pointed at the sky, her feet at the ground, and wouldn't get whiplash. Unless the landing was hard enough to smash the whole apparatus, but the trailrunner was programmed with preset tolerances, and its computer brain translated "maximum speed" as "maximum *safe* speed." Too bad. Sometimes it was fun to be a little unsafe.

Bianca didn't bother with opening the gates, just leapt nimbly from junkheap to junkheap and sailed over the top of the wall. The sensors it used to detect the environment could tell which structures made stable launching points, and which would collapse under its weight. Bianca whooped when they cleared the wall, full of the joy of motion, but she did wish she'd thought to put on goggles. She'd never been in the trailrunner when it was going this fast before, and her eyes were watering. She kept her mouth firmly shut against the possibility of swallowing bugs. She *did* like the feeling of the wind streaming through her hair, though.

She landed on the path outside the gates and didn't even slow down, just rushed toward the village, legs a whirring blur. There was that meandering road, but the trailrunner didn't bother to stay on that for long: it had a local survey map and a compass, and it took the most direct possible route instead. Bianca raced across the high meadows, leaping over rock walls and fences, dancing down rocky slopes, never stepping on a field under cultivation (Torvald knew better) but ducking low and hurtling through the trees of the orchard on the Glinnis farm. The trailrunner reconnected with the road not far from town, startling groups of people walking or riding on bikes or trundling along in various forms of transport, come down from their own scattered farms and holdings to answer the call. Some people shouted at her: "Torvald, slow down," and, "I wish I had one of those," and, gratifyingly, "Is that Bianca *Xing*?"

Bianca leaned hard to the right, as the trailrunner dashed off to the side of the road to avoid the traffic, picking up speed, so she arrived well ahead of the other newcomers. The mech slowed down a bit as it approached the central square, an open green space surrounded by the village's largest buildings: the elegant arched roof of the Halemeeting hall, the imposing two stories of the burgher's house, the general store with its wide porch full of chairs, and the dusty and neglected façade of the Traveler's Rest, an inn and way station hardly ever used since they didn't attract many visitors, and weren't on the way to anywhere in particular. At least the alarm wasn't going off anymore. As loud as it had been up at the mech farm, she couldn't imagine how ear-splitting it would have been right here at the source.

The mech stopped at the edge of the square, since Bianca hadn't specified a particular destination. The trailrunner hummed quietly to itself as Bianca stared at the Halemeeting hall. Something had changed. It was a small change, but it felt big.

Someone had climbed up to the roof of the hall and put a pole up there, and on top of the pole there was a big flag now, all black and trimmed with silver, with a red circle in the center, like a planet hanging in a starless void.

CHAPTER 3

"Bianca!" Her mother hurried over from the porch of the general store. Her hair was pulled back in a hurry, and she was wearing trousers and a work shirt – she'd never come to town looking so disheveled, but *things were happening*, weren't they? "What are you doing on that thing?"

Bianca directed the trailrunner to park itself on the side of the road and shut down, then clambered out of the seat. "Torvald let me borrow it." She hated how sulky and defensive her voice got around her ma. Bianca was old enough to be pair-bonded, so why did she always feel like a child when the two of them talked? *Maybe because I still live in her house and eat her food and mostly wear clothes she made me*, Bianca thought. Could you really grow up when you were still in the same place, and in the same context, where you'd spent so long as a child?

"Torvald isn't coming?" Her mother seemed distracted, her eyes skittering up to the flag and then back down to Bianca's face again.

"He said he had too much work to do. He said I should go, and tell him what happened. We… we saw a ship go by overhead, and–"

"We did too," she said. "I did, anyway, your father just heard it. Oh, Bianca." She put a hand on her daughter's arm. "I'm so nervous. What does it mean? What does that *flag* mean?"

"I don't know." Bianca squeezed her hand. "Let's go in and find out." She looked around. "Where's Dad?"

"He couldn't leave the caprids – they were all out grazing."

"How can he think about livestock right now?" Bianca said. "There are *aliens* here!"

Her mother looked at her like she'd grown an extra head. "Aliens or not, we still have chores to do, don't we?"

"I guess so." It seemed like something this big should transform the whole world, all at once, but that wasn't how things worked, was it?

By now others were drifting toward the Halemeeting hall. The interior was one big room, with ranks of benches arranged in curving rows to face the stage at the far end. This was the place where weddings and wakes were held, dances and festivals, auctions and trials (not that there'd been a crime worthy of a trial in Bianca's lifetime). There was also a small weekly fellowship meeting and a big monthly one, just so people on the far-flung farms and orchards could remember they were part of a community, with people around to help them through the hard times and celebrate the good. In theory, the Halemeeting hall could hold just about everyone within fifty kilometers, though Bianca had seldom seen it more than a third full. She thought it might get a lot closer to capacity today.

Bianca and her mother took seats near the front; her mother's eyesight wasn't very good anymore. The burgher was there, fine yellow sash across her chest. Her family was charged with maintaining the Halemeeting hall, and they owned the general store, too, and were in more frequent contact with neighboring communities than anyone else. The burgher helped organize the Five-Year's Fair, when everyone from the six nearest villages gathered in a distant field and built a temporary festival city, trading food and art and fine goods and, quite often, mingling and falling in love and bonding with strangers. A few people almost always left the Fair to make their homes in other settlements, and before today it was the most exciting thing in Bianca's world. The next Five-Year's Fair was in the spring, and she'd been toying with the idea of falling in love with someone from as far away as possible, or convincing herself she had, just for an excuse to live in a new place... but she knew the other settlements were much like her own, just in a slightly different configuration of hills and valleys, so what was the point? That fear that every place would look the same was the same thing that kept her from putting on her best shoes and filling a sack with food and setting out on her own. Darit was just *Darit*, and how could it satisfy her when there was so much more beyond? Wherever she went, her eyes would still be drawn to that dark spot in the sky and the wonders it promised.

"So many people," her mother said. Bianca looked behind her and goggled. Every bench was full, and there were other people *standing*, lining the walls! There must have been three hundred people there! She'd only seen that many at once at the Fair, and even there they weren't all jammed in together, breathing and shuffling and muttering. The sound of the crowd was like the susurration of waves against rocks.

The burgher stood up on stage and cleared her throat. "Everyone!" she said. "Thank you for coming to the call." The acoustics of the hall were perfect, and Bianca could hear the strain in the woman's voice. She was the richest person in town, and she'd always seemed effortlessly in control, but today... *Things are happening*. "Some of you may have noticed, ah, something strange in the sky earlier..."

Someone stepped out of the wings and onto the stage. He was not just a stranger, but *strange* – wearing shiny black clothes, his skin an unhealthy-looking bluish hue, his mouth set in a hard line. He walked across the stage, stiff-backed, boot heels clicking on the boards. He stood beside the burgher, then turned his head to stare at her. He was half a meter taller than her, and she was not a small woman. She shrank away, then hurried to a seat behind him on the stage. The man followed her with his gaze until she was seated, then looked back at the crowd.

He sniffed. "I am Undercommandant Voyou." He spoke in the local language, but his accent made it sound like he was building a wall of rough stones. "It is my privilege to welcome… what is the name of this charming settlement again?" This last to the burgher.

"We – this is Lowcliff, it's–"

He returned his attention to the room. "Lowcliff. Welcome, denizens of Lowcliff, to the glorious and eternal Barony of Letnev. No longer will you suffer lives of lawless anarchy. The Barony has returned to reclaim Darit. You are home."

"What do you mean *reclaim*?" someone shouted.

"I did not intend to take questions," Voyou said. "Impertinence is not appreciated in the Barony. But, because this is new to you, and you are simple country folk, unaccustomed to the uses of power, I will answer. This planet was once a mining colony, a cherished possession of the Barony of Letnev. We lost track of you for a little while – as you can imagine, we had more pressing concerns than this place – but the Baron remembers you now. He has reached out his hand, and gathered you to his bosom. Your… burgher, is it? She will explain to you what this means in terms of taxes and so on. Glory to the Barony." He turned smartly and walked off the stage.

The audience waited until he was out of sight before they erupted.

The burgher stood and called for silence. "I know!" she said. "I know. I was just as surprised as you are. I've heard from Highcliff and Midcliff and some of the other towns we trade with on the wireless, and they've all had visits like this too. I think these, ah, Letnev are visiting every settlement on the whole planet."

"Why are they here?" someone called.

"We're still figuring that out," she said. "They don't seem to *want* much, apart from making us put up a flag, though they said they're doing a survey and will announce any, ah, necessary reallocations of resources."

"We've always governed ourselves just fine!" That was Bianca's mother, and Bianca was almost proud of her.

"I agree," the burgher said. "My hope, my *expectation*, is that these Letnev won't care much about us in particular, or how we run things here. We can go on as we always have, more or less, with some… some small changes. They're imposing a tax, to be collected twice a year, from every household. They want a tenth part of whatever we produce."

The crowd roared at *that*, with shouts, curses, and, "Let them come and take it!"

"They will come and take it," the burgher said grimly. "I have no doubt of that. They… showed me some of their weapons."

"They're just bandits!"

"Worse," the burgher said. "They're the government."

"What do *we* get out of this?" someone called. "If they're our new leaders, what are they offering us?"

"Protection," the burgher said. "From the Barony's many enemies. Who are now our enemies, since we're a Barony colony world. I *know*!" She held out her hands, trying vainly to quell the uproar. "I don't like this any more than you do! Maybe they'll lose interest and go away! Maybe they won't even bother to *send* tax collectors for a few bushels of wool and baskets of apples! They…" She closed her eyes. "They wanted me to tell you, specifically, that they are forgiving all of our back taxes. Meaning, they won't try to collect what they say we owe from all the years we've been out of their control." She gave a jagged, broken little laugh. "Which is good, because as near as I can tell, that's been *thousands* of years, and that's… that's a lot of taxes. It could be worse, people. They could have burned our farms. Or even just nudged the orbital mirrors out of true by a few degrees, and turned our little bubble of green into frozen tundra. They could kill us all without even firing a shot–"

"Why would they do *that*?" Bianca called. "Why slaughter a caprid when you can get milk and wool from it for years? We're just livestock for the Barony now!"

"Better to be alive than dead, Bianca Xing," the burgher snapped. "What did you want me to do? Tell them *no*? I hear the burgher of Reachway did that, and they cut off his head and put it on top of their flagpole!"

The crowd had no reply to that. The burgher contained herself. "I'll… I'll send word if there's any more news. For now, just… go on as you have. And hope this all blows over." She slumped and went backstage, instead of walking out down the aisle and shaking hands and slapping backs like she did at Hale-meetings.

"So," Bianca's mother said, "that's that, then. You'd better get that mech back to old Torvald and fill him in on how things are, I reckon. I'll see you at the house after."

"Yes, Ma."

She put a hand on her daughter's knee. "Be careful, Bianca. I know I always say that, but this time, really, be careful. There are strangers out there."

"Reclaimed?" Torvald shook his head. They were sitting in his bunker, him in the chair, Bianca sprawled on her back on the hard bunk. "No, this world of ours was a colony all right, but it belonged to the Federation of Sol, not the Barony of Letnev. The Federation, that's where most of the humans are, or at least were, back in the old days. Just look around – we're *humans*, not Letnev. Sure, we look similar, blue skin and odd proportions aside, but they're *aliens*. Who are they trying to fool?"

"Everybody," Bianca said. "They're trying to fool everybody. I can't believe I saw an alien for the first time and it wasn't even amazing. It was just awful. Why couldn't this Federation have come here? I bet *they* would have offered me a ticket to the stars."

Torvald went *hmm*. "As I recall, the Barony and the Federation didn't get along too well. When things fell apart, they did some of the fiercest fighting just amongst themselves. Maybe the Barony beat the Federation, and think that gives them some rightful claim to this place? Not that they need a claim, really, if they've got ships and guns." He sighed.

"I don't understand." Bianca stared at the ceiling. She couldn't see the sky, but she knew right where her triangle of stars was. "I thought there was an empire, one big community, back then. Why would they fight each other?"

"An emperor is a king of kings, and an empire is a bunch of nations all stuck together under a single ruler. That doesn't mean they all *like* being together. You like some of your neighbors more than others, don't you? Same thing. Just on a bigger scale. Some of those nations joined the empire because they wanted to share in the power, or they wanted to be protected, but some of them were forced to join, or threatened into joining. Any system that big and complicated and full of tensions is bound to fall apart eventually, and when it falls, it makes a mess." He swiveled back and forth in his chair. "But knowing a little bit of history doesn't change the price of wool, does it? I'm the only person on the whole planet, maybe, with evidence that Darit wasn't really a Barony colony world, and even if I told the world, it wouldn't make a difference. The Barony would just mark me as a troublemaker, and that wouldn't be good for me."

"Ships and guns," Bianca said. "I can't believe we got invaded by aliens. That we got conquered. And that the invasion is so boring and stupid! I've read stories about this sort of thing, but it's not like there's a resistance I can join or anything."

"We'd be flies resisting the swatter, I'm afraid," Torvald said. "You're sitting in the most technologically advanced place on all of Darit, maybe, and I wouldn't be a match for even one of their shuttles."

"Maybe there's some sort of super-weapon, buried out in the forest? Something to let us fight back?"

"Maybe," Torvald said. "This was an important place, once. I guess that's why the Barony is here – there's still precious metal in those mines, just too deep for us to reach with our technology. If you find some super-weapon, though, keep it to yourself, or you'll get a lot of people killed. We don't have any tactical genius generals around here. We don't even have any soldiers. In a situation like this… we mostly just have to hope the boot on our neck doesn't get too heavy."

"I don't want to be a coward, Torvald."

"You aren't, Bianca. You're brave, and you're a romantic, and I want you to stay alive so you can keep being both."

"The world has changed, though. Doesn't that mean we have to change too?"

He looked at the ceiling for a long moment, then sighed. "Probably so, Bianca. Whether we want to or not."

Nothing *did* change, though, apart from that flag on the Halemeeting hall. Occasionally a ship flew overhead, but none landed, and no more alien visitors came to the village. There was a lot of shouting at the next few Halemeetings, but after six weeks without any contact from the Barony of Letnev, people mostly settled back into their old patterns, and hoped they'd been forgotten by the new masters. Bianca's hope and excitement at seeing the first ship go by had turned to fear and then, to her great annoyance, back into boredom.

Until the day a Barony ship landed at her parents' farm.

CHAPTER 4

Heuvelt Angriff – former treasure hunter, lapsed gentleperson adventurer, current reluctant criminal – was trying to get drunk, but he wasn't having much luck. He shook a fistful of coins at the bartender, a sorrowful-looking Winnaran. He squinted. Maybe the bartender wasn't sorrowful. Maybe Heuvelt was just projecting again. "Look, these coins are from the Xxlan system, and according to the treaty the Hylar government has with the Xxcha Kingdom, that means they're also legal tender on Jol-Nar and any associated colony worlds, and since Elekayne is a Hylar colony world, that means you have to–"

"No cash," the Winnaran bartender repeated, then pointed to a sign behind her that presumably said "No cash" in whatever language it appeared in. The bartender glanced around the bar, which was deserted at this time of day, and apparently decided to take pity on Heuvelt, because she placed a small glass on the bar before him.

Heuvelt tossed the contents back eagerly, expecting the burn of liquor, but it was just water. He sighed. "Thank you."

The bartender leaned forward and said, "I think the cash prohibition is stupid too, but we had a gene-plague last year. One of the ways it got spread around was through infected surfaces, and everyone is still being careful about unnecessary contact. Don't you have a credit account? Doesn't have to be with the Universities of Jol-Nar. We're hooked into all the major data systems, and we even have decent exchange rates for Letnev or Naalu currency."

"I am having… difficulty accessing my accounts." Heuvelt stared at the luminous, worthless discs in his hand. Xxcha money was pretty, but you couldn't eat beauty. "I was the victim of identity theft. I returned from a deep space exploration several months ago and promptly found myself arrested and accused of various horrible crimes. Only the fact that I don't resemble the perpetrator who used my name kept me from being thrown into a prison camp."

The Winnaran wiped the bar with a rag. "That's a real sad story."

Heuvelt nodded enthusiastically. "It *is*. Thank you for appreciating that. If you find yourself moved by sympathy, you could–"

"The real bad guy didn't have that big scar down his face, I take it?"

Heuvelt winced. He'd been reckoned a handsome man – almost *too* handsome, some of his lovers had told him: how could you trust a man with those teeth and that hairline and a chin like that all at the same time? But his former best friend and former first mate, Dob Ell, had left him with a long knife scar that started just under his right eye and took a wandering path down his cheek and over his jawline toward his neck. He was lucky to have both eyes in his head and all his blood inside him. "He didn't, no. One of the Hylar prosecutors said all humans look alike and I'd scarred my face as a disguise, but there was DNA evidence to exonerate me, fortunately."

"You could get that scar fixed," the bartender said. "I know a Hylar surgeon who does top-notch reconstructive work. Though, now that I think of it, yeah, all her humans *do* kind of come out looking the same."

Heuvelt bowed his head, hoping to make the scar less noticeable. "I tried. I wasted some of the proceeds from selling my old ship on a plastic surgeon. I looked like my old self… for a day. Then the scar came back. It seems I was cut by an Yssaril shame-blade. Have you ever heard of those?"

"Can't say I have."

Heuvelt slumped lower on his stool. "Some of the Yssaril tribes use them back on their homeworld, during their feuds. Sometimes it isn't enough to kill an enemy, you see. You want them to carry the mark of their defeat with them for the rest of their lives instead. So they take the sap from some horrible swamp plant and boil it and mix it with the venom from some reptile and coat a blade with it, and any wounds given with that blade create a scar that has *memory*. I don't know how it works. Something about the toxins on the blade promoting collagen degradation. The surgeon said I should be grateful. Without his intervention, the wound would have just kept opening up on its own, never quite healing, for the rest of my life. This bright meandering line across my face is the best medical science can do for me."

The Winnaran chuckled. "I'm sure some people will find it appealing, though they'll wonder why you don't get it fixed, and assume you *want* to look dangerous. Wearing a scar is, in its own way, a weird kind of vanity, don't you think?"

"I hadn't thought about it. So now I'm scarred *and* vain. I used to just be vain."

"And broke, apparently. If you were cleared of wrongdoing, why didn't you get access to your accounts back?"

"An excellent question," he said. "It turns out, once your accounts are frozen, they take a long time to get *unfrozen* again." There had been precious little in the accounts anyway, since Heuvelt's parents had cut him off for "being an incorrigible wastrel" and stopped replenishing his funds. "As a further complication, I was wanted by both the Universities of Jor-Nal and the Barony of Letnev. Their different alliances and reciprocal business arrangements, taken together, encompass most of the systems where a human is likely to visit or do business. I'm having trouble establishing new accounts – there's a flag on my name, apparently. I'm told a fancy Hacan lawyer could sort it all out for me, if I could afford one, but I can't."

The Winnaran looked to the left, and looked to the right, and confirmed once again that the bar was empty, except for a human sleeping with his head on a table in the back. "Give me the coins. I'll buy your drinks on my account."

Heuvelt was moved by the kindness, even though he suspected the bartender drank for free, and would simply pocket the coins as profit, but as long as the end result was booze inside him, he was happy. "Thank you."

"We have a range of alcoholic beverages safe for human consumption. What are you drinking?"

"Do you have anything that started out life as corn?"

"That's one of those plants humans like, isn't it? I thought they made syrup out of it."

"You can make *lots* of things out of it. Including sweet, brown liquor."

"I have sweet brown liquor," the Winnaran said. "Well. Brown-ish. I think it's made of algae. That's the best I can do."

"I'm sure it will suffice."

The Winnaran poured him a small glass of something too dark and syrupy to be mistaken for bourbon, but it *was* brown-ish. Heuvelt took a sip and winced; it was sweet, too, repulsively so, with a distinct hint of cinnamon. It tasted like something that should be poured over pancakes. "This is alcohol?"

"It's fifty-five percent alcohol, according to the label on the bottle."

A hundred and ten proof, then. That cheered him up. "Thank you. Maybe something… less sweet for my next round."

The bartender nodded and wandered off down the bar, busily attending to nothing much, probably just tired of his company. Heuvelt was getting used to that. When had he become a bore? Probably when his stories stopped being about recent adventures and became about old grievances instead. "Rotten thieves," he muttered into his glass. "Ruined my life." That was a comforting idea, though it wasn't true. Having his identity stolen hadn't made his old friend and family retainer Dob Ell attack him with a knife. His fortunes had been circling a black hole even before his accounts were frozen, after the ruinous expense of his failed deep-space exploration. He'd had visions of discovering new rich worlds, ancient alien artifacts, perhaps a previously unknown species of alien, and returning a hero. Instead he'd found radiation, rocks, and betrayal, and he'd returned the next best thing to a pauper.

Dob Ell had stabbed him the *very day* her scheduled monthly stipend failed to arrive: as soon as she was off the payroll, the illusion of friendship and the reality of a lifetime of resentment had become manifest. His parents had hired her to watch over him when he was a mere child, and he'd assumed a bond of love had grown between them. He'd called his parents to tell them about the attack, hoping they could take some vengeance on his behalf, but they weren't talking to him anymore. The second underbutler who took the message had laughed at him and said, "Of *course* she attacked you. She was paid to guard your body, and I can't imagine a more thankless or tedious job."

And so, scarred and betrayed, he'd been forced to sell his pride and joy, *The Lady of Misrule*, an exceptionally beautiful long-range cruiser he'd emptied his trust fund to buy as a university graduation gift to himself. (He hadn't technically graduated from university, but he'd stopped going, which was close enough.) Oh, the times he'd had in that ship, plying the spaceways with Dob Ell and a series of attractive humanoids! He could have lived the life of a dashing adventurer for decades if he hadn't decided to get so ambitious. "Ambition is poison!" he called to the bartender.

She ignored him. Perhaps she couldn't relate. She worked the morning shift in a dingy bar on a Hylar colony world that was mostly desert (and as the Hylar were mainly an aquatic species, that meant it wasn't a colony world held in high esteem), so it was possible she'd never sipped the poison of ambition, personally.

He'd gotten a lot of money for the *Lady of Misrule*, and used the proceeds for living expenses and to purchase a far less beautiful ship, the *Show and Tell*. It was a fast courier retrofitted with extra cargo space, and Heuvelt had planned to use it to establish a business for himself as a high-end transporter of luxury goods. He'd even hired a crew. Why not? He knew *lots* of rich people from the Federation of Sol, the Jol-Nar, the Emirates, even the Mentak Coalition and the Yin Brotherhood, because his parents were well connected in those circles. He might as well exploit their good name.

He hadn't counted on the difficulties his not-fully-expunged criminal record would cause when it came to getting licensed and insured, though. No one would hire him for legitimate work, so he was forced to take on less savory jobs. The sort that paid in cash, and brought him to planets like *this*.

Where the hell was his contact, anyway? His crew – sorry, his *partners* – Ashont and Clec were waiting for him back on the ship, and while he didn't think they'd steal the *Show and Tell* and leave without him, he had trouble trusting anyone fully after his experience with Dob Ell.

The door swung open, and a Hylar came clomping in on six mechanical legs, its real body a tangle of tentacles floating in a dingy soup of fluid inside a translucent tank. The alien approached the bar and stood beside Heuvelt.

The bartender started toward them, then thought better of it and withdrew. Oh, good, so the illicit nature of their business was *that* obvious. What a comfort.

"You are Mr Scar?" The Hylar's voice grated out of a metal box on the front of the containment suit.

Heuvelt sighed. He certainly hadn't chosen that *nom de crim*, but some Saar drug dealer had called him that, and it stuck. People didn't have much trouble identifying him, at least, though it wasn't like there were a lot of potential criminal contacts in this particular dingy bar at this particular dingy hour. "That's me. You're Mr Slosh?"

The artificial voicebox gave a harsh, uninflected series of ha-ha-ha sounds. "I chose my name when I heard yours."

"Most clever," Heuvelt said. "You have my money?"

"You have my data-stick?"

"Right here." He reached down for the briefcase by his stool and opened it up. There were dozens of data-sticks inside, all different colors, jumbled together. "It's one of these."

"Which one?"

"Give me the money and I'll show you."

The Hylar grabbed the briefcase instead and tried to run for the door. Annoying, but not unprecedented. None of the data-sticks were the one Mr Slosh's employers actually wanted, and once they figured that out, they'd have to slink back to Heuvelt and pay a "we're sorry we tried to screw you over" premium to get the *real* one–

"Stop right there!" The sleeping human in the corner leapt up and became very much an awake human, and one armed with a long and complex energy rifle. "Jol-Nar Data Enforcement Agency!"

Oh, no. The last thing Heuvelt needed was an *actual* criminal record on top of his accidental one. He dropped to the floor and started looking for a likely table to hide under as more agents came rushing in through the door, humanoid and Hylar both.

That's when Mr Slosh triggered some kind of smoke bomb. The bar filled with thick, inky black clouds, but there was still a little clear air near the floor, so Heuvelt crawled along on his belly toward the restrooms.

The cloud really was thick and blinding, but didn't seem to be nerve gas, or at least, not one that did anything untoward to humans. He knew some Hylar had ink sacs, used in the old days to release clouds in the water to let them evade predators, and it seemed Mr Slosh had replicated the effect for use on dry land. The data enforcement agents weren't shooting blindly, at least. They must be pretty well trained.

Heuvelt stuck close to the walls while he crawled, so no one stepped on him, though he saw some boots and mechanical feet go by. He reached the restroom door and slipped inside. The air was clear here, relatively speaking, though it didn't exactly smell *good*; this was a multicultural colony world, and various sorts of aliens had relieved themselves of waste here since the place had been cleaned last. In deference to the stench, though, there was a small window, and since this bar made you pay in advance for drinks, there weren't even bars on said window to stop patrons from escaping without paying their tabs.

After glancing behind him to make sure no one was watching, Heuvelt climbed up on a trash bin and peered out at a tantalizing strip of horrible arid desert ground. There were various data enforcement agency vehicles parked here and there, but no actual agents in sight, so he might just wriggle out of this.

He got his head through the window okay, but his shoulders gave him a bit of trouble until he twisted himself around at just the right angle, and wriggled a bit. Hadn't he possessed considerable dignity once upon a time? Better undignified than imprisoned, though.

He was halfway through the window when someone grabbed his ankles and hauled him out. He managed to cover his head so he didn't get a concussion when he slammed into the trash bin and bounced onto the ground. He landed on his back, groaned, and looked up at the Winnaran bartender, who stood over him, aiming a slim black kinetic sidearm at his chest. "Did I not tip you well enough?" he croaked.

She reached into her shirt and pulled out a badge hanging on a chain.

"Ah," he said. "As my father used to say when mother caught him canoodling with one of the gardeners, 'All right then, it's a fair cop.'"

"I'm sorry," she said. "It really *was* a very sad story."

"And getting sadder all the time, don't you think?" Heuvelt said.

CHAPTER 5

Bianca and her family had just settled down to supper when they heard the sounds: first the terrified bleatings of the caprids out back, followed by a roar-like gale force wind rushing through trees. Bianca's parents looked at one another, wide-eyed, across their small wooden table, but Bianca leapt to her feet and rushed for the door. She did grab a heavy walking stick on her way out – curiosity didn't entirely override good sense.

The ship she'd seen fly over the mech farm (or one just like it) was settling down in front of her house. Its presence in her front yard was as incongruous and disturbing as seeing a snake on her pillow. In the course of landing, the ship crushed the metal watering trough and obliterated an ornamental flowerbed her mother had put in during some of her rare free time.

Up close and unmoving, the ship was, if anything, *more* menacing: gleaming black with silver highlights, and covered in cruel barbs, hooks, spikes, and spines, as if it meant to tear apart the very air as it flew. In general shape, it reminded her of a diving predator bird, and its lowered, beaked head was pointed right at her front door.

That beak dropped open, and a ramp extended to the ground. The man from the Halemeeting hall, Undercommandant Voyou, walked slowly down the ramp, looking around as if inventorying the farm for auction. His eyes marked Bianca, but he seemed to take no more notice of her than he did of the house, the barn, or the trees. When he reached the bottom of the ramp, he adjusted his black gloves, wrinkled his nose like he smelled something foul, and opened his mouth.

"You're going to have to pay for that," Bianca said. She stood with the walking stick leaning over her shoulder in a deliberately casual way.

"What?" Voyou seemed as baffled as he would have been had a tree stump or a caprid talked to him.

Bianca was pleased to see him taken aback. She pointed with her stick, and Voyou turned to look where she indicated: at the water trough, crumpled under one of the ship's legs, and the flowers ground to mud and mush. "You should have looked where you landed." She clucked her tongue. "That's going to cost you."

He narrowed his eyes. "You–" He stopped, took a breath, and said, "On behalf of the Barony of Letnev, please accept my apologies. Be assured, your parents will receive recompense. If it's any consolation, the only other nearby landing zone my pilot deemed acceptable was the field near your… livestock… and I chose this location instead, since I did not wish to risk upsetting your animals."

Now it was Bianca's turn to be taken aback. "Oh. Ah. That's… thank you. Why are you here?"

Her parents emerged then – they'd taken the time to change clothes, Bianca saw, her father in a clean shirt, her mother with a Halemeeting day dress pulled hastily on. "Don't be rude, Bianca." Her father's voice seemed calm, but she knew him well enough to detect the undercurrent of anxiety. "How may we help you, Undercommandant Voyou?"

He puffed up. "I am – ah. You recall my name. Yes."

Bianca was pleased to see him bumped off his equilibrium again. These Barony people certainly had shiny tech, and Torvald said they were a major galactic power (or had been), but if things didn't go the way they expected, they wobbled like newborn caprids. Or maybe she was overgeneralizing about their species. She'd only met the one, after all.

The alien said, "You are Keon and Willen Xing, Bianca's parents?"

Bianca felt a chill. She didn't like this man knowing her parents' names. Her mother and father shared a glance, then nodded mute confirmation.

"Excellent," Voyou said. "You ask how you can help me, but in fact, I am here to help you. May I come inside? I'm afraid it's all rather complex."

"Are we in any trouble?" her mother said.

"Trouble, Madame Xing? Absolutely not. Indeed, you may be the luckiest people on this planet. Except, perhaps, for your darling daughter."

Kind words and compliments. They just seemed wrong, coming from the undercommandant. Bianca thought of a snake on a pillow again.

Her parents exchanged one of their infuriating pair-bonded-people-telepathy glances. When Bianca was little, she'd thought they could *really* read each other's minds, and only realized later that they'd simply been together so long they knew one another's habits of thought. "You'd better come in," her mother said. "Can we get anything for your crew?"

"No, they are amply provisioned." Voyou made a gracious half-bow and gestured that they should lead the way.

"Why are we lucky?" Bianca fell into step behind him.

He leaned a little closer to her, and spoke low. "Your parents are lucky because we are going to give them a great deal of money. *You* are lucky because you get to leave this latrine of a planet."

"What–"

"All will be explained." He patted her arm. In a friendly way! Looking at him, you'd think his only interaction with a peasant like her would be hitting her in the face with a riding crop if she got in his way while he was crossing the street.

Having an extra adult in the house made the small space seem terribly crowded, but the undercommandant said, "What a charming home you have," and took a seat on the long wooden bench at the table like he was settling onto a cushioned settee. "I see I interrupted your dinner. I am terribly sorry. Please, feel free to eat while we talk."

Her mother hurriedly set a plate before him – root mash, a few thin slices of dried caprid meat, a sorghum cake – but he demurred. "I am so sorry, the biology of my people, it's just different enough from humans that your food tends not to agree with us. It looks and smells delectable, however, I assure you. I would welcome a glass of water, though, if such is available?" Her father rushed to comply.

Bianca pulled his plate toward herself and chewed on some of the dried caprid while staring at him directly. That seemed to make him nervous, which she found exceedingly interesting and wished to know why.

Her parents didn't eat. They just stared at Voyou, like they were waiting to see if he might do a trick, or bite someone. "We've heard some interesting stories, about your daughter," the undercommandant said. He picked up the cup of water, gazed into it, and then put it back down without drinking. Bianca couldn't imagine what the problem was. That water was fresh from the rain barrel. There hadn't even been any bugs in it last time she checked, and they always picked those out anyway. "Would you tell me a little bit about how Bianca became part of your family?"

Her father glanced at Bianca, coughed, and said, "Ah. Well. It was almost nineteen turns ago now, I think, right, Willen?"

Her mother nodded silently. What was that look on her face? Bianca thought she'd seen every possible expression either of her parents was capable of producing, but the way Ma looked now was calculating? Speculative?

"I was out in the eastern forest," her father went on. "We were having a real hard go of things that year. Lost half our flock to heartstone, and the crops were only just middling. I went out to gather mushrooms, hoping for some to eat, maybe a few to sell. There's always good foraging, bird-of-the-wood, green lady, witch fingers, especially after a hard rain–"

"This was soon after a hard rain?" The undercommandant's attention was fixed on her father like a laser tracking sight.

"Hmm? Oh, yes, a big storm, blew over trees that had stood for two hundred years. There was flooding down the valley, a bridge even washed out, and I mean a good bridge, stone and all, not a plank someone had thrown across a gap. We haven't seen a storm like that since, thank the moons."

Voyou nodded like this was confirmation of something he'd suspected. Who cared about the weather twenty years ago? "You were gathering mushrooms, in the forest, you say. But aren't those forests dangerous for a man alone?"

Her father nodded. "They can be. But I went in the middle of the day, when the nightclimbers are deep sleeping in their holes and boles."

"I'd heard there were other dangers in these woods," the undercommandant said. "Relics of a past time, that can cause people to sicken and die, or suffer more immediate hardships."

"That sort of thing happens," her mother said. "And none of us wants to see it happen to our children, so we make sure they know how dangerous the woods can be. But…" She looked at her husband.

He picked up the thread. "When someone digs up something dangerous, it's the talk of the town for years afterward. Such things are rare, is what I mean. It could be we overstate how likely the danger is. In truth, I can't remember the last time someone picked up a glowing piece of glass and died puking with their hair falling out. Not since I was a child myself." He looked at his daughter. "We didn't really mean to mislead you, Bianca, it's just–"

"I know," Bianca said. "I know you made the forest sound scarier than it is. I've been halfway an apprentice to old Torvald for years now, and half the stock at his mech farm was scavenged from the forest. I've even gone foraging with him once or twice, but just on the edges – don't worry."

"Please go on," the undercommandant murmured, apparently fascinated by this familial back-and-forth.

Bianca's father blinked. "Ah. I just mean, I felt fairly safe going to gather mushrooms. Back then I had a walking stick with a jolt-tip on it. Do you know what that is?"

"I would assume some sort of electrical discharge weapon."

"That right," he said. "Torvald fixed it up for me. I figured if I ran into anything nasty, I'd give it a spark and drive it away. As for the other dangers… I know well enough not to pick up glass that shines all blue or yellow or green on its own, or to go digging around the edges of any bit of metal I see poking up out of the ground."

"Did you see any metal poking up out of the ground that particular day?"

"Oh, no, no." He shook his head and held up his hands and Bianca thought, *Wait. He's* lying! He'd looked flustered in exactly the same way when he tried to convince her that her pet felid had run away, when really she'd been eaten by a nightclimber. "No, nothing out of the ordinary happened. I just filled my basket with bird-of-the-wood and such, and then I heard this squalling. Sounded like a child in trouble, so I followed the sound. There she was, baby Bianca, just laying naked on the forest floor, crying her lungs out, and it's lucky I found her before a predator did–"

"I am offering you an opportunity to revise your account," the undercommandant said. The worst part was, he didn't even sound menacing. He sounded *kind*. "I understand, this is the story you've told for so long, perhaps it has come to replace the truth, even in your own mind. But I'm afraid the truth is what I must have."

"I don't know what you mean." Her father twisted a napkin in his hands. "I found Bianca in the forest, just like I said."

"You did find her in the forest. That I believe." The undercommandant had one hand under the table. It emerged, holding a sleek black weapon, some kind of sidearm, an energy pistol or flechette gun or something else Bianca had only read about and never seen. He rested it on the table, not pointed at anyone. "You did not find her 'just like you said,' however. The truth, please."

He glanced at his wife, and the undercommandant barked, "You need not look at her! Look at *me!*"

Bianca gripped the knife by her plate, but the undercommandant noticed the movement, and his weapon shifted – pointed now at her mother. "Mademoiselle Xing, I would not advise that. You might very well bury that blade in my throat – you seem to me to possess the will, and I respect you for it. But I would surely discharge my weapon in my dying moments, and then there would be two bodies here, instead of none. Listen. Your parents have not told you the truth about your origins. Aren't you curious?"

Bianca didn't release the knife, but she did glance toward the end of the table where her parents sat. "What is he talking about?"

"We… we just didn't want you to feel different, Bee," her mother said.

She'd always felt different, in a hundred ways. "Different *how?*"

"You're a very special young woman," Voyou said. "More special even than your parents know. Why don't you tell us the *true* story, Monsieur Xing? Then, when you're done, I can fill you in on some context you might be missing."

Her father looked down at his plate for a moment. When he looked up, there were tears shining in his eyes. "Bee, it doesn't matter where you come from. You're our daughter, and you always will be. You're *ours.*"

"The story, please." The undercommandant put the gun back in his lap and returned his hands to the tabletop. Bianca carefully put her knife back down beside her plate. Even when she exhaled, she still felt somehow like she was holding her breath, every muscle tensed in anticipation. There was some secret in her life, and it was about to be revealed.

"As best I remember," her father began, "it happened like this."

CHAPTER 6

Keon Xing was a man with only a few things to call his own: he had a little house, a half-sick flock, a few fields of crops all torn up from a storm, and a wife who'd once been happy and beaming and full of life, but who spent more and more time now crying, or just gazing off into space. She loved him, and she loved the farm, but most of all she wanted to share that love by starting a family… and try as they might, they couldn't seem to have a child.

She blamed herself, though Keon told her she shouldn't. He'd done a fair bit of scavenging in his youth, going deep into the forest in search of ancient remnants to sell to the mech farm, and he thought he might have been exposed to something that made him sterile, or at least diminished the likelihood of having children. The wise woman said it might be that, or "Maybe just bad luck." The life of a small farmer on Darit certainly had enough of that.

Keon went out that morning to forage for mushrooms, yes – with the crops beat up by the storm, they needed all the food they could get – but he also went out because he needed some time alone, and thought his wife might like some as well. Willen had been so excited just a few days before, thinking they'd finally hit lucky, and they'd start a family at last… but it turned out she was just late on her monthlies, and there was no baby on the way. She'd put on a brave face, but he'd seen her shoulders move up and down with silent sobbing as she pulled weeds in her little flowerbed. He couldn't stand to see that, so he fled, and in his own sadness and distraction, he looked up and realized he'd gone much deeper into the woods than he'd intended. Subconsciously trying to put distance between himself and his troubles, maybe.

Now that he was in the forest, though, beneath the dense and dripping trees, he felt guilty about leaving Willen alone in her grief. *What kind of man am I?* he thought. *I can't give her a child, can't comfort her in her sadness, can't–*

He shook it off. Keon was a practical man, and he could at least bring home supper. There was some bird-of-the-wood right there, yellowy-orange shelves of fungus clinging to a tree that had fallen over in the storm. There must have been a kilogram or more of the mushrooms, and they really did taste a lot like poultry when you cooked them right. He filled the basket he carried on his back, and, somewhat cheered, continued to forage.

He climbed up a hill, slow and careful because the slope was muddy and partly washed out, but the erosion had exposed a lot of roots he could use as handholds. When he got to the top he found a patch of green lady mushrooms, bright and still damp from the rainwater sifting down from the trees above. He hummed happily as he plucked the stems and caps and put them in the basket. Once he was done, he straightened up, stretched his back, and looked across the gully before him–

Something was buried in the hillside across the way. He caught a flash of light on glass, and the gleam of metal. That hillside had also been torn up by the storm, but even more so: a tangle of uprooted trees lay at the base, tumbled down from the ridge, resting now amid piles of mud. The root system of those trees had been holding all the soil in place, and with so much washed away, the secret at the heart of the hill was revealed.

Keon's own heart fluttered. He wasn't sure what he was looking at, what kind of forgotten tech, but whatever it was, it was *big*. Size wasn't everything – power cells weren't very large, and they were about the most valuable thing you could find – but Torvald over at the mech farm paid for scavenged metal by weight. A find like this might not save the farm, but it sure would slow the rate of failure considerably.

Keon set his basket down and carefully picked his way toward the metal gleam. A stream of water still ran along the bottom of the gully between the hills, about a meter across and shallow, the remnant of what must have been a great flood the day before. He stepped across, climbed over the mess of fallen trees, and finally reached the exposed hillside. Using both hands, he brushed away the mud from the surface, trying to reveal the full extent of his find.

He uncovered a rectangle of shining metal, two and a half meters high by a meter and a half wide, with a plate of square glass set in the middle, just above his head height. The glass was milky, and he couldn't see anything behind it, but he realized with surprise that there might *be* something behind it, because this surely did look like a door, didn't it?

People found ancient vehicles sometimes, shuttles and trucks, and maybe this was an unusually large example. Or maybe… maybe it was something else. There were always rumors of hidden spaces below the forest, secret tombs or vaults in the more fanciful stories, or just rooms the long-ago inhabitants of Dar-it had built to keep supplies dry or hide from storms, in the more plausible legends. There were ancient tales of plucky youths finding caves full of treasure and making their fortune, though no one knew anybody it had actually happened to.

Keon looked for a handle and couldn't find one, but he did find a crack where the door didn't quite sit true in its frame. Even the best-built artifact of the olden days would fail when left out in the weather for hundreds or thousands of years. That crack could mean everything inside would be buried in mud, but metal was metal, dirty or not, and Keon was up for the hard work of excavation if it meant saving his farm.

Keon's jolt-stick was made of stout metal, and would serve as a pry bar. He hesitated, thinking of the dangers that sometimes accompanied old tech, but he was an experienced if out-of-practice salvager. If he saw anything glowing or oozing mysterious liquids, he'd back away fast and just sell Torvald the location of the place instead. He'd make less money that way, but it was an adequate fall-back plan.

Settled in his mind, Keon worked the end of his bar into the crack beside the door and heaved, then moved the stick a few centimeters down and heaved again. He worked his way along that seam, using all his weight and strength and leverage, and when he'd worked his way through about three-fourths down the crack, he heard the *pop* of a seal breaking and a hiss of air. Maybe the inside wasn't going to be so muddy after all; the door was loose but not broken.

After that, he was able to work the bar deeper into the crack, and a few more hard, grunting heaves got the door open enough for him to squeeze through the gap. He peered through first though. The space beyond was dark, and he was nervous – he didn't have anything with him to make a light – but no animals could have gotten in to make their lairs inside, and it wasn't like whoever'd lived in this place hundreds or thousands of years ago would still be lurking around. Nothing could live *that* long, no matter how good their tech was. He didn't be-lieve in ghosts, either, not since he was young.

My eyes will adjust, he thought, and squeezed into the hill.

Adjustment proved unnecessary, because when he entered, lights came on, and hidden machinery hummed to life. Keon froze, overwhelmed first by the sudden brightness and then by all the things it revealed.

The room was as big as his whole cottage, and the first thing he noticed was the skeleton on the floor. Keon had seen such remains before – a flood had un-earthed sections of the old graveyard when he was a boy, and there'd been bones strewn for a kilometer afterward – but never one all together like this, still in the shape of a person... or something like a person. This one was on its belly, one arm down by its side, the other reaching over its head, legs cocked at funny angles. Whoever it was had fallen down and never gotten up again. There were metal straps and bits of old cloth crisscrossing the skeleton – the remnants of clothes or jewelry, or both, maybe? How long had this body been here? And what kind of body *was* it? The shape of the head was all wrong for a human, too thin and too bulbous, and something about the proportion of the limbs was strange too. There were aliens in the galaxy, everyone knew that, but Keon never expected to see one on Darit, alive *or* dead.

I'm a grave robber, Keon thought with something like horror. He stepped around the skeleton and took in the rest of the space. The room contained a met-al table, with a stone bowl and cup on top, all coated in a layer of dust. There was a metal frame in the corner, low and rectangular, and after a moment Keon real-ized it was a cot, its sleeping surface long since turned to dust. There were crates full of cans and tins, probably food, but Keon would never be hungry enough to risk opening something *that* ancient. There was probably nothing inside except dust by now anyway.

All that was basically ordinary. The back wall of the chamber was something else, though. It was covered from the ceiling halfway to the floor in shiny black surfaces, screens like the one in the burgher's house, each a meter long on each side. Beneath the screens there was a sort of ledge, or maybe desktop, covered in switches, dials, knobs, and lights. Those lights were all lit up now, some steady green, most pulsing orange, a few red and flashing rapidly. As he watched, some of the oranges turned green, and some of the reds went orange. Were they changing because of him? He hadn't touched anything!

There were eight screens in three rows: three along the top, three along the bottom, and in the center, just one on the left, and one on the right. That left a space right in the center, and it was glass, too, but instead of being blank and black like the screens, it was transparent. At first Keon thought it was just a different kind of screen, but when he stepped close, he saw it was more like a window. There was a chamber beyond, the same dimensions as the window, and maybe two meters deep. There were things protruding from the walls and ceiling of that little compartment: nozzles, maybe, and shining rods that came to sharp points, and oily-looking eyeball-sized hemispheres. Keon couldn't even begin to imagine what any of it was for. Even Torvald would scratch his head, Keon reckoned. He'd never even heard tell of such things.

Keon glanced down at the console. All the red lights were gone now, and as he watched, the last orange one turned to green.

Then all the screens lit up, some scrolling with symbols that were meaningless to him, others displaying colored bars, a few showing the progress of zig-zagging lines. The machinery behind the clear glass started to move, rods turning slowly, hemispheres emerging from the walls to reveal themselves as spheres, nozzles sliding back and forth on hidden tracks. Keon leaned forward, hands on the ledge, to get a closer look–

Something gave beneath the palm of his hand, and he leapt back, horrified. A panel had slid open on the console, revealing a square button, and he'd put his hand *right on it* – he'd pushed the button down! What had he done? What if this was some kind of weapon?

A bright drop of blood shone on the end of his fingertip, and he put it in his mouth and sucked it instinctively, then pulled his finger out and stared at it, a sick feeling roiling in his guts. What if he'd just been poisoned?

Nothing happened, though. The lights continued to pulse green, and the other screens continued to display data that was entirely incomprehensible to him. One of the colored bars started to rise, and one of the others shrank, which suggested something was happening, but he couldn't know what. The blood was troubling. Maybe he'd just brushed his finger on a sharp burr of metal, a little accidental lancet too small to see. He'd wash the wound out with icewort when he got home and wrap it up good and hope it didn't get infected, or worse.

Assuming he didn't die from that little prick, this was a life-changing find. Whatever this place was, it was unimaginably valuable. He'd gone way beyond making up for a bad harvest and a sick flock. Once he brought this out, and started selling it to Torvald… he'd be wealthy by the time he was done. Indeed, he'd have to sell it in bits and pieces, because otherwise Torvald wouldn't be able to afford it all. This place could set Keon and Willen up for life.

For an undertaking like this, though, he'd need tools, and equipment. He could borrow a drone from the mech farm – he'd been meaning to do that anyway, to pull some stumps and expand the back field, so no one would think twice about it. He would come back here tomorrow and start taking this place apart, breaking it down into components he could transport.

Back outside, he dragged some of the smaller fallen branches around until he'd covered up the door in the hillside. He was pretty far out in the woods, and thought it unlikely anyone else would stumble on this place. On the way out, he carved a few discreet markings on tree trunks so he'd be able to find it again, his head spinning with visions of his glorious future.

When he got home, Willen didn't notice his good spirits, absorbed as she was in her own troubles. He couldn't give her a child, maybe, but he could give her a better life, of plenty and comfort. Maybe they could afford a journey to distant Tallmount, where they were supposed to have all manner of fancy medical machines – could be the doctors there could sort out this whole fertility thing once and for all.

He decided not to tell her about what he'd found. He was being superstitious, not counting his caprids before they were lambed, because he didn't want to risk handing his poor wife another disappointment. He made a big show of cooking up the bird-of-the-wood just the way Willen liked it, hoping that would explain his irrepressible smiles. *We won't have to eat forage anymore after this*, he thought.

The next day, he borrowed a mech and went out to the woods. The machine walked along after him on its four nimble legs, pincer-arms dangling at its sides until it was time to pull or lift something, its body nothing but storage space and a few sensors to keep it from walking into things.

Keon made his way back to the bunker, only consulting his trail signs once or twice to confirm he was on the right track – the path was burned into his memory. He had a tool satchel, and he was already planning out how to take apart the console to get at all the valuable wire that must be inside, and to remove the screens without cracking them. Maybe he'd even hang one in his *own* house, and be as fancy as the burgher was–

When he stepped inside, the screens looked different. Now some of them showed different views of a newborn baby – her puffy red face on one, her body as a whole on a second, her curled fist on a third. Three other screens showed the *inside* of her body: the shape of her bones, her organs, her brain. The remaining two screens were just those incomprehensible symbols, scrolling by.

Keon walked forward, baffled. Who was that girl? He leaned over the console and peered through the little window at the center of the screen, careful not to touch anything this time.

The machine somehow sensed his approach anyway, though, because the window turned out to be a door, and slid aside into the wall.

The tiny baby girl in the compartment there sucked in her first breath of Dar-it's air, and let out a great whooping cry.

CHAPTER 7

"You found me inside a *machine*?" Bianca said.

"It was a miracle," Willen said. "*You're* a miracle."

"You never told anyone about this place you found?" Voyou said to Keon.

Her pa shook his head. "When I found the baby… Bianca… I knew I couldn't tell. People would ask questions, wouldn't they, if I found a baby *and* a bunch of old tech on the selfsame day, or even in the same year? Plus, I don't know how to explain it, it seemed ungrateful to tear apart the place that gave me a daughter. Breaking up a miracle to sell it for scrap. Does that make sense? I just took Bianca home… I showed her to Willen, I showed her our *daughter*… and the next day I went back. I stepped inside the bunker again, but the lights were off, the screens dark, the chamber where I found Bianca empty. I was a little afraid there'd be a new baby in there every day."

"No," Voyou said. "The machine was made to incubate just a single child. What did you do next?"

Keon shrugged. "I used the mech to jam the door shut, then I made it shift about a ton of dirt and buried the hillside again. I shoved all the fallen trees up against the hill, and turned that place back into the grave it used to be. Before I left, though, I said 'thank you' to that alien skeleton. I don't know who he was, or what he was doing there, but if he's the one who made it possible for me to have a family, I'll give him thanks every day."

Voyou nodded, once, apparently satisfied. "This version of events accords with our own analysis. I needed to hear your story, in case there were unexpected elements, but I am pleased to say there was nothing of concern."

"Why is no one talking about the fact that I was *made* by a *machine*?" Bianca's mind spun with horror and wonder, confusion and dismay. "Does this mean I'm not even *human*, am I even a person, am I some kind of machine?"

"You are biological," the undercommandant said. "That machine was a sort of incubator. You were tucked away inside it, nearly ready to be born, frozen in a sort of stasis field. You would be there still, if your father had not activated the machine and completed the process of your birth."

Bianca frowned. Her father hadn't described an incubator – they had one of those for caprids who were born too early. The thing he described had machine components, nozzles and manipulators, and what were *those* for? But she didn't have any other explanation. What was the alternative? That the chamber had somehow *made* her? Printed her out? What kind of technology could, what, *fabricate* a baby, and in the course of a single night? She'd never heard of technology like that, even in the stories she'd read.

She'd ask old Torvald about it, though. Wow, would *he* be astonished by all this!

"You know about the machine?" Keon asked Voyou.

"Of course I do," the Letnev said. "My people built it, after all, when they first ruled this planet."

Bianca opened her mouth to say, "But you never ruled Darit," and only just stopped herself in time. She knew the Barony had never controlled this world, but only because Torvald's database knew, and he'd never forgive her if she revealed that secret, especially to their new alien overlords. Was Voyou lying, or confused? Or was he right, and Torvald's database wrong?

"I bring you glad tidings," Voyou said. "Your daughter is very special. She is, to put it in simple terms, a princess of the Barony of Letnev."

That astonishing assertion was met by a long beat of total silence, and then Willen said, "*What*?"

Voyou sat back in the chair and laced his long fingers over his stomach. "It is an interesting tale, and one with deep roots in the history of our people. As you may know – though perhaps not, given how remote this world is – there was once a single galactic empire, ruled by a race of cruel oppressors known as the Lazax. My people rebelled under the yoke of their rule and fought for our freedom, inspiring many other worlds and peoples to do the same. The Lazax empire did not fall quickly, but it *did* fall, and even now we continue to rebuild what was lost in that time of turmoil. That's why we've reclaimed your planet. The Barony of Letnev is positioned to found a *new* empire, and gathering in all of our lost worlds is an important part of that process."

"What does any of this have to do with me?" Bianca said.

Voyou gazed at her with a benevolent smile. "During those tumultuous days, there were, of course, factions, even within the Barony. Some people remained loyal to the Lazax emperors – contemptible lapdogs, unworthy even to be called Letnev, but they possessed power and influence. These divisions expanded into the aristocracy, with some nobles siding with the empire, and others with the revolutionaries. The nobles fought with the tools they always had: private armies, assassination, hostage-taking. There happened to be one nobleman, highly placed in our society, who was also a brilliant scientist, adept at all matters biological. He was loyal to the revolution – indeed, he was a hero of that war. His wife was pregnant, and very nearly ready to give birth to the family's only heir, when he was attacked by his cowardly enemies. He fled, his wife dying from her wounds, his unborn child's life in grave danger as well. He vanished from our history then, and we all believed he was dead, his line and legacy extinguished... until we reached this planet and began our survey. Our sensors picked up the same bunker your father found – fortunately, it was close to the surface and its seal was broken, or else we might have missed it entirely. Such places are often shielded from detection, you see, when their systems are intact." Voyou leaned forward, smiling at Bianca with his small, even teeth. "We found the skeleton. We found the incubation chamber. We accessed the computer systems there, and have spent the last weeks analyzing the data. That skeleton belongs to your *true* father, the nobleman and scientist Ranulph Malladoc – we have confirmed this definitively. You are also the daughter of Adeliza Malladoc, a noblewoman in her own right, who must, sadly, have passed away en route to this remote place, where your true father took refuge. Your father took you from her dying body and placed you in stasis."

"I waited in that cavern to be born for thousands of years?" Bianca said.

Voyou nodded. "So it seems. Your father was a scientist beyond compare, even for one who lived in that age of wonders – his brilliance is what made him a target for his enemies, of course."

Bianca shook her head. "I don't understand. Why did he keep me locked away in some machine? Why not just let me be born, and raise me?"

"These are excellent questions, and display the sort of keen mind I would expect the heir to the Malladoc name to have. Sadly, the records we found were incomplete, and partially corrupted. Based on what we could read, and our own extrapolations, I suspect your father intended to wait until things were safe for him at home before bringing you fully to term. Doubtless he wished to raise you in the Barony, rather than in this savage place. Before he could return home, though, some tragedy befell him. We do not know how he died. His remains were far too old to provide useful information. Perhaps he suffered wounds himself in the escape. Perhaps it was something as simple as an infection. Or–"

"She doesn't look anything like the Letnev," Willen broke in. "Her skin isn't blue. This doesn't make any sense!"

"That skeleton didn't look much like you either," Keon said with a frown.

"Do not humans come in a variety of hues and shapes?" Voyou smiled. "The Letnev are the same. Oh, most of us have a bluish tint these days, but some are far paler. The Lady Malladoc doesn't resemble *you* much more than she resembles *me*, does she? Why, to an alien eye, you might not even seem the same species – she is smaller, her skin and hair differs from yours, and so on. Over the course of so many thousands of years, a species must be expected to change its appearance somewhat. I assure you, your adopted daughter is the very epitome of beauty, by the standards of imperial-era Letnev."

"So, she's a princess." Keon crossed his arms. "Fine. What does that mean?"

The undercommandant spread his hands. "It means her life is about to change, and infinitely for the better. While the noble families no longer possess the absolute power they once held in Letnev society, the Lady Malladoc *is* the heir to great estates and wealth."

"Surely after thousands of years there'd be nothing left," Willen said.

"You too show a keen mind!" Voyou said. "The Malladoc assets were indeed dispersed, when their line was believed to be finished, but Barony inheritance law is complex, and your daughter had many other powerful relatives. Portions of at least a dozen assorted estates have been held in escrow while a legitimate heir is sought. Those will be hers. I have also mentioned the Barony's ongoing attempts to recover *old* property and holdings, like the planet Darit. Some of the properties scheduled for reclamation are the rightful property of your daughter."

Bianca stared at him. "Wait… do you mean I'll own houses, and fields, and things?"

"My lady," Voyou said. "I do mean that, but I don't mean *just* that. I mean you'll own islands. I mean you'll own continents. I mean you'll own *moons*."

Moons. "If I were reading this in a story," Bianca said, "this is the part where I would 'faint dead away in shock.' But I've never felt more awake in my life."

"You want to take Bee away from us?" Willen said. She took Keon's hand and squeezed it tight.

Voyou shook his head. "I would not dream of *taking* a lady of her stature anywhere she did not wish to go. But, yes, she does have the option, if she wishes, to join me on my ship. I have informed my superiors of her presence, and they have authorized me to take her to one of her ancestral properties."

One of my properties. "Undercommandant," she said. "This is a lot to think about. If I go, can I take my parents with me?"

They looked even more terrified at the prospect of *that* than they had at the possibility of losing her, she realized, but then, they actually liked the rhythms of life here, and found the sameness comforting in a way Bianca never had.

But Voyou was shaking his head. "We cannot accommodate your parents on our ship, I'm afraid. Normally we wouldn't take on any passengers at all – the *Grim Countenance* is a Barony military ship, not a transport vessel – but these are special circumstances. An exception has been made for you, my lady, but only for you. Once you are settled, of course, you can send for your parents if you like. You'll have ample resources to send more comfortable transport for them." He looked around the room. "Or, if your parents prefer to stay here, you can make sure they are amply provided for, and live in comfort forever."

Bianca leaned forward. "I'm going to need an advance."

Voyou looked at her blankly. "I'm sorry?"

"You're proposing to take away one-third of the labor force of a working farm," Bianca said. "My parents will have to hire help if I leave. They'll need to be compensated for that." Her mother and father looked from her to the undercommandant and back again like they were watching a spirited game of bounceball.

"Surely you're of marriageable age, and would be leaving the farm soon anyway?" There was a gleam in Voyou's eyes that made her think, improbably, that he was *enjoying* this, but then, you probably didn't get to run a planetary annexation team if you didn't enjoy sparring, even of the verbal kind.

"Any pair-bonding arrangement would involve a reciprocal work exchange," Bianca said. "My partner's family would provide labor or tangible goods to balance the benefits of me joining their family. That's simple economics. Surely if I have such vast resources coming to me soon, compensating my family for the cost of my departure should be trivial?"

Voyou leaned back and crossed one leg over the other, then laced his fingers together over the knee. "I am authorized to make such arrangements. I must say, you're very practical and level-headed for someone who just had her entire understanding of her world and her self transformed."

"I grew up on a farm," Bianca said. "You can look up at the stars as much as you want, as long as you remember to shovel all the dung first." She glanced at her parents. "We'll need to talk this over as a family."

"Would, say, ten minutes suffice? The *Grim Countenance* is leaving shortly."

Bianca snorted. "Don't be ridiculous. Even if I decide to go, I'd have to make arrangements, say my goodbyes, pack–"

"There is nothing here that you *need*, believe me. We can provide all–"

"Even if you'll feed and clothe me, there are matters of sentimental value."

Voyou sniffed. "Sentimental? That's not a very Letnev thing to say, but then, you weren't raised among your people, so it's understandable." He rose. "I can give you, mmm, seven local hours, and even then, you'll have to come to town to catch the shuttle."

"You want her to leave home in the middle of the night?" her father burst out.

"Where I am from, Monsieur Xing, it is *always* the middle of the night. And yes. That is when the *Grim Countenance* is departing this system." He smiled faintly. "Don't worry, there will be Letnev officials stationed in all the villages. The Lowcliff governor will be moving into your burgher's house, I believe. If you wish to send a message to your daughter, you may contact him, and receive any replies in the same way." He bowed smartly to Bianca, turned, and walked out of the house.

The Xings sat, silently, as they listened to the shuttle spin up its engine, roar, rise, and gradually fade to silence, except for the distant bleating of the caprids.

After a beat of quiet, her father burst out, "Bianca, you can't go!"

Bianca looked at him, an almost physical pain in her chest. "Pa…" she began, but her mother put her hand on his arm instead.

"Our little Bee was always going to fly away, Keon," she said. "I half expected to wake up some morning and find her gone a-wandering, with just a note left behind."

Bianca reached across the table and took their hands. "I love you both. But… I think I need to see what all this means. If I really am what he says, then I can help the family, help the farm, help all of Darit, even. And if the truth is something else, if this story he told us is *just* a story, I should find out why they lied."

"Maybe it's true," Keon said. "What that man said, it does explain things, about the… birthing chamber, or whatever it was. I'm sorry we never told you the truth about how we found you, Bianca. We just, we wanted you to feel like you *belonged.*"

She'd never felt like she belonged, but not because of anything her parents had done. There was just something waiting for her out there in the stars. She'd always known it. Now she might find out what. "You did make me feel that way," she said. "You always did."

"What will you do with your last hours?" her mother said. "Say goodbye to Grandly?"

Bianca had never been as attached to Grandly as everyone else, including Grandly, wanted her to be. "Maybe," she said. "But I have to go see someone else first."

CHAPTER 8

"Your majesty." Torvald puffed on a foul-smelling pipe, the stench of which not even the advanced air filters in his bunker could fully neutralize. "Your *Baronic* majesty? Is that the adjective?"

"They didn't give me a book of protocol." Bianca flopped back on Torvald's cot. Her parents had fussed over her and cried and put together a care package of her favorite jerky and dried fruit and so forth for hours, and Bianca didn't have much time left before she had to go to the village to catch her ride off the planet. "What do you make of all this?"

"Hmm?" Torvald said. "Oh, you mean their story, and you being a princess and all? Total nonsense."

Bianca stared at the shiny metal curve of the ceiling and sighed. "Yeah. I thought so, too."

"For one thing, Darit was never a Barony holding. I dug deep enough into the database to confirm my recollection for real and for sure. We were part of the Federation of Sol, the bitterest enemies the Barony of Letnev had. There's no way an aristocrat from the Barony would have hidden out on a planet full of humans, even in the midst of a civil war, unless he was some kind of traitor who'd allied himself with the humans, and then the Barony would hardly be welcoming you back, now would they? If that part of the story is a lie, and it is…" He shrugged.

"Then there's no reason to believe any of it," Bianca said. "But if I'm *not* a secret princess, why do they really want me?"

"Something to do with the non-standard nature of your birth, I'd guess," Torvald said. "Could you do me a favor, Bee?"

"What?"

"Stand up there and lift up your shirt, just enough to show me your belly."

She sat up on the bunk and glared at him. "The last person who asked me to lift my shirt was Grandly, Torvald, and I was fool enough to do it for him, though I didn't get much out of the experience myself. Why do *you* want me to do it? You've never been creepy before."

Torvald burst out laughing, which she found reassuring. "Bianca, you don't have to worry about that. For one thing, you're an ill-tempered irritant, and for another, you're an infant, but the main thing is – have you ever wondered why I don't have a wife and a whole mess of children around here? My romantic preferences lie in *other directions*, if you see what I mean."

Bianca's face warmed up. She herself was attracted to men and women and androgynes, but she'd never thought of old Torvald being attracted to *anyone*, because he was *old*. "Gross. Fine. You'd better have a good reason, though." She lifted up her shirt, just enough to show her stomach.

Torvald peered at her, then nodded and puffed his pipe. "You've got a navel."

"*Everyone* has a navel," she said.

He shrugged. "It suggests their story isn't entirely caprid-shit, is all. The database says it is indeed possible to grow a baby from scratch in a laboratory, but if you never spent time in a person's womb, that means you never had an umbilical cord, and then you wouldn't have that little dimple full of lint on your stomach. That suggests you *were* inside a mother at some point, even if that mother wasn't a Letnev aristocrat." He cocked his head. "Unless."

"Unless what?"

"Oh, nothing, I've always had a twisty and treacherous sort of mind."

"Out with it, old man. I can't go into space wondering what you're not telling me."

"I keep thinking about the way your pa cut his hand," Torvald said. "A drop of blood on his fingertip, and the next day there's a baby. A *human* baby, as far as we can tell, though skin color aside, our species does look enough like the Letnev that's it's hard to tell."

"You think the machine, what, took a sample of my father's blood and used that as a blueprint to make me?"

Torvald shook his head. "You'd look more like your ma and pa if that was the case. That skeleton watching over the machinery *wasn't* human, though, and it doesn't sound like it was Letnev, either. Why would you turn out to look so human, in that case? What I'm wondering is, did the machine take a sample of your pa to find out what the local people are made of? What if the birthing chamber used that information to tweak your design parameters, to make sure you'd conform to local norms, physiologically speaking? If that's the case, you looking like a human is just a good disguise, and that belly button you've got there might just be a convincing detail the machine added on."

Bianca frowned. "That seems like a stretch. You're always telling me the simpler explanation is usually the right one."

Torvald shrugged. "I'm just wondering out loud, that's all. But Bianca, whatever you're caught up in now, it's not simple, so maybe my old saws don't cut as well in this situation. This whole thing is so strange, there's not a simple explanation to cover it. I sure wish we could run a test or two, though, maybe peek into your genetic code and see what's going on there, but I don't have that capability down here. The nearest place with decent medical facilities is days away, too."

"I wish I could just believe them." Bianca slumped. "It's such a *nice* story. I'd love to be a secret princess. What if they want to cut me open or something? Maybe I should run away and hide."

"If they really wanted to find you, they would," Torvald said. "They wouldn't even have to look that hard, would they? They could just burn your parents' farm, or kill one of them and broadcast word that they'd kill the other if you didn't come home."

Bianca shuddered. "Would they really do that?"

"The head they put on a spike a few villages over wasn't a cultural anomaly, unless the Letnev have become a more peaceful and relaxed race since my database was last updated. But as for cutting you open… I think you can rest easy there, Bee. If they wanted to hurt you, they'd have just snatched you and been done with it. Nobody here could stop them, after all. If they wanted to look at your genetic code, they could have plucked a hair or come up with some excuse to take a blood sample. No, whatever they want from you, they need your cooperation to do it, or they wouldn't have spun you such a tempting tale."

"Maybe I'm the daughter of a *human* aristocrat, and they want to ransom me back, or something."

"Maybe," Torvald said. "Maybe someone in the Federation of Sol, if it even still exists, gives enough of a damn about family history from thousands of years ago to make that worth the Barony's while." He took another puff. "I'd enjoy reading a novel about something like that, sure enough. No matter what the truth turns out to be, though, you're getting what you always wanted, albeit in something of a roundabout way. You're leaving all the caprids and mud behind and going to the stars."

Bianca nodded, but with a sour face. "I never thought about everything I'd *miss*!" she cried. "Pa's cooking, Ma's songs, nights sitting around the fire reading, even visiting *you*, old man. I'll even miss Grandly, a little, looking at me with those big eyes like he's a caprid hoping I'll give him something to eat. He made me feel special and important, anyway."

"Grandly won't be the last one to look at you that way, Bee. And you're some kind of special and important anyway, it seems. You just have to find out what. I've got a little gift for you." He reached into the front pocket of his overalls and fished out something that glittered: a ring of some moon-bright polished metal. "Why don't you slip this on? And if the Barony people ask about it, tell them it's a promise ring from your beau or something of the sort."

Bianca took the ring and held it up to the light. Pretty, in a plain way. "I'm not sure we're ready to get engaged, Torvald. I have some concerns about your ability to support our inevitable brood."

"Me, support you? I was thinking the other way around. Why else would I want to marry a princess? You can keep me in the manner to which I wish to become accustomed." He grinned. "That ring's a piece of old tech, taken off a skeleton found beneath a tree uprooted in the last real big storm. Damnedest thing I've ever seen. That skeleton had been in the ground so long the roots of the tree had grown all through the ribs. I thought the ring was just a bit of shiny and took to wearing it myself, and I'd fiddle with it sometimes, twist it this way and that. One day, I twisted it just right, and fried the insides of a mech I was repairing." He leaned forward. "I assume the ring was used for self-defense. Wear it on your finger, and twist it *all* the way around, counterclockwise, exactly three-hundred-sixty degrees, no more and no less. I put a little scratch in it on the side there so it's easier to tell when you've gone all the way around. Do that, and the next thing you touch with that hand will get one hell of an electric shock. Enough to overload a machine or paralyze a person, according to my voltmeter. Somehow the ring shields the wearer from its effects, so don't worry about hurting yourself, just others. It has a little integrated battery that I have no idea how to recharge, and think it only has a jolt or two left in it. I hope you'll never need to use it, but if there's ever a proper emergency, maybe it'll give you an edge the cause of that emergency won't see coming."

A piece of tech like that, a remnant of a lost age, was worth a year's supply of food at least, and Torvald was just giving it to her. Tears welled in Bianca's eyes, and she dashed them away, then slipped the treasure onto her finger. She held out her hand and tilted it to and fro, as if she was a girl admiring a real promise ring. "In that case, sir, I accept your proposal." She frowned. "Torvald, you've got such treasures down here… this ring, that database… if the Letnev found the bunker where I was born, or made, or whatever, won't they find this one?"

"I asked the database that, too," he said. "There are working countermeasures in place to keep this bunker shielded from detection, and the tons of junk upstairs should baffle their sensors even further. They only found the chamber where you were born so easily because it was cracked open and exposed to the air. I don't think they'll notice me down here." He shrugged. "Which isn't to say I don't *worry* about them noticing, but the Letnev were so excited about finding the place you came from I hope they got distracted from looking too closely for anything more."

"You should clear out anyway," Bianca said. "Pour concrete in the opening to the elevator, so if they *do* find the bunker you can pretend you didn't even know it was under your house all this time."

"That is a wise proposal, and if it makes you feel better, I can tell you I'll consider it." Torvald rose. "I reckon you should be on your way to the up-and-out. It's been nice knowing you, Bianca Xing. I'll give you the same advice my father gave me the first time he sent me out to the woods to search for salvage on my own: 'Be careful, but not too careful; be bold, but not too bold.'"

She stood up too, and started to twist the ring, then stopped herself. *That* was a habit of fidgeting she'd better not fall into. "You talk like I'm never coming back, Torvald. Of course I will. Whether I'm a princess or something else, I'll come back."

"I believe you intend to, and I hope you will, Bee. But the world is big, and you're going beyond the world, into something a whole lot bigger. You don't need to make me any promises, except to take care of yourself as best you can."

He embraced her and kissed her on the cheek, his whiskery chin tickling her. He'd never done that before. Torvald pulled back and winked. "Go on, then. Make a name for yourself, earn your fortune, conquer the galaxy, or whatever other damnfool thing you've got a mind to do."

The ride back up in the elevator was long, and the walk over the dark hills to her house was longer still. All three moons were up, so it was bright, but she knew the way well enough to traverse what obstacles there were even in total darkness. She wouldn't be traveling paths that familiar again for a long time – if ever. She was going where everything was new.

When she reached the field closest to her house, and saw the lights still burning there, waiting for her, she stopped, and looked up at the sky, and the black patch between that triangle of stars. *I'm on my way*, she thought.

Her parents went with her to the village – there was no stopping that – but otherwise there was no seeing-off party. They'd acceded to her wishes and promised not to tell Grandly or anyone else she was gone until tomorrow at the earliest. The village was sleeping, except for the shuttle from the *Grim Countenance*, crouched like a predatory insect in the clear space behind the Halemeeting hall. They had wrestling matches and dances in that spot when the weather was fair. Everything really had changed.

Voyou emerged from the shuttle, strolling down the ramp to meet them. "Right on time, even though as far as I can tell no one has an accurate clock on this entire planet. The punctuality is appreciated. Perhaps it's your Letnev heritage asserting itself."

I'm no Letnev, Bianca thought, but she only smiled. "I learned to be on time from my parents. It's only polite. And we don't need clocks. We have the sun, the moons, the stars, the animals, and our bellies, after all."

"All quite alien to my experience, I'm afraid," Voyou said. "Except for my belly. We should really get going. Say your farewells and come aboard."

Bianca hugged and kissed her parents, and admired them for not breaking down; they'd done plenty of breaking down earlier, but it wasn't as if they would exhaust their supply of worry anytime soon. They bore up, though, and soon Bianca lifted her small knapsack, waved, and walked up the ramp to whatever her future held.

CHAPTER 9

Heuvelt sat in his cell and contemplated his dinner. There was a mound of something gray that smelled like fish, and a mound of something green that smelled like brine, and a mound of something yellow and gelatinous that smelled acidic. He had his doubts about whether any of it was meant for human consumption. The tray itself honestly seemed more edible than anything on top of it.

The Winnaran bartender-turned-officer walked in and peered at him through the bars, her arms folded across her chest. She still wore her pull-tab necklace, which he'd assumed was an affectation for her undercover role, but now she was dressed in a sleek, black, well-fitted uniform.

"Hello," Heuvelt said. "Have you come to bring me my change? I paid *far* too much for that drink."

She smiled. "Your story checked out, Mr Angriff. You really did have a run of terrible luck, though it seems a rich kid like you could have bought your way out by now."

"I am in my thirties, officer," he said. "In human terms, that no longer qualifies as a 'kid.' I also no longer qualify as 'rich.'"

"How did you get mixed up with a data smuggling operation?"

"I have no idea what you're talking about," Heuvelt said. "I merely went to a bar to have a drink, and a strange Hylar tried to steal my briefcase full of empty data sticks. I tried to get away from the chaos that ensued, and you hit me in the head with a sink. Be glad I'm not a rich kid anymore. Rich kids have voracious lawyers."

She nodded. "You're right. We checked all those data sticks, and there's nothing on any of them, so we don't have any legal grounds to keep you."

He stood up. "I'll be going, then?"

She smiled. "We were *going* to process your release, but it's all a bit complicated, because of how muddled your history is. It seems you're still technically a wanted criminal in the Barony of Letnev – their bureaucracy takes forever to update their records, and they really hate admitting they were wrong about anything. While we don't have an extradition arrangement with them, my superiors think this could be a good opportunity for a trade. We give them something they want, and we get something we want, like that."

Heuvelt slumped. "I see. Please, tell me what action I can take to inspire your superiors to release me instead of handing me over to a notoriously punitive militaristic nation."

"You're pretty smart, for a rich kid. If you happened to know the location of a data stick with stolen cryptographic keys on it, the sort of thing that a criminal consortium might pay medium-good money for, why, we'd be so busy and excited by the news that we'd probably forget all about handing you over to the Letnev."

"Perhaps there might even be a reward for this information?"

"I've always found that freedom is its own reward, Mr Angriff."

"Have you really?" Heuvelt knew when he was beaten. He had lots of practice. He gave her the coordinates of the buried data stick, and she went away. Four hours later she returned and personally escorted him out of the facility, into the cold, dark, desert night.

"You're free to go, Mr Angriff."

He looked around. "Go *where*? What happened to my sand-skidder?"

"Your vehicle was impounded. It won't be processed and ready for release for eight or ten weeks. But it's a lovely night for walking, isn't it?"

"A lovely night for many things." He gave her his most charming grin, which was a shadow of its former self, but not without some lingering potency. "What's your name, officer?" She really was quite attractive, and perhaps *something* could be salvaged from this disaster.

"My name is Sergeant Get Off My Planet and Never Come Back."

"I suppose that means you won't let me buy you a drink?"

"You already bought me a drink, rich kid. I kept all your coins, remember?" She sauntered back into the long, low building, and Heuvelt was alone.

The authorities had returned his comm bracelet, at least, so he called the *Show and Tell*, half expecting an "out of range" error message. That would be a suitable new chapter in the saga of Heuvelt Angriff, outcast scion of the Angriff Industries fortune, gentleperson adventurer turned scurrilous rascal: stranded on a desert planet controlled by an aquatic race, with the local criminal element doubtless highly motivated to show him the opposite of hospitality.

To his pleasant surprise, the growling voice of Ashont, his Rokha first mate, said, "Heuvelt? Are you all right?"

"I am alive," he said. "I suppose that counts. Can you come pick me up?"

Once he was back on board the *Show and Tell*, Heuvelt just wanted to retreat to his cabin with his last bottle of sorghum whiskey, but he had to debrief his crew first. Ashont and Clec were waiting for him in the galley – together, of course, because they were *always* together.

Ashont was Rokha, and Clec was Naaz, but of course the species were seldom spoken of as individuals: they were the Naaz-Rokha Alliance, physically dissimilar aliens who shared a culture and history as well as a symbiotic relationship that Heuvelt sometimes envied, when he wasn't feeling too misanthropic: the Naaz-Rokha never had to be alone. Oh, it wasn't like they were physically or psychically bound together, but by culture and preference they seldom spent much time or distance apart, and it must have been a comfort, knowing you could really trust someone like that. Heuvelt absently touched the scar on his face.

Ashont was a panther-like humanoid, all sleek black fur and round green eyes and bright white canines. Heuvelt's family had pet cats growing up, and it was tempting to think of Ashont as a giant housecat… but her eyes had round pupils, not slit ones. Ashont had helpfully explained that cats with slit pupils were ambush predators, and cats with round eyes were "Active predators. We chase down our prey." The Rokha were relatives of the lion-like Hacan, but evolved in the jungle rather than desert or savannah climes, and the two species had diverged countless millennia before and didn't share much in the way of culture anymore. The Rokha were known as mercenaries, and for most of their history had been nomadic wanderers, traveling from place to place and job to job, without a homeworld to call their own. That changed when they met the Naaz.

Clec often rode around in a sort of open-weave harness Ashont wore on her back, but at that moment, the Naaz was perched on her shoulder. Clec was diminutive, smaller than a human toddler, with four arms, a bulbous head, and large eyes. Two of the arms clung to Ashont, and the other two were busily disassembling some small engine component. Clec was Heuvelt's first mate *too* – they'd insisted on sharing the rank equally, as their peoples shared everything – but in practice Ashont was the pilot and navigator and Clec was the ship's engineer. The Naaz were a highly intelligent race, adept at science and engineering, but they had a long history of falling prey to powerful oppressors. In ancient times their homeworld had been invaded by a Winnu corporation, then conquered by deserters from the Federation of Sol, and so on, changing hands countless times over the centuries, their people always under the heel of a new overlord who wanted to exploit their world and their population, until the Naaz finally had enough, and hired the vast Rokha military army. With the help of those famous soldiers, the Naaz finally won their freedom, and they offered the nomadic Rokha a place on their homeworld in exchange. Their reasons had doubtless been practical: a way to keep the army without paying mercenary prices, and to make the Rokha more invested in defending their now-shared homeworld. Yet, somehow, that pragmatic arrangement had blossomed over the centuries into a true shared culture.

Heuvelt found their history astonishing. The Naaz looked like something the Rokha would hunt for sport, but the two species were by now so closely associated that if you saw one without the other, you knew a terrible tragedy must have occurred. Even on their homeworld, they lived in mixed households, a Naaz couple and a Rokha couple cohabiting together and rearing one another's young collectively. Heuvelt didn't like to imagine what it was like for such a species to *date*, but maybe it was all arranged marriages or something. He'd deliberately never inquired about the details of Naaz-Rokha love lives.

"I take it things went badly?" Clec said.

"It could have gone worse, but it went bad enough." He sat down and told them the tale of woe.

Once he was finished, Ashont clucked her tongue and put a bowl of protein mush in front of him. "Eat. They never feed you right in jail." She treated Heuvelt like he was one of her cubs, sometimes, but right now he didn't mind.

"We have the half of the payment we were given up front for the delivery," Clec said. "So we can, at least, afford the fuel to get off this planet. We need to line up another job, though, and soon."

"We should be transporting a hold full of ice-mink furs, or sun-spice, or the singing beads of Halcyon-IV," Heuvelt said. "Not grubbing around like lowly smugglers."

"We are smugglers," Clec said. "Not lowly ones, though. Excellent ones. I'll point out, you did your job exactly as you were hired to do, except for the last bit, and that was outside your control."

"Carrying any cargo at all is a waste of our time and talents," Heuvelt grumbled. "We should be exploring new worlds in search of treasure, seeking our fortune among uncharted stars!"

"It's hard to seek your fortune that way if you don't already have a fortune to start with," Clec pointed out. "Financing that kind of expedition isn't cheap. How about we make some more money this way, and then we can go... out there." She waved one of her nimble-fingered hands vaguely skyward.

"Or not," Ashont said. "Treasure-hunting didn't work out so well for you last time, Mr Scar. Making an honestly dishonest living will be good for you. It builds character."

"I have quite enough character already, thank you. If anything, I have too much." He looked up from his bowl. "I was a day late returning, and didn't send you any messages. Why didn't you two leave me?"

Clec and Ashont glanced at each other, and Heuvelt sensed that a vast quantity of information was silently shared in that look. Ashont was the one who spoke. "Our people understand loyalty, Heuvelt. We aren't like Dob Ell. We won't betray you."

"We also won't spend your entire life pretending to be your best friend when, in reality, we were just paid to do that by your parents," Clec added. "So we won't have any pent-up decades of grudges to take out on you when those payments stop coming. See the difference?"

"Now that you point it out, the distinction does seem clear."

"We are *partners*," Ashont said. "We own half the ship, and you own the other half, and we are stronger together. There was no question of us leaving you."

Clec made a noise of agreement. "We were already tracking down your location and planning a jailbreak, in fact. I'm glad we didn't have to follow through. Even my best calculations showed only a seventy-three percent chance of success. But we would have tried."

Heuvelt lowered his head so they wouldn't see the tears welling in his eyes. They were a fine crew, and more than that, they would be his friends, if he let them. Did he dare hope they might someday become… family? His own family had always been cold, until they cut him off, and then that cold had plunged further, to absolute zero. His closest other relationship, with Dob Ell, had proven to be a sham. "I don't have much practice with this sort of thing," Heuvelt said. "But I will try to be worthy of your loyalty."

"Good," Clec said. "You can start by not arguing when we tell you what we have to do next."

"What's that?"

"We need to take that job from Sagasa," Ashont said.

Heuvelt groaned. Sagasa was a Hacan who ran a shady shipyard, scrap, and salvage operation near Vega Major. Nicknamed "The Disciplinarian" , Sagasa was trustworthy as far as criminals went, but he was also famously unforgiving when it came to failure. Ashont was connected to him vaguely through a series of cousins, and an offer for a high-speed transport job had come through recently. Clec and Ashont had argued in favor of accepting the job, but Heuvelt had resisted, because working for the Disciplinarian meant fully immersing himself in the criminal world, a fate he still half-hoped to avoid. "There has to be another job we can take."

"Not one this simple and lucrative," Clec said. "More importantly, this job would lead to *more* jobs."

"It's basically the work you planned to do when you first bought this ship," Ashont added. "We'd just be transporting high-end goods for wealthy clients."

"I meant wealthy *legitimate* clients."

"Legitimate rich people are just criminals successful enough to manipulate governments and bribe lawmakers," Clec said. "Sagasa is practically a government of his own."

"We could take a vote," Ashont said.

"You two always vote together," Heuvelt said. "You only own half the ship, so you should only get one vote anyway."

"Then we'd always have ties," Clec said. "We'd never get anything done. This way is much better."

"I vote yes," Ashont said.

"Me too," Clec said.

Heuvelt sighed. "I suppose it's unanimous, then."

"I do so like it when we're unified in purpose," Clec said.

• • •

A basic tenet of the freight business held that there was nothing worse than traveling with an empty hold, so they picked up some replacement parts for decommissioned Hylar vessels from a nearby wholesaler trying to clear out a warehouse. If nothing else, Sagasa would pay them *slightly* more than the parts had cost – enough to cover the fuel it took to get to his scrapyard, anyway.

The trip to Vega Major required a jump through a wormhole, and Heuvelt always got nauseated during those – space-time distortions were bad for his digestion – so he hunkered down in his cabin while Ashont and Clec handled the transit.

Heuvelt stared at the bulkhead above his bunk and thought about the future. He didn't want to be a smuggler. He wanted to see *new* things, stand on planets that no human had ever seen before, smash open alien crypts and plunder the contents, make first contact with new species – do something important, exciting, and meaningful. As a child he'd had every material comfort, but he'd grown up feeling empty and without purpose. Losing those material comforts hadn't suddenly imbued him with any sort of suffering-based enlightenment, though; now he was just empty and purposeless and *poor*, which was even worse. Was it so much to ask, to be rich *and* feel like your life had a purpose?

Ashont and Clec never seemed to worry about such things. They just got on with the job at hand. Heuvelt would have to try and do that too. Focus on the now, and the future would come… or maybe, at least, he could stop thinking about it so much.

"We're here," Clec called on the comms.

Heuvelt made his way to the front of the ship and gazed out at what appeared to be the aftermath of a vast space battle, but was, in fact, just Sagasa's scrapyard: hundreds of ships ranging from seemingly intact to blackened wrecks and every state in between. He'd never seen so much broken metal in one place. "There's a space station in the middle of all that?" he said.

"Quite a nice one, too, from what I hear," Clec said. "But we won't be visiting it today. Sagasa is sending a ship out to meet us, take our spare parts away, and deliver our package."

"There's one interesting thing," Ashont said. "When Sagasa heard we were traveling with you, he said he'd throw in a complimentary refuel, 'as a way of making things square between us.'"

"What does *that* mean?" Heuvelt said. He'd never had any dealings with the Disciplinarian.

Clec replied. "He also said, 'Tell Angriff I thought he was dead when I sold his ID to those pirates.'"

Heuvelt widened his eyes. "*Sagasa* stole my identity?"

"We told him the whole identity theft issue was still causing you problems," Clec said. "Sagasa offered to purge your name from the remaining criminal databases as a bonus if we complete this mission early, and with the fuel he's giving us, that shouldn't be a problem."

"Oh, I see," Heuvelt said. "He ruins my good name, but he offers to *fix* it, as a reward! Isn't *that* nice."

"By the standards of Sagasa the Disciplinarian, that is beyond nice," Ashont said. "I told him we would be most grateful to accept his offer."

"Your name wasn't all that good to start with anyway," Clec said. "At least you'll be able to get a proper credit account again."

"Then I could begin my legitimate courier business!" That was a happy thought.

"There's more money to be made being illegitimate," Clec said. "Especially if we get more jobs from Sagasa."

"Which means we could go on a treasure-hunting adventure that much sooner," Ashont added.

"But whatever you want," Clec said.

"We're easy," Ashont said.

Heuvelt recalled his recent decision to focus on the present. "Let's just complete the job in front of us. What are we delivering, anyway?"

"Sagasa just said 'biological materials'," Clec said. "We're taking them to a space station run by a member of the Yin Brotherhood."

"Huh," Heuvelt said. "'Biological materials' could be a euphemism for so *many* horrible things. And as for the Yin, I have to confess, I know it's an irrational prejudice, but I find clones a little bit creepy. Don't you?"

They shared another one of those information-rich glances, mostly inscrutable to Heuvelt. "You should probably let us handle client relations on this one, then," Ashont said.

CHAPTER 10

The interior of the shuttle was just one long room, with a pilot and co-pilot seated up front, two rows of three seats each in the middle, and bulky storage lockers running along the walls on either side. Voyou was already seated in the front row, strapping himself in. "Stow your gear there." He pointed to an open locker. "I'm pleased to see you didn't bring any livestock with you."

"You seem very cheerful, Undercommandant." She put her bag into the bin and secured the compartment – it latched just like the feed bins at home – and then sat down in the same row, with the middle seat empty between them. The straps here were different from those used in the trailrunner, of course, but the design was intuitive enough: you slipped a metal tab into a slot and there was a click when it locked, with a simple button-push to release it.

Voyou nodded. "Have you noticed it's never properly dark on your planet, Lady Malladoc? The sun… well, I was prepared for the sun. We have a special lotion to protect us from its rays, my uniform hat has a brim, and I have lenses in my eyes that adjust to keep me from being blinded. But I thought, when the sun went down, there would be something resembling *darkness* – not the case. Those moons! Three of them. Far too many moons, and all shining, all night long."

"Sometimes just one or two are visible, and there are a few nights when they're all below the horizon at once," Bianca said.

"Do your people revel in blessed peace then?"

She shook her head. "Those are festival nights. We light big fires. Part of an old ritual, I think, meant to call the moons back? But now it's just an excuse for a party."

Voyou shuddered. "I cannot understand such an impulse. To be surrounded by darkness is to be safe and secure and home. Do *you* like the dark, my lady?"

She was neutral about the dark. There were times it was nice, and times it was inconvenient. "My favorite part of the sky is the blackness between the stars."

The undercommandant was quiet for a moment, and then he barked out a laugh. "Perhaps you really *are* Letnev."

"So I'm told." The shuttle began to hum, far more muffled from the inside than the outside. She looked around, wishing for windows – the only ones in the ship were those up front. It would be nice to see the world shrink beneath her. The Letnev, it seemed, were not keen on looking outward. The shuttle lurched, but after that there was no sensation at all.

After (presumably) rising in silence for a few moments, she said, "Is it true there's no sun on your world? A friend of mine told me he'd heard that."

"The homeworld of the Barony, Arc Prime, has no star. We are not bound to a single system, locked in orbit, as other planets are. We are free to go wherever our ambitions take us."

"How do you live on a planet with no star? Isn't it cold?"

"Rather," he said. "We do not live on the surface, as a rule – it is inhospitable, even for a people as hardy as ours. We live in vast caverns underground, warmed by our planet's core."

"What do you eat? How do you *breathe*?"

"Oh, we have immense fungus farms, of course, and these days we have colony worlds to supply other resources. As for breathing, there is a plant called Ao, a blessed wonder, that grows in great profusion throughout the tunnels and caverns, supplying ample oxygen."

"I can't imagine living in such a place," Bianca said.

"You needn't necessarily settle on Arc Prime, my lady. There are many colony worlds under the Baron's care, and while I find most of them inhospitable, they might be more to your liking. You don't even have to live in the Barony, though once you see all we have to offer, I can't imagine why you'd want to live anywhere else."

"Where are we going now?" Bianca asked.

"Our immediate destination is known only to the captain," he said. "But I gather we'll be returning to civilization soon, and the restoration of your birthright will shortly follow."

"So, you aren't in charge of the ship, the *Grim Countenance*?"

He grimaced. "You flatter me, lady. No, I am merely one of several undercommandants sent to ensure a smooth transition of power during the annexation. I was given stewardship of the eastern half of this continent, though I have been reassigned to assist you instead. Perhaps I might someday command a vessel as fine as the *Grim Countenance*. Bringing you home should help my career immeasurably."

"What's the captain like?"

"Complicated," the undercommandant said. "Only a few members of the crew, the senior officers, have even seen her. She relays her orders remotely, or through subordinates. She prefers a level of anonymity. Some say she likes to dress as a common soldier and mingle with the crew, so she can see what's *really* happening on the ship."

"Wouldn't that sort of thing make everyone nervous and paranoid?" Bianca asked.

"I prefer to think it fosters an atmosphere of continual excellence." He craned his head, apparently checking to see if the pilot and co-pilot were paying attention, and then leaned over to whisper in Bianca's ear. "We hear rumors about her, though. They say she once ran a research facility, and when a leading scientist tried to defect to the humans she led a commando team to recover the traitor. When recovery proved impossible, the captain killed the traitor personally, and then kidnapped a scientist from the Federation of Sol to replace her. They say her favorite training exercise is to clear an entire deck of a ship and lock herself down there with a soldier, one armed with the best in Letnev technology, while the captain has only a knife. If you survive the experience, she puts in a good word for you with her superiors. As far as I know she hasn't organized any such exercises since I joined her command, but then, the annexation schedule has been very demanding."

"She sounds… formidable," Bianca said.

"All the Letnev are formidable. The captain is something else again, if the stories are true."

"I don't suppose I'll meet her?"

"I wouldn't count on it. She did instruct me to tell you that you are most welcome on board. That's not a sentiment she ever extended to me."

"How kind of her." Bianca's curiosity was piqued, but life would probably be easier if she *didn't* meet someone Voyou clearly found intimidating.

Voyou pointed toward the front of the ship. "There, look through the viewport, and you'll see the *Grim Countenance*, one of the many glories of the Barony."

Bianca turned her head and watched as a large, dark shape loomed larger still against a backdrop of blackness. "It looks like a muddy caprid," she blurted, and Voyou reared back as if she'd slapped him.

"Why in the dark do you say *that*?"

Bianca put a hand to her mouth to stifle a laugh. "I'm sorry, I just – it has all those, what, those curly bits–"

"Those are spikes." His voice was as cold as winter mud. "Our thorn ships strike terror into our enemies and ensure proper respect from our vassals."

"I'm sorry, I didn't mean anything, it's just, well, our caprids have that curly wool, you know, and sometimes there's a storm and they get all muddy, and then the sun comes out and the mud dries, and they end up covered with all these curving spiky sort of things and… well… it just struck me, that's all. The resemblance."

"I would refrain from mentioning that comparison to anyone else, my lady." Voyou sounded less affronted now, and more resigned. "The rest of the crew might not understand your charming country ways. Oh! Speaking of which. When we dock, I'll throw a cloak over you, and we'll rush you to your room, hidden from sight."

That sounded like something you'd do to a criminal, not a princess. "Why?"

"You are a lady of the Letnev aristocracy, a distant cousin to Baron Daz Emmicial Werqan III himself, and when the officers first get a glimpse of you, you should appear suitably regal, don't you think?"

Bianca looked down at herself. She was in her best Halemeeting dress, flowy white with little blue flowers stitched around the hem, and it was as clean as it could be. "What's wrong with what I'm wearing?"

"Nothing at all, from the local perspective. But you are now entering a world where the perspective is different. Wider. Unless you don't want new dresses and jewels and shoes?" He gazed at her with wide-eyed innocence, not an expression his face was suited for.

"I suppose I can at least *look* at them," she said.

Because of the cloak – it was more of a blanket, really – thrown over her head, she didn't get to see much of the *Grim Countenance's* hangar bay, which was too bad, since her knowledge of spacecraft came largely from novels and most of those were extremely old. As Voyou and the co-pilot guided her blindly along, each holding one of her elbows, she could hear banging, thumping, sizzling, grinding, and shouting, which suggested the hangar bay was a busy place, and not much fun.

Then again, maybe there was no fun to be had on the whole ship. She had delivered herself into the hands of people who put heads on spikes to make a point. She'd seen the Letnev as a means to an end, a way to escape Darit and set off into the galaxy (and, eventually, reach that dark spot in the sky that called to her), but she hadn't dwelled on the fact that she'd be in their custody and care for an indefinite interval. The Letnev were less a stepping stone and more of a way station. She'd just have to keep her head down and her eyes open, learn what she could, and wait for her moment to leap free if their true plans for her turned out to be unacceptable.

A tiny part of her hoped against hope that they *were* going to take her to a palace on her very own moon. Surely the world could be like stories *sometimes,* couldn't it?

Her escorts led her into a quieter portion of the ship. She hoped they'd reach their destination soon and that it wouldn't turn out to be a dungeon or something. It was hot under the cloak, which smelled like engine oil. "I must say, you're navigating the gravity here very well," Voyou said, his voice only a little muffled.

"What do you mean?"

"The artificial gravity on the ship is set at a slightly higher intensity than Darit's. I was afraid you'd find it uncomfortable."

Now that he mentioned it, she supposed she was working a little harder to walk than usual, but it was no more strenuous than making her way uphill, and she tended to leap up slopes anyway. "I've always been in good shape. Ma says I have enough energy for two girls."

"Oh, to be so young." Voyou was puffing a little. "Those weeks on your planet made me soft, and *I* certainly feel the extra weight. I'll have to get back to the gym soon. My exercise regime has suffered lately."

"I've heard of exercising," Bianca said. "I think the burgher's son used to stretch, and lift buckets of rocks and things? The rest of us … we just work, mostly. That seems like exercise enough."

"You need never work again, my lady," he said. "You can simply relax in splendor and comfort for the rest of your days."

That sounded awful. Bianca liked having things to do. Oh, it would be nice to be able to *choose* which things she did, and if she never had to shovel another heap of dung that would be fine, but a lifetime of indolence didn't appeal. She wanted to go places and do things. "How nice," she said.

"We've arrived." The co-pilot whipped the cloak off her. They stood before a gray metal door set in a gray metal wall. The light here was grim, with a lot more red in the spectrum than she was used to. She looked left and right, and saw more doors set at intervals along a narrow corridor in both directions. The overall effect of the place was claustrophobic. *They live in caverns,* she thought. *Being all squeezed and cramped probably makes them feel at home.*

"Touch the door, please – just press your hand against it, anywhere at all," Voyou said.

Bianca did as she was bid, the metal cold beneath her skin. The door made a grinding sound and then gave off a chime.

"There, now it's keyed to you," Voyou said. "Simply touch the door, and it will open to you."

"No one else?" Bianca said.

"*Almost* no one else. The security team has access, and the political officers, and of course the captain, but none of them would come in uninvited unless there was an emergency. Why don't you go in, familiarize yourself with your room, and get some rest? I'll be along to fetch you when it's time for breakfast. I'll bring your bag to you then too."

"Why can't I have it now?" There was nothing in the bag she really needed, but on the other hand it contained literally everything she owned.

"Luggage from the surface is subject to mandatory inspection. Your planet is full of filth and parasites and such, after all." Voyou bowed, then turned and walked away, co-pilot at his heels.

Bianca touched the door again. It swung open, and she stepped into a dim chamber of unknown dimensions. The door shut behind her, turning the dim into total darkness. Bianca swore softly. Could the Letnev see in the dark? Probably. Where were the lights?

"Hello, Bianca," a voice said in her ear, and Bianca screamed and swung her fist.

CHAPTER 11

Far from Darit, far from Elekayne, far from the path of the *Grim Countenance* or the course of the *Show and Tell*, far from any other inhabited or even habitable place in the galaxy, someone stirred in his slumber, deep underground. This was only the second time in two decades the sleeper had moved toward wakefulness, and before that he had not stirred for millennia. Things were *happening* now. A quickening was underway.

The sleeper's shrouded world was remote, but not unreachable. A series of relays hidden in asteroids, comets, and dead stars formed an invisible chain between his world and Darit; a chain that existed for the sole purpose of delivering simple supraluminal messages to the sleeper.

Two decades earlier the first message had arrived, and it said simply: *The child is born.* The sleeper swam up from the depths of his stasis to think, *Oh? Already?* Though he'd been awaiting that signal for millennia, his sleep was deep, and dreamless, and the passage of time was irrelevant to him in almost every way. Nothing that happened in the galaxy while the sleeper still slumbered had any meaning at all, of course. Because none of it would last for long after he woke again.

Now, nineteen years later, a second message came: *The child is on her way.*

The sleeper was not capable of smiling, but he felt pleasure.

There would be no more messages from distant Darit. The next alert would come from somewhere much closer to his silent world.

It was not yet time to wake, so the sleeper sank back into his long slumber, but as the darkness closed in around him, he thought: *Soon.*

CHAPTER 12

Bianca's fist didn't connect with anything, which was disappointing. She crouched and held up her hands. "Who's there?"

"I am Ayla," the voice said, smooth and uninflected. "Your artificial learning assistant. Would you like to turn on the lights?"

"Yes."

"Say 'lights.'"

"Lights?"

The room was hardly flooded with brightness, but it was illuminated by a red-tinged wash, revealing a space slightly smaller than her bedroom back home. There were storage cabinets just above head-height, a seat that folded down from the wall, and a door as long as she was tall set into the far wall. She didn't see a bed. That wasn't promising. Did the Letnev sleep standing up, like caprids, or was she expected to bunk on the floor?

There was no sign of whoever had spoken to her. Was this something like Torvald's database, then? A voice in the wall? "You said you're a … learning assistant?"

"That is correct. I am programmed to answer your questions and begin teaching you the rudiments of the Letnev language."

"Are you a mechanical intelligence, then? I've read about such things."

"True machine intelligences are rare in Barony space," the voice said. "Artificial intelligences often develop goals that are in opposition to the glory of the Barony. I am programmed to answer your questions and begin teaching you the rudiments of the Letnev language, as well as the most common trading argot."

"Yeah, you said," Bianca muttered. Ah, well. So much for making a mechanical friend. She'd sometimes talked to the caprids in the fields when she was lonely or needed to work things out in her mind, and talking to a robot wouldn't be any stranger than that. Although … she thought of Torvald telling her to be careful. A robot that could talk could also listen, couldn't it? It could even record what she said, or transmit her words in real time to a listening Letnev soldier. She'd have to watch her tongue. "Where am I supposed to sleep?"

"Your bunk folds down from the wall automatically during the designated rest interval. The Letnev are an industrious people, and do not require constant access to a bed, as some of the lazier races in the galaxy do."

"How about a bathroom? Or is the elimination of waste also something only lazier races do?"

"Hygiene facilities are located behind a wall panel, and may be accessed at will."

"That's something. Are there any other hidden amenities?"

"A desk with a terminal can also extend from the wall. The information accessible by the terminal is primarily in the Letnev language, however. Machine translation options are available, but since Letnev is the most sophisticated and nuanced tongue in the known galaxy, such translations are inherently inferior."

"I see." Bianca sat on the hard chair. The benches in the Halemeeting hall were more comfortable. "This room is pretty small. Is it some kind of jail cell?"

"This is the second-best cabin on the *Grim Countenance*," Ayla said. "Only the captain's is more spacious and luxurious."

Ah. She would have to adjust her interpretation of "palatial splendor" to fit Letnev standards. Her supposed estates were probably holes in the ground. Still, if this really was the second-best cabin, they were treating her like she mattered. "I was promised dresses," she said.

That long door on the wall swung open, and revealed a closet half again the size of the rest of the cabin. Bianca doubted it was intended as a closet – it was probably a guest bedroom or office or something – but she approved of the transformation. The closet held racks of hanging garments in rich dark colors, and a shelf full of shoes in similar hues. The inside of the door was studded with pegs that held necklaces, earrings, and bracelets, all glistening with gems in red and black and a blue so dark it was *almost* black.

Bianca's lips parted and she said "Ooohhhh," quite involuntarily. She reached out to touch one of the dresses – it was deep red, and shimmered like flowing water – and then stopped. "I need a shower before I touch clothes this nice."

A section of the wall slid aside, revealing a tiny pod with a showerhead on the ceiling and a drain on the floor. That thing off to the side must have been some kind of toilet. She hoped Letnev anatomy was roughly congruent with her own when it came to using *that*. Bianca slipped off her dress, which suddenly seemed very shabby, and stepped into the pod. "How does this work–"

Water – not freezing, but also not warm – beat down on her from above in tiny stinging streams, and soap or something like it sprayed her from all sides. She shrieked and spun as jets of water started coming from the sides, too, and even up from the floor. Okay. This wasn't some horrible malfunction. This was just how the thing *worked*.

She stopped, closed her eyes, and let the water pound her – it was invigorating, once she got over the surprise. After a few moments the water stopped, and warm air blew on her from all directions. "A *hot* shower, I should have said!" she shouted, just as the drying wind cut off.

"Hot showers are an indulgence," Ayla said. "The Letnev are a practical people, and this is a warship."

Bianca opened her eyes, and screamed again, because someone was in here with her–

No, it was just *her*, reflected in a wall that had become a mirror. Except, looking closer, she realized it was a screen, because it didn't show her reversed, the way a mirror would.

"I need to brush my hair," she said, annoyed that her luggage was being pawed over by Barony lackeys. A panel in her reflection slid open, and a tray emerged, holding the most beautiful hairbrush she'd ever seen, its silver back elaborately engraved with swirling designs. Bianca took the brush and ran it through her hair, meeting far less resistance than she usually did. "Is this some sort of magic brush?" she said.

"It has an auto-detangler setting," Ayla said. "It works by creating tiny bursts of sonic energy. The Letnev take proper grooming very seriously. An orderly appearance reflects an orderly mind."

"Everything is going to be a lesson on the nature of the Letnev with you, isn't it?"

"I am programmed to–"

"Yes, yes, I know." Bianca stepped out of the shower and considered her new wardrobe. She found a drawer that contained undergarments – they, at least, were simple and familiar, though of higher quality than her own – and gazed at the dresses. "Am I really supposed to dress like this all the time? These are nicer than bonding ceremony dresses back home. A ball gown every moment of every day seems excessive."

"You also have access to crew-standard clothing, stripped of uniform insignia, if you would prefer."

"Well… maybe tomorrow. It can't hurt to try something on for now." She selected the deep red dress and wriggled into it. The cloth seemed to shift and adjust to fit her better. "Is this stuff *alive*?"

"The Letnev value efficiency," Ayla said. She then spoke in some language Bianca didn't understand, full of harsh glottal stops and noises like throat clearing. "Taking measurements and creating bespoke garments tailored for an individual is needlessly time-consuming. Instead, that dress is made of smartcloth, capable of adapting to your particular needs." More incomprehensible phrases. "The skirt can divide itself and become leggings, if that is preferable." More guttural talk.

"Are you repeating everything you say in Letnev?"

"Yes." Then: Something like *Yechh*. "We have begun your language instruction." More Letnev followed. Bianca recognized the word for "we" this time, assuming word order worked the way in Letnev it did in her own tongue, which was probably a big assumption. She actually didn't know how other languages worked; she'd never been exposed to any.

"Carry on, then," Bianca said. Ayla made another wall into a mirror and Bianca played around with the dress. Stroking the cloth in a certain way could make the sleeves extend from caps to full-length, and smoothing the skirt just right could turn it into leggings, as promised, and with a little more effort she could even make leggings beneath a shorter skirt. The bodice was adjustable, too, from low-cut to so modest it made it hard to breathe. The cloth wasn't totally mutable – the fall of the skirt and the nature of the hem were limited, and there were only a few styles she could coax the rest of it into; nothing asymmetrical, for one thing. "This dress has weird limitations."

"It is smartcloth designed for Letnev aristocracy," Ayla explained. "It is programmed to always adhere to current fashions, or timeless elegance." Her repetition of her statements in the Letnev language continued.

"So I won't be able to look like a fool, no matter how hard I try. That's comforting. Show me the shoes."

The shelf slid forward, and she chose a pair of pumps that matched her dress. "These heels are absurd." They were easily six inches high. The burgher back home had a pair of heels; she'd worn them in her bonding ceremony, and still talked about how bad her feet hurt at the end of the night.

These heels were adjustable, it turned out: they shrank down to a mere inch, and Bianca laughed. "That's handy."

"They can be any length you choose, or even become flats," Ayla said. "But they are equally easy to walk in at all heights, with auto-stabilizers built in, and they will make constant micro-adjustments to ensure you do not blister or experience discomfort."

Bianca strapped the shoes on, and even though they looked wonderfully impractical they were the most comfortable things she'd ever had on her feet. She did a few twirls, as best she could in the small space, then admired her legs in the mirror. "I guess the life of an aristocrat isn't so bad. Tell me about the ways of the Letnev elite, Ayla."

"We are a true meritocracy, where the strongest and smartest inevitably rise to great heights in the Baron's service."

Bianca frowned. "That doesn't sound like a system with much room for hereditary aristocrats, which is what I'm supposed to be."

"While even those from humble origins may rise to great heights through diligence or brilliance, it is no surprise that the most prominent families produce the most impressive offspring, and so the great families of the Barony maintain their positions and justify their power through the continued excellence of their–"

"Right," Bianca said. "The burgher's son back home always has time to study, and plenty to eat, and he's the healthiest and best-educated person in the village. That kind of excellence just runs in the blood, huh, Ayla?"

"I am afraid I do not understand the question."

"That's all right. I understand the answer." Bianca's belly rumbled. "When do we eat?"

"Breakfast is in approximately one standard hour."

"How long is that in Darit time?"

"I do not understand the question. There are twenty-five standard hours in a standard day, and ten standard days in a standard week, and four standard weeks in a standard month, and ten standard months in a standard year–"

Her door chimed, and a screen appeared on its inner surface, revealing Voyou. He was smiling, and it still looked out of place on him. "Are you ready, Bianca?"

"Almost." With a few smoothing touches and tugs she turned the dress into the leggings-and-short skirt arrangement, and clicked her heels together to turn the shoes into flats. She was a lot shorter than the Letnev around her, but she refused to compensate. She glanced at the jewels, thinking it would be silly to wear something like that to breakfast, though it would probably be good to get into the habit of wearing the jewelry all the time, wouldn't it? Then she'd have some ready wealth at her disposal if she had to strike out on her own unexpectedly. She plucked a bracelet of dark red stones from the wall and closed it around her wrist, then went to the door. Voyou's eyes widened when he saw her. "I clean up all right, don't I?" she said.

"The style suits you, my lady," he said, offering a half-bow. "Are the accommodations satisfactory?"

"They're as good as it gets, aren't they? Unless you're planning to kick out the captain and give me *her* room."

"I would hesitate to make such a suggestion."

"Is it breakfast time already?" she said.

"Soon. Will you accompany me?"

"I don't know how to find my way around on my own yet, so yes." He set off down the corridor, and she fell into step beside him. "Did the lights get brighter?" They seemed less red, somehow, and she could see more clearly now.

Voyou glanced at her. "The illumination level is set to Letnev military standards, and is unchanging."

"Maybe my eyes are adjusting, or something." She was getting used to the gravity difference, too. It no longer felt like walking uphill – just taking a stroll down to the village.

"That must be it," Voyou said. They turned down more identical corridors, and finally reached a door twice the size of her cabin's. The door slid open as they approached, revealing a gleaming white room, with pedestal beds and mechanical manipulator arms clustered along the ceiling and poking out of the walls, all folded up and waiting. She thought of her pa's description of the birthing chamber.

"What's this place?" Bianca said.

"The medical bay." A Letnev wearing a transparent face mask and a white uniform emerged. She was taller, thinner, and paler than Voyou, and her eyes were bright and avid. The overall impression was that of a predatory insect adapted to hide in the snow. "I am Doctor Archambelle. I will perform your medical assessment. Disrobe now."

Before Bianca could object, Voyou snapped, "Show some respect, doctor. This is the lady Malladoc."

The doctor cocked her head, then bowed. "My apologies, lady. *Please* disrobe now."

"Why do I need a medical test? I feel fine."

"You come from a backward planet, lady. Your body doubtless contains countless parasites, viruses, bacteria, toxins, and other harmful elements. You may have a genetic predisposition toward disease or organ failure. We will scan for, and correct, any such problems."

Bianca looked at Voyou, who was, she realized with mild horror, the closest thing she had to a friend here, unless you counted Ayla, who was no more a person than old Torvald's database was. "Don't worry," he said. "Doctor Archambelle is the head of our medical team, and the captain's own personal physician."

She sighed. She could kick up a fuss and argue, but she was enmeshed in the might of the Letnev military now, and she wanted them to *keep* being nice to her, after all. A medical examination made sense. They'd even inspected her bag for foreign contaminants; of course they'd want to inspect her too. She slipped off her shoes and began to pull at the straps of her garment.

"I'll be back to pick you up for breakfast." Voyou retreated from the room, leaving her alone with the doctor.

Bianca had never really been subject to a doctor's care before – there was a woman who set broken bones and another who knew the herbs that broke fevers and soothed nausea, but Bianca had never been sick or injured a day in her life. She had a sense from her novel reading that doctors were aloof and dispassionate, but this woman wasn't that; she looked positively eager to start poking and prodding and scanning Bianca. *She probably just loves her work,* Bianca thought, and climbed up on the pedestal bed as the doctor directed. "Will this hurt?" Bianca said.

"Letnev medical science is the greatest in the galaxy," Archambelle said, which didn't really answer the question, did it?

CHAPTER 13

Severyne Joelle Dampierre, captain of the *Grim Countenance* and provisional governor of the newly annexed planet Darit, was watching Bianca Xing's medical examination on a screen when her door chimed with Undercommandant Voyou's pattern.

"Enter," she snapped, and the undercommandant came slinking in, overly deferential as always. "My *personal physician*?" she said. "As if I'd let Archambelle touch me." The woman was a doctor, and an entirely competent one, but healing wasn't really her specialty. "She'd probably start vivisecting me out of habit."

"I was trying to set the girl at ease."

Voyou stood at attention, and Severyne didn't bother to set *him* at ease. "I must admit, you do seem to have a rapport with the creature."

He shrugged infinitesimally. "I am a slightly familiar face in a wildly unfamiliar place, captain. Someone surrounded by the unknown will cling to the known, however scant the connection."

"A reasonably astute observation," Severyne acknowledged. Voyou was really quite capable – he'd run his portion of the annexation flawlessly, and even dealt with this… unexpected side mission… with aplomb. Severyne wasn't in the habit of doling out compliments to underlings, however. Negative reinforcement was much more effective, in her experience. "I just hope Archambelle can turn up something useful about this girl. Did you see the way she reacted to the gravity here?"

"More the way she failed to react, captain, but yes."

Severyne had deliberately cranked up the artificial gravity several percentage points above normal – not in her own cabin, of course, but everywhere else – in an attempt to make the girl feel weak and overwhelmed and dependent upon her arrival… but Bianca Xing had skipped along the corridors like she didn't even notice, even as Severyne's own crew visibly sagged under the strain. "That thing she said earlier, about the lights changing – are her eyes *actually* adjusting to conditions here? That quickly?"

"It would seem so, captain."

Severyne leaned back in her chair. "I don't like it when my tools are so unpredictable."

"The entire situation is unprecedented, captain. But I have no doubt you will handle it with grace and efficiency. You certainly worked out the best way to get her here without any complications."

Severyne turned back to the screen, where Archambelle was poking the girl with needles, presumably not just for her own amusement. "However unusual her origins, Xing is still just a young woman with big dreams from a backward place. Once you gathered some data regarding her personality, it was easy to tailor a story that would appeal to her. Of course she wants to believe she's the lost heir to a great fortune, with the whole galaxy her playground. Who in her circumstances wouldn't want that?" Severyne touched her terminal, pulling up the preliminary results of the medical exam as the machines hidden in the medical bay's walls scanned their patient. The Xing girl seemed entirely human so far, but she had to be more than that, didn't she? "The map and the key," Severyne muttered.

"What's that, captain?"

"Nothing," Severyne said. "Dismissed. See that she's treated with all due pomp and honor when you feed her."

"Captain." He clicked his heels, turned smartly, and exited.

Severyne rubbed her temples, a show of exhaustion and weariness she would have never indulged in while a subordinate was present – or a superior, for that matter. This was her first mission as captain of the *Grim Countenance*, and it should have been relatively simple. Her brief was to subjugate one of the old colonies of the Federation of Sol as a way of sticking a metaphorical thumb into the eye of their human rivals. Severyne was happy enough to comply. During her career, Severyne had met only a single human she didn't entirely loathe, and even her, Severyne had *partly* loathed. As a result, she had the same instinctive antipathy toward Bianca Xing that she did for the rest of the population of Darit… but she wasn't even sure the girl *was* human, or not entirely. Severyne was curious to see what Archambelle found. The doctor wasn't Severyne's superior, but she wasn't her subordinate either, and the latest orders from Barony high command were to "aid the doctor in her researches." They were, the captain had to admit, very *interesting* researches, with significant implications if Archambelle's suspicions were true.

The *human* factor was troubling, though. So much depended on that young woman with her head full of dreams.

"The map and the key," Severyne said again, louder this time since she was alone, and gazed at the sleeping girl on the screen.

The call that changed Severyne's mission came from one of the survey ships, out searching for ancient human weapons hidden on Darit. The locals might choose to stage an uprising, after all, and it would be preferable if they didn't come armed with anything more deadly than sticks, rocks, and gunpowder. There was always the chance of finding buried treasure on these colony worlds, too – caches of wealth or resources, embarrassing old secrets – though the Federation of Sol hadn't been present here for millennia, and the odds of turning up anything interesting were low.

Severyne's first officer, Richeline, buzzed her private comms. "Captain, one of the survey ships found something unusual in Undercommandant Voyou's sector."

A two-headed sheep, perhaps? Severyne thought. *A gourd of astonishing size?* "Brief me in person," she said, on the off chance that it was something relevant.

Richeline sidled into the room; she always moved like an assassin creeping up on her target, even when in plain sight. Severyne liked her as much as she liked anyone: Richeline was poisonously ambitious, but her ambitions didn't overlap much with Severyne's. She wanted to lead covert specialist kill teams, and had only requested a post on a pacification ship to polish the "leadership skills" section of her file. Severyne had no interest in being an assassin. She wanted to be the person gathering intelligence and *dispatching* the kill teams. Why get blood all over her own boots?

"Take a seat." Severyne gestured at the chair on the other side of her desk, which was, she knew, the single most uncomfortable seat on the ship.

Richeline perched on the edge of the chair (the least painful option), her uniform perfect, a tiny scarlet teardrop insignia on the collar her only deviation from the standard: only survivors of the Battle of Three Lions were permitted to display that pin. Severyne had looked into her file and knew Richeline had been knocked unconscious by the first sonic bombardment at that battle, and had awakened on a hospital ship with no memory of the previous three days, but she *had* survived the engagement, which technically entitled her to the pin, and suggested she was lucky, at least. "Thank you, captain. I know you didn't want to go down to Darit at all, but… this might benefit from your personal involvement."

Severyne's exact words had been, "I don't intend to set foot on that human-infested ball of excrement," and she'd meant it, but now she was intrigued. "Do tell."

"May I?" Severyne granted Richeline access to one of her screens, and bright clear footage appeared: someone walking through a dreary forest, toward a steep, muddy hill.

"This is from one of our surveyors? Why did they land?" The survey ships were supposed to fly low, scanning the ground for signs of buried technology, with search teams to follow. They weren't supposed to land and poke around personally.

"Extraordinary circumstances," Richeline said. "I authorized it."

Severyne grunted. That level of initiative was within her remit as first officer. Severyne didn't want to be bothered by every little thing, after all. Nevertheless, she paused the playback. "Why?"

"The surveyors picked up readings inconsistent with human technology…

inconsistent, indeed, with *any* known technology. What they found is older than the human colonization of this planet."

"What do you mean? I thought Darit had no native sapients?"

"It didn't," Richeline said. "Someone else came here, a long time ago, and built… a sort of laboratory."

"Who? Do you mean… the Lazax?" Those aliens were the former rulers of the galaxy, now degenerate and debased, but at their height they'd possessed incomprehensible powers.

Richeline licked her lips. "Ah. No. Older."

"Older? Who are you talking about?"

"Have you ever heard of the Prophecy of Ixth, captain?"

Severyne frowned. "Ixth? That's the promised land, where the Letnev will someday dwell in blissful, perfect darkness? Why are you talking about children's stories, Richeline?"

Richeline cleared her throat. "It's more than just the Letnev. Almost every culture in the galaxy has legends about the lost paradise world of Ixth. The tales are older than the Lazax, and they pop up *everywhere*."

"That's because people everywhere are fools, Richeline, and would rather imagine a paradise waiting for them in the future than do the hard work of creating their own paradise here and now."

Richeline seemed to change tack. "How much do you know about Doctor Archambelle, captain?"

"I know she asked me to get her human test subjects from Darit so she could vivisect them and see how they'd diverged anatomically and genetically from their cousins in the Federation of Sol," Severyne replied. "That told me everything I *need* to know about her."

"I served with her on a prior mission," Richeline said. "She is a scholar of the body, yes, but also of antiquity, and a believer in the powers of ancient, lost science – technology so advanced that its users would seem like gods to us. She believes Ixth is a real place, and a treasure trove of technological wonders powerful enough to transform the balance of power in the galaxy."

"Oh. She's a lunatic, then."

"I'm… not sure, captain. Archambelle's studies have led her to remote dig sites on forgotten worlds, and she has pored over old scrolls, tablets, databases, and drives that expand on the prophecy of Ixth. She has even, she says, seen some remnants of their technology. Before we began our survey, she took me aside and asked me to report any *peculiarities* we found to her. When I asked what sort of peculiarities, she specified exactly the sort of readings we found in that forest."

Severyne didn't allow herself to react. So, Archambelle had a secret mission, hidden within Severyne's own. That was irritating, though hardly unprecedented among her people. Wheels within wheels was the norm. "And you promptly shared your discovery with the good doctor?" Severyne didn't try to keep the ice from her voice.

"No, captain." Richeline shook her head firmly. "This is your ship. You decide who receives information, and why. I just wanted to place what you're about to see in context. This place… it may be a relic of a truly forgotten age. Archambelle says she believes an ancient, almost forgotten alien race *created* Ixth, and that they may have also come to Darit."

Why would ancient powerful aliens ever come here? Severyne silently resumed the video playback. The surveyor approached the hillside, and directed a many-armed utility drone bobbing along on anti-gravity thrusters to clear the dirt and mud away. The machine worked furiously, scooping and scraping, until a portion of a metal doorway was revealed. Bright metal was overlapped by duller sheets of steel, crudely welded on. "Someone tried to seal this place up," Severyne said. "One of the locals must have found your ancient relic before you. There won't be anything of value inside by now, I'm sure. It's all picked over by grave robbers."

Richeline didn't answer, just inclined her head at the screen, as if to say: *keep watching.*

The utility drone tore away the metal patch and hauled the door open, metal bending with a grinding squeal. The camera view moved in, with the surveyor shining a light into the space beyond. The light was swiftly made redundant, though – when the surveyor stepped inside, the chamber illuminated, revealing a wall of screens and dials and lights, a control console… and a skeleton on the floor.

"Interesting," Severyne said. "Are the remains human? No, I can see they're not." The surveyor ducked down to look at the body, and its head was bulbous and misshapen, its limbs oddly proportioned. "What is it?"

"I don't know," Richeline said. "We can ask Archambelle, if you like. Anatomy is one of her passions."

Severyne grunted. The surveyor stepped over the body, moving closer to the console. If he *touched* anything in there, she would have his skin peeled off–

But he knew his work. He merely panned his camera slowly around, taking in the whole room. "What is that little window?" Severyne said. "In the center of all the screens?"

"We don't know," Richeline said. "But look, here it comes–" The screens lit up and began to scroll unfamiliar glyphs, startling the surveyor, who hastily retreated from the hidden lab, if that's what it was, and back to the forest. The video ended.

"Was that gibberish on the screens supposed to mean something to me?"

"When I was with Doctor Archambelle on that other mission, at a remote dig site… we saw screens with glyphs a lot like those, captain. I can't be sure, we'd have to check with the doctor, but… I think it's a language used by these ancient aliens Archambelle talks about."

Severyne grunted. "I will go to the surface in one hour. The site is to be secured until my arrival. Tell Archambelle I require her company for a visit to Dar-it, but don't give her any further information. You will have command of the *Grim Countenance* while I am gone. Do not use that command to do anything at all."

Richeline bowed her head. "Yes, captain."

Severyne flicked her fingers. "Dismissed." Richeline departed, and Severyne sat in the dimness of her office for a long moment, thinking about the deep past and the uncertain future.

CHAPTER 14

Not long after her meeting with Richeline, Severyne set foot on the surface of her colony world for the first, and, she hoped, last time. Darit smelled, and it was much too bright, and the gravity was different, and there were bugs. Severyne hated each new problem she noticed slightly more than the last, due to the cumulative effects.

Her shuttle landed as close to the mystery site as possible, but reaching the location still required a long slog through leaf mold and mud, beneath spindly trees that made ominous whispering sounds in the wind. The whole place would have benefited greatly from a raging forest fire. Severyne could have piloted an all-terrain vehicle through the filth instead of walking – there were numerous forms of ground transportation available, fast-moving nimble things designed for putting down all the insurrections that hadn't happened – but she refused to show anything like weakness.

Besides, Archambelle clearly hated walking through the dirt even more than Severyne did, so that was a pleasure. *Her* uniform was bright white, and showed the muck rather more starkly than Severyne's blacks. They had four armed guards with them, faceless in their reflective dark helmets, and the soldiers formed a square with the doctor and the captain in the center. In theory, the locals could use their knowledge of local terrain to wage effective guerilla warfare, and such precautions were standard for an officer visiting a newly annexed area. In practice, the natives seemed more baffled by the arrival of their new masters than combative. They'd never really been ruled before, apparently. They didn't know what to make of the experience.

They reached the hillside – Severyne recognized it from the video – and there were two surveyors there, armed with energy weapons, a utility drone patrolling around them. Archambelle started to rush forward, and Severyne cleared her throat. The doctor paused, looked at her, and sighed. "Really, captain, I am eager to look inside."

"I can't imagine why," Severyne said. "All I told you was the survey team had discovered something anomalous, and I wanted you to take a look. It's almost like you expected to find something here."

"Isn't it?" Archambelle said brightly.

"I wondered why someone of your standing and experience was sent along on an annexation mission. I assumed you'd done something to enrage one of your superiors, and once I spent a little time with you, I was confident I'd guessed correctly. But you came to Darit for a reason. You were expecting to find something like this."

Archambelle stared at Severyne for a moment, sucking her teeth. It was a disgusting habit. "Expecting is too strong a word," she said at last. "*Hoping*, perhaps. Fortunately, I have enough influence in the right circles that hope was enough for me to secure the assignment."

"What are we walking into?" Severyne said.

"I am not entirely sure," Archambelle said. "But if we're lucky… we might just find the keys to paradise."

"Someone else gave me a vague and poetic answer to a serious question, once," Severyne mused. "He had twice as many kneecaps before he did that as he did afterward. Try again. If you don't answer me to my satisfaction, you aren't setting foot inside that chamber."

Archambelle scowled. "One call to my friends in the Barony–"

"How would you place such a call?" Severyne said. "Not from the surface of this planet, certainly, and I'm afraid you may need to stay here indefinitely. I understand some of the locals have parasites and fungal infections, things like that. Your skills are definitely needed. Try again."

"You are *not* my superior officer, Severyne. I don't take orders from you."

Severyne picked up a stick and whipped it viciously through the air a few times. "That's true. Of course, everyone in a position to get you off this planet *does* take orders from me. Or were you going to walk back to the *Grim Countenance*? Try. Again."

The doctor sighed. The guards and surveyors were stoically pretending to ignore the friction between their superior officers. "Fine," Archambelle said. "Have you heard of the prophecy of Ixth?"

"Of course. Hasn't everyone?" The entirety of her knowledge, apart from the half-remembered fairy stories she'd mentioned to Richeline, had been acquired from a database query earlier that day, but Severyne hadn't attained her rank by showing weakness.

"I have a theory about Ixth. I think it belonged to, or was at least somehow associated with, an ancient race known as the Mahact. It may even have been their homeworld."

Severyne kept her face impassive. To profess belief in one outlandish imaginary thing was an eccentricity; to believe in two was pathology. "The Mahact are just a story, Archambelle. They were supposed to be, what, ancient wizards or something? They're no more real than the Ebon Witches or cave ghosts or the Strangleman."

"I believe the stories of the Mahact are rooted in fact," Archambelle said. "They were powerful gene-sorcerers. Mad tyrants. Terrors of the galaxy in ancient times, long before the Lazax empire rose. They twisted the bodies of their enemies to amuse themselves, and did the same to their servants to make them more useful. They could enslave other species with a glance. The Mahact hated everyone, and hated each other, and released horrific technologies into the galaxy in pursuit of incomprehensible feuds, or just for fun. Then the Lazax stepped in, an upstart race full of ambition and ferocity. The Lazax defeated the Mahact, killed every last one of them, and took control of what remained of their dominion, including the imperial seat on Mecatol Rex."

"Or so they claimed," Severyne said. "Sounds like propaganda to me – 'Oh, be grateful, citizens, we saved you from the scary star wizards.' It's nonsense."

Archambelle sighed. "Many scholars share your view, but I believe the Mahact were real. I think it's safe to say they were terrors, and that any single member of that strange race possessed more technological power than the entire Barony does today."

"You'd better hope one of these guards isn't secretly a political informant," Severyne said. "Good citizens, like myself, know that *no one* could be greater than the Barony."

Archambelle waved that away. "You must rise above such concerns, captain. Some things are beyond politics, and the stakes are much higher than personal ambition now. Not that personal ambitions can't be satisfied in the process." She gazed at the broken door of the ancient chamber.

"The Mahact are long dead … but the wonders they created remain, waiting for worthy successors to claim them, and use that power to found a new empire."

"On Ixth, you mean?"

"Yes. If I'm right about Ixth being the homeworld of the Mahact, it is a graveyard now, a monument to a dead race … but there are treasures in those tombs. If we can locate Ixth, and loot that technology, the Barony will become what we always claim to be: the most powerful faction in the galaxy, rightful inheritors of the throne of Mecatol Rex, destined to be the new rulers of a single galactic empire."

"Ruling a single galactic empire didn't work out well for the Mahact *or* the Lazax," Severyne pointed out.

"True," Archambelle said. "But the Letnev are superior to those filthy aliens in every respect except technological might. We would run the empire *properly*." The doctor *was* a patriot, then – just one whose loyalty was so unquestioned by the higher echelons that she could indulge in petty critiques of the regime.

"You have some plan to find Ixth, then?" Severyne said. "A plan that, inexplicably, has something to do with an old Federation of Sol colony world like Darit?"

"The Mahact were secretive, paranoid, covetous – we can't expect to find a map leading straight to Ixth. They would have hidden any such map, broken it into pieces, disguised it with a cipher. But if someone very smart, and very dedicated, put enough pieces together, followed enough clues… they might find the way."

"You think there's such a clue here?" Severyne slapped at a bug on her neck. Biospheres were repulsive. She couldn't wait to get back to space.

Archambelle smiled. "Oh, yes. I have found certain artifacts I believe to be of Mahact origin, and fragmented files, largely corrupted, but with suggestive lines of code intact. Mentions of a map that could lead to a hidden treasure planet – a planet that *must* be Ixth. My colleagues and I have been gathering those hints for more than a decade, translating them, and looking for clues. One such clue pointed to this world, Darit, as 'the key to the key.'"

"I thought we were looking for a map. Now we're looking for a key?"

"We're looking for both. And sometimes, instead of a map, there's mention of a 'navigation system,' or simply 'a compass.' Maybe we're looking for all three. Or one thing that serves all three functions. Perhaps we need a map or a compass or both to find Ixth, and a key to open it. I don't know. But… I think the secret might be there." Archambelle pointed to the door in the hill. "May I *please* take a look?"

"Fine," Severyne said. "Since the future of the Barony and the fate of the galaxy is at stake." She glared around at the guards and surveyors. "None of you heard *any* of that, all right?"

"Yes, captain!" they chorused, with acceptable levels of zeal. Severyne decided not to have them all executed to keep the secret safe. Likely there was no secret at all. This was probably just a vault full of mud and crawling things.

Archambelle slipped through the crack in the door, and light spilled out. Severyne followed, more carefully. She looked around the interior, and found it much as it had appeared on the video. The only notable difference was the scent, which was rather musty and stale. She crouched and looked at the skeleton on the ground. "What manner of creature was this?"

The doctor spared it barely a glance. "The physiology is unfamiliar to me. Some unknown species, then. Almost certainly one of the many slave races of the Mahact, sent here to hide the key. But where is it? *What* is it?" She went to the console and began manipulating knobs and dials, causing the incomprehensible characters on the screen to change.

"What am I looking at?" Severyne peered into the square compartment at the center of the screen array, with its odd nozzles and manipulator arms, some with crusts of organic effluvia on the tips. "Is this some kind of… biomatter printer?"

Archambelle groaned, staring at the streaming characters on the screen. "That's exactly what it is. I'm looking at the logs, and this machine… it made an organism. I shouldn't be surprised – that's what the Mahact *did*. They were wizards with flesh, gods of genetic engineering. Some say they could even create life from non-life. Our scientists can't even create living *wood* from raw chemical components, let alone animal life, but this machine made… wait. It sampled a dominant local species, which based on a glance at this DNA code is clearly human, and then created an organism based on that template, with… frankly incomprehensible additions, hidden inside the genome. Lines of dormant code, strange strings of RNA, chemical signatures that make no sense inside a living creature. They should be totally inert. Though I suppose if they combined with some sort of catalyst, internal or environmental… or maybe there's a kind of internal timer, counting down…"

"What are you talking about?" Severyne demanded. "You're saying this machine created a person? A human person?"

"It created something that *looks* human," Archambelle said. "But only because it sampled a human's DNA to create a template. If the machine had sampled a Letnev instead, the child would look Letnev, and if it had sampled a Hylar, the child would have fins instead of legs."

Severyne looked into the compartment. "This machine built a child?"

"It would have been an infant, at the beginning," Archambelle said. "Something small, showing perfectly ordinary human development, most likely. I wonder if it's a sort of camouflage, so the child would blend in with the local population? But underneath, the child would be… something other than human. I don't *know* what, but – wait. There's a message in the archive. A brief note that was apparently displayed, hmm, approximately nineteen standard years ago, when the child was first… printed? Decanted?"

"Settle on the nomenclature later," Severyne said. "What did the message say?"

"This a loose translation, mind you, but it says, 'The child is the map and the key.'" Archambelle slammed her fist on the console. "The map and the key! The path to Ixth must be hidden in the child, probably written in its genetic code!"

"Mmm," Severyne said. "Can you make the machine print us another child?"

Archambelle shook her head. "This device was meant to do one thing, and it has done it. The reserves of organic material are spent, and I can't begin to imagine what to refill them with. I suppose the Mahact who created this chamber expected one of their operatives to find it and decant the child. I'm sure one of *them* would know how to decipher the secrets hidden in the child's blood."

"It all seems a bit involved," Severyne said. "You'd think they could just write the directions down."

Archambelle shrugged. "Maybe it's not that simple. There could be complicating factors we can't imagine or hope to understand. The ways of the Mahact can be incomprehensible. They were as gods to us, captain." Archambelle's eyes were wide, and she gazed around the chamber with a reverent intensity Severyne found troubling. Zealotry had its uses, but Severyne preferred not to be so close to it, in case it exploded and made a mess. "You can't expect to understand everything the gods do." She sagged. "But some stupid human found this place, nearly twenty years ago, and triggered the machinery. The child is lost. The map, and the key, lost."

Severyne sniffed. "I imagine we can find it. The number of humans in the immediate area numbers in the hundreds, not the thousands. Small communities gossip, and everyone knows everyone else's business. The human who discovered this place probably burst into the nearest tavern and shouted 'Who wants to buy a mechanical baby?' Even if she showed more discretion than that, there would still be rumors. Mystery infants appearing in the absence of pregnancies always start people talking – such things are either a scandal or a miracle, and people love both. I'll have Voyou make some inquiries, and see what we can find out."

Archambelle perked up. "Yes, captain, it's of the utmost importance, this supersedes all other elements of your mission–"

"The child could be dead, of course," Severyne mused. "Is that a problem? I think they bury their dead here, instead of sensible, efficient cremation, so we might be able to recover bones with some viable DNA inside."

"If it comes to digging up a corpse, I'll wield the shovel myself," Archambelle said. "But alive is better. Alive and cooperative is *much* better. I don't know exactly what form the code will take, and the message says the child is the key as well as the map – what if it has to be alive to activate the wormhole, perhaps via some sort of sophisticated biometrics? What if the child has to speak some phrase, something programmed deep in its memory, that will come to mind only when the child reaches the appointed place? We simply can't know until we arrive… wherever it is we're going."

"So we need to find a local mysterious foundling, now a young adult, and convince them to accompany us to an unknown destination, ideally of their own free will, since if the child decides to fight us, they could ruin everything?"

"Yes," Archambelle said. "When you put it that way… it sounds like rather a difficult challenge."

"Nonsense," Severyne said. "Once Voyou tracks down this human compass of yours, and does a little research, I'm sure I can come up with the right lie to elicit the desired outcome."

Severyne's comms buzzed with Archambelle's priority call, and Severyne shook off her memories and answered. "Well? Have you completed your preliminary examination of the girl?"

"I have." Archambelle's voice was dull. "There's nothing in her blood. Nothing in her tissue. I examined her hairs under an electron microscope. I looked at every inch of her body, in case her freckles and moles formed some kind of star chart. I examined her fingernail clippings and the underside of her tongue and every other part of her, inside and out. I found no code. No sign. No ciphers, no secrets, no coordinates. Nothing at all."

"That's not good," Severyne said. "Did you ask her about the yearning?"

"What?" Archambelle said. "What yearning?"

Severyne sighed. "You didn't read the dossier I compiled on her, did you?"

"Why would I? I was interested in *her genetics,* not the details of her life or the psychological profile you used to concoct your silly secret space princess story!"

"If you'd read the file, then you'd know about our princess's yearning, so I suggest you take a look, doctor." Severyne shut down the comms and sat smiling in the dark. She knew she should focus on the success of the mission, especially since Archambelle's very powerful friends back home had called to make it *Severyne's* mission too… but seeing Archambelle frustrated was still something to savor. "Speaking of the secret space princess," she said to herself, and switched on the hidden cameras in Bianca's room.

CHAPTER 15

Bianca repeated the Letnev words Ayla had just spoken. She couldn't imagine why she'd ever *need* to say "These mushrooms are too pungent," but the phrase was now lodged in her mind, along with hundreds of others. She'd never tried to learn a foreign language before – everyone she'd ever met spoke *hers*, though people from the most distant valleys rounded their vowels in a peculiar way – and, it turned out, she had a knack for it. At least, she assumed so, judging by the fact that she was already doing what Ayla called "third-year lessons" just a few days into her studies. Maybe the program was intended for small children? The machine didn't show any surprise at her progress, but then, surprise was probably beyond the scope of Ayla's programming. Bianca was also, simultaneously, learning the trading tongue used by most of the species who used spoken language at all when they had to deal with one another; that language was far simpler, with logical rules and a more limited vocabulary, and she'd basically mastered it already.

Bianca had been back to the doctor three times, and had every fluid she could produce drawn out of her (including some she'd never even heard of – what was a lymph, anyway, and who knew she had fluid in her *spine*? That one had pinched a little). She'd been prodded, poked, scraped, scanned, exposed to various wavelengths of light, and endured having every inch of her body examined through a hand-held magnifying glass, wielded by Doctor Archambelle personally. "What are you doing that for?" Bianca had asked.

"Looking for unusual moles," the doctor said. "You've been on a planet, under a sun, and people of Letnev heritage are vulnerable to skin cancer in such conditions. Your health seems perfect, however." The doctor didn't sound very happy about the good news, but then, the Letnev, as a rule, were not a joyful people. They had so many wondrous things – high technology, the freedom of the stars, citizenship in one of the great societies of the galaxy – but as a group they seemed less cheerful than the humblest farmer on Darit.

Ayla said, "You have progressed to the year four curriculum. At current rates of language acquisition, you will achieve full fluency in Baronic Letnev in two days. Would you like to begin the next lesson?"

"No, not right now." Bianca flung herself down on the bunk and looked up at the ceiling. She was *bored*. She was sick of studying languages, the Letnev "entertainment" videos and texts available didn't merit the name (it was all patriotism and shooting, with very little kissing and cleverness), and she'd already written two letters to her parents and three to old Torvald, which Ayla assured her were being transmitted. At this point, she'd even welcome another round of medical tests, just to get out of her cabin.

She was free to walk around the ship, but guards trailed her everywhere, because "elites must be protected," which made her feel awkward, and the ship was pretty dull anyway. She'd been to the engineering deck and the bridge and the navigation room and all of them sparked a million questions, but no one would *teach* her anything, except the hydroponic gardener, who'd been happy to talk to her for an hour or so yesterday about farming techniques on a spaceship versus a planet. Bianca had made one or two obvious-seeming suggestions for improving crop yields and the gardener had acted genuinely stunned by her ideas, though she supposed he was just being nice and humoring her; if it was obvious to *her*, it must be obvious to everyone, right?

Funny how she'd never had any ideas about farming back home, but maybe the change of scenery had inspired her mind to look at things from a different angle.

She'd also discovered a knack for computers. With a little digging around, she discovered there *was* surveillance in her room, though it was intermittent and usually brief – spot checks rather than constant vigilance. Maybe the Letnev spied on *everyone* that way. Even so, she managed to create a loop of her napping under the covers that she could run while she did things she doubted the captain would approve of. She'd had a lot of fun exploring the ship's various databases, learning all sorts of fascinating technical details about spacecraft, though there were restricted areas where the security defeated her efforts to explore… at least so far. The officer files in particular were heavily encrypted, and her attempts to satisfy her curiosity about Voyou, Archambelle, and the captain were stymied at every turn. She was getting better and better at understanding the architecture of the Letnev systems, though, so in time–

Someone knocked at her door, and Bianca sat up and said, "Come in!"

Doctor Archambelle entered, wearing the strained expression that passed for a smile with her. "Greetings. May I sit?" Bianca gestured grandly to the fold-down seat, and Archambelle perched on its edge.

"Is everything all right?" Bianca said. "Did the tests show something wrong?"

"No, nothing we didn't expect," she said. "Your health is excellent. But I was perusing your file recently, and read something I wished to ask you about."

"You have a file on me?"

"Yes, of course. When we began to suspect your true identity, Undercommandant Voyou made certain inquiries on Darit. While many people were understandably reluctant to talk to a member of the Letnev military, he managed to glean some information about you through diligent efforts."

Bianca felt a chill. "Did he threaten people?"

"I believe his chief motivational tool was bribery, actually. Don't worry, we didn't learn anything embarrassing or salacious. Several people he interviewed did mention your, ah – 'yearning'?"

Bianca couldn't help it: she blushed to her roots. She'd stopped talking about her obsession with the sky when she got older, of course, but as a child she hadn't realized her fixation was strange, or that other people *didn't* feel the way she did. In a small community, hungry for any gossip, people remembered, and they talked. "Yearning. It sounds like something from a love story when you put it that way."

Archambelle looked at her, alert and attentive. "Could you describe the experience to me?"

Bianca looked down at her hands, twisting the edge of her blanket. "Oh, it's just, ever since I was little, I sometimes find myself looking at the sky. Day or night, it doesn't matter, and my eye is drawn to different parts of the sky at different times. I feel this… well, 'yearning' is a good enough way to put it. Like I was supposed to *go* to the place where I was looking. Like I belonged there. My parents said I just had wanderlust, itchy feet, things like that. But when I got old enough, I realized I *wasn't* looking at different parts of the sky. I was looking at one particular spot in the sky – it just moved around throughout the year. It was easiest to point out on summer nights, because there's a triangle of three stars, not especially bright or useful for navigation, and as far as I know we don't even have special names for them. When I see those stars, I just feel this need to go there." Some nights she would stand and stare so intently that she lost track of time, only blinking herself back to true consciousness when dawn arrived. She wasn't even looking at the stars, exactly, but at the center of the triangle they formed, where there was nothing to see at all… but that sounded too ridiculous to admit. "Do you think that yearning means something?"

"We'll do a neurological workup," Archambelle said. "Sometimes compulsions to go to a particular place are caused by parasites."

"*Parasites?*" Bianca was aghast.

She nodded enthusiastically. "On Darit there is a parasite that lives inside small insects. It gives those insects an overpowering desire to climb *up*, and so the insects trundle up a blade of grass, to the very tip." She made a little walking motion with her fingers. "Of course, once they're on the end of a blade of grass, your caprids come along to munch the grass, and eat the insect along the way. That suits the parasite fine, because it needs to continue its life cycle in the belly of a caprid. The parasite lays its eggs inside the animal, and when the caprid defecates, those eggs are evacuated as well. Insects crawl through the fecal matter, and in so doing, they pick up the parasites, which infect the insects, and compel them to climb, and so the cycle continues."

Bianca made a gagging face. "You think I'm drawn to those stars because there's some kind of parasite inside me? What kind of parasite needs to complete its life cycle in a distant star system?"

"Do you have a better theory?" Archambelle snapped. Bianca narrowed her eyes, and the doctor winced. "Apologies, Lady Maladroit."

"It's Malladoc," Bianca said frostily.

Archambelle blinked. "Isn't that what I said? We'll do a few more tests, just to rule out anything dangerous, and if we do find a parasite, we'll deal with it. You're in good hands." The doctor hurried out, and Bianca flopped down on her bunk again.

Then she stared at a spot on the bulkhead, beyond which, she knew – she just *knew* – those three stars shone. They were getting closer. She knew that, too.

"There you have it," Severyne said. "Find out where those stars are and set a course for them. I'm sure you'll find your wormhole gate there."

"I will investigate the issue," the doctor said. "Perhaps this yearning of hers is relevant, though more likely it's a meaningless epiphenomenon. Even if she is being guided to those stars, there's nothing to say they're our actual destination – they may be merely signposts or markers."

Severyne shrugged. "At least now you're *fully* informed." She chuckled. "I did like the bit about the parasite."

Archambelle grinned back, and for a moment Severyne very nearly liked her. Then the doctor remembered herself and scowled. "I did see something new in the girl's medical records."

"Oh? What's that?"

"As I said, there was no cipher in her genome that we could detect. One part of her genetic code is particularly rife with incomprehensible data, though, and while perusing her latest scans, the sequencing looked *wrong* to me. Still baffling, but in a different way than I remembered. I assumed I was simply mistaken, but that's rarely the case, so I compared her newest genetic sample to the first one we collected." Archambelle clenched her fists. "The code was *different.*"

"Your latest sample was corrupted, then?"

"No! I double-checked, and triple-checked, I *octuple*-checked, and the sample was fine. The girl's genetic code is actually changing."

"By the endless dark, what does that even mean?"

"I have no idea what it means," Archambelle said. "But it makes me think, perhaps the secret hidden in her genes is not a static message, but something dynamic. Maybe it's a timer, or a counter. Or the secret could be hidden in the nature of the *change* – a message being revealed only gradually."

"I see. Does this insight bring you any closer to deciphering that message?"

Archambelle opened her mouth, closed it, opened it again, then sighed. "No. I hate to admit no, but I think we need to contact an outside consultant."

"Outside, doctor? As in, not Letnev? But we are the best, the brightest, the greatest, without equal–"

"All true," Archambelle said. "But there are certain individuals outside the Barony with highly specific skill sets that could prove useful."

"Who are we consulting, then?"

"His name is Brother Errin."

"Ah. One of the Yin Brotherhood, I assume?"

Archambelle nodded.

"Why do they call themselves 'Brother This' and 'Brother That'?" Severyne complained. "They're all male anyway, and I never heard of one who claimed a gender other than 'man', I assume because of their odd religion. You'd think the 'Brother' bit could just be taken as read."

"Every culture has its oddities," the doctor said. "Except for the Letnev, of course. Brother Errin is something of an outcast among his people – a brother exiled from the brotherhood, as it were. You are aware of the Yin's deep preoccupation with genetic matters, I assume?"

Severyne nodded. The Yin Brotherhood were all clones of the founder of their order, a human named Darien Van Hauge. Cloning was frowned upon even now, and in that scientist's time, under the Lazax empire, it had been outright illegal. That hadn't stopped his research, and he became a master of the forbidden craft. When his family died, Van Hauge went mad with grief and made a child from his own seed and one of his dead wife's eggs, and then proceeded to clone that egg. The cloning process had two flaws, though: one caused a genetic predisposition to Greyfire, a disease that disfigured the flesh before killing the victim, and the other resulted in a total inability to create female clones. Over the centuries, the clones in what became the Brotherhood of Yin had continued tinkering with their own genome, but so far they'd failed to solve *either* problem, though they'd managed to make the Greyfire less lethal, if no less disfiguring. These days the Brothers most grotesquely altered by the disease were considered "blessed," and formed the ruling councils of their people, while the "untouched" went out to deal with the other races of the galaxy, since their presence was considered *slightly* less off-putting.

Severyne didn't have any issues with the disfigured – that sort of thing couldn't be helped, and a physical infirmity reflected nothing meaningful about the affected individual. Ideals of "beauty" or "normality" were culture-bound and subjective anyway. Severyne found zealotry off-putting, however, and every time she'd met a member of the Brotherhood they'd gone on about the wonders of their founder and the majesty of the egg they called "Yin" and considered the embodiment of some kind of "feminine principle," and *that* was tiresome and repulsive.

"This Errin knows more about genetics than you do?" Severyne asked.

"Oh, yes. Does it surprise you to hear me admit that? There are only half a dozen people in the galaxy who can rival my expertise in these matters. Errin happens to be one of them, and he's the one who's easiest to reach. His quest to remove the flaws in the Brotherhood's cloning process led him to study ancient accounts of the gene-sorcery of the Mahact." She leaned forward, clearly fascinated by her own knowledge. "One story says the Lazax forbade cloning under their rule *because* the Mahact made such extensive use of the technology. Others say that propensity for clones led to the downfall of the Mahact. They were so jealous and selfish they didn't like to have children, but instead made cloned thralls of themselves. Some legends say the Mahact could even move their minds into the bodies of their clones, though that strikes me as an *actual* fairy tale. Errin's studies strayed into areas the Brotherhood found unsavory, his experiments were denounced, and he was cast out… which didn't stop him from doing his research. He continued his studies, just more unfettered than before. He still wants to help his people, whether they want that help or not."

"That's zealots for you," Severyne said.

"Errin's work may give him a special insight into the nature of the girl's changing genetic code. Perhaps he can decipher what I cannot."

"Fine. Give me the details, and I'll have Richeline set a course for his doubtless horrifying bio-lab. You can meet with him by yourself, though. The last time I encountered one of the Brotherhood, he wouldn't stop talking about how 'ineluctably feminine' I was, and I don't need any more of *that*."

CHAPTER 16

The direction of Bianca's yearning changed, suddenly and dramatically, which meant the ship was charting a new course. She wondered where they were going, and why they were going somewhere other than wherever they'd been going *before*, but her guards were uncommunicative, Archambelle wasn't answering her messages, and Ayla had no insight, of course.

Bianca passed the morning doing years five and six of the Letnev language study. Apparently, she'd attained fluency. Languages weren't that hard, really. It was all just sounds paired with meanings. Now she was learning to read the Letnev language, which was even simpler, despite the unfamiliar alphabet, since there were far fewer characters than phonemes. The sound each character represented changed according to the context of the characters around it, that was all, just like the language she'd grown up speaking. Maybe next time she'd learn the written and spoken versions of a language (or two) at the same time, just to give herself a *bit* of a challenge–

Ayla spoke up, unprompted: "I have received permission to share the star charts you inquired about," she said.

That made Bianca sit up. She'd asked for the charts ages ago, and been refused, because "navigational data is classified," which was baffling – how could a simple map of the sky be a secret, when anyone could look up and see it? She'd tried and failed to hack into the navigation system herself, though she thought in another day or two she'd get in – now it wasn't necessary.

Why had the Letnev changed their minds? She wondered if her odd conversation with Archambelle about her "yearning" had something to do with the sudden reversal of policy. "Show me."

One wall became a screen, depicting a night sky that was at first just a profusion of stars but that she soon recognized as the view from her own farm. "Those stars." She pointed to the trio of lights that always drew her attention when she looked up – and to the space between them, where she so desperately wanted to go. "What are those?"

The screen zoomed in closer, though they just remained points of light. "Those stars are known as Burgis-A, Burgis-B, and Eekhout."

"What's out there?"

"Nothing of note," Ayla said. "The Burgis star systems include no habitable planets, and the gas giants there were deemed poor candidates for resource extraction. Eekhout has never been formally surveyed, but imaging indicates no planets of any kind in its orbit, only asteroids."

"What about right *there*?" She pressed her finger into the center of the triangle. "What's in that empty space?"

"Only more empty space, Lady Malladoc."

Bianca shook her head. "There has to be something!"

"There are no objects noted in my database, though there are presumably uncharted areas."

"That's not very helpful, Ayla."

"I always try to be helpful, my lady."

"Try harder." Bianca slumped on the bunk, frustrated. For all her yearning, she still didn't know what she was yearning *for*, and it troubled her that the ship was no longer moving in the direction of those stars.

She was tired of all this "Lady Malladoc" business too – she'd gone from "wouldn't it be wonderful if it were true" to accepting the whole thing was total nonsense. The Barony doctor had done so many medical tests on her it was clear they were trying to figure something out, not just assess her health, but what? She hadn't left her family, her planet, and everything she knew just to be kept in the dark and fed shit, like one of the Letnev's beloved mushrooms. If they needed her for something, they could at least tell her *what*, if they expected her cooperation.

"Message Doctor Archambelle, Ayla. Tell her I want to know what all these tests are really for. Tell her, if she isn't honest with me, I won't help her anymore."

"Message sent, my lady."

"Let's see what she has to say to *that*," Bianca said.

"The girl has grown suspicious," Archambelle said. "She no longer believes your space-princess story."

Severyne yawned. She didn't require much sleep, but she needed some, and the doctor had interrupted her scheduled downtime with an urgent request for a meeting. "So? The story was only meant to entice her on board and into our control anyway."

"You don't understand. She has threatened to stop cooperating. If I just needed access to her blood and tissue her cooperation would be irrelevant, but we don't know what reaching Ixth will require from her. If she refuses to help us, she could make our mission difficult or impossible. She is demanding answers, captain."

Severyne yawned again, more widely. "Then give her answers."

"You want me to tell her the *truth*? That her genetic code contains a treasure map hidden by ancient alien gene-sorcerers?"

The captain rolled her eyes. "I didn't say give her *correct* answers. Or complete ones. She's seen through our lie. Admit to that, and tell her a *new* lie, and she'll believe that's the truth, because of course we wouldn't try to deceive her twice.

The names Ixth and Mahact won't mean anything to her, but you can tell her… oh, tell her that Darit was never really Letnev territory at all. Hide the lie inside as much truth as possible. Tell her… Darit was a Federation of Sol territory, and the humans hid the location of some great treasure cache in her genetic code. Say we need her to lead us there and breathe on a biometric lock or something, and that we'll split the treasure with her. Do I have to think of everything?"

"That might work," Archambelle said. "I don't think the girl considers me trustworthy, though."

"Send Voyou. He's the closest thing she has to a friend here, and he's excellent at lying to humans. He did an admirable job of that on Darit."

"So there you have it." Voyou spread his hands. "I know my superiors misled you, Bianca. That was wrong, and now the captain *knows* it was wrong. They were afraid you'd be unwilling to travel with us if you knew the truth, and concocted a story to gain your trust. They tricked me too. I can only offer my sincere apologies on their behalf, and convey their promise to be truthful with you in the future. While you aren't, technically, a princess of the Letnev, once you take possession of your share of the Federation treasure we hope to recover you might as *well* be – you will possess wealth beyond imagining."

"I'm going to need something in writing." Bianca crossed her arms and glared. "The Letnev are great believers in law and rules and order, aren't they? That's what my language-and-culture bot tells me. So, I'll require a contract, specifying the terms of this split, and the rights and responsibilities of *both* parties." She wanted to say all that in Voyou's native language – Letnev was almost poetic when it came to the subject of binding agreements – but she'd decided to keep her degree of fluency a secret, just in case. Sometimes the Letnev spoke in their own tongue within her hearing, and they might be more discreet if they knew she understood them.

"I'll take your request to the captain," Voyou said.

He rose and departed, and Bianca made her way to the gym. She'd started working out recently, using the weights and resistance machines, and she could feel herself getting stronger and more flexible. This time, in her frustration, annoyance, and anger, she piled more and more weight on the bar as she did deadlifts. She grunted, lowering the bar, and noticed a gargantuan Letnev staring at her. "How someone so small lift thing so big?" he sputtered in the trading tongue, accent heavy and diction broken.

She grinned. "I grew up on a farm. When one of the caprids had a kid, I lifted the baby over my head. I kept lifting that kid over my head every day and when it was full grown I could still lift it, as easily as I had that first day." That was a lie, of course, but it was a story she'd heard about a muscle-bound boy she'd seen at one of the festivals, and she'd always found it delightful in its unlikeliness.

"I must find one of this kid," the bodybuilder said.

Bianca returned to her room so she could shower in private – the Letnev tended to sneak glances at her when she used the communal showers in the gym, which was probably because she was *human*, a completely different *species* than them, and not because they were in awe of her royal nature. Although to be fair, she didn't know what the crew had been told about her – Voyou claimed he'd been deceived about her nature too. They probably thought she *was* some kind of elite. It was much easier to tell hundreds of people the same story than to expect all of the people on board to keep a secret, after all. Or perhaps the captain hadn't told them anything at all. The Letnev weren't big on sharing information, she'd come to learn. They were an elitist military hierarchy with a strong streak of bureaucracy. She smiled. Those were all terms that would have been mostly meaningless to her a month ago, since none of them had much bearing on her life on Darit.

It was amazing the things you picked up in the course of learning a new language, since you couldn't achieve true fluency without understanding the cultural context of the tongue. For instance, the Letnev *liked* darkness, and they found tunnels and caverns comforting, and those qualities were reflected in their idioms – instead of "over the horizon" they said "beyond the chasm," and instead of "the sky's the limit" they said "we venture into the endless dark," and other things like that – "bright stars" was a mild curse. It was odd how she'd never thought about the nature of language this way before. Like so many things lately, the insights just came naturally the moment she gave a subject any thought at all.

When she got to her cabin, Voyou was waiting outside with a woman Bianca hadn't met before. "This is First Officer Richeline," Voyou said. "She is the captain's right hand, and she came to bring the contract personally."

"Are those *paper*?" Bianca had seen paper books at the Halemeeting hall, but they weren't common. Almost everything was digital, even on Darit.

"They will be scanned and entered into the central database, of course," Richeline said. "But we begin with paper. We are traditionalists in the Barony. Shall we go over the terms?"

Bianca showed them into her cabin, and they folded down her desk and clustered around it. The documents were printed on thick, heavy paper, festooned with seals and sigils. The text was in her own language, alongside the Letnev tongue, and Voyou assured her the words were as identical as possible. Bianca could read Letnev well enough by now to spot-check and confirm that for herself, fortunately. "What's this about a seventeen percent split?" Bianca said. "That seems impossibly low."

"I am authorized to go up to twenty-one percent."

"How about twenty-one percent for *you*," Bianca said.

Voyou and Richeline conferred furiously in Letnev, and Bianca listened in; they were arguing about what the captain would accept, and what the *Baron* would accept, and finally Richeline said, "Twenty-five percent, and you get to keep all the clothes and jewelry you have received. Understand, twenty-five percent of the treasure we expect to acquire will be enough for you to buy your own *system*."

"What if the vault is empty, though?" Bianca said. "We're going to need to set a minimum floor for my compensation, regardless of the value of monies and goods recovered – I can't possibly do all this purely on spec."

Another furious conference, this time with expressions of shock from Richeline that a simple farm girl was so adept at negotiating, and speculation that she must have been in charge of haggling for animal feed or something back home. In truth, Bianca had never had much to do with the business side of things, but it seemed she had a knack. She was discovering all kinds of knacks lately. Anyway, even if the deal had struck her as perfect, she would have argued several points. The Letnev didn't respect anyone who didn't bargain hard and negotiate for every possible advantage. Their words for "contract negotiations" and "total war" were close cognates.

They agreed on a minimum level of compensation, and set deadlines for when she'd be released from the contract if they failed to find this treasure (she didn't want to be stuck roaming the galaxy on the *Grim Countenance* for years if the search proved fruitless). She even negotiated a better deal for Darit in terms of the colony world's tax burden, though it meant giving up some things she could have gotten for herself.

In one of their huddled conferences Richeline insulted her rather colorfully, but Bianca didn't let so much as a hint of comprehension slip. She filed away the phrases for later, though. Ayla's teachings had been remarkably short on profanity. Fortunately, the meaning was clear enough in context.

After three hours, they finally had a contract they could all agree upon, and they signed with great flourishes and then scanned the contracts and uploaded them.

Richeline's collar was undone and her hairline was sweaty. She gave Bianca a stiff bow. "That was as satisfying a duel as I have ever fought, Miss Xing. And I'd say we *both* drew a little blood."

Bianca almost said, "A battle without blood is like a day in the sunshine," but that was a Letnev idiom, so instead she said, "I think you got the best of me, but you've been doing this a lot longer."

"Your performance was more than creditable," she said. "Doctor Archambelle will be in touch about your next round of tests, and yes, she will discuss the results with you, as the contract requires." Another bow and she left, Voyou following at her heels.

Bianca flung herself down on the bed and smiled. She'd finally taken control of her destiny, and it felt good.

"She believed you?" Severyne said.

Richeline nodded. "She thinks the contract is legitimate, yes."

"As a resident of a Barony colony world, she is entitled to protection under our laws. It would be a valid contract… if I sealed and witnessed it, of course." Severyne tore the sheaf of papers in two and tossed them into the matter recycler.

"It was clever of you to make sure that detail was omitted from her lessons on Barony contract law, captain," Richeline said.

"I don't need you to tell me how clever I am, Richeline."

"She's even more clever than you realize," Voyou said. "The captain had me alter the same pertinent information in the ship's legal database, even though Bianca doesn't have access to those files, just in case. We've made a few other redactions elsewhere in the system, and planted some false information here and there, too, including in the personnel files."

"Why would you bother to do all that?" Richeline said.

Severyne didn't have to explain herself, but sometimes it was useful to let your subordinates know you'd already dealt with problems they hadn't even considered yet. "The girl spends too much time in her room, using her tutoring program. Remedial schoolwork isn't that interesting. I suspect she's been using her terminal for other things, and poking her nose into places it doesn't belong."

"You think she's hacking our systems?" Richeline said. "Without leaving a trace? How? She has no training. The computers on her planet are probably made of dung and corn cobs."

"Nevertheless. Caution costs nothing. The girl has shown surprising capabilities, time and again. I'd rather not be surprised further. Speaking of… what was your assessment of her language skills, Richeline?"

The woman made a sour face. "We negotiated as if the contract were real, as instructed, even when speaking in our own language, but she showed no interest or attentiveness when we spoke Letnev. I insulted her, also as instructed, and she showed no reaction. I'm sure she has a few words of Letnev, but no one can become fluent in the great tongue so quickly, no matter what her system says. She's probably using a dictionary program to cheat on the tests she takes, or else the system is just poorly calibrated."

"Those are possibilities. She did negotiate well, though, for a human." Severyne had briefly regretted not taking part in the ruse – it would have been enjoyable to spar with the girl. Severyne was withholding direct contact with Bianca, though, in case she *really* needed to step in to fix things at some point. It was better if the captain remained a figure of shadow and menace in the girl's mind. That left more possibilities open.

"Oh, she did all right," Richeline said. "I'm sure her bargaining skills come from all those years trying to get a better price for turnips. You know what people in gravity wells are like."

"I suppose. Be discreet around her anyway, in case she understands more than you think. As I said–"

"Caution costs nothing." Richeline didn't roll her eyes, but Severyne could tell she *wanted* to.

"Remember that. Dismissed."

Once she was alone again, Severyne called up what scant information the Letnev database had about the world of Ixth. She was beginning to think they might actually see the place, and wanted to be prepared if they did. Archambelle seemed to think there would be miraculous technology and priceless artifacts lying around unattended, just waiting to be picked up by anyone who happened by, but in Severyne's experience nothing worthwhile happened *that* easily. Everything worth getting came at a cost; the key was to make sure someone *else* paid it. "I nominate Bianca Xing," she muttered.

CHAPTER 17

Bianca spent the journey to the space station mostly alone in her room, studying with Ayla, trying to find out more about the galaxy in general, and hitting a lot of "data redacted" and "that information is outside the scope of my programming" responses. The history of the Barony was officially an unbroken string of victories, and that seemed unlikely for a culture that was at least thousands of years old. Even her hacking skills didn't help – there were odd gaps wherever she looked. The Baron didn't want his own people learning the truth about their heritage either, it seemed.

She did eventually finesse the systems enough to break into the encrypted personnel and medical files, though there wasn't much of interest there – not the juicy secrets Bianca had hoped for. Archambelle's parents were doctors from the Letnev homeworld, and her life was a boring series of schools and residencies and fellowships. Voyou's first name was Orist, he'd been born on a remote outpost moon, and he was allergic to some medication Bianca had never heard. Riveting stuff.

The captain's name was Rania Jennis Dampierre. Her file was heavily redacted, full of sections blacked out and marked "classified" and "state secret," which suggested she was potentially interesting, but Bianca couldn't find out exactly how. At least now Bianca knew what the mystery woman looked like, since there was a photo in the file: the captain was at least as old as Torvald, white-haired, stone-faced, and she had a cybernetic left eye with a red pupil. Bianca didn't think she'd seen that face around, but maybe the captain wore one of those full-face masks when she secretly mingled with the crew.

There were occasional other distractions. Voyou dropped by more often than he used to, and played one of the Barony's favorite games with her – spiralstone, a strategic and tactical combat simulator traditionally played with stones on a circular board marked out with spirals, but played more often these days via holographic interface. When they first started playing Voyou warned her not to get discouraged if she lost a lot, because the game took a lifetime to master, and he was ranked in the top five thousand players in the Barony.

He was so easy to beat that Bianca soon started losing intentionally, in different ways, without him realizing she was failing on purpose, because that was more challenging than playing in a more straightforward way. She'd played some similar games back home with old Torvald, and had only beaten *him* about half the time, so she knew she wasn't some sort of unrivaled gaming savant. Maybe he was ranked in some kind of amateur league, or just bending the truth to impress her. Did he *like* her? He'd never done anything creepy or even flirtatious, so maybe not.

Occasionally Voyou accompanied her to the mess hall, a welcome change from eating alone in her room. She was still the subject of glances from the rest of the crew, but not as many as before. They'd grown more accustomed to the aristocrat – or alien – in their midst.

One day, an ensign bumped up against their table by accident and knocked Voyou's teacup off the edge. At the moment of impact Bianca's perception of time… changed. As the cup tumbled toward the floor, spilling its mushroom tea, everything seemed to slow down, the cup drifting down as slowly as a feather. Bianca reached out and effortlessly plucked the cup from the air, and even scooped up the tea in midair before it could splatter on the floor. Voyou stared at her, and some of the other officers actually applauded. "Fast reflexes, my lady."

Bianca shrugged, trying for nonchalance. Later, in her room she experimented, trying to trigger that bizarre perceptual shift by knocking small objects off her desk. She couldn't make the time dilation happen again, and wondered if it was a protective reflex, an unconscious and reactive ability, like flinching away from a blow. If it happened again, she'd try to analyze the experience more closely, because if she *could* control her perception of time, it would be all sorts of useful.

Her yearning worsened as their journey continued to take her away from those three stars, but Voyou assured her the scientist they were on their way to visit would give them the insight they needed to complete their journey. When Voyou arrived at her door that day, she booted up the game, but he shook his head. "Not this time. We're approaching Brother Errin's station. We should be there in an hour or so, if you'd like to get dressed. Are you excited to visit your first space station?"

Bianca shrugged. "I assume it's going to be a lot like being on a spaceship, only without the engines making the deck vibrate."

He chuckled. "This is a military vessel, and short on amenities. I think you'll find the Tree of Grace rather more pleasant."

"The station is called the Tree of Grace? Why?"

"Get dressed and you can see for yourself."

Bianca put on her favorite red smartcloth dress and shoes and went out to the corridor, following Voyou down in a lift to an observation deck she'd never visited before. The room was circular, with windows on all sides. Even the floor was translucent, and she felt like she was floating in the void.

Something else floated in the void, beyond the windows, and it *did* look like a tree – a silver one, uprooted and suspended in the air. The station had a central trunk with symmetrical arrays of modules at the top and bottom, like branches above and roots below.

"Brother Errin is one of the galaxy's leading experts on biological matters," Voyou explained. "He became wealthy by treating genetic disorders in prominent members of various species. They say he helped a major Naalu leader overcome her infertility problems, and she gifted him with this crystal space station, retrofitted inside to suit human habitation."

Bianca glanced away from the vista to look at Voyou. "Brother Errin is human?"

"He's cloned from human biological material, anyway. The Yin Brotherhood consider themselves distinct as a species, though, and I imagine their biology has diverged a lot from that of baseline humans by now."

Bianca pressed her hand to the glass and gazed out at the station. "It really is beautiful."

"The Tree of Grace is hopelessly impractical and needlessly ornamental by Letnev standards, but I've spent enough time in foreign service to know that our aesthetics aren't universal. I do think it looks like it would shatter if you tapped it with a small hammer, but the Naalu build whole cities out of crystal, so I'm sure it's stronger than it looks. We should head for the shuttle."

Voyou, Richeline, and Archambelle accompanied Bianca, along with three guards in their faceless helmets. The shuttle was smaller than the one that had taken her from Darit up to the *Grim Countenance*, and Voyou explained that this one was meant strictly for ship-to-ship (or -station) transfers, and wasn't meant to land in atmosphere. One of the guards sat in the front, but apparently there was no real piloting to be done – the shuttle computer talked to the station computer, and the guidance and docking happened automatically.

They let Bianca sit in the co-pilot seat, so she had a good view as the crystal branches grew larger. Their shuttle approached one of the uppermost modules, shimmering like it was made of diamonds, and docked. There were various clanks, hisses, thumps, and whirrs, but soon enough all the connections were secure and pressures equalized, and the shuttle door opened. Two of the guards went ahead, as if they expected an ambush, and then Richeline strode out. Archambelle stuck close to Bianca's side, and Voyou brought up the rear.

The inside of the station wasn't all diamond sparkle, but it was pleasant: plush carpets on the floors, walls a soothing shade of greyish blue, corridors dotted with little niches that held flowering plants or climbing vines. The lighting was indirect but full-spectrum, a welcome relief after the dim redness of the Letnev ship. Voyou squinted, and Archambelle slipped on a pair of dark glasses.

A towering figure stepped into the corridor from a side room. She had a cat-like face and long sand-colored hair in complex braids, and wore a robe intricately embellished with ornamental knotwork. "Greetings," she purred. "I am Kyrria, Brother Errin's representative."

"Why does he need a representative?" Richeline said. "We came to see the scientist, not the secretary."

Kyrria smiled, or at least, Bianca supposed it was a smile; she showed off a terrifying array of teeth, anyway, with long curving canines.

"She's a Hacan, right?" Bianca whispered to Voyou. Ayla had provided Bianca with very little information about the other inhabitants of the galaxy, but she'd been able to access a children's book called *Rivals to the Barony* that included brief descriptions of other species, including the Hacan, though the alien in the picture had been holding a curved sword and a severed head and had blood smeared all around her mouth.

"That's right," Voyou murmured. "If you shake hands with one, count your fingers afterward."

Bianca suppressed a gasp. "They eat *fingers?*"

"What? No. Or, I suppose they might – who knows what they eat? I just mean, they're famous negotiators and traders."

"Oh. I thought they went around beheading people all the time."

"Not in my experience," Voyou said. "Though it can't hurt to be watchful."

Bianca wondered what else in the children's book was inaccurate or slanted. Perhaps the Hylar weren't really building doomsday weapons on the bottom of the sea, and the Gashlai didn't destroy planets because they liked how pretty the explosions were, and the N'orr weren't desperate to lay their eggs in Letnev abdomens. The book had been rather alarming for a work aimed at children, but Bianca supposed many of them had a taste for the bloody and the macabre. She certainly would have devoured a book like that if she'd found it at the Halemeeting Hall.

Kyrria was explaining herself. "So you see, Brother Errin has little patience or interest in matters of the world, preferring to dwell wholly in the realms of science… but, alas, tissue vats and chemical printers and genomic scanners cost money, and I make sure he has all the resources necessary for his work. *That's* why I'm here. We're still waiting for your consultation, and we'll need it before you go any deeper into the Tree of Grace."

"You haven't paid them yet?" Archambelle glared at Richeline, who winced.

"I submitted all the paperwork, and the captain expedited things, but you know how the procurement office can be. Let me see what the holdup is." She stepped off into a niche beside a plant and began jabbing furiously at a hand terminal.

Bianca took a step forward and cleared her throat. "Hello," she said to Kyrria. "Why is this place called the Tree of Grace? The tree part I can see, but…"

The Hacan looked down at her from a great height, then crouched so their eyes were at the same level. "Brother Errin is a member of the Yin Brotherhood. They come from the Lael system, and Errin grew up there, in the Lucas monastery. The monastery stands on a place called the Hills of Grace, and though Brother Errin has parted ways with his fellows, he still considers himself part of their sacred order. He says if he cannot live on the Hills of Grace, he will carry the spirit of the place with him, and so he named this station in their honor."

"That's lovely," Bianca said. "Thank you for explaining."

"You have such nice manners," Kyrria said. "How did someone so polite end up in the company of the Letnev?"

"They kidnapped me under false pretenses," Bianca said. Voyou coughed so loud it sounded like he was choking.

"That sounds like the Barony," Kyrria said amiably. "I'm not in a position to rescue you, though I can reach out to the human authorities if you'd like. It's possible they might intercede, especially if it annoys the Barony."

"That's all right," Bianca said. "We worked things out. We negotiated the terms of my cooperation."

"Your contract was signed by all parties?" Kyrria said.

"Oh, yes, of course."

"And properly wit–"

Richeline stepped between them, though there was hardly space to do so, and waved her terminal in Kyrria's face. "There, the transaction is complete, if we can *please* get on with the examination?"

The Hacan showed her teeth again, then checked her own terminal. Once she was satisfied, she bowed her head. "Right this way. Brother Errin is waiting in his lab."

Properly wit? Bianca thought. *What did she mean?* She must have stood with her brow furrowed for too long, because Voyou took her elbow and guided her along the corridor.

Brother Errin's lab was all gleaming metal surfaces and white tile, and the man himself looked just like plenty of other humans Bianca had met, though his head was entirely bald and his skin was an unhealthy, grayish sort of pale.

"The clients from Letnev are here," Kyrria said.

Errin was standing at a workbench, staring into a complex device mounted beneath an array of lenses. He looked up and blinked. His eyes were large and moist-looking, he sniffed constantly, and overall he reminded her of a sick caprid. Maybe not terminally ill, but you'd want to keep him away from the rest of the flock until he got better. "What? Who?"

Doctor Archambelle pushed herself forward. "Brother Errin. You remember me, I'm sure. Araminta Allencourt Archambelle?"

"Archie?" He squinted.

Bianca couldn't *actually* hear the doctor grind her teeth, but she certainly sensed it. "That is… what you sometimes call me on the forums, yes."

"Can't remember all those other names," he said. "Too many, too long. Come and look at this, it's remarkable, a specimen recovered from a bog, have you ever been to a bog? Horrible places, squishy, look." He grabbed the doctor by the arm and manhandled her over to the scope, practically pressing her face against a set of lenses. "See, I know what you're thinking, it's just *Ascaris lumbricoides*, but look closer and it's *not*, do you see the ring pattern there, it *can't* be, doctor – what you're looking at is a worm unknown to science!"

"That is fascinating, Brother Errin." Archambelle stepped away and straightened her jacket. "I brought the woman I told you about. The one with the, ah, genetic anomaly?"

Errin cocked his head, then slowly followed her pointing finger. "Strange. Strange, strange, strange. I reviewed your samples and they are, something, what's the word. Strange." He walked in a slow circle around Bianca, the guards and other Letnev moving aside to give him room. He reached out and touched Bianca's hair, poked her shoulder, and sniffed at her elbow, and she tolerated all of that, but when he grabbed her lower lip and pulled it down and looked into her mouth, she shouted "Hey!" and he jumped backward.

"Apologies!" His voice was much too loud. "So much time in the lab, I forget myself, yes, would you believe I used to work in the diplomatic corps, ha, me? Scientific liaison, I was, they brought me to talk to the scientists when we visited other nations, so much talking." He shook his head. "Wasn't for me. Wrong path. Had some shocks. Met the Creuss! The Ghosts, you know them?"

The children's primer hadn't mentioned anyone called the Creuss, and Bianca didn't believe in ghosts, so she shook her head. Errin didn't seem to notice. "The Creuss, that was hard, I kept it together, for a while, did my job, went to parties, smiled and nodded, but I had nightmares. Every time I went to a new place, I thought, will a Ghost be there, asking me things, 'Where is music?' and 'Would you vapor?' and 'Why electric meat?' I retired. I say I retired. I was not retiring. I made a fuss, I made a scene, I was taken away, then I *went* away, and here I am."

"I see," Bianca said. "That must have been very hard for you."

Errin gave a solemn, big-eyed nod. "Now, here, I do the work. I don't go anywhere anymore. The same place every day. New people, yes, sometimes, but the same place. My Tree is solid. My Tree won't come apart. It won't turn into a ghost under me." He clapped his hands together in front of her face. "You! An interesting anomaly, hmmm, yes. Let's get you scanned and see what's happening inside you. *You* don't stay the same, oh no, you don't dissolve, or haven't yet at least, but you certainly change." He hurried over to a console and started pressing buttons, and parts of the wall slid open, revealing person-sized glass cylinders, shelves of vials, and gleaming robot arms tipped with alarming attachments.

Bianca sidled over to Archambelle. "He's insane."

"Well, yes," Archambelle said. "But within very predictable parameters, which is functionally identical to being sane. He's good at his work, the best at his work, and that's all that matters. If there's a way to decipher the secrets inside you, he'll know them."

"Take off all your clothes!" Brother Errin shouted.

CHAPTER 18

"I'll just escort the rest of you outside," Kyrria said. Archambelle started to object – "We are *colleagues*, I'm sure Brother Errin wants me here to assist" – and the Hacan simply picked her up, as easily as Bianca would have lifted a teacup, and carried the doctor, stunned and silent, out of the room.

Voyou patted Bianca on the arm, rather awkwardly. "You'll be all right," Voyou said. "He's, ah… a professional."

"Just do as you're told, Xing." Richeline beckoned to the guards, who followed her and Voyou out of the lab.

Bianca disrobed. She was chilly at first, but the lab must have warmed up or something, because a moment later she was perfectly comfortable. At least her weeks undergoing Archambelle's tests had given her lots of practice being naked around a stranger… though Brother Errin was stranger than most.

He turned, looked at her, nodded, then returned to his console. "Archie believes in fairy tales, you know. Ancient aliens, former masters of the galaxy, experts in cloning and genetic manipulation. The legends say they were experts on *everything*, super-scientists with everyday conveniences that violated the laws of physics as we understand them, and cities that soared impossibly high and delved impossibly deep. Supposedly the Mahact could make almost anything. Archie thinks they made *you*." He looked at her again, and this time there was a shrewdness and clarity in his eyes she hadn't noticed before.

"Wait. Who are the Mahact?"

Errin clucked his tongue. "What did the Letnev tell you?"

Oh, no. "Which time?"

"All the times, please. I'm curious."

Bianca told him the first story, about her being the heir to a lost fortune, and the "truth," that she was the child of a human aristocrat with a treasure map hidden in her genetics. "But I guess that's not true either?"

Errin shook his head.

"Then, what am I?"

"Something new in the galaxy, I think," Errin said. "I thought Archie was losing her grip, and believe me, I *know* about losing your grip, but I've seen your test results and who could have made you *but* the Mahact?"

"I still don't know who they are," she said.

Errin nodded. "According to old stories, ones almost no one remembers and even fewer people believe, there was once a great empire ruled by a cruel and brilliant people called the Mahact…" Errin told her about the aliens and their purported genetic mastery, and how Archambelle's research led her to Darit, and how the Letnev hoped she would lead them to the treasure world of Ixth. "Archie thinks Ixth might have been the Mahact homeworld, or maybe just one of their holdings. If you could find it, that would be remarkable. The legends of my people say that on Ixth we'll finally find the secret to cleansing our genome, and even creating female clones."

Bianca took in everything he'd told her and finally said, "Why did the Letnev lie to me? Why not just tell me the truth about this Ixth?"

"Bianca. They need you to find Ixth. You don't need *them*. If you knew the truth, there would be no reason for you to travel with them. You could make your own way, and leave the Letnev behind. They brought you here because they hoped I could tell them your secrets so they wouldn't actually need *you* anymore, either. But don't worry. They're going to be disappointed, because I don't think I can give them what they need."

"But they're supposed to work *with* me. We have a contract!"

"Oh, do you? I'm sure that's all right then. I'm sure the Letnev would never try to deceive you."

Bianca slumped. "Should you be telling me all this?"

"I was, in fact, forbidden to tell you any of this, but the Tree of Grace is *my* domain, and I think it's only fair you know the truth of your nature. You are a miracle of sorts, Bianca. And you're being exploited."

She nodded slowly, then said, "You aren't as insane as you seemed to be earlier, are you?"

He lowered his head and sighed. "When I act mad, it's not an act. My mind expands and contracts. It comes and goes. But when the wind is right, I *can* tell a knife from a nightjar. Sometimes I think, when the Creuss made that station come apart, they made part of *me* come apart, too…"

"Who are these Creuss you keep talking about?" Bianca said.

Brother Errin shook his head rapidly. "No, no, no, that's a tale for another telling. We're not talking about *those* bogeymen this time, we're talking about the Mahact. The Creuss don't care about flesh, they care about energy, but the Mahact, they were supposed to be *sculptors* of flesh, wizards with it, gods with it, even. And yes, they did, they did make you. I didn't say so to Archie, not straight out, because she's insufferable when she knows she's right, but looking at the data she collected, and the fragments of unknown provenance she's gathered over the years, it's clearly all connected. The mark of Mahact handiwork is all through you, their little signature touches, their embellishments, their elegance. Elegances? All of those."

"If you already studied my samples, why am I standing naked in your lab?"

"Because you are not a static problem, Bianca Xing, you are a dynamic one, and I wished to see how you *changed*. But yes, come, stand here." He beckoned and gestured and led her to the wall where the tiles had slid away, indicating a circular podium only a little shorter than Bianca. "I need you to get on the scanner, I have a stepstool somewhere, wait, it's just–"

Bianca rolled her eyes, bent her knees, and jumped up onto the platform from the floor. She straightened, turned around on the podium, and resisted the urge to do a curtsy or take a bow.

Brother Errin looked at her, then at the podium, then at her again. "That is... not a record. No. Not quite a record for highest vertical leap by an unaugmented human at this level of gravity. But it is *close* to a record, and the person who set the record was *much* taller and *much* more muscular and–"

"I'm in good shape," Bianca said. "It's nothing." But she was blushing. When she'd jumped up onto the platform, it hadn't *felt* like a big deal – she'd just instinctively known she could do it – but she certainly hadn't leapt that high back on Darit. *Nobody* had. She must have cleared, what, a hundred and twenty centimeters, straight up.

"The Mahact made you well," Errin said. "You are not an unaugmented human. Not really human at all. You're something new. Or something new wrapped around a core of something very old. Please stand as still as you can. Commencing scan."

Bianca froze herself in place and held her breath, but more than that, was her heart even beating? Wouldn't she die if it didn't beat? And ... shouldn't it be harder to hold her breath? Doing so wasn't even a strain, not like when she'd competed with the other children to dive to the bottom of the pond to retrieve rocks – that had been hard, and she'd come up gasping. She felt no need to gasp now.

Am I changing? The thought had occurred to her before, several times, but always in the back of her mind, always quiet, always quickly dismissed. What Errin said about her being a *dynamic* problem, though... that made the thought louder. Maybe she really was getting stronger, faster, and smarter than she had been before. But how? And why?

Violet light shone from the walls, and she hoped it wasn't radioactive or anything. "Lift your arms, please. Hmm. What an interesting vascular system."

"People are always telling me that," Bianca said.

"I wonder, if I made a clone of *you*, if the clone would retain your polymorphic qualities. I suspect there are failsafes in place..."

"You don't have my consent to make a clone of me." Bianca crossed her arms and glared down at him.

"Noted." He put on a pair of square-rimmed glasses and began drawing in the air, probably interacting with some kind of virtual display... or else the wind was blowing the wrong way again, and he was mad.

"What are polymorphic qualities?" she said. "What does that mean?"

"I am under strict instructions to discuss my findings only with Archie and the woman who scowls so much." His eyes were unreadable behind lenses full of flickering light. Before she could object, he continued. "I refused to sign anything to that effect, of course, so I can say whatever I like. You are the subject of the examination, so you're entitled to know my findings. Most people, in most species, are born with their genetic code essentially fixed. Sometimes things can change that code – radiation and toxins can damage DNA, or dormant sequences can be activated by environmental factors, and of course individuals are born all the time with random mutations, which survive in successive generations if they turn out to be useful adaptations… or useless but not especially detrimental. Traumatic experiences can cause a change in gene *expression*, though that only alters the phenotype, not the underlying genotype – that's known as epigenetics, and allows a parent to pass certain heritable traits to their offspring. Often they're traits they wouldn't *want* to pass on, but it's not optional. And, of course, with the tools available to us, courtesy of science, we can alter DNA at will, though the results are often unpredictable. Does all that make sense?"

"It does." Ayla had been allowed to give her texts on basic biology, at least. She hadn't even needed to hack the systems for that.

"Good. Your DNA isn't like everyone else's. Your genome is changing, constantly, without recognizable environmental causes or the deliberate actions of anyone, including yourself. Your phenotype – that is, your actual observed physical characteristics – have remained fairly constant, but only on the most superficial level. You look basically the same, is what I mean: you haven't grown wings or started glowing bright green. But when I look a little deeper, I find significant changes in your bone density, muscle mass, blood volume, synaptic activity, and other systems that aren't apparent to the unaided eye. You've changed a lot since Archie first scanned you on the *Grim Countenance*."

"So I am getting stronger," Bianca said. "Thinking faster, too. Doing everything faster. Remembering things better. I thought I might be, but it just… seemed impossible."

"It is certainly unprecedented in my experience. If we could make a serum that does for others what your body does naturally for you, we'd be rich enough to buy whole systems."

"I retain the intellectual property rights to any technology derived from the study of my body," Bianca said.

"True enough in the Barony," Errin said. "Provided you aren't in a subordinate client relationship and have full legal status, which you don't. Anyway, this isn't the Barony. Not all jurisdictions have the same rules, and some places have no rules at all. Those are the places where the most interesting science gets done." Bianca glared at him, and he winced. "But don't worry. I don't care about wealth, and I don't think I could replicate the miracle of you anyway. You are the product of Mahact technology. I can look at your genetic code, and see what it does, without having the faintest idea about how to replicate that effect.

A worm might sense the vibrations of a spacecraft passing overhead, but that doesn't mean the worm can invent space travel. All right, you can jump down now."

"My body started changing when I left my homeworld." Bianca leapt easily from the podium and accepted the thin white robe Errin held out for her. "Why?"

"You're being prepared for something." Errin bustled over to a console and began calling up data on several of his screens. "I have no idea what. The changes aren't just altering your physical characteristics. There's another part of the code, linked to the deepest parts of your brain, where the instincts and the autonomous systems live. Your file said something about a 'yearning'?"

Bianca nodded. "I look at the stars, and I feel a strong desire to go to a certain place."

"Hmm. Perhaps it's similar to the way some migratory species feel a need to travel when the weather changes."

"That's nicer than Archambelle's idea. She thought it was like a parasite, changing my behavior for its own purposes."

Errin smiled. "Archie does have a certain point of view, doesn't she? I have examined the mechanism of the yearning, and have reached certain conclusions. I will have to share those conclusions with the Letnev, since that is why they hired me, but I do not have to share all the other details of my examination with them. Do you understand?"

"You mean, you're not going to tell them how I'm changing?"

"I am not. I do not know their ultimate intentions for you, but I do know they're meddling with forces beyond their ability to comprehend *or* control. You have been chosen for something – no, you have been *made* for something – and Archie and the rest think they can control that process. But I'm not sure the creations of the Mahact can be controlled. They're all dead now, exterminated by the Lazax, but if the stories are to be believed the Mahact were prepared, once upon a time, to destroy the galaxy in order to demonstrate their refusal to bow to those they considered lesser races. The Letnev share the arrogance of the Mahact without as much justification. If they try to push things too far, they may bring ruin. If I tell them how strong you are, I fear they will hobble you. When the time comes, Bianca Xing, you might need your new strength and speed and cleverness to ensure your own survival."

Before she could reply, he punched a button on the console, and the lab's doors slid open. Kyrria walked in, the Letnev delegation following. "Well?" Archambelle said. "What were your findings?"

"Have you deciphered this map hidden inside her genetic code?" Richeline said.

"Are you all right, Bianca?" Voyou asked, and she smiled at him and bowed her head in assent.

The guards didn't say anything, just hung back in a little cluster, unreadable in their blank facemasks.

"There is a no map," Brother Errin said. "Bianca is more like a metal detector. Beep beep beep, yes? Or a radiation sensor. She can feel when she is going in the right direction, and when she is getting closer to her destination."

"There must be a way to extrapolate from the data and figure *out* that destination!" Archambelle said.

Errin shrugged. "There may be a sort of counter hidden inside her, or a complete set of directions, or even something like coordinates, though we don't know how to read these ancient cartographic measurements, so they wouldn't do much good. Given enough time – on the order of years – and computational power, yes, there's a chance I could find out where her yearning will take her, or perhaps I could bioengineer an organism that glows or screams or hisses when you're headed the right way… but there is a simpler solution, yes?" The Yin scientist looked around expectantly, and they all looked back at him blankly. Brother Errin sighed. "Why don't you just *ask* Bianca which way you should go, and follow her directions?"

The Letnev delegation stared at him for a long moment. Then Archambelle and Richeline burst into furious outrage at once: "Absurd," "impossible," "give control of our navigation to a *human*," "not even part of the chain of command," "you don't ask the test subject to run the test," and other objections along those lines.

Bianca cleared her throat, and then did it again, louder , and then said, "Quiet!" She smiled at them sweetly as they scowled at her. "We have an agreement, don't we? A partnership?"

"Yes," Richeline said, rather sullenly, Bianca thought.

"Then I don't see the problem. I'll talk things over with the navigators on the *Grim Countenance*, and we'll set a course." They wanted to use her? Fine. She'd use *them* instead. She'd make the Letnev take her to the source of her yearning, and when she got close to Ixth, she'd escape and make her own way to the planet, and seize the treasure for herself. Ha. She'd show them all.

"We can't go wandering all over the galaxy on the say-so of a human," Richeline said.

"We both know I'm not human," Bianca said. "Not really. You wanted a treasure map. I *am* the treasure map. Now you don't want to follow the map's directions?"

Richeline looked at her, dead-eyed and cold. "I'll have to consult with the captain."

"Of course you will," Bianca said. "I'd like to the meet the captain soon, too. As the most important person on this mission, it's really time I stopped talking to subordinates."

Kyrria made a low rumble that was probably a laugh.

Archambelle didn't care. She was arguing with Brother Errin, who was shooing them toward the door. "Yes, Archie, I'll send over my data, but it won't tell you anything I didn't – it will just illustrate the wisdom of my advice."

Kyrria led them back to the corridors. Archambelle and Richeline went first, heads together in furious conference, followed by Bianca and Voyou, with the guards at the rear. Voyou walked beside her, murmuring, "Very impressive, Bianca, it's good to see you asserting yourself and recognizing your value," and she wanted to shush him, because the doctor and the first officer were exchanging angry words in Letnev, and she wanted to hear them. Then she realized she could just split her auditory focus, taking Voyou's bland affirmations into one ear and the more interesting discussion into the other.

"It doesn't really matter," Archambelle was saying. "Let her think she's in charge – let her play the space princess again, strutting around the command deck in her fancy red dress! Once we reach our destination, you can hand her over to me for vivisection as planned. *That* will shut her up, apart from all the screaming."

"She thinks she's so smart," Richeline seethed. "But she doesn't even realize the contract she signed is a sham. As if we'd let some alien science experiment extort us that way."

"Lower your voice," Archambelle said. "She speaks a *little* Letnev, we think, after all, so better to be discreet."

Oh. Bianca's plan to use the Letnev suddenly seemed ill-advised. If she let them get close to this Ixth, they might decide they were close *enough*, and kill her. Plus, how could she travel with them as she had before, knowing the depth of their deception, and their plans? Bianca thought for a moment. She considered angles, velocities, the dimensions of the corridor, the distance to the shuttle, and, the true x factor: her body's new capabilities. A little time dilation would have been welcome, but she still couldn't enter that state deliberately, so she'd have to settle for speed, strength, and the element of surprise.

After a few milliseconds, she was satisfied with her calculations, and she spun. As she whipped around, she elbowed Voyou in the face, his nose crunching beneath the blow. She whipped an energy rifle out of the hands of a startled guard, used her momentum to strike a second guard across the face with the gun butt, then dropped and struck out with her leg, sweeping the two guards still standing off their feet.

She didn't want to fire the rifle here – what if it punched a hole in the wall and exposed them to vacuum? – but she'd always been good at throwing things, even back on Darit, before her improvements. She ejected the rifle's energy cell and then hurled the weapon at the back of Archambelle's head.

That was a tactical mistake – she hated Archambelle more, so she'd aimed for her, but Richeline was a bigger threat. When the doctor hit the floor, Richeline spun and rushed straight at Bianca, without hesitation. The look on her face was *gleeful.* Bianca tossed the energy cell at her face, but Richeline just ducked and dove for her.

Bianca did a standing vertical leap, higher even than the one she'd done in the lab, and when Richeline passed below her Bianca dropped, both feet slamming into the back of her neck. Richeline landed with a gasping cry, and Bianca bent her knees and launched herself onward, down the corridor, toward the towering form of the Hacan. Fighting *her* would be a different proposition; the Letnev were big too, but they didn't have those fangs or those claws.

But Kyrria just stepped out of the way, putting her back to the wall. "No one paid me to stop you, child. Best of luck to you."

Bianca made it to the shuttle and got inside, sealing the doors. She scanned the documentation and figured out how to take manual control. She started the engines, but the station wouldn't release its docking clamps. She could manually force the *shuttle's* clamps to release, but that was only half the issue.

People began hammering on the shuttle doors, trying to override her locks with various priority codes she had to frantically counter. There were no weapons on board, no escape pod, nowhere to go from here. Maybe if she put on an environment suit, she could spacewalk, make her way to another portion of the station, somehow get inside, hide in the service tunnels, but she couldn't get *out* of the shuttle, because there was only one door, and it led to an airlock full of angry enemies.

The Letnev, she knew, were not a very trusting people. Their technology was full of spyware, remote overrides, and countermeasures meant to enforce obedience and punish non-compliance. On the shuttle, it turned out those countermeasures consisted of anesthetic gas, triggered remotely from the *Grim Countenance*, she assumed. Once the vents began hissing, Bianca filled her lungs with clean air, and then she held her breath.

It turned out she could hold her breath for thirty-seven full minutes. *Is that a record for a human, Brother Errin?* she thought, and then she opened her mouth and inhaled, and sank into blackness.

CHAPTER 19

"We've been waiting here for over an hour!" Heuvelt shouted into the comms.

"We're terribly sorry," the Hacan's voice purred. "We've had a small… security issue. The situation is nearly resolved, and then you will be allowed to board the station."

Heuvelt cursed and stomped back to the galley, where Ashont and Clec were playing a card game. Heuvelt had no idea how that worked, because Clec was perched on Ashont's shoulder, and could see all the cards in her hands, but apparently the Naaz was scrupulously honest when it came to playing games. "They treat us like our time is worth nothing," Heuvelt said.

"'A small security issue' could be a euphemism for all sorts of horrible things," Ashont said. "A terrorist attack by genetic originalists, a lab-grown monster eating the staff, a disappointed client waving around an energy rifle… anything really."

"So you're saying I shouldn't be in such a big hurry to climb onto the Tree of Grace," Heuvelt said. "I suppose you're right. Even if it's nothing as dramatic as you describe, there are Letnev on board, and they still want to arrest me for crimes I never committed." He paused. "Don't you want to know how I surmised there are Letnev on board?"

"The giant Barony warship floating a few klicks away, all covered with unnecessary spikes, was my first indication," Clec said. "The presence of a Barony shuttle, covered in smaller unnecessary spikes, in one of the other docking modules confirmed my initial findings."

Heuvelt picked at a peeling piece of the tabletop's laminate. "Yes, that's what gave it away for me too."

"Well spotted, though, captain," Ashont said. "You still get credit." She slammed down two cards, one depicting some kind of snake twisted into a sigil and the other a curving fang. "Serpent's Tooth! Ha! The initiative is mine!"

"I am sure you cheat," Clec said. "I don't know *how*, but you must."

Heuvelt looked at the screen in the galley, showing a map of the system. "After we finish this delivery, I say we head to that moon there and spend some of our profits."

"I didn't know we had profits," Ashont said. "I thought we were looking at offsetting some debt at best."

"We can afford a few *drinks*, Ashont."

"Mmm. That particular moon caters to medical tourists who come here to consult the Yin," Clec said. "Since he doesn't let friends and family stay on the Tree of Grace overnight, just patients, there are luxury accommodations and entertainments for all the relatives and hangers-on. The amenities on that moon are expensive, is what I mean to say."

"Then we can afford *one* drink," Heuvelt said. "I call dibs on said drink."

"Oh, there are always bars for the pilots and security staff and valets and corset-lace-tighteners and scale-polishers and mandible-cleaners," Ashont said, shuffling the cards. "We can find some affordable entertainment. The captain's right. We should celebrate our change of fortune. We'll get a lot more work from Sagasa after this job, and with the captain's record cleared we'll be able to pass through Letnev space without worrying about it more than anyone *else* does."

"Did the two of you just disagree with each other?" Heuvelt said.

"No," Clec said. "Ashont makes good points. What you just witnessed was the process of us discussing a topic and then coming to agreement. We do that a lot. You just don't usually pay attention."

Heuvelt went back to the cockpit to wait for someone to open the airlock. He had a crate full of who-knew-what grotesque biological material in his cargo hold, and he just wanted to hand it over to the mad scientist, go on his way, and reap his rewards. Working for someone like Sagasa was troubling, but if it got his record cleared and allowed him to give up this furtive half-fugitive lifestyle, and make progress toward his dreams of exploration again, it was all worthwhile.

I can't wait for life to get simpler again, he thought.

"We could threaten to torture her parents," Voyou said. "She's clearly very fond of them."

"That is an option," Severyne said. "I am certainly not above compelling obedience, but there are drawbacks to the technique. For one thing, we'll have no idea if Bianca is telling the truth or leading us astray. Since we don't know where we're going, or what might be required from her in terms of activating mechanisms or opening vaults or what have you, she could lead us on indefinitely."

Richeline rubbed the back of her neck where Bianca had stomped on her. Severyne had watched that part of the video twice, her annoyance slightly tempered by amusement. What a leap! The young woman clearly had hidden capabilities, including fluency in Letnev, since overhearing Richeline's comments about the sham contract was the only reasonable explanation for the timing of her escape attempt.

Richeline growled. "I say we just cut off one of her hands and tell her we'll cut off the other if she doesn't take us where we want to go, and fast."

"Same problem," Severyne said. "We can't give her a ticking clock, because for all we know the journey will take years. Besides, now she knows we don't plan to let her live after we're done with her. We also don't know the extent of her physical capabilities, so torturing her effectively will be a difficult series of trials-and-errors, with more of the latter than we have time for. Especially in light of Archambelle's theory about her pain management."

"What theory?" Richeline said.

"No one reads the whole files," Severyne sighed. "Really, you can't just skim the precis." She leaned back in her desk chair and fixed Richeline with the full weight of her disappointment. "Tell her, doctor."

The doctor was still a little groggy from the meds she'd taken after the blow to her head, but her gaze sharpened as she spoke. "I think Bianca can control her pain receptors, though perhaps not consciously. I deliberately did some painful procedures, to test her reactions, and after a brief wince she evinced no further distress, and I detected reduced conductivity in her nerves. Very targeted, very selective. Inflicting pain on her is likely to be difficult. As for maiming her, yes, that could be highly motivating, but I have also noted astonishing capabilities in terms of tissue regeneration. I have not gone so far as to cut off one of her hands, but if I did, I suspect it would grow back. I also have other concerns about compelling her cooperation through force."

"Such as?" Severyne said.

Archambelle shifted in her chair, unable to find a comfortable position, by design. No one in Severyne's presence should be too relaxed. The doctor said, "What if Bianca is developing mental powers in addition to physical ones? We know there are species who can read minds, project thoughts, even dominate the wills of others. What if the Mahact seeded those abilities in her? Perhaps she beats Voyou when they play spiralstone, not because of her superior tactical skill, but because she can sense, perhaps unconsciously, what's in his mind, and knows what moves he plans to make in advance?"

"That's certainly something new to worry about," Severyne said. "Though her tactical acumen is obviously impressive, for a farm girl. She bested a first officer, an undercommandant, a ship's doctor, and three marines in hand-to-hand combat."

"We didn't think she posed a threat!" Richeline said. "We'll be much more careful going forward, you can believe me—"

"Going forward *where*? We've already established that any attempt to compel obedience could backfire. Archambelle says the girl's genome and volatile brain chemistry mean our usual drugs to weaken human wills are unlikely to do any good."

"We keep having to switch sedatives," the doctor said glumly. "The gas that knocked her out the first time didn't work the next time, and the anesthetic we used instead failed the time after *that*. Her body is learning to shrug off everything we use against her. It won't be long before we're reduced to bashing her in the back of the head with a rock if we want her to stay unconscious, and obviously that has certain inherent dangers."

Severyne nodded. "This girl was designed by the Mahact, or whomever, to operate with independence and reach her destination. We spent all this time poking and prodding and trying to decipher her secrets, when Brother Errin has it right: we should have just asked her where she wanted to go, and gone along with her. We've spoiled any chance of that now, thanks to you two babbling fools."

"So what, then?" Archambelle demanded. "Are you saying the mission is a failure?"

"Of course not." Severyne rolled her head around on her neck, limbering up for what was likely to be a very strenuous few days. "I'm saying it's up to *me* to fix things, as usual. Here's what we're going to do."

Bianca woke up with a groan, her head all fuzzy and her eyes all blurry, but two blinks later she felt sharp and in focus again. She was stretched out on the floor in a bare, dimly lit room with some sort of flickering energy field in the place of one wall. The brig, then. And she wasn't alone.

The person she wasn't alone with was Letnev, but her hair was loose and messy around her face, a level of disarray Bianca had never witnessed in the crew before. The woman had a split lip, still a little bloody, and her close-fitting black uniform was askew, one sleeve torn. The woman sat on the floor, back against the wall, legs folded up so her knees were close to her chin. She frowned at Bianca, and spoke in the trading tongue. "What did *you* do to get locked up, princess?"

Bianca had no intention of talking to any Letnev in any language ever again, so she took a personal inventory instead. She was wearing her smartcloth dress, and she still had on her silver ring, so *that* was a surprise they wouldn't be prepared for if need be. They'd taken her shoes away for some reason, but she'd grown up running barefoot across rocky fields, so that was hardly debilitating. Otherwise, she had… well, just what she took with her everywhere. Strength and speed that wouldn't surprise her captors as much next time, and her mind. Those advantages would have to suffice.

The brig didn't have beds, just niches in the wall that were slightly more padded than the floor. Nothing she could wrench free to use as a weapon. Otherwise, the space was entirely bare. *So* bare, in fact, that, huh…

"You're wondering where you're supposed to shit?" the woman said. "That sleeping cubby in the middle isn't a sleeping cubby. You can tell by the smell. There's a hole, and suction. Crawl in there if you need to do your business. I'll avert my eyes from your aristocratic nethers, my lady." She cackled.

Bianca carefully examined the walls, looking for a seam she could pry open – she only had her bare hands, but they were strong, and her nails seemed to be unbreakable lately. There was nothing, just smooth metal. She growled in frustration.

The other prisoner was amused. "My people are apex jailers, and this is the cell where they keep enemy combatants, princess. We are secure. You aren't going to find a handy ventilation duct to crawl through. That's storybook stuff."

Bianca dropped down to the floor, thinking furiously, but her mind was like a vehicle stuck in the mud: the wheels spun, but there was nothing for them to dig into, so none of her thoughts got any purchase or took her anywhere. She cursed, elaborately, in Letnev, a combination of oaths she'd picked up from listening in on the cargo bay workers.

Her cellmate cackled again. "You swear like a toddler. You can't use *eshin* as a verb, that would be like saying, hmm, 'you assholing scum,' ha."

"Oh, shut up," Bianca said. "I know you're just a spy here to watch me."

"Watch you do what? Sit here and pout? My report back to my superiors is going to be *scintillating*." She worked her jaw, winced, and spat a tooth out onto the floor. "Seriously, princess, why are you locked up in here? What crime could *you* have possibly committed? A grievous breach of aristocratic etiquette? Did you use the wrong spoon at dinner with the captain?"

Bianca let her annoyance bubble up. "I've never even *met* the captain."

"Lucky break there. She's the worst. So what, then? Did you drop a stitch in your embroidery?"

She ground her teeth. "No. I assaulted three guards, a doctor, an undercommandant, and the ship's first officer, and tried to steal a shuttle."

The woman whistled. "Why did you do *that*? Was the thread count on your sheets too low for your tastes? Why would a princess like you–"

"I'm not a princess!" Bianca roared. "I'm a *prisoner*, and I was a prisoner *before*, but once I realized I was a prisoner and tried to get away, they made me a *real* prisoner."

The woman was silent for a long moment. "Oh. I see. You mean to tell me the officers lied to us about the aristocrat in our midst? Barony officials, bending the truth?" She smirked. "Truly unprecedented. I've never heard of such a thing before. You've shattered my worldview and dashed my illusions to splinters. Or shards. Whatever illusions break up into. I'm sad to hear you aren't a princess, though. I thought I must be pretty important if they put me in here with the likes of you."

"Why are you here?" Bianca said. "I know you're a spy, but I assume you have some elaborate cover story, and I could use the entertainment."

"Oh, yes, I really commit to my role. That's why I had to spit out a tooth just now, for *verisimilitude*. Listen to you – you think you're so important. They have cameras and microphones. Why would they need to punch me in the face and put me in here to listen to you whine? You're not the supermassive black hole at the center of the galaxy, princess – not *everything* revolves around you." The woman leaned her head back against the wall and appeared to go to sleep.

So what if she was a spy. That didn't necessarily mean Bianca shouldn't talk to her – maybe she could get *her* to let something slip, some piece of information that could help Bianca out of this situation. It wasn't like she had a lot of other avenues to pursue just now. If the woman tried to pump her for information about which way her yearning wanted them to go, Bianca simply wouldn't give her any. *I'll secretly and expertly interrogate* you, she thought. "All right," she said. "You're right. I've had a difficult day. I apologize. My name is Bianca. What's yours."

The woman cracked open one eyelid. "You can call me Sev, princess." Then she closed her eye again, and a moment later started to snore.

CHAPTER 20

It was difficult to convincingly pretend to sleep – faking the right kind of breathing was famously tricky – so Severyne didn't pretend; she actually went to sleep. She'd slept in worse circumstances, after all, and in more dangerous company.

Severyne woke up, not too much later, and smacked her dry lips. "Water!" she shouted. "Do you idiots want me to die before you get the chance to execute me?" She looked over at Bianca, who was sitting against the far wall hugging her knees to her chest, but didn't say anything to her. People didn't appreciate things that came too easily.

So far, Sev thought she'd done a good job with the girl. She didn't know if Archambelle's speculations about Bianca's possible psychic abilities were plausible or not, but for all they knew the girl could detect minute changes in breathing and heartbeat and blood pressure too, and might be able to sense when people were lying to her. Severyne had learned long ago that you could lie a lot without actually *lying*; you just said carefully chosen true things, and let people draw the conclusions you'd led them toward. You could even say some of your deep dark secrets straight out, and as long as you used a sarcastic tone, people would believe you meant the opposite. Avoiding outright lies while speaking to Bianca might not be necessary, but it couldn't hurt, and the challenge kept Severyne's mind focused.

"Will they bring us water?" Bianca said in a small voice.

Severyne yawned. "Oh, probably, eventually. As a rule, Barony officials don't let people they're planning to execute die of thirst. Why give their prisoners the easy way out? They must want to keep you alive too, if they kidnapped you and made up a whole elaborate story. Do you know why they really want you?"

Bianca ignored that. "Why are they going to execute you? What did *you* do?"

"Oh, lots of things." Severyne walked to the forcefield wall separating them from the corridor, and freedom, or at least, *relative* freedom; even if they escaped the cell, they'd still be on a Barony warship, after all. Though maybe not for much longer. "I got my start working in security – not standing by a door with a pulse rifle, my scores were too high for *that*, but managing teams of guards in a secure facility. Everything was going well, and my career was on the rise, when there was a regrettable incident and we lost a high-value asset. In the aftermath, I was reassigned to the *Grim Countenance*." All that was true. It was just that, in reality, she'd turned that regrettable incident to her own advantage, and the re-assignment had been a promotion to captain of her own ship. "Once I got here, I kept clashing with high-ranking officers, especially first officer Richeline. We had a lot of disagreements and, well, today I called her a babbling fool." All true. "Do you know how the Letnev feel about insubordination?"

Bianca nodded. "Section nineteen-c, paragraph g, of Barony military code says the penalty for willful insubordination is confinement to quarters, docking one cycle's pay, and a level-three formal public apology."

Severyne blinked at her with unfeigned surprise. "You memorized the military codes?"

She shrugged. "I get bored easily. The codes were one of the only things I was allowed to read in my room that didn't have any redactions. Lately, when I read things, they sort of stick in my mind."

"Huh. Do you remember what it says about *striking* a superior officer?"

Bianca laughed. "Detention, court martial, execution. Is that what you did?"

Severyne spread out her hands. "You see me standing here in this cell, don't you?"

Bianca nearly smiled. "It looks like Richeline got a couple of hits in herself."

That she had. Richeline had definitely seemed to enjoy hitting Severyne to complete her "fellow prisoner" disguise. The captain hadn't expected to be hit hard enough to loosen a tooth, but she could get it replaced later, and it did help sell the whole story. Severyne had refused painkillers, because as a real prisoner she wouldn't have received any, and she wanted to be as convincing as possible. A little pain – all right, a medium amount of pain – was a small price to pay to win Bianca's trust and complete the mission. "Richeline is trained in combat, and it shows. I understand why she was in such a bad mood when we had our little interaction now, if you roughed her up earlier."

"I guess we're both here for the same reason, in a way," Bianca said. "Except I don't think they plan to execute me. They want something from me." She paused, and it was such a *deliberate* pause that Severyne knew it was a trap. If she started probing about *what* the Letnev wanted from her, Bianca would suspect her even more of being a spy.

But Severyne's plan didn't rely on Bianca telling her anything, really, so she ignored the bait, and dangled a little bait of her own instead. "Screw them," Severyne said. "Why should you give them anything they want? I used to think the Barony was a true meritocracy, but I've been forced to serve under enough fools to know it's not that simple." She sat down next to Bianca, leaned in close, and whispered, "I have absolutely no intention of being tried and executed. I'm getting out of here."

"I thought you people were apex jailers?"

"Oh, we are. Nobody has better prisons. But do you know the weakest part of any system?"

"People," Bianca said.

"That's right. We can't break the walls, but we can break the *people*. Like I said, I worked in security, so I have some insight into these operations. I'm familiar with the duty rosters and shift changes and security procedures down here, too. I should be. I drew them up myself."

"Wait – you were in charge of the same brig they *put* you in?"

Severyne shrugged. "I oversaw security for the whole ship, yeah." As captain, that was true; the real security chief reported to her, after all. "This is the most secure brig they've got. It's not like the guards would set me free just because they used to work for me – personal loyalty only goes so far, and once you get locked up and scheduled for execution, you tend to lose your influence."

"So what's your plan?"

Severyne looked away. "I, ah, well, I, you see, I…" She didn't have to pretend to be uncomfortable. Talking about this really did bring up all sorts of complex feelings, including but not limited to guilt and shame. "I have a sort of history. With humans. Human women. *A* human woman. I was on a mission once, with a woman from the Federation of Sol, and we… became close. I know, we're ancestral enemies and all that, but we had a common interest that forced us to work together for a time, and professional respect grew into something more. That sort of thing is frowned upon in the Barony. It's seen as perversion. Worse, a violation of Barony values. It's like fraternization with the enemy, but more repulsive."

"There's no regulation against interspecies intimacy in the military codes," Bianca whispered.

"There's not a specific regulation against chopping up your mother and making her into soup, either, because there doesn't *need* to be – everyone knows it's simply not done."

"So, what? You want to *fraternize* with me? This is a very elaborate way to be creepy, Sev, and I don't like it."

Severyne wrinkled her nose. "You are far too young for me, princess, among other drawbacks too numerous to list. But I know the camera angles, and we can make it look like we're getting intimate without the necessity of actual contact. Believe me, the guards will come in with stun batons to break things up quickly if they think we're kissing. Witnessing a grotesque perversion of Letnev purity will probably make them a little careless – both guards on duty tonight are especially straitlaced."

Bianca laughed. "Why not? Say we lure them in. What then?"

"We beat them up. I wouldn't rate our chances high in a fair fight, but you say you took out three guards, so maybe you'll impress me. If it doesn't work…" She shrugged. "I'm already going to be tried and executed. It's not like I can get in *more* trouble for trying to escape."

"Say we do defeat the guards. Then what?"

"Then we hope Richeline hasn't gotten around to changing my security codes yet, so I can cancel any alarms and open the security doors and get to the shuttle bay."

"What if she *has* changed your codes?"

"Then I'll use Richeline's officer-level codes." Severyne grinned. "The security officer is the one who *generates* those codes. Sure, you're not supposed to look at them, let alone memorize them, but who knows what people get up to when no one else is watching?"

"It sounds pretty risky."

"My other plan is to fake a seizure, and try to escape when the medical team comes."

"I've read about that kind of thing in stories," Bianca said. "Actually, lots of stories."

Sev scowled. "Some things are classics for a reason, princess. Anyway, I like the first idea better, because I'd only have to punch guards instead of guards *and* medics, and you'll help with the punching, but like I said: when you're going to die anyway, every risk is an acceptable risk. If you're so valuable, they won't hurt you even if we fail. But maybe you'd prefer to stay, negotiate with the captain, try to make a deal–"

"They don't honor deals anyway." Bianca's voice shook with bitterness. Severyne felt a tiny bit bad about that. This all could have been handled differently. It had simply never crossed Severyne's mind to deal with the girl *fairly*, on an open, even-handed basis; the stakes were too high, the path too uncertain, and, after all, Bianca was just some human farm girl from a worthless mudball, not worthy of any real consideration. By the time Severyne started to respect the girl and understand her true capabilities, they'd gone too far down the road of deception, and well, here they were. But this road, however twisty, could still lead them to their destination. "Let's do it. At least this way I'll get to *hit* someone."

"Wonderful," Severyne said. "I hope you're as good at fighting as you claim to be. All right, you sit there, let me cuddle up close beside you. Good, now, lean *this* way, a little and I'll bow my head, here, and my hair will hide our faces. Go ahead and put your hand, ugh, on my hip there, all right, and the other one on the back of my neck ..."

They weren't *actually* kissing, but their faces were very close together, and it still felt more intimate than Bianca had been with anyone except Grandly, a few times, when the stars were bright and the moons were high and her blood sang in her veins. "Move your hands a little," Sev whispered. "Look passionate." Bianca did her best to comply, pretending she was in the throes of lust like the heroines she'd read about, but it was hard to feel those feelings when she was nose-to-nose with an alien woman. (But, she supposed, Grandly wasn't really the same species as her either. Was anyone, since all the Mahact were dead? But she wasn't quite Mahact, either.)

"No touching!" a voice grated harshly over the loudspeaker. Sev's hand briefly left its place on Bianca's shoulder, then returned.

"What did you just do?" Bianca whispered.

"I made an obscene gesture," Sev said. "I'll teach it to you later."

Boots came thumping down the hall – *three* sets of them, Bianca could hear, not two, as Sev had expected. Maybe she didn't know the rota here as well as she claimed, or they'd changed things up to confuse her, or they'd brought an extra guard because they knew what Bianca was capable of. Ha. Probably that one.

Bianca didn't expect this plan to work, not really, but trying something was better than waiting around for someone *else* to do something.

There was a buzz as the wall of energy came down, and Sev let go of Bianca and turned her head. With her view now unobstructed by the Letnev woman's face, Bianca could see two masked guards and first officer Richeline, all three holding black batons that crackled with blue sparks of energy at the ends.

Richeline stepped forward, a bruise dark around her eye. "A pervert as well as a violent insubordinate," Richeline said. "And you, Bianca – I thought better of you. When the guards first called me, I thought the traitor was molesting you, but no, apparently you're a willing participant!"

"It's boring in the cell, Richie," Sev said. "We had to entertain ourselves somehow. How's your eye?"

"How's your *neck*?" Bianca added, wanting to get in on the fun.

Richeline growled and stepped forward, baton at the ready.

Sev did a diving somersault, grabbing for Richeline's legs, doubtless intending to take her down – but one of the guards got a boot in, kicking her in the side and throwing her off course. Sev tried to scramble to her feet, but the guard hit her with a stun baton in the neck, and she jolted, eyes rolling back, and went limp.

So much for two against two. Now it was three against one.

Bianca almost felt bad for the three.

CHAPTER 21

Bianca still thought Sev was probably a spy and this was all a ploy to gain her trust. Participating in a doomed escape attempt would create a bond between them that would lead to shared confidences, and eventually Sev would encourage Bianca to cooperate with the Letnev... or, perhaps, Richeline would offer to spare Sev's life as a "reward" if Bianca helped them find their treasure world.

None of that mattered, though. If this was all a sham to manipulate her, Bianca would show them what a bad mistake they'd made trying to play her. While Richeline and the guards were distracted by their efforts to incapacitate Sev, she rose smoothly to her feet and kicked out Richeline's knee. The first officer squawked, dropping, leaving Bianca with a clear shot at the guards. They were impressively armored, but they needed to be able to move their heads around on their necks, so their throats weren't as well protected as the rest of them. (There weren't any body armor specs in the databases Ayla could provide, of course, but one bored afternoon Bianca had idly hacked into a security database and perused some of the technical manuals.) She stiffened the first two fingers of her right hand and jabbed straight into the most vulnerable spot. Poking the guard that way felt a lot like pushing her fingertips into a pudding. He gasped and fell down, writhing and grabbing his throat.

Richeline was slumped on the floor, but she was still conscious, and still a threat. She hit Bianca with the stun baton, jamming it right into the muscle of her calf, but apart from a faint tingle, Bianca didn't feel anything. She plucked the baton from Richeline's hand and used it like a club to smack the other guard across the facemask when he came at her, rather slowly since he was now trying not to trip over Richeline, Sev, *or* his writhing compatriot.

His mask shattered under the blow (the stun baton came apart in Bianca's hand, too), and he howled, blood running out from under the mask – a fragment must have cut his cheek. He stumbled around the cell in a very distracting fashion, so she kicked out one of his knees. She picked up his baton and zapped him in a now-exposed part of his neck, and that was him sorted out.

Fighting was pretty easy, it turned out: mostly just physics and anatomy, with a bit of psychology thrown in, and synchronizing three disciplines at once presented no particular challenge. Richeline was trying to crawl away, but Bianca looked at her and shook her head, and the first officer sank back, staring at Bianca and breathing hard.

Severyne sat up then, rubbing her face and blinking. "Wha? You took them all out yourself?"

"I am not taken *out*," Richeline spoke through clenched teeth. "This is absurd. You're on a secure deck. There's no escape."

"Sure there is," Bianca said. "You're going to escort me to a shuttle."

"I can fly us out of here," Sev said.

"I've read the manuals," Bianca said. "I can manage. If you really are a prisoner, I'm sorry, and I wish you luck with your escape. But you could be a spy, trying to trick me, so I'm going to take Richeline as a hostage and make my own way out of here."

Sev reached over, picked up a shard of the guard's broken mask, and stabbed it into the side of Richeline's neck.

The first officer screamed, clapped a hand to the shard, and tried to drag herself away on a broken knee as blood welled out all around her fingers. Sev kicked Richeline hard in the ribs, making her roll over and curl up. She glared at Bianca. "A *spy*?" she shouted. "Do you still think I'm a spy? Would a spy do *that*?" She kicked Richeline again, and the first officer huddled into a ball at the center of a spreading pool of blood.

Bianca stared at her. "I… no. I guess not."

"Shall we go, then?"

Bianca nodded. With Richeline dying – she was really dying! Bianca had never seen a person gurgling their last like this, only livestock, and this was *very* different! – Sev was the only one with the necessary access codes to get them out of the brig.

Sev picked up a stun baton in each hand, then tore a gauntlet from Richeline's arm. The first officer made a desperate sighing sound and clawed at her with the hand, but Sev idly kicked her arm away. She stalked off down the corridor, and Bianca hurried after her, happy to leave the scene of carnage behind. Sev didn't have Bianca's strength, speed, or reflexes, but she had a will to strike hard and without mercy that Bianca knew she couldn't hope to match and that she didn't *want* to match, honestly.

"You're lucky Richeline's baton malfunctioned," Sev called over her shoulder. "If we'd *both* gone down, that would have been the end of us."

"Yes," Bianca said. "Really lucky." She wondered, though. Her body was good at lots of things, lately: that impressive Mahact handiwork. Maybe she could just ignore the effects of a stun baton now. She had no doubt a knife wielded with sufficient force would cut her, that a laser would burn her, that a ball of superheated plasma would put a hole through her body, but she suspected she could shrug off a lot more than anyone supposed.

"Here." They reached an imposingly solid door at the end of the corridor. Sev strapped the first officer's gauntlet onto her own arm and slid her fingers across it until the door slid open. "Perfect. She never changed the default code used to unlock the gauntlet. Very sloppy. She should be written up for that. Not that her permanent record matters much now, I suppose, with her dead on the floor of the brig." She tapped the gauntlet. "With this, we can get anywhere on the ship, as long as we move fast."

"Where are we going?" Bianca said.

"I haven't thought any farther than 'off the ship'," Sev said. "You don't have any contacts in the Lue-Hel system, do you?"

"I only know people on one planet, and it's a long way from here."

Sev grunted, stepping out of the corridor into some sort of security station, with a curved desk, a row of monitors, and a rack of silver and black weaponry sealed behind a forcefield like the one in their cell. "Can you use a gun?"

"My father taught me to use a kinetic rifle, a few years back, when there was a drought and the nightclimbers expanded their territory."

"Same principle." She waved her hand, and the field over the rack of guns shimmered, responding to the gauntlet. The ship thought she *was* Richeline now. Sev took down a long black gun and handed it to Bianca, then took one for herself, and tucked a sidearm into her belt, too. "These are better than a kinetic rifle, though. You don't have to account for recoil, so it won't bruise your shoulder."

I don't think I bruise so easily anymore, Bianca thought. She looked over the rifle, and its mechanisms were readily apparent to her. In fact, she saw two or three ways she could improve it to boost its power and accuracy, if she had the right tools and a few minutes to work on it, but now wasn't the time.

"The main hangar bay is too crowded." Sev tapped on a terminal at the security desk, consulting various screens. "But there's a secondary launch bay where we keep the survey ships. They aren't made for long-distance travel, but they can handle vacuum and atmosphere both. We'll need to switch ships as soon as we can, so the more flexibility the better. Let me spoof a security alert to get the guards in the secondary launch bay to leave their posts… Done. Let's move."

Sev set off without hesitation, and Bianca followed close behind, gun at port arms. "Aren't you afraid someone will see us?"

"I checked our route. There's no one along our path right now but cleaning drones. I looped the camera feeds, too. That won't fool anyone who looks closely, but we can avoid triggering any automated alerts."

"You act like you've done this before."

Sev snorted. "I was trained to *stop* this sort of thing. I've done countless simulated jailbreaks, escapes, rescues, hostage situations, you name it. There are ways to ruin my plan, but only if they've got someone smarter than me running things, and by definition, they don't. The person who's in charge of security now is no match for me."

"I've never been in this part of the ship." Bianca looked around with interest. The corridors here were more bare and austere, and more cramped too. She heard the rumble and whirr of machinery hidden by doors and access panels on all sides.

"Why would you come down here? It's where we keep the cargo, the noisy boring machines, the air scrubbers, the matter recyclers, all the unlovely infrastructure of long-haul space voyages. And the prisoners, of course. No reason to give them deluxe accommodations. Here, this way."

Sev scrambled up a ladder, and Bianca shifted the rifle on its strap so it hung on her back, then followed. She looked up, Sev's feet just inches from her face. There was blood all over one of her boots. "Did you have to kill Richeline?" Bianca said.

"You were going to take her with you instead of me," Sev said. "That was a choice *you* made. I simply responded in the only tactically sound manner."

Bianca frowned. "Then why are you *still* with me? Once you took Richeline's wristband, you could have left me behind."

Sev emerged at the top of the ladder into an even more cramped space, some kind of service corridor, and gestured for Bianca to hurry up. When she answered, it was in a whisper. "I don't know what you are exactly, princess, but you tore through those guards like they were made of lace. Maybe you're some kind of vat-grown supersoldier who had her memory erased, or Brother Errin crammed you full of military implants, or maybe you're something else I could never hope to understand, but you are a definite asset. I forgive you for trying to leave me behind. *That* was tactically sound too, and it's why I stabbed Richeline in the neck: so you'd believe I *wasn't* a spy, and that we're in this together. How about we stay in this together, at least until we get far away from the *Grim Countenance* and Letnev space?"

Bianca considered. Sev definitely knew more about the galaxy than Bianca did – she hadn't even known this was the Lue-Hel system! – and that expertise could prove useful. Plus, if Sev didn't care where she went, and she just wanted to get *away*, then maybe she'd be amenable to traveling to the source of Bianca's yearning. She still intended to go there, and see what she was meant for. She didn't want to go on the end of a Letnev leash, but it would be easier to make her way with company than all alone. "That works for me."

"Then let's go. Through here." Sev crept forward, then waved her gauntlet at a door. It slid open, revealing a guard who stepped back in surprise. Sev launched herself forward, attempting to bowl the man over, but he was huge, and she bounced off his armored legs instead. She swung one of her stun batons, and he caught her arm with one hand and her throat with the other. Sev swung her other baton at the guard's head, but he kept his chin tucked, taking the blows on the solid back and sides of his helmet, and not the more fragile faceplate.

Amazingly, he didn't seem to notice Bianca at all, but then, he was understandably focused on choking the life out of Sev. Bianca slung her energy rifle around her body, took aim at his center mass, then shifted and squeezed the trigger.

The rifle emitted a beam of reddish light – Bianca knew no portion of the energy that emerged needed to be in the visible spectrum, but she assumed it was probably useful for soldiers to see if they were firing straight. The beam passed through the soldier's ankle, nearly detaching his foot from his body. He howled, dropped Sev, and fell backward. Sev gagged, spat, and drew her sidearm, pointing at his head.

Bianca blurred across the intervening space and batted the gun out of Severyne's hand. "He's *down*! You don't have to kill him!"

The guard wasn't even screaming, just moaning; probably going into shock, though he shouldn't bleed out since the beam had cauterized the wound on its way through.

Sev scowled at Bianca, baring her teeth, and Bianca thought she might lash out, but instead the Letnev woman nodded. She stooped to pick up her handgun and put it away. "Strangle me," she muttered, looking balefully at the fallen guard. "Yesterday he would have *saluted* me."

"A couple of months ago, the most unpleasant thing I ever had to do was shoveling caprid shit," Bianca said. "Things have changed for both of us."

"Ha. True enough." Sev strode down the hallway toward a large set of doors. She waved her wrist gauntlet, cursed, and then punched in a code. One of the doors lurched open half a meter, and Sev said, "Hurry, they're going into lockdown, I don't know how long before they cancel these codes!" She squeezed through the gap, and Bianca followed. They were in an airlock. The door behind them closed, and Sev cursed at the door on the opposite side, finally convincing it to open a crack.

Once they squeezed through that, they were in a small hangar, with three of the birdlike shuttles. The far wall was open to the stars, a shimmering forcefield standing between them and the void… and freedom.

Sev ran toward the nearest ship, punching inputs on her gauntlet, and the shuttle lowered a ramp. They raced onto the ship, and Sev slid into the pilot's seat and began punching at the controls.

Bianca sat beside her, watching the ship's external camera feeds on the co-pilot screens. A guard was trying to squeeze through the gap in the door they'd used, but in her bulky body armor, she couldn't quite make it. She stuck a sidearm through the crack instead and started firing at their ship. "They're shooting at us!" she shouted.

"Might as well throw rocks at a moon," Sev said. "Those weapons can't hurt this ship, and I locked them out of the main hangar controls, so they won't be able to scramble fighters to come after us until they untangle my code. Still, I don't like being shot at. I could turn on the maneuvering thrusters and cook her in her armor…"

"*Don't*," Bianca said.

"I won't. I was just saying I could. See how merciful and noble I can be, princess?" The survey ship rumbled and rose up from the deck. "They'd better get back into that airlock and shut the door if they don't want to suck vacuum, though." Sev manipulated the controls, and the shimmering wall of light before them vanished. Bianca kept one eye on the external camera feed, and was relieved to see the arm pull back and the airlock door close.

The ship rumbled. Sev moved a slider on the hovering visual interface, and they shot out of the *Grim Countenance* and into the dark. The shimmering crystal beauty of the Tree of Grace floated out on their left, but they were headed the other way, toward dark, and stars… and the source of Bianca's yearning.

Sev said, "There. If we survive the next hour without being blown up by Barony fighters, I'd say we have a chance at living at least, oh, say, another week." She rose and entered the main compartment, where she began stripping off her torn and bloody clothing. Bianca averted her eyes, then thought to look at her own clothes, but her smartcloth was pristine, stain-resistant and self-cleaning. None of the blood or dirt or grease of their escape had stuck to her.

"Where are we headed?" Bianca called.

Sev returned to the cockpit, pulling on a plain gray sweatshirt over matching pants. "There's a moon nearby, where wealthy visitors to the Tree of Grace stay sometimes. I'm sure I can find another ride for us there." She pulled her messy hair back into a tight ponytail and secured it in place with an elastic band. When she was done, she still looked like someone who'd been in a couple of fights recently, but less like someone who'd *lost* them all.

"Sev, I couldn't have gotten away without you. Which isn't to say I approve of everything you did along the *way*, but… thank you."

"Mmm. You really don't like killing, do you, princess? That's odd, since you have a real knack for causing mayhem."

"I'll defend myself," Bianca said. "I'll fight for my freedom. If I had no choice, maybe I could kill. But that guard, all those guards, were just doing their jobs."

"Their *jobs* were imprisoning you. Doesn't that make you angry?"

"They had their orders," Bianca said. "If you're a Letnev, orders are all you have, and if you don't follow them… well, you know. Look at your own situation. Now, if we're talking about the people who *gave* the orders, I might not be so forgiving if I ended up in a room alone with the captain."

"It might surprise you to know captains have to follow orders, too," Sev said. "So do admirals. So do the heads of the great families. The only person in the Barony who never has to take orders from anyone is the Baron. But if he declared tomorrow that the Letnev should become a pacifist nation, devoted to doing good works for the downtrodden people of the galaxy, he might find out his rule isn't quite as absolute as he *thinks* it is, and we'd owe our fealty to a newly elevated Baron by the end of the week – one who supports the true Letnev way of life. We *all* follow someone's orders."

"I don't," Bianca said.

"Huh," Sev said. "I guess you don't. Neither do I, now. No one to answer to. No one making demands. Thinking about living that kind of life, honestly, it makes me a little dizzy."

"I hope we both have a lot of time to get used to it," Bianca said. And yet… was she really as free as she claimed? There was that yearning, wasn't there? A compulsion to visit one particular bit of the sky. Who'd given her *that* order, and why?

What if she'd escaped one tether, only to discover she was at the end of another, much longer one?

She'd just have to go and see. And if she arrived at her destination and found a hand holding the other end of that leash, she'd just have to see about biting it off.

"Do you know where you want to go?" Bianca asked. "I mean, longer term?"

Sev shook her head. "The only life I've known is the Barony military. I've got access to a little money, enough to keep me going in the short term. After that, I guess I'll try to find work as a soldier-of-fortune or something. I have some useful skills."

"I could use some help," Bianca said. "I think I could even make it worth your while, on the other side."

Sev cocked her head. "Oh? Do tell, princess."

There was a lot to tell – about the Mahact, about the compass in her head, about the fabled world of Ixth… but she started where it began. "I have this… Dr Archambelle called it a *yearning*…"

CHAPTER 22

"Are we going to steal another ship once we get to that moon?" Bianca asked.

Severyne couldn't tell if the idea excited or bothered the girl, so she chose a neutral response. "We'll assess the situation when we land. We have more immediate concerns. Help me get this panel off." Severyne pried at a part of the cockpit console that wasn't meant to be opened from this side; even jamming in a probe as hard as she could, she couldn't get it to flex more than a millimeter or two.

Bianca reached over and popped off the metal square without apparent effort. "What are you doing?" She peered inside at a tangle of wire and dull metal components.

"There's a transponder under here. Barony tracking technology. They like to know where their ships are. The tracker is integrated with the propulsion system, so if I remove it, then the ship stops flying. I can't do anything about that, but I think I can stop the tracker from *reporting* it's been tampered with, and make sure it keeps broadcasting its location even once I remove it from the ship."

"How does that help us?"

"We'll put this tracker on another ship after we land, and send the Barony chasing after *them* instead of us. Should buy us a little extra time." Severyne delicately snipped at wires. This was all theater, of course – there was a tracking chip in her body, and anyway, she wanted to be followed. But she performed the alterations as carefully and accurately as if it really mattered, because it was safest to treat Bianca as if she were omniscient and omnicognizant. It was doubtful that she could discern the workings of complex machinery from a mere glance but–

"Not that one," Bianca said. "That goes into the navigation system, but then it continues on to the communications array, see? You need to jump that wire instead, peel away the insulation and attach those clips here and here."

"I didn't realize you had an engineering background," Severyne said.

"Oh, just watching my father work on machinery around the farm. But I pick things up quickly."

A primitive tractor on a backward colony world had as much in common with a Barony starship as a candle had with a star, but no matter. It was good to know her caution had been warranted. "There," Severyne said. "That should buy us a little time later."

•••

The luxury moon was called Glamarij, and it orbited a blackened cinder of a planet. "What happened there?"

Severyne glanced at the dead husk of a world. "War."

They glided down toward the surface of the moon without being challenged, skimming over low scrub. "This moon has an atmosphere?"

"It's a bit thin and inhospitable, but yes. The inhabitants of that planet started a terraforming process here before they destroyed themselves. We'll land soon."

"We weren't allowed to dock at the space station without permission," Bianca said.

"Oh, we can't get anywhere *good* without permission here, either," Severyne said. "We can land on the surface, but the underground galleries and pleasure domes are less accessible. This is the unfashionable side of the moon, where the servants and crews congregate, so we'll fit right in." They crested a low mountain range, and Severyne said, "Oh, good, we can set down there."

She pointed to a hexagon marked out on the ground in glowing lines. Other hexagons were scattered across the greenish-gray surface of the moon, many of them occupied by ships of varying shapes and sizes. "We're allowed to park in any open hex. The locals will impound the ship eventually, when we fail to pay our docking fees, but we don't need this shuttle anymore anyway." Once they were settled on the ground, Severyne deployed the ramp, then popped out the transponder they'd tampered with earlier. The ship blared an alarm, but only briefly, and then the vessel's lights went out.

Severyne had to suppress a gasp. In the sudden darkness, Bianca's eyes began to glow, a faint blue that quickly faded. Was it some adaptation that helped her see in the dark? What *was* she?

They walked down the ramp and stepped onto the moon's surface. The air was breathable, if a bit astringent. "I'm so bouncy!" Bianca jumped into the air in the low gravity and did a full pirouette as she drifted back down, laughing joyously. Severyne had experienced the same joy in movement, at times… but usually those movements involved hitting people with things.

"That ship should do." Severyne nodded toward a vessel a few hexes over, larger than theirs, with a crew lugging cargo crates on board. "They look like they're on the way out. Do you want to distract them, or hide this?" She held up the transponder, still blinking its little telltale light.

Bianca frowned. "Won't the Barony shoot them when they catch up?"

Severyne sighed. "You're so concerned for others. Once the *Grim Countenance* gets within range, they'll realize it's not our ship, and shooting won't be necessary. They'll be fine."

Bianca grunted. "I'll do the distracting, then. I like meeting new people." She turned and bounded toward the workers, shouting, "Hello, I just got here, it's wonderful, can you tell me, is there anywhere good to *eat* around here?"

Severyne tuned out the prattle, slipped around the far side of the ship, and crouched by one of the landing gears. She had a small pressurized can of sealant on her belt, sufficiently strong to bind the transponder to the gear. She sprayed, attached, and counted to ten slowly for the sealant to dry. She wiggled the device. Hmm, still a little loose. She'd better–

Severyne sighed. She had to act like all these evasive maneuvers were real in front of Bianca, but she didn't have to *believe* it was real. She gave the transponder a last squirt anyway and then sauntered around the ship. "Amina, stop bothering those people, they have work to do. Forgive my hireling. She's new."

The Xxcha lugging a crate rumbled, "It's fine. She's charming. Enjoy your visit."

"They told me where to get *pie*," Bianca said. Severyne led her away, toward a cluster of low domes beyond the landing zone. Bianca leaned closer and said, "Why did you call me Amina?"

"I knew an Amina once. It's the only name, other than Bianca, that I know for sure is plausible for a human."

"Secret identities! What should I call you?"

"Whatever you like, as long as it's a Letnev name." Might as well indulge her.

"Genevieve, I think," Bianca said. "That was the name of one of the great Barony generals I read about. We'll call you 'Gen' for short."

Severyne couldn't help but be flattered. Genevieve Lamorte was a legendary general who'd crushed a dozen uprisings with effortless aplomb. She frowned. "You actually *are* charming. Where did you learn to be like that?"

"I don't know," Bianca said. "It's just… Look, I really thought you were a spy earlier. I almost left you to certain death, and I feel terrible about that. I've decided I'm going to treat people like they really are the way I wish they were. Sometimes I'll be disappointed, but you know what? I bet a lot of people will rise to the occasion."

"You're so… *human*."

"Tell that to Brother Errin," Bianca said. "What's in the domes?"

"Places that sell various intoxicants, probably. Along with places to sleep off their effects."

"Yay!" Bianca said. "But I guess we aren't getting intoxicated?"

"We are not. We are going to find intoxicated people to take advantage of instead."

Heuvelt sat drinking in a corner of a bar on Glamarij. Ashont and Clec were a few tables away, playing cards with a Winnaran and a Saar. They were only betting with toothpicks taken from the bartender, but apparently the toothpicks represented the honor of their respective species, and Heuvelt did not feel capable of representing humanity in the manner his people deserved. He stared at his hand terminal, where two windows were open. One window showed their credit balance in the ship's account Clec had opened (since accounts with Heuvelt's name on them tended to get frozen or seized), and the other displayed a Barony of Letnev fugitive bounty database.

The first window was very nice. The Disciplinarian had paid quite well for their delivery, with a bonus for swift completion. He paid so well that Heuvelt wondered what, exactly, they'd handed over to the twitchy little Yin scientist, but it was probably better not to know. The *Show and Tell* was actually operating in the black again.

The second window was… less nice. Heuvelt was still listed as a "fugitive alien of interest" with a note to "contact Barony officials immediately if you know his whereabouts." The Disciplinarian said that alert would be expunged, but it might take a few days for the system to update, Barony bureaucracy being what it was. The Letnev weren't offering a reward for him anymore, so he doubted anyone would bother to turn him in – most species didn't feel a need to do the Letnev any uncompensated favors – but the sight of those Barony vessels back at the Tree of Grace still had him twitchy and on edge.

Which is why, when a Letnev woman strode in, glaring around the bar, he froze.

Her eyes didn't linger on him for very long, though, before she stomped toward the bar, moving like she wanted to kick the floor to death with every step. *Then* Heuvelt noticed the woman she'd come in with. Young, slender, pretty, wide-eyed and smiling, and *human*. Why in the galaxy would a human and a Letnev be traveling together? The species had a long and extensive history of enmity, stretching back to the collapse of the Lazax empire, if not earlier. The human ambled over to Ashont and Clec's table and said, "Ooh, what are you playing?"

"Where I'm from, we call it Kiss-Kill," Ashont rumbled. "The Saar call it Song and Scream, and I don't know what Winnu call it."

"By its proper name," the Winnaran said. "Traitor's Tongue."

"May I watch?" the young woman said. They assented, and she sat down, perched on the edge of her chair. She wore a red dress that should have been out of place in this working-class bar, but somehow she seemed perfectly at ease, and the motley group around her was at ease with her in return.

Heuvelt couldn't stop staring at the young woman. There was something strangely captivating about her, and it wasn't just her beauty (when it came to lust, he was mostly attracted to men, though as a rich spendthrift with a taste for adventure he'd dabbled considerably more widely).

The Letnev woman walked over to the table, looked down, and said, "Are you playing for money?"

The other players exchanged glances. "We're playing for honor."

"I don't have any of that to spare," the Letnev said. She put a small glass in front of the human. "You get this one, Amina. Just *one*. Don't accept drinks from strangers, no matter how nice they are. If they're nice, in fact, be especially suspicious."

"Good advice," Ashont rumbled.

"I'm going to the bathroom," the Letnev said. "Lesson one of space travel: never pass up the chance to use a toilet someone else has to clean."

"Yes, Gen." The girl beamed at her. The Letnev scowled and stomped off toward the back of the bar.

Heuvelt watched her go. Was she really just going to the bathroom, or was it a ruse? Maybe she was a fugitive hunter, setting a trap to capture him. Or maybe she was just a loyal Barony citizen, but she'd recognized him, and gone off to call the authorities to turn him in. He looked around, scanning for the exits, so he'd know where to go if heavily armed Letnev shock troopers burst into the bar–

He shook his head and took a deep sip of his liquor. He was being paranoid.

Heuvelt went back to watching Amina as they dealt her in for their next hand. "Oh, I think I picked up the basics from watching," she said airily. Heuvelt doubted that. It was a twisty game, all bluff and double-bluff and cards that changed value depending on the placement of other cards around them. He'd been taught six times, and still made beginner's mistakes. Ah well. As long as they had fun. Everyone deserved a little fun every once in a while.

"Stop whining," Severyne snapped. "You're alive, aren't you?"

Richeline's face flickered on Severyne's stolen wrist gauntlet. The first officer – now acting captain, since she'd lived – had an immense bandage wrapped around her neck, and wires and tubes running into her body, but she was sitting upright, and she was lucid. Too lucid for Severyne's taste, honestly. "I just didn't expect you to *stab* me, captain!"

"I had to improvise. That's part of being a field operative – you should know that, since your dream is to run covert teams. I knew there were soldiers watching us, and that they'd send medical help as soon as I left. You were never in any danger." Richeline had been in a great deal of danger, of course, but Severyne could lie all she wanted while talking to *her*.

The woman wasn't done venting yet, though, apparently. "Archambelle said if you'd stayed even a minute longer, I would have bled out."

"That's why I didn't spend the extra minute, Richeline. Now, please, *focus*. Things are going perfectly on my end. The girl actually *asked* me to help her find Ixth – I didn't even have to plant the seed in her mind." She scowled. "I am curious how she knows the name of her destination, though, and how she learned about the Mahact. She is distressingly well informed."

Richeline groaned. "It must have been Brother Errin. He refused to sign any confidentiality agreements, but Archambelle said we should go ahead with the meeting anyway. I knew it was a mistake."

"It is what it is," Severyne said. "We can only go forward. Is my new ship ready?"

"Yes. We contracted with the mercenaries through the intermediary you suggested. They had a team in the system, and they just landed on Glamarij. How did you get Sagasa the Disciplinarian to vouch for you? A Hacan crime lord and a Barony captain, it's… not a connection I'd expect."

"Oh, I have connections everywhere," Severyne said. That wasn't really true, but the connections she *did* have were valuable. "Once we give Bianca a proper scare, we'll flee toward the landing zone, 'hijack' the mercenary ship, and lock up the crew. Then we'll escape, and Bianca can set a course for us. You just hang back and follow at a discreet distance until we get wherever it is we're going. Once we've reached Archambelle's magical wonder planet and all the locks are open, the mercenaries can throw off their chains and subdue the princess for me. Understood?"

"Yes, captain."

"Good," Severyne said. "Give me two minutes, and then send in the shock troops."

CHAPTER 23

"I'm really sorry," Bianca said again, raking the last of the toothpicks toward her. "It's just beginner's luck."

"You can't be a hustler," the big teddy bear said, voice all a-growl. "We weren't playing for money, and we certainly aren't going to start *now*."

"Oh, I just enjoy games, and making new friends." Bianca picked up one of the toothpicks and began chewing on it.

Sev emerged from the bathroom, glanced around, and beckoned to Bianca.

She stood up, offering her hand to Strig (the teddy bear), and to Gretla (the Winnaran), and Ashont (the kitty with the little four-armed person on her shoulder), and to Clec (the little four-armed person). "It was lovely to meet all of you."

"Very nice to meet you, too, Amina," Ashont rumbled.

She walked to the bar, where Sev was leaning with studied casualness. "Are we leaving, Gen?"

"I hope." Sev drew Bianca in close and spoke into her ear. "Did any of those gamblers mention plans to leave soon? We could follow them, and persuade them to let us borrow their ship." She patted her waist, where her sidearm was hidden under her sweatshirt.

"Gen, they're my *friends*. I bet they'd help us if we just asked."

Sev snorted. "Faint hope. Oh, you're charming enough to get us a ride off this rock, no doubt, but we need a ship we can take anywhere we *want*, so we can explore this… what did you call it?"

"My yearning."

"Yes. That. You're not charming enough to convince someone to give us a ship for free, I'm afraid, so we'll have to proceed by other means."

Bianca sighed. "I suppose you're right. I just hate to strand anyone here."

"This is a civilized place. If they're professionals, their ships are insured against theft. They'll be fine." She looked past Bianca, toward the door. "So, again, are any of your new friends departing Glamarij soon?"

Ashont and Clec were planning to leave shortly, she knew – they'd just landed here to refuel and resupply and "get a little R&R."

"I suppose after we find the treasure, I can repay them for the trouble," she said.

"Repay who?" Sev asked.

Bianca started to point out Ashont and Clec, and then time slowed down, the same way it had when the cup fell in the mess hall, but far more extreme. The sounds of the bar, the drinking and boasting and grousing and flirting and slurping and clattering, all elongated and stretched and dropped in pitch. The movements of the people around her stopped almost entirely, until she was surrounded by a room full of mannequins.

Last time, this power had manifested so she could prevent the very small disaster of a broken teacup. What disaster was it meant to prevent this time? What danger had her subconscious noticed, and acted to protect her from?

She looked at the open door and saw a shadow. Two shadows, actually, overlapping. The shadows were moving quickly, far quicker than anything *else* here, though they still crawled. Someone was rushing into the bar. That probably wasn't good.

Bianca stepped away from Sev, discovering that she could move at normal speed. She picked up a bottle from the bar as she went by – not glass, but a heavy metal vessel, containing some potent brew not meant for human consumption. The floor was crowded with patrons, now frozen in place, and cluttered with tables, so she just stepped onto an empty chair and used it as a launching pad to leap over the whole crowd. (Fortunately, the ceiling was high enough for such a maneuver, though the top of her head only cleared it by a few centimeters.)

She landed near the door just as the first of the Barony shock troopers cleared the entryway. Bianca dropped, spun, and swept his legs out from under him, and he fell forward in slow motion. The trooper behind him came at her, and, since Bianca was already crouching, she swung the metal vessel at his knee.

Just at the last moment, she pulled the strike, following a quick mental calculation. Force equals mass times acceleration, after all, and her acceleration must be a *lot* faster than it currently appeared. If she hadn't pulled back, she thought she would have torn his whole lower leg off – it would have been more like blowing off his kneecap with a shotgun than hitting him with a bottle.

As it was, his knee crunched, and he began his own slow fall. Bianca stood up, and then stepped back, giving herself some room to operate. Two more guards approached, one of them raising a weapon at her – not a lethal armament, she noted, but some kind of tranquilizer gun, meant to subdue.

She threw the bottle at his gun hand, then stepped toward the other soldier while the bottle was still making its way through the air. She had to reach over the first two troopers (who were still slowly collapsing to the floor) to shove him in the chest, sending him flying back into yet another trooper beyond him.

Their bodies moved slow, slow, like drifting snow. Last time, the time dilation had stopped when the cup was saved, and the danger was done – but the danger here was ongoing, wasn't it? This state wasn't likely to end on its own anytime soon, but she needed to get Sev out of here, and that was hard when she was a statue.

Bianca turned her ever-more-powerful attention to the contours of her own mind, seeking to understand the mechanism. How could you seize control of a process that happened without thought? There were ways. Breathing was an automatic function, but you could *choose* to exert control, to hold your breath, to stop and start... or how about changing the focus of your eyes from something up close to something far away? That happened by itself too, but you could blur your vision at will if you wanted... Ah. There. The process had been opaque to her when the teacup fell, but now she could understand. Brother Errin was right. She was changing all the time. Bianca exhaled, walked over to Sev, and then bid time return...

Heuvelt jerked his head up at a sudden explosion of violence by the front door. His hand went to the knife at his belt – a gift from Dob Ell that he hadn't thrown away, because even though their friendship was over it was still a good blade. He couldn't tell what was happening exactly, but bodies were falling, and people were screaming. After a moment, his brain caught up to his eyes and made sense of what he was seeing – those were Barony of Letnev soldiers, in their terrifyingly blank face masks and black body armor.

Someone *had* seen him, and turned him in, and the Barony was coming for him! He couldn't tell what had happened to their ranks, whether they'd been attacked or if one of their weapons had gone off by mistake, but the commotion might allow him a few crucial moments to escape.

"Ashont, Clec, come on!" Heuvelt leapt up from the booth as his crewmates shoved back from their table and rushed to join them. "Through the back!" They followed as he hurried toward the doors leading to the kitchen. Heuvelt had spent enough time in bars to know that door would inevitably lead to some sort of back alley or service entrance or loading dock – they certainly didn't take the trash out or bring the kegs in through the front door, after all.

He was surprised to see the human and Letnev women – Amina and Gen – rushing toward that exit too. What were they running from?

They all piled up in the rear of the kitchen while a human in a dirty apron shouted at them. "It's locked!" Gen shouted, hammering her fist against the door. She spun toward the cook, drawing a gun, and said, "Open this door!"

He shrieked and ran away, and Gen swore, then pointed the gun at Heuvelt. "Who the hell are you and what do you want?"

"I- I- we..." Heuvelt had never been good at expressing himself when he was figuratively under the gun, and it turned out he was even worse at doing so when the gun was literal.

"I've got it." Amina kicked the door, and it *crashed off its hinges*, banging against the wall of the hallway beyond. Was the door made of lightweight plastic or something? It had certainly *looked* solid enough. Amina rushed through, and Gen followed.

Heuvelt looked at Ashont and Clec. "Very strange," Ashont rumbled.

"They went through there!" a voice shouted from the bar behind them. Heuvelt swore and ran through the opening, his crewmates following. They pelted down the service corridor on the other side, Gen and Amina just a few steps ahead. Someone yelled at them to stop immediately, so Heuvelt ran faster. Gen looked back at him without breaking stride and shouted, "Why are you following us?"

"I'm not!" he called. "We're just running away in the same direction!"

"Why are you running away?" Amina called.

"Because there are Letnev soldiers *chasing* us!"

"They're chasing *us*, you fool!" Gen said.

Oh. Could that be possible? Surely not. Such a thing would constitute good luck, and Heuvelt no longer believed in that. "I don't think so!" he said. "I'm a wanted man in the Barony!"

"Us too!" Amina said. "Only we're wanted women!"

"Go away, leave us alone, you're slowing us down!" Gen shouted.

"How can we be slowing you down when we're behind you?"

"Stop chasing us or I'll shoot!" the Letnev howled.

"No, don't!" Amina said. "This is perfect! Ashont, Clec, strange man – let's all go to your ship!"

"*What?*" Gen shouted.

They escaped the building and slammed the external door behind them. "I don't know how to lock it!" the human (who ran pretty fast, for an old guy) cried out, furiously pushing his fingers against an access panel.

Bianca touched his shoulder and gently pushed him aside. She was learning to be gentle, now that she could so easily break things accidentally. She squinted at the panel, punched in a rapid sixteen-digit code, and then smiled as the lights went red and bolts slammed home. "There. I remembered the factory settings, and they didn't change. The door thinks there's atmospheric decompression on this side. It won't open without a command override from the station administrators now."

"There's *atmosphere* out here," the man said. "Why would there even be a code to indicate decompression?"

"This facility uses standard hardware and software," Clec said. "The same doors are used on space stations and habitats all over the galaxy. But there are dozens of manufacturers – how did you know the factory codes for *this* one?"

Bianca shrugged. They were the same sort of doors used on the *Grim Countenance*, and she'd perused a technical manual on one of her visits to the engineering department, until they chased her off. The next time she came down, the terminal with those files had been locked. It had taken her almost a full minute to unlock them. "I must have picked them up somewhere."

"Our Amina has a mind like a wastebasket that never gets emptied," Sev said. "It's been a displeasure meeting you. We'll be on our way now–"

Bianca shook her head. "They've got a ship, Gen. I'm sure they want to leave in a hurry. We should go with them, instead of taking our chances on finding a ride elsewhere."

Sev opened her mouth as if to object, then looked toward the ranks of parked spacecraft in their neat hexagons. Her shoulders slumped. "Fine. We can work with this. Take us to your ship."

"You weren't *invited*," the human said, drawing himself up and crossing his arms over his chest.

"She's the reason you aren't in Letnev custody right now, Heuvelt," Ashont said. "Even if those troopers weren't chasing us specifically, they would have been happy enough to pick you up as a bonus." The panther-woman showed off her teeth in what was surely meant to be a smile. "*I'm* inviting her."

"Seconded," Clec said from her shoulder.

Heuvelt sighed. "I–"

Something slammed hard against the door on the other side.

"Go!" Sev said. Ashont and Clec set off running, weaving through the parked ships, and the others followed. They arrowed toward one particular vessel, on the far edge of the lot, and Bianca was surprised to see it was a fast courier, though retrofitted to add extra compartments on either side of the main body – it looked like a wasp wearing saddlebags.

A signal pulsed out from Clec toward the ship, and – Wait. Bianca wondered how she knew that. Apparently, she had another new ability, bubbling up from the depths. She couldn't exactly *see* the beam of energy, but she could sense it, from its origin to its direction. Now that she knew to pay attention, she could sense a whole overlapping array of signals, crisscrossing the facility and the ships. She could pick out individual signals and trace them from source to destination. She shook her head. There would be time enough to ponder this new sense later. Clec's pulse triggered a mechanism on the ship, and a boarding ramp slid down as they approached.

"Get us out of here!" Heuvelt shouted, the last one on board, the ramp rising under his feet as he ran. Ashont and Clec were already moving to the front, the engines engaging in reply to more signals from Clec.

"We'd better strap in," Heuvelt said. "Things get a bit bumpy on the *Show and Tell* when we take off in atmosphere."

"Your ship is called the *Show and Tell*?" Sev said. "That is a ridiculous name."

Bianca smiled and turned toward her. "Your old ship was called the *Grim–*"

She stared at Sev for what felt like a long moment (it was, in fact, barely a microsecond), then snatched the knife from Heuvelt's hip, knocked Sev's legs out from under her, and leapt atop the Letnev, blade raised.

CHAPTER 24

"Report!" Richeline barked. Voyou winced, and he wasn't even on the receiving end of her bad mood.

The shock trooper's head filled the screen at an odd, tilted angle, as seen from the camera on a wrist gauntlet. "Xing disabled half a dozen of my people. We need immediate medical attention–"

Richeline pointed at the bandage bulging around her neck. "I *told* you to be careful around her."

"We didn't have time to be careful, captain. She attacked us before we even came through the door."

"Remarkable," Archambelle murmured. "If we could replicate her transformations, the military applications–"

"Shut up," Richeline said. "Not you, trooper. Continue your report."

"Xing fled, as planned, along with some bystanders from the bar, who we assume were frightened by the violence. Those few troopers capable of movement pursued her all the way to the facility's external door. The door was sealed before we could continue pursuit, but we'd chased them nearly as far as we were supposed to, anyway."

"Are you expecting congratulations? Following your orders exactly is the bare minimum I expect, squad leader, and you didn't even manage to do *that*."

If he looked chastened, Voyou couldn't tell; those full-face masks were useful for hiding emotions. He wished *he* had one. "Understood," the trooper said. "We're in some trouble, here, captain. The local security forces aren't happy with an unauthorized action on their moon–"

Richeline slapped the terminal, and the squad leader's head vanished from the screen, replaced by a map of the moon's surface, with a blinking dot moving slowly from left to right. "What in the bright stars are they doing over *there*?" Richeline said. "Their rendezvous with the mercenary ship is on the other side of the facility, but the captain is going the wrong way. No one is chasing them anymore, so they should be heading straight for the extraction point. The whole *point* of sending in those troopers was to herd Xing in the right direction and make her jump onto the first available transport."

"I'm sure the captain knows what she's doing," Voyou said loyally. He wasn't sure why he was even part of this executive team – probably because he was the first person on board to meet Bianca, and the only "friend" she'd had on board, which made him, rather laughably, the closest thing they had to an expert on her psychology. He didn't think he'd be able to add much of value, but no Letnev would turn down an opportunity to sit closer to the seat of power. In this case, *very* close: they were in Captain Dampierre's ready room, the most secure place on the ship for monitoring a clandestine operation.

"Spoken like someone the captain never stabbed in the neck," Richeline said.

"Wait. Where did her signal go?" Archambelle shoved her face close to the screen, as if perhaps the little blinking dot had merely gotten smaller and fainter, instead of completely disappearing.

Richeline hissed and pulled the doctor away. "Stop it. Maybe I just need to reboot the monitoring system." She tapped at the terminal for a moment, squinted, then shook her head. "No good. We've lost her."

"What does that mean?" Voyou asked.

"It means we can't track her anymore." Richeline sat back in her chair – the *captain's* chair, and, to be fair, she was acting captain, but Voyou still wouldn't have dared to sit there in her place. "As for *why* we can't track her... it could be a malfunction, I suppose. *You* implanted the tracker, Archambelle – what are the odds you botched the job?"

"Nil," she snarled. "That tracking device is so simple it's barely capable of failure." The doctor didn't look good, in Voyou's opinion. She'd always been pale, even by Letnev standards, but now she looked somehow waxy, too. She must not be sleeping much, or not very well when she did. "We deliberately chose the most foolproof device available. The tracker doesn't even have a separate battery. It's passively powered by Severyne's own body heat – oh." The doctor sat down and stared at the least interesting wall in the cabin.

"So that means if she died," Voyou said, "then the tracker would die too? Once she, ah, cooled off?"

"One outcome I did *not* consider was the death of Captain Severyne Joelle Dampierre," Richeline said. "I honestly thought she was too mean-spirited to die." She shook herself. "All right. The mission goes on, even if the captain doesn't. Let's scan the moon, and interdict and search any ship that leaves. Our runaway princess has to be *somewhere–*"

A Letnev face appeared on the screen, the image bordered by the flashing red that indicated an emergency override message. "Captain, the Glamarij authorities are demanding we collect our troopers and immediately leave the system."

"What? Who are they to give commands to a Letnev warship? We could bomb their moon into shards!"

"They, ah, have excellent orbital defenses, captain. They've also jammed our scanners and communications equipment – indeed, *everyone's* communications equipment – so we can't reach out to the Barony. I think they're concerned about public relations, considering their wealthy clientele, and they have the newest Hylar tech, so we can't overcome their jammers, except by traveling outside their range." The bridge officer cleared her throat. "We've also received a message from Lord Alicante's personal secretary asking, quote, 'Why are you bothering her Lordship's dear friends the Glamariji?'"

"When you say Lord Alicante…"

"The Baron's second cousin, yes, captain."

Richeline closed her eyes. Voyou was very glad he didn't have her job. "Fine. All right. Get me the Glamarij – whoever is in charge here – so I can apologize for the misunderstanding. Let them know we were pursuing a wanted terrorist, and there was no time to go through proper channels. Send a shuttle to pick up our troopers." She blanked the screen and slumped back in her chair.

"What *now*?" Archambelle said. "We can't simply give up! That girl holds the key to securing Letnev supremacy, throughout the galaxy, forevermore!"

Richeline shrugged. "I'm not the one who killed the captain. More's the pity."

"We can't follow her as planned," Voyou said. "But don't we know where she's going? Those three stars she always talked about, right?"

Richeline sat up. "That's true. Archambelle, what are the coordinates for that empty bit of nothing in the sky?"

"Coordinates? There are no coordinates! She pointed at a bit of darkness! The center of a triangle made by three stars that aren't even all that close to each other, astronomically speaking."

"So we don't have coordinates," Richeline said. "We have a direction, and that means we have a heading. What wormhole gate gets us *closest* to those stars?" She looked at Voyou. "That question was directed at you, Undercommandant. You're in charge of surveyor teams, so you're the closest thing in this room to a navigator."

Voyou wasn't flustered. The captain – could she really be dead? – had flayed him with words on a regular basis. Richeline couldn't compete. He consulted his wrist gauntlet. "There are two possible gates nearby, one controlled by the humans, the other by the Naalu. The Naalu will let us pass for a price, but the humans won't let a Letnev warship pass through for any price."

"Fine. Send word ahead to the Naalu, with a photo of Xing. Tell them she's a wanted terrorist and we're offering a reward for her apprehension. Maybe we'll get lucky and she'll try to use that wormhole too."

"And if not?" Archambelle said. "We just, what, aim for a vague point in the distance and hope we happen to cross paths with the girl?"

"We're headed to the middle of nowhere," Richeline said. "No one goes there, because there's no *reason* to go there. If we find any ship in the vicinity, odds are it's hers."

"I detest this plan," Archambelle said. "But I cannot think of a better one."

The screen blinked on again, with the same apologetic bridge officer, bordered in override red. "The premier of Glamarij is on the line."

Richeline made a shooing gesture at Voyou and Archambelle. "Get out of here. I have to practice diplomacy now."

Voyou didn't much like Archambelle – she looked at you like she was guessing how much your organs weighed – but when engaged on a secret mission, one had to find camaraderie where one could. "It's a shame we didn't put a tracking device on Bianca," he said once they were in the corridor.

"We did. Three times. The first two were simple subcutaneous implants, placed secretly in her back. I found the first tracking chip on the floor outside her cabin. The second one, I found on the floor of the corridor, halfway between the lab and her rooms. The third time, I told her I needed a deep tissue sample, and jammed a needle in as far as I dared." She sighed. "I found that tracking chip under the examination table – it never even made it outside the lab. Her body simply expelled the devices, so quietly and efficiently that I don't think Bianca even noticed."

"She's a remarkable woman," Voyou said.

"Mmm. She is a compass and key that will lead to a world of wonders. Her only value is utilitarian and scientific."

Voyou could hardly think of a suitable reply to that, so he moved on to another topic. "Do you really think the captain is dead?"

"As a scientist, I am reluctant to draw conclusions based on a single piece of indirect evidence, but I am also capable of assigning probabilities to various explanations. There *are* other reasons the tracker could have failed, but Severyne's death is the most likely. It's a shame. She didn't believe in the mission, not the way I do, but she would have pursued our goals to the death anyway, simply because that *was* the mission."

"She did," Voyou said.

"She did what?"

"Pursue our goals. To the death. It seems."

Archambelle made a sour face. "I wish she'd pursued the mission a bit *closer* to the goal first."

"Be careful with that." Severyne scowled at the Naaz as she sewed up the shoulder gash Bianca had inflicted on her. Clec had a delicate touch, at least. "Did you stitch up that human's face, too? I don't want a big ugly scar like *he's* got."

Clec, hovering in a little anti-grav harness, made a clucking sound. "I think it gives Heuvelt's face character. And no. That wasn't my work. This shouldn't leave a mark once you've healed."

"Back on my ship they would have smeared on some medical gel and healed my wound seamlessly. You're using a needle and thread? Barbaric."

The door to the tiny medical bay – really just a closet with a reclining table, a first-aid kit, and some rudimentary medical machinery – slid open, and Bianca sidled in, eyes downcast. "Back on your ship, they were going to put you to death," she said. "No amount of medical gel would have fixed that."

"Did you *have* to tackle me, princess? Really? You could have told me what you had planned."

Bianca shook her head. "Once I realized there was a tracking device inside you, I knew we had to cut it out and destroy it right away. If the ship had actually taken off while that device was active, the *Grim Countenance* would have been able to figure out our heading, and then it would have been easy to tell what vessel we were on – I had to act immediately."

That was all true, and it was also why Severyne really wished Bianca had noticed her tracking chip ten minutes later.

"I was very careful, really, and I made the smallest incision I could."

"How did you know they were tracking me?" Severyne allowed a little of her genuine dismay to come through, since she could play it off as pain from her wound. When Bianca had leapt on her with that knife, Severyne was sure it was all over – that Bianca's psychic abilities had blossomed, and she'd seen the truth of Severyne's treachery. But then Bianca had flipped her over and cut the tracker out of her shoulder instead.

"I just… I can tell when there are signals going back and forth, from machine to machine, system to system. That's new, or anyway, I just realized I can do it. When I saw signals coming out of *you*, I knew it had to be a tracker. I'm just glad we found it. Now we've got a real chance at getting away."

Yes. Getting away on *the wrong ship*. They should have been on board a mercenary vessel, crewed by Severyne's hired freelancers, pursued at a respectable distance by the full might and majesty of the *Grim Countenance*. Instead, they were on a ship with a crew who were, apparently, fugitives from Letnev justice. Bianca really was off the leash.

Not entirely, though. Severyne was still here. She'd just have to complete the mission herself.

She reached out and snatched the hovering Naaz from the air, grasping its four flailing limbs, two in each fist. "Tell your captain we're commandeering his vessel," she said.

For the second time that day, Bianca hit her.

CHAPTER 25

Severyne rocked back when Bianca smacked her arm, and Bianca winced – she hadn't meant to apply that much force. Clec went spinning out of Severyne's grasp, and suddenly her four arms were glistening with tiny metal spikes – weapons, though Bianca wasn't sure what kind. She stepped between Clec and Severyne. "Stop! Clec, I apologize, our original plan was to hijack a ship, *but,*" she turned and glared at Severyne, who was rubbing her arm. "*But,* that won't be necessary, because we can make an arrangement that benefits everyone."

Clec lowered her weapons. "If I tell Ashont what you did, she will bite your face off," Clec said. "And I tell Ashont *everything.* Amina, if you wish to have a discussion with us, you must first lock her up." She sent out a signal. Bianca watched it pass through the door.

A few moments later, Heuvelt appeared, holding a pair of shackles. "What's going on here?"

"This Letnev uses violence as a first resort," Clec said. "It is best if we curb her negative impulses before she gets hurt."

"Amina could kill you all in the space of three heartbeats," Sev said. "That's three of *your* rapid little heartbeats, Naaz."

"But I *won't,*" Bianca said. "Everyone, please, calm down." She spread her hands, smiling, and to her surprise, Heuvelt and Severyne both appeared to relax, their muscles loosening, their eyes softening and then going glassy. What was happening?

"I must ask you to stop generating soporific pheromones," Clec said.

Bianca blinked. "Am I? Did I?" She stopped doing it, and only in that moment did she even realize what she'd done, or that she could control it.

"I have detected an anomaly in the atmosphere, yes. My personal filtration system prevented the chemicals from affecting me, and I'm instructing the ship's filters to do the same." The Naaz bobbed before her in the air. "How did you even *do* that? With cross-species compatibility!"

"I didn't mean to!" Bianca said. "I'm so sorry, really. Can we just… talk?"

Heuvelt snapped the shackles onto Sev's wrists. "Oh, yes. We should definitely talk."

"Why did you shackle her, Clec?" the Rokha growled.

"Because I know you won't bite someone in chains," the Naaz said.

"Using my own ethical framework against me is unfair."

"It may be reasonable to bite her later," the Naaz said. "We should try to gain a better understanding of the situation first, though." She turned, fixing her eyes on Severyne and Bianca. "Why were you fleeing the Letnev?"

Severyne placed her shackled wrists on the table. Playing the prisoner had been rather more enjoyable than actually being one. The galley was small, and five people crowded it, even when one of those people was so small they perched on another's shoulder. "Do you want to field this one, princess?"

"Sev is on the run because–"

"Who's Sev?" Heuvelt interrupted.

Severyne sighed. "I am. And the princess here is Bianca. We were using assumed names earlier, but I suppose it hardly matters now."

"I see," Heuvelt said. "I disapprove of false names, for personal reasons, but… do continue."

"Sev struck a superior officer," Bianca said, "and was sentenced to death. She helped me escape the brig on the Barony ship. I'm so sorry she grabbed you, Clec, really, we just didn't have time to discuss changing our plan, it's my fault–"

"Why were you in the brig?" Ashont said. "Does it have anything to do with your ability to dispatch half a dozen Barony shock troopers in mere seconds?"

"Yes, are you some sort of augmented soldier?" Heuvelt said. "A Barony experiment meant to infiltrate Federation society or something?"

"I'm not any kind of soldier. I'm… well… I'm a compass. And a key. But mostly I'm just a person."

"Explicate," Clec said.

To Severyne's considerable dismay, Bianca told them her entire life story, from her father discovering the secret lab up to their escape to Glamarij, and all points in between. Some of it, like Bianca's early fluency in Letnev, Brother Errin's revelations about her true nature, and her hacking her way to free rein in the *Grim Countenance* systems confirmed the worst things Severyne had suspected. She congratulated herself on her paranoia, though; Richeline had thought planting the fake personnel file was an unnecessary precaution, but if she hadn't, Bianca would have seen a photograph of the real captain, and the whole ruse would have failed.

"I do not know about these Mahact," Clec said, "but I have heard of Ixth. A world of impossible wonders."

"I've heard of Ixth too, in adventuring circles," Heuvelt said. "A world with rivers of liquor and trees made of gold. But tales of Ixth are like those stories about the lost colony world of the Hylar, filled with forgotten technology, or the Muaat City of Diamond – they're just *stories*."

"The Mahact were real," Bianca said. "They made me. They're remaking me, even now. I don't know why, but the Letnev thought I was created to lead people to Ixth. They thought following me would make them rich and powerful.

If you help us get where we're going... I can make you rich, instead. Will you help me?"

"We'll have to discuss this," Heuvelt said.

Bianca nodded. "Of course! Sev and I can wait. Ah..."

"My cabin is fine," Heuvelt said. "Please don't remove her shackles."

"I don't even have the key or the code," Bianca said.

"I think we all know that would not prevent you, if you wished to set her free," the Naaz said.

Bianca blinked. "Oh. I suppose that's true. Of course I won't." She rose, and Severyne followed her. They went into Heuvelt's room, with its unmade bed and pile of dirty clothes in one corner, and the door closed after them.

Severyne wrinkled her nose. "This place is vile." She shook her shackles. "Will you get these off me?"

"I think Ashont would hurt you if I did. I could smell she was serious."

"Oh, you can smell intent now?"

"Sometimes." Bianca sat down on the edge of the bunk. "Really, Sev, you didn't have to grab Clec like that. I listened to them while we played cards – they're doing deliveries these days, but by preference they're explorers and treasure hunters, trying to make money to outfit their next expedition. We can *be* that next expedition."

"I apologize," Severyne said. If she couldn't have her own loyal crew on hand, the next best thing was dumping *this* crew out an airlock, but it seemed that wasn't going to happen, either. What could not be changed must be accommodated. "I was acting in what I believed to be our best interest. That trick with the pheromones, did you know you could do that?"

"I really didn't." She sounded miserable. "I don't want to make *anyone* do things they don't want to do."

"I don't know much about these Mahact, princess, but you sure don't sound like you inherited your morality from them. According to the legends, they liked taking and making slaves, ruling by force, and destroying anyone who opposed them."

"Just because I have some of their power doesn't mean I have to use it the way they did. I'm afraid of my own capabilities, Sev. With all the things I can do, I have to be extra careful, don't you see? Sometimes I think it would be better for me to forget all about my yearning and go live on some little planet out of the way somewhere. But I have to know what's in that dark space behind the stars. I thought when I got closer, the need would diminish, but it's actually gotten stronger. It's like being hungry, or thirsty, or exhausted – it's a desire beyond thought, deep in my body. I know the Mahact programmed this need into me, but I need to know why."

"What if it's something bad?" Severyne hadn't thought much about that question before. She was a pragmatist. She had her orders, and knew the purpose of her mission, and she would do everything she could to fulfill it. Archambelle was irritating, but she was also brilliant, and there was no reason to doubt her theory about Bianca's provenance and purpose. But it was all speculation, based on fragments of ancient lore and assumptions that could be faulty. The only way to truly know Bianca's purpose was to follow her and watch her fulfill it.

Severyne's first field operation had gone disastrously awry, and given her a glimpse of cosmic horrors beyond her capacity to imagine. She really hoped that sort of thing wasn't going to become a pattern.

"Then I'll do my best to use it for something good instead." Bianca glanced at the closed door. "How long do you think it will take them to decide?"

Severyne snorted. "Bianca. Really. What is there to decide?"

"What is there to decide?" Clec said. "If we refuse to help her, Bianca could disable all of us, lock us in the cargo bay or jettison us from the airlock, and take our ship for her own. If we cooperate with her willingly, we might actually make a profit instead."

"I concur," Ashont said. "Working with her is the only practical approach."

"So, we believe her story?" Heuvelt said.

"It's so outlandish, it's hard to believe it's a fiction," Ashont said. "Surely a liar would have concocted something more plausible. The Letnev certainly wanted her for something. Plus, we saw what she did in that bar, and even on our ship – she *is* something more than human."

"It's all very hard to credit," Heuvelt said. "But it won't be the first time I've chased a hint of a whisper of a rumor into the depths of space." He smiled. "Let's do it."

Ashont cocked her head, and Clec made a sort of strangled sound. "Wait," the Naaz said. "You agree?"

"All I want is to be a treasure hunter," Heuvelt said. "I didn't lay awake in bed as a child and dream about transporting freight – that was simply a necessity for survival. This is a chance to get back to what I love. Seeing the light of unknown stars on new worlds. Cracking open vaults and looting the treasures within. Walking where no human has trod before. That's what I was *made* for. To be honest, I'm delighted this strange woman hijacked our ship. Otherwise, what – we'd be doing more deliveries for Sagasa, ad infinitum?"

"Helping a Letnev fugitive – *two* Letnev fugitives – isn't going to help your legal situation," Ashont said. "If they find out we're involved in this, Sagasa won't be able to scrub you from their systems."

"I have spent too long driven by fear," Heuvelt declared. That fact had recently struck him with the force of epiphany. "Look at Bianca – barely an adult, from a nowhere planet, taken from her family and friends, used against her will, abused and experimented upon, and what did she do? Did she sulk on the outskirts of a system waiting for paperwork to go through? No. She seized control of her destiny and struck out into the unknown, to *seek* her destiny. She *inspires* me."

"Are you sure there aren't any more strange pheromones floating around?" Ashont said.

"None at all," Clec said. "This is all him."

"It's unanimous, then," Heuvelt said. "Set a course for the nearest appropriate wormhole."

"There's a Federation of Sol gate that will get us in the right direction," Clec said.

"And we won't have to worry about running into any lurking Letnev there," Ashont added.

"I'll go give our guests the good news." Heuvelt stood up, smiling. He didn't do that much anymore – smiling made the muscles in his face contract around the scar, and the skin felt tight there as a result, which usually wiped any brief sign of happiness off his face. This time, though, he didn't care. He'd resigned himself to a life of shuttling to and fro, running errands for criminal scum. But now, *now*, he was on a mission of greatness, chasing a chance at wonder once again.

Granted, things hadn't turned out very well last time he tried that, but what kind of explorer would he be if he gave up forever after the first time he got lost?

CHAPTER 26

The Federation of Sol ran an efficient port, and, according to Heuvelt's grumbles, charged accordingly. Bianca sat in the cockpit, watching the ships bustling to and fro, taking in the strange convex shape of the space-time anomaly at the center of all the traffic. "Why does the wormhole *glow* that way?"

"There is nothing I'd call a glow in any of our visual spectrums," Clec said, hovering over the pilot's chair. "I think you're seeing things we can't see again."

"That's a shame," Bianca said. "It's so beautiful."

The *Show and Tell* transited the wormhole without difficulty. Bianca slowed down her subjective time sense as they passed through – she could do that at will now – but the transition still happened almost instantaneously, and she didn't gather any useful data. She'd have to think about wormholes more. They were interesting. The whole fabric of space-time… it seemed like there were possibilities there.

They emerged on the far side of the wormhole, where there was comparatively little traffic, and all of it headed in the same direction. Heuvelt stepped into the cockpit and nodded at Bianca. He looked a little queasy. "That's step one on our journey of who knows how many steps."

Bianca pointed at the departing ships on the viewscreen. "Where are they headed?"

"Toward the Zaxony system, mainly," Clec said. "It's the nearest point of interest, a Federation of Sol colony built in the ruins of a star-shell left behind by some lost civilization. There's a joint project with the Hylar government to research the structure's origins and find new applications for the tech. Beyond that, there's a colony world called Whiteraven, which I'm told is a nice place to live, except for all the bone-colored terror birds trying to rip you to pieces. Is that where we're going?"

Bianca shook her head and pointed. "We're going that way. What's over there?"

"Nothing," Clec said. "At least, as far as anyone has noticed in any recorded survey."

The door opened again, and Ashont stood on the other side, Severyne lurking nearby, hands still shackled. They couldn't all fit in the cockpit.

"Should we resupply?" Heuvelt said. "The administrative station for the wormhole can provide most of what we need, but it would be nice if we had some idea how far we were going. I don't suppose you can be more specific than saying 'that way', Bianca?"

She considered. "We're *much* closer now. Drastically so. That wormhole really made a difference. Hmm. I know how far we've traveled, and I know how much more intense my desire to reach our destination is now, and if I plot the change in my internal state against our movement in space, I can extrapolate an end point to the curve–"

"You don't have any telemetry data," Severyne interrupted. "You don't have records of ship speeds or course headings, nor do you know *this* ship's capabilities. How can you extrapolate anything?"

"I glanced at navigation screens on the *Grim Countenance*," she said. "I perused star maps. I read through this ship's manual this morning, so I know the specs. I was sitting right here when coordinates were discussed. I remember it all well enough. It's just a question of putting the data together."

"How can anyone possibly remember that level of detail?" Heuvelt said.

"I… just can," Bianca said. "Do you trust me?"

"Trusting you is the entire basis of this expedition," Clec said. "So it doesn't seem to be optional."

She closed her eyes, and a three-dimensional map of this sector of the galaxy filled her mind. She drew curves across her vision and watched them converge. She opened her eyes. "At top speed, it will take us seventeen days to reach our destination. But I don't know if that's our *final* destination. Maybe it's just the first stepping stone."

"You're saying there might be a wormhole there," Sev said.

"There may be. Or maybe just directions, or a trail marker, pointing to another place. I just don't know. Sev, do you want to stay here? Or on the shellworld? You just wanted to escape the *Grim Countenance*, and I feel terrible asking you to risk your life this way. You never set out to be a treasure hunter."

"Though there is no more noble calling," Heuvelt said.

"Not many more interesting ones, at least," Ashont said.

Sev grinned. "Being free is one thing, princess." She rattled her shackles. "Isn't it better to be free *and* rich? Besides, now I'm curious about these Mahact of yours."

"Very well," Heuvelt said. "We'll outfit ourselves for a journey of indefinite length. I've done *that* before."

"We'll outfit ourselves for a journey of depressingly finite length, actually," Ashont said. "We didn't get paid *that* much for our last job. We did some repairs based on the assumption that we'd be getting more work from Sagasa soon, too."

"Oh, that's all right," Bianca said. "I have authorization codes. We can charge whatever we need to the Barony, or rather, to one of the officially neutral sub-accounts they use when it's necessary to make payments to organizations they don't have diplomatic ties with."

Sev made a choking noise. "*What?*"

"I hacked the ship's financial system, just to see if I could." She shrugged. "When you see something nested under ten levels of encryption and dig through those and see the words 'covert operations budget' in the metadata, well, that sort of thing grabs your interest."

"The Letnev will *know* someone defrauded them," Sev said. "They'll know we came this way. Use those accounts, and we might as well still have tracking devices on us."

Bianca cocked her head. "They'll know we came this way anyway. They know the general heading of my yearning, after all, and this is one of the obvious wormhole gates to use. A flagged transaction won't tell them anything they don't already know. They just won't know where we went *from* here. We can lay a false trail, I bet – Heuvelt, when you're getting supplies, talk about your plans to explore the uncharted regions of space beyond Whiteraven."

"That might possibly work," she said.

Bianca beamed. "Sev, coming from you, grudging admiration is like a kiss on the mouth and a whoop of joy all rolled up in one."

Bianca loved her time aboard the *Show and Tell.*

When she'd first caught sight of Heuvelt, sitting alone in the bar on Glamarij, she'd made the sort of swift (and usually accurate) assessment her mind automatically generated these days: a once-formidable man, handsome and privileged, fallen on hard times – slipping into middle age, nursing his bitterness, and fixated on his failures and scars. She didn't think her read on him was wrong, exactly, but it was incomplete. Heuvelt Angriff had simply been a man out of place, and miserable there, but now, he was back in his element: right or wrong, wise or otherwise, he was pursuing his passion again, and being on a treasure hunt animated him, made his spirit bright, and turned his whole bearing boisterous and warm.

She'd been worried, at first, that Heuvelt would be creepy – he was a human man, after all, and she'd met plenty of those on Darit who wouldn't let a little thing like a two-and-a-half-decade age difference stand in the way of flirtation or attempts at even greater liberties. Heuvelt had never even needed a brush-off, though, either because his tastes didn't run that way, or because, as seemed increasingly obvious, he looked at her more like a younger sibling than anything else.

Bianca didn't know if she reminded him of someone from his earlier life or if she was the little sister he wished he'd had, but they clicked, and spent a lot of time together laughing as they told each other stories about their homeworlds. Their upbringings could not have been more different, which made the swapping of experiences more interesting for both of them. He called her "farm girl" and she called him "rich kid" , and he told her about exploration techniques and she tried to teach him to be slightly better at cards.

Ashont and Clec were complete in themselves, but Bianca got to know both of them too: as the members of a relatively less powerful polity, they had strong opinions about all the various factions in the galactic political arena, and Bianca absorbed their perspectives as fast as they could share them. For their part, the duo was amused and amazed by Bianca, and they frequently played games to test her capabilities – throwing multiple objects for her to snatch out of the air, blindfolding her and making her identify various objects through the synergy of her other senses, cranking up computer games beyond their maximum speed settings and watching her reflexes keep up just fine anyway. Ashont liked to recite long passages of literature in a foreign language into one of her ears while Clec whispered technical specs into the other, and they'd marvel as she recited them back, one after another at first, and then alternating word-by-word, letter perfect every time. "You could make good money on the entertainment vids," Ashont said. "If the whole being-a-fake-space-princess thing doesn't work out."

"I'll keep that in mind," Bianca said.

Sev was… not blossoming, but she was, at least, not engaged in open hostilities anymore. She sulked a bit, and didn't talk to anyone except Bianca, but *their* talks were fascinating. Sev was more than willing to answer questions about security protocols, how to exploit flaws in systems (people, Bianca knew, but Sev explained *how* to exploit people), and to share her opinions on assorted military matters. Bianca had the persistent sense – based on another synergy of senses – that Sev was hiding something, but really, a woman like that probably had *lots* of secrets.

One night, Sev loosened up sufficiently to share some of Heuvelt's liquor – Letnev biology was roughly compatible with that of humans, at least when it came to getting intoxicated. Bianca got tipsy and told her about her first time (pretty much her only time, with Grandly, which is what led to him following her around all moon-eyed).

"My first time was nothing to speak of," Sev said. "Just another girl in the dorms. Lots of us did that sort of thing, just to calm the hormonal distraction so we could focus on our studies."

"You've never been in love? I thought I was in love with Grandly, for about five minutes, but it was just the *idea* of being in love."

"The Letnev are more about strategic interpersonal alliances than love, princess. But…" She sipped brown liquor from her tumbler and grimaced. "There was one person."

"That human you fraternized with?"

She winced. "Ah, that memory of yours, princess. Yes. Her name was Azad. She was fascinating, and challenging, and profoundly irritating – she made your company positively soothing in comparison. Still. I am glad we shared what we did. Knowing her opened up my understanding of the world. But we could have never worked out. I'm glad our involvement ended before it became even more disastrous."

"Doomed romance is even *more* romantic, in a way," Bianca said.

Severyne threw her head back and laughed until tears rolled from her eyes.

"What?" Bianca said. "*What?*"

"Sometimes, princess, you're so fast, and so smart, and so strong, that I forget you're also *so young.*"

Bianca grinned despite herself. "It's nice to hear you laugh, Sev, even if you *are* laughing at me."

"It's a cold, dark universe, princess. We should all take laughter where we can find it."

It was fourteen days into the journey before Severyne felt safe making contact with her people.

Bianca was sleeping, and careful experimentation had revealed that she didn't snap instantly awake when a signal went past. Severyne wriggled her way into the ship's communication system so she could piggyback on their emergency beacon and its powerful supraluminal broadcast capabilities. She wouldn't be able to engage in an actual *conversation* with Richeline and Archambelle and Voyou, but she could update them on the ship's destination… assuming they'd had the good sense to traverse the obvious Naalu wormhole and head in the known direction of Bianca's yearning. If not, Severyne would be broadcasting to empty space. She didn't like depending on the competence of her underlings, but she had no choice.

Severyne recorded and sent her transmission, before scrubbing all evidence of the message. Then she waited, crouched in the corridor beside the access panel she'd tampered with. After ten minutes, when no one came to jettison her into space, she crept back to the hammock she'd strung in the port side cargo hold.

Heuvelt slept in the starboard hold, and if the connecting doors were open she could hear him snoring. Bianca was sleeping in the captain's bed, because Heuvelt was a polite host, but that politeness didn't extend to Severyne. She was meant to be grateful they'd taken the shackles off her a mere three days into the journey. Bianca had finally convinced them that "Sev is trustworthy, even just on the basis of her naked self-interest!" That was certainly true, to a point. She would help Bianca and her pet menagerie fulfill their mission, up to the moment it diverged from her own. There was no reason to be a treasure hunter when you could just follow the treasure hunters and steal what they found, after all.

She looked at the hammock with great distaste, and went instead to the cockpit. Clec was there, as she was most of the time. Naaz didn't sleep much, apparently, and while Ashont slept frequently she didn't do so for very long at a time. Severyne dropped into the co-pilot seat and said, "Anything going on?" Casual, casual, always casual.

"Nothing at all. No one has even tried to tear my arms off in over a week."

"I said I was sorry."

"You never did, actually."

Severyne sighed. "I meant to. That sort of thing doesn't come easily to me. So: I apologize for laying hands on you."

"Apology accepted. Why did you strike your ship's first officer?"

Severyne didn't have to watch her words as carefully with Clec – there was no reason to think the Naaz could detect a lie – but she was in the habit now. "Richeline is arrogant, self-important, and irritating."

"These are qualities you detest? In anyone other than yourself, I mean?"

It could have gone either way. Once upon a time, a jab like that would have made Severyne bare her teeth and strike back, verbally at the very least. She'd been through a lot, though, and had been jabbed more ruthlessly by experts. She was able to laugh at herself a little now, and so that's what she did: or chuckled, anyway. "I have nothing against arrogance, as long as it's justified. I don't think I'm arrogant at all. I simply have … a clear-eyed self-regard."

"You can't be all bad. Bee seems fond of you."

"The princess doesn't have many friends. She becomes overly attached to those she does have. Even if we aren't worthy of her regard."

"She's extremely pleasant, for an unstoppable, genetically engineered killing machine."

"She's not engineered for killing, I don't think." Severyne decided speaking freely here would do no harm, and might ingratiate her, a little, with Clec and thus the rest of the crew, which could be useful when the time came to betray them. "I think her capacity for violence is a side-effect. If it was just about murder, the engines in her DNA would have her spewing neurotoxins or producing biological weapons instead of bliss-inducing pheromones. She's engineered to do something *else*, and the ability to defend herself is just a way of making sure she survives long enough to do whatever that is."

"Was she always so bright and quick? She pumped me for everything I know about space flight, physics, and galactic history and culture, and it's not because she needs to know anything, she just has an endless hunger for information. I think she's read every piece of media we have in the ship's database, and the other day I caught her consuming audio-visual media at thirty-two times the standard playback speed – how can she even follow it when it plays that fast?"

"Time doesn't work for Bianca the way it does for us. That's how she took down armed shock troopers without any combat training. She's not a particularly skilled warrior. She's just so much faster than everyone else that it doesn't matter. A clumsy blow can knock you down just as well as a graceful one, if you can't dodge or block the strike."

"I hope those kind of reflexes aren't a prerequisite for survival wherever we're going."

"Me too," Severyne said. "Though we could actually trust Bianca to go in on her own, and bring back whatever treasures she finds, and share them out as agreed. Isn't that remarkable? I've never known anyone like her."

"I think you're right," Clec said. "She seems so... well, good. But I think the flip side is, she expects her allies to behave just as honorably. If someone disappoints her, and she loses her temper and acts impulsively? I wouldn't want to be on the other end of that fit of pique."

Severyne kept her breath steady. She was afraid that was a hint, and that the Naaz would casually say, "By the way, I intercepted your transmission," and then things would turn very violent very fast.

Clec didn't say anything like that, though; instead, she said, "I'm picking up something on the long-range sensors."

"A planet? A moon?"

"Can't tell. Maybe an asteroid, but there's a lot of metal in it. Could be a ship, but if so, it's derelict – no energy signatures. We'll be close enough for a visual scan in a few hours."

"I knew this trip was going too smoothly," Severyne said.

"You make a good partner for Bianca," Clec said. "Someone needs to provide a counterbalance to her optimism and good cheer."

CHAPTER 27

Another message arrived.

This time, when the sleeper woke, he remembered who he was: Kor Noq Weer. A name to inspire terror, once upon a time, even among those who trafficked in terror. A name synonymous with rogue, with renegade, with apostate, with traitor. But that name had outlasted so many others, hadn't it?

He took in the message, sent by a nearby relay. The child had passed through a wormhole, it seemed, closing the distance between them greatly, and soon she would reach the World of Stone. From there, she need only traverse the gate, and open the tomb, and fulfill her purpose.

After so many uncounted millennia spent patiently waiting, things were moving fast, now – very fast.

Soon the name Kor Noq Weer would be known and feared across all the worlds of the galaxy again.

CHAPTER 28

"A wrecked ship." Heuvelt gazed at the viewscreen with everyone else. "When I was a teenager, I went hiking in the wilderness. I forced my way through the brush, broke trail along the bottom of an overgrown ravine, climbed up a cliff face, and reached the summit of a rock tower, with absolutely breathtaking views in every direction. Except right at my feet. Do you know what I saw right at my feet?"

"A beer can," Ashont said. "You've told this story before."

He sighed. "Sev and Bee haven't heard it. The point is, there's a unique sort of disappointment in going to a place you think is wholly undiscovered and realizing someone else got there first and left their junk behind."

"The more pressing question is who *wrecked* that ship," Sev said. "I've never seen damage like that before."

The ship actually looked a bit like a crumpled can, Bianca thought. It had probably been graceful, once, shaped like an arrowhead or a predatory bird in flight, but it had been crushed. "Do you know what kind of ship that is, Clec? I didn't see anything like it in the *Show and Tell*'s database, or the *Grim Countenance*'s, either."

"Its design is unknown to me," Clec said. "Would anyone like to go over and see what's inside? Whatever destroyed the vessel doesn't seem to be lurking around at the moment."

Bianca, Heuvelt, and Sev suited up for the spacewalk. "You could probably go outside without a suit on, Bianca," Heuvelt said over their comms. "Given everything *else* you can do."

"I can hold my breath for a long time," Bianca said. "But that wouldn't help with the moisture on my eyeballs and tongue vaporizing instantly, or my lungs exploding from the pressure change, and then there's the solar radiation… let's just say I'd rather not test my capabilities that way unless I have to."

The outer airlock door opened. Bianca had never done a spacewalk before, and the experience of stepping out of the ship into the void was dizzying, exhilarating, and astonishing, but by now her yearning was so intense she had to fight her urge to use her little propulsion pack to send her off past the wreck, toward the point of her mysterious desire. She was tethered to Heuvelt and Sev, though, so they pulled her along to the ship and didn't even notice her urge to fly away alone.

They reached a huge gash in the hull of the wreck, and Heuvelt shone a light inside. Debris floated around the interior, the artificial gravity as dead as everything else. They eased into the ship. The corridors were a little larger than they were on most human or Letnev vessels, but the contents of the compartments weren't too alien – there were hammocks, even, though they seemed to be spun of some cocoonlike silk material. There was a galley, with unfamiliar foodstuffs, preserved by the airless vacuum – pale blue eggs, bits of gray meat sealed in plastic, bundles of stalks and flowers and stems.

"They were humanoid, judging by the clothes in this locker," Heuvelt said. "Let's take a look at the bridge. Maybe there's some data to be recovered."

Bianca reached the bridge first, so she was the one who found the bodies. The front of the bridge was open to vacuum, the viewscreen cracked right down the center, and a hole torn in the hull big enough to walk through upright, so the two crew members must have died quickly. Unlit consoles ringed the room, controls for systems that had been catastrophically damaged.

The floating aliens were humanoid, insofar as they were bipedal and had two arms, but they had wickedly curved beaks, and heads covered in feathers, though they seemed devoid of wings. They both wore uniforms with unfamiliar insignia at the shoulders, six jagged quadrangular segments of alternating size arranged around a central point to create a sort of starburst shape. "Bird people?" Bianca said. "I didn't know there were bird people."

"It's a big galaxy." Sev floated past the corpses, toward one of the control panels. "I wasn't aware of any avian humanoids with the capacity for space travel, but I'm no xeno-anthropologist. Unless a species is powerful enough to be a military threat, or unlucky enough to live somewhere with resources we need, the Barony isn't concerned about keeping track of every sapient species." She worked at the computer for a while, then shook her head. "Even if I understood their technological architecture, this is all hopelessly broken." She looked at the deep dents on the ceiling and the floor, where the metal had been deformed under some terrible pressure. "It looks like somebody picked up this ship and squeezed it in their fist. Have you led us to the land of spacefaring death giants, princess?"

"Your guess is as good as mine."

Sev grunted and sailed out of the bridge, down an unfamiliar corridor.

"How long ago do you think this ship was destroyed?" Bianca asked.

"It's hard to tell," Heuvelt said. "Nothing rots in vacuum, and I have no idea if this ship is state-of-the-art for bird people, or a quaint antique. I think we should probably proceed very carefully from here. If the place we're headed is as valuable as you think, it could well be protected. We might be looking at the aftermath of a security system being triggered."

"I'm supposed to be the key, though," Bianca said. "Surely they won't crush *me*?"

"Let's hope they won't crush the people standing next to you, either." Heuvelt spun around slowly, taking in the bridge. "There's nothing here for us. No information, and nothing I'd call treasure. We should continue on our way. We'll be wherever we're going in a few days now, if your calculations are correct."

It took them a while to find Severyne – she'd gone to the engine room, she said, to see if there was anything worth salvaging, but the technology was so different from their own, she soon realized it was pointless.

The three of them returned to the *Show and Tell* and continued on their way, the crew overall more subdued, and more watchful.

But they were more watchful in the sense that they were looking *out* for potential threats from the outside, which is why none of them noticed that Severyne had a souvenir. She'd carefully wrapped an item she found on the wrecked ship in a layer of alien hammock fabric and jammed it in the crack between her back and her suit's propulsion pack. While everyone was getting out of their suits on the *Show and Tell*, she managed to slip the salvaged item out of the gap and into her waistband, and made her way to her own little corner of the ship, a hammock strung among heaps of supplies.

Nestled safely behind a pile of crates, she slid the object out of her waistband and unwrapped it.

Severyne had found a weapons locker near the engine room on the alien ship, and there had been many lovely things inside: rifles of an unfamiliar curving design, and graceful sidearms with multiple barrels, and even something like an archer's bow, but with integrated sights and no visible ammunition, which made her wonder if it fired energy bolts of some kind.

Most interesting, though, was the symbol she saw carved into all their hilts or stocks or barrels. She had no idea what the symbol *meant*, but she'd seen it before: it was one of the glyphs Archambelle had shown her. A symbol of the Mahact. Archambelle hadn't said anything about the Mahact servants including bird people, but her information was hardly complete. Perhaps these were Mahact weapons. Or, perhaps they were the weapons used by those who *opposed* the Mahact. There were hash marks beside the symbols, three lines on one weapon, four on another, two on a third, all clearly scratched there by hand. Were they tallies, perhaps, of enemies killed by those weapons? There was no telling how old the ship was – the dead might have been soldiers in a war that ended untold eons ago. Those guns probably wouldn't work after all this time, anyway, even if Severyne could have gotten one off the ship unobserved.

But there was a knife, with a blade curved like a raptor's beak, the edge shimmering with its own faint blue light. The hilt was etched with that same symbol, and there were easily a dozen hash marks carved around it. This might be a blade that had tasted Mahact blood – or whatever they had instead of blood – many times. Best of all, the knife was small enough for Severyne to sneak it out.

Would the knife hurt Bianca? She wasn't sure, and in truth she hoped she never had to find out, given how formidable the girl had proven to be, but Severyne believed in taking advantage of opportunities when they arose, and this knife was a gift from the universe.

She found some canvas and used the blade to cut it into strips – the weapon was gratifyingly sharp, having lost none of its edge during its long interval of disuse. She used some epoxy resin to bind the canvas into a sheath, and fixed the sheath to the inner waistband of her pants. Now the knife could rest comfortably, hilt nestled into the small of her back. Maybe it would stay there.

The blade was just a contingency, but Severyne felt so much better when she had one of those at hand.

"It's today," Heuvelt said. "Isn't it today? You said it would be today."

"We're very close," Bianca said, for the third time that morning. She sat in the co-pilot's chair, while Ashont and Clec ran the ship. Their scanners were stretched to the limit of their range and sensitivity, and they revealed: nothing.

If she shuffled through the *Show and Tell*'s external cameras, Bianca could still see the three stars that had formed that triangle encompassing her yearning, but each one was off in a different direction now; one behind, one above, one below. They formed no discernible pattern from this vantage, transformed into unrelated points of light. Everything was a matter of perspective, wasn't it?

They *were* close – she could feel that. Doubt crept in, though. What if she was being drawn to a place that had *once* held something of value, but now held nothing at all? What if her yearning led her to a wormhole that had been disabled millennia ago by the victors in a forgotten war? The lab her father Keon found her in was so *old*. Maybe her whole existence was meaningless. She could be a compass leading them to a city that was not just ruins but entirely vanished. A distress beacon on a dead ship, still pointlessly beaming out a cry for help. A key to a door that had turned to dust in some forgotten epoch.

"We've got enough food and fuel to get back where we started easily enough." Heuvelt's dolorous tone belied the practicality of his statement. "No great loss, apart from time." He sighed. "I suppose Sagasa always needs more–"

"What is *that*?" Ashont pointed through the viewscreen.

"What?" Heuvelt peered. "I don't see anything. Magnify?"

"It's a light," Bianca said. "There's a *light* shining out there!"

"Whatever it's shining out of must be tiny," Clec said. "I'm not picking up any objects in that direction at all. Let me see what I can do with the visual sensors."

That distant yellow point of light leapt forward, growing in the screen, and now they could see the contours of some solid object illuminated by its backscatter, the surface smooth. "Some kind of asteroid?" Bianca said.

"It can't be!" Clec said. "I'd be picking it up on my sensors… here, let me try something, if I move the ship so the object occults one of those distant stars, I can examine the lensing and – wait. It eclipsed that star way too fast. That doesn't make any sense, the object would have to be *huge*." Clec buzzed around like an agitated fly. "That's a planet. Or something the *size* of a planet. But it doesn't show up on our sensors. How does an *entire planet* not show up on our sensors? There's no stealth technology in the galaxy that can do that! If we hadn't seen the light, we might have been caught in its gravity well before we even *noticed*."

Bianca gazed at the absent planet, and a feeling of serenity descended on her like a blanket in the coldest winter. She released an audible sigh. She felt like she'd spent the past twenty years being thirsty and had finally taken a drink.

Hungry, and had finally eaten.

Asleep, and was finally awake.

"We're here," Bianca said.

CHAPTER 29

First they orbited the planet, and did a visual survey, which didn't tell them much: the surface was mostly smooth, and black or dark gray, with occasional large irregularities that might have been structures or the remnant of structures. The planet was either an unnatural object created in a colossal feat of engineering, or a planet with no star that had been transformed for unknown reasons.

There were no lights or signs of habitations, save for the single yellow beacon.

The *Show and Tell* didn't have a shuttle – it was too small – so they had no choice but to descend to the surface on their own. "I'll have to land entirely by eye," Clec said. "We can't use the automated systems, because they don't think there's any land below us at all. If we miscalculate our angle or velocity… well, it won't be good for us."

"Let me pilot the ship." Bianca was perfectly serene.

"Have you ever flown a ship like this before?" Heuvelt asked.

"She hasn't," Sev said. "But she'd never defeated a squad of Letnev shock troopers until the first time she did. If she thinks she can land us safely, she can."

"I can." Bianca sat down in the pilot's chair, looked over the controls, and switched the system to manual. She began a slow descent. "There's no atmosphere, or if there is, it's very thin – I'm not hitting any turbulence at all."

The ship felt like an extension of her body. Flying it was no more difficult than walking down a set of steps. Bianca guided the *Show and Tell* gently in the direction of the light, which proved to be a luminous orb set atop a cyclopean structure made of stone blocks, like a step pyramid.

Bianca set the ship down so gently they barely felt the impact. She smiled beatifically at the crew crowding into the cockpit. "Shall we take a walk?"

"Is this the destination?" Sev said. "I mean, is this the treasure planet? Ixth?"

Bianca shrugged. "It's the place I was meant to go. If I'm meant to go somewhere else after this, that will be revealed. But from what Doctor Archambelle said, no. I don't think Ixth is seventeen days' voyage away from a known wormhole. That seems too easy. So, this may just be a stepping stone."

"Which isn't to say there won't be things to loot here, I trust," Heuvelt said.

"Oh, there may be valuable artifacts," Bianca said. "But the knowledge we stand to gain will be worth far more."

"I am aware it's possible to sell knowledge," Heuvelt said, "but the collectors *I* know are more interested in objects."

"I'll get the blowtorch and the wrecking bar," Ashont said.

Once they were all suited up and ready to deploy the ramp, Bianca turned to face them. "Maybe I should go in alone, at first? Just in case?" She didn't want to leave her companions behind, but she didn't know what waited for them in this strange place.

"You can take the lead," Sev said firmly. "We'll give you a little space, but you can't possibly think we'd let you go in there alone."

Tears welled in Bianca's eyes, and she threw her arms around Sev. "You're such a good friend." She stepped back, blinking – you can't wipe away tears with a space helmet on – and then straightened her back. "I'll do my best to protect you all, no matter what we find here."

"We know you will," Heuvelt said.

Clec lowered the boarding ramp, and they descended to the surface of a world made of stone. The gravity here was higher than it was on the ship, and Bianca noticed her friends stumble, but it barely registered; the difference in gravity was just another piece of data. The structure topped by the light was only a hundred meters or so away, and Bianca strode toward it confidently, with full faith that her destiny would reveal itself.

Then she stopped, holding up a hand to call the others to halt. "The structure is transmitting… or, no, wait, it's receiving… there's a signal going *into* it."

"A signal from where?" Sev asked.

Bianca turned her head, following the lines of force, and went *hmmm*. "It's communicating with the *Show and Tell*."

"I want to say 'that's impossible,'" Clec said. "Because my encryption protocols are very good. But I am willing to believe a lost civilization of super-intellects can break them, I guess. It's not as if we have any valuable secrets hidden in our data banks."

"I'd rather an alien entity didn't seize control of my ship!" Heuvelt said.

"We can always do the necessary sabotage to convert the *Show and Tell* to fully manual control," Ashont said. "Bianca has demonstrated she can fly instruments-only. Actually, she barely even had instruments."

"The transmission has stopped," Bianca said. "I guess we keep walking?"

"It is better to act than to wait and be acted upon," Sev said. "Lead on."

Bianca closed the distance to the pyramid by half, but then the beacon lit up in that other spectrum again. "It's transmitting again–" she began.

"Greetings, child of the master, and her companions." The voice was low, rumbling, and broadcasting on their comms channel. "Forgive my intrusion into your ship's systems. I had to ascertain what language I should use to speak to you."

"Who are you?" Bianca asked.

"I am Tyrolian the Gatekeeper. I understand you are known as Bianca Xing, honored heir. May I call you Bianca?"

"I… yes, of course. This is not what I expected."

"I am sure you have many questions. I have answers."

The peace that had flooded through Bianca was overtaken by excitement. She was talking to – what, one of the Mahact? One of their servants? And that title, the Gatekeeper, suggested there was a further destination beyond this one. "We–"

"I have a question," Sev said. "Did you have anything to do with a crushed spaceship we found en route to this planet?"

The low, rumbling voice laughed. "You are one of the… Letnev, isn't it? Mmm. Your people were still hitting each other with rocks in your caves when my master was at his zenith, shaping galactic affairs. *Your* questions do not interest me."

Bianca cleared her throat. "These are my friends, Gatekeeper. Without them, I never would have made it here."

"Apologies, honored heir. I will address them with greater respect, if that is your desire. But the point stands: my purpose is to assist you in your journey, not to answer the idle queries of your companions."

"It's not idle, though," Bianca said. "*Do* you know about that ship?"

"I did not encounter the vessel personally, as my duties keep me here, on the surface. But some of my, you could say siblings, patrol this system, and yes, they destroyed that ship."

"Why?" Bianca said, but she was afraid she knew. "Because they weren't *me*? Do you kill anyone who comes here except the honored heir?"

"Not at all." The Gatekeeper's tone was soothing. "No one has ever landed here before – no one has been *drawn* to this particular point in space, as you were, and the World of Stone is not easy to discern. We only lit the beacon when we sensed the shape of your mind. But occasionally ships pass through this region, and we allow them go about their business unmolested, so long as they do not interfere with the World of Stone, or the machinery within."

"What made the ship you wrecked any different?"

"That was a scout vessel send by the Argent Flight. They are old enemies of my master, and all the Mahact. They may have been following rumors or whispers about the existence of the World of Stone, or perhaps it was a cosmically unlikely coincidence. My associate disabled their ship before they could reach us. Be assured, Bianca, that we do not take life lightly. But the Argent Flight… they are implacable fanatics, dedicated to continuing a war that ended millennia ago, and they would not hesitate to destroy this place. If they knew about *you*, your death would be the best possible outcome. They have weapons made to destroy the Mahact and their creations, and that destruction is painful."

"Creations like me," Bianca said.

"Indeed. And like myself, and my cohort."

"Maybe we can continue this discussion inside?" Bianca said.

"Yes, it would be disappointing to be killed by a random stray micro-meteor," Heuvelt said.

"Inside?" the Gatekeeper said. "What do you mean – oh. I see. No, there has been some confusion."

The step pyramid began to move, rotating on its base as the stones shifted their positions. The movements weren't drastic, but they changed the shape of the thing in significant ways, and after a moment Bianca was no longer looking at a temple of blocks: she was looking into an immense face made of planes and angles.

The pyramid was no pyramid at all. It was a stone head, bigger than the *Show and Tell*. It opened immense eyes, and they shone with blue-green light.

"I'll stand up," the Gatekeeper said, and began to rise.

"The crew has questions, acting captain," Voyou said.

"You can just call me 'captain'," Richeline snapped.

"Yes… captain."

"You said 'acting' under your breath, didn't you?"

"Yes… captain. About those questions. A representative asked me to share their concerns with you during our next meeting."

Richeline groaned. Voyou stood at attention before her, because she hadn't told him he could stop, even though she was slumped in the captain's chair at the captain's desk with her head in her hands. The bandage was off her neck, and she was mostly healed, except for a shiny scar she'd chosen not to have removed because, she said, "It serves as a useful reminder about the nature of the chain of command."

"Questions," she said. "They have questions? I have questions. Like how in the light I'm supposed to find an unknown ship in a search area that spans millions of kilometers or more. But fine. What are *their* questions?"

"Just what you'd expect, captain." He managed to swallow the "acting" entirely that time, though it took an effort, and he hoped the *real* captain never found out. He still couldn't really accept that Severyne was dead. His mind simply wouldn't retain the information. Maybe if he'd seen a body… though maybe not even then. Pretending to be dead just to find out what people might say about her afterward seemed like something the captain would do. "We've been following an erratic course for more than two weeks, with no stated mission or goal. We are crewed by loyal Letnev soldiers, of course, and they'll do what they're told, without question, but in addition to troopers, the crew also includes surveyors, linguists, mining engineers, all sorts of planetary annexation specialists who aren't accustomed to this sort of open-ended assignment."

"They'd better *get* accustomed, or they can see how they like taking spacewalks without environment suits on. They should realize that on an 'open-ended assignment' like this I don't actually *need* surveyors and mining engineers."

"I'm sure they do realize," Voyou said. "I imagine that adds to the general anxiety. The half rations don't help. They also want to know when the captain is coming back." Officially, Severyne had been recalled to the home world to update the Baron personally about the state of their annexation efforts, but that was a flimsy sort of lie, and only the most prone to propaganda believed it.

"The captain is dead," Richeline muttered. "Long live the captain. Is there anything *else*?"

"Well. Yes. The crew is also wondering where the 'princess' went. There are all *sorts* of rumors about Bianca at this point – including that she's the one who stabbed you in the neck. One popular notion is that she attacked you and escaped, and you vowed revenge. When the captain refused to let you chase after Bianca, you killed her, and seized control of the ship to pursue your mad obsession."

"That's the plot of *The Lord and the Liar*!" Richeline finally lifted her head. "They think I'm reenacting a two-hundred-year-old *opera*?"

"In the absence of any other narrative, I'm afraid so. If we told them something – anything, really – they'd feel better."

"Tell them we're in pursuit of a terrorist bent on the destruction of the Letnev people. Tell them *she* killed the captain, because she almost certainly *did*."

"Really?" Voyou said. "You want to go on the record, officially, that the captain is dead?"

"Of course she's dead! She must be dead! What else could have possibly–"

A red-bordered emergency call appeared on the screen, and a bridge communication officer said, "We have received an encrypted message for you, captain."

"From the Barony?" Richeline said. Voyou knew she hoped she was being recalled. She was ready to give up this whole mission as a waste. Archambelle was still fanatical about it, but she was mostly being fanatical alone in her quarters these days.

"We're not sure where the message came from, captain – it arrived from an unremarkable quadrant of space, presumably sent from a ship – but it has top-level authorization keys."

A moment of silence. Then: "Send the message to my desk."

A flashing icon blinked on her screen.

Voyou stared at it. "Is that… could it be…?"

"Call Archambelle," Richeline said. "We might as well all watch it together."

The doctor arrived, even more disheveled than the last time Voyou had seen her. She'd been poring over her database of Mahact artifacts and translations, desperately seeking some detail that would narrow down their search parameters, and she hadn't been eating or sleeping much. "What is it? Did you find the girl? Did you find *anything*?"

"Something found us." Richeline activated the message.

The captain's face appeared on screen, half hidden in shadow. "Hello, devoted underlings. I know how much you've missed me. You'd better come and join me, don't you think?"

CHAPTER 30

Heuvelt had seen extraordinary things in the course of his many journeys.

He'd watched twin suns twinkle through the geysers of the living silver fountain on Abadona Eight.

He'd ridden the last train out of the poisoned city of Thammux, and turned in his seat to watch its towers collapse behind him as the local government bombed their own seat of power in a desperate (and futile) attempt to stop the logic plague.

He'd kissed one of the most famous entertainment vid actors in the world in the viewing gallery of a luxury Supernova Tour liner as a star imploded just on the other side of the transparent forcefields.

He and Dob Ell had skied over icy plains beneath red-and-gold aurora, and blasted their way into an icy temple complex devoted to the dead gods of a cold-blooded species rendered extinct by climate change. Once inside, they navigated corridors mosaicked with scenes of reptilian warriors fighting their implacable furry enemies, dodged pit traps and spike traps and arrow traps, and reached the central chamber where a statue of a saurian king ten meters high presided over dust and spiders. (Someone else had gotten there first and stolen the statue's jeweled scepter and orb, but still, what a thing to see.)

He'd seen his whole life, and all its extraordinary wonders and glories, flash before his eyes when Dob Ell came at him, snarling, shame-blade in hand, so in a way, he'd seen all those remarkable things *twice*.

But all those wonders paled in comparison to seeing Tyrolian the Gatekeeper rise. The ground shook beneath their feet, throwing all of them off balance, except Clec (who hovered) and Bianca (who simply compensated, shifting her weight as the ground lurched). The great being raised all four of its arms out of the ground, seams in the planet's surface revealing themselves to be merely the edges of the Gatekeeper's immense fingers and limbs. Those hands *were* big enough to crush a ship, and Heuvelt looked fearfully back at the *Show and Tell*, afraid it would be swallowed by a crack in the ground, but its portion of the planet seemed stable. This wasn't an earthquake, really, as much as it felt like one. It was more like someone climbing out of a hole.

The Gatekeeper's immense chest rose up from the surface, a chiseled blank of stone threaded with lines of shining metal. "There," the Gatekeeper said, resting one set of immense elbows on the ground. "I don't suppose I need to stand *all* the way up. You have some sense of my stature now, and I would hate to inadvertently step on any friends of the honored heir."

"What *are* you?" Bianca craned her neck to look up at the now-distant stone face. "You said the Mahact made you, but… how?"

"The creation of Titans is complex and difficult," the Gatekeeper rumbled. Though his head was far above them now, he still spoke to them through their comms, so the voice was intimate and close. "We can reproduce ourselves, though with great effort, and the process requires long periods of dormancy. The Mahact could create us more easily, but they did not share all their secrets with us. We are living beings, of stone and steel, created to serve the Mahact. I was created to serve a *specific* Mahact: my master, and your maker, honored heir."

"But *why* did he make us? I don't understand what the point of all this is! Why arrange for me to be born on a distant planet, to look like a human, to draw me here – what is the goal? Why am I here?"

Heuvelt winced in sympathy at the anguish in Bianca's voice. He'd often wondered what the point of *his* life was, but he could accept, ultimately, that there was no inherent purpose to existence – he was responsible for making his own meaning. Bianca was different. She'd been created for a reason, and she deserved to know what that was.

"I wish I could ease your mind, honored heir," the Gatekeeper said. "I know only my own part in your journey. I was charged to wait, and watch, and listen. To protect this place, until the honored heir arrived. And, once you arrived, to send you through the gate."

"Where does the gate lead?"

"To the abiding home of the master."

"Who is this master?" Bianca said.

"Kor Noq Weer," the Gatekeeper said.

Bianca didn't say anything for a moment. Then: "I don't know who that is."

"Kor Noq Weer was a great scientist, philosopher, and shaper of destinies," the Gatekeeper said. "His name rang through the stars even at the height of the Mahact empire. He found this planet, near a wormhole, and shaped it to his liking. He created the machinery that closed the wormhole, and that will open it again. He made me, and he made *you*, and I know he considered you the greater creation, simply because of the nature of my orders: to honor and protect you at all costs. Whatever he intends for you, it must be something great."

"Is Kor Noq Weer still alive?" Bianca said. "I thought all the Mahact were dead?"

"I do not know," he rumbled. "I was assigned my duties long ago, and the master was very ill, even in those days. Perhaps he has passed on, but left instructions for you. Or perhaps he waits, dormant, in stasis, to share some final words with you before he passes on. Who can say?"

"I have so many more questions," Bianca said. "What is Ixth like? What do the Mahact *look* like? Was Kor Noq Weer… nice?"

"I will tell you all I know. We can converse while I set the machinery in motion to reopen the wormhole gate."

Heuvelt looked to the sky. There was no evidence of a wormhole yet, and no telling where it would appear. He glanced around at his companions. Clec and Ashont were circling around the immense torso of the Gatekeeper, communicating on their private channel; probably wishing they could pry the valuable ore out of that immense body. Sev was – huh. Where was she? He looked back toward the ship in time to see her disappear up the ramp. He opened a channel to her. "Sev? What are you doing?"

"I'm thirsty and my suit reservoir is empty. I'll be right back."

"Ah, of course." He realized he was speaking to an empty channel – she'd cut the comms as soon as she finished speaking.

Heuvelt didn't trust Sev. He'd confessed this to Bianca once, and she'd only laughed. "I don't blame you. She tried to squish Clec!"

"It's more than that. She has a secretive nature, don't you think?"

"I spent some time on a ship full of Letnev. Believe me when I say Sev is open and welcoming compared to most of them."

"Mmm. I suppose you're right. I find it difficult to trust anyone since Dob Ell. Though Dob was always kind, even deferential, sometimes even fawning, before she betrayed me, so you'd think I'd be more inclined to trust someone abrasive like Sev."

"After all you've been through, of course it's hard to let your guard down," Bianca said. "But if your walls are too high, nothing good can get through them, either."

Heuvelt's walls were nothing compared to Sev's, though, and he still had profound doubts about her. He walked toward the ship, filled with a sudden and irrational terror that Sev would turn on the engines and fly away, stranding them here with the Titan. The fear didn't make any *sense*, but knowing that didn't dispel it.

The interior of the ship beyond the airlock was pressurized, but he didn't bother to take his helmet off – why waste the time? He crept up the ramp, moving toward the galley, where their water stores were kept. Sev wasn't there. He moved quietly down the corridor to her sleeping area. Maybe she had her own supplies stashed away there. He certainly had all sorts of assorted bottles in *his* makeshift quarters.

He walked in to find her crouched behind a pile of crates, speaking into her wrist gauntlet. Her helmet was off, so he could hear her words: "… about to open a wormhole, so if you're anywhere in the vicinity, you need to get here *now*. You'll have to transit the wormhole quickly, because there are these giants made of stone here, and they can crush spaceships as easily as you'd crumple a piece of paper–"

She must have sensed his presence and simply pretended not to, because she spun and knocked his legs out from under him. He went down with a *whump*, landing on his side, and Severyne rolled him face down, then knelt on his back.

She was doing something there, messing with his pack, poking at the back of his suit. He tried to open a comm channel to call for help, but only heard dead air – Severyne had torn out his transmitter wires. He tried to rise, but she wrenched his arms behind him, pinning his wrists together, and he couldn't get enough leverage with his knees alone. Maybe he could roll her over, shake her loose, flee the ship, wave his arms–

Things began to get sort of… swimmy. He gasped for air, but air didn't come. She was doing something to his oxygen supply! She was going to kill him – he was going to die – he'd been *betrayed again,* and worse, if she meant him harm, that meant she might try to hurt *Bianca,* and Bianca could fight anything, but only if she knew she *needed* to fight.

Heuvelt's life passed before his eyes again, but curiously, only his life from the *last* time he'd been sure death was imminent – when Dob Ell came at him with the shame-blade.

His life since then was a shorter but rather more depressing span, with a lot more drinking and sulking… but at least the most recent parts of his existence resembled something like the life he'd dreamed of living.

I wish I'd gotten to see Ixth, he thought, and then slipped into the dark.

Once the man was unconscious, Severyne restored his air supply. She didn't think she'd deprived him of oxygen long enough to give him permanent brain damage. *But then again, would I even be able to tell?*

The meddling fool. Bianca was so distracted by the Titan that Severyne decided she could risk slipping back to send another transmission to the *Grim Countenance,* but she hadn't counted on Heuvelt following her.

This situation was annoying. Severyne simply couldn't be found out yet – not before she made it through the wormhole. If Bianca realized Severyne *was* a spy, she wouldn't even have to perform the execution herself: she could just ask Tyrolian to pick Severyne up and make a fist. This situation could be salvaged, though. She opened her comms. "Something's wrong with Heuvelt! I think his suit malfunctioned!"

"What?" Bianca shouted, and Ashont and Clec said "Coming" in unison.

By the time they all crowded through the airlock, Sev had Heuvelt in the reclining chair in the tiny medical suite. A mask over his face fed him oxygen, and his system was filled with sedatives, though Severyne had deleted the logs that would reveal the last part.

Ashont growled "Move," and crouched beside Heuvelt, looking at his medical data scroll past on a screen. "He seems stable. What happened?"

"He was face down, and wasn't moving." Severyne was careful, as always, to avoid outright lies. Bianca was watching her far too closely as she spoke. "His air supply wasn't working properly, but I got the oxygen flowing again, and then brought him here. He hasn't woken up yet, but I think he'll be all right."

"Those suits are all overdue for maintenance," Clec said. "It's my fault. I prioritized ship repairs."

"We all agreed that was the best way to allocate funds," Ashont said. "The suits were still within acceptable range. I'll take a look at his to see what happened."

"I'm afraid I may have damaged his suit," Severyne said. "I was agitated, and I took it off him in a hurry."

Ashont growled at her and stomped off.

"I don't know enough about human health issues." Clec hovered before Heuvelt's face. "Is it normal for them to stay asleep like this? Should I give him stimulants and wake him up?"

Severyne did not reach for the knife hidden in the small of her back, but she was prepared to.

"The body can take time to recover," Bianca said. "I knew a boy who almost drowned, and they saved him but he didn't wake up until the next morning. I think we should let Heuvelt rest. Sleep helps humans heal."

"He'd be just as happy sleeping through a wormhole transit anyway," Clec said. "Those always make him feel ill."

"I need to go talk to the Titan," Bianca said. "Will you all be okay here?"

"We'll prepare the ship for the journey," Clec said. "I hope Heuvelt wakes up before we get to Ixth. He'd hate to miss that."

"Time will tell," Severyne said. Heuvelt might need to suffer a fatal accident later, but if she could keep him sedated until they reached Ixth, and the *Grim Countenance* actually showed up, that might not be necessary. For now, she didn't want Bianca distracted by grief. She might still have crucial work to do. The possibility of encountering a *living* Mahact, even one in stasis, seemed incredibly unlikely. If they did, Bianca was probably the only one of them capable of dealing with such an entity… if anyone could.

Heuvelt's interruption had cut Severyne's transmission short. She'd planned to mention that Mahact name, Kor Noq Weer, to Archambelle, in case it had ever come up in her research.

Oh well. It probably didn't matter.

At just that moment, Archambelle was taking one of her naps, a brief interval of restless slumber snatched in between long hours spent poring over research.

Quite by coincidence, she'd just read a fragmentary account of one of Kor Noq Weer's more infamous genocidal exploits, the Cleansing of the Barred Spiral.

She was having a nightmare about it, in fact.

CHAPTER 31

The Titan picked Bianca up in its hand and raised her high. The beacon shining on his forehead cast light into the darkness, and she could see other shapes dotting the planet's surface. She clung to the Gatekeeper's fingers and gazed down. The *Show and Tell* looked like a toy from up here. "Are those shapes on the ground more Titans?"

"Some, yes, slumbering and dormant. Others are raw materials for future additions to our ranks. Kor Noq Weer's plans are unknown to us, but we stand ready to serve in whatever capacity his design requires."

Machinery rumbled deep beneath the surface of the World of Stone. Bianca could sense the meshing of great gears, the turning of axles, the thrum of wires, the resonance of crystals. Her expanding senses could feel a change in the sky above them, too. A shimmering. A quickening. A throwing open of locks. "The wormhole will open soon, won't it?"

"Oh, yes."

"Have you seen the other side?"

"I have not. I was created here."

"Then you've never seen Ixth?"

"I have never seen Ixth. I understand it is a place of great and terrible beauty."

She frowned. "Is Ixth where I'm going? Is that where the wormhole leads?"

"My apologies, honored heir. I assumed that was your destination, because you suggested as much. But Kor Noq Weer did not tell me where the gate leads."

"We assumed we were going to the Ixth, but it's just a guess. What if that gate just leads to another stepping stone along the way?"

"Kor Noq Weer is wise, and you must trust in his design."

"I suppose that is, literally, true. I don't have much choice." She paused. "Gatekeeper, did you notice the ship down there sending a transmission a little while ago?"

"I did, honored heir."

"You didn't send it? Through the ship, or something? Like a message to Kor Noq Weer?"

"No, honored heir. I thought one of your friends was sending a message to someone on your behalf."

"No," Bianca said. "Not on my behalf." Her mind was a terrific engine, capable of correlating disparate points of information and drawing conclusions ranked by probability. But she had to pay *attention* to those conclusions for them to do any good. She had to accept them. If she ignored them – willfully ignored them, even – then her capacity for deductive and inductive reasoning was wasted.

Now, unfortunately, some of the probabilities were so high they could no longer be dismissed.

The machinery beneath them fully engaged. A veil of darkness shimmered away, and a shining sphere revealed itself: the four-dimensional point in space-time that marked the end of a wormhole.

"The gate is open," Tyrolian said. "My work is done."

He lowered her to the ground. "Thank you, Gatekeeper."

"To fulfill one's purpose is the greatest pleasure in life, honored heir. I hope you will experience the same joy soon."

Bianca walked to the ship, where her friends – and one person she'd really hoped was her friend – waited.

"We're so close." Richeline was stunned. "We could be there in less than an hour, and if we hadn't gotten that message, we still would have missed it entirely. Voy-ou, have the navigator set a course."

Voyou sent orders from his gauntlet. He wasn't technically in a position to give orders to the bridge crew, but everyone knew he was the acting captain's unofficial message-carrier, dogsbody, and helpmeet now.

"Giants made of stone," Archambelle muttered. "I've heard of them. Titans, they're called – 'the statues that serve,' sometimes, 'the sleeping giants,' 'the stones that grow.' Some kind of robots, we all assumed. Definitely Mahact. And a *wormhole*. It's just as we thought: a secret passageway to Ixth."

"This will make my career." Richeline was smiling for the first time in weeks, and Voyou thought she looked ghastly. "I assumed this was all a waste of time, but Severyne actually came through. The Baron will make me leader of my own covert operations team for sure after this."

"You think too small," Archambelle said. "Once we have the power of the Mahact at our disposal, the petty wars and covert operations that so excite you will cease to matter. The Barony will have the power to crush our enemies and impose our will on the entire galaxy. Our empire will be eternal."

"It will be good to have the captain back, too," Voyou said.

Richeline glared at him. "Do you find my leadership lacking, Undercommandant?"

What leadership? Voyou thought. She was just following the plan Severyne had provided for her. He bowed his head meekly. "Of course not. I merely respect the chain of command, act– captain."

"See that you respect *my* command first and foremost," Richeline said.

The transit through this wormhole was no different than the first one Bianca had experienced, which was disappointing, somehow – there should have been the bang of drums, the sound of horns, at least a crash of thunder. Instead, there was a silent and nearly instantaneous moment of disorientation, and then they were on the other side.

"We're in a completely uncharted region," Clec said from the pilot's chair. "This star field doesn't appear anywhere in the navigational database. Let me pan around for – oh. Look. There's a planet. At least this one shows up on our sensors."

"I don't think it's really a planet," Bianca said. She could sense, somehow, that the dark shape in the distance was a *made* thing. The World of Stone was a planet shaped to Kor Noq Weer's whims. This place, on the other hand, was a whim created in the shape of a planet. "More like a giant space station."

Their destination was an immense sphere of metal and ice, dotted here and there with towers as tall as mountains, and one immense black stone obelisk at the pole that made those towers seem like toothpicks in comparison.

"Is this Ixth, then?" Sev said. "It's supposed to be an *actual* planet, right?"

"I'm not sure," Bianca said. "Maybe this is just another–"

She gasped, then doubled over, bracing herself against the console as her whole body shuddered. The full-body muscular contractions were accompanied by a lightheaded feeling, and her blood sang in her veins. "Oh, oh, oh, something – there's something – oh, this makes the yearning feel like nothing at all, this–" She looked up, and now she *could* see the lines of force rising up from the planet, the signals beaming from the towers to the ring of satellites she'd just now noticed, and all that energy streaming – into *her*. "I can feel… this world is like a big machine, some kind of computer, and I'm the user *and* the interface, all at once. I think I can… Look."

She raised her arms, and the lines of force shifted. The tops of all the thousands of towers on the surface burst into jets of sputtering blue flame, and then those flames burned gold.

The surface of the planet was suddenly illuminated, with vast patterns of concentric circles intersected by radiating lines, drawn across the sphere in strokes of light. The new brightness revealed further complex patterning across the surface that resembled circuitry, or a grid of city streets. The towers began to smoothly move, sinking into the surface, but the flames at their tops kept burning, and the circles and lines grew even brighter.

"What did you *do*?" Clec said in awe.

"I am the key." Bianca pointed to the black obelisk. "And that is the door."

"Unless it's the head of another stone giant or something," Sev muttered.

Bianca shook her head. "No. I can *feel* it. That's our way in. And far below, I'll find my heart's desire."

"Which is what, exactly?" Sev asked.

"I have no idea," Bianca said. "I can't wait to find out."

•••

"Fire the torpedoes! Prime the railgun! Launch the fighters!" Richeline screamed. The *Grim Countenance* was a warship with a full complement of small fighter vessels on board, and a squadron of those flew out now, toward the pair of impossible-seeming ships trying to stop them from reaching the wormhole. "Why are their ships shaped like giants?" Richeline said.

"They *are* giants," Archambelle said. "Titans capable of independent space-flight! They're extraordinary. Imagine what the Barony could do with a fleet of *those*? They could fly to a planet, land on the surface, and lay waste to the enemy. No crew would even be required."

"Trying to put us out of a job, doctor?" Voyou did his best to keep his tone light, but the spectacle on the viewscreen was terrifying. The Titans were a third the size of the *Grim Countenance* itself, and they were reaching out and crushing the Barony fighter ships with their immense hands.

"Oh, stars, what is *that*?" Richeline pointed toward the dim shape of the World of Stone – an anomaly invisible to their sensors. "Is there something climbing *out* of that planet?"

Archambelle leaned close to the screen. "Another Titan," she said. "Bigger. It must have been growing for a *long* time."

"Get us through that wormhole *now*!" Richeline shouted at the bridge crew.

The camera view switched, the wormhole looming before them – until a Titan sailed into their field of view. The *Grim Countenance* was too big for the Titan to simply crush like it had the fighters, but Voyou had no doubt it could do murderous quantities of damage anyway.

"Fire the railgun!" Richeline shouted.

The *Grim Countenance* shuddered. The railgun was meant for disabling enemy warships, and it was basically a simple kinetic weapon: a dense ball of shot, accelerated along a rail that ran the full length of the *Grim Countenance*'s hull, and fired at a small but sufficient fraction of the speed of light. High mass, very high acceleration: immense force.

The shot struck the Titan and sent it spinning away from the gate with a new hole in the center of its chest.

Voyou cheered, and Richeline did too, but Archambelle kept staring at the screen. "The Titan is still moving. Look at that. Arms waving around, legs kicking, thrusters in its feet still firing. Perhaps they don't have anything analogous to vital organs at all. I – wait. Stop. I'm still looking–"

They passed through the wormhole, leaving the few surviving fighter ships behind. Richeline didn't even say anything about them, or their sacrifice. Their pilots must feel so abandoned.

Oh well, Voyou thought. They probably won't have to feel much of anything for very long.

•••

Bianca did the piloting again, guiding the *Show and Tell* toward the monolith. This planet *did* have an atmosphere, but she was deft enough with the controls that the descent wasn't too bumpy. "This atmosphere is breathable for all of our species," Clec said, consulting readouts. "That seems... unlikely."

"Those towers we saw did something to the air. I think I told them what I needed, and just didn't realize that's what I was doing." Bianca guided the ship down, and the irregularities on the surface turned out to be structures of different sizes and shapes, but with no visible doors or windows. The buildings were covered with glyphs, though – Mahact writing, she assumed. She couldn't read the words, but it felt like she *almost* could: like there was a blurry film across her vision, and if she only stopped and rubbed her eyes for a moment, all would be revealed.

She set the ship down on a clear spot, near the base of the monolith. A set of gleaming black-and-gold-flecked steps, just slightly too big for a human to climb comfortably, led up to the top of the obelisk, which must have been five hundred meters high. She turned in her chair. "Ashont, Clec… I think you should stay here with Heuvelt. If he wakes up alone, who knows what he'll think? Even if we left him a message, he'd try to come in after us, and it might not be safe."

Ashont sighed. "Yes. I was thinking the same thing. We can't leave our injured cub behind. Not now."

Bianca patted her furry shoulder. "It will make me feel safer, knowing you're here to watch over him. We don't know where we are, or what dangers we might encounter. I'll stay in comms contact as long as I can, though I think I'm going pretty deep, so don't worry if I lose connection."

"I'm hearing too much 'I' and not enough 'we,'" Sev said. "I'm going with you."

"My Sev." Bianca touched her hand. "Dear Sev. I knew you'd never leave my side."

"We have exploration packs prepared," Ashont said. "Anti-grav harnesses for those hard-to-reach places, respirators, water, flares, distress beacons. It's a shame Heuvelt isn't awake. He loves all that stuff. There's nothing he enjoys more than climbing into a weird hole in the ground and looking for wonders."

"We'll take lots of pictures," Sev said.

Bianca helped Sev into her pack, then shouldered her own. "It means so much to me, Sev, the way you made my mission your own."

Sev shrugged. "I like to keep busy. The worst part about being locked up in the brig was the boredom. This gives me something to do. Besides. I admit. I am curious about what we're going to find down there."

"I'm sure it will be worth the work and wait," Bianca said.

They passed through the airlock and marched down the boarding ramp. The gravity was lighter here than it was on the World of Stone, and Bianca went bounding up the steps that led to the top of the monolith. Sev came after her, more slowly, but steadily. "How many of these stupid steps are there?"

Bianca glanced at the height of the step before her, then the height of the monolith. "Two thousand-one-hundred-seventy-four," she said. "But every journey begins with just one, right?"

"I don't mind the first step," Sev said. "It's all the ones that come after. Why don't we use our anti-grav harnesses and fly up there?"

Bianca shook her head. "Come on, Sev. We came all this way. Where's your sense of occasion?"

"You're one of those people who enjoys delayed gratification, aren't you?"

"I'll take gratification any way I can get it," Bianca said. "But sometimes it is a little sweeter when you have to wait."

"Why is that planet *glowing*?" Richeline said. "Archambelle, is Ixth supposed to glow like that?"

The doctor stared at the screen for a long time. When she turned toward the others, her eyes were wider than Voyou had ever seen them.

"I don't know what that is," she said. "But it is not Ixth."

CHAPTER 32

At the top of the stairs they faced the monolith, a blank wall of smoothly gleaming black stone, with flecks of gold that seemed to float deep inside.

Bianca walked across the short landing and pressed her hand against the wall. "I'm here," she said, her breath puffing out against the stone. Some combination of her touch, her voice, and the air from her lungs set ancient machinery in motion, and the stone split vertically right down the middle, each half swinging silently inward, revealing a small chamber beyond.

"Ashont, Clec, we're going in," Bianca transmitted. "It looks like some sort of elevator."

"Keep us updated as long as you can," Ashont said.

Sev and Bianca stepped into the chamber, and a segment of the wall lit up with incomprehensible twisty symbols. "Are those buttons?" Sev said. "Which one do you press?"

One of the glyphs glowed more brightly, and sent tendrils of force through the air toward Bianca, invisible to Sev. "This one." She put her hand against the symbol, and the floor began to drop smoothly down, the ceiling and the spill of light from outside receding until they were lit only by the glow of the symbols on the wall, which somehow moved down with them.

"How did you know that was the right symbol?"

"I know lots of things, Sev. More and more every minute."

Sev went *hmmm*. "Do you think this Kor Noq Weer is really waiting down there?"

"I'm really not sure. There's *something* down there. Something I'm supposed to see. Something I'm supposed to do." She watched spirals of invisible energy swirling all around her. This whole planet was a ship of sorts, she realized; and more than that, it was a shipbuilding facility, and a weapons factory, and more. It was not just a world in itself, but the seed of a greater world to come.

She closed her eyes, and it was as if she moved through the darkened caverns and endless tunnels that riddled the sphere, a bodiless roving point of view. There were incubators here too. The same sort of machinery that had created *her* body waited deep below the ground, on a much vaster scale. Once she offered up a sample of herself, this place could make more of her. Bodies like hers, anyway. Bodies like hers was *now*, with all these new capabilities she barely understood. Enough new bodies to populate this planet. Enough to field an army. But to what end?

"Do you know *what* you're supposed to do yet?"

"Something glorious," Bianca murmured.

They rode the rest of the way down in silence.

"What do you *mean* it's not Ixth?" Richeline said.

Archambelle was chewing on the ends of her hair and staring off into space. "It's a Mahact artifact, I'm sure, but... There aren't many descriptions of Ixth, but there are a few, and it's not like this. Everyone says it's a paradise world, and this... it's some kind of giant space station, can't you tell?"

"The scans definitely indicate something other than a natural planet," Voyou agreed. "Our sensors can't penetrate the surface to a very great depth, but even within those limits we've detected all sorts of tunnels, chambers, and cavities down there. No signs of life, though. Maybe this world is abandoned. The lights are on, but no one's home."

"The dead outpost of a dead race," Richeline said.

"A necropolis," Archambelle said. The idea seemed to cheer her up. "A *city* of the dead. A tomb that we can raid. So, it's not Ixth. We misunderstood, or we were misled. It's still a Mahact world, and it's glowing, and that means it's still *operational*. I'm sure we can find something here to give the Barony the kind of edge we're looking for. Maybe we'll even find directions to reach the *real* Ixth. We won't know until we go inside."

Richeline sighed. "You know the captain's in there already. She must be. If Bianca's the key, the captain is the one who turned her. She might have killed the princess already by now."

"The captain certainly wouldn't wait for us to arrive," Voyou agreed. "She's so decisive."

"I'll bring my research assistants," Archambelle said. "Richeline, call up a full complement of soldiers. We'll need them to..." She gestured vaguely. "Carry stuff."

"I'll bring my best surveying team," Voyou said. "We might as well start making maps of the place."

"Just a small, manageable party of thirty people or so," Richeline said sourly. "It's practically a commando squad. I'll get a shuttle ready."

Heuvelt sat up, gasping, and tore the oxygen mask from his face. Ashont was there, petting him with her immense paws, making soothing sounds, but he shouted over her. "Sev attacked me! She's a traitor, a Letnev spy, Bianca is in danger!"

Ashont immediately slammed the comms panel by the door and shouted, "Bianca, do you read me? Bianca, are you there?"

Only static crackled in reply. Ashont lowered her hand and shook her head. "They descended a while ago. Bianca and Sev. We've lost contact."

"Descended into *what*?" Heuvelt said.

"The depths of the alien planet, or planet-sized space station, maybe, that we landed on while you were unconscious. Ixth, or whatever."

"That's all Sev *wants*, is access to this place, this power! She'll kill Bianca if we don't stop her!"

"Bianca is hard to kill," Ashont said. "But if Sev took her by surprise… hrm. Yes. All right. We'll go in after them. We were just waiting for you to wake up anyway. Clec! Did you get all that?"

"I did," Clec said over the comms. "But we have a bigger problem. A Barony warship, all spikes and cannons, just came through the wormhole, and it's hovering above the planet now."

"Sev made a transmission before she attacked me. She must have been calling *them*. They were following us the whole time!" Heuvelt rose, cursing as he tore off various bits of diagnostic equipment, to a chorus of squawking machine alarms. "Clec, get our ship out of sight, and then we're going after Bee."

The elevator stopped at last, opening onto a corridor hacked roughly into black stone, lit by fist-sized glowing crystals protruding at random intervals from the ceiling and walls. "It's very rustic down here, isn't it?" Severyne said.

"Who can judge the aesthetics of the Mahact?" Bianca strode along, Severyne at her side.

The tunnels weren't particularly small – they could walk abreast with plenty of room, and the ceiling was a meter above their heads – but Severyne still enjoyed the comforting weight of rock all around her. "This reminds me a little of home," she said.

"I read all about your homeworld," Bianca said. "The Letnev don't even have a word for 'claustrophobia.'"

"I had a bit of trouble comprehending the concept, until someone explained it as the opposite of agoraphobia. *That* I can understand."

"Maybe that's why the Letnev are so obsessed with controlling everything," Bianca said. "It all stems from their basic fear of wide-open spaces."

"You're smart these days, princess, but psychologically assessing an entire culture is a stretch, even for you."

"It's just a hypothesis," Bianca said. The corridor split, one path angling right, the other left. Bianca didn't even break stride, just bore right, and when the path split again, she went left, and when it diverged into three possibilities, she went straight.

"Your yearning is guiding us now?" Sev said.

"Hmm? Oh. Yes. It's a maze down here. This world is remote and hidden away, but it's still possible someone could stumble across it, and I get the sense it's sort of vulnerable, when it's not fully operational. If some explorer or treasure hunter like Heuvelt found it, they could ruin everything. Whatever everything entails. Plus, if enemies ever invaded in force, the layout would frustrate their attempts to take control. This is the safest path. The others are more dangerous."

"A tomb full of traps, then? Marvelous."

Their "safest path" led them to a room with no floor, just a pool of bubbling, hissing liquid, with a few pillars of black stone sticking out of the goo, spaced several meters apart. There was no ledge around the sides, and the ceiling was so far above it couldn't be seen. "Even on the proper route, there are little challenges like this," Bianca said. "Places that are tricky to navigate, unless you have the right capabilities."

"Ah. I see. You jump from pillar to pillar. A bit pointless as a deterrent, since I have an anti-grav harness in my pack."

Severyne began rummaging for it, but Bianca shook her head. "It won't work. There's a dampening field here. None of your tech will work, actually."

Severyne frowned. She tapped at her wrist gauntlet, but it was just a piece of jewelry now. "Oh. Well. Leaping to and fro is all well and good for you, but how do I get across?"

"Do you trust me?"

"I do." Severyne didn't hesitate. She wasn't trustworthy, but Bianca was.

"Great. Hold on tight."

"Wait. What are you doing?"

Bianca picked up Severyne, pack and all, and held her in her arms. Without even taking a running start, Bianca jumped from the edge to the first pillar. She didn't pause there, either, but sprang off to the next, and the next, and the next. A few terrifying seconds later, they were safely on the other side, and Bianca deposited Severyne gently on the floor. "There."

Severyne looked back at the bubbling acid – if it was even something as simple as acid. "Don't get killed in here, princess, or I'll never make my way out again."

"Oh, I don't know, Sev. You're pretty resourceful. You escaped one prison, didn't you?"

"Letnev security has nothing on the Mahact, it seems."

They followed more branches, and Sev did her best to keep track of their route, but it was hard, especially when they spiraled down a corridor that went past several identical doors leading to descending ramps before Bianca picked one that looked just like the others.

They reached a room filled with a greasy-looking green fog, the borders of the mist perfectly, eerily regular. Bianca stuck her head into the fog, sniffed, and pulled back. "It's harmless to you unless you inhale it. Put on the respirator – that's not a machine, just filters, so it should work even with the dampening field. But hold your breath and close your eyes just in case, okay?" Bianca picked Severyne up and ran her through the fog, too.

She carried Severyne when she leapt from a platform into an opaque swirl of cloud and landed, barely bending her knees with the impact, some ten meters down.

She raced with Severyne through a corridor where spikes thrust out of the walls at intervals that seemed perfectly random to Severyne but must have revealed their pattern to Bianca and her time-slowing perception.

She stepped between Severyne and a wall that spat a dozen tiny needles, all embedding themselves in Bianca's back instead. "Pull those out for me, will you, Sev? But put on your gloves, and careful, don't touch the tips. From the smell, it's a toxin that would unravel your DNA, like suffering acute radiation poisoning."

The next obstacle was a long room full of bubbling fluid again, but this time, there was a metal cable about three meters overhead. "I guess I jump up, grab that, and then make my way across hand-over-hand," Bianca said.

"Should I climb on your back and just hold on tight?" Severyne opened her pack. "Actually, there are climbing harnesses in here. We could clip them together, and then–"

"That won't be necessary," Bianca said. "This is as far as you're going."

Severyne thought about acting confused, but she could tell from the look on Bianca's face that the time for all subterfuge was past. "I see. When did you figure it out?"

"I sensed a transmission back on the World of Stone, sent from the *Show and Tell*. Then, moments later, Heuvelt had an accident that conveniently knocked him unconscious." She shook her head. "It was too many data points. I couldn't ignore the obvious conclusion anymore. You are a spy."

"Why not take me out on the ship, then?" Severyne said. "Why bring me here?"

Bianca shrugged. "I know you're dangerous. I saw what you did to Richeline. I didn't want to risk you hurting Ashont or Clec or Heuvelt in those close quarters. I figured I'd take you down here and strand you instead."

"You could have just killed me, and then I wouldn't be a danger to anyone." She shook her head. "But you don't have the will. You'd rather let the Mahact do the killing for you."

"Oh," Bianca said. "You think I'm being weak. No. I wanted to bring you to the very edge of fulfilling your mission, and then watch it crumble before your eyes. I'm being cruel, Sev, because I'm very, very angry, and very, very hurt."

"I see." Severyne smiled. "In that case, I'm very, very impressed."

"I don't care."

"You don't? I have a reputation for being difficult to impress. I'm surprised you didn't hear about that, with all the time you spent with my crew."

Bianca frowned. "Your crew?" It clicked. "Wait. *You're* the captain?" She groaned. "You faked the personnel files, just so you could trick me later? You knew I was hacking your systems all along?"

"I make a point of knowing everything," Severyne said. "Be flattered. The Barony sent the very best to look after you." She dropped her pack and reached for the Argent Flight blade tucked into the small of her back. The knife wouldn't help her now – Bianca could take it from her in the space of an eye-blink, since her only hope at besting the woman was by surprise – but she'd rather die in a fight than sit here waiting to starve.

Bianca staggered away when Severyne brandished the blade, shading her eyes with her hand as if something was blinding her. "What – where did you *get* that horrible thing?"

Severyne looked at the knife, which didn't look any different to her than it had before, but all *sorts* of things looked different to Bianca than they did to everyone else, didn't they? Severyne took a step forward. "This doesn't have to end with you dead, princess."

"Don't call me that," she spat.

"Fine. Miss Xing. I think we can reach a mutually agreeable accommodation. Your death doesn't benefit me. Your life could. What do you say?"

A sudden, blistering wind blew through the room, and it carried a voice that spoke in the tones of a crackling fire: *She says no.*

CHAPTER 33

"We're going to use ropes *and* anti-grav harnesses going down the shaft," Heuvelt said. "I don't want to risk my life to any single form of technology, new or old." They used the harnesses to carry them to the top of the stairs, and once they attained the summit, they drove pitons into the stone landing outside the doors. They attached ropes to those, and dropped them down the seemingly bottomless elevator shaft. There was no telling what awaited them below, but Heuvelt had done blind descents before. He usually enjoyed them. If he hadn't been worried about Sev stabbing Bianca in the back, he would have rather enjoyed this whole experience.

Clec and Ashont readied their ropes, though Clec was merely strapped to Ashont – their fates, as always, so closely aligned they functioned as one. They'd parked the *Show and Tell* a short distance away, in a small square surrounded by taller structures, out of sight and, with luck, at least partly hidden from sensor detection by all the sources of heat and vibration in the walls. This whole planet was a machine, and it seemed to be revving up. Maybe, when and if they climbed out again, they'd still have a ship, instead of a smoking bombed ruin where a ship *used* to be, courtesy of the Barony vessel overhead.

They dropped down the shaft with their anti-grav harnesses, at least until those harnesses abruptly stopped working ten meters from the bottom, sending them all slamming into the wall on their ropes. Heuvelt groaned, but then shouted, "Vindication! The old ways are best!" From there, they rappelled down.

At the bottom they unclipped their ropes and went down the corridor, Heuvelt dabbing the wall with a marker when they reached the first branch in the passageway. He put on a specially tinted monocle and grunted in satisfaction. The mark was invisible to the naked eye, but glowed violet when seen through the lens, and because it was a function of chemistry and optics, whatever tech-dampening field had killed their anti-grav harnesses didn't interfere. He didn't want to get lost down here, but he didn't want to leave the pursuing Letnev a series of trail markers, either. "Which way?" he asked.

Ashont sniffed, then pointed right. "Bianca went that way. Not long ago, either."

"Bless your miraculous nose," Heuvelt said, and they set off.

•••

In the end, a detachment of thirty-six people landed on the new world, because Archambelle had more research assistants than anyone had realized, all carrying various sensors and instruments. The surveying team carried flares, ropes, laser rangefinders, and other useful tools. The soldiers carried guns.

Archambelle touched the glyphs etched all over the walls of the nearest structure. "This is … a sort of life story. Or more like … a series of boasts. An extremely lengthy epitaph? You! Postdoc two! Scan these glyphs!"

"What do they say?" Voyou asked.

"Tales of conquest, enemies crushed, plans enacted, discoveries discovered, inventions invented. There's no mention of this great conqueror's name, though."

"Would the name mean anything to you if you saw it?" he asked, genuinely curious.

"Some names would. Tales of a few individual Mahact have survived. The great ruler Vertar Auran Oublis. The mad renegade Kor Noq Weer. The brilliant scientist Callam Harran Coulis. Others."

"This is rather fancy for a tomb," Voyou said. "Maybe we will find something valuable."

"Let's go!" Richeline snapped. "We can do a proper survey after we secure the princess and find the captain."

Richeline, Archambelle, and Voyou each gave orders to their individual commands, then joined together, the three of them leading the way up the steps to the obelisk. Richeline and Voyou had to help Archambelle up. She hadn't yet recovered from her research binge. "Why don't we just use anti-grav?" Richeline muttered. "Ascend right to the top?"

"We are on *Mahact land*," Archambelle said. "This is a momentous occasion. When I tell my colleagues about this journey, I intend to tell them that I *walked* up all two thousand or however many steps it turns out to be."

"You walked up some of them, anyway," Voyou said. "It doesn't seem like you're walking up *quite* as many as I am, though."

The soldiers, lacking any sense of ceremony, floated up the steps in their harnesses, moving at a slow and stately pace behind their leaders. The surveyors and research assistants didn't have anti-grav harnesses, so they just huffed and puffed and climbed at the rear.

Their party reached the top and looked at the ropes, and Richeline cursed. "Why in the brightness did the Mahact build this giant tower, just to have it descend so far below ground level?" she said. "Because of *ceremony*?"

"The ways of the Mahact are not ours to understand," Archambelle said. "Just to exploit. All right, who's helping me down here? I need to see *everything*."

Kill her, my child, the voice said.

Bianca couldn't take her eyes off the horrible knife in Severyne's hand. The weapon seemed to poison the light around it, twisting and distorting her vision, and it somehow also *stank*, but the stench was in her mind more than her nose. Was it some kind of radiation? Worst of all, the presence of the blade seemed to cut off Bianca from her extra senses: she couldn't detect the flow of energy around her anymore, or even tell which way she was supposed to go – the yearning that had guided her to her maker's side was gone, and she felt bereft.

Strike! the wind blew. *She is slow! Show me what you can do!*

The voice was in her head, and she knew it belonged to her maker, Kor Noq Weer. Rumors of the extinction of the Mahact, it seemed, were greatly exaggerated. His words weren't quite irresistible, but they were certainly *motivating*, and unlocked the paralysis the sight of Sev's strange weapon had caused in her. She had to get that horrible *thing* away from her. If it touched Bianca's flesh, she feared she would simply start to come apart.

Bianca slowed time. That didn't work as well as it should have, either, but even at half capacity her powers were formidable. She darted around Sev, calculating the best way to strike. She wanted to kill the traitor, rip her head off, throw her in the acid – to punish her for the crime of making Bianca think she was her *friend*. Killing her would have been easy. Indeed, moving at this speed, a strike of any force would kill Sev, unarmored as she was. It would honestly be harder *not* to kill her.

Bianca could do hard things, though. She remembered the ring Torvald had given her, meant as a self-defense of last resort. Now it could be an instrument of mercy.

Bianca twisted the ring the way Torvald had taught her, then reached out as slowly as she could, and gently cupped her hand around the back of Sev's neck. The ring sent a jolt of electricity into Sev, and Bianca let time resume its normal flow.

Severyne dropped the horrible knife – it went spinning toward the edge of the chasm – and collapsed in a boneless sort of heap. "Thank you, Torvald," Bianca muttered. She still wasn't a murderer, despite Sev's goading. Maybe she could *continue* not murdering anyone, despite her maker's gleeful urging. She quickly frisked Sev for weapons, but all she found was the sheath she'd kept that horrible knife in.

"What *is* that thing?" She looked at the knife and shuddered. Once, on Darit, she'd turned over a rock and seen a squirming nest of wriggling things, all mandibles and legs and eyes, and she felt the same instinctive revulsion at the sight of that blade.

A weapon made to kill Mahact. Vile thing. Cast it away.

Bianca crept up on it. The hilt wasn't horrible, just the blade, so she gingerly grabbed the hilt and shoved the knife into the sheath she'd taken from Sev. Once that blade was hidden from sight, she was able to exhale, all the tension running out of her, and her powers returning.

Is it gone? the wind demanded. *I can't sense it anymore. Come to me, my child. My heir. Come to me, and we will make the Mahact live again.*

"Is that what we're doing?" Bianca said.

What else? Kor Noq Weer replied.

"What else?" Bianca muttered. She leapt up to grab the cable and swung hand-over-hand across the chasm, toward her destiny.

Ashont was strong and agile enough to jump across the pillars in the acid room, Clec on her shoulder, and she carried a line of strong cable with her. Heuvelt clipped his climbing harness to that line, then pulled himself across the chasm, the fumes stinging his eyes all the way. The acid stench had worried Ashont, but she was able to pick up Bianca's scent well enough on the other side.

They wore their respirators and shut their eyes as they raced through the room full of green fog. Heuvelt was certain they'd step into a spike-filled pit at some point in their sightless rush, but apparently the Mahact believed in using one trap at a time.

When they reached the platform above the clouds, they lowered Clec on a rope to make sure it was safe, then dropped ropes and rappelled down to the next level.

The corridor full of spikes would have been impassable, but Clec was small enough to crawl along the floor, below their scything passage. She located an access panel – "Even deadly spike traps need to be *serviced* occasionally" – and yanked out wires until the blades stopped moving. Then it was just a question of carefully climbing under, over, and around razor-edged spears. Heuvelt had done more difficult things… but not often.

They saw the needles glistening on the floor of the next room and knew to be wary. They threw objects from their packs – canteens, unlit flares, nutrient bars – across the motion sensors until the walls ran out of ammunition, then jumped over the ankle-deep glittering carpet of deadly projectiles.

After that, they found Severyne, sitting with her back against a wall. She rose slowly to her feet when they entered. "Heuvelt. Are you here to thank me for sparing your life when I could have so easily taken it?"

"How could you betray Bianca?" Heuvelt roared. "I should throw you in that acid!"

"I didn't betray anyone," Sev said mildly. "I'm loyal to my people, the Letnev. Without them, Bianca would never have reached her destiny. She would have pair-bonded with a farm boy named Grandly, had some babies, and died of dysentery or ergot poisoning or whatever they die of on Darit. I'm the real captain of the *Grim Countenance*. That means I'm the one who took her off that planet and gave her the stars. Me, personally, *I* did that, and all I required from her was a share of what she found. She wasn't willing to give me that."

"She told us a different story," Ashont growled.

"Yes, well, her perspective differs in certain key respects," Sev said. "I wouldn't have let the doctor vivisect her. Not as long as she kept being useful, anyway. But look where she led us. This isn't a treasure planet. This is a tomb, and if we're not careful, it could be our final resting place, too. Oh, and it's a *haunted* tomb, by the way – there's a living Mahact down here somewhere, whispering words of murder on the wind. We thought we'd loot this place and take its wonders for our own. We thought the original owners were long gone. Instead, I fear all we did was wake them up."

"I have no interest in anything you have to say," Heuvelt declared. "Where is Bianca?"

"Where do you think, you cretin? On the other side of that bubbling pool of acid."

"Then we're going that way too. Ashont? Help me up?"

"Don't mind me!" Sev called as the panther-woman boosted the human up to the cable above the pool. He clipped his harness to the line and began to work his way across. Ashont growled at her, Clec made a rude noise, and then the Naaz and Rokha followed. "I'll be fine here!" Sev said. "You're going *toward* the mad genetic sorcerer! I hope that works out for you!"

"I," huff, "never," huff, "liked her," Heuvelt said, grunting his way across the chasm.

"I would have bitten her face off," Ashont said behind him. "But she's so awful I'm afraid I'd get face poisoning."

"I hope her crew finds her," Clec said, "and they all fall into the acid together."

"I am beginning to think we should have gone right instead of left at that first branch," Voyou said. He blinked blood out of his eye. It wasn't his blood. It belonged to one of the research assistants, he thought. That one had sprayed *everywhere.*

"The Mahact… left is the more sacred direction in their culture, according to my research, so I thought…" Archambelle was fairly bloody too. She'd lost her right arm from the elbow down when they passed through the room Voyou thought of as the Chamber of a Thousand Blades, but one of the surveyors had a self-tightening tourniquet that had kept her from bleeding out. A tourniquet couldn't help that same surveyor when his head got sliced off in the Room of Electric Whips, though.

"We can hardly go back now," Richeline said. Her eyes were wide, and she brandished a weapon she'd salvaged from the last soldier (he'd died in the Hall of Biting Mirrors, Voyou thought, or maybe it was the Burning Salon; after a while, the deaths all ran together). "That third chamber is sealed, the walls slammed together, there's no getting through anymore."

"I go back and forth on what to name that one," Voyou said. "Do we call it the Chamber of Crushing? Or maybe something simple, like the Pestle? It killed half the troopers in one smush. I'd say it earned a bit of distinction."

"Shut up, shut up, shut up." Richeline's eyes darted in all directions. "You're supposed to be a *surveyor*, so survey us out of this. Do we go left, right, or straight?"

"Hmm. I predict that left leads to horrible death, straight leads to unimaginably horrible death, and right leads to incomparably unimaginably horrible death. But maybe I got those reversed?" He laughed, but even to his own ears, it sounded more like an unhinged titter.

"Forward," Richeline said. "The princess has to be here somewhere."

"Yes," Voyou said. "Somewhere to the *right* of that first branch, if I had to guess. Don't you think so, Doctor Archambelle? Doctor?" He nudged her shoulder, and she fell over. "Oh," he said.

Richeline stared down at Archambelle. "What? We put a tourniquet on her wound!"

Voyou pointed at the small of Archambelle's back, revealed by her collapse. Her white uniform was matted black with blood all across the base of her spine. "It appears she suffered another injury that went undetected. In the Shrapnel Parlor, if I had to guess. I got a piece in my hip there myself. I do hope the shards aren't poisonous."

"We're getting out of here, Voyou," Richeline snarled. "I am *not* dying here."

"You want to die just ahead of here, then?" he asked. "We only survived this far because we always took the rear, and sent other people ahead of us so they triggered the traps first. Now it's just us."

She grinned. It was a horrible grin. She pointed the rifle at him. "That's true. You're right. That really was a successful strategy. This time, *you* go first." He didn't move. "Come on!" She prodded him in the chest with the barrel of the weapon.

"Go ahead and shoot me," he said. "That would be a much more pleasant way to die than being eaten by acid from the feet up, like postdoc number two, or dragged into the ceiling by mechanical arms like that trooper, or slammed between spiked grates like my best cartographer was. Please. I'd shoot myself if I had a gun."

"Coward!" Richeline said. "Fool! You can sit here and wait to die, but I'm getting *out*. I am a professional, I trained for this, I am the best of the best, I am the captain of the *Grim Countenance* and I will not be defeated!" She ran off, choosing the straight-ahead corridor.

"Acting captain," Voyou muttered. Then he heard her scream. Briefly. "Former acting captain," he corrected, and tittered again.

CHAPTER 34

Bianca pushed her way through a set of tall golden doors and entered the central chamber, a suitable resting place for a sorcerer king. The room was octagonal, the walls filled with shelves and niches, and the floor crowded with pedestals, all holding precious objects – the sort of things that Heuvelt would have taken great delight in looting. Jewels in every color, some as big as her fist; a tiny silver bird that hovered in the air above a plinth; model spaceships made of precious metals; golden cups; crowns, necklaces, gauntlets, rings; a full suit of armor, glimmering with forcefields and strange energies; daggers with gems in the hilts; an orrery depicting an unknown solar system; figurines of fanciful animals carved in substances like ivory and jade; and more.

They were like the grave goods buried with ancient kings in some cultures, Bianca thought, to make their afterlives more comfortable. Except… this king wasn't dead. "Kor Noq Weer?" she called.

The center of the room held an immense chest on a raised platform, with a lid of shining silver metal, filigreed all over in gold. When Bianca spoke, the lid began to slide to one side. She could see the lines of force flowing through the chamber, the machinery that engaged to move the lid, but those lines were much fainter and harder to discern than they had been before.

A figure sat up from his resting place inside the chest – or was it a sarcophagus? He wore robes so purple they were nearly black, intricately patterned around the sleeves, neckline, and cowl with glyphs picked out in shining white wire. His face was shadowed in the deep hood. His hands, hidden in bulky gloves, gripped the sides of the sarcophagus, and he hauled himself to his feet. He was humanoid, though much taller than Bianca herself. Tubes and wires snaked up from the interior of the chest into his sleeves and hood, and he tore them away, letting them drop, hissing and writhing and spurting acrid fluids.

The foot end of the sarcophagus folded down and extended to form a ramp, and he walked down it to the floor… rather unsteadily, she noticed.

He's old, Bianca thought. *He's frail.* "I wasn't supposed to take this long to arrive, was I?" she said. "You thought I would get here a lot sooner than this."

"Plans." The voice was a croak, not at all the strong tones the wind had carried to her before – they must have been generated by some of the strange technology in this place. And here she thought the god-king had actually been *shouting* his encouragements to murder. "Plans seldom work out as intended. That is why we have contingencies. Redundancies. *You* were a backup plan for a backup plan, in fact – and yet, here you are, the one that actually came through. What is your name, child?"

"You don't know?"

"I cannot read your mind. Not without special equipment. I knew you were coming – I sensed your arrival, and the World of Light woke up when it detected your brainwave patterns, designed to interface with its systems, just like my own. I scanned your ship's database to learn your languages, and what sad and rudimentary things they are. But your thoughts, secrets, and memories – those are your own."

"My name is Bianca Xing."

"Welcome, Bianca Xing, to your destiny."

"Why am I here? I don't understand. I came all this way, and I *still* don't know why."

"I'll tell you," Kor Noq Weer said. His voice was getting stronger. "I do, after all, love to talk about myself." He shoved a delicate crystal sculpture off a pedestal, sending it shattering to the floor, and sat down, the effort of standing too great for him, it seemed. "What do you know of the Mahact, child?"

Just what Brother Errin had told her. "They ruled the galaxy, a long time ago. So long ago almost no one remembers them. There was a rebellion, and they were all killed. Or we thought so. We didn't expect to find this place. We were looking for a paradise world, maybe the Mahact homeworld, called Ixth."

"Of course you were. I told the servant who built your incubator to spread those stories, and it seems some fragment of his work survived through the eons. The Mahact did rule, and ruled well, until it all started to fall apart. Our leaders encouraged us all to band together, to crush the rebellion, but I could tell our empire was doomed. The old ways had failed us, or else the upstarts would have never made any headway at all. I knew the Mahact needed new leadership." He put a gloved hand to his chest. "They needed *me*. So I formed my own faction, supported by like-minded people, and clones, and our various servants. I sought to overthrow our leaders and take control of Ixth. I dabbled in forbidden practices in pursuit of those goals."

"What kind of practices could be forbidden to the *Mahact*?"

"Gene warfare, mainly," he said. "Oh, we had no problem using those techniques against our enemies or subjects – destroying or rewriting DNA was part of our standard approach to governance. But it was forbidden to use those powers on the *Mahact*. I did so anyway. I just wanted to hurry along the inevitable collapse of my world's leaders, so I could take over, and rule the galaxy properly. I was making progress. Many victories. Others called them massacres, but, well. Semantics." He sighed, a sound like a death rattle. "But, sadly, there was an accident. A wasting disease meant to destroy my enemies instead infected my allies… and eventually myself. I knew, then, that I could not defeat my enemies.

But!" He held up one finger. "I could outlast them. As I said, their doom was inevitable. Just too slow for my tastes. I caused the World of Light to be created, in a remote part of the galaxy, accessible only by a wormhole I controlled, with the aid of my Titans. I installed myself here with all the necessary elements of conquest. Shipbuilding facilities, cloning tanks, weapons. I set in motion various plans to awaken me when a suitable interval had passed, so long that the Mahact were forgotten, and no longer considered a threat. Then *I* would return, and take control of an unprepared galaxy. Sadly, my plans all seem to have gone awry... except for you. Even your arrival took far longer than expected. My stasis systems were beginning to fail. Another three or four centuries, and I might even have died."

"So, I'm just, what? A living alarm clock?" Bianca said. "I'm here to wake you up?"

"You serve multiple purposes, as all good components do. You were designed to blend in with the local population in terms of gross morphology, adapting to suit whatever society you found yourself in, while remaining Mahact on the inside. You would be able to travel in disguise, as it were, gathering intelligence about the state of the galaxy – indeed, you would have a relentless drive to learn all you could about culture, politics, technology, and military matters. Did you not find it so?"

"I just thought I was a curious person."

"I *made* you to be curious. I also gave you the ability to defend yourself, to win, to conquer – and instilled in you a profound urge to reach this place. Your body and mind are, if I may say, the height of my art. Once you'd gained the necessary data, you would come to this place, a world closed to everyone else, and awaken the World of Light. I was already stirring, alerted by certain arcane systems to the fact of your quickening. I've just been waiting for your arrival."

"What if I'd been born after you were already awakened by some other process?" Bianca said. "What if I'd followed my yearning all the way out here, and found you already gone, departed centuries before?"

Kor Noq Weer laughed. "Then you would have been disappointed, I suppose."

"I don't think I could possibly be any more disappointed than I am right now." She crossed her arms. "I don't understand, though. You're still dying. Am I supposed to continue your work after you pass?"

The Mahact rose, and spread his arms. "Sweet Bianca Xing. *I* am not going anywhere. I could not clone my damaged body, no. So I used all of my art to create something new: a body possessed of Mahact capabilities, hybridized with alien DNA to create a more robust whole – one immune to the wasting disease that targets my people. That body you're walking around in belongs to me. I designed it. And now, I intend to take possession."

She fell back a step. Were those dim lines of force changing direction? Flowing into her? No, oh no. "You can't do this."

"Of course I can, Bianca. Your brain is specifically designed to accommodate the architecture of my thoughts, and the World of Light, my greatest invention, is an engine that will allow me to transfer my consciousness into your form. My mind, in that exquisitely engineered body! I will be strong again. Fast. And capable of moving unnoticed among the denizens of the galaxy, in your alien guise. Everyone will look at me and see a harmless human girl. It's delicious, isn't it?"

"What will happen to *me*?" Bianca imagined herself trapped in his desiccated husk of a body and shuddered.

He chuckled, wet and soft. "Have you ever reformatted a hard drive, Bianca? Repainted a wall? Those are not perfect analogies, but close enough. I'll retain your memories, all that useful intelligence you gathered, but your personality will be erased. Except, perhaps, for the odd ghost and shadow of data bleeding through. The occasional fleeting memory. Perhaps an occasional dream, of what it was like to be Bianca Xing, before she ceased to exist."

Bianca set her feet. "What makes you think I'll allow this? You said it yourself. I'm fast. I'm strong. You can't force me to, to hook myself up to some machine."

"Hook you up? Bianca. The whole World of Light is the machine. And as for the process…"

It's already started, his voice said, but this time it came from inside her own mind, like an intrusive thought.

Kor Noq Weer rose and stripped off his gloves, revealing fingers twisted into claws. He spread his arms wide. "The vessel is prepared. Come to me. We need only embrace to complete the transfer."

"No." She gritted her teeth. "Never."

"It doesn't have to be an embrace. Any sustained touch will do. My hands around your throat, for instance."

"I won't let you take my body from me!"

You have no choice, Kor Noq Weer said. *You are part of the machinery. A mere component. You are programmed to obey. You want to reach for me – you yearn for my embrace. Don't you?*

She did. She wanted to fold herself into those outstretched arms, just like she'd wanted to travel to the dark place at the center of that triangle of stars, just like she'd wanted to descend to the heart of the World of Light. It was more than a desire. It was a drive. She took a step toward her maker, and then another, and another.

He started to close his arms around her.

Bianca's yearning to accept his embrace was powerful, but it wasn't impossible to resist. Not anymore.

Not since she'd put the sheathed blade she took from Sev in the small of her own back, the smartcloth of her dress helpfully forming a pocket the perfect size and shape to hold it. While the blade was covered, it didn't make her sick or disoriented, but its proximity did somewhat dull her connection to the machinery of the World of Light and the intensity of her compulsion to obey her maker.

As she stepped into Kor Noq Weer's arms, she reached behind her and drew the knife. She had to grit her teeth against the sickening vertigo that seized her when she exposed the blade, and even so she stumbled into the Mahact sorcerer. His body was light, frail, a bag of sticks, and they went down together in a heap. He hissed, sensing the blade, but wrapped his arms around her more tightly, his claws scrabbling for any centimeter of bare skin, so he could complete the transfer.

Bianca wriggled around until she freed one arm, then jammed the knife into Kor Noq Weer's chest. She had no idea if the Mahact even had hearts, but it seemed likely there was *something* vital in there. She pulled the knife out, though exposing the blade made her guts seize up and her vision blur.

She stabbed again, and again, and again, even as Kor Noq Weer screamed in her mind: *No! No! You're mine, you're mine, you're mine!* One of his bare hands closed around her throat and started to squeeze, but it was just a spasm, and a moment later his grip went limp and his ancient claw fell away.

The lines of force around Bianca snapped, the delicate whorls and toruses and arcs of energy vanishing from her senses. The deep machinery she felt thrumming all around and through her shuddered, and stalled, and then died. The resulting silence was the silence of an undiscovered tomb.

The last of her strength ran out of her, and Bianca collapsed atop Kor Noq Weer. *I am me*, she thought. *I am still me.*

The lights in the chamber went out. A moment later, so did the light of Bianca's consciousness.

Everything went dark in the chamber where Severyne sat, the crystals dimming and plunging the room into darkness. A moment later, everything went silent, the thrum and hum and vibration of the engines deep inside this planet-sized machine subsiding.

Interesting. Severyne rummaged in her pack until she found a chemical light. The Letnev had excellent night vision, of course, but they needed at least the occasional stray photon to work with, and there were none here. But maybe, since the machines had stopped… She strapped on an electric headlamp instead, and, wonder of wonders, it turned on, shining a beam that illuminated the acid pit. *That* kept bubbling. No power source necessary there beyond its own chemical reaction, apparently.

Hmm. If the planet was turned off, though, how long before the breathable atmosphere dissipated?

Severyne checked her anti-grav harness… and it worked too. Whatever jamming technology the mysterious Kor Noq Weer had in place had definitely stopped working.

She carefully made her way back through the tomb, retracing her earlier journey, using the harness to float over obstacles as necessary. The crew of the *Grim Countenance* should have come to rescue her by now, but of course she had to do everything *herself*, didn't she? Richeline would catch the rough side of her temper once Severyne got back. Speaking of, she'd better steal the *Show and Tell* quickly, just in case Heuvelt and his merry band came crawling out of the depths again.

When she reached the first corridor, the one that led to the long shaft up to the surface, Severyne heard *singing* from the branch Bianca hadn't taken. The Letnev weren't much for music, apart from martial tunes, and this was a soldier's marching song. She considered, then crept a little way down the passage, until she saw a light.

The bearer of the light must have seen hers, too, because it stopped. "*Captain?*" a voice cried out in disbelief.

"Oh, it's you, Voyou." She sniffed. "You went the wrong way, I see. Where's everyone else?"

"They didn't make it, captain."

"What, Richeline and Archambelle too?"

"I… yes, captain. I was there when they died. Archambelle first, Richeline soon after."

"Hmm. Did Archambelle get dissolved in acid or anything?"

"No, captain. It was blood loss. Her body is back in–"

"Well go and *get* her," Severyne said. "We can do without Richeline's remains, but this whole idea was Archambelle's, and the inquiry will go much easier for us if we can demonstrate that her wild ideas got her killed." Severyne paused. "That was an order, Undercommandant."

"Yes, captain!"

Severyne waited for a while, gnawing on a protein bar, until he came floating back, dragging Archambelle's corpse. She dangled, slack, in her own anti-grav harness, tethered to Voyou's waist by a rope. Now that he was closer, she got a good look at his face. "You've got blood all over you."

"Yes, captain."

"How many people were in your little expeditionary force?"

"Thirty-six, captain."

"And you are the sole survivor?"

"Yes, captain."

"You know, Voyou, you may be due for a promotion. Come on. Let's get out of here."

"Is… did you… what about the princess?"

"Bianca Xing is dead."

Voyou didn't speak as they returned to the main corridor and reached the bottom of the long shaft. There was no light shining at the top, now, just more darkness. This place had seemed like a necropolis before, but now it was dead in truth.

"How did Bianca die?" Voyou said.

Severyne grunted. They began to rise up the shaft in their harnesses, holding onto the dangling ropes, just in case. "I didn't *see* her die, directly, but she must have. This whole world came to life when she arrived, somehow activated by her very presence. Now it's all dark. I suppose it's possible she's alive, but her death is the most likely explanation for why a planet-sized machine would turn into a chunk of dead metal."

"When your tracker died, we thought you did too, but you were still alive," Voyou said, seemingly to himself.

"What are you going on about?"

"Nothing, captain. So, the mission is a failure, then?"

"The point of the mission was to ascertain whether Bianca Xing could lead us to valuable Mahact artifacts. My report will say no: she led us to a hole full of death traps, and it killed everyone who came near it, and then shut itself down when Xing died. I suspect Archambelle's one-armed corpse will have a chilling effect on the enthusiasm of her colleagues. The Barony may send engineers here in case there's something they can salvage, but I doubt they'll have much luck. That's if the Titans on the other side don't seal the wormhole and cut this place off again. Frankly, I hope they do. I hate it here."

"Oh, darkness, the Titans – what if they're waiting for us on the other side? They nearly tore the *Grim Countenance* apart when we arrived!"

"We'll deal with that if it happens," Severyne said. "Don't we have enough current problems without worrying about future ones? The Titans were tasked with preventing anyone except the princess from passing through that wormhole. I doubt their orders require them to stop anyone who comes *out*. My expectation is, as long as we leave them alone, they'll leave us alone, too."

"I hope you're right, captain."

"Oh, Voyou," Severyne said. "Haven't you realized yet that I'm essentially *always* right?"

CHAPTER 35

Heuvelt shouted, "Bianca! Bianca, where are you?"

Everything had gone dark and silent a little while ago, but their tech started working again at the same time, and Ashont could still smell Bianca's trail, so they soldiered on. That trail led them here, to an impressive set of golden doors, standing ajar. Heuvelt squeezed through and shone his light around the inside. Ashont and Clec came in after, and Clec rose up near the ceiling in her harness, shining lights down and illuminating the cluttered space.

Bianca was on the floor, her arms wrapped around what appeared to be a bundle of filthy rags. Heuvelt rushed to her and pulled her into his lap. The rags proved to be the corpse of some unknown creature composed mostly of rotten meat and dust.

He looked for Bianca's pulse, and breathed out in relief when he found one, but it was rapid and thready, her breath shallow and uneven. He pulled up one of her eyelids, and her pupil didn't respond to light. Heuvelt was no physician, but he knew that was a bad sign. "Bianca? Are you all right? Bianca?"

"She appears to be comatose," Clec said.

"We have to get her out of here, back to the *Show and Tell*."

Ashont put a heavy paw on his shoulder. "We will. Of course we will. But Heuvelt… you have to prepare yourself–"

"She'll be fine," Heuvelt said. "She just had a shock. She'll come out of it."

"She was linked to this place, in some way beyond our understanding," Clec said. "Now that this place has stopped functioning–"

"She. Will. Be. Fine. Help me get her out."

"You don't want to look around quickly, to see if there's anything worth pillaging?" Ashont asked.

"I'd be afraid anything we took from this place would sprout needles or teeth or stingers and kill us in our beds," Heuvelt said. "Besides, I didn't get into treasure hunting for the *treasure*. I was born with treasures aplenty, and they never fulfilled me. One needs money to live, of course, but what does one live *for*? Adventure! Excitement! To challenge oneself and test one's limits!"

"I'm fine with just the money," Ashont said.

"Me too," Clec said.

"So I'm just going to grab up some of these jewels and figurines," Ashont said. "In deference to your pure love of the work for its own sake, though, Clec and I will gladly keep your share of any profits."

He looked down at Bianca. She seemed stable enough. "Now that you mention it," Heuvelt said, "I do have room in my pack for a bauble or two. Why don't you hand me a couple of those crowns?"

They hooked an anti-grav harness onto Bianca and made their way out. They paused in the chamber where they'd left Severyne. "Do you think she made it out of here?" Ashont asked.

"I think that woman could survive anything short of a direct railgun strike," Heuvelt said. "I just hope she isn't crouched in a corner with a knife, waiting to gut us."

She was not. They made it to the top of the long shaft and emerged onto the planet's surface, where the air was noticeably thinner, and the wind furious. *This must be what it feels like when an atmosphere starts to shred away*, Heuvelt thought.

There was no sign of the *Grim Countenance*, or any Letnev at all. Severyne must have given up the whole expedition as a bad job. Heuvelt wondered what his legal status with the Barony was now. Probably, not good. Ah, well. He was used to it, really, by now.

"I hope Sev didn't bomb our ship on the way out," Clec said.

"Thank you for that cheerful thought," Heuvelt said.

Their ship was unmolested, though the ground beneath it was beginning to tilt. It seemed the structural integrity of the false planet was beginning to fail, chambers and tunnels collapsing now that load-bearing forcefields had flickered off.

They got Bianca on board and hooked into their rudimentary medical suite. While Clec and Ashont took the shuttle up and headed toward the wormhole – mercifully still open – Heuvelt looked at the suite's readings.

He'd feared – expected, really – to see no brain activity at all, but instead he saw quite the opposite: Bianca's brain was incredibly active, but in a disordered and erratic way. The medical suite recommended immediate medication to stop the life-threatening seizures Bianca was having. Except she wasn't having seizures. She wasn't moving at all, apart from the occasional flutter of her eyelids.

They passed through the gate. There were two Titans hovering on the other side, including one with a large, rough, circular hole through its center mass.

The Gatekeeper's voice spoke over the ship's public address system. "Honored heir. You have returned. What did you find? Do you have new orders for us?"

"Clec, transmit on the open channel," Heuvelt said. He cleared his throat. "Gatekeeper, the heir was hurt on the other side of the wormhole. She is unconscious. We're… quite worried about her."

A moment's silence, and then, "I see. Our remit is to protect the heir. Bring her here."

They piloted the *Show and Tell* toward the World of Stone. "I don't suppose you destroyed a passing Barony warship a little while ago?" Ashont asked the Gatekeeper.

"Their vessel emerged not long ago, and departed at great speed. We saw no reason to interfere with their exit."

"I can think of a few reasons," Ashont said.

They made a rather rougher landing than Bianca had managed, and once they settled down the surface of the planet began to shift, the ground rising up around them, curving above them, and enclosing them in a dome like a vast hangar. "They're pumping breathable atmosphere into this space," Clec said.

"Bring her outside," the Gatekeeper said.

Ashont and Heuvelt got Bianca onto a floating stretcher and carried her down the boarding ramp. The domed hangar was brightly lit, like an operating theater. A small Titan, only a meter or so taller than Heuvelt, and glittering like onyx, waited for them. The Titan gestured toward a stone plinth rising out of the floor. "Place her there," it said.

They put Bianca down, and the Titan gazed at her, then touched her temples with its fingertips. Those hands could have crushed her skull easily, but they moved with impossible gentleness. "Ah. There is a battle within her. Another mind is attempting to take over her body."

"What?" Heuvelt said.

The Gatekeeper's voice rumbled in the air. "It seems Kor Noq Weer did not intend his heir to receive his estate, but instead, to provide a vessel for his mind."

Heuvelt frowned. "He wanted to steal her body?"

"He created her body, human. He merely wanted to take ownership of what he made."

"How do you feel about that?" Heuvelt said.

"I believe it is monstrous," the Gatekeeper said. "If I could prevent such a possession, I would – and since I was tasked to protect the heir and aid her in her journey, there would be no conflict with my orders if I did. But, there is nothing I can do to stop this. She must fight on her own. The psyche of a young woman, pitted against the mind of one of the most powerful Mahact to ever live. I do not know who will prevail."

"I believe in Bee," Heuvelt said. "She'll open her eyes again."

"She may," the Gatekeeper said. "The question is, who will be looking out of them?"

They stood. They watched. They waited.

Bianca was back on Darit, but something terrible had happened. The Halemeeting hall was a burned shell, the ruins still smoking. The burgher's house had collapsed in on itself, the walls covered with strange mold. The trailrunner was overturned in the street, legs kicking randomly, sparks shooting from the joints.

She blinked, and she was somehow back at her family farm, only where the house should have been there was a black obelisk instead, solid and sealed. The caprids were all dead in a heap and covered in flies. A stench of burning metal came from the direction of Old Torvald's junkyard, and a black cloud covered that whole quarter of the sky.

Also, the sun was the color of blood, and all three moons were on fire. "That's a bit much," Bianca said. "Where are you, maker?"

The obelisk split open, and Kor Noq Weer emerged. He was wearing the armor she'd seen in his chamber, flickering with blue light, resplendent and mighty. But he stumbled when he approached, and wove an unsteady path toward her. The obelisk vanished behind him, replaced by her family home, cozy and undamaged, smoke rising from the chimney.

"You're barely even here," Bianca said. "Look at you. You didn't get your whole mind into me. You're like… we have these insects, bees, they're fat and yellow and black, good little pollinators. They have stingers, but they're really meant for killing other insects, not hurting people or animals. When the bees sting a person, the barbs get caught, and the poor little creatures end up disemboweling themselves when they pull away, leaving the stinger behind. That's you. You're just a broken-off piece of poison."

Those stingers can get infected if they aren't removed, though, can't they? He spoke in her mind, even though, in the truest sense, they were already in her mind. *You stopped the transfer, it's true, but there's enough of me here to make sure you never wake up again.*

"What's the point of that?"

Kor Noq Weer's face was hidden – she'd never seen it, she realized – but even so, she knew he was looking at her with contempt. *The point is* revenge, *of course!*

"You tried to take my body, but you couldn't. In a way, you should be proud. You made me. You made me so well even *you* couldn't defeat me."

You are a tool that turned in my hand. An experiment gone wrong.

"Perhaps we can reach some mutually agreeable accommodation," Bianca said, echoing something Sev had said to her. The woman had broken her heart, but still, her approach was worth a try. "You can guide me, advise me, and we can work together to fulfill our mutual–"

I would sooner die than negotiate with a lesser being.

"Would you rather spend a subjective eternity bickering here in my mindscape?"

I will grind you down. I am eternal. I am implacable. I am stone.

"And I'm flexible," Bianca said. "You made me that way. I'm far more adaptable than you are, Kor. I can change myself to solve whatever problem faces me – I can change my body. I can change my brain. I can change my *mind*. And in here, that means…" She glanced up at the sky, and the flames wreathing the moons snuffed. The clouds rolled back, and the smoke blew away over the sea. "I can change the *world*."

Kor Noq Weer ran toward her, but she made the ground split open with a glance. Mechanical arms reached out of cracks in the earth, grabbing his limbs, pulling him down, and he shrieked in outrage. She cocked her head, remembering what the Gatekeeper had said about his illness, and his hood fell away, revealing flesh that melted and bubbled, necrotized and sloughing off. More mechanical limbs – the hidden treasures beneath Darit's surface – grabbed at him, pulling him down, tearing off pieces of his rotting body in the process.

Bianca understood that this was all analogy. She was altering the landscape of her own *mind*, capturing and isolating the rogue psyche that was trying to take control. He'd made her too well. Maybe at his height she would have been unable to resist him, but he'd overestimated his own strength. Even so, she wasn't sure if she could fully eradicate him, but she could bury him deep.

You cannot destroy me. His whole body had been pulled underground now, and only the sockets where his eyes had been held guttering lights. *I am too vast, too full of knowing, my stratagems span eons, my wisdom is eternal–*

"I'll hold onto whatever bits of you are useful, don't worry." She snapped her fingers. The chasm snapped shut, crushing his skull, scattering fragments across the newly solid soil.

Eternallllllll, his voice whispered on the wind, but the words trailed off, and faded.

Bianca sat down cross-legged on the solid ground of her own mind, and looked for a while at the moons in the sky. She felt a yearning now, too, but it was different than the one Kor Noq Weer had planted inside her.

Now what she yearned for was home.

A little while later, back on the World of Stone, Bianca opened her eyes.

CHAPTER 36

Torvald looked at the components scattered on his workbench and whistled. It was the damnedest thing: that morning, a whole bunch of pieces of inert technology in his scrapyard just all of a sudden *woke up*. Mysterious boxes started beeping. Inscrutable cylinders began to hum. Fans turned, and solenoids clicked, and indicators lit up. As best he could figure, some kind of remote power station had come online, and dormant systems were sending messages across the planet again. He wondered if the Letnev surveyors had stumbled on some ancient control center deep in a dead mine and gotten it up and running again. *I wish Bianca was here*, he thought. *She'd have a good old time figuring out what all this junk does.*

His alert system beeped. Someone was at the gates – he'd disabled the automatic opening system, because not all his visitors were welcome anymore. He sure hoped it wasn't another tax collector. He'd already given them pretty much all his best aluminum. The Barony had an endless hunger for resources, and Torvald had yet to see what they offered in return.

He went out into the scrapyard and pressed the remote that made the small door in the gate swing open.

"Open the big doors!" a voice called. "I'm bringing something in!"

Torvald frowned. That voice sounded familiar, but… He made the larger gates swing wide.

There was a spaceship parked beyond the gates, one that looked a little like a bug wearing saddlebags, but that wasn't what drew his eye. There was some kind of three-meter-high *robot* standing there, only it was made of black stone that glittered–

A woman ran toward him. She wore a red dress with a skirt that fluttered, and there was some sort of tiara glittering on her head.

She was just a few steps away before he recognized her, and shouted, *"Bee!"*

She flung herself into his arms, squeezing him and laughing in his ear. "Torvald! That's 'Queen Bee' to you, old man."

He took a step back, but kept his hands on her shoulders as he looked her up and down. "You look different, your local majesty, but I can't quite say how."

"A lot of things have changed," she said. "I'll tell you all about it." The immense stone figure stepped forward, and Torvald craned his neck. "What's this?"

"This is my friend, Natrion the Vigilant. He looks out for me. Doesn't like to be far from my side."

"I'm pleased to meet you," Torvald said. The immense figure nodded. Maybe more than just a robot, then.

Torvald touched Bianca's tiara, straightening it a little from where it went askew during their hug. "Did you turn out to be a space princess after all?"

"More sort of a king," she said. "But I abdicated the throne. The world they offered wasn't much to my liking. Too big. Too ugly. Too dangerous. I closed it up behind a broken wormhole, where it can't do any harm." She cocked her head, and her eyes got a little faraway, like she was listening to words Torvald couldn't hear. "But there's another world that *does* interest me. Darit."

"Since when? You couldn't wait to get away from here."

"I just never appreciated it properly before." She gazed around the scrapyard. "Sometimes you have to go away from a place so you can come back and see it with fresh eyes, I guess." She linked arms with Torvald and began to lead him toward the ship, the tall fella following at their heels. "Tell me," she said. "Have the Letnev been bothering you much?"

"More than I'd like."

"I have some ideas about how to encourage them to move along. Undo their annexation. Bother someone else for a while."

"Bee, are you talking about fighting the Barony? That seems like a tall order, even with your big friend's help."

"Oh, a couple of his siblings came with me too," Bianca said. "They're in space, hanging out beyond the orbit of the moons. They're a little bigger than Natrion here, and they'd draw too much attention if they came down to say hello. We have other resources as well. Darit has all kinds of fascinating things buried under the surface. It was a valuable colony world, once upon a time, with rich mines, and it has planetary defenses to suit. Most of them still work, I think. I can see all the connections now, all the lines of energy and force. It's just a question of altering the flow. I think I can even increase the radii of the habitable zones, connect the settlements better, so you don't have to bundle up in tundra gear to get from place to place."

Torvald whistled. "Did you have something to do with all this machinery waking up again, Bee?"

She looked over at him, and her eyes twinkled. "I always did have something of a knack for tech, didn't I? That's gotten a lot stronger lately. Just like the rest of me."

"Even so… the *Barony*…"

"It won't be easy," Bee said. "But it turns out my original destiny was to conquer the whole galaxy. I figure it shouldn't be *that* hard to liberate and protect one little world."

ACKNOWLEDGMENTS

Thanks again to Marc Gascoigne and the whole Aconyte team, especially Lottie Llewelyn-Wells and my editor Paul Simpson, and to the Twilight Imperium creative team too. And look at that cover by Scott Schomburg! Thanks to my agent Ginger Clark and the whole Curtis Brown team too.

In my personal life, especially in these pandemic days, my wife Heather Shaw and son River help keep me steady. I also rely on Ais, Amanda, Emily, Katrina, and Sarah – I hope I get to see them all in person a lot more soon. My fellow writers are always there for me, and Molly Tanzer especially offered great insight and support on this project.

And thank you, readers, for joining Bianca on her journey. I'll see you next time. (You may not have seen the last of Severyne, either.)

THE VEILED MASTERS

For my brother and sister

CHAPTER 1
TERRAK

I am recording this chronicle so that, in the event of my capture and inevitable death, the truth might still come out. I have been accused of a monstrous act, and I am innocent of that crime… although I can't claim to be innocent in a general sense. (Those failings I do possess, and there are many, I will admit to whenever relevant.)

This is how my troubles began.

I stood on the highest floor of Shilsaad Station, at a huge wraparound window overlooking the frozen nova. I swirled a cup of Hacan sunwine and did my best to project an air of knowing, benevolent wisdom. One of the junior diplomats from the Mentak Coalition, a human with high cheekbones and elaborately razor-cut hair named Coralee, strolled over to me, holding a fluted glass of something no doubt less potent than my own libation. The Mentak were organizing this event, so she had more reason to stay sharp than I did.

"Ambassador Terrak," she said, leaning against the railing at the viewport. "I was hoping for the chance to speak with you privately."

I towered over the human by two-thirds of a meter, and surely weighed at least twice as much as she did, but she didn't shy away from me or exhibit nervousness the way many humans do when in such close proximity to my people. The Hacan superficially resemble a nearly extinct predator from the ancestral human homeworld, a large feline called a "lion". Being seen as reminiscent of an intimidating but noble beast can be useful at times when dealing with such people, but this human wasn't from Jord, or even the Federation of Sol. She'd grown up in the multiracial mélange of the Mentak Coalition, which meant she'd lived alongside Hacan her entire life.

The Mentak Coalition was an oddity in the galaxy, with so many different species living closely together in some approximation of harmony. Now her government wanted to expand that coalition to encompass other cultures, including mine, in a grand alliance – and, amazingly, the plan might even succeed. The purpose of this gathering was to discuss final details regarding the rather grandly named "Greater Union", and ours was just one of many preliminary meetings leading up to a major multi-faction summit on the Coalition homeworld of Moll Primus, where the treaty would, in theory, be formally signed. Assuming everything didn't fall apart before that, anyway. Convincing several proud and ancient cultures, some of whom had clashed in the past, to join together in a single grand enterprise was a delicate operation. I was a bit cynical about the whole idea. The Greater Union seemed to me like the sort of plan that would take tens of thousands of hours of collective work in order to achieve, at best, a largely symbolic outcome. But diplomats have to keep busy somehow, and at least such endeavors keep the drinks flowing.

"Am I so famed as a conversationalist?" I said. Before she could answer, I gestured to the vast blur of the frozen nova beyond the viewport, the star stilled forever at the moment of explosive expansion. The nova's true brightness was hidden behind an array of shells, shields, and lenses, so it was possible to look directly upon the stalled stellar devastation. "What's your theory?"

"About the frozen nova?" She shrugged. "Some ancient civilization tried to harness the energy of an exploding star, and that's what remains of their solar battery."

"Ah, the exploitation hypothesis." I swirled my golden wine. "I favor the survival theory myself – that the ancient aliens were local to this system and put the star in stasis to preserve their homeworld from destruction."

She cocked her head. "Surely a civilization capable of halting the expansion of a star and wrapping it in perpetual forcefields could simply pack up and move to a system that *wasn't* about to fall prey to a supernova? It's not as though stars explode without warning – these local aliens would have had time to prepare."

"You underestimate the appeal of defending one's homeland," I said. "Some people are sentimentally attached to the cradle of their civilization, even once that civilization has expanded throughout the galaxy. A homeworld is about heritage, and the root of one's identity as a people. Maintaining that connection can be very important."

Coralee snorted. "Are you making a political point? Since I'm the descendant of prisoners on a penal colony, and grew up on a space station alongside a dozen other species, that means I can't understand cultural identity?"

I blinked at her. "Burning sands, no. I think you overestimate both the subtlety of my wit and my interest in offending you." That statement was half true.

"Oh, I'm not offended." She sipped from her glass, glancing up at me and smiling. "I have great loyalty to my people, ambassador. That loyalty just doesn't have anything to do with our shared connection to any particular ball of dirt and water. Moll Primus is still the center of the Mentak Coalition, but it was our prison, too, long ago, so our relationship with the homeland is… complex. Instead, I'm loyal to our ideals – freedom, of course, but also forging something new and strong from disparate pieces. That's what we're trying to do with the Greater Union."

"I am in sympathy with your stated goals," I said. "But the decision to join was made without my input, so my position never mattered much." I bowed my head. "I am, of course, a humble servant of the Emirates of Hacan… but to be frank, I'm here mostly for the drinks and the chance to catch up with old friends."

"Don't be so modest, Ambassador Terrak. You're a man of influence."

My official title was "Ambassador-at-Large", which was to say, I wasn't ambassador to any place in particular, but represented the Emirates of Hacan in various places and situations as necessary. I did occasionally advise my government on matters of trade, and certainly I had highly placed friends and contacts… but it was no secret I'd secured my largely ceremonial title (and the very real diplomatic privileges that came along with it) by bribing the right officials. Wealth is the source of power, after all, political and otherwise; this is true throughout the galaxy, though only the Hacan acknowledge it openly.

We have a saying back home: "Money is the blood of the world". If money ceases to flow, the world dies. I've spent a lot of time among the other factions and have gradually come to realize they *really mean it* when they insist wealth matters less than diplomacy (as if influence can't be purchased), or military might (when bigger and better weapons can always be bought), or the pursuit of knowledge (which is inevitably used to make money). I used to think those people were naïve. I've come to accept that they're simply *alien*.

My diplomatic credentials accompanied me wherever I roamed, and I led an enjoyable life drifting from one embassy party to another, tagging along on official missions to interesting places, and engaging in a little light favor-trading and bribe-taking here and there. You have to spread around a few credits at strategic moments in order to foster the smooth flow of interstellar trade, after all, and I am one of the people who knows just who to approach, and how to appease them. The purpose of this meeting was ostensibly to discuss the details of free trade areas and cultural exchange programs among Union members, so it was within my sphere… but in reality, everyone from every invited faction was looking for advantages they could gain or weaknesses they could exploit. With a space station full of diplomats and politicians (and, no doubt, a few spies), how could it be otherwise?

I shook my head, mane swaying. "I have contacts in various government offices and can occasionally convince a minister of procurement to look favorably upon one supplier or another. I've been known to arrange an off-the-record meeting with this official or that. But whether the Emirates will join this Greater Union of yours, and what sort of terms will be settled on regarding commerce and so forth… *those* decisions are far above my level."

"Every voice that joins the chorus makes the song that much stronger," Coralee said. "We value your support. We'll all be safer, and richer, if the Greater Union goes forward."

I raised my cup to her. "Your people pour an excellent libation, so consider yourself well on your way to winning me over."

"I'd hoped to appeal to you as a businessman. We've all had trouble with the L1Z1X growing bolder, and the corrosive swarming of the Nekro Virus, but there are also these strange new threats that have arisen recently. These nightmarish invaders on the edge of inhabited space… the stranger-than-usual behavior of the Creuss… the so-called Titans taking over that old mining colony planet… this mysterious information broker on that remote station, buying up influence for reasons no one can ascertain… they all pose a threat to the smooth operation of commerce, don't you think? If we band together, we can form a united front, and stand as one against the coming chaos."

"The nature of the galaxy is change," I said. "And in chaos, there are opportunities for profit. That's something the Mentak Coalition understands. Your raider fleets are always poised to seize the moment when the moment passes by, hmm? I'm not the only one who finds it… peculiar… that you would ask to make alliances with people you have historically boarded and robbed."

She sighed. "Even if you think the Mentak are all pirates, you can see why we'd want to defend the civilized galaxy against existential threats. Pirates prefer nice, predictable trade routes to prey upon. We've all heard the stories of remote worlds being wiped out by mysterious invaders from who-knows-where. No one benefits from that sort of… disruption." Perhaps sensing that this grim turn in the conversation was unlikely to please me, she suddenly grinned. "Besides, we can still ambush and pillage the Letnev. We'd never give up *that* pastime."

"Nor should you." I happened to spot a familiar silhouette across the room – my old friend Qqurant, of the Xxcha, with his distinctive red-and-white striped shell pattern. "If you'll excuse me, I see someone I need to speak to."

Coralee didn't put her hand on me, but she did shift her body to block my smooth escape. "Can we count on your support, ambassador?"

"My support is not worth as much as you seem to think, Coralee, but as I said, I am in sympathy with your goals, and will certainly say as much if anyone bothers to ask."

She hardly seemed satisfied, but she nodded and stepped aside, sparing me the necessity of gently picking her up and moving her.

I strolled across the circular room of windowed walls, the floor dotted with small groups of people, weaving mechanical servers, and hovering drone-trays. Everyone was dressed in their cultural finery: Xxcha shells gleaming with embedded jewels, humans in shimmering gowns or sleek suits, Hylar in elegant mobile tanks (and, in one case, a delicate silvery exo-skeleton; undersecretary Jhuri was one of the amphibious sub-species who could breathe air unassisted), Hacan in formal robes or sashes (the latter a bit daring and modern; that's what I wore, of course), and even a few Yssaril, those being less inconspicuous than usual so no one would trip over them.

The Xxcha Kingdom, the Federation of Sol, the Universities of Jol-Narr, the Emirates of Hacan, and the Yssaril Guild of Spies: if the Mentak Coalition got its way, those factions would join them to form the core of the Greater Union. I'd heard rumors the Mentak had also reached out to the Saar, the Naaz-Rokha, and the Brotherhood of Yin, but if so, those groups hadn't sent any representatives to this particular summit. That was fine by me; the Saar are depressing, the Yin are zealots, and the Naaz-Rokha are just strange, even if the Rokha *are* distant cousins of my people, genetically speaking. My sources told me the Coalition had also attempted to contact the Naalu Collective, through intermediaries in the Yssaril Guild of Spies, who maintained a relationship with the reclusive serpent-folk. The Naalu were aloof, as always, and ignored the call entirely. Just as well. The snakes were said to possess telepathic powers, and I loathed the idea of someone messing about with my mind.

I angled toward Qqurant, who was standing in a corner, holding a tankard and staring at nothing. The Xxcha was a minister of cultural affairs, promoting the art of his people across the galaxy by arranging tours and exhibitions. He was by all accounts an accomplished poet himself, though Xxcha poetry doesn't do much for me; too much water and trees and mournfulness, not enough fire and blood and sex. I wondered what was wrong with him. Qqurant was one of the most animated and gregarious Xxcha I'd ever known. It wouldn't be fair to call him the life of a party – Xxcha don't tend to get drunk, stand on tables, and perform impromptu dances – but he could usually be seen trundling from one group to another, dropping in gravelly witticisms and making wry comments that punctured pomposity and made everyone relax and interact more as *people* than as Representatives of the State. Qqurant and I had known each other for thirty years and been to literally hundreds of these functions together, and I'd never seen him looking so abstract and remote.

"What's wrong, Shelly?" I said. He lifted his beaky face toward me, his eyes glassy and vague. He usually called me "Whiskers", but instead, after a long pause, he said, "Greetings… Ambassador Terrak." A pause. "I hope." A longer pause. "You are having. An enjoyable evening."

I glanced around, and we were out of earshot, so I moved closer. "Blazing stars, Shelly, what's wrong? You've got something on your mind and no mistake. Are the girls all right?" Shelly had been widowed twenty years ago, but he had two daughters, the twin stars his world orbited around.

"The girls… my daughters… they are well. Continuing their studies. Thriving in their… chosen fields. It is kind… of you to. Inquire. After them." Qqurant wasn't quite looking at me. He didn't seem to be looking at *anything*.

I couldn't understand why he'd be so cold and distant. "If I've done something to offend you, old friend…"

Now his gaze focused on me. "Oh. No… please. Accept. My apologies. I have… been ill. Nothing to worry… about. I will be. Fine soon. If you will… excuse me." He toddled away from me but instead of leaving, or talking to someone else, he just took up another solitary post on the other side of the room, watching the others, or else watching nothing at all.

How very strange. I spied another familiar face, a Federation of Sol trade representative named Lillith, just detaching herself from a group of laughing, red-faced humans. She wore a rather daring arrangement of metallic rings held in place by antigravity generators or magnetic resonances or something, and wires woven through her long red hair made her tresses undulate as if in the wind. Lillith tended to dazzle those who weren't used to her, and it took a *long* time to get used to her, which allowed her to make deals that were usually lopsided in her favor. "Lil, you look absolutely bizarre tonight."

She swiveled toward me, smiling. I was taller than her, of course, but she had the long, lean build of someone born outside a gravity well, and she was wearing remarkable heels, so she could nearly look me in the eye. "Terrak, you old reprobate! Is your sash edged in *blue*? What would the revered sages say if they saw you dressed like that?"

"Nothing I haven't heard before." I took her elbow and steered her away from the ears cocked our way. "Have you talked to Shelly tonight?"

"No, I haven't seen him yet, is he here? I never go *looking* for Qqurant, he always bulldozes his way up to me – you know how he is."

I nodded. "Yes, usually. There's something off about him tonight, though. I've never seen him so… distant isn't even the word for it." I gestured with my glass to where Qqurant stood, like a powered-down robot. "He wasn't even like this right after his partner died. He just threw himself into his work then. Have you heard anything that might explain the change?"

Lillith put on a face of concern, but I could see the cogs whirring behind her eyes, trying to figure out how a lapse in Qqurant's focus could be turned to her faction's benefit, but one reason Shelly and Lillith could be uncomplicated friends was because their spheres of influence didn't overlap much. "Not at all. The poor thing. I'll check on him myself, and let you know if I hear anything. I do hope he's all right. I always say he's one of the only truly good souls you're ever likely to meet in our world."

I reared back in mock offense. "What about me?"

Lillith chuckled. "When it comes to goodness, we're not worthy to polish his shell, and you know it."

I thanked her, turned, and almost tripped over an Yssaril I hadn't seen standing so close. You don't usually see Yssaril unless they want you to; that's why the tiny humanoids make such good spies. "Did I overhear you express concern about Minister Qqurant?" she said, voice low. She spoke in my native language rather than the intergalactic argot, which surprised me, though I don't know why. Yssaril operatives are good with languages. Eavesdropping is useless if you can't understand what you overhear. This one was wearing the uniform of station security.

"I was just inquiring after the health of an old friend," I said blandly in the trader's tongue.

She nodded, and switched languages without a blink, and with those large eyes of theirs, you'd notice a blink. "The minister is fine. Just very busy."

How curious. The Xxcha don't make as much use of the guild of spies as other cultures do, favoring open diplomacy over covert evidence-gathering, and anyway,

Shelly didn't have anything to do with the kind of operations the Guild would be involved with. "I don't believe we've met before. I'm Ambassador Terrak."

A pause. "This one is Kote Strom."

"And how do you know Shelly?"

"Through… work." She took a half-step away. "I only wanted to reassure you. Do not worry. The minister is fine."

"I am *deeply* reassured." I put a little growling purr into the last word. "Let me reassure *you* on that point."

The Yssaril scurried away, disappearing behind a group of people conversing. How bizarre. I pride myself on knowing what's going on behind the scenes, but there were clearly forces at work here doing things I didn't understand for reasons I couldn't currently imagine. I'd just been warned off investigating Shelly's odd behavior, which, of course, only strengthened my resolve to do just that.

I did a slow circuit of the room, looking around for Shelly, who'd moved on from the last spot. I saw him at last, standing with a peculiar, hunched posture. Was that a *shimmer* beside him, like an Yssaril doing their don't-notice-me trick? Shelley abruptly turned and walked toward the lift platform that led to the complex below us – to the guest quarters, dining halls and meeting rooms of this convention center and luxury hotel.

I considered following him. It wouldn't be difficult to come up with some pretext to tag along after him. But… what could I hope to accomplish? I'd achieve as much by talking to a stone wall. Something was going on. Was Shelly trying to give me a message by behaving so strangely? The way someone being held captive might say something wildly out of character when answering the door, as a way of signaling that something isn't right, but they can't speak freely? Perhaps my old friend was in trouble. True, he was a cultural minister, not involved in anything more dangerous than rivalries among musicians, but he still walked the halls of power… and the halls of power were filled with trapdoors and pitfalls.

I moved to one side of a crystalline kinetic sculpture, shielded from the eyes of most partygoers and all the security personnel, and pressed an invisible button on one of my bracelets. I subvocalized: "Catriona, I want you to look into a Xxcha cultural minister named Qqurant. Medium-depth investigation, do pattern-matching against the database of known behaviors, and send me a chart of any recent anomalies, particularly financial or intimate-relational. Look into an Yssaril named Kote Strom, too, just a basic dossier, assuming you can find anything – she's here as station security but I wonder if she might be Guild of Spies." I sent the message. It would be encrypted, and then transmit itself disguised as signal noise in routine communication traffic emitting from the space station, to be snagged by one of my consultant's many automated agents. Catriona was a freelance data analyst, and while no one is better at market research, her skills are highly transferrable when it comes to other matters as well. If something was going on with Shelly, assuming it wasn't something happening entirely inside his ellipsoidal scaly head, I'd know soon enough.

I slipped back into my usual role, all bonhomie and knowing smiles, and circulated throughout the party until it was time for our formal dinner. I ended up at a table with Lillith, so that was fun – she was filled with scandalous tales about old acquaintances. The meal was… peculiar. The Mentak Coalition's culinary tradition is one of fusion, of course, since all the different species living together there had shared their own delicacies for centuries. Our hosts proudly served us dishes that were *almost* familiar, but also all wrong. I'd requested the Hacan-style meat dish, and received a platter of roast caprid, which was all well and good, but the chop was crusted with ground-up arthropod bits and served atop entirely the wrong sort of grain, and worse, the grain was stained deep purple with some kind of discharge from a cephalopod's ink sac. Lillith stared at her plate in open horror. She'd opted for the fish – people who spent as much time at the Universities of Jol-Nar with the Hylar as she did were basically required to develop a fondness for seafood, if only out of self-defense – and the seared protean eel set before her was *technically* a fish, though it looked more like a snake with vestigial fins, and its head was still attached, too. The less said about the sticky reduction dribbled all over it, the better.

Fortunately, the cheese course included several edible varieties, and if you brushed the odd seeds off the bread, that wasn't so bad either, so we didn't starve. Shelly wasn't present at the dinner, despite having the most robust appetite of any Xxcha I've ever met, and I didn't see Kote Strom, either, though that didn't mean she wasn't around. I inquired with one of the Mentak officials circulating the room about Shelly's whereabouts and she said, "Oh, the minister had some urgent business to take care of, but he'll rejoin us for the morning sessions."

Hmm. After the inevitable speeches, I declined several offers of after-dinner alcohols and vapors and teas, claiming I had some reports to go over, and took a lift down to the floor where my room was located. In truth, I wanted to see whether Catriona had found anything about Shelly yet.

I entered my room and turned to face the door to engage the lock. That's when something slammed into the back of my knees, knocking me off balance. I caught myself against the door and tried to turn, but something swarmed up my back. A moment later a hand slammed my head against the wall hard enough to make my vision swim with black dots, and I sank to my knees. My head rang like a bell, and there was pain, but it felt far away. I hadn't been in a fight for a long time and wouldn't have thought someone so small could hurt me so badly. Sometimes it's less about might and more about leverage. I tried to rise, but…

I'll have to pick this up later. My benefactor is shouting questions at me, and when someone saves your life, it's polite to answer.

THE FAITHFUL I

Qqurant lay on the floor of his room, adrift in a peaceful cloud. Thinking was difficult, lately, but then, he was called upon to think less and less. In the early days of his conversion, Qqurant had needed to use his wits, to improvise, to charm and wheedle and insinuate – he was given missions to complete, yes, but he was granted great latitude when it came to *how* he completed them.

Now, he had almost no freedom. He was no longer given missions; he was barely even given tasks, except to be careful, and not arouse suspicion. The last few… days? Weeks? Had been a bit of a blur. Had he seen Whiskers tonight? That old… no, the thought slipped away, as thoughts so often did now. Qqurant didn't mind. He was still permitted to serve, still rewarded for his service, and so, all was right in his world.

That familiar voice, or chorus of voices, spoke in his mind. *<Our faithful servant. We are sorry to see you so diminished.>*

Qqurant stirred. "My… guides?"

<We are here. We have need of you. One final mission.>

"My… pleasure. To. Serve."

<You must make a call,> his masters whispered, and Qqurant was happy, because such a task was still within his ability, and active obedience was the greatest bliss.

CHAPTER 2
TERRAK

My rescuer is satisfied, and amusing herself while we complete our journey, so I'll resume my account. I would like to send out these missives as I go – Catriona would see they reached the right listeners – but I don't dare risk giving my position away. Catriona never answered my request for information about Shelly, which makes me wonder if my oh-so-encrypted messages were intercepted. If so, I don't dare break my silence now, when half the galaxy is looking for me…

When I was attacked in my room on Shilsaad Station, head slammed into the door, I growled, fight-or-flight chemicals flooding my system and dispelling my daze. I struggled up from my knees, but the person on my back yanked my hair hard, forcing my head up. A small, long-fingered hand holding a slim black canister appeared on the edge of my vision. Was it poison? A gas to render me unconscious? I didn't want to find out. The weight on my back wasn't heavy, and I flung myself hard to one side, trying to shake off my unwelcome passenger, and falling to my knees again in the process. The canister went flying, bouncing across the floor and out of sight, and small arms locked tightly around my neck.

I was *not* going to be strangled to death in my hotel room. I pulled at my attacker's arms, but despite their diminutive size they were too strong to dislodge, so instead I concentrated on gaining my feet. Once I was upright, I spun and slammed my back against one of the walls as hard as I could, crushing my assailant between my own body mass and the station's bulkhead. The attacker hissed in my ear, but their grip loosened, and I stepped forward, ready to slam myself back again. Instead the figure dropped from my back and scurried away – or so I assumed, since I saw only a shimmer in the air as my door opened and then closed again.

When your attacker is invisible, it's probably Yssaril. Kote Strom? I rubbed my throat, but though it was sore, I detected no real damage. My assailant clearly hadn't been trying to kill me – a blade while I was sleeping would have accomplished that much more easily. What was the purpose, then? To drug me, and take me somewhere else, for some unknown purpose? That thought disturbed me the most, in some ways. I have devoted much of my life to being the insider, to having control over my own small sphere of influence, so being at the mercy of mysterious forces chilled me to the heart. I am in the business of knowledge and influence, and I currently had neither.

Best to correct that and learn what I could. I picked up the canister from the floor. The cylinder was small and black, barely the size of my thumb, with a simple push-button and nozzle on top, and a toggle to open or close the valve. There were no markings or indication at all regarding what substance might be inside. I pushed the safety toggle closed and tucked the canister away in one of the hidden pockets in my tunic. I considered whether or not to call station security. This attack had all the makings of an international incident, and I wasn't sure I wanted to be in the middle of one of *those* as they involve far too much paperwork and long, tedious meetings that detract from the more enjoyable things in life.

A melodious chime sounded from the ceiling. "Ambassador Terrak, you have a message," the room's expert system said.

"What is it?"

A pause, and then a recording of Shelly's voice played. "Old friend… Whiskers… I need your help. Please… come to my room… so I can. Explain. I am on Azimuth Deck… room four. Hurry. As soon. As you… get this." He still sounded strange, but if he was in trouble that could be explained by stress and fear. So. Shelly had gotten mixed up in something, and in the course of asking about his welfare, I'd mixed *myself* up, somehow. Whatever was going on, it was serious to send an Yssaril operative to try and gas me.

I sighed. This summit had seemed so uneventful, and I hadn't been prepared for this level of excitement. But the Hacan have a saying: *There's no use arguing with the desert.* Protest all you want, but the sun will still beat down on you, and the drifting sand will bury you while you complain about the injustice of it all. Sometimes you just have to deal with things as they are. Was someone trying to disrupt the Greater Union? The idea wasn't universally popular, but how could Shelly possibly impact it one way or another? Not to disparage my old friend, but his role in the Kingdom of Xxcha simply wasn't that important.

I considered bringing a weapon, but only ceremonial ones were allowed at the summit, mostly for photographs, and those aren't any good in a fight. My own dune spear – a traditional Hacan weapon – had *never* been wielded in a fight, though I looked quite dashing with it across my back. I decided to leave the spear in the closet; walking around the station with a weapon was sure to draw comment. At least I always have my claws.

I went into the hallway, keeping my eyes open for shimmers in the air. I didn't see anyone suspicious, or actually anyone at all, on my walk to the lift – most of the delegation was probably drinking and talking and making the little side deals that keep international relations interesting. I descended to Azimuth Deck and walked down another empty corridor. Room four was at the end of a hallway – and the door was ajar.

I growled and pushed the door fully open, wishing I *had* brought my dune spear. "Shelly?" There was no answer, and the lights inside were dim. I stepped into the suite's foyer. There was a little sitting room with a chair and stool and a table straight ahead. No sign of Shelly, or anyone else. I turned toward the sleeping quarters, and the door was standing half-open there, too.

I pushed the door wide and looked inside.

Shelly was dead on the floor at the foot of his sleeping pod, his head twisted at a horrible angle… but not because his neck was broken. No, his head was pushed aside by the haft of a spear sticking out of his body. Someone had inserted the point of the spear at the base of his neck, in one of the few places not protected by the shell, and shoved the weapon down, doubtless destroying all sorts of vital organs on the way. How could you even manage such an attack, unless the victim simply sat there and allowed it?

I was so stunned, it took a moment for me to realize the spear looked familiar. It had a red jewel set in the base, and the haft was wrapped with dark blue cloth – the colors of the Emirates of Hacan diplomatic corps. That was *my* dune spear. Someone had stolen my spear from my room and killed my friend with it. Which meant–

"Burning sands." I turned just in time for three people in station security uniforms to rush into the room pointing sidearms at me.

I raised my hands and lowered my head. I'd been in a number of unusual situations over the course of my life and career, but this was the first time I'd ever been framed for murder.

Station security put me in a room. It wasn't a cell – Shilsaad Station was essentially a convention center, not a detainment facility – but it was obviously the closest thing they had, just a table and a couple of chairs and bare walls, with a camera high up in one corner, watching me. I should have been mourning my friend, but I confess, I was a bit more preoccupied with the idea of how to save my own skin… and figuring out who could possibly want to frame me for such a crime. I had enemies, but none of the sort who'd go to these lengths. Time enough for grief when all this was cleared up… or, I supposed, while I was sitting in a prison cell somewhere.

I wondered which branch of officialdom would arrive to interrogate me. The station was owned by a Federation of Sol corporation, so it would probably be their police, but the Mentak Coalition was running this summit, so maybe they'd jump in, or it could be Xxcha, since one of their people was the victim. I wondered how long I'd have to sit here before the various interested parties worked out their jurisdictional issues and sent someone in to ask why I'd murdered my friend of three decades.

It took less than an hour, and when she arrived, she wasn't any of the people I might have expected. She was a human, dressed in a station security uniform – they're white and gray, and make their people look more like custodial staff than the teeth and claws of authority, but again: it's a hotel and convention center. They don't get a lot of murders. She stepped inside and shut the door, and then gave me a grin. I grinned back, because my spirit was not broken, and my teeth are a lot longer. She dropped into the chair on the other side of the table and relaxed, like she was a princeling on a throne. "So. Terrak. How's it going? You need anything?"

"I need to contact the Hacan diplomatic corps so they can send an advocate. As I told your colleagues when they first brought me in."

She snorted. "I meant more, like, do you need a drink of water, or to take a leak, or whatever."

I sighed. "No. I don't."

"Great." She reached into her pocket and removed a small black canister.

I reached across and pinned her wrist to the table, her hand still wrapped around the spray bottle. *Another* attacker? Was all of the station security compromised? If so, my prospects for escaping this situation were even more dismal than I'd realized.

She laughed and patted my gripping hand with her free one. "Relax, big guy, I'm not here to blast you in the face. This is the canister you had in your pocket when they took you in – I filched it out of the evidence locker. Which is really just the security head's *personal* locker, where she keeps a spare shirt and stuff, so it wasn't too hard to get open. Amateurs, right? The security team on this station is *not* equipped to deal with somebody sticking a big spear through a guy. The real authorities are on the way, though. Federation of Sol investigators from the colony world we're orbiting." She looked at my hand, still pinning her wrist. "Go ahead and take the canister and let me go, so we can discuss your options." She opened her fingers, and the canister rolled across the table toward me.

She was clearly not your average security guard. I let her wrist go, picked up the canister, and tucked it away again. It was my only evidence that someone had done anything untoward to me, and I wanted to protect it. "What are you talking about? What options? Who are you?"

"I'm Amina Azad. That's not the name on my official identification, but hey, why should we have any secrets between us?" She laced her hands together on the table. "You've stepped into a big ugly mess, Terrak. Fortunately, I can get you out of it. If you want to help me clean it up, that is. I could use a person with your resources and connections."

I barked a laugh. Was she a spy from another polity, or just an opportunist who wanted to turn my disaster into her personal gain? "My diplomatic credentials aren't much good now that I've been accused of murdering a cultural minister, and I rather doubt I'll have free access to my bank accounts."

She shook her head. "I asked around about you. You know *lots* of people – maybe even as many as I do – and because you've helped a lot of them get richer over the years, they're all happy to see you whenever you come around. Most of my old friends hate my guts, I'm sad to say, and in this part of space, I don't have many people I can reach out to. As for money – come on, Terrak. A guy like you keeps all his money in *official* banks? I don't believe that."

I cleared my throat. "Well. I've made a few arrangements over the years, yes. For tax purposes. But…" I glowered at her. "I'm not *paying* you."

"I'm not asking you to. Funds aren't currently a problem. I was just making a general observation. I believe in honesty and transparency between friends. We should be friends. You sure could use one."

"Who *are* you?" I had suspicions. I've met a few covert operatives in my time. They can be very smug, because they really *do* know more about what's going on than you do.

"I told you who I am. I think what you mean is: what do I *do*? The answer is, I clean up messes. Discreetly. And if I can't be discreet, I can at least be deniable."

Interesting. "You're telling me you're a covert operation? For the Mentak Coalition? Or the Federation of Sol?"

She made a sour face. "Ugh. Don't talk to me about the Mentak Coalition. You'd think a bunch of pirates and convicts would be more fun. I was born on Jord, but I haven't been back in a while. There's a great big beautiful galaxy out there, and the stars are all the home I need." She pointed at the canister. "Let's focus on your immediate situation. Someone tried to spray you in the face with whatever's in that tube. If they had, I'm pretty sure one of two things would have happened. Either you would have been killed, and replaced with some kind of double, maybe a clone or an android or something, I'm not sure. Or you would have been mind-controlled, hollowed out, and turned into a puppet. One of those things happened to your buddy Qqurant. Don't you want to know which one? I do. I'd like to get a read on the contents of this canister – is it knockout gas, or poison, or some kind of nanotech brain-rewiring stuff, or what? That little spray bottle is the first bit of actual *evidence* I've gotten my hands on regarding this conspiracy. We need to find somebody reliable and trustworthy who knows their way around a chemistry lab to analyze that evidence and see where the information takes us."

"What do you mean, Qqurant was replaced? What *conspiracy*?" Conspiracies are mostly imaginary, in my experience. People aren't that organized, they're terrible at keeping secrets, and they're generally too wrapped up in their personal drama to really commit themselves to collective action, even for nefarious reasons. Most attempts fall apart quickly.

She shrugged. "Maybe not replaced. Maybe brainwashed. I'm not sure yet. I thought about hanging around for the autopsy results, to see if there's anything weird about your dead friend's body, but then I'd miss my chance to recruit you, and a partnership seems more useful. Besides, if I'm being totally honest, I'm not as good at waiting as I should be. I'd rather be making moves."

"You want to recruit me into some investigation you're conducting. Because of my connections." At that moment, I should have been sleeping. I was supposed to wake up in a few hours, have a lavish breakfast, and attend a breakout session on the establishment of free ports. I was not supposed to be sitting in an interrogation room with someone who claimed, in a nebulous and deniable way, to be a spy.

"For your connections, sure, but also because you're highly motivated." Azad leaned forward. "You asked too many questions, Terrak. You got overly nosy. The bad guys tried to compromise you, the way they did Qqurant – the way they've compromised a *lot* of others, believe me. When they couldn't turn you, they fell back on plan B: frame you for murder. You were found standing over the corpse of a known associate, killed by your own decorative spear. If they faked that much, they can fake whatever other evidence they need, but I doubt they'll go to much effort. Why would they? There's no reason to think you'll survive long once you're in custody. If I was running their operation, I'd make sure your transport shuttle had a fatal fault. Or maybe you'll get knifed in the holding facility on that colony planet below us, in a random act of violence. But maybe not. Maybe the puppetmasters will get a few guys to pin your arms and legs while they blast another canister of whatever this is right in your face, and then clear you of all charges, and send you out to do their work."

That was a lot of maybes, but I didn't find any of the options reassuring. I was, however, thrilled to be in the company of someone who at least *claimed* to know what was going on. If I could orient myself, and figure out what the stakes were, perhaps I could find a way to extricate myself from this situation… and maybe even to profit from it. (Unlikely, I know, but I'm a trader at heart, and we can never stop looking for angles.) If she'd just stop being so damnably *vague*. "What work? What's the goal of this supposed conspiracy?"

Azad shook her head. "Wish I knew. I'm supposed to find out. All I know is, the puppetmasters have compromised people in your government, and the Federation, the Coalition, the Universities, the Kingdom, the Guild, everybody involved in the Greater Union. Not just that, but they also have Letnev agents, which makes me think they're involved in the alliance the Barony is putting together, the Legion. Somebody with connections like that could do all kinds of damage."

If this supposed conspiracy could pull the strings of two great opposing factions, they could do almost *anything*. Alter the entire financial structure of the galaxy. Manipulate supply chains, corner markets, vertically integrate every known industry, create multiple monopolies. They could starve any system they wanted, metaphorically *and* literally. You don't have to control the levers of power. Just the people who can reach those levers.

She shook her head. "Sorry. I'm heading off into spirals of speculation."

Same here, I thought.

"That's the problem with investigating a mysterious conspiracy with tendrils in a dozen polities," Azad said. "It tends to be distracting. So, let's focus. You're the latest victim of the conspiracy, and lucky for you, I just happened to be here when you got victimized, pursuing the same lead you stumbled on."

"You were looking into Qqurant?"

"You aren't the only one who noticed he was acting strangely. I've got a shortlist of people who've almost certainly been compromised, and Qqurant was on it."

"Why kill him if they controlled him?"

"Who knows? Maybe things reached the point where Qqurant was more useful to his new masters dead." She squinted. "I think we have about fifteen minutes before the actual cops show up and start asking you polite questions, or hitting you with sticks, or whatever it is they do in this jurisdiction. Do you want to wait around for that, or do you want to leave with me?"

I barked a laugh. "Flee the charges? Become a fugitive? That's the option you're offering me?"

She shrugged. "Fleeing is just step one. Step two is, you help me uncover the conspiracy. Prove your innocence. And maybe save the galaxy. But it's up to you. I could be a lunatic, and this whole murder charge could be a big misunderstanding that gets cleared up as soon as the lawyers get involved. Maybe a few hours from now you'll be walking around free, instead of on your way to getting murdered or mind-controlled. What do *you* think is most likely to happen?"

"Something was… very wrong with Qqurant." *Had* he been replaced by some sort of imposter? That didn't seem quite right. I thought it *was* Shelly, but profoundly traumatized, mentally broken, going through the motions of life and only barely managing that. A wave of despair rose up at the thought of my clever, quick-witted, murdered friend, and I pushed it down. I had to focus on keeping myself alive. "*Very* wrong."

She nodded. "We think he was one of the earliest… whatever. Replacements. Puppets. The early ones, they aren't as convincing, and they seem to get more glassy-eyed and vague and mumbly as time goes by. Maybe the puppetmasters were still working out the glitches with their brain-stealing or body-copying technology or something. The conspiracy started small, compromising people who didn't have a lot of personal security, but who went to *meetings* with the really important players, you know?"

I could see it. "Qqurant doesn't have a lot of power, but he works with people who do."

"Exactly. Maybe your buddy had his own little canister and sprayed it in the faces of his more powerful friends. The puppetmasters turned people like Qqurant, and used them to turn *others*, and so on up the ladder. I'd sure like to know how exactly they're compromising their targets. Seeing what's in that canister might help."

"How do you *know* all this? Where did you get this shortlist of candidates?"

"I am a trained investigator with very smart and well-connected bosses." She rose. "I'm also leaving. Are you coming with me, or are you going to sit there and hope for the best?"

I am, as a rule, a careful person. I study data. I do market research. But, in the end, whatever the numbers say, my decisions ultimately come down to my instincts. Not because I fetishize intuition, but because I trust that my mind is conducting calculations, analysis, and synthesis beyond the level of my conscious understanding. I've walked away from deals that looked great on paper and embraced ones that seemed questionable, and usually, my decisions worked out. Ninety percent of the time, anyway. Maybe eighty-five.

My instincts now were telling me to go with this woman. The worst case if I did was becoming a fugitive from justice, and that was pretty bad. If I stayed here, and she was right… the worst case was ending up dead, and that was much worse.

Except, no. The *worst* case if I stayed was being transformed into a hollow shell of myself and used as a pawn, like Shelly had been.

I stood up.

Azad grinned at me.

Azad had an array of useful override codes, including ones I was pretty sure only the chief of station security should possess. A facility like Shilsaad Station has many public-facing areas, but it also has myriad places the average visitor never sees: service corridors, maintenance tunnels, freight elevators, laundries, kitchens, pantries, and storage rooms. That's the world we passed through now: far less polished but far more functional, full of clanging and rushing and shouting, laughter and loafing and low conversation, stains and scuffs and doors that stuck a little before they slid open. Everything glamorous is built on grimier foundations.

We did not creep through the corridors silently. Azad led me openly through rooms filled with workers of various species, occasionally nodding and smiling at them, but mostly just breezing by. I learned long ago that if you walk with confidence and intent, you can reach all sorts of interesting places without being challenged. Her wearing a security uniform probably didn't hurt. I admired her brashness, though I couldn't share her confidence. Word must have gotten around about the killing, and there weren't *that* many Hacan on the station, so surely someone would wonder…

But no one did. At least, no one that made a fuss about it where we could see. Probably because no one would believe an escaped prisoner would walk around so openly. We made it to one of the hangars, where the station's dart-like security ships were located. The small ships were only big enough for two or three crew members, and were theoretically a last line of defense if the station came under attack… but in practice they mostly did escort duty for dignitaries on larger ships entering and leaving the area.

"We're escaping in one of these?" I said when she approached one of the fighters. "Surely the station has ways to track their own ships?"

Azad stopped, turned, and stared at me, eyes wide. Her hand went to her mouth, trembling. After a moment, she whispered, "No. Oh, no. I never thought of that. How could I be so *stupid*? After all the years I've spent as a covert operative! Thank Sol I had an elderly merchant here to warn me, or I would have made a terrible mistake!"

I sighed. "Yes. Fine. Point taken."

"Good. Get in the ship, big guy."

"For the record, I'm only *middle-aged* for my species," I grumbled as I obeyed.

THE FAITHFUL II

Kote Strom, head of security on Shilsaad Station and devotee to the great work, sat on the floor with her back against the wall in her quarters and communed with her masters.

Since taking the sacrament, Kote did not feel pain as keenly as she once had, so the sore spots from Terrak slamming her against the wall were only distant aches. The shame of failure hurt far more. "I am sorry, guides, for how things went with the Hacan. Your contingency plan has been enacted, though. Terrak has been framed for the death of Qqurant, and will meet with an accident on the shuttle tomorrow." A misgiving – actually, a pair of misgivings – surfaced in Kote's mind, and because her masters were generally gentle and seldom showed anger, she dared to broach one. "Was he really such a threat, to require such extreme actions?"

The answer emanated through her mind. *<We made inquiries among the faithful. Terrak pretends to be a simple trader, but his influence extends through many factions, like root tendrils hidden in the soil. He is a creature of connections, and if he continues to ask questions at this delicate time, and spurs his associates toward deeper investigations, the faithful might be exposed. Terrak must be thoroughly discredited and removed. We cannot allow anything to endanger the summits on Moll Primus and Arc Prime.>*

"Yes, but… a murder at this meeting is *already* disruptive, isn't it? The Xxcha Kingdom is threatening to leave the negotiations–"

<When Terrak is dead, they will be satisfied. Any who are not satisfied can be bribed or otherwise soothed. The crime will become simply another point in the negotiation – while the discovery of our influence would end the alliance entirely.>

"Yes, guides. I see now."

<Something further troubles you. Let us ease your mind.>

A soothing wave passed through Kote as the sacrament released all the best chemicals in her brain, and she relaxed against the wall as tensions she hadn't realized she was holding bled away. Eyes half-closed in bliss, she said, "Qqurant. I killed him, and he didn't resist, but he barely seemed to understand what was happening. When he recruited me, he was so sharp, and so clever. I understand that he became a… liability to the great work, and had to be removed, but what caused that change in him? Why did he become so… hollow?"

<He was one of the first to accept the sacrament, and our guidance,> the voice, or

voices, said in her mind. <*After so much time spent in our service there was a certain amount of… degradation. Personality decay. Diminished faculties. It is regrettable.*>

"Will that happen to me?" The prospect didn't worry Kote, exactly, but it seemed, to some distant part of her mind, important.

<*We have refined our techniques and continue to work on the problem. You will last longer. But more importantly, you will last long enough. And even if your mind or body fail, perishing in the service of the great work is more noble than to live for nothing, is it not?*>

"Yes, my guides," Kote murmured, and shivered with the ecstasy of purpose and service.

CHAPTER 3
FELIX

Felix Duval – captain of the cruiser *Temerarious*, leader of the covert operations team nicknamed "Duval's Devils", witness to the infamous "fractured void" experiment, rising star in the Mentak Coalition military – woke with a groan as his cabin lights flashed red and a siren shrieked at him from the ceiling speakers above his bunk. Those were emergency signals. There should not be an emergency here. They were parked in their ship outside Shilsaad Station, doing transport duty for a dignitary visiting the Greater Coalition summit. The biggest crisis around here should be running out of canapés.

He fumbled for the comm-switch beside the bed, but some override protocol had already turned on the viewscreen. Felix blinked into the bulbous face of his superior Fololire Jhuri, the dignitary in question, Undersecretary of Special Projects for the Mentak Coalition. Jhuri's chromatophores were flushed with the yellows of irritation. "Wake up, Felix. Things are falling apart, and we need you to pick up the pieces."

Felix sat up on the side of the bunk and rubbed his face. This was supposed to be his rest-and-recovery shift, and he'd prepared for it by having a drinking competition with Calred, his ship's security officer. (Felix lost, but he didn't mind; he played for love of the game.)

Rubbing his face wasn't working, so he slapped his own cheeks a couple of times, and that helped. He also found the switch that turned off the alarms, which helped more. "Sir. Yes. Present. What?"

Hylar didn't really sigh, not even the amphibious sub-species like Jhuri who could live in air or water, but Felix had grown up among the aliens, and he recognized the body language equivalent – chromatophores shifting to red, tentacles twitching. "Focus, Felix. This is important. Someone murdered one of the Xxcha delegates."

What, here? He looked out the window, at the spindle of the station and the frozen nova beyond. It was hard to imagine someone had died violently in that graceful structure, set against such grandeur. Wait. What did Jhuri want him to do about it? "I'm not much of a detective, but I guess I could–"

"We know who did the killing," Jhuri said. "A Hacan trade ambassador named Terrak. He was taken into custody almost immediately. But then he escaped."

Ahhh. That made more sense. "So you want me to catch him?"

"That's the idea, yes."

Felix managed not to grin; grinning after hearing some fancy official had died was inadvisable. But that disaster meant he had something to *do*, besides sitting here waiting for Jhuri to finish negotiating things, and that was a reason to be cheerful. Felix was happiest when he was in forward motion, in pursuit of some difficult-to-achieve goal, overcoming challenges and engaging in derring-do in the company of his trusted crew – wait. He had a horrible suspicion.

"Will you be joining us?" Felix asked. The *Temerarious* had transported Jhuri to the summit and having the boss on board for that long was weird enough. Usually, the undersecretary set the mission parameters and then sent Duval's Devils to do the job, with the understanding that if anything went terribly wrong, Felix and his crew were pretty much on their own. That was life in the clandestine services. Actually taking their handler on a mission would be… distracting.

Fortunately, Jhuri gestured in the negative. "No, I'll provide operational support remotely as needed, and I'll be in touch a *lot* more than usual."

Ah, well, that was fine. There were always ion storms or technical difficulties to blame communication delays on if Jhuri became too intrusive.

"This situation requires a delicate touch," the Hylar went on. "My superiors are worried this will delay the treaty signing, the Federation is running around shouting because it happened on one of their stations, and the Kingdom… well, you know the Xxcha don't scream and throw things, but they're very, very unhappy. Speaking of, there's going to be a temporary addition to your crew."

Felix frowned. He'd had a horrible suspicion about the wrong thing. He ran a three-person team – himself, Calred, and his first officer, the Yssaril Tib Pelta – and they worked beautifully together, a smoothly calibrated team. He didn't want help or need a babysitter. "If I'm pursuing a fugitive, shouldn't I… start pursuing? This hardly seems like the right time for new crew member orientation."

"We don't even have a direction to point you in yet, Felix. We only just realized Terrak is gone, because the security logs were tampered with – he must have had inside help, which suggests an organized plot, maybe one meant to disrupt the Greater Union, rather than a crime of passion or some personal grudge."

"I still don't see–"

"An Xxcha was killed, Felix," Jhuri said. "The representatives of the Kingdom are insisting – politely, but implacably, you know how they can be – that an Xxcha be included on the mission to hunt Terrak down. They want to be sure you're properly invested and motivated."

"Ah," Felix said. "I guess that makes sense. You're Hylar, I'm human, Cal is Hacan, Tib is Yssaril – add an Xxcha and we're like the Greater Union in microcosm, right?"

"The optics of a team like that are good. And since the overall optics are otherwise terrible, we'll take all the good we can get. I won't say the success of the Greater Union depends on the swift apprehension of Terrak, but… let's just say it would help."

There were a few Xxcha with the Mentak Coalition delegation at the summit, and Felix tried to think of who they'd send with him. "It's not Rrimiel, is it? She's a good systems analyst but she goes *on* and *on* about hydroponic agriculture – we get it, you like lettuce, but that doesn't substitute for a personality–"

"It's not one of our people," Jhuri said. "The ambassador from the Kingdom is sending their personal bodyguard. Her name is Ggorgos Skal."

Felix had known many Xxcha, but they were from his culture, not the Kingdom itself, and while all the various species that called the Mentak Coalition home retained elements of their ancestral cultures, they had more in common with each other than with the modern offshoots of their common ancestors. The denizens of the Kingdom were famed for their diplomacy, their measured approach, their thoughtfulness, and their calm in the midst of chaos. Felix wasn't sure how any of that would be much help in a chase, when speed and rapid responses were requirements. There was something strange, though… "Hold on, did you say Ggorgos Skal, two words? The Xxcha have surnames now?"

"The second name is a sort of qualifier, or signifier," Jhuri said. "Not all the Xxcha use them, and they're not quite ranks, not quite titles… but sometimes they're a job description, or a status revealer – they might translate as 'senior' or 'doctor' or 'the wise' or 'the younger' or other things."

"So what does Skal mean?"

"Ah. You know how the Xxcha are renowned for their placid natures?"

"I do."

"Every culture has its exceptions," Jhuri said. "As best I can tell, 'Skal' means something like 'the righteously violent.'"

"Oh. Well. I can't wait to meet her," Felix said.

Felix stood in the hangar bay of the *Temerarious* with Calred and Tib Pelta. Calred had recently returned from a rest-and-relaxation rotation, and still had colorful beads woven into his mane from the beach resort. (Such decorations were a violation of Coalition Navy uniform order, but part of the fun of being a covert squad was a certain looseness when it came to the niceties of military protocol. Felix himself often kept the top button of his uniform jacket undone.)

They were discussing their new crew member, of course.

Tib Pelta, who was pragmatic by nature, said, "OK, but who's in *charge*?"

"I am," Felix said.

"Jhuri is," Calred said.

Felix sighed. "Well, yes, *ultimately*, but Jhuri gives out the missions, and I decide how to complete them."

"Sure, but this… murder turtle… is outside your chain of command," Tib pointed out. "Is she going to be a good soldier for you, or try to boss you around?"

"She can *try*," Felix said. "But this is my ship, and I make the decisions."

"All the decisions that Jhuri delegates to you," Calred said.

Felix glared. "Which is most of them."

"It could be good, having someone new on board," Calred said. "Maybe she plays cards. Maybe she plays cards *badly*."

"You probably shouldn't cheat someone who has 'righteously violent' in her name," Tib said.

Calred smirked. "I've never met a Xxcha who intimidated me. Someone who hides inside a shell at the first sign of trouble isn't intimidating."

"What about Qqmel?" Tib said. Qqmel was an Xxcha from the Mentak Coalition who ran with the raider fleets and had a shoulder-mounted autocannon; he tended to make a striking impression.

Calred went *hmm*. "All right, Qqmel, I'll grant you, is a little daunting, but Qqmel is a hardened raider, not the babysitter for some ambassador."

"The shuttle's docked," Felix said.

They stood at approximations of attention while the airlock cycled up to pressure. They were meeting a representative of another faction for a difficult cross-cultural mission, and Felix wanted to make a good impression.

Ggorgos Skal emerged from the airlock, carrying a heavy-looking black duffel bag in one clawed hand. Felix swallowed a gasp. Calred made a small sound of surprise that he turned into a cough. Tib Pelta said nothing, but the Yssaril were good at hiding their reactions.

The Xxcha, as a species, resembled immense bipedal tortoises, though in place of hard shells, they had artificial onces, "exocarapaces", in a variety of designs. Some were painted, some studded with jewels, some smooth and gleaming, some pocked by kinetic fire or scorched by energy weapons in battle with the marks left as badges of honor. Ggorgos's exocarapace was beautiful, in a menacing sort of way: a matte black structure made of interlocking hexagonal panels, constructed of some material Felix couldn't immediately recognize, but which he assumed was highly armored. Her head was scarred, and one eye had been replaced with an embedded metal monocle where an oval lens glowed faintly yellow. "Felix Duval. Captain." Her voice was a rasp, as if her vocal cords were damaged.

Felix realized he had no idea of her rank, or how to refer to her, so he fell back on the basics, and hoped he wouldn't give offense. "Ggorgos Skal. Welcome aboard. We look forward to working with you."

Ggorgos just stared at him, then flicked her eyes – one black and gleaming, one yellow and shining – toward the others. "Calred. Security officer. Tib Pelta. First officer." A grunt. "Duval's Devils." Her rasp made the name sound like a joke, or a mockery, or maybe Felix was just feeling overly sensitive. She gazed at them for a moment, then said, "I need to stow my gear."

"I'll show you to your–" Felix began.

She slung her bag at his feet. "Just put my bag there. You can show me the bunk later. First, I need to review the ship's armaments. Calred, take me to the tactical board."

Felix looked down at the bag. No. This wasn't happening. "Listen. We're perfectly happy to have you on board, but I'm the captain here–"

"A high official of the Xxcha Kingdom was assassinated," Ggorgos said. "I will apprehend the killer. You are my support staff."

"I don't think so," Felix said.

"Your thoughts do not interest me. Check with your superior. He must not have explained the situation clearly enough, or perhaps you simply failed to listen. Calred, take me to the security console now."

Calred glanced at Felix, who sighed. "Go ahead. I'll call Jhuri and get this straightened out."

Ggorgos ignored him, just waited impatiently for Calred, until the Hacan shrugged and beckoned her down the corridor.

"She's nice," Tib Pelta said. "Almost makes me miss Thales."

Felix shuddered. Their first covert mission had involved ferrying a truly vile human scientist halfway across the galaxy. "No one is *that* bad."

Jhuri's face appeared on the screen in Felix's ready room. "Ggorgos says *she's* in charge here. Can you set her straight, please?"

"Ah." The Hylar's chromatophores flushed a deep purple. "She is, broadly speaking, in a technical sense… correct."

Felix closed his eyes for a moment. "You might have mentioned that." All he'd ever wanted was to have his own command, and the opportunity to do his nation proud (ideally while enjoying a bit of excitement along the way). He was in the military, and no stranger to taking orders, but to be supplanted on his own *ship*, by someone from an entirely different faction? That was hard to swallow.

"I was hoping it wouldn't be necessary. I just finished a call where I sadly failed to make any headway. When the Xxcha first suggested that Ggorgos lead the mission, we pointed out that we had our best people on the case, and her presence wasn't necessary at all. We thought adding her to your crew was enough of a compromise, but the Xxcha ambassador is… rather implacable. It's like arguing with a very polite stone. The Xxcha are really bothered by this. I gather Qqurant was well liked by a lot of important people. We're counting on the diplomatic ties the Xxcha can provide to make the Greater Union a success, and if they pull out, the whole enterprise could fall apart."

"But to be demoted on my own ship, Jhuri!"

"If Ggorgos tells you to fly into a black hole, you have my permission to mutiny. But as long as her plans are reasonable and tactically sound, why not go along with them? One of their people got killed on our watch, Felix. We can't undo that, but we can try not to make it any worse."

"Understood." Felix clicked off the comms, took a deep breath, and fastened the top button of his uniform. He was an officer of the Mentak Coalition, and he would comport himself with all appropriate dignity, even if, inside, he wanted to stomp his feet and punch the bulkhead.

"I think we got off on the wrong foot," Felix said.

Ggorgos, standing over a navigation panel, grunted.

The two of them were alone on the bridge. Calred was doing a manual check of the torpedo bays because Ggorgos had seen a number on a readout that wasn't perfectly optimal, though it was within acceptable range. Tib was off reviewing the dossier they'd been sent about Terrak's history and known associates so they could try to guess where he might head for sanctuary.

Felix went on, "There was some confusion, on my part, about our arrangements, and I ... apologize for that."

This time he didn't even get a grunt. "Set a course for the Rantula sector, captain."

Felix frowned. "I thought we didn't know which way Terrak went?"

"I received an intel update a moment ago. I'm sure the Coalition will have one for you shortly. In the meantime, set the course. Every moment we fall behind is a moment a killer enjoys freedom."

Felix doubted being on the run was very enjoyable, but he took the point and went to the navigation terminal. While he was laying a course, he got the *ping* of a priority update from Jhuri: *Proceed to the Rantula sector.* There was a lot of supporting data included – information about a missing security ship, accounts from other vessels who'd seen a vehicle that couldn't be accounted for by local traffic control – but Felix just skimmed it. "Ggorgos," he said, "would you share your intelligence from the Kingdom with me as soon as you get it? Just so we're all working with the same information at the same time?"

"I see no reason to refuse." The Xxcha didn't look up from her panel, but it was a start.

"We can be more than transportation for you, Ggorgos. We want to catch Terrak as much as you do."

"Doubtful," Ggorgos said. "I will be in my quarters." The Xxcha stomped off the deck.

Felix sank into the captain's chair and sighed. He pulled up the information Tib had compiled on Terrak and the dead cultural minister. Maybe he'd find some useful insight that he could present to Ggorgos. He'd gone from running the ship to trying to find ways to impress the person who was *now* running the ship. The great virtues of the Mentak nation were resilience and adaptability. They were descended from prisoners, transported to a distant planet, considered outcasts and pirates, but they'd united, and risen to the heights of influence and prestige in galactic civilization. If their great founder Erwan Mentak was able to unite the disparate, feuding species of Moll Primus into a unified whole, overcoming their tribal affiliations and old prejudices to make something new, then surely Felix could get along with one brusque and zealous Xxcha. The important thing was the mission.

Also, the sooner Felix *finished* the mission, the sooner he could get rid of Ggorgos.

As Felix perused the details, though, he realized the crime made absolutely no sense. Terrak was by all accounts interested in two things: money and pleasure – and even the money was mostly a way to facilitate more pleasure. The Mentak Coalition had invited Terrak to the summit because he had an outsized level of influence with the leaders of the Emirates, considering his status and rank, because he was a lightly corrupt favor trader who was good at making friends. Felix's bosses thought Terrak could be wined, dined, and wooed into supporting favorable trading terms within the Greater Union, and to bring along some of his highly placed friends. Terrak had seemed happy to enjoy the thinly disguised bribes… until, for some reason, he'd murdered a random Xxcha cultural minister. Terrak and the victim were old friends, so maybe there was some personal reason for the violence hidden in their deep history, but it was hard to imagine what. If Terrak had planned to kill Qqurant, he could have done it in a more subtle way, so it must have been a crime of passion… but if it was a spur-of-the-moment assault, how could you explain that someone was prepared to smuggle Terrak off the station? That suggested planning, even a conspiracy, but to what possible end? To disrupt the formation of the Greater Union? Why would Terrak want to do that so badly he'd sacrifice his own good name and freedom to the cause? Unless someone was just using Terrak for that purpose.

Felix sent a note to Jhuri: Are we sure Terrak is the actual killer?

The response came quickly: He was found standing over the victim, with his spear stuck in the dead minister, so it sure looks that way.

Could be a frame-up, Felix sent. Part of an attempt to disrupt the Greater Union, maybe.

We're considering the possibility, Jhuri said. We're not idiots over here, Felix. The simplest way to find out what's going on is for you to find Terrak and ask him.

If I can keep Ggorgos from killing him first.

Jhuri replied: By all accounts, Ggorgos never kills anyone until she's finished with them first, and she likes to take her time.

"Uh, Felix?" Tib said over the comms. "I think you should come look at this. I found something Shilsaad Station security missed."

Felix went to Tib's office. Her specialties were infiltration and intelligence gathering, and she also had a natural affinity for data analysis. Her office was wall-to-wall screens, and they displayed a dizzying array of data, from loops of video to blown-up still photographs to pages of text with sections highlighted and color-coded according to some arcane system of Tib's own devising. Tib herself sat in a swivel chair in the center of it all, fingers manipulating a tablet in her lap.

"What did you find?" Felix moved a pile of binders off a chair to sit beside her.

"A human member of station security disappeared at the same time Terrak did, and the current theory is that she's the one who helped him escape. Her name is… some human name, it doesn't matter. I assume it's a fake anyway, though so far, the identity stands up to scrutiny, so it must be a really good fake. There are some weird gaps in the station's personnel files – all photographs of her are gone, along with any security footage that might have shown her face."

"She's a professional, then," Felix said.

"You could say that." There was something peculiar in Tib's tone, and Felix knew bad news was coming. "All Jhuri sent us was a description of the woman, and you know how useful *those* are. If she cut and colored her hair and put on high heels and a baggy coat, she wouldn't match the description anymore. I was annoyed by the lack of photos, though, and you know how I get when something annoys me."

"I annoy you, and you became my lifelong best friend."

"OK, the *other* way I get. Stubborn and mildly obsessive, I mean. I kept digging through the station systems and found out the employees set up a secret social media intranet. It's basically a forum for gripes about management and guests and so on. There are some photos there, very informal, including a group shot from some junior officer's going-away party a week before the summit." She tapped her terminal, and one of the screens filled with a crowded shot of about thirty people holding drinks and laughing and jostling each other, some caught frozen in mid-dance-step. "I ran facial recognition to match all the people at the party with the photos in the personnel files," Tib said. "Everyone was accounted for… except one." More tapping at the tablet, and the photo on the screen zoomed in and cropped, isolating a single face, turned partly away from the camera. It was a human woman, her hair buzzed short on one side, her mouth thrown open in a laugh, and–

Felix groaned. "No. It's not. It can't be. It's just a superficial resemblance. Right?"

"All humans look basically alike to me," Tib said. "So, I pulled up one of *our* photos from ship security and ran a comparative analysis. That picture on the screen isn't very high quality, so I can't be absolutely sure, but I got an eighty-seven percent probability match." She sighed. "I'm pretty sure the mystery guest is Amina Azad."

Felix put his head in his hands. Amina Azad was a covert operative from the Federation of Sol. She was a dreadful combination of the unpredictable and the implacable, wickedly good at improvising, and a joyful sower of chaos and confusion. She'd once pursued him across the galaxy, and with the help of an equally horrible Letnev officer named Severyne Dampierre, she'd even seized control of the *Temerarious* for a while. If Felix had to pick, of the two of them, he'd honestly rather face Severyne again – sure, she'd stab him in the neck too, but at least she wouldn't crack jokes while she did it.

"We'd better tell Jhuri," Felix sighed. "We should also tell Ggorgos. I asked her to share information with us, so that should go both ways."

"By 'we' I assume you mean 'you'," Tib said. "Talking to Ggorgos makes me nervous. When she looks at me it's like she's running down a list of ways to dismember me."

"The burdens of captainhood," Felix muttered.

Not much later, Ggorgos stood in Tib's office, reviewing the data, while Jhuri's face watched from another screen. He'd set up an office on Shilsaad Station, and there was a large fern and a bad painting of a beach in the background. "This Azad," Ggorgos said at last. "She is employed by the Federation of Sol?"

"Not officially," Jhuri said. "She's a former naval officer who left the service many years ago to become an independent security contractor. Unofficially, we know she was employed as a deniable asset by the Federation a few years ago, when Felix tangled with her. She may have actually become a freelancer since then, or she could still be working for the Federation. I'm making inquiries with my counterparts among the humans, but the nature of deniable assets is that the people in charge have a tendency to deny them."

"A Hacan and a human conspired to murder one of my compatriots at a diplomatic summit. We must ascertain whether they did so at the behest of their governments, or for reasons of their own." This was a very long speech for Ggorgos.

"I can't imagine that the Emirates of the Federation directed Terrak and Azad to do this," Jhuri said. "Both those nations have fairly good relations with the Kingdom, and if they wanted to disrupt the Greater Union, they could just pull out of the treaty."

"Governments are not monolithic," Ggorgos said. "There are factions within factions. Perhaps Azad and Terrak represent minority members of their respective governments who wish to see the Greater Union fail. When we apprehend them… we will ask."

"You can't believe anything Amina Azad says," Felix offered. "She's treacherous. And by all accounts Terrak tells lies for a living. He's a trade ambassador with a fondness for bribes."

"I am adept at extracting the truth," Ggorgos said.

"Torture doesn't actually work," Tib said from the corner. "People just tell you what they think you want to hear, so you'll stop hurting them."

"I am aware." Ggorgos's voice was even frostier than usual. "I have experienced torture, at the hands of skilled practitioners. I have my own methods. They have proven effective." She clomped out of the room.

"She's charming, isn't she?" Felix looked at Jhuri. "Do you know how she, ah… got to be the way she is?"

"Her service record is sealed," Jhuri said. "Apparently everything from the moment she enlisted to the day she was assigned as the ambassador's bodyguard is a state secret. I think you can assume she's good at her job, though."

"I'd better make sure we do ours just as well, then. Do we have any idea why Terrak is headed to the Rantula system?"

"Amazingly, yes," Jhuri said. "He has two known associates there. One is an agricultural exporter who specializes in fruit. We think he's an unlikely target. The other is a professional liaison and information broker called the Facilitator – no one's even sure what species they are, or if they're an individual at all. They connect people with other people for a living."

"What, like hired killers, professional thieves, things like that?"

"Certainly," Jhuri said. "But they facilitate legitimate business meetings, too. If you desperately need an audience with someone you have no way to reach, the Facilitator can help, for a price. That's how Terrak knows them – our murderous Hacan can secure audiences with certain Emirate officials, especially in the economic departments, so he's part of the Facilitator's network."

"This Facilitator sounds like the kind of person who could help you disappear," Felix said.

"Or hire you to disrupt a diplomatic summit," Tib said.

"Or first the second, and then the first," Jhuri said. "The Facilitator operates out of a little moon in the Rantula system. That's where you're headed. We don't advise bursting in and blowing things up – the Facilitator is the kind of person you pay off, not the kind of person you beat up – though the specific tactical approach is at Ggorgos's discretion."

"Shouldn't you be telling Ggorgos all this then?" Felix said.

"She knows," Jhuri said. "She received substantially the same intelligence from the Kingdom about half an hour ago, as best I can determine. Their diplomatic connections make them *slightly* faster at finding things out than we are, and they tell Ggorgos everything before they mention any of it to us."

Felix ground his teeth. "She told me she'd share."

"Did she really?" Tib said.

"Well, not in exactly those words," Felix admitted. "She said she couldn't think of a reason *not* to share."

"I guess she must have come up with one," Jhuri said.

THE FAITHFUL III

Kote Strom snarled at her subordinates one last time, slammed the door to her office, and crawled underneath her desk, where it was quiet, and dark, and she could try to think. She had failed the guides, not once, but twice, and *that* was a pain that made her whimper.

<*What has happened?*> the voice in her head said. <*We are too distant to taste your thoughts directly. You must tell us what causes your distress.*>

"Terrak has escaped. We do not know how. Someone helped him. One of my… one of my own people, we think, though we don't know why."

<*He must be captured and killed.*>

"Yes, of course, but I'm not in charge of that operation, guides – station security is in some disgrace now, as you might imagine, with a murder and an escape in the space of barely a day. The Mentak Coalition and the Xxcha Kingdom are coordinating the pursuit. The operation is still being run from here, and as a professional courtesy they're giving me updates, so I can, at least, keep you informed. They've sent a team of operatives to pursue Terrak and his accomplice."

A pulse of pain shot through Kote's head, making her clutch her skull and moan. <*We must have one of the faithful on that ship!*>

"We do, we do!" Kote said. "I checked. If you reach out, you'll find one of us on a ship called the *Temerarious–*"

Calm flooded her mind, and she slouched in relief.

<*Yes, we see. Good. Terrak cannot be allowed to tell his story or share any of his speculations. Our operative will kill him on sight.*>

"There is, ah… another problem. The canister that holds the sacrament was stolen from my locker. I fear Terrak has it."

A long silence, and then, in a voice as chill as the void: <*We see.*>

"If they find someone to analyze the sacrament, they might be able to trace–"

<*The implications are clear to us. We will take further steps to ensure Terrak's capture.*>

"What steps, guides?"

<*We have other faithful nearby, with other resources. We will mobilize them as well. This Terrak will be pursued from many sides. Escape will be impossible. The great work will succeed.*>

"What shall I do, guides?"

<*Don't make any more mistakes,*> the voice said, and a cascade of pain – needles, teeth, acid, ice – poured through Kote's brain, leaving her curled on the floor of her office… but she was grateful even for that.

She was, at least, still permitted to serve.

CHAPTER 4
TERRAK

"Off to see the Facilitator, then?" Azad said, piloting the little ship through the void toward the Rantula system.

"It seems like an obvious destination for a fugitive and his mysterious benefactor." I'd figured out how to make the co-pilot's seat recline and was resting with a cloth over my eyes.

"Probably not so mysterious anymore. I covered my tracks as best I could, but the Greater Union people will be highly motivated to track us down, and sadly, I've had some past interactions with the Mentak. If I missed a photo, somebody there will recognize me."

That was mildly interesting. I lifted the cloth from my eyes and looked at her. "What was the nature of those past interactions?"

"It's all double-secret classified," Azad said.

"Ah."

"Fortunately, I don't give two craps about that. What happened was, my bosses sent me to steal a guy from a Coalition colony world. The Coalition didn't like that, and they stole him *back*, and then I had to go and steal him *again*, and it was a whole thing. This one Hylar, Jhuri, he was my opposition on that operation. I actually saw him at the summit."

"I am familiar with him," I said. "He has a very vague job title, something about 'special projects', but everyone assumes he commands squads of elite black ops assassins."

Azad snorted. "Maybe he does. I didn't meet any. Just some jerks with a fast ship and better-than-average luck."

"They got the best of you, then?" That wasn't comforting.

She shrugged. "It's more like we all failed *together*. I walked away and kept my job at the end, and looking back, parts of it were pretty fun. Like, I met this girl–"

"Please spare me tales of your romantic adventures," I said.

"Your loss. It's a good story. Two people from different worlds, brought together by circumstance, forced to work as a team, finding common cause in a shared enemy… it's a whole enemies-to-lovers-and-then-back-to-enemies-again sort of thing."

"I'm sure it would make a wonderful serial drama, but I'm more concerned with my future than your past, Azad."

"Fine, be like that. So we'll drop in on the Facilitator – I never met the guy, are they even a guy, or like a consortium, or what?"

"They are a shining black obelisk with a speaker in the side, usually," I said. "I have never seen them or heard their unaltered voice. That's how they operate. In the shadows."

"An entity after my own heart," Azad said. "I love shadows. That's why I set so many fires – you get lots of shadows cast in the light of burning things."

"Let's try to keep any burning to a minimum. Anyway, I just said going to see the Facilitator would make sense. That's why we aren't actually going to *do* it."

Some people are hard to read because they're impassive and blank. You have to watch them carefully to catch fleeting micro-expressions that give away their thoughts, and those are wildly different for every species, not even counting variations within cultures and subcultures. Amina Azad obscured her true feelings in a different way; she was incredibly expressive, always showing *something,* usually a variety of malign delight, and the trick was looking deeper to see what her *true* feelings were, always hidden by the tricksterish mask. I didn't know her well enough at that point to tell if I'd truly surprised her.

She cackled and said, "Beautiful, I love it. Anyone who gets a sense of our bearing and looks at your known associates will assume that's where we're going. So, what's the *actual* destination?"

"My other usual contact in the Rantula system is an agricultural importer and exporter. He has contracts with many colony worlds with fruit orchards, and I've helped him make some useful connections, especially selling his wares to Federation ships in this region of space. Humans are vulnerable to a vitamin deficiency disorder called scurvy, and while there are supplements that can help, your people generally prefer fresh fruit to dry pills."

"Ooh, yeah, scurvy is nasty. Has all kinds of gross effects. Your teeth fall out, your joints go to hell, you're irritable – which is a natural response to having your teeth fall out and your joints hurt, probably, but even beyond that. Do you know what the wildest symptom of scurvy is?"

"I'm sure you'll tell me."

"Scurvy stops your body from producing collagen," she said. "In humans, and maybe Hacan too, collagen is the stuff scar tissue is made of. So, in advanced cases of scurvy, old wounds you thought were totally healed can *open back up again.* It turns out, you never truly recover from the damage you take in this life – you're never *really* as good as new again. You carry your wounds with you forever, and the best you can hope for is that they get hidden away."

I thought about that. "I feel like you're trying to make some kind of philosophical point."

Azad cocked her head. "Nah. That doesn't sound like me. I don't need philosophy. I just do stuff. Thinking about why would only slow me down. Anyway. You were saying. We're going to see your fruit guy? Does he do chemical analysis on the side?"

"We are not, and he does not. I'm sure if anyone realizes we're heading to the Rantula system, they'll send someone to check his warehouse, too. I want to avoid my known associates entirely."

"We're going to an *unknown* associate then. Those are my favorite kind."

"Yes. But I met her through the, as you say, my 'fruit guy'. Lonrah is a chemist, a Hylar, who makes her money from the production of bespoke recreational drugs."

"Ooh."

"Her most expensive wares can be tuned to individual brain and body chemistry, for a variety of species. She acquires many of her raw materials, rare botanicals and organic compounds, from my agricultural friend. I made contact with her years ago, and meet her surreptitiously, under the cover of other appointments."

"Ha, so you're a drug dealer, too?"

"I will sell anything there's a market for," I said. "Assuming there's some profit in it beyond the merely monetary. The Quieron's personal facilitator is a connoisseur of unusual psychedelics and euphorics, and my partnership with Lonrah allowed me to strengthen my relationship with him."

"The Quieron is like the king of your people, right?"

I growled. "The Quieron is an elected representative who speaks for the united emirates of the Hacan and resolves disputes among the clans. We do not have *kings.*"

"OK, I didn't mean to stick a thorn in your paw. Take it easy. I knew your shady connections were going to come in handy. This Lonrah can take a look at the stuff in that canister and tell us what we're dealing with, right?"

"That is my hope," I said.

"How do we get a message to her?"

"I generally just turn up," I said. "She's an agoraphobe, so she's always home."

"Why is it called Huntsman's Moon?" Azad asked as we followed the bored traffic controller's instructions to a designated landing zone.

I shrugged. "I have no idea. Probably named after some early settler."

"It's a good thing I don't believe in omens, or I'd say this is a bad one. If there's hunting going on, I prefer to be the predator, and right now, we're mostly the prey."

I had discovered, to my chagrin, that I rather enjoyed Azad's company. She had that human brashness and impulsiveness that can be so invigorating (when it's not irritating), but she'd also proven herself a capable operator. Getting me off that station could not have been easy, but she'd made it look that way. She was worthy of my respect, though not, as yet, my trust. I believed we had a common enemy, at least, and that would have to do for now.

Azad settled the ship onto the surface at the end of a row of other vessels. She'd done something to disguise the ship's transponder, so in theory, we wouldn't be immediately identified as escaped fugitives. "If you need anything from the ship, grab it now. We're going to have to find another ride off the moon."

I spread my hands. "I appear to be fully packed."

"We are traveling pretty light. Maybe we can find you another spear at least."

"I am not particularly adept with spears. We carry them mostly for ceremonial purposes."

"Sure, but when you're a two-and-a-half-meter-tall lion-guy with a polearm on your belt, you don't *have* to be good with it, because nobody bothers you anyway."

"That has been my experience," I agreed. "But it's hardly a priority. We won't need to menace Lonrah to get her help."

We disembarked. I wouldn't miss the cramped little ship, though I missed my *own* vessel, the *Afterparty*. I wondered if I'd ever see her again.

Huntsman's Moon had a breathable atmosphere, though the air was a bit thin and acrid – typical of terraformed worlds engineered to sustain the lives of as many different species as possible.

"Not much of a skyline, is it?" Azad looked at the low cluster of buildings a few hundred meters away from our landing zone.

There were only two major cities on the moon, each near a pole, where water and ice was most plentiful. We were in the northernmost city, Missulena, the oldest settlement on the moon. "Large portions of the city are still underground, and there are even a few domed areas left, from before this place had breathable air. The domes are now full of atmospheres we'd find inhospitable, neighborhoods set aside for those species who don't cope well with what we're breathing."

Azad tilted her head back. "Nice view when you look up, anyway. I grew up near a gas giant, Meginstjarna, so having a huge storm-world hanging over my head always comforts me."

The planet we were orbiting, Tegenaria, was a swirl of orange and blue clouds, and filled nearly a quarter of the sky. No one lived there – the clouds were full of leviathan aliens, unintelligent but hostile, and since they weren't good to eat and their bodily fluids had no useful properties, no one bothered with the planet much. With seventy moons, there was plenty of other real estate available, and you didn't have to rig up floating cities on any of them.

"Did you just reveal something about your personal life?" I said as we walked toward the city.

"I'm an open book! I was trying to tell you about my *love life* before you shushed me earlier. If you're curious now, there was this Letnev–"

"Again, please. My sensibilities are too delicate. Let's just go see Lonrah."

There was a transit hub near the landing area, and Azad used a smart ring to acquire day passes for us. "Aren't you worried about leaving a data trail?" I asked her.

She snorted as we pushed through the gate, both of us with hoods up to disguise us from any security cameras, and joined the small crowd waiting on the platform. The travelers were mostly humans with a smattering of Hacan and the odd representative of other species. The station was pretty, with cream-colored pillars carved with representations of the local moons. "I've got a bunch of accounts under a bunch of names and corporate designations, and the ring cycles through them. The encryption is really robust, but even if someone cracks it, they won't find anything useful. My resources are more limited than I'd like – my bosses don't trust me *that* much – but I can safely buy us train fare."

The local mass transit system was less a train and more a series of windowed pods that hovered in magnetic fields, but fair enough. I consulted a wall map – not having a personal terminal, tablet, gauntlet, or even ring of my own was annoying – and found the right place on the platform to wait. Lonrah lived in a distant, industrial part of the city, and since our journey took place outside regular commuting hours, we were alone in our pod. Azad amused herself by reading the graffiti aloud while I sat on a padded bench with my elbows on my knees and my head in my hands, massaging my temples.

The worst part about running for your life is how simultaneously tense and boring it can be. There's a lot of time spent just moving through space, or waiting to do so, with nothing to occupy the mind but one's terrible predicament. Azad said there was a vast conspiracy at work, one that had wormed its way through multiple governments, and that conspiracy was after *me*, because I'd been unlucky enough to stumble into the middle of their operation. Now my only hope for survival was to unravel that conspiracy. No one with knowledge of my official resume would have selected me for a mission like *that*. I had to hope Azad was right, and that I could prove useful to her investigations... because if I *wasn't* useful to her, I had no doubt she would cheerfully abandon me to my fate. There wouldn't even be any malice in the act. I thought she liked me, in fact... but she was a professional, despite her jocular air.

The pod hissed to a stop, and we disembarked. This station was rather less pretty, a low-roofed structure, open to the air on all sides, with trash blowing across the platform. We went through the exit gates, and Azad raised an eyebrow at me. "I don't think we'll have much luck getting a pedi-cab out here, but I can try to steal some ground transportation."

"Lonrah's lab is within walking distance." The air was chilly, and I wished for a heavier coat. I'd have to make Azad use some of her untraceable funds to get me a change of clothes, at least, before we left; there were Hacan shops here. I took off my sash and stuffed it into a pocket. Such an accessory was appropriate for the summit, but here, it would just look like I was trying too hard. The rest of my clothes were unexceptional apart from their fine quality, but they were wrinkled, and would become rank if I wore them too much longer.

We set off along the pavement, past the blank facades of warehouses and fabrication plants and empty lots that were nevertheless warded with chain link and razor wire. After half a kilometer, I led Azad down an alley between two brick buildings to what looked like a large utility box, marred with graffiti and scratches.

I pressed a few seemingly random locations on the box, and the front panel popped open, revealing not wires or controls but a tiny elevator. I squeezed in, and Azad joined me to make it an even tighter squeeze. The doors closed, and we waited.

"Who's your friend, Terrak?" a speaker in the ceiling said. Lonrah's artificial voicebox had a metallic edge. She thought it made her sound menacing, and if you didn't know her, it probably did.

"Her name is Amina Azad," I said. "She's helping me with a problem. We have need of your professional services."

"I heard you murdered someone, Terrak," Lonrah said. "That doesn't sound much like you."

"News travels… faster than I anticipated," I said.

"Oh, it's not trending at the top of the feeds or anything," she said. "I just have alerts set up for basically everyone I've ever met. Because you never know. Knowledge is power and all that."

"I am innocent," I said. "You might be able to help me prove that."

She was silent.

Azad closed her eyes. "Terrak, if you brought me to someone who is going to *turn you in—*"

"Come on down," Lonrah said, and the elevator lurched into motion.

"I wasn't worried about her turning me in," I said. "Lonrah was expelled from the university on Jor for some of her more unconventional experiments. Now she works in areas that are at best quasi-legal and at worst forbidden in major systems. As a result, she doesn't like authorities very much."

"You are an actual *literal* government official," Azad pointed out.

"Yes, and that fact was always something of an impediment to true intimacy between us. I think Lonrah will like me better as a fugitive."

The elevator opened into a long narrow room lined on both sides by shelves filled with jars, which were filled with various things, many of them disgusting.

"This place looks like a museum of medical oddities crossed with an herb shop," Azad said.

"Lonrah collects unusual biological samples, and studies them to see if they have any useful properties. She found the cure for Gungar's Rot in a clump of swamp mud – I think selling that pharmaceutical patent is the way she secured initial funding for her operation. These days, she's less interested in curing unusual fungal infections, and more interested in turning brains into fountains of pure bliss."

"A noble form of employment," Azad said.

We proceeded between the shelves, across the polished floor, made of black stone with little starlike specks of white. Chosen because of how pretty it looked on psychedelic drugs, I'd always assumed. I ducked through a beaded curtain, into a little anteroom lined with shelves full of tea canisters and boxes of crackers and cookies. The next doorway was covered by a plastic flap that unsealed with a *schloop* and then sealed back closed after us. A few short steps through the plastic umbilicus took us to a matching doorway at the other end. "Uh, do we need to be in clean-suits or something?" Azad said. "I'm getting bio-weapons-lab feelings here."

"No," I replied. "This is just a safeguard. She keeps the nastier things well contained. As for any contamination we might bring in – well, if we tracked in some horrible pathogen, Lon's sensors would detect them, and she'd probably be very excited to examine them."

We went on into the lab, a far sleeker, cleaner, and better-lit area than we'd seen so far, with worktables and glass-fronted cabinets and mysterious silver and white equipment everywhere. Lon was small even for a Hylar, and she sat nestled in a mech suit nearly as big as my body, fitted with an array of articulated limbs tipped with delicate pincers and assorted diagnostic equipment.

"Terrak! And your new friend. What can I do for you?" She worked delicate levers with her pseudopods and marched the suit toward us.

"What have you got in the way of human-compatible combat drugs?" Azad said before I could answer.

"Oh, all sorts of stimulants, focus drugs, pain blockers, sensory boosters, the works."

Azad grinned. "I'm gonna want some of all of those."

The idea of Azad on *stimulants* was rather alarming – humans were energetic as a rule, and she was already an extreme outlier on their scale – but I liked the idea of her investing in combat drugs. That meant, if it came to fighting, she'd be the one to leap into action, allowing me to observe, which was the position I preferred.

Lonrah glanced at me. "I can take a blood sample and get started on some personalized items, sure. It'll only take an hour or so to analyze your samples and chem-print the product."

"That's it? You didn't have to take a break from being a fugitive to make introductions for this kind of transaction, Terrak. I thought it was going to be something *weird*."

"We'll do the weird stuff while we wait for my drugs to be ready," Azad said. "You tell her about the canister, Terrak. I'm going to check out some of these news stories she mentioned and see what I can glean about the state of the investigation." She found a battered crate labeled "DO NOT SHAKE" to sit on, and stabbed at her gauntlet, pulling up the feeds.

I showed Lon the canister. "Someone attacked me and tried to spray me in the face with this. I fought them off, and they escaped. Not long afterward, I was framed for murdering one of my oldest friends. I suspect these events are connected."

One of her mechanical arms uncurled and took the canister from me. "So, you'd like to know what they tried to spray you with. Could just be poison, or something to knock you out, right?"

"Could be," I agreed. "But… we have another theory." I opened my mouth to tell her about how strangely Shelly had acted, and Azad's theory that people were being brainwashed or replaced, but Lonrah held up one of her fleshy pseudopods in a "stop" gesture.

"Don't tell me," she said. "I don't want to be influenced. You can't go around prejudicing the *science*."

"You might not want to, ah, risk inhaling any of it–"

She flushed the colors of amusement. "You'll be shocked to hear I have protocols for dealing with unidentified and potentially deadly substances, Terrak. Let me draw some of your friend's blood, and then I'll get into analyzing this."

"Can I borrow a terminal?" I said. "I'd like to check the feeds myself, and see how much trouble I'm in."

"I don't think you're going to like it at all, actually, but feel free," she said. "My server room is just through that door, and there's a terminal you can use."

I spent a rather demoralizing hour reading about myself. There were quotes from some of my colleagues, expressing shock and dismay, but not nearly enough of them were insisting I must have been framed or was obviously innocent of these scurrilous charges. Being found standing over a corpse with your own spear sticking out of the body tended to dampen such doubts, apparently.

Azad was amusing herself, instead of amusing herself with *me*, so I had nothing to do but read about my perfidy. Azad's name was left out of the accounts, and indeed, there was no suggestion that I'd had help escaping at all, least of all from station security, though I was sure the authorities knew. They were just holding that information back, probably because it made *everyone* look bad.

There were lots of pieces speculating about how my vicious and senseless crime might impact the plans for the Greater Union, with somber quotations from the Xxcha Kingdom and the Mentak Coalition. I was wondering about that myself. It seemed like such a scandal was obviously bad news for the alliance, but at least one respected columnist said: "This Terrak is clearly on the payroll of cowards opposed to the Greater Union. The fact that such treacherous people are opposed to the treaty is a strong argument for moving forward as planned. If we let this disrupt the Union, then we're letting terrorists like Terrak win." I mused, not for the first time, that writers of political opinion pieces could make almost any event an argument for whatever they wanted.

I returned to the lab. "Azad. Who do you think is behind this conspiracy? If they're manipulating the prospective members of the Greater Union, *and* of the Legion, they must belong to some other faction, right? Trying to diminish the effectiveness of those alliances?"

"Like maybe one of the great big bogeymen your Union is supposed to protect against?" Azad said. "Could be. The N'orr don't do subtlety. I've met the Creuss and they're spooky as anything, but I feel like they'd be more likely to fill your guts with frogs or turn you into a cloud of radioactive glitter or something than enact a complex plan based on social engineering. The L1Z1X … maybe. Their whole thing is cybernetics and the mindnet. I'm open to the possibility."

"There are rumors of other forces … nightmarish creatures attacking the edges of the galaxy, though who knows if they even exist …"

"Oh, they do," Azad said. "I've even seen them. But though some of them look a little like spiders, they aren't exactly delicate web spinners. And, yeah, I've considered the other rumors. I'm pretty sure the Mahact are imaginary, and the Titans are more the brute force types, if the stories are true."

"How about this shadowy information dealer I've heard rumors about? No one knows anything about their true motives, and they're rumored to have agents everywhere."

Azad nodded. "Yeah. That's a possibility I'm considering. One of many, honestly. But I think you're starting off from a faulty premise anyhow."

"In what way?"

"It sounds like you think the conspiracy is trying to disrupt the Greater Union and the Legion, and I've got my doubts. Some of the people I'm pretty sure have been compromised are the ones pushing hardest for those treaties. So, ask yourself: why would someone want to bring all those factions *together*? Don't assume it's an outside group, either. It could be one of the member states of either organization, trying to manipulate the rest. Or it could be some totally unaffiliated bad actors. We just don't know enough yet."

Lonrah reappeared through a door in the rear of the lab. I am not a master of Hylar body language, but I could tell immediately she was troubled. "This is very weird," she said. "How much do you know about the Arborec?"

I shuddered. "More than I'd like." I'd met a lot of species in my business. None had disturbed me so much.

Azad went *hmm*. "They're just about the most *alien* aliens we're actually able to talk to, even compared to the Creuss. Sapient plants. It's pretty impressive they managed to build spaceships, honestly."

"They're native to a planet called Nestphar," Lonrah said. "They're plants, yes, but it's more than that – the Arborec are composed of many species, some ambulatory and some not, with many grown for specialty purposes, but all symbiotically and telepathically linked by a planet-spanning cloud of spores. They call that connection, shared by all living things on the planet, 'the Symphony'. It's better to think of the Arborec as a conscious ecosystem than as a species in the conventional sense."

"So, your basic hive-mind sort of thing," Azad said.

"In a sense, but they can send out representatives who have a sort of temporary individuality, called the Letani. Those are the ones who make contact with the rest of the galaxy's inhabitants, and they carry a miniature version of the Symphony with them, generating their own spore field to allow communication beyond Nestphar. When they return home, I gather they're sort of absorbed, giving the Symphony the knowledge and experience they acquired while they were elsewhere."

"I was in a room with an Arborec representative, once, during a trade negotiation," I said. "It was one of the most unnerving experiences of my life." (And not just because the Arborec barely understand the concepts of ownership or property.) "The Arborec can't speak, by word or gesture – they only communicate telepathically among themselves. So, when they have to talk to other species, the Letani acquire corpses, and reanimate them through some… fungal alchemy, and use those bodies as mouthpieces. It's horrible. Talking to the *corpse* of someone, puppeted around, their original consciousness gone…"

"Yeah, I've heard of those, the Dirzuga," Azad said. "Somebody I know had to… eliminate one, once, to disrupt… well, it's not important. The Dirzuga was using a human body. My colleague stabbed her, and the Dirzuga didn't even react, just stared at her, and then said, 'This is a new sort of conversation'. So, then he started cutting off limbs and stuff, and the Dirzuga kept saying 'Please provide context for this interaction', and honestly it came down to fire and acid to clean the whole mess up." She crossed her arms. "I assume we aren't just sharing our best weird alien stories, though. What's in the canister, Lonrah?"

"Spores," she said. "An engineered variant of a fungus called Arzuga. I've only seen a sample of Arzuga once before, collected by a friend of mine and smuggled to me in the greatest secrecy."

"What's so special about Arzuga?" Azad asked.

"That's the fungus the Arborec implant in the brains of dead bodies to create the Dirzuga."

THE FAITHFUL IV

Doctor Astin Canner wasn't sure what the point of this autopsy was. He stood over the exam table in Shilsaad Station's tiny pathology lab, a space he'd hardly ever had to use before, and which, in his opinion, he didn't really need to use *now*. The victim, some Xxcha cultural minister, had been killed by a spear, which was unusual, but easy to diagnose. The weapon was thrust down vertically through the victim's main body cavity with substantial force, causing massive trauma to the minister's internal organs. The crime hardly needed further investigation, at least when it came to determining cause of death.

But that intense-looking Hylar, Jhuri, had insisted on a thorough examination of the body, and the Xxcha Kingdom officials had agreed, so here Canner was, taken away from his usual duties. Canner was human, but an expert in xenobiology, which was a good fit for the head of medicine on Shilsaad Station, where so many aliens congregated, although the full range of his expertise was seldom called upon. Usually, all Canner had to deal with was bumps, bruises, and the sort of viruses that liked to spread through convention center crowds. Doing an autopsy was admittedly a diversion, but not a pleasant one. He *liked* things simple. That's why he'd taken this job.

There were some intriguing peculiarities, though. The toxicology screening had turned up drastically elevated hormonal levels in the victim's blood – mostly chemicals associated with pleasure and calm, oddly enough, rather than the fear-chemicals you would have expected in someone who was murdered by a spear. Canner didn't know what to make of that data. Jhuri said the victim had exhibited odd behavior, possibly even signs of dementia, on the evening of his death, so maybe there was some sort of issue with brain function that indirectly caused the anomalous readings.

Canner's bone saw whirred, and in a few moments, he had the top of the victim's skull ready for removal. He twisted and pulled away the bone cap, set it aside in a sterile tray, and angled the light to shine on the minister's exposed gray matter.

He hadn't seen the inside of an Xxcha's head since his fellowship, but even someone with no experience at all would have known something was *very* wrong here. For one thing, the gray matter wasn't gray. The dead Xxcha's brain was threaded through with green tendrils, almost mossy in spots, and there were tiny red bulbs nestled in some of the folds. The bulbs looked like miniature versions of the air sacs produced by some aquatic plants like kelp. He let out a low whistle. "Poor creature would have been dead soon even without a spear through the neck," he murmured. It must be some sort of exotic fungal infection. He'd certainly never seen anything like it. Perhaps he could write a paper about it…

Canner picked up a shining steel probe and gently prodded one of the sacs – and it burst with a surprisingly loud "pop", spraying gold-green motes all over Canner's face shield. He gasped and stumbled back. Spores! Some kind of fungal infection! He had his transparent shield, and a mask over his mouth and nose that should keep him from breathing anything in, but damn it, the spores were in the *air*. He'd have to seal the room, go into quarantine until the spores could be identified, notify his second-in-command to take over operations until–

"Welcome, doctor," a voice said from beneath the autopsy table.

Canner frowned and crouched, and station security chief Kote Strom shimmered into visibility. "What are you doing here?" Canner asked.

Kote launched herself at him, knocking him to sprawl on the floor. She knelt on his chest as he gasped, more shocked than hurt. She wrenched the face shield from his head, then tore the mask from his face.

He rolled over – she was tiny, and her weight couldn't hold him – and scuttled away on his hands and knees. "What are you *doing*? There's an infectious agent in the air here!"

"There's a *sacrament*," she said.

Canner looked at her, baffled and alarmed. She was holding up his face shield, still dusted with spores, with its speckled surface parallel to the floor. She took a deep breath and blew across the shield, sending motes spiraling into his face – his nose, his mouth, his eyes, his mucous membranes.

Canner fell back, coughing, as black spots danced before his eyes. He had to get to the eye wash station, had to take anti-fungal drugs, had to notify his colleagues–

<Shhhh,> a voice – or chorus of voices? – whispered in his mind. The sound was faint at first, but soon became clearer. *<Be at peace. We are your guides.>*

Canner slumped to the floor as his brain unleashed its finest chemical vintages in a sustained rush. Once, before medical school, Canner had accepted a mysterious pill from a man he had a desperate crush on, some designer drug that stimulated the pleasure centers of the brain, and he always remembered it as the most profound physical enjoyment he'd ever experienced, an all-consuming sense of total euphoria.

That pill was nothing compared to this. This was bliss, and peace, yes, but it was also *purpose*.

<Will you be faithful?> his guide whispered.

"Oh, yes," Canner said eagerly. "Anything."

<We are engaged in a great work.>

"What can I do to help?"

<You can start by getting rid of all this evidence,> the guides replied.

CHAPTER 5
SEVERYNE

Severyne Joelle Dampierre – captain of the Barony of Letnev battleship *Grim Countenance*, famed fugitive hunter, highest-ranking survivor of the catastrophic expedition to the World of Light, rising star in the military – sat in a meeting and stifled a yawn.

She sat in a room full of other Letnev captains – most older than her, and largely a bunch of puffed-up toads, deeply uncomfortable in the presence of people they couldn't order around, since they spent most of their time wielding (locally) absolute power on their ships. She despised nearly all of them.

The one advantage was that they weren't with her in person, so she didn't have to smell their various exhalations. Severyne was actually in her ready room on the *Grim Countenance*, immersed in a holographic representation of a meeting room in a government installation beneath the city of Goz (which was already deep underground) on the Letnev homeworld of Arc Prime.

When the call went out to so many high-ranking members of the military, speculation among the captains was rampant. With the imminent formation of the Legion, the treaty organization led by the Letnev in response to the Greater Union, there must be major plans afoot. Were they finally launching all-out war against the Federation of Sol, aided by their new allies? Had the Baron crafted a plan to seize control of Mecatol Rex, and re-establish the empire the Lazax had incompetently lost so long ago? Was the prototype Dark Star – the newest generation of the Letnev version of the Gashlai War Suns – finally operational, and ready to lead the Legion vanguard into battle? Severyne had even found herself caught up in the whirl of speculation.

The lights brightened – though not much, of course; they were Letnev – and a figure shimmered into view on the stage at the front of the room. A mechanical voice said, "Prepare for a briefing by Lady Immental, high admiral of the Prime Fleet."

Everyone straightened up in their seats, even Severyne. Admiral Immental was her boss, but she'd never actually received an order from the woman, or indeed even seen her. In rank, Immental was just below her cousin, the Baron, in the government's hierarchy. If she was here to address them directly, something serious was going on.

The admiral was tall for a Letnev, her back perfectly straight, her uniform so pristine it might never have been worn before, her expression a cool snarl of disdain. She stood before them, hands clasped behind her back, and surveyed the gathering, her eyes resting a moment on each and every one of them. When those dark eyes fixed on Severyne, she had to resist the urge to squirm a little in her chair, even though the woman was actually millions of kilometers away. Severyne seldom found anyone impressive, let alone imposing, but Immental was everything a Letnev official should be, and everything Severyne wished to someday be herself.

"Captains," Immental said at last. "The balance of power in the galaxy is about to radically shift. You've all heard about the negotiations I'm leading on the Baron's behalf, to form a treaty organization with our natural allies against our most persistent rivals. You are here now to learn the part *you'll* play in the Legion's formation. But first… a few words about why the Legion is so necessary."

This should be interesting. Opinions among Letnev officers were sharply divided on the issue, and as far as Severyne could tell, most of the military was opposed to the idea of a treaty. The Letnev were the most capable, most accomplished, and most powerful civilization in the galaxy – why would they bother to ally themselves with lesser races? Severyne herself was relatively open to the idea, having collaborated usefully with people of other species on occasion in the past, but even she was a bit leery of the proposed members of the alliance.

"You might ask yourselves, why would we ally ourselves with lesser races, including factions we've clashed with sometimes in the past?" Immental said. "The reason is simple: our enemies gather against us." Images began to appear on the screen behind her: the twin worlds of Jor and Nal, superimposed with the head of an impassive Hylar; the hated blue-green globe of Jord, overlaid with a sneering human face; the yellow haze of the three principal desert worlds of the Emirates, beneath a hooded Hacan figure, canines bared; the twin planets of the Xxlak star system, a beaked Xxcha squinting disdainfully above them; and finally the shrouded orb of Moll Primus, surrounded by a pirate fleet, inset with a scheming human face and a shifty Yssaril: the Mentak Coalition and the Guild of Spies. "These are the likely members of the so-called Greater Union, led by the Mentak." Her voice dripped with the appropriate scorn. "Their propaganda *claims* it is a strategic alliance, to allow them to join forces against new threats in the galaxy." She shook her head. "They cite fairy tales of the Mahact Kings and the Titans, and rumors of strange new aliens in the outer systems. Obvious nonsense."

Severyne still didn't shift in her chair, but it took some effort. The Mahact Kings… well, she found the idea of their return plausible. Not so long ago, she'd been lost in a deathtrap of a world *created* by one of the Mahact, and where there was one, there might be others. As for the mysterious aliens, she'd heard the same rumors of misshapen monsters descending on remote worlds and outposts. The creatures described in those fragments sounded disturbingly like the entities she'd glimpsed through a rift in space when the rogue scientist Thales attempted to create an artificial wormhole. She'd turned in her reports on those events – slanted, certainly, to show her in the best light, but accurate in their essentials – so Immental must know the threats she cited weren't "obvious nonsense", though the details were highly classified.

Immental paced back and forth, boots clicking. "Why do they gather together, then, if not to defend themselves against these imaginary threats?" She stopped and looked at the holographic audience expectantly.

Severyne knew the answer the admiral probably wanted and was never above a little light favor-currying. "To strike against us!" she called.

Immental nodded. "Precisely. The human government on Jord has long sought to destroy us, in retribution for the humiliations we heaped on them during our many past conflicts, but they could never hope to defeat us alone. We believe the humans reached out to their cousins on Moll Primus and convinced the Mentak Coalition to organize this alliance under a flimsy pretext. The Xxcha still hold a grudge against us for our occupation of Archon Ren. The Hylar are envious of our technological prowess and wish to take our secrets for their own. The Hacan want to seize our colony worlds and all the natural resources and trade opportunities they represent. The Guild of Spies, well… they work in the darkness, and they hate us for our mastery of the dark. All of them despise us, and the true goal of this Greater Union is nothing less than the *annihilation of the Barony itself.*"

Now the captains murmured, and a few even cursed and pounded fists on their desktops. Severyne made a point of looking just as outraged as the rest, but she didn't truly feel it. She had no fondness for the Federation of Sol *or* the Mentak Coalition, but she thought the admiral's presentation of the facts was at least as slanted as Severyne's own reports tended to be. Still, the Greater Union would certainly be a threat to Barony interests, even if their actual focus wasn't the devastation of Severyne's entire species. Maybe Immental was just trying to get the captains fired up.

"Can we defeat such an alliance?" Immental said. "Can we stand against such an array of implacable enemies when all their resources are ranged against us?"

"Yes!" screamed one of the captains, and this set up a whole round of shouting: "For the Barony!" "Letnev reign supreme!" "Death to the humans!" Immental looked at the room coolly, her own thoughts impossible to guess, and gradually the hubbub wound down and the room settled into silence.

A silence that Severyne broke. "Of course we can't defeat them," she said. "They would crush us."

Now *every* eye in the room was on her, some of the older and more hidebound of the captains (which was a relative term – the default was old and hidebound anyway) gasping or scowling or muttering about disloyalty and treason.

"Elaborate," Immental said.

Severyne sighed and stood up. "We'd make the war *cost* them, of course. No one is better at inflicting pain on enemies than the Barony. But if all five – six, counting the Yssaril – factions truly focused on annihilating us, we would have no hope. The balance of power in the galaxy depends on *imbalance*. No one faction is capable of gaining the upper hand over the others. We have all spent the past several decades busily consolidating power and looking for advantages, even small ones, that would allow us to exert sufficient power to force the other nations into accommodation – to turn them into vassal states, so that we might eventually found a new empire to rival the one the Lazax squandered. If our enemies have changed tactics, and are instead *cooperating*, that balance will shift. The Letnev could destroy any one of those factions, with effort. We could, I daresay, destroy two of them, though it might ruin us in the process. But five? With the help of the spies as well?" She shook her head. "I'm sorry, admiral. You will find no greater patriot than myself. But if we were strong enough to crush the Hacan, the Hylar, the Xxcha, the humans, the Mentak Coalition… we would have done so already, and the Baron would be at ease on the throne of Mecatol Rex."

That was heresy, more or less, Severyne knew, but she was ultimately supporting the admiral's point, so she wasn't worried about ending up in a reeducation facility.

Well. Not *overly* worried.

"Captain Dampierre is correct," the admiral said simply.

If the Baron's cousin and their superior officer said something, it probably wasn't treason, so the captains all murmured their agreement. "Well said," the one seated nearest Severyne grunted, though he looked like he could taste his own stomach acid while he said it.

"Faced with such a threat, how can we defend ourselves? How can we retaliate?" Immental looked straight at Severyne.

The answer was, depressingly, obvious. "We form our own strategic alliance," she said. "We form the Legion."

The admiral smiled, thin-lipped, but on her face, it was a show of strong emotion. "That's correct."

The captains cheered. Severyne resisted rolling her eyes. They really did bend whichever way the political winds blew.

"Who will we allow to join our Legion? While negotiations are still ongoing, we can confirm some. First, the Embers of Muaat. No one hates the Hylar more than the Gashlai, and they were eager to join us – they know once the Barony is destroyed, they would be the obvious next target for the Greater Union."

And we could use their War Suns, Severyne thought, since the Dark Star program seems to be infinitely delayed.

"The Sardakk N'orr, too, have no love for the squids, and they have also agreed to join us." Various nods and sounds of approval arose in the audience. The Sardakk N'orr were savage monsters, of course, but their skill at violence was unmatched, and it was better to be on their side than against them. "We have also received a… surprisingly positive response from the L1Z1X."

That set off a different tenor of muttering. They'd heard *rumors*, but to have them confirmed was still troubling. The L1Z1X were a mystery in many ways, but they were generally held to be abominations, the corpse of a once-great race brought to lurching life with cybernetic implants and other horrific forms of technology.

"I know," Immental said. "I find the notion of cooperating with such creatures… unpleasant as well. But the L1Z1X have secrets of Hylar technology that could prove useful, and they have a history of enmity with the Hacan that we could exploit. When faced with a threat like the Greater Union, we must be open to extreme measures." Immental went on, "You assembled captains represent the best and darkest of the Barony military. You will each be sent on a mission to meet with representatives of our new Legion. You will finalize any outstanding points of negotiation – I will provide guidance as necessary – and will further act as honor guards and escorts for the leaders of the other factions. We will all gather for a summit on Arc Prime, attended by the Baron himself, who will sign the treaty and formalize the alliance."

Severyne wrinkled her nose. Babysitting duty? Dreadful. She just hoped she wasn't getting sent to the L1Z1X. The rumors said the people they murdered were the *lucky* ones.

"You'll all receive your individual orders shortly," the admiral said. "You are dismissed."

The captains flickered out of existence as their holographic connections were severed… but Severyne's connection stayed live. The image of the admiral approached her and said, "Captain Dampierre. A word?"

"Yes, admiral." Severyne attempted to remain serene as she rose and stood at attention. Being singled out by an officer of Immental's rank was either wonderful or terrible; there was no inbetween.

"You showed an admirable gasp of the political and strategic realities today," Immental said.

"I have spent some time in the field, and among our enemies," she said. "It gives me a broader perspective than the one visible solely from the captain's chair."

"Indeed. It's your field work that interests me now. I have a special mission for you."

Severyne felt a stir of interest. She'd expected to be sent on a mission of diplomacy. This was potentially more intriguing.

Immental said, "Two days ago, at a Greater Union meeting, a Hacan trade ambassador named Terrak brutally murdered a Xxcha cultural minister. Terrak subsequently escaped with the aid of unknown co-conspirators. You will take the *Grim Countenance,* capture this Terrak, and bring him to me."

Severyne waited, but there didn't seem to be anything else forthcoming. "If I may ask, are there any further details you can share?"

"You will be sent a dossier, though I have already presented you with the essentials."

Severyne composed her next words carefully. Speaking to an officer of Immental's rank was like piloting through an asteroid field scattered with hidden mines. "Of course, admiral. I am honored to be selected for this mission and will fulfill my duties with zeal. But in order to ensure my success, it would be helpful if I knew… some things that might not be included in a standard dossier."

The admiral fixed her with a gaze that could have melted tantalum. Seen up close, there were little flecks of green in her irises. The fidelity of the simulation was really remarkable. "Such as?"

"Admiral, if I may. You chose me for this mission because I have some experience hunting down fugitives, I assume?"

She sniffed. "Some rate your abilities in that area highly. You tracked down the defector Shelma and her associate Thales, yes, for all the good that did. What a disaster." The admiral clucked her tongue. "And you managed to prevent the Xing girl from escaping our grasp, though, again, that mission hardly ended in glory for the Barony."

Interesting. Severyne had gone from favored captain to barely tolerated failure in the span of two sentences, and all because she'd dared to ask a question. That just made her want to know the answers more, but she made every effort to appear abashed and defensive. "Those failures could not be laid at my feet, admiral. I acquitted myself as well as–"

"Yes, yes." Immental flapped a dismissive hand. "The general assessment is that you kept both situations from getting any worse than they might have, though I personally prefer officers who triumph, rather than those who merely mitigate disasters."

"I myself would enjoy an assignment where triumph was possible, admiral," Severyne dared.

Immental stared down her nose at Severyne for a moment… and then her lips quirked in the suggestion of a smile. "You were forced to correct the errors of incompetent superiors on both those missions, weren't you, captain? Fortunately, this time, *I* am sending you on the mission, and I am anything but incompetent."

Severyne was curious about the admiral's attempts to manipulate her emotionally by whiplashing Severyne in and out of favor. Most officers of her rank wouldn't have bothered.

Immental said, "To answer your question: yes. You are the closest thing we have to an expert at hunting down fugitive aliens. What's your point?"

"The reason I am good at what I do is because I make a study of my targets, admiral. I knew Shelma from her time on the facility where I served as security chief, and learned all I could about Thales, and the Coalition crew assigned to protect him. As for Bianca Xing… my success with her was based *entirely* on my understanding of her psychology. Essentially, admiral, if you want me to capture this Hacan, I need to know everything I can about him – including why we're interested in him in the first place. If he murdered this Xxcha, and disrupted a summit of the Greater Union, it seems we should thank him, rather than pursue him."

The admiral looked around, then gestured for Severyne to come close. Immental removed a small black box from her pocket and pressed a button. A low hiss filled the air, and the light seemed to shimmer. "Anti-surveillance technology," the admiral explained. Severyne wondered who she could possibly be keeping secrets from in a bunker on Arc Prime. "Is your location shielded against surveillance?"

"Certain," Severyne said. That was true. No one surpassed her in the logistical applications of paranoia.

"What I'm about to tell you is classified above your level, Captain Dampierre, but I am authorized to reveal the information on a need-to-know basis… and you make a good point. You'll do better work with more data. We want the Hacan because he works for us. He has been a spy in our employ for many years. We sent him to disrupt the Coalition. But rather than follow our escape plan, he fled the station in the company of an unknown individual. We don't know who Terrak is with, or, more importantly, who they *work* for. He is trying to escape not just his murder charges, but to escape his responsibilities to the Barony, and, of course, we cannot abide that."

Severyne nodded. "I understand."

"Terrak will doubtless use resources unrelated to his Barony connections to flee. But perhaps knowing his nature will offer you some insight into his character that will prove useful."

"If you tell me *why* he worked for the Barony, it will," Severyne said. "His motives will reveal much about his nature. Did he help us for ideological reasons? Because we had some leverage over him? Or because of greed?"

"Greed, of course," the admiral said. "We paid him for information. You know how corrupt the Hacan can be."

"Of course, admiral. I'll begin my pursuit immediately."

"We'll send all available information to your ship." Immental turned off the shimmering field, gave Severyne a nod, and severed the holographic connection.

Her ready room flickered back into visibility, and Severyne allowed herself a sigh. It was rather early in the day to become tangled in a web of so many falsehoods.

Severyne sat in her ready room sipping moss tea while Undercommandant Voyou – who had, improbably, become her closest confidante on the ship, which was also to say, in her life – processed the information she'd just shared with him.

"I'm fairly sure I'm not supposed to know data classified at that level," Voyou said.

"I'm fairly sure 'classified data' was a lie anyway," Severyne said.

Voyou took that in, then nodded. "Could you explain why you think so, captain?" Severyne liked Voyou because he was competent, loyal, and had no desire to stab her in the back (literally or metaphorically) in order to take her job. He was also the only other survivor of the disastrous mission to the interior of the World of Light, the Mahact death trap where Severyne's *last* mission involving aliens had gone horrendously wrong. The two of them had gone through something together, and come out the other side alive, and while Severyne certainly didn't *need* Voyou, she could grudgingly admit it was nice having someone around to listen while she talked.

She said, "The admiral claims the Hacan was in our employ, spying on the Greater Union for money. Does that seem plausible to you?"

"Greed is a reasonable explanation for treachery, especially among the honorless, duplicitous races," Voyou said.

Severyne waved her hand. "Yes, of course, but think it through. Would Terrak have murdered another delegate at the summit, merely for money? This was no covert assassination – it was a showy, public mess. Would he kill someone that way, knowing it would destroy his life and make him a fugitive?"

"I see. What good would his wealth do him if he had to leave his entire life behind?"

"Yes. Plus, our Baron… well… the government purse strings…"

"Our rulers are not famously generous paymasters, you mean," Voyou said.

"Exactly. Let's say this Terrak is solely and fanatically motivated by a desire for money. A corrupt Hacan trade ambassador would have many other opportunities to get rich, from graft, skimming, and kickbacks. Anyway, he fled from us after the killing, so if it was murder for hire, he didn't even come to collect his balance. It makes no sense."

"If the admiral had said we'd co-opted this Terrak through blackmail, that would be more believable," Voyou said. "But even then, what secret could we know about him that would be worse than becoming a fugitive murderer?"

There was a reason she kept Voyou around. He was intelligent, and was willing to say things to her that might get him in trouble if a political officer overheard. "Yes. I think the admiral had to answer me on the spot, and just fell back reflexively on the stereotype of Hacans as obsessed by commerce. Her explanation makes perfect sense, if you don't think about it for more than two seconds." Severyne sipped her tea. "Oh well. This isn't the first time we've gone on a mission based on incomplete, or indeed outright false, information."

"The fact that Admiral Immental herself lied *personally* to your face, virtually speaking, is even rather flattering," Voyou said.

She very nearly smiled. "I am appropriately complimented. At any rate, it doesn't matter – the orders are lawful, and the mission is clear. We will track and capture this Terrak."

"And… perhaps… find out the truth along the way," Voyou said.

She sipped the last of her tea. "Well. Sometimes such things are unavoidable."

THE FAITHFUL V

"I speak for the Baron," Immental said.

<To a point,> the voice whispered. *<But we wish him to speak for us.>*

"The level of paranoia the Baron has regarding security… he is so very cautious. Even I can't get close enough to administer the sacrament, and we've known each other since we were children. His guards are never alone, so they can never be corrupted."

<There will be opportunities to turn the Baron, during preparations for the summit on Arc Prime.>

"Perhaps, guides," Immental said. The summit would involve changes in routine, which could provide opportunities. But the idea of taking action that might be construed as – well, as *treason* – was powerful enough to cause a twinge of discomfort, even in the sea of bliss that accompanied her devotion to the guides.

Her masters sensed her hesitation. *<You fear that your cousin would not want this. You fear that he would kill you if he knew your loyalty was to us, and not him.>*

"Yes, guides," she murmured.

<But think of it this way, faithful one: you are giving the Baron a great gift. Isn't your life better now, in our care?>

Immental thought of her existence before she took the sacrament. Striving, scheming, and the exercise of naked ambition; playing her rivals against one another; jockeying for her cousin and supreme leader's favor; amassing as much power for herself as possible. In retrospect, all those enterprises were hollow and empty. Immental had wanted to rule, but now, she knew, true pleasure came from service and devotion. "My cousin… he serves *no one!*" She spoke with the force of revelation. "He has no idea the joy that could be his! If the bonds of duty mean anything to me, then surely it is my duty to share the wonder of the sacrament with my Baron!"

<Yes. You will give him our blessing, and the great work will proceed.>

CHAPTER 6
AZAD

"They're turning people into *Dirzuga?*" Terrak said, obviously horrified at the prospect.

Azad shook her head. "No, that can't be it, or not exactly. You've seen Dirzuga – you can tell they're corpses. They don't blink, they don't breathe, they don't move or speak naturally at all, and they don't seem to remember who they were in life. They're basically ventriloquist dummies. I know Qqurant was a little out of it at the meeting, but he wasn't a walking corpse, and plenty of the people who've been compromised don't show any level of impairment at all."

"These samples aren't *exactly* the same as the spores I've seen before, anyway," Lonrah said. "They've clearly been altered, though I couldn't say exactly how."

"Give me your data," Azad said. "I need to make a call."

"To *whom?*" Terrak demanded.

"This isn't some personal crusade I'm on," Azad said. "I'm going to report to my bosses and see what they can make of all this." Lonrah transferred the data, and Azad sent it via encrypted channels, then ducked into a side room for privacy.

When her boss made contact, Azad said, "The mind-control stuff is made of Arborec spores, it looks like. Some modification of the process they use to reanimate corpses. Maybe the spores have been altered to turn *living* people into puppets, but puppets who retain their memories and at least a semblance of their personalities."

Pause.

"Yeah, I spiked you the data, so you can get your science types to look into it."

A longer pause.

Azad sighed. "Well, no, I doubt it's the Arborec. I mean, they're *plants*, they barely even interact with the rest of the galaxy, right? They trade with us, but otherwise, they just keep to themselves, doing… plant stuff. They don't strike me as likely prospects for the secret masters of the galaxy. Nobody even thought about inviting them to the Greater Union *or* the stupid League of the Beleaguered the Letnev are putting together. The Arborec are a power, sure, but they're not a major player in the great game of empires, and nobody gets the sense they really want to be."

A much longer pause.

Talking to the boss was so weird, mostly because it wasn't really *talking*. Azad could have carried on her half of the conversation without saying a word aloud, but she didn't trust her thoughts to stay inside the lines. Better to put her thoughts into words, and be sure she conveyed what she intended, and nothing else.

She grunted. "Sure, but it can't be that hard to get your hands on the spores. The Dirzuga are around. They probably leak the stuff out of every orifice. And once you get some spore samples, they're just plants. Anybody could grow more, tweak them, do some genetic engineering… I don't know. My shortlist would include the Hylar, since this sounds a lot like mad science, and the Brotherhood of Yin, since it sounds like *biological* mad science. The Letnev have a lot of experience with mushroom stuff, too, don't they? This discovery doesn't narrow down the 'who' much, admittedly, but it's something. At least it's a 'how'. We can stop looking for evidence of android duplicates or light-based mirror-neuron manipulators and focus on the spores. You can get your people started on some kind of anti-fungal antidote, right?"

Brief pause.

"Ha, really? What a busy little bioweapons lab you must have." Azad had worked for a lot of people and organizations, but her current employers kept surprising her with the depth and breadth of their resources.

Pause.

"Sure, sure, tweaks, tailoring, I get it. How long?"

Pause.

"Hmm, all right. Terrak's friend can probably produce whatever we need if you send a recipe."

Pause.

Azad was getting a headache. Long conversations with the boss tended to cause those. "That's fine. I enjoy Terrak's company, he's got more contacts than I do in this sector, *and* he's highly motivated to uncover the conspiracy. Why?"

Pause.

Ooh, that idea was nasty, even by her standards. She didn't like it. Fortunately, she had operational authority, so she could brush the suggestion off. "Ha. I mean, yes, we do need a subject, but Terrak has uses beyond acting as a talking petri dish. We can find someone else to experiment on. People will do anything for money. Terrak might object to the testing protocol, though."

A longer pause.

Azad chuckled. "True enough. Once he finds out the alternative is even worse, I'm sure he'll go along."

CHAPTER 7
TERRAK

When Azad returned from the restroom, I said, "Lon thinks, given a few weeks, she might be able to engineer an antidote–"

Azad waved her hand. "Not necessary. I've got people working on the problem, and they'll have answers for us a lot sooner than that."

Lon swiveled in her exoskeleton. "What are you talking about? We just found out what we're dealing with, and even with more resources than I have here, tailoring something to combat these spores will take time."

Azad sat back down on her crate and grinned. "If you're starting from zero, sure. But my employers have already been working on ways to counteract Arborec spores. That's how the big plant monsters *talk*, after all, and you know how much the military likes being able to disrupt enemy communications. You can't use signal jammers on people who don't use signals, so my employers explored other possibilities. They already have a way to neutralize Arborec spores. Of course, they'll have to tweak the recipe, since these spores have been altered, but they seem confident they'll have a working recipe soon. I told them we had access to a compounding pharmacy and chemical supply company all rolled up in one; that's you, Lonnie. Name your rate. Feel free to charge us double for the rush job. My bosses can afford it."

I wondered who her bosses were. The Federation of Sol seemed most likely, still; they were always anticipating future conflicts. My more immediate concern was my colleague's safety, though. I turned to Lonrah. "Are you willing to do this?" She was a professional, and no stranger to shady business practices, but this was a different order of complication, and I wanted her to be sure she understood what she was getting into. "You didn't ask to be dragged into my troubles, and you've already helped so much. The forces arrayed against us seem formidable." Azad scowled at me, but I ignored her.

"I'll do it for you, Terrak," Lonrah said. I felt an unfamiliar surge of warmth. She paused. "Also… for triple my usual fee."

Azad laughed. "It's not my money, so sure. We've got some time to kill, though. What do you do for fun around here?"

"Immersive sims, usually," Lonrah said. "It gets a bit cramped down here, so I like to spread my pseudopods in simulated realms."

Azad said *hmmm*. "There's a non-zero chance we'll be attacked by hostile forces at some point, so I shouldn't fly off into a virtual reality right now."

I closed my eyes briefly. I knew there was a possibility that agents of the conspiracy would track us down and take violent action against us, but hearing Azad state that so matter-of-factly made the dread less abstract and more concrete.

"I would rather not have my lab attacked at all," Lonrah said.

"I don't want to cause you any trouble," I said. "I don't think anyone can connect me to you, but… it's not impossible. Maybe we should find another place to wait, Azad."

Azad shook her head. "If the bad guys – or the local authorities, who are probably working for the bad guys, whether they know it or not – figure out you two know each other, they will come *here*. Wouldn't you rather have us around to protect you if that happens, Lonnie?"

"I don't want some military melee in my laboratory, Azad. I'd rather be able to truthfully say that you aren't here, and I don't know where you are, if the authorities ask."

"Ha. OK. Maybe we can work out a compromise. I get the feeling you're operating a little bit in the gray, legally speaking. So, is there a back way out of here? A secret escape tunnel? Something we can slip out of, if the opposition shows up at your cunningly disguised front door?"

"There is," Lonrah said. "But it's made for me to use as a last resort, so… its usefulness to you depends on how long you can hold your breath."

I groaned. I never liked getting wet. Hacan aren't meant to *submerge*. But if it was a choice between discomfort and death – or, worse, the loss of self and subjugation to the will of another – it was no choice at all, really.

We passed the time waiting for Azad's employers to reach out in various ways. Lonrah studied the spores, which she found fascinating and horrifying. I brooded over news reports about my perfidy, and composed messages to friends and colleagues I didn't dare send. Azad slouched in a corner with headphones on, watching a screen and occasionally giggling. I wondered what she was watching. Zany spaceship crashes? The galaxy's funniest reactor meltdowns? People cooing at cute alien fauna, which subsequently ate them?

Finally, she took her headphones off and said, "I've got a recipe for you, Lonrah. Can you make this?"

Lonrah trundled over in her exoskeleton and took Azad's tablet, peering at the information on the screen. "Oh, I see, they're combining an array of anti-fungals with hunter-killer phages… oh, that's intriguing, there's a neural growth stimulator, I guess to repair any–"

"Do you have the *ingredients*?" Azad said.

Lonrah looked up. "Hmm? Oh. Yes. What I don't have I can synthesize in a few hours. I have no idea if this will actually work on your… spore-zombies, or whatever… though. It seems plausible, but you won't know for sure until you test it."

"Can't you just see how the cure affects the spores you have here?" I asked. "From the canister?"

Lonrah fluttered a pseudopod. "Sure I can, but killing the spores in a jar is different from killing them in someone's *brain*, without also killing, or even damaging, that brain in the process. I could destroy the spores with acid or bleach, but I wouldn't recommend injecting that into an infected person's brain."

I slumped. "Ah. Right. I have no idea how we can test—"

"What's the delivery mechanism?" Azad cut in.

"It will need to be injected," Lonrah said. "Into a vein, not a muscle."

"I was hoping for an aerosol," Azad muttered. "Failing that, a needle I could just jam anywhere at all. But it is what it is." She stood up. "OK, Lonnie, you get to work making the magic juice. Terrak, let's you and me take a walk."

I frowned. I knew by now that Azad always had plans within plans, and that she wasn't reliable about sharing them in advance, or even while they were happening. I'd never liked surprises, but *Azad* surprises were even worse. "Why? Where are we going?"

"We're going to see someone who can help us with our testing problem. I think, for now, we can still leave by the front door."

We walked the industrial streets, and Azad wasn't any more forthcoming about where we were going, or why. "I didn't think you knew anyone on this moon," I said.

"Oh, I make friends real easy."

"What aren't you telling me?" I demanded.

"About a million things. Listen, it'll be easier if I just show you."

"Easier for *whom*?"

"Easier for me, Terrak. I'm always about making things easier for me."

We wound our way through filthy alleys, occasionally passing vagrants – humans bundled in rags, mainly, but also a Hylar splashing in a dirty puddle and muttering to himself, and a couple of Saar sitting on splintered pallets who bared their teeth and hissed at us until I growled at them and sent them scurrying into the shadows.

"Is your contact homeless?" I asked when we walked through a little settlement made of tarps and packing crates built along the back of a warehouse.

"Probably," Azad said. "That would be ideal." I would say that's when I started to have misgivings, but that would belie the fact that I'd been having those all along. I was horribly afraid she intended to abduct a homeless person and infect them with spores just so she could test the antidote. If she tried that, I would have to stop her, and it would be both the end of our partnership and spoil my best chance at proving my innocence.

We turned a corner and then walked around another warehouse, until we reached a weed-filled vacant lot. Azad grabbed my arm. "Right there. I think that's our guy."

She indicated an elderly, slow-moving Hacan wearing a blue tarp for a cloak. He was hunched over, prodding at the ground with a stick. He grunted, leaned forward, and picked up the butt of a cigar someone had discarded, sniffed it, and put it in his pocket.

"Go on," Azad said. "Say hi."

"Why?"

"Because it's polite," she said. "Don't be prejudiced, Terrak. Any of us could end up where that guy is."

I sighed. Azad was clearly not in the mood to be helpful. I approached the old fellow and said, "Hail, elder."

He startled, then scowled, then growled. "My patch," he snarled. "Mine."

I showed my palms in a gesture of peace. "I don't want your…" I lowered my hands. This was ridiculous. "Azad, what is the meaning of this? Why are we talking to this man?"

She sauntered over. "I thought it'd go more smoothly if initial contact was made by someone from his own socio… cultural… somebody who's the same species, is what I mean, but I guess he's just generally cranky. Well, who can blame him?" She reached into a pocket, and I moved between her and the elder.

"I won't let you hurt him, Azad." If she had a stun gun or a tranquilizer gun, she'd have to hit me with it first, and at least then the old fellow would have a chance to run for it. I have no illusions that I can save everyone, or even *anyone*, but I had to at least try when the potential victim was right behind me.

Azad cocked her head, then chuckled. "Let me sidebar with my associate for a moment, sir." She stepped a little distance away, and I had no choice but to follow. "You thought I was going to take a test subject by force. I get it. I'm not even opposed to the idea in principle, but just logistically, who wants to drag a huge unconscious guy all the way back to the lab? I've got money. He's got desperation. We're a good match."

"I will not be party to this, Azad. You want to infect an innocent person with a mind-control drug? That's monstrous, even if you *do* offer to pay him."

"We're going to cure him after we infect him, Terrak. Come on. That's the whole point. We have to make sure this recipe works. Look, maybe you're feeling some sort of species solidarity with this old wreck, and I understand that, but it's really for the best if our subject is Hacan. Maybe the spores in that canister are multi-purpose and work on anything with a brain, but it's possible they were tailored for your specific biology, so our test subject should be as close to your biology as we can get."

"The idea is monstrous, Azad."

She sighed. "OK, Terrak. Just so you know, refusing to help means you're volunteering to be the test subject yourself. Infecting you is actually the obvious choice – these spores were meant for you in the first place. My employer suggested using you right away, but I said, 'Nah, Terrak's useful, we're in this together, we're a team'. Did I make a mistake? Are we *not* a team?"

I thought things over and raised my hands. "We are a team. I just... wish there was another way." Maybe the old Hacan would refuse. If not... I'd have to figure out something else.

"Hey, I'd love to get an ethics committee involved in this too, but we're on the run and we have limited resources. I understand your reluctance, I really do, but the old guy will be *fine*. My people do good lab work. Tomorrow he'll be good as new and a whole lot richer. OK?"

It wasn't OK, but I stepped aside.

"G'off my patch," the old Hacan snarled at us again.

Azad stepped toward him and said, "Sir, we're recruiting paid test subjects for a clinical trial. I can't go into *too* many details, but it's an experimental drug designed to combat certain cognitive deficiencies."

The old fellow glared at both of us. "Can't do those trials anymore," he muttered. "Won't take me. Not healthy enough. Pre-existing whatnot. Mucks up the results." He turned his head and coughed raggedly, as if to demonstrate.

"That is not a problem in this case," Azad said. "It's a study about mental function, and you seem sharp enough to me."

"The drug is *very* experimental," I said pointedly.

"Which is why the payment is *very* high." Azad reached into her pocket again and came up with a credit stick, then pressed the button to display the shockingly high balance. The Hacan leaned forward, squinted, gasped, and then tried to snag the stick, but she danced out of the way. "Now, now," she said. "You get this one when we get back to the lab, and you get another one just like it after the trial."

"How long will this take?" he said.

"What, you've got somewhere to be? I don't know, probably not more than a day."

He looked from her, to me, and back to her. "You'd pay me that much for a *day*? What's the catch?"

Azad surprised me. She said, "You could die. Your brain could melt out your ears. I'm not saying it isn't a gamble, but that's why the payoff is so big."

He looked at me, and suddenly, there *was* some fellow feeling in his eye; this was a human, making an outlandish offer, but I was a fellow son of the desert, and he wanted to believe he could trust me. "Is this for real?" he said.

I sighed. "Yes. Especially the part about you maybe dying." Except it could be even worse – he could be possessed by a mysterious conspiracy, his volition removed, his will lost forever.

He laughed, harshly. "I deal with *maybe dying* every single day. I'll do it. Where do I sign?"

Azad smiled. "We're more streamlined than that. Paperwork just slows us down. Let's just take a walk back to the lab."

"Who is *that*?" Lon asked over her hidden speaker when we reached the utility box.

"A volunteer," Azad said. "Bring us down."

The Hacan smelled rather ripe in the open air, and worse in the jammed confines of the elevator. We took him into the lab, which he glared at suspiciously.

"You can just hop up on this table here," Azad said.

"You gotta put me under," the Hacan said. "I get medical anxiety. I'm not drug-seeking. People always say that. I'm just going to freak out if you put needles in me and I know about it."

"Why are we putting needles in him?" Lonrah said, trundling over in her exo-suit.

"We're going to dose him with the spores, and then see if our cure works on him," Azad said.

The Hylar was silent for a moment. "Sir? Did they explain…"

"Brains melting out my ears maybe? Yeah." He hopped up onto the table and reached out a hand. "Credit stick now."

Azad handed it over, he pocketed it, then lay down on the table and closed his eyes. "I've done worse for less," he muttered.

"See? A volunteer," Azad said. I stood nearby, arms crossed, glowering.

"I still don't know if I'm totally comfortable…" Lonrah said.

"Nothing is more important to me than your comfort," Azad said. "Wait, no, I meant, nothing is *less* important to me." She stalked over to me, beckoning Lonrah, until we were out of the old Hacan's earshot. "Don't you two get it? Some unknown group is out there using *mind control spores* to infiltrate major governments. Terrak, your buddy the cultural minister didn't have his claws on the levers of power, but he routinely met with people who did. That means he could have sprayed military or political leaders in the face in some executive bathroom, or slipped some spores into the punch bowl at a fancy party, or who knows what? We have no idea how widespread this conspiracy is, and we've only identified a few high-ranking officials in various factions who we're *pretty* sure have been co-opted, based on behavioral analysis and other info. If we can cure them? That changes everything. It means we have a chance at stopping them, exposing them, and actually saving people. We don't know what their plans are, but traditionally, conspirators who infiltrate the highest echelons of intergalactic power don't do it for *nice* reasons. Yes, shooting this guy in the face with spores and then jamming experimental drugs into his veins isn't nice, but he volunteered, and sometimes we have to be nasty to save the galaxy. Really, I am being as *nice as I can be* under the circumstances."

"I feel like I should clap," I said. "What a rousing speech. I understand the stakes, Azad."

"I'd prefer wholehearted effort over grudging cooperation, but whatever." Azad flapped her hand. "Put this guy under and put him in some kind of containment and then we can introduce the spores."

"We don't know how the spores work," I objected. "What if he links up with some malign intelligence and attempts to murder us all? Or spies on us? We don't know how any of this works."

Azad rolled her eyes. "Hence the sedation. I was going to suggest it if he didn't. We'll strap him down, too, just in case he wakes up with super-spore-strength or something. I'll even cover his eyes so they can't use his eyeballs for remote viewing. Terrak, don't worry. I secure people all the time. I've got this."

"And what if he dies?" I demanded again. "We have no idea if this will work!"

"He took the job," Azad said. "Again, the job is *yours* if you'd rather take it instead. Otherwise, shut up."

I shut up.

Once the old Hacan was in blissful sedated slumber, I helped Lonrah set up a tent of overlapping sheets of transparent material over the table. Azad eyed the arrangement critically. "Is that thing spore-tight? I really don't want to inhale any of this stuff."

"I work with dangerous pathogens on a regular basis," Lonrah said. "I cured—"

"Yeah, yeah, I get it. Sorry." She shuddered, a rare sign of weakness, and I wondered if the reaction was genuine, or just another layer of subterfuge. Maybe Azad was subterfuge all the way down. "I just get a little twitchy when it comes to stuff like this. Germs, viruses, spores, all that kind of thing. Give me an enemy I can blast or punch or bite, you know? These invisible tiny monsters don't play fair."

"I think we're ready." Lonrah wheeled over a glass box with manipulator arms on the inside and hooked it up to a flexible tube that led into the tent. "We can trigger the canister inside the containment chamber, and the spores will be pulled into the tube and the tent. And then… well, we'll see what happens."

"We think whatever happens works fast," Azad said. "We're really curious about how exactly it happens, though. Do the spores just make the subject pliable, and then a handler gives them instructions? Do the spores somehow *program* a set of behaviors? Do the victims have a mission, but personal agency when it comes to fulfilling that mission? Or is it some kind of telepathic thing?"

"The Arborec communicate through their spore fields," Lonrah said. "They can only talk to each other when there's a certain concentration of spores in the vicinity. That's the whole reason they have the Letani – those have a degree of individuality, but more than that, they're mobile communications platforms, carrying a cloud of the spores with them wherever they go. But these spores aren't exactly the same as the ones the Arborec use to communicate, or the ones that activate the Dirzuga, so these victims might not be… networked the same way."

"Enough speculation," Azad said. "Let's make observations instead."

Lonrah crossed the room, opened a secure container, and removed the canister of spores. She turned toward the tent and the sleeping innocent within. As I watched her, I thought, *There is a better way.*

Then I snatched the canister from her, darted across the room to her bio-waste incinerator, opened the hatch, and dropped the spores inside.

THE FAITHFUL VI

Lillith was losing money every minute she spent on Shilsaad Station, which was generally the worst thing she could imagine, but in this case, it wasn't even the most annoying part of the situation: the confinement was. She paced back and forth in her (admittedly lovely) rooms, waiting to be released. The whole station was under lockdown, with no indication of when it would end. Her own government wanted her to be released, and the other factions were doubtless applying pressure too, but murder investigations took precedence.

She'd expected this to be a pleasant and profitable meeting, and an opportunity to set up even more lucrative deals she could finalize during the Greater Union summit on Moll Primus, and instead it had turned into a nightmare of death and absurdity. Harmless, charming old Shelly dead, and Terrak blamed for it? What nonsense, how absurd–

"I understand you spoke to the Hylar investigator, Jhuri," a voice said, and Lillith spun. There was an Yssaril standing in the corner of her bedroom, watching her with those enormous eyes.

"How did you get in here?" There were representatives from the Guild of Spies at the summit, and some as part of the Mentak delegation, but she didn't remember meeting this one. There were often Yssaril around you *didn't* see, though.

"I'm the head of security for the station, Kote Strom." She gave a little bow. "I can get in everywhere."

Lillith realized she *had* met Strom before, during the immediate chaos of the killing, but hadn't recognized the Yssaril out of uniform. Why *was* she out of uniform, and wearing that plain gray coverall? "What do you want? I've already talked to the authorities and told them everything I know."

"That's why I'm here. Because of the answers you gave to certain questions." Strom sidled a bit closer to her. "I understand you told Jhuri that Terrak was innocent, and that Qqurant seemed disoriented at the party the night he died."

"Yes? So?"

"So, I'd like you to… refine your statement. Tell Jhuri you were mistaken, speaking out of misguided loyalty, and that you've realized the error of your ways, and accept that Terrak committed this heinous crime."

Lillith snorted. "You want to tamper with the investigation? Under some circumstances I might be amenable, if the price was right, but Terrak is my friend, and Shelly was, too. I'm afraid this is one case where my conscience makes me incorruptible."

"Oh, I'm not proposing a transaction." Strom came a little closer still, in that sideways, insinuating way.

Lillith understood that sneaky people had their uses – she'd made a lot of money from information acquired by the Guild of Spies – but it was still unsettling to have someone sidling up to her like she was a pocket to be picked. She moved a step away.

Strom said, "I want you to willingly change your story, because you know it's the right thing to do."

"Why would I do that?"

"Look what I have here." The Yssaril held up a closed hand.

Did the little toad have some real proof that Terrak was responsible? Lillith didn't want to believe it, but she leaned down to look just the same.

Kote uncurled her fingers, revealing… an empty palm. "What do you think of this?"

"What, of nothing at all?"

"It's small, but it's there." The Yssaril leaned forward and blew across her own palm, and Lillith blinked at the puff of air in her eyes. The room was dim, but she'd seen something swirl off Strom's hand. Oh, stars, she'd heard about people being poisoned by radioactive dust, but surely such an attack would poison Kote too? She staggered back as her head began to spin–

<Shhh,> a chorus of voices, speaking as one, whispered to her. *<Be faithful.>*

Lillith's body trembled. How had she ended up on the floor? It didn't matter. Nothing mattered except the clouds parting in her head, letting the light suffuse her. She moaned as she pressed her cheek against the carpet, which suddenly felt soft as velvet.

Lillith heard Strom say, "I will need more of the sacrament, guides, if you wish me to recruit further. I had to harvest that dose from the ambassador's brain, and it was barely enough."

<All will be well,> the voice whispered to Lillith, and she knew in every fiber of herself that it was true.

CHAPTER 8
FELIX

"There are almost a hundred moons in this system, and only half of them are even developed," Felix said. "Why did this Facilitator go to the trouble of building a space station? It's not like there's a shortage of available real estate."

"Paranoia," Ggorgos said. "Desire to control every aspect of the environment. Long-term security, too. It's not uncommon for polities to retroactively declare that any natural object in a given system is its sovereign territory, which doesn't go well for the people already living there."

"I suppose if you can afford it, building your own station is worth it for the peace of mind." Felix was beginning to relax a bit around Ggorgos, and Ggorgos, for her part, had become a bit more talkative and slightly less intense since they'd reached the Rantula system. *She's just driven*, he'd decided. Now that they had a lead to pursue, Ggorgos had a place to direct her dark energies, rather than letting them spill over onto everyone else.

They'd received permission to dock their shuttle at the Facilitator's station, which saved them the trouble of insisting with threats of missiles and so forth. That was good. Making too much noise would draw the attention of the local authorities, such as they were. The Rantula system was ostensibly independent, a loose affinity group of moons with a distinct commercial lean toward "specialty goods" – things that could be produced here and exported elsewhere, unencumbered by pesky local regulations. The rumor was that the Hylar supported the system on an off-the-books basis, but there was also a nearby wormhole that led to Letnev-controlled space, so maybe they had a hand in things here, too.

The Facilitator didn't provide specialty goods; they provided specialty services. "Concierge to the stars," Felix muttered. "They say the Facilitator can get anything, for a price."

"It's a sound business model," Ggorgos rumbled. "If there's something you *can't* get, you simply claim the client can't afford it, and your mystique remains undiluted."

Only Felix and Ggorgos were on board the shuttle, as far as the Facilitator knew. Calred had wanted to come, expressing an unusual degree of eagerness to do field work. He was usually happy to stay on the ship, but he said after serving as a transport service for Jhuri, he was eager to do something more interesting.

Felix had to leave Calred behind, though. If he'd come along, that would have left the *Temerarious* uncrewed… since Tib Pelta was secretly on board the shuttle, too, ready to slip unseen and stealthily through the station to search for signs of their rogue Hacan.

"The station looks like a sort of black crystal knife, doesn't it?" Felix enhanced the view of the Facilitator's facility as they approached. The station was a simple structure: a central spike, with the pointed end at the bottom (relative to their position), with a wider disc surrounded by windows near the top. The whole structure was oddly faceted and threw off counterintuitive sparkles in the illumination of the star, the planet, the nearby moons, and even the shuttle's lights.

Ggorgos grunted. "Like the ceremonial daggers your ancestors used to cut out the hearts of sacrificial victims."

"*My* ancestors?" Felix said. "That doesn't sound like my ancestors. I'm sure my ancestors were lovely. Wait. Why do you have conversational knowledge of ancient human murder techniques?" Actually, upon reflection, that didn't really surprise him.

"I used to be a xeno-anthropologist," Ggorgos said.

That *did* surprise him. "Why did you go into that line of work?"

"I sought to refine the Kingdom's diplomatic efforts by developing a deeper understanding of the alien cultures we dealt with."

"Really. If you don't mind me asking, how did you, ah… transition from that field of study into your current line of work?"

"I had several difficult interactions with the alien cultures I studied," Ggorgos said. "Those experiences altered my worldview. Now I pursue diplomacy by other means."

"I see." Felix looked at her scars, and wondered what other marks might be hidden beneath her carapace. That kind of trauma would have altered his worldview, too.

The station's docking system sent approach instructions, which the shuttle's computer handled more or less automatically. They approached the center of the spike, where a forcefield wall covered a small hangar bay. The station wasn't immense, but it was pretty big for something owned by a private individual. Of course, it was possible the Facilitator was some kind of consortium. No one really knew.

The forcefield shifted to admit them, and then the shuttle settled to the floor inside. A Rokha wearing a white dress with gold cuffs – a striking look against her void-black fur – approached, arms raised in welcome, as Felix and Ggorgos descended the ramp. Felix looked around, and there was the Naaz, a tiny four-armed creature zipping around on a small hovering platform. The Rokha and Naaz species were closely intertwined, almost symbiotic; they shared a homeworld, and even when they went abroad in the galaxy, you seldom saw one without the other.

The Rokha bowed. "Honored guests. I am Makena." She gestured to the Naaz. "This is my partner, Craic."

The Naaz zipped past them – Ggorgos swiveled to keep an eye on her – and then said, in a buzzing voice, "We did not realize you were bringing a third guest. Hello, friend Yssaril."

Felix managed not to wince. The little Naaz must have some kind of tech that enabled her to see through the natural camouflage of Tib's people.

Tib shimmered into visibility and stepped forward to stand beside the others. "This is my first officer," Felix said. "She decided to come along at the last minute."

"All are welcome!" Makena said. "Come. The Facilitator has only a brief window open in their schedule, but when they heard both the Mentak Coalition *and* the Xxcha Kingdom were requesting an audience, how could they possibly refuse?"

"Very civic-minded," Felix said. Ggorgos grunted, and Tib snorted.

"Please, follow Craic."

As they walked through the hangar, Felix was keenly aware that they were being led by an alien floating in what might very well be a miniature mobile weapons platform, while there was an immense humanoid panther at their backs. "I'm surprised you didn't check us for weapons," Felix said.

"We politely asked you not to bring any," Makena said. "Surely we can trust you?"

"Of course," Felix said. "I just wouldn't expect you to rely on trust."

"I am not worried overmuch for my own safety," Makena said. "And the Facilitator is in no danger from any of you."

While it stung a bit to be dismissed as a threat, Felix had to admit that the Facilitator had something of a home court advantage here.

They were led to a rather nice lift, all dim lights and glittering black walls. "What is the station made of, if you don't mind me asking?" Felix said as they ascended. "I've never seen material like this before."

"Something developed by the Gashlai," Makena said.

"They use this material as armor on their War Suns," Craic added.

"The Facilitator helped the Embers with a… tricky negotiation… and this was the reward they offered," Makena said. "I gather it's the only significant quantity of the material in existence outside Gashlai space."

"I'm surprised people aren't constantly trying to chip off samples to take home for analysis," Felix said.

"That would be rude," Makena said. "Our clients are never rude to the Facilitator."

"It's also rather resistant to chipping," Craic said.

The elevator doors opened, and they were ushered into a round, windowless room, completely empty except for a chest-high (to Felix) pillar of the same glittering, faceted material. "The Facilitator will see you now," Makena said.

Felix looked around. "Will we see the Facilitator?"

Makena and Craic didn't answer, but simply withdrew to the elevator. The doors closed behind them.

"The walls are full of scanners," Ggorgos said, peering around through her artificial eye. "That pillar is entirely opaque to my sensors, though."

The pillar said, "Let a mysterious entity keep a few secrets, would you?" The voice was soothing and neutral, neither low nor high, and clearly artificial.

"Where are you transmitting from?" Ggorgos said.

"No preliminary niceties? All right. It's hard to say where I'm transmitting from. The signal bounces around a bit, and I'm always on the move. It's so hard to keep track. If you'll allow *me* the niceties: welcome, Ggorgos Skal of the Kingdom of Xxcha, and Captain Duval and First Officer Pelta of the Mentak Coalition. I have had no contact with Terrak since the commission of that heinous crime."

"How did you know why we were here?" Felix said.

"Knowing things is half my business, captain. In this case, though, I didn't even require informants, just deduction. You're an international delegation of military personnel, dispatched from a space station where a murder was committed by one of my known associates. I was expecting you sooner."

Ggorgos said, "Did you help arrange Terrak's escape?" Her voice was flat, without particular menace, which was somehow even more menacing than a roar would have been.

"I did not."

Felix sighed. "If you knew we were coming, and knew you had nothing of value to tell us, you might have saved us the trouble of actually coming all this way."

"You *will* tell us everything you know," Ggorgos said. "Your station is impressively armored, but you made the mistake of letting me *inside* it. And–"

"And your carapace is full of drones loaded with horrifying quantities of explosives, yes, I know."

Ggorgos seemed taken aback. "You should not be able to scan beyond the surface of my shell."

"I can't, but I can scan information archives. You were once captured on a Letnev science colony, thoroughly searched, and taken to their secure facility, which promptly exploded. You walked out of the wreckage. You've done the same trick a few other times. Given the patterns of the explosions I've studied, there were multiple ignition points, and in most of those cases you didn't have time to place multiple bombs yourself, so: drones. Threatening me is silly. If you disrupt my operations, *so* many powerful people will be very unhappy with you. Anyway, it's unnecessary. I am susceptible to bribes, not threats."

Just like Jhuri said. "So, you *do* have useful information?" Felix said.

"I do. You have identified two known associates of Terrak's in this system: myself, and an agricultural importer-exporter, correct?"

"You answer *our* questions," Ggorgos said. "You don't get to–"

"Yes," Felix said. Ggorgos glared at him. "That's right. I assume you know something we don't?"

"There is a third associate."

"Tell us who." Ggorgos was vibrating, with rage or eagerness or probably some combination of the two.

"If I give you the information you need to find this associate, what will you give me in return?"

"If you obstruct the lawful investigation of the murder of a member of the Xxcha Kingdom–"

Felix rubbed his forehead. "Ggorgos, a word?" He turned his back on the pillar, and Ggorgos glared before stepping up beside him.

"There's no *privacy* here, Duval. Why are you turning your back on a pedestal with a speaker inside it?"

"For my own psychological comfort, Ggorgos. This is a situation that requires finesse, and possibly a bit of charm, and the soft skills of an equitable negotiation. Perhaps you should let me handle things?"

"Handle them *swiftly*." Ggorgos stomped across the room to stand by Tib Pelta, who was staring off into space, looking bored, which probably meant she was thinking hard.

Felix turned and faced the pillar. "Facilitator. What would you like in exchange for this information?"

"I'm so pleased you asked!" the Facilitator said. "I'd love to have the full unredacted dossier on the Thales affair."

"I have no idea what you're talking about," Felix lied. "Pick something else."

"That's all I want that you can offer. Unless… you'd like to offer me a favor?"

"What kind of favor?"

"Mmmm… for this information… a small favor. Nothing that would compromise your mission, threaten your life, or endanger the interests of the Mentak Coalition."

"I am going to need something more specific than that, Facilitator."

"We're talking about you taking a package from one place to another and making sure no one looks at the contents, including yourself. That sort of thing. You wouldn't even have to go very far out of your way. A secure courier with military credentials is a useful thing to have."

Well, if it was only smuggling, that was fine. "Agreed. Who's the third associate?"

"I am not entirely sure."

"Bombs," Ggorgos said in a voice like lead. "I have so many bombs."

Felix winced. He wouldn't have offered a threat of mass destruction at this juncture, but Ggorgos clearly had her own way of doing things.

"Please, don't be so dramatic," the Facilitator said. "The vagueness of my information is the reason why you only had to offer me a *small* favor. Here's what

I know. Terrak tried to cover his tracks, but he often went to Huntsman's Moon when he visited the system. He visited an industrial area on the outskirts of the northern city, but I can't narrow his destination down beyond a two-kilometer radius. It's hard to track someone on foot in such a desolate neighborhood, and since no one was *paying* me to spy on Terrak, I didn't allocate very many resources to the problem. There are half a dozen plausible groups or individuals in that area he could have been meeting with – various engineers and scientists doing work that would be frowned upon in more closely regulated parts of the galaxy."

"That's all you know?" Felix had been hoping for something more. The exact location where Terrak was hiding out, and the details of any security he might have, and why Amina Azad was involved in all this, and, well, lots of other things, really, in a perfect world.

"I just narrowed your search area from seventy moons to six addresses on *one* moon. I'd say I know plenty. I can offer more, though: Terrak frequently visited the moon immediately after meeting with the importer-exporter. I have a high degree of certainty that Terrak met this unknown associate *through* the fruit seller, so if you go ask *him–*"

"Let's go," Ggorgos snapped. "If you have further details, Facilitator, send them to our ship." She stomped out.

Felix bowed to the central pillar. "A pleasure doing business."

"One last thing, captain?"

Ggorgos and Tib were on the elevator, and the doors closed when Felix turned back to the pillar. "What's that?"

"Terrak is probably innocent," the Facilitator said. "I have run multiple simulations, and my confidence level is around ninety-two percent. Terrak is mildly corrupt, yes, but he's much smarter than most people realize. Anyone can be a killer, if pushed the wrong way, but it's highly unlikely Terrak would have committed such a violent crime in such an obvious way."

"People have psychotic breaks," Felix said. "There are crimes of passion. It happens all the time."

"My model accounts for those possibilities, captain. But do people who have psychotic breaks then stage unlikely jailbreaks with the help of unknown associates?"

"If he's not the killer, then he was framed. Who'd want to do that?" Felix said.

"I have no idea."

Felix sighed. "I'm just supposed to apprehend Terrak and bring him to justice. The courts can determine his guilt or innocence."

"If he's being framed, captain, it's because someone wants to discredit him, or remove him from the field of play in a game you don't even know is happening. That means Terrak knows something, or can do something, to disrupt the plans of people who are happy to commit murder. Terrak is frustrating those efforts by going on the run. If he is the victim of a conspiracy, do you think the conspirators will give him the opportunity to testify in court, or even tell his version of events to the authorities? My models suggest he is likely to meet with an accident soon after you apprehend him. What precisely *are* your orders, captain?"

Felix frowned. "I told you. Apprehension. Terrak won't come to any harm while he's in my custody." There were all sorts of mysteries and uncertainties swirling around this business, but Felix was sure of his *own* orders and intentions, at least.

"Mmm. Even if you don't intend to do him harm yourself… can you say the same, with certainty, about everyone else on your crew?"

Felix scowled and, like Ggorgos before him, stomped out of the room in a foul temper.

The fruit seller – a Hacan so physically imposing he made Calred look slight – went flying across the warehouse and crashed into a pile of crates. Wood splintered and broke, and small round green fruits rolled across the warehouse floor. Felix picked one up, took a bite, and frowned. "Sour," he said, and spat it out.

"It's a *lime*, Felix," Tib said. "I'd think you'd recognize it. You see slices of them on the rim of your glasses all the time."

"I assumed it was some sort of exotic fruit," he said. "Since this is an alien fruit warehouse."

"Limes *are* alien and exotic to the Hacan."

"Point," Felix said. They were standing off to one side while Ggorgos ran the… interrogation, for want of a better word.

Ggorgos advanced on the fruit seller, who stood up, groaning. The Hacan put up his fists, still game to fight, though he was a bit unsteady on his feet. "I will ask you again," Ggorgos said. "Tell us the identity of Terrak's other contact."

"You can't come into *my* place of business–"

Ggorgos moved faster than Felix would have expected for someone so heavily armored and shoved the Hacan sprawling back into the crates. Felix wondered if there were cybernetic or chemical enhancements at work. Or… maybe *all* the Xxcha could move that fast if they wanted to, and simply didn't bother, since they were generally an easygoing and phlegmatic culture?

"Answer me," Ggorgos said. Some of the faceted panels of her exocarapace slid open, and small sleek drones rose up, hovering, pointing various nozzles and barrels at the Hacan.

The fruit seller closed his eyes and covered his head. "All right!" he shouted. "It's a Hylar chemist, her name is Lonrah!"

"Why would Terrak go see a chemist?" Tib said.

"No clue," Felix said. He was trying to convince himself he didn't *care* if Terrak was innocent or guilty – that the issue was outside his mission parameters. Unfortunately, Felix had never been good at staying strictly within mission parameters. "Her name is on the list of possibilities the Facilitator gave us, though."

"Back to the ship!" Ggorgos said, and headed toward the shuttle.

Felix and Tib walked over to the fruit seller and helped him up. "Sorry about all that," he said. "You obviously shouldn't call this chemist and warn her, or my Xxcha colleague will be very unhappy."

"Who cares about that?!" he bellowed as he rose. "Look what she did to my warehouse! And my employees!"

Felix looked around. There had been a certain amount of… wastage, in terms of smashed crates and pulped fruit. And a couple of the warehouse laborers, who'd attempted to act as ersatz bodyguards, were moaning on the floor by the door, though they didn't seem irreparably damaged. Felix said, "You can invoice the Mentak Coalition Embassy on Rex for any damage or medical costs. You can pad the invoice by, oh, fifteen percent, and I'll vouch for its accuracy. All right?"

The fruit seller stood to his full height, nearly a meter taller than Felix, and gazed down at him. He showed his canine teeth. "Twenty percent," he said.

Back on the *Temerarious*, they filled Calred in on their adventures, and set a course for Huntsman's Moon. "Will you let me come for *this* mission?" Calred asked. "I've got a new rifle I haven't had a chance to point at anyone yet."

"I've had enough field trips for the day," Tib Pelta said. "I'll stay on board. Also, I doubt Ggorgos has a tactical plan in mind that would make use of my special abilities. She's more run-and-gun than stealthy sneaking."

Ggorgos was standing at the navigation panel, glaring at it, as if doing so would make the ship go faster. "Your security officer may join us," she said. "His marksmanship record is adequate."

"*Adequate*?" Calred said. He held several fleet records for sharpshooting.

"You have to understand, coming from her, that's the highest possible praise," Felix said. "I *dream* of being adequate."

"I need to make a call." Ggorgos left the bridge.

"I should fill Jhuri in on things, too," Felix said, and headed to his ready room.

"The minister's autopsy didn't turn up anything unusual," Jhuri said.

"Did you expect it to?" Felix said. "I thought, well, big spear through the neck, it all seemed pretty clear."

"I was troubled by the reports of the victim acting strangely before the murder. I thought there might be something there, but we got nothing from toxicology, and no unusual findings from the pathologist, so… maybe the ambassador was just having an off night. Something strange did happen, though. I was questioning the other guests about Terrak and met a woman from the Federation of Sol who's known him for years. In our initial interview she told me, very adamantly, that Terrak was never violent, had a wonderful relationship with the victim, and was certainly innocent of the crime."

"I heard much the same from the Facilitator," Felix said.

"Let me finish. This woman, Lillith, came back to me a few hours ago and said she had a confession to make. Now she claimed that, actually, things had been terribly strained between Terrak and Qqurant, and they'd had a serious falling out. She didn't know the details, but said Terrak and Qqurant had gone from friendly to frosty to vicious in recent months. She said she'd overheard arguments between them that included threats of violence. She told me she'd lied earlier because Terrak was an old friend, and she didn't want to see him in trouble, but that her conscience had been bothering her, and compelled her to come forward with the truth. Her conscience! She's a *trade* representative!"

Not a type famed for their ethical inflexibility, Felix thought. Combined with the Facilitator's claims, it was looking more and more likely that the official narrative about Terrak wasn't the whole story. "What do you think it means?" Felix said. "Was Terrak framed? Did someone reach out to Lillith, and, what, bribe her to change her story?"

"A murder that brazen and obvious is a truly stupid crime," Jhuri mused. "And everyone agrees Terrak is anything but stupid. Slightly corrupt, a bit lazy and self-indulgent, but a sharp operator all the same. I don't know what's going on, Felix, but I'll be very interested to hear what Terrak has to say when you get him in custody."

"Assuming Ggorgos doesn't shoot him first."

"See that she doesn't, Felix. I'll be in touch if I find out more." Jhuri cut the connection, and Felix went to prep his gear for their visit to Huntsman's Moon.

CHAPTER 9
SEVERYNE

The *Grim Countenance* had just transited the wormhole and set a course for the nearby Rantula system when Severyne received a call from the admiral.

"We have new information," Immental said without preamble. "Our rogue asset is currently believed to be on a small satellite called Huntsman's Moon, visiting a chemist."

"It will take us a few hours to reach the moon," Severyne said. "But we'll scramble a landing party as soon as–"

"No, the Mentak Coalition has a team closer, attempting an apprehension. You will take up a hidden position near the moon. Be prepared to capture Terrak if the Coalition team fails."

"And if they succeed, should I take Terrak away from them?"

"That won't be necessary. We have… other plans in place if the Coalition captures him."

Severyne wondered what that meant. There was no love lost between the Barony and the Mentak Coalition. Did Immental have double agents embedded with the Coalition?

"Just head for the moon and await further instructions," Immental said.

"As you command, admiral."

Immental's face vanished from the screen. Severyne looked across her desk at Undercommandant Voyou. "What do you think?"

He considered the question with his customary seriousness. "I think we are operating with too little information for me to think anything much at all."

"I don't like serving as the safety net for a bunch of Mentak pirates. But we do what we must." She waved her hand. "Go set things in motion. Let me know if there are any noteworthy developments."

A few hours later, Severyne's research on Terrak was interrupted by a call from Voyou on her private priority comms. "We're in sensor range of Huntsman's Moon, captain. We've identified the Mentak Coalition vessel, a cruiser that's currently registered as a diplomatic transport ship. It's odd, but it seems you set a flag in the system? You wanted to be notified if we ever encountered this particular ship–"

Severyne groaned. "Don't tell me it's the *Temerarious*."

"Are you familiar with the ship, captain?" Voyou asked.

"You might say that," Severyne said. "I stole it, once."

THE FAITHFUL VII

"Filthy Gashlai." Captain Rayonner ran a finger beneath the collar of his uniform, sweat running down his face. "Why do they keep it so abominably hot in here, eh?"

Undercommandant Misericore said, "The Embers are savages, sir." She did her best to look uncomfortable, too, though since taking the sacrament she didn't feel extremes of heat or cold as much as she once had. She didn't feel extremes of any kind, really: she was too fully at ease in the sure knowledge of her purpose. Misericore was, ostensibly, a representative of the Barony of Letnev, here to escort the Gashlai leaders to their summit on Arc Prime… but she was really here in service to the guides, to fulfill her small part of the greater plan. She burned with the desire to please her masters.

Since traveling through the wormhole to the Gashlai system, she'd lost intimate contact with the guides, but they'd warned her that would happen: she was in wild lands, now, beyond their caring cultivation. Once she returned home, she was assured, she would once again hear them whispering in her mind, and in the meantime, she had her instructions. The guides didn't have a presence in this system, apart from Misericore and a couple of other faithful elsewhere in the delegation. For some reason, the Gashlai were incompatible with the sacrament. She felt so very bad for them.

Captain Rayonner strode to the small observation window in the wall of this bare room on the tiny, cramped station. Misericore dutifully followed him, hands clasped behind her back to mirror his own posture. This station was where the Embers met with the more flammable biological species, since their home planet Muaat was inhospitable for most organic beings.

"Look at those things." Rayonner was gazing at the War Suns in orbit above the burning sphere of Muaat, far beneath them. The Suns were dark, thorny orbs, surrounded by swarms of lesser ships coming and going. In truth, the War Suns seemed less like ships at all, and more like space stations – cities of the void, but cities full of weapons, capable of moving great distances under their own power. Other species had variations on the theme – the Barony's own Dark Star program was their latest iteration – but the Gashlai War Suns were legendary. "This whole place used to be shipyards for the Hylar, when the Gashlai were their slaves. The Embers took the technology and turned it against their old masters. Ha. The squids should have known better than to play with fire, eh?" Misericore murmured agreement.

The large doors at the end of the room slid open, and three Gashlai entered, wearing their golden Ember suits. In truth the containment systems were less like suits of armor and more like small, armored vehicles, bristling with sensors and manipulators. The Gashlai were creatures of energy, and small windows set in their armor revealed the glow of molten matter and the flicker of flames within. Misericore wasn't sure if the placid faces gazing at them from each suit were the true faces of the Gashlai, or masks of some kind. The one in the lead spoke in a voice like water sizzling on coals, "You may call me Molash. I am a Flame Warden and speak with the authority of our leaders."

"Molash?" Rayonner scowled. "We're supposed to meet with, eh, what is it, Molt, ah, Sha, lah, ta–"

"Cease defiling my true name," the Warden interrupted. "It does not fit properly in your wet mouth. I have offered you a name of convenience – one that you *can* pronounce."

Rayonner stiffened. "Yes. Very well. I have come to formally extend the Baron's invitation to your ruling tribunal to join us on Arc Prime for the upcoming summit, to sign our treaty and join the Legion as a member state, with full partner status. In the meantime, my crew includes various negotiators and lawyers and advisers and the like, so we can settle all those little details in advance of the meeting."

The Warden said, "I know why you are here. My leaders have agreed to this alliance, in principle, but if I may make a personal observation… it is unlike the Letnev, to seek alliances. The Wardens have found the entire process rather surprising."

Rayonner said, "The Baron, in his wisdom–"

Misericore cleared her throat. Rayonner looked at her. "Captain, if I may?"

Rayonner was here because of his legendary military status – at the helm of the *City Imperishable* he'd razed the colony world of Pax Agricola – but Misericore was present because of her diplomatic skills, and because she'd studied the Gashlai. "Carry on," the captain said.

"May your flame burn eternally, Warden," she said, in her best approximation of the Embers' language. No Letnev could duplicate their tongueless tongue perfectly, but she had practiced.

The Warden made a hissing sound that Misericore knew was a chuckle of amusement. "And yours as well, Letnev. Or, what do your people say – may the dark embrace you?"

"Just so, Warden." She cleared her throat. "It is true that the Letnev are a proud people, and accustomed to making our own way in the galaxy. But we face an unprecedented threat. Our old enemies, the humans, have joined with your ancient foes, the Hylar. We know the humans seek to spread throughout the galaxy until every world is subsumed in their cultural hegemony. We also know the Hylar care only for the expansion of their technological power. The humans view the Letnev as an obstacle to their expansion. The Hylar view your people as a natural resource, theirs to exploit, which is even worse."

Molash sizzled in agreement.

"The Hylar have joined forces with the humans, expanding their coalition, and it is only a matter of time before they seek to regain that which was lost. This Greater Union will bring overwhelming force to bear, and pick off their old rivals, one at a time… unless we can form a united front and strike them first. The Gashlai have been unable to take revenge on the Hylar for their crimes against your people, because your forces are too evenly matched. If you join with the Barony, and our other allies…" She let a small smile touch her lips. "Then you will see the seas of Jol and Nar *boil.*"

"We have heard these explanations before, of course," Molash said. "But it is meaningful to us, to hear them in person, where we can better judge your sincerity. I… find your position compelling." The Warden turned to face Rayonner. "We are also pleased that such a distinguished figure was sent to bring this message and escort our leaders to Arc Prime."

"Eh?" Rayonner said. Anything that didn't directly involve warfare usually failed to keep his attention for long.

"I have studied the burning of Pax Agricola with great interest, captain," the Warden said.

Rayonner brightened, as he always did when the subject of past glories, or the prospect of future ones, came up. "Oh, you liked that, did you? Let me tell you something that *wasn't* in the reports, I think you'll enjoy this…"

Rayonner didn't care about anything but war, Misericore thought, which was very sad; she pitied anyone who lacked her own sense of purpose in service. The guides said there was no need to give Rayonner the sacrament, though.

War, after all, was the only thing they *needed* the captain to care about.

CHAPTER 10
TERRAK

Azad groaned. "Terrak, you idiot, that was *so stupid*, I cannot get over how stupid that was."

I expected her to scream at me, punch me, or even shoot me, but after that initial complaint, Azad was all business. Either she was incredibly pragmatic, or she was saving her revenge for later. I greatly hoped it was the former. She turned to Lonrah. "Do you have any samples of the spores left? Can you, I don't know, replicate what was in that canister?"

"No," Lonrah said. "My analysis was destructive. The samples I took are wholly inert."

"Right. Any chance of recovering something useful from inside that incinerator?"

"It wouldn't be a very good incinerator if there was. The spores… they're all gone."

"I hope that warm glow of righteousness I assume you're feeling right now keeps on comforting you when the entire galaxy is engulfed in war, Terrak," Azad said.

"You said you knew the identities of compromised individuals." I'd given this some thought, in the moments before I acted. I couldn't ruin her plan without proposing an alternative.

Azad frowned. "Yeah, we have a list of a few, with a reasonably high degree of certainty."

I spread my hands. "Then let's go test the cure on one of them. If it doesn't work, we're no worse off than we are now, and if it does work, we've made actual, measurable progress against our enemy, and enlisted new allies to our cause, since I'm sure they'll be grateful to be free. That's a much better plan than injecting a random subject snatched off the street."

Azad rubbed her temples. "The problem, Terrak, is that highly placed government officials who've been co-opted by an enemy conspiracy are *harder to tranquilize and strap to a table* than random subjects snatched off the street."

"If your work was easy, Azad, everyone would do it. Plus, I am perfectly comfortable helping you execute this plan, so it's better for our partnership."

"I should execute *you*. 'Partnership'. What do you bring to this operation, besides impulsiveness and unreliability?"

"For one thing," I said, "I can get us on a ship and off this moon."

"I can, too," Azad said.

"My way won't involve theft or murder."

She wrinkled her nose. "OK. That's probably better." She rolled her neck around on her shoulders. "All right. I'm not big on revenge, or on holding grudges. I'm a believer in dealing with the world as it is and changing with the conditions on the ground instead of complaining that everything isn't exactly how I'd like it to be. That said … if you screw me around like this again, Terrak, I will turn you into a fur rug. Do you understand me?" There was no grin now, no playfulness, and I glimpsed a core of ice within her.

I nodded. "I understand. As long as you understand that I won't condone causing unnecessary harm to innocents."

"You want us to inject mystery drugs into generals and political leaders and industrialists, Terrak." Azad rolled her eyes. "We might have to hurt some nice people to get close enough to the bad people to find a vein."

I shrugged. "Military personnel, bodyguards – they know danger comes with the job. That's different from what you wanted to do with this elder."

Azad shook her head. "People who draw lines like that just baffle me. My line of work is hard enough – why set up a bunch of artificial barriers to success? 'Oh, no, I can't do *that*, I have to stay inside the lines' – why? We're not on a sports field here. All that matters is outcomes. But, sure, fine. I've been burdened with people like you my entire career. I'm used to it. Adaptability." She pointed at Lonrah. "You, get me as much of the cure as you can make, and some syringes and such." She pointed at me. "You, think about ways to make me as happy as possible for as long as possible going forward." She pointed at her own chest. "Me, I'm going to go call my bosses and tell them, oops, there was a lab mishap, the spores got destroyed, and we're going into the field to seek a new test subject. Because if I told them the truth, they'd have me kill you, Terrak. See how nice I am? Maybe they can advise me on the best target for your experiment." She left the room.

I released a slow breath. "I was not at all sure I'd survive that."

"Since you did, can we please get this unconscious Hacan out of my laboratory?" Lonrah said.

I picked him up from the table and took him back to the field where we'd first found him. No one paid me any attention on that part of the journey, either. The old fellow blinked up at me when I let him down, and growled halfheartedly. "What? Did you finish? Where are my brains?"

"Inside your head and unharmed. The experiment was canceled, but you have still been paid." I slipped another credit stick I'd pilfered from Azad into his hand. "Be well, elder."

"My patch," he grumbled. "Get off it."

When I returned to the alley that led to Lonrah's lab, I had a nasty shock.

The utility box that hid the elevator was surrounded by a group in tactical armor that included a human, a Hacan, and an Xxcha. The Xxcha was cutting into the box with some sort of large grinding implement, the blade showering sparks.

I drew back before any of them noticed me, and stood around the corner of the adjacent warehouse, back against the wall, my mind racing.

Well, not racing so much as just thinking, "Oh, no," over and over.

CHAPTER 11
AZAD

Azad finished her call. She hadn't actually lied to her boss – that wasn't really a thing she could do – but she'd successfully argued for Terrak's continued usefulness. "At least let me use him to get off the moon, OK?" She'd insisted on operational independence for this mission, so it was her call anyway, but she preferred not to be in opposition with the people who paid the bills.

She returned to Lonrah's lab to find Terrak and the Hacan vagrant both gone. She groaned. "Did he wander off? He's supposed to be making me happy. Going off on his own does not make me happy."

"I asked him to remove the subject." Lonrah approached, carrying a slim black case, zippered shut. "This contains the cure. I made enough for about a dozen doses, though it will vary a bit depending on the species of the subjects – you don't need to give as much to an Yssaril as you do to a Hacan. There's also a drive inside with the recipes, and any disreputable chemist should be able to create more. None of the required components are terribly exotic, though the neural growth promoters are expensive."

"Money, I've got. What I need is a more reliable partner."

"Terrak is extremely flexible, morally, when it comes to matters of commerce," Lonrah said. "But he has a few clear bright lines when it comes to people. It's an unusual combination, and he's not as rich as he could be if he didn't care about hurting anyone, but I admit, it makes him more pleasant to be around, and more comfortable to do business with."

"Baffling," Azad said. "You're all just baffling." She took the bag. "Tell me Terrak will be back soon. That he isn't taking the old guy to a rehab facility or setting him up in a hotel or something–"

An alarm blatted, and Lonrah hurried over to a console. "Oh, no. We have visitors upstairs, and they are wearing very shiny black armor."

Azad cursed. She used one of her very best special occasion curses. "Stall them. And then show me that back entrance you mentioned."

Lonrah pressed a button and said, "Can I help you?"

"You will," a voice crackled back over the loudspeaker. Azad thought it sounded like an Xxcha.

"Is this Lonrah?" a human male voice said. It sounded vaguely familiar… "We'd, ah, like to speak to Terrak."

"I don't know who that is," Lonrah said.

Azad shook her head. The soldiers up there clearly already knew Lonrah was acquainted with Terrak, so a more nuanced lie was really called for. Amateurs.

A sigh. "Look," the voice said. "Could I just speak to Amina Azad for a moment?"

The Hylar looked at her, and she looked back at the Hylar, and then, despite herself, Azad began to laugh. She'd just realized where she knew the man's voice from. This was extremely poor operational security, but it was too amusing *not* to answer him. She reached out for the intercom button. "Is that Felix? Of all the moons in all the galaxy, you land on mine?"

"What can I say, Azad? I have extremely poor luck. I also have a question. Would you like to explain why a Federation of Sol operative is helping a murderer escape justice?"

Azad snorted. "First, who says I'm a Federation of Sol operative? You never proved that. You always put the 'ass' in 'assumptions', don't you, Felix? This guy. I can't believe we even have a prehistoric proto-human common ancestor. Second of all, Terrak isn't a murderer. He's the victim of a conspiracy. So, I have a question for *you*: did the bad guys get to you yet? Are you a puppet? Or are you just mindlessly following orders like usual? Wait, that's just a different kind of puppet–"

"I follow my orders with great mindfulness, Azad." He still sounded so smug and sure of himself. The Thales affair really should have knocked some of that confidence out of him, but apparently Felix had mistaken the fluke of his survival for evidence of his own competence. "What conspiracy are you–"

"Enough." That first, harsher Xxcha voice cut in. "You will surrender yourself, and Terrak."

Azad laughed. "Felix, why don't you tell them how likely that is?"

"I cannot guarantee your safety if you do not comply," the Xxcha said.

"That's fine. I can't guarantee yours if you keep bothering me." She turned off the intercom. "OK, Lon. As much as I'd love the opportunity to punch Felix in the face, the situation isn't *quite* what I'd like it to be, tactically, for that kind of fun. Let's see this escape route. And patch my comms into your intercom system so I can listen to what's happening here after I'm gone, all right?"

CHAPTER 12
TERRAK

I went back to the empty lot, where the Hacan was now upright, and said, "Hello. Could I make you an offer? I'd like to buy your garment."

He laughed at me and said, "Consider it a gift. I can buy something better." He pulled off the filthy tarp and threw it at my feet. I wrapped it around myself and nodded my thanks.

I made my way to the outskirts of a homeless encampment, one where broken-down Hacan sipped from green glass bottles, and a few Saar scuffled at the dirt, and a N'orr missing half its limbs lurched along, picking at a pile of trash and putting occasional finds in its mouth. One of the other Hacan shuffled over and offered me a sip of his beverage, and I took one, to be hospitable. The drink bore the same relationship to the fine sunwine I'd enjoyed on Shilsaad Station that a lump of regurgitated gristle bears to a prime-cut caprid steak.

That said, I'd drunk worse, and enjoyed it less.

I couldn't do much at the moment, so I just waited. When the Coalition thugs departed, I'd figure out what to do next. Azad would likely get out all right – there was an escape route, after all, and anyone who caused as much trouble as she did was probably adept at escaping it. I hoped she'd find me again. Despite our recent disagreements over the best way to proceed, we still had a common goal, and she was a resource I could use.

If she didn't come back, I supposed I would try to make my way to one of my hidden caches – I'd always considered the possibility that life might turn against me, and had prepared contingencies, after all – and just lay low for a while. But I had higher hopes. I wanted to find out who'd destroyed my life. I wanted to destroy *theirs*.

I took another sip. "This is marvelous," I said, and handed the bottle back to my new friend.

CHAPTER 13
AZAD

"Of course I don't have any breathing apparatus," Lonrah said. "I can breathe fine underwater."

Azad looked at the pool of black water in the floor. They were in a tiny concrete-lined space hidden behind a false panel in the back of the server room – they'd had to move a rack of machines just to get access. What they'd gotten access to looked a lot like drowning to death. "Yes, but you deal with all sorts of chemicals, so you must have *something*."

"I have various filtration systems, but none that would help you breathe down there. I have an attachment dome for my exo-suit that I can fill with air or water, and I use that sometimes when I work with especially volatile materials, but even if we could cram you inside the bubble, it wouldn't fit in the escape tunnel."

"Great. How far is it to the other end?"

"About five hundred meters."

Azad tried to do some math – how fast could she swim underwater, how long could she hold her breath – and gave up because even without all the variables the answer was obvious. "Five hundred meters is very far. I will die."

"I *said* the usefulness of this route depended on how long you could hold your breath."

"No human can hold their breath that long. Or a Hacan either!"

"It's not a water pipe," Lonrah said. "It's an old smuggler's tunnel that flooded. It's not full of water the whole way – there are places where the roof caved in, with air pockets, so you can pop up and get a breath here and there."

"I don't suppose you have a map or a list of the precise locations of these pockets?"

"I've tried this tunnel exactly once, Azad, and I just swam through it. I didn't make a map. There are no branches or anything."

"Right. That's something, I guess. At least I won't take a wrong turn." She looked at the still pool. "The alternative is staying here, and probably dying at the hands of *Felix Duval*, and I can't abide that. Better to drown like a rat. OK." She was prepared to swim, wearing a tank top and shorts and shoes that were pretty much just extremely tough socks. She checked her belt and the vest she'd strapped on, its waterproof pouches full of the cure and her other possessions, such as they were. "Thanks for all your help, Lonrah."

"I didn't do it for you. I did it for Terrak. And also for science."

Terrak. At least Azad didn't have to listen to him complain about the swim. She hoped he was OK. He was savvy enough not to wander into the middle of a commando raid, anyway, and with luck he was laying low nearby instead of running as far and fast as he could. If he was still in the vicinity, she'd find him. Assuming she survived her escape. "That's still very noble, Lon. I pretty much only do stuff for money."

"I'm… surprised you didn't kill me."

Azad cocked her head. "Why would I do that?"

"To keep me from telling those soldiers up there what you're doing. You didn't even make me promise not to tell."

"Why make you tell a lie? Of course you'll tell. But killing you wouldn't be very good manners, after all the help you've given us. Listen, though. The puppetmasters aren't as polite as I am. You should run. In fact, you should swim, along with me, right now. Show me where those air bubbles are."

Lonrah said, "My whole *life* is in this place, all my research, everything–"

And Terrak had said she was an agoraphobe. Oh well. Azad had tried. Sometimes people didn't understand the danger they were in until the danger fully closed around them. "Suit yourself. But you might end up locked in a place a lot less pleasant." Azad gave a little wave, took a breath, and dove straight down.

The water was cold, which was unpleasant. Azad hadn't done a lot of swimming growing up – it wasn't a common form of recreation in orbit around Meginstjarna – and though she'd learned to move in the water well enough during her military training, being underwater never felt good or natural, even when it *wasn't* cold and dark.

Once Azad kicked her way down into the tunnel proper, she was glad she hadn't bothered with a careful calculation of lung capacity and swim speed, because conditions in the field were worse than anticipated. For one thing, the tunnel was narrow, and her hands slammed against the sides, slowing her progress; she mainly propelled herself by kicking. She swam as close to the top of the tunnel as possible, which meant she bumped her head a lot, but she couldn't risk missing an air pocket. Just when her lungs had transformed into two burning coals in her chest, her head broke through the top of the water. She spun, sticking her face into the dark gap above, and sucked in deep breaths. The air was scented with stone and water. Better than sewage, anyway. She took another breath and went down again.

She proceeded that way, rapidly losing track of how far she'd gone. After that first long stretch, the crumbled spaces at the top of the tunnel were more frequent, and then the water level gradually sank as the tunnel angled upward, which helped. She walked the last dozen meters, the water dropping from neck deep to chest to waist to knees. There was light ahead of her, just a faint glow filtering down from above. The water was only ankle deep when she reached a rusty maintenance ladder, the bottom rungs slick with mildew, and climbed up. There was a hatch on top, but it was just made of wood – hence the light, filtered between the slats – so she was able to heave the cover up and out of the way.

She emerged in an empty lot full of weeds, looked around, and laughed out loud. It was the same field where they'd captured the old Hacan, though he'd moved on, apparently. She clambered out, soaking wet in the bright sun. After stretching for a moment, she turned her earpiece back on. She was hooked into Lon's intercom and could hear the audio from her lab's surveillance system. Mostly what she heard was various thumps and screeches. Not terribly informative.

She went looking for Terrak. He was annoying just lately, but overall, he'd been more help than hindrance. If he was telling the truth about being able to get them a ship, she'd even forgive him for throwing their spores away. As long as it was a ship with good heating.

CHAPTER 14
FELIX

Ggorgos pried the hidden elevator shaft open, but there was no elevator car there, of course. "We should have brought antigrav harnesses or something," Felix said, peering down into the depths.

A panel popped open on the back of Ggorgos's shell, and a spool wrapped with black cable topped with a folding grapnel emerged. "Secure the end," she said, pulling some of the line loose and handing the hook to Calred.

The security officer dutifully wrapped the cable around the utility box and hooked it into place, giving it some hard tugs to make sure the grapnel would hold. "All set."

"Give mother a hug," Ggorgos said, opening her arms wide, her tone so entirely deadpan that it took Felix a moment to realize she was making a joke.

"You're being funny now?" he said.

"Descending into the lair of my enemies puts me in good spirits. Come." She beckoned again, and Calred and Felix awkwardly stepped into her embrace. Felix didn't like the idea of clinging to a large tortoise being lowered into a pit – the chances of slipping and falling seemed too great – but her shell shifted, panels popping open to reveal molded carbon handholds. "Grab on tight," she said, and once they assured her they were secure, she stepped into the shaft.

The cable unspooled steadily, lowering them to the bottom of the shaft – it wasn't that deep, in the end, more basement-level dwelling than proper subterranean lair. Ggorgos used the same cutting tool that had opened the ground-level doors to cut through the roof of the elevator car and dropped down. She opened the doors – that only required pushing a button – and rushed out into a long, narrow room lined with shelves full of bottles and jars. Calred and Felix came behind her, weapons up, Calred holding an energy rifle, Felix a kinetic sidearm. There was nothing and no one to shoot at, but also no trip wires or exploding things, so Felix decided to call it a win.

Ggorgos dispersed her drones, and they went zipping through the space, disappearing through an open doorway at the end of the room. After a moment, she grunted. "One hostile present. Not Terrak or Azad."

"Azad was *here*," Felix said.

"Was I?" Azad's voice crackled over the intercom. "Or was I just broadcasting remotely? Go easy on Lonrah. She was just doing a little business. And Felix – listen to what she says about the conspiracy, OK? You're on the wrong side, which isn't unusual for you, but this time, you're even wronger than usual."

"Azad, damn it, where are you?" Felix glared at the ceiling, but no one answered.

A Hylar in an exo-suit stomped in, escorted by a buzzing group of drones. "Hello, unthinking tools of state-sanctioned violence."

"Where is Terrak?" Ggorgos demanded.

"I have no idea. He left a little before you all showed up, to run an errand. I expected him back by now, but… I imagine he saw you, or the hole you put in my elevator doors, and decided not to hang around."

Ggorgos cursed, and several of her drones zipped back up the shaft. "I'll search the local area. Duval, see what useful information you can get out of her." She returned to the shaft and zipped back upward on her line.

I hope the elevator still works, Felix thought. He turned to Calred. "Why don't you see if you can get into her security system, take a peek at the archive, and make sure Azad and Terrak aren't hiding under a floorboard or something?" Calred gave a lazy salute and pushed past Lonrah, moving deeper into the lab.

Felix smiled at the Hylar. "So, Lonrah. What's all this I hear about a conspiracy?"

CHAPTER 15
SEVERYNE

A message came in from Immental, in text form this time: *Our targets have evaded capture. They may attempt to leave the moon in an unknown vessel. Be on alert.*

"Oh, good, we're looking for an unknown vessel," Severyne said. "There's never any shortage of those." She sent back a reply: *Acknowledged.*

The *Grim Countenance* was the sort of ship people tended to notice, so they were hiding in the shadow of an uninhabited satellite, with unostentatious probes dispersed to keep watch over Huntsman's Moon and relay sensor data back to them.

How was Severyne supposed to find the right ship? Stop them all and search them? The local authorities wouldn't be happy about that, and neither would the *Temerarious*, once they noticed she was here.

She notified the bridge crew. "Monitor all traffic from Huntsman's Moon. Our fugitive may try to depart soon, and we don't know what vessel he'll use. Hack the local traffic control system and look for anything anomalous – departures ahead of schedule, reports of vehicle theft, life sign readings that don't match crew manifests, *anything*. If our quarry gets away, I will be very upset, and you all know what happens when I'm upset." Severyne had encouraged the rumor that if any of her subordinates displeased her, she would take them down to the training deck, turn off all the lights, and hunt and kill them for sport.

The rumor wasn't true, of course. She never actually killed any of them. That would generate far too much paperwork.

THE FAITHFUL VIII

Fleet Captain Harlow – retired leader of the Mentak Coalition raider fleet, renowned politician and military strategist, and one of the first to be blessed by the sacrament – lay unmoving in her bed.

Her two longtime, devoted aides stood by her bedside. "I don't see how she'll be able to attend the summit," Callis said. "She's supposed to be right up there on the dais, as one of the architects of the Greater Union, but there's just less and less of her here every day."

Wallich nodded. "I caught her wandering in the garden yesterday. That's why I strapped her down. She almost fell into the fishpond. She seemed to think she was back in the battle of Tegenaria, on the bridge, and the fish were Letnev ships. She couldn't understand their fleet formation, she said. She thought it was some new tactic."

"She doesn't seem to be in any pain, at least."

Wallich shook her head. "No, of course. The guides would never allow her to suffer."

Callis and Wallich had been a devoted couple before they joined the faithful; now devotion to anyone but the guides seemed pointless. Callis oversaw the grounds of Harlow's estate, and Wallich oversaw the house, and they shared a cottage that was nicer than any home they'd lived in before joining Harlow's staff. The three of them were the only sapient beings in residence on the entire continent of this remote, automated agricultural world. The place got lonely sometimes, but Harlow had wanted a quiet retirement after a career filled with political and literal battles.

The isolation made hiding Harlow's decline easier, of course. The fleet captain had always been sharp, quick-witted, decisive, and hilarious. Even in retirement, she'd had a thousand hobbies and projects. She often said that after devoting her career to conflict, she wanted to spend her last years learning the pastimes of peacetime. Her favorite activities ranged from word puzzles (she excelled at them) to logic games (even better) to painting (she was very bad) to sculpture (she was worse) to cooking (she had Wallich make edible meals afterward), and there were always new books and media streaming into the database as she sent out requests for material to help explore her latest interests.

Harlow kept up an extensive correspondence, too, maintaining the myriad connections she'd made in her career – the same connections that had made her so valuable to the guides. Keeping *those* communications going without raising suspicion was the hardest part of Harlow's decline. Wallich had found a program that could scan a database of material and produce plausible new entries in a series, and they'd used that on the captain's vast archive to generate new letters, but every one of them had to be reviewed and tweaked and personalized. Wallich forestalled video and voice calls with claims of mild illness or technical difficulties, but they both wondered how long the charade could last. "Someone will come to check on her," Wallich said. "She's supposed to arrive early for the summit on Moll Primus, and when she doesn't show up, someone will come, no matter what excuses we make."

"We have a little sacrament put aside," Callis said. "Enough to bring an unwelcome visitor or two into the fold."

"What if there are more than one or two?"

"Then… the guides will tell us what to do. Won't they?"

"Of course," Wallich said. "Of course they will."

It was hard to worry much, when the sacrament was doing its work to ease their minds. They were both so happy the fleet captain had taken them into her confidence and allowed them to join her communion. Callis had screamed so much, when she saw Wallich twitching and spasming on the ground, but she simply hadn't understood what was happening. She'd sobbed, later, when she gave thanks for the blessing of the guides.

Still. Seeing the captain decline like this – first forgetting things, then going blank for longer and longer stretches of time, and finally lapsing into delirium and catatonia… it was disturbing enough that occasional spikes of unease broke through the comfort of the sacrament.

Wallich reached out and found Callis's hand, their fingers entwining out of the habit of years. "Trust in the guides," Callis murmured.

CHAPTER 16
TERRAK

Azad squatted down next to me. She'd acquired an old brown coat from somewhere and jammed a tattered hat down tight over her ears. "Thanks for not fleeing the moon without me," she said. No one glanced twice at her, though everyone in the camp had surely noticed her arrival. She was the only human here. Hiding your true feelings and reactions can be a useful survival skill. Excessive curiosity was probably not an advantage in this sort of place.

"I saw those soldiers…" I trailed off. I was going to ask, "Did you kill them?" but I didn't actually care much about that. "Is Lonrah all right?"

"Last time I saw her, yeah. I was slipping out the back door, which was really more of a filthy tube full of water, but any exit is better than none. I doubt the Coalition goons will rough her up much. I know the leader, a little, from a past operation, and he doesn't have the stomach for real nastiness. She'll be questioned, but nothing worse."

"You're assuming this leader you know is still the person you *used* to know," I said. "What if he's been co-opted, too?"

"In that case, bad news for Lonrah," Azad said. "But as far as I can tell, the puppetmasters are targeting people with high-level political or military connections. Felix Duval is a field operative. He doesn't usually get close enough to anyone important to spray spores in their face, either. He may have been turned before being sent after us, I guess, but it's hardly necessary – the cover story about you being a remorseless murderer is perfectly adequate justification for pursuit."

"Poor Lonrah," I murmured. "I never meant to get her into trouble."

"She's definitely got trouble. That said… I called the local authorities and told them Mentak Coalition soldiers were conducting unauthorized operations in the city. I sent them some of Lonrah's footage of soldiers in tactical gear, cutting into private property. I imagine the Rantula security forces will be along…"

Three ships screamed overhead, just black-and-white streaks, moving low, making trash swirl around the alley and provoking curses and shaken fists from the people in the camp.

"…right about now," Azad said. "That should keep Lonrah from getting *immediately* murdered, even if there are spore-zombies in her lab. If she has any sense, she'll run before the puppetmasters can get to her."

I hoped she would, but she hadn't left her lab in years, and I was afraid inertia would overcome good sense. There was nothing I could do about it. We could only move forward. "Do you have the cure?"

She patted the side of her coat. "Sure do. Your plan is still the least bad option. We should move away from the nexus of police activity. You said you could get us a ship?"

"I can. But first: tell me where we're going? Who's the nearest subject we can test the cure on?" I still didn't like the idea of injecting people with an untested cure, but at least our future subject was *already* infested with mind-control spores, and it was worth the risk if we could save them.

"I've been giving that some thought. From here we can most easily reach a wormhole leading to Barony territory. There's a Letnev captain who's been really vocal about supporting the Legion, despite a career spent as a frothing xenophobic warmonger, extreme even by Barony standards. If someone like *that* starts talking about the need for a strategic alliance with filthy aliens, important people will listen, because things must be serious. I'm about ninety-nine percent certain he got turned, and he was just on the other side of that wormhole, last I heard… but I don't like our odds. He'll be tough to reach without more guns or connections. I don't suppose *you* have secret allies in the Barony?"

"No. It's hard to make friends with the Letnev. They are not a friendly people." I'd encountered a few in my diplomatic career. They were not, as a rule, charmed by my sparkling wit.

Azad smirked. "Oh, you might be surprised. Under the right circumstances, some of them can be very friendly."

I firmly decided not to ask any follow-up questions. "Do we have another option?"

"We're not too far from another wormhole that leads to a Mentak Coalition system. It's kind of a backwater… but there's this one Coalition fleet captain there. Retired, so she's not on a battleship or locked away at the center of some facility bristling with energy weapons. She's just enjoying her dotage on a colony planet. We think she was one of the first people the puppetmasters compromised, because she quit fishing or quilting or whatever she was doing down there, and started calling in favors and taking meetings with various colleagues who were still active in politics. She would have been easy for the puppetmasters to reach and turning her would open a lot of doors. Not long after her sudden return to politics, the whole Greater Union thing started to gain momentum, and she's considered one of the architects behind the idea."

I mulled that over. "She does sound like a better choice. I still can't understand why the conspirators would try to create both the Greater Union and the Legion. They're oppositional forces – the Legion only came about because the Letnev are paranoid and assume the Union exists to target them."

"Both sides are planning big summits, one on Moll Primus and one on Arc

Prime. You know how these things are, they can fall through or get postponed infinitely, but it looks like they're both going to happen, and soon. That means a bunch of very important people, including heads of state, will be all together in a couple of concentrated areas."

"So, the conspirators want to compromise them as well? If you could pull the strings of the rulers of major nations…"

"Sure, you could do some stuff with that. But even absolute tyrants have limits on their behavior. If the Baron of Letnev suddenly said, 'Hey, let's throw our support behind some other random faction for the throne on Mecatol Rex', he'd probably have a terrible accident the next day and some cousin would step in to steer the people back to the old path."

"Assassination, then," I suggested. "The conspirators put agents in place to kill all those leaders at the summits, so they can take advantage of the resulting chaos?"

"My bosses give that scenario a pretty high degree of probability. I'm not an analyst. I just steal things and blow stuff up. Maybe if the cure works, we can get some answers out of this fleet captain. She's become a lot quieter recently, like her part of the plan was done."

"Tell me about her retirement home. We can get to her there?"

"Oh, sure. She's on a planet called Entelegyne. Fertile and boring, mostly home to automated agricultural systems. The place produces food for a bunch of Mentak Coalition worlds. It's close to a wormhole, convenient for shipping, but it'll take us a few days or a week to get there, depending on what kind of ship we get."

"Which wormhole is it?" I asked. She told me. "I think I can get us a ship there."

She rubbed her hands together. "Good. I'll drive."

I laughed. "About that…"

CHAPTER 17
AZAD

"It will be fine," Terrak insisted. "I've used this method to transport various items before." Azad started to object, and he held up his hands. "Don't worry, no one local knows about the arrangement, not Lonrah, or the Facilitator, or my importer/exporter friend. It's all arranged remotely with a dispatcher I have a deal with. Even *she* doesn't know when I'm putting contraband into a given shipment."

They were in the belly of a mostly automated cargo ship, inside a pressurized container that was half-filled with live plants housed in transparent cubes with their own inbuilt light sources and water systems. They hadn't talked to any-one on the way here, just crept to the spaceport, where Terrak had used various codes to get them through the security gates and onto the ship. That part was good. The part Azad didn't like was the idea of traveling as cargo.

Terrak kept trying to convince her. "This vessel is going in the right direction, and in six days it's stopping near the correct wormhole to drop off a delivery. We'll need to pick up another ship to traverse the wormhole and reach Entele-gyne, but by then we won't have such… fervent pursuit… and will have more options." Terrak pulled the container doors shut, and they sealed with a hiss.

"This is a wonderful plan that won't work at all," Azad said. "We've got no sup-plies, or access to any. We don't have water, so a few days into this six-day journey, we'll be dead. We also don't have any food, unless these plants are edible, but hey, starving takes longer than dying of thirst, so I'm less worried about that."

"Humans die after a few days without water?" Terrak said. "My people evolved on a desert world; we can do rather better. But that's not an issue. Why do you think I looked in three other containers before choosing this one?" He knelt by one of the plants and used one of his fingernails – rather stronger than a human's – to pry off a back panel of the containment cube. He twisted some-thing, then removed a bulb-shaped reservoir with a tube sticking out of it. "Pure water, for the plant's internal irrigation system. There are gallons and gallons in here." He slurped on the tube and grinned, pleased with himself.

Azad wasn't so pleased. "Fine, so we won't die of thirst. We have bigger prob-lems."

"As for food–"

"I'm sure you have some solution," she interrupted. "Maybe one of the five hundred other containers in here is crammed full of raw seafood. I don't *care*. Being alive and well is actually our problem. There's only supposed to be one living person on a ship like this! The backup redundancy pilot, and he's only along for the ride in case the automated systems have a catastrophic failure. If Duval's crew or anybody else is in orbit looking for us, they're going to scan for life signs and compare the findings to crew manifests, and then flag any anomalies for investigation. We're anomalies. Even if we get past them, we're still going to hit a couple of customs checkpoints on this route, and the authorities there *will* scan for life signs, *because* ships like this get used for smuggling."

Terrak looked at her patiently, and Azad suddenly found herself wondering about him and his capabilities. She'd determined early on that Terrak was in over his head and unwilling to admit it to himself. She'd pegged him as a reasonably canny merchant and diplomat who foolishly thought his social and negotiating skills had equipped him for life on the run. Among people of all species, there was a tendency for older, successful people to believe that, because they were experts in a given field, that made them experts in *every* field. Such people tended to blunder around in clouds of hubris. Maybe Terrak was doing that, and his confidence was totally unfounded, but he was certainly looking at her like he had a handle on this situation. How could that be? Someone like him shouldn't be comfortable in circumstances like this.

"If you're done assuming I'm a fool," Terrak said mildly. "no one is going to detect our life signs." He reached into a pocket and removed two capped auto-syringes. "I had Lonrah mix these up for us. I've used this technique when I've needed to… help people reach distant places without being noticed."

Azad groaned. "Are those stasis drugs?"

"They'll drop our body temperature and slow our heartbeats and other electrical activity enough for standard life sign scans to miss us, *and* we won't need to eat or drink while we're in hibernation. These doses are calibrated to keep us down for five days, which will give us a day of consciousness to rehydrate before we need to do anything too active. The ship is stopping to make a delivery at a small station where they won't care about anomalous life signs, or anything else, as long as you pay your fees, so we can get off there and find our next mode of transport."

"I apologize for misjudging your competence," Azad said. Apologies were the kind of thing diplomats cared about, right? It didn't cost her anything to say some words. But then, Terrak was proving he wasn't an average diplomat. Her intel said he was a little shady, but she was beginning to wonder if he wasn't downright criminal. The skillsets of professional thieves and smugglers often overlapped meaningfully with her own, after all. She hated any plan that involved loss of control, but they weren't exactly swimming in options. "I don't know about being unconscious here, though. It's a perfectly good plan, assuming nothing goes wrong. If somebody does board this ship looking for us, we won't be able to run or fight."

Terrak spread his hands. "I am open to alternative suggestions. But decide soon – this ship is scheduled to depart shortly."

Azad sighed. "Fine. Hibernation it is. I can't believe I'm injecting myself with mystery juice some squid gave to a guy I barely know. But I've done stupider things for a mission. Let me call my bosses and tell them I'm going to be out of contact for a few days."

She pushed her way through the plants until she reached the far end of the compartment and sat with her back against the wall. She closed her eyes and waited for the connection to click into place. "Hey, boss," she said into the expectant silence. "I'm going to be out of contact for a little while…"

CHAPTER 18
TERRAK

Azad mumbled to herself at the other end of the cargo container as I moved the plants around to clear some space for us to stretch out. I prefer not to sleep on metal floors, but at least I'd be so profoundly unconscious that I wouldn't be uncomfortable… until I woke up. If you've ever experienced decreased circulation and felt that pins-and-needles sensation when you move the affected limb… imagine that in *every* muscle of your body, and you'll have a sense of what it's like to emerge from this sort of stasis. It's not pleasant, but this was the best solution I could come up with in the time I had. You have to be adaptable and willing to improvise if you want to succeed.

Azad returned, and I said, "How are things back on Jord?"

"I wouldn't know. I don't usually talk about the weather or local politics."

"Are your handlers on board with the new direction our mission is taking?"

She laughed and sat on the floor, leaning back against a couple of plant boxes, looking instantly at ease. "They're results-oriented. They let me run things as I see fit, with their full support, as long as that support is completely deniable and untraceable. The moment I fail, they stop being happy with me, and I pretty much cease to exist as far as they're concerned. They've arranged for me to get my funds replenished when we hit the station by the wormhole, though. I don't have any useful contacts in that area, so I'm not sure how we'll get a ship, but money will help."

"Oh, I know some people," I said. "I know people almost everywhere. That's why you keep me around, isn't it?"

"Also for the titillating conversation and the access to exciting drugs."

The ship rumbled around us, and there was a lurch as we lifted off. Traveling through the atmosphere and pulling out of a gravity well was always a little bumpy. "We'd better get sedated," she said. "In case anyone is lurking in orbit scanning for life signs."

I complied, removing a small case that held two syringes, one marked with Azad's initials, and one with mine. I didn't want to mix them up. Hacan and human physiology differ, and I am a *lot* bigger than Azad. "Don't accidentally kill me," she said. "Don't kill me on purpose either, now that I think about it. We're probably the only hope to save the galaxy, and also I'd like to get paid."

"We are in accord." I handed her the syringe. "Do you know how to use this?"

"I've had to take my share of combat drugs in the field. Nobody's even shooting at me right now. I can manage."

I took my syringe, and we settled ourselves as comfortably as we could among the plants. I watched Azad until I realized there was no way she was going to inject herself first. She probably wanted a few minutes to rifle through my pockets before she went into hibernation, to see if I had any *other* surprises hidden away from Lonrah's lab. That was fine. I'd expected as much, and there was nothing on me that I didn't want her to see. I seated the needle in a vein, depressed the plunger, and winced at the sensation of cold that flowed into me. Then I put the needle away and settled onto my back. "See you in a few days, Azad," I murmured, already feeling myself pulled down, down, down.

CHAPTER 19
FELIX

"Conspiracy," Lonrah repeated. "I thought you were going to ask me where Terrak and Azad went."

Felix said, "Do you *know* where Terrak and Azad went?"

"No."

Felix shrugged. "I didn't expect you would. It hardly seemed like they'd tell you their plans and then leave you behind to tell someone else. So, instead, you can tell me the things you *do* know."

"Are you a spore-zombie?" Lonrah said. "You don't seem like one, but then… I'm not sure I'd be able to tell."

"What, exactly, is a spore-zombie?" Felix was aiming for an earnest and curious tone. He was not a professional interrogator, but he vaguely remembered something about the importance of building rapport and a sense of trust. In this case, that meant humoring a very strange Hylar.

"You have no idea what's going on here, do you?" Lonrah said. "Or else you do, and you're pretending… Ugh. This whole situation is so exhausting."

"Consider me clueless." Felix leaned against the doorframe and crossed his arms. "I'd love to be enlightened. Maybe you can spare yourself a charge for aiding and abetting a fugitive if you help me out now."

"The Mentak Coalition has no authority in the Rantula system! We're independent."

Felix shrugged. "Such things can generally be worked out. This system does have trade relations with the Coalition, and with trade comes diplomacy. I'm sure the local authorities would hand you over if we asked nicely. But it doesn't need to come to that. I've heard rumors about a conspiracy that Terrak is involved in. If he's not working alone, that would be useful information–"

"Terrak isn't working *for* the conspiracy, he's working against it. Only because they gave him no choice, by framing him for murder."

Felix considered for a moment, then said, "Let's say I believe you. Terrak is innocent. He was framed because he stumbled onto some secret. What *is* that secret?"

"How much do you know about the Arborec?" she asked.

The answer was… almost nothing. The Mentak Coalition was the most diverse of the major polities, with numerous alien species sharing citizenship and a common culture, but there were no Arborec involved. He only knew what he'd learned at the academy and picked up in passing. "They're telepathic plant creatures. I've never met them… it… one of their representatives, though I hear they're a bit gruesome. Why?"

Lonrah's pseudopods fluttered nervously as she spoke. "After Terrak started asking questions about his friend's odd behavior, someone broke into his room and tried to spray him in the face with a canister. I examined the contents of that canister and found spores similar to the ones the Arborec use to create their Dirzuga – the walking, talking corpses they use to communicate with other species. Terrak and Azad believe someone has altered those spores to allow them to work on *living* people. Either to brainwash them into compliance, or to outright control their minds, turning them into puppets. Azad rescued Terrak and stole the canister of spores because she's investigating who's behind the whole thing. She believes the conspiracy has compromised agents in most of the major polities, both in the Greater Union and among the Letnev and maybe other members of their Legion."

"That's… quite an accusation," Felix said. It was a totally ridiculous story, but the fact that it was so ridiculous almost made him more inclined to believe it; surely a liar would come up with something more plausible? "Do you have any proof?"

"I have my analysis of the spores."

"Could I analyze them myself? Or have one of our people do it, rather?"

She flushed the color of dismay. "The samples were destroyed."

"That's convenient."

"No, it really *isn't*, because there's an armed man in my lab demanding them. I don't have the spores, but I do have the recipe for a possible cure, provided by Azad's bosses."

Felix whistled. "That is… all extremely interesting." What would Jhuri make of this story? It sounded outlandish, but then, Felix had discovered to his dismay that sometimes outlandish things were all too true.

"It's more than interesting, it's *terrifying*," Lonrah said. "Unknown individuals are controlling the actions of powerful people all over the galaxy, for reasons we don't understand!"

"I do recognize the gravity of the situation," Felix said.

"That's nice. I wish that made any difference. Knowing about this conspiracy won't help you."

Felix frowned. "I'll contact my superiors, and we'll look into your claims–"

The Hylar spasmed her limbs in what Felix recognized as a laugh. "Then you'll get murdered or turned into a spore-zombie yourself. Terrak basically just said, 'Does anyone know why my old friend is acting funny?' and hours later the old friend was dead and Terrak was wanted for murder. If you ask your superiors to launch an investigation, you'll be next."

Felix sat down on a crate. "Well. When you put it that way…" He enjoyed chasing fugitives through space, matching wits against villains, and concocting stratagems to best enemies in battle. Why didn't he get to do more of *that*? Why did he always end up in these strange, gray, complicated, mysterious situations? "I suppose I'll have to investigate these claims myself."

"That's a good idea. But… do you trust your crew, captain?"

"Of course." To say Felix trusted Calred and Tib with his life would have been an understatement. Tib was his best friend from childhood – they'd grown up together on space stations, joined the military together, and apart from an interval when Tib was undergoing special training in infiltration, they'd even served together. He hadn't known Calred as long, but they'd been on the *Temerarious* together for years, and the Hacan had proven an invaluable ally, bold and brave and willing to improvise. But then… there was Ggorgos. "Mostly."

"Mostly may not be enough." Lonrah sounded almost sad about it. "And even someone you trust completely could have caught a face full of spores in some dark alley. Your crew might not be the people you knew anymore. They may have different loyalties."

Felix shook his head. He didn't want to believe that, and decided he'd think about it later. "Enough. Give me the data on this supposed cure."

"Planning to pre-emptively inject it into the veins of your crewmates?" Lonrah said. "Not a bad idea… except the antidote hasn't been tested yet. We didn't have any infected subjects."

Felix frowned. "Then… assuming your story is true… Terrak and Azad must be going to find test subjects. Do they have a list of supposedly compromised people?"

"Probably, but they didn't tell me where they were going, and I didn't ask. I think I've come to the end of my usefulness, captain." She offered him a small data stick. "This contains the information on the pathogen I found, and the formula for the possible cure. I don't know what good any of that will do, but I wish you well."

Felix slotted the data stick into his tablet, revealing an array of tables and charts and a terse report. There was also a photo: a small vial, filled with little green specks. Could those tiny green flecks really – what? Rewrite your brain? Make you into a puppet? He put the data stick away. "We'll be out of your way soon, Lonrah. Thanks for your cooperation. I think our official involvement can end now."

Felix went looking for Calred and found him working at a console. "Turn up anything useful?" he asked.

Calred sighed. "Nothing. Lonrah has a security system, but large swathes of it have been wiped. Amina Azad covering her tracks, I imagine." The big Hacan looked away from the screen and down at Felix. "Did you get anything useful out of the squid?"

Felix hesitated, but just for a fraction of a second. "I'm afraid not. I–"

"This is the police!" An amplified voice boomed through the lab. "Come out with your hands up!"

"Oh, dear," Felix said. "I think it's time for diplomacy."

THE FAITHFUL IX

Canner wasn't exactly frustrated; it was impossible to be frustrated with the guides, as they were the source of all that was good and worthwhile in the universe. But at times they seemed to have difficulty grasping matters that seemed simple enough to him. "No, it's not an issue of tissue degradation. The physical structures of the brains of your faithful are essentially unharmed by your interventions."

< Then we do not understand. The faithful gradually lose efficacy after receiving the sacrament. In some, the progression is slower, and in others faster, but in every case, decline has proven inevitable. Our earliest converts are bedridden now, and almost entirely insensible.>

"As I said, it's a matter of overstimulation, great ones." Canner sat at the desk in his medical office, buoyed by the constant cloud of happy chemicals that had suffused him since his conversion. He had files of brain scans and blood test data before him, all gathered through the network of the faithful and sent to him for analysis. Their fellowship boasted many politicians and members of the military, but very few scientists, and Canner had been tasked to deal with the intractable problem of mental decay among the faithful.

"Your sacrament provides bliss when we please you, and a constant sense of well-being, and the sure knowledge that our service is meaningful and essential. The experience is *glorious*. But… the brains of humans, Hylar, Hacan, Xxcha, the Letnev, all the species you have seen fit to bless – they are adaptable things. Neural pathways can be rewired, new pathways created, and we *are* rewired to better serve you… but there are trade-offs. There are troubling long-term changes, but even short-term… surely you've noticed that even new converts seem to lose a certain degree of creativity, and the ability to adapt to unforeseen situations? Thinking very deeply, without getting distracted, becomes harder for us, too."

< The faithful look to us for guidance. Perhaps… slightly more than is ideal.>

"I would never presume to say so, guides!" Canner spoke with absolute sincerity. "In addition to those very mild deficits, however, your followers also develop a tolerance to the effects of the sacrament, and that resistance intensifies over time."

<Resistance? Do you suggest that the faithful wish to defy us?>

"Not consciously, guides!" Canner was terrified of offending his benefactors. "I'm sure all the faithful, like myself, are delighted to serve you. The path forward has never been so clear, and when I think back on my life before, I see only a gray haze of poisonous ambition and resentment. Now everything is bright and clean. You have our minds. But our *bodies*… those are, to an extent, autonomous things, beyond the direct control of our minds. Our brains become resistant to specific forms of pleasure, when those pleasures are experienced too frequently and intensely. Hormones become depleted and take time to be replenished. Receptors can become overwhelmed and cease to bind to chemicals as strongly as they once did. Our bodies also have myriad methods to resist what they perceive as, ah, invaders."

There was no answer from the guides, but there was a sort of expectant silence.

"As time goes on, and the impact of the sacrament begins to wane, the faithful become… less faithful." A distant part of Canner's mind was shouting at him: *Listen to this, listen to yourself, don't you* understand? That part of him was easy to ignore. He hadn't been faithful for very long and had only experienced the positive effects of the sacrament. "They begin to return to their old selves – their flawed, terrible, selfish selves – and as a result, the sacrament increases its efforts, in order to prevent the faithful from straying, and regain the lost equilibrium. The growths in their brains create analogues to the hormones and other chemicals that have been depleted and increase stimulation in other areas of the brain as well. As a result, the faithful do remain devoted, but then, they develop a tolerance to that *new* level of stimulation… and so the stimulation must increase again. As the chemical interventions grow more powerful, mental functions diminish."

<Why do they diminish?>

Canner sighed. "Basically, their brains become so flooded with bliss-inducing chemicals that other functions are overwhelmed. Motor control begins to fail, first on a fine level, and then a gross one. Their underlying personalities and skills vanish beneath a rising tide of chemicals. Eventually all that is left is a vague and hazy sense of compliance and well-being, but without the ability to make independent decisions." Or, indeed, casual cocktail party conversation. "The autonomic functions persist, so they breathe, and their hearts beat. They remain faithful, too, of course! The sacrament sees to that. Their faith just… isn't good for much anymore." *That same decline will happen to me,* Canner thought, and a spike of clarifying terror flooded his mind before being washed away by the release of counteracting chemicals to keep him calm. He sighed contentedly.

<We understand,> the guides said. *<How can this problem be dealt with?>*

Canner shook himself out of his brief, blissful reverie. "What? Oh. I can't think of a way, really. You could counteract the soporific effects with stimulants, I suppose, but that will also make the faithful more resistant to the sacrament's soothing effects. Essentially, all of the faithful are on intense doses of recreational drugs, and long-term users of those sorts of drugs… generally suffer ill effects. In the absence of the sacrament, even the most far gone of the faithful would improve, and with time and therapy and medication most would recover fully. But, of course, their lives would be empty and meaningless, and none of us would wish for that."

<No solution,> the guides murmured. <*That is unfortunate. But we have time. If the plan is not interrupted, we have time.*>

"Will you tell me, guides, what is the nature of the great work?" Canner had never been more eager to know anything. "What is the glorious future we are helping usher into being?"

<*You will see, faithful one. The old stars will be extinguished, and new stars born, and the void itself will seem to burn.*>

"Beautiful," Canner murmured, and sank into the blissful haze of a job well done.

CHAPTER 20
SEVERYNE

"Nothing, captain," Voyou reported, face impassive on her screen. She was in her office, and he was reporting from the bridge. Everyone worked better there when she wasn't obviously watching them. She made most of her crew nervous. She even made Voyou nervous, but at least he'd gotten better at not visibly wincing when he had to give her bad news.

Severyne made a sound of disgust and leaned back in her chair. "What about that cargo ship? It's big enough to hide an entire pride of Hacan."

"We detected only one life sign, and we confirmed that was the pilot," Voyou said. "There's no sign that the fugitives have left the moon."

"The admiral's reputation does not suggest a great tolerance for failure, Voyou."

"No, captain. It does not."

"Hmm. What are the Coalition forces doing now?"

"They've just returned to the *Temerarious*. They did not appear to have any prisoners with them, and they were escorted off the moon by local security forces – there was some jurisdictional argument there, it seems."

Severyne smirked. That was amusing, at least.

Voyou continued. "We're monitoring communications from the *Temerarious*, and they haven't sent any messages out of the system. If they'd succeeded in capturing or killing Terrak, I'm sure they would have sent word back home by now."

"Give me *something*, Voyou, or you'll find out the admiral isn't the only woman who doesn't like failure."

"I was already aware of your feelings in that area, captain. We did find the place where Terrak and his escort landed on the moon. We were able to obtain security footage from the port, including one fairly clear image of the human assisting Terrak, though she did a remarkably good job of avoiding the direct view of the cameras. We're going to run her through our databases. Perhaps if we identify her, we can better understand Terrak's plans."

"Let me see," Severyne said.

Voyou's face vanished from her screen, replaced by a still image of a human woman's face, half turned away.

Severyne stared. She hadn't seen that face in some time, but it hadn't changed much. Her features were sharp, and her expression faintly amused, like the world was a joke only she truly understood. "I know her." Severyne's voice croaked, and she cleared her throat before continuing. She'd never expected to see that face again. She ruthlessly suppressed the feelings that welled up when she did. "That woman is a Federation of Sol covert operative named Amina Azad. I have crossed paths with her before."

"The Federation is helping Terrak escape?"

"It makes sense, if Terrak is one of our operatives, attempting to defect," Severyne said. "Of course he would go to our most hated enemy for help."

"But, ah…" Voyou clearly didn't want to say, 'but we thought the admiral was lying to us' on a Barony communications channel, even a supposedly private one like this.

"Yes," Severyne said. "But." What was going *on*? Why was Azad involved? And – Severyne did her best to suppress a flutter at the thought – was she going to see her again in person before this was all over?

Severyne sat back and drummed her fingers on the arm of her chair. Finding out Azad was part of this had briefly knocked her mind off track – the woman *did* have that effect on her – but she was still Severyne, so she almost immediately began to calculate angles and points of leverage and ways to turn this information to her advantage. After a moment, she smiled. The admiral would not approve of her idea… but the admiral would approve of success, by whatever means. As long as you won, nobody really cared, after the fact, *how* you'd won.

"Desperate times," she murmured. "Voyou, open a channel to the *Temerarious*, would you? Tell the captain an old friend would like to have a word with him."

"Are… you sure?"

"Have you ever known me to be unsure, Voyou?" she said, still gazing at the image of Amina Azad's face, nowhere near as clear on the screen as it always was in her mind.

CHAPTER 21
FELIX

Felix was in his cabin, tucking Lonrah's data into a locked drawer, when Ggorgos appeared on his screen, transmitting from the bridge. "We are being hailed by a Letnev cruiser," Ggorgos said. "Why are we being hailed by a Letnev cruiser?"

"How would I know? What does the message say?"

"It is from a Captain Dampierre of the *Grim Countenance*," she replied. "Requesting to speak with you personally."

Felix would have been only slightly more surprised if he'd heard it was the ghost of his dead grandmother, but he didn't let that show. He was having to hide a lot of things just lately, and he didn't like that. "Why don't you put her through and I'll find out what she wants?"

"You would simply... converse with an enemy?" Ggorgos radiated disapproval.

"Was there a formal declaration of war between the Mentak Coalition and the Barony of Letnev that I don't know about?" Felix asked. "I don't always read my memos very carefully, I confess, but I think I would have heard about that. Besides, conversing with an enemy is one of the best ways to learn things about them, Ggorgos."

Ggorgos didn't scowl, or blink, or anything at all. "If you receive any information pertinent to the mission, you will share it with me at once."

"We share everything, don't we, Ggorgos?"

The reptilian face vanished from the screen, replaced by the hard features of Severyne Joelle Dampierre. Felix hadn't seen her in years, since the disastrous Thales expedition ended, a mess they'd somehow all managed to walk away from alive. "Sev!" he said with as much bonhomie as possible. "Still zipping around on the old *Grim Countenance*, I see, and with a face to match. This must be homecoming week, because I *just* spoke to–"

"Amina Azad," Severyne interrupted. "I received reports that she was in this system. You've had contact with her, then?"

"I've been fine, Sev, thanks for asking."

"Amina. Azad. Tell me what you know about her location and trajectory, and I will be on my way."

Felix shook his head. "Why are you looking for her?"

"She is wanted for crimes against the Barony of Letnev. When we received reports that she was sighted in this system, I was nearby, and was dispatched to retrieve her."

"Huh. I thought after Thales completely failed to revolutionize space travel, you and Azad parted as friends. Or, if not as friends, then at least not as hated enemies who would pursue one another across the galaxy–"

"The Barony is not forgiving, Duval. Neither am I. Why are *you* pursuing Azad?"

"Ah, well, you know, the same reasons you are, probably–"

"Hmm." Severyne glanced off to the side. "I have received additional information. Azad is in the company of... an escaped murder suspect, one Terrak, who killed a diplomat at a Greater Union summit." Her face stopped being impassive. Now she was doing her version of a smile, which was even worse. "Did someone disrupt a meeting of your little club, Duval? And they sent *you* to bring the killer back? They must not want him very badly. But why is Amina Azad helping this Terrak? She works for the Federation of Sol, which, as I recall, is a *member* of the Greater Union. Could your entire alliance be falling apart, riddled by factions, plotting against one another? The Federation *is* treacherous – we could have told you that. Humans seek only their own advancement and dominance in the galaxy–"

"Unlike the loving altruism of the Barony of Letnev, yes, yes." Talking to Severyne was exhausting. He'd enjoyed spending years not doing it. If only there were a clear way to get rid of her now. "I can neither confirm nor deny that I'm in pursuit of Terrak, but you're an intelligent person and secure in your own judgment, I'm sure."

"I have no interest in the Hacan," Severyne said. "You, I assume, have no particular interest in Azad."

"She *is* aiding and abetting a fugitive, but... she is a secondary target at best, I will admit." Felix could see where this was going, and he didn't like it, and he especially didn't like that he was probably going to agree to it.

"Then we will join forces," Severyne said. "Share information and resources. When we capture the fugitives, you will take this Terrak, and I will take Amina Azad. I trust these terms are acceptable?"

"I'll... have to run them by my superiors," Felix said. He would, but it was all just going through the motions. Severyne was relentless, and it wasn't like she'd stop going after Azad if he told her she wasn't allowed. If he agreed to a partnership, at least she'd be less likely to shoot at his ship *too*.

Severyne snorted. "They keep you on a short leash, then, Duval? I have authority to complete my mission in whatever way I deem most expedient."

"Then I'll leave you to revel in your freedom for a little while and get back to you soon, all right?"

He'd barely cut the connection when Ggorgos reappeared on his screen. "Well?" she demanded.

"The Letnev are in pursuit of Amina Azad. Which, before you object, does make a degree of sense – Azad was involved in an operation a few years back, one I have firsthand knowledge about, where she crossed paths with the Barony. Captain Dampierre has a personal grudge against Azad." A personal something, anyway. Their relationship was complicated in ways Felix preferred not to think about, but he figured it was best to keep it simple for Ggorgos. "Dampierre suggested we join forces to track down Azad and Terrak – she'll take custody of the former, and we'll get the latter."

Ggorgos said, "This proposal is–"

"Not yours to allow or forbid," Felix said. "This is a joint mission, and while you were given the lead, I do get some input. I'm going to contact Jhuri now."

It took a few moments for the automated assistant on the other end of the line to track down Jhuri, who appeared to be peering into a portable terminal in a hallway somewhere, the view bouncing around. "Felix! Did you get him?"

"Negative. Terrak has either gone to ground on the moon, or he's escaped. The local authorities are doing a thorough search, but… if you ask me, they're gone, offworld and on to their next destination."

"What destination? Those contacts in the Rantula system were our only lead!"

"Maybe not our only one." Felix had given this a lot of thought. He had to trust *someone*, and Jhuri – despite being a professional liar and spymaster – was someone he trusted. After all, Jhuri wouldn't have mentioned a theory about a conspiracy if he was part of said conspiracy, would he? "I questioned the Hylar chemist Terrak and Azad met with, and she told me quite a story…"

Felix filled Jhuri in about the spores and Lonrah's claims. The view on the screen stopped bobbing as Jhuri ducked into an empty conference room. "If this is true, Felix… I've had to deal with double agents before, but this is beyond that. No amount of poring over financial records can uncover someone who's been compromised by mind-control spores instead of money." He considered. "I *can* sift through some databases looking for anomalous behavior, at least among high ranking Mentak Coalition personnel. There's no point in controlling someone's mind if you don't make them do things they *wouldn't* normally do. The trick will be mining that data without anyone noticing what I'm up to."

"You believe this conspiracy idea could be true, then? Not just paranoid fantasy?" Having someone he respected say this *wasn't* insanity would go a long way toward assuaging Felix's own doubts. It sounded like a delusion, but if so, it was an increasingly widespread one. Morever, he'd once seen a hole ripped in the fabric of space-time, revealing monsters from another reality on the other side, so he'd learned not to dismiss even outlandish ideas out of hand.

Jhuri gestured uncertainly. "Nothing Terrak did makes any sense, and I can't see why Amina Azad would be involved… unless this conspiracy business is true. Then events begin to form a pattern. The conspiracy theory is certainly worth looking into, with extreme caution. Trust no one else with this information. Send me the data on this supposed cure via an encrypted channel."

Great. The worst-case scenario had just gotten a lot worse. Now they had to uncover and uproot a vast conspiracy? The "vast" part would presumably make it easier to uncover… but harder to uproot. "Will do. There's one other thing. I was recently contacted by Severyne Dampierre on the *Grim Countenance*. She's in the Rantula system. She says she's after Amina Azad, pursuing her for crimes against the Barony, and she asked to join forces since we're in pursuit of a different member of the same duo."

"Her arrival right now is awfully convenient," Jhuri mused. "If she's part of the conspiracy, she could be after Terrak too, to silence him."

"Jhuri, how do you know *we* aren't part of the conspiracy, even unwittingly? What if we were sent after Terrak to silence him? We don't know much of anything about Ggorgos, beyond the fact that she's terrifyingly competent. What if the Xxcha insisted she come along because they needed someone compromised by spores on my crew, to make sure Terrak has an accident before he can tell us what's really going on?"

"I have considered the possibility," Jhuri said grimly. "For the time being, we *all* have the same goal: get our hands on Terrak and Azad. So… sure. Team up with Dampierre. We know she has a history of cooperating with her rivals to achieve a common goal – her partnership with Azad caused you enough trouble during the Thales affair. This time *you* can enjoy her company. If she gets any leads, follow them. I'll start sifting through the data here. If Terrak and Azad need test subjects for their cure, they'll be looking for someone they believe is compromised, as close to the Rantula system or nearby wormholes as possible." He flushed the Hylar equivalent of a resigned sigh. "It's a good thing I am extremely good at data mining."

"Be careful, Jhuri. If there is a conspiracy, there are people on Shilsaad Station who are part of it. They tried to turn Terrak and destroyed his reputation when they couldn't. Don't let them get to you too." Lonrah's suggestion that someone on Felix's crew could theoretically be compromised had stuck with him and made him worry about literally everyone he knew and trusted.

"I have years of practice at being paranoid and mistrustful, Felix. Don't worry about me. Keep *your* eyes open. If Lonrah's story is true, anyone could be infected, even people you've known your entire life."

"When I became a secret agent, I didn't think it would involve quite *this* many secrets," Felix complained.

CHAPTER 22
SEVERYNE

Duval contacted Severyne directly on an encrypted line she'd provided. "All right, you have a deal." His face looked slightly less smug than she was accustomed to, which pleased her. "We have reason to believe that Terrak and Azad have left the moon."

"Why were they on the moon in the first place?" Severyne said. "We understand they met with a chemist. Why?"

Felix hesitated, briefly, but long enough to make Severyne suspicious. "Just making contact to acquire supplies, as far as we can tell. We questioned the chemist. She didn't tell us anything useful."

"I see." Out of the screen's view, Severyne tapped out a message to Voyou on her wrist gauntlet: *Secure the chemist and bring her here. Quickly and quietly.* "Do you have any idea where our fugitives might be headed next?"

"Nothing definite. This is the only system of any significance that's reachable without traversing a wormhole. The closest wormhole leads to Barony territory – I'm guessing that's where you came through. The next nearest leads to a region that's a mix of independent systems and Mentak Coalition space. Terrak and Azad are probably headed to one of those. I can cover one, and you can cover the other? I guess it's obvious which of us should do which."

"You want us to stand watch over wormholes? That's not much of a plan, Duval." Not that she was surprised. Duval was adequate in a fight and capable of following a straight line to the end no matter how arduous the journey, but he didn't have her skill at thinking around corners.

Felix winced. "You're not wrong. I'm hoping for a more solid lead soon. Our analysts are working on the problem, and if they come up with something, I'll let you know. You'll do the same for me?"

Severyne showed her teeth. "Of course. We're partners now." She would share anything it benefited her to share, of course. She trusted he would do the same on his end.

"That is an outlandish story," Severyne said to the Hylar across the table in one of the *Grim Countenance*'s more pleasant interrogation rooms. (This one didn't even have a drain in the floor, and there were no alarming stains on the walls.)

Some people said that outlandish stories were more likely to be true because a liar would try to come up with a more believable tale, but Severyne assumed that liars were aware of that interpretation, and willing to take advantage of it.

Lonrah said, "Agreed. I'm getting pretty tired of telling it."

Voyou, sitting beside Severyne, shook his head. Most of his experience was in annexation, and he was often the officer sent to break the news to the denizens of a given planet or moon that they were part of the glorious Barony of Letnev now, and by the way, their taxes were extremely overdue. He could switch between veiled and overt threats with ease, which made him better at talking to people than Severyne was. She generally dispensed with the veils entirely. "You really expect us to believe there's some spore-based conspiracy, not just in the Greater Union, but in the *Legion*?" Voyou said.

"I don't expect you to believe anything. The fact that you scooped me up when I was trying to flee for my life might lend my story some credence, though." The Hylar sounded totally defeated. That, more than anything, made Severyne inclined to believe her – or at least to think the Hylar believed her own story. "Look, I can only definitively tell you two things: what Azad and Terrak told me, and what I saw when I did my analysis of the spore sample."

"A spore sample you conveniently no longer possess," Voyou pointed out.

Lonrah undulated. "People keep saying that's convenient. It is *less and less* convenient. I gave you my analysis. That's the best I can do. The spores themselves were incinerated."

"You told all this to Duval?" Severyne asked. She wasn't surprised Felix had kept this conspiracy rumor from her; she was just surprised she hadn't realized he was hiding something. Perhaps he was improving at the "covert" part of being a covert operator.

"I'm not good at keeping secrets from people with a lot of guns," the Hylar said. "So yes."

Voyou turned to Severyne. "I don't suppose Duval gave you any hint of this conspiracy story, despite our so-called partnership?"

"No," Severyne said. "But then, he hardly would, since I might well be an agent of said conspiracy. I would be cautious in his position as well." She thought about the situation, then turned her attention back to Lonrah. "It is irrelevant whether the conspiracy is real or not."

The Hylar waved her pseudopods in a gesture that Severyne assumed was meant to convey outrage or disbelief. "What? If the leaders of major polities, including your own, are being manipulated, that's *irrelevant*?"

"For my purposes, yes. I am chiefly interested in trying to find Amina Azad." That was true; it just wasn't the whole truth. Severyne preferred her lies to contain as few falsehoods as possible. She was in fact *deeply* interested in whether the conspiracy theory was true or not, and talking to Amina Azad would help her figure that out. Azad was a professional liar, but Severyne knew her better than most, and was confident she'd be able to judge Azad's sincerity. "That is my mission. What matters to me is, does *Azad* believe in this conspiracy? You think she does?"

"She's absolutely committed," Lonrah said. "She has no doubts. She even kidnapped a Hacan vagrant to infect with the spores so she could test her cure, before Terrak stopped her – he's the one who destroyed the spores. That's why they need to find another test subject, someone who they already know, or strongly believe, is compromised."

"Did they tell you their candidates?"

"No. I assume they discussed it after they escaped. Assuming they even did escape together. I don't know where Terrak went."

"Azad is quite capable," Severyne said. "If she wished to find Terrak again, I'm sure she did. Hmm." She waved her hand. "All right, put her in a shuttle back to her little moon, Voyou."

"Should we, ah, really…"

"Release her? She has been cooperative. Killing those who cooperate discourages future cooperation."

"Of course, but if she spreads this ridiculous tale…"

"What do we care?" Severyne asked. "The galaxy is full of conspiracy theories."

Voyou nodded. "As you say, captain."

"I'm not interested in talking about this anymore anyway," Lonrah said. "Don't worry about that. If I never hear the word 'spore' again it will be too soon."

Severyne got a priority call from Admiral Immental not long after Lonrah was gone. "Report," the admiral demanded.

"It's been an interesting few hours," Severyne said, and filled her in completely, omitting no detail. Her doubts about Immental had taken on a new heft and seriousness, and Severyne wanted to see the admiral's reaction to the conspiracy theory. When she finished, she said, "It's quite a delusional notion, isn't it, admiral?"

"I'm not interested in some squid raving about spores." Immental scowled through the screen.

Dismissing the whole idea out of hand, then. Interesting. You didn't become a Barony admiral without being paranoid, and if Immental was… uncompromised… Severyne would have expected at least a few follow-up questions about the supposed conspiracy. Still, there was a lot going on. Perhaps the admiral was simply preoccupied. The information was inconclusive.

Immental said, "I'm more concerned about this alliance you've formed with Duval."

Severyne sniffed. "'Alliance' is a strong word for our arrangement. I will use him as long as he is useful and discard him the moment he ceases to be. Unless you forbid our association?"

Immental sighed. "I was warned your methods were unconventional… but effective. I won't stop you if you think Duval can be useful. In fact, I can see how he might be. We have recently received intelligence suggesting that Terrak is headed for a Mentak Coalition colony world, on the other side of a wormhole near your location. If Duval accompanies you there, he can smooth things over if any local authorities notice your presence."

"Where did we acquire this new intelligence, admiral?" Severyne asked. If there *was* a conspiracy, one that had agents among the Barony *and* the Mentak Coalition, there would, presumably, be sharing of information among them… but the admiral had many sources, including legitimate spies. Still inconclusive.

"We have many sources," the admiral snapped. "It doesn't matter. All that matters is, the tip is credible. Contact Duval and let him know, if you insist." She closed the connection.

Severyne lay down in her bunk and gazed at the ceiling. The time had come to work this through as far as she could.

Assume there was a conspiracy; make that an axiom upon which to build a theorem. Suddenly, her superiors had a lead, when there was no lead before. How? Had members of the conspiracy received word that Terrak and Azad were looking for a victim to test their cure on, and figured out the most likely nearby candidate, someone who was compromised and probably on Azad's list? That seemed plausible. The puppetmasters didn't need to bother with data mining or behavioral analysis or anonymous tips. They already *knew* who the closest compromised people were. So: how did the puppetmasters know that Terrak and Azad had a cure they needed to test? Someone must have told them.

Severyne ran down the list of possible sources. Lonrah knew; Severyne and Voyou knew; and Duval knew, as did anyone else he'd told. That's where her list had to break down. Lonrah might have told others, after all. And Duval had probably told his handler, at least. Had he also told his potentially compromised crew? Or had one of them learned it independently? Duval hadn't been alone in Lonrah's lab, after all. Someone could have overheard them or monitored the conversation.

Disappointing. Severyne possessed insufficient data to make a solid determination. Anyone, other than herself, could be the leak; even Lonrah could be compromised, and engaged in some elaborate double-bluff. That was the problem with vast and shadowy conspiracies. If you believed in them, they made every shadow into a threat, which rendered accurate threat assessment impossible.

The more pressing question was still whether Immental was part of this conspiracy, or if she'd simply received information from a compromised source, without understanding its nature. The admiral could be a great ally, or her most dangerous enemy. If there *was* a conspiracy, and it stretched *that* high, the Barony itself was under threat. Severyne couldn't allow that. The Barony was not just her beloved homeland; it was the theater for her career and personal success.

Severyne would have to proceed without trusting anyone… except, hilariously, Duval himself. Not that she intended to be fully open and honest with him, but she was at least fairly sure he didn't have a brain full of spores.

Ah, but no, Felix wasn't the only one she could trust. There was Amina Azad, too: she was fighting the conspiracy, not part of it, though Severyne didn't doubt Azad had her own personal agenda.

Severyne's feelings about Azad were the most complex she had about anyone or anything. Azad had saved Severyne's life, and threatened it; made her growl in frustration, and cry out in ecstasy; and, in the end, altered Severyne's entire conception of herself. In a sense, her brief, tempestuous relationship with Amina Azad had made Severyne into the person she was today: an officer working out in the field, rather than a bureaucrat manipulating her way up the chain of command on some remote Barony science compound. "Perhaps I'll get the chance to thank you in person before we're through, Azad," she murmured.

She sent a message to Duval: *We have a lead.*

He replied promptly: *Really? I wonder if it's the same one we just received…*

THE FAITHFUL X

Mmaranor, the head of the Xxcha delegation on Shilsaad Station, double-checked that the doors of his suite were locked before reaching out to his masters. "Wise ones, your suspicions have been conveyed to Captain Duval through channels he will not find unusual. The *Temerarious* will make all due haste for Entelegyne and apprehend these vile criminals. They should reach their destination in a few days."

<Terrak must not be permitted to use his poison on our faithful.>

Reading the tone of the guides was difficult – telepathic communication was very strange overall, though, oh, it felt so *good* to be spoken to by the wise ones – but Mmaranor thought they seemed… concerned. "Is it truly possible to break our holy connection?" Mmaranor asked. "I can think of nothing more terrible."

<Our power is great, but the forces arrayed against us are fiendish. We will not take chances with the great work. If Terrak does poison the fleet captain, and turns her against us, she might reveal crucial details that could yet be disrupted. The plan must proceed until the final summits are held.>

"I will do all I can to assure its success."

<There is something else on your mind. What troubles you?>

"Wise ones," Mmaranor said. "Earlier today, I was in a meeting, and my… my mind wandered. I lost track of time, and over a minute passed before I returned fully to myself. Everyone stared at me, waiting for me to answer a question I hadn't even heard. I am somewhat worried–"

<Worry not, for you are faithful,> the guides said, and waves of bliss obliterated all Mmaranor's concerns.

CHAPTER 23
TERRAK

I opened my eyes in the shipping container. The interior wasn't dark, because of the lights shining in the containment vessels of the plants stacked all around us.

I groaned as I tried to sit up and turn my head. Every joint resisted me, like the hinges of a rusty grate. I was surprised not to hear an audible squeal when I moved. Eventually I managed to roll over on my side, fumble one limp hand toward the bulb of water I'd set aside and maneuver the straw into my mouth. I took small sips, resisting the urge to gulp the fluid down, knowing I'd only give myself a sick stomach if I overindulged now.

After that I spent long minutes on my back, waiting for my muscles to stop complaining. I finally gave up on that hopeless wish and started gently massaging my sorest parts instead, even though my hands were plenty sore themselves. After a long time – longer than last time I took hibernation drugs; age was creeping up on me – I got to my feet and went to look at Azad.

She was resting on her back, looking like a fresh corpse. Her skin was waxy, and she didn't appear to be breathing. I hoped she wasn't actually dead. She had skills I could use, but it was more than that. I wasn't exactly growing fond of her, but I was certainly getting used to her, and having her around was better on many metrics than being alone. I can work by myself, but I don't relish solitary struggle – not the way I used to. Another symptom of getting old, probably.

I'd had Lonrah configure Azad's dose differently from my own. I told her to keep Azad down for five days. For me? Four and a half. Hibernation drugs aren't exact, and I knew that time could shift in either direction by a few hours, but I'd get at least a small interval when I was awake, and Azad wasn't.

I searched her. She had a standard earpiece, for local comms, but that was all. How had she called her handlers in the Federation of Sol (or wherever) before we took off? Sure, her comms could be routed through a ship or a station's system to reach more distant contacts, but not without leaving a trace, and there was no way she would have risked piggybacking on the container ship's system to make a call. Did she have a more sophisticated comm system implanted in her skull? Such things weren't unheard of, but they weren't likely for an undercover agent, who might be subject to scans that would reveal the tech.

It crossed my mind that maybe Azad wasn't talking to her handlers at all. Maybe she didn't *have* any handlers. Maybe she was mentally ill, with a persecution complex and delusions of grandeur, and she'd dragged me along into her insanity, convincing me her worldview was real. That was a depressing idea to contemplate. I didn't *really* believe it – the conspiracy explained too many otherwise inexplicable things, and Lonrah's data on the spores supported that interpretation – but I couldn't shake the image of Azad just sitting in a corner, talking to herself, lost in labyrinths of the mind.

I shook off the idea and continued my search. Azad really didn't have much on her – just what she carried in that vest of hers and at her belt. The drugs from Lonrah. Her folding tranquilizer gun, and an energy pistol. Credit and data sticks. A wicked folding knife, lockpicks, a handheld codebreaker, and a lighter. The only item that seemed remotely personal was a small and much-folded printout of a photograph of a Letnev woman's face. It looked like a frame grab from a security camera. I frowned at it for a long time. I had no idea who the woman was. The Federation and the Barony were ancient and implacable enemies, so perhaps the woman was Azad's nemesis? She seemed like the type who might have a nemesis.

Well. That all turned out to be basically pointless, but I had to try. I've gotten as far as I have in life because I am always keen to acquire useful information.

I put everything back just the way I'd found it. Then I settled down, and thought, and dozed, and generally waited for Azad to wake up. She finally did, a bit earlier than I would have expected. Once her groans were sufficiently loud, I made a few sounds of waking myself. "Good morning," I said, pretending to yawn. "How did you sleep?"

"I feel like I just plummeted into the atmosphere without a ship or a suit." Her voice was a dry rasp. "And my mouth tastes like some kind of animal took a crap inside it."

"Wasn't me," I said. "Though I will have to relieve myself at some point, once I get this water into me."

"Water. Yesssss." She rolled over and groped for the bulb she'd prepared before going to sleep, and slurped hungrily. After a thoughtful belch, she stood up and went through a series of stretching exercises. Her movements appeared much more effective than my own attempts to work the kinks out had been. "So, I've been thinking," she said.

"When? In the five minutes since you regained consciousness?"

"My mind is always working, Terrak, even when I'm sleeping. You've never woken up with the solution to a problem just waiting there for you on the top of your thoughts?"

"I suppose I am familiar with the phenomenon. What solution did slumber afford you?"

"Mmm, the details are still a little hazy. Let's talk over our situation, and maybe the fuzzy bits will clear up. So. Lonrah probably told everything she knows about us to anybody who asked, right?"

"I am sure she cooperated with the authorities, yes," I agreed. "We are friendly, but not so friendly she'd risk imprisonment or worse to protect me."

"So, she told them all about the conspiracy, the spores, the cures, everything."

"Hmm. She probably told them we believed there was a conspiracy, at least. I don't know if she believed us, honestly, and she probably wouldn't have admitted it if she did."

"She more than likely told somebody who's been compromised – there might even be somebody on Duval's crew. The puppetmasters have to be following your case pretty closely, so if that information got passed on anywhere, I'm sure they picked it up." Azad did a series of moves that involved squatting and flinging her hands out in front of herself over and over. Just watching her made me tired. "So much for the element of surprise. All the bad guys knew before was that you were on the run, with help from a mysterious benefactor. I'm usually more of a mysterious malefactor, but this role works for me too. Now, though, we have to assume the puppetmasters know we're onto their scheme, and actively seeking to oppose them. That changes the whole nature of the relationship."

"Really?" Terrak said. "We were being relentlessly pursued anyway."

"Now we're being relentlessly pursued with malice, and, I hope, just a little bit of desperation." She switched to jumping jacks. "Assume they know we have a possible cure and need to test it. You don't become an interstellar puppetmaster by being stupid, so they've probably guessed we're going after the fleet captain. At the very least, they'll know it's a possibility, and take precautions."

"Not necessarily. They don't know about your data mining, the anomalous behavioral comparisons, or that you have a list of people who've likely been compromised."

"Probably not, but they know there's an opposition now, and an organized one, so I'm sure they can guess. We whipped up a cure fast, which suggests a certain level of competence on our part. The Mentak fleet captain is the nearest person who's gotten weird recently. Trust me, they'll be keeping an eye on her. That's the way to bet, anyway. I doubt we can just stroll in, snatch her up and inject her full of the cure."

"I must admit, I'm glad you didn't realize all these problems earlier," I said. "You probably would have killed Lonrah to keep her quiet."

Azad snorted. "Of course I realized all this earlier. The only reason Lonrah is still alive is because just killing her wasn't sufficient, and I didn't have time to cover our tracks. Duval's Devils showed up at her lab, and I had to flee. I could have blasted Lonrah after she showed me her escape hatch, but I didn't have time to wipe her data banks or clear out all her surveillance footage, so there was no point. The puppetmasters would have found out about us and the spore sample and the cure anyway." She smirked. "Lonrah actually asked me why I didn't kill her. I said it was bad manners." Her face went serious again. "I hope she took my advice and ran as fast and far as she could, though. Maybe the cops barging in gave her enough time."

"Calling them was an actual kindness," I said. "It made me like you better."

She waved a dismissive hand. "Nah, I was just sowing discord and confusion among my enemies." She grinned. "Which is basically my idea for how we'll get our hands on this fleet captain."

"Do tell," I said.

"First, give me some more information about this station we're sneaking onto."

CHAPTER 24
AZAD

Chelicera Station catered to travelers going in and out of the wormhole, which meant it specialized in supplies, food, booze, and entertainment, the latter encompassing everything from immersive holo-suites to dancing to prizefighting to intimate companionship (and sometimes combinations of some or all of the above).

The station was independently operated, run by a protégé of the infamous Sagasa the Disciplinarian, a Hacan crime boss whose tendrils expanded into numerous systems. Azad had dealt with Sagasa in the past and was confident that someone schooled in his business methods would nurture the kind of environment where she could do business.

Sneaking off the ship wasn't difficult – everything was run by autoloaders, so they just walked out of the cargo bay past the robot forklifts and onto the bustling docks. Azad stopped at a public terminal and refilled her credit sticks with the promised funds from her employers, then tossed a handful of sticks to Terrak. "That should cover your part."

Terrak frowned. "I have concerns about your plan."

"What do you mean? My plan has *two prongs*. That's one more prong than I usually bother with. Confusion to our enemies is always a solid tactic. You go ship-shopping and make the recording. I'll get busy recruiting."

She sauntered off in search of a couple of desperate idiots. There were always plenty of those on a shady station like this. She went to the closest bar and looked around but didn't see what she needed. Fortunately, there were other bars. She needed a human woman and a male Hacan, the kind of people who'd accept a windfall without questioning why their garbage luck had finally turned…

Three bars later, after marking a few possibilities, she found something she hadn't dared hope for: an existing set. Way in the back, a Hacan and a human sat together in a booth, looking extremely glum. She decided to give them a shot; if it worked out, she'd only have to make her pitch once.

Azad slid into the seat next to the woman and said, "Let me buy you two a couple of drinks." The Hacan was older than Terrak, with a scar on his muzzle, and the woman was younger than Azad, but they were both close enough at a glance.

"We don't have any money for you to scam off us," the woman said. "We can't even afford our port fees."

"Then you should be happy I'm buying you drinks." She gestured to a passing server and said, "Two more of whatever they're drinking, and something twice as expensive for me." She tapped the server's ring with her own and winked. "Plus a little something extra for your efforts."

"What do you want from us?" the Hacan rumbled.

"We won't do any weird stuff," the woman said.

"Well…" the Hacan said. "I mean…"

"Nothing weird. I want you to leave this station on a better ship than the one you arrived in, that's all."

"You want us for your crew?" the woman said. "You don't even know us."

"I am hiring a crew, but I won't be on the ship with you. I just want you to deliver something for me."

"Smuggling? Why pick us?"

"Because my known associates all got compromised, and you're total strangers, who can't be traced back to me. I'll pay you ten percent up front, and the other ninety percent on delivery."

"Ten percent of *what*?"

Azad grinned. By the time people started asking questions like that, you had a deal; it was just about nailing down the details.

After Azad concluded her business, she went over to the bar and picked up a napkin. "Do you have something to write with?" she asked the bartender.

CHAPTER 25
TERRAK

Buying a small, fast ship was surprisingly easy. After some discreet inquiries, I found a captain with significant gambling debts sitting in a public corridor, staring blankly at a wall, and offered to solve all his problems. He took me to his vessel, the *Vermilion*. The ship was a smuggler's dream, small and swift and sleek, with more cargo space than you'd expect, and faster engines, too. He transferred ownership to a false corporate identity Azad had already prepared.

I went into the *Vermilion*'s cockpit, fiddled with the controls, and figured out how to make a recording. Once I was sure the screen showed everything I needed it to – Azad had been very specific about the background we required – I gazed directly into the camera, and I told my story.

When I was done, and all the necessary arrangements were made, I joined Azad on the station. "I wish we could have taken the *Vermilion*," I said, watching the sleek machine depart through one of the station windows, a dart made of night.

"What have you got against the *Nine-Tenths of the Law*?" Azad said. "It's… well… it has a working propulsion system. And seats. There's a window. Who could ask for anything more?"

"I could." I turned and looked down at her. "How long before the message starts to broadcast?"

"I programmed it to launch for an hour from departure, and it'll run on a loop after that until it gets out of range of the station here. Sagasa's cousin is happy to amplify and rebroadcast basically any signal we want, for a price. He didn't even ask what we were planning to transmit. I love the free market."

The *Temerarious* lurked in space, as stealthy as could be, between the wormhole and the nearest inhabited object of any size, Chelicera Station. They'd been here for two days, and Felix was getting antsy.

Having Undercommandant Voyou on board didn't help. The Letnev officer was unfailingly polite and formal, but there was a current of mockery running underneath every interaction, like Voyou thought he was better than the Mentak Coalition crew – which he doubtless did, since a sense of superiority was the Letnev national pastime. Voyou strolled around the ship, making conversation, inquiring about everyone's work and pasts, and somehow managed to never reveal anything at all about himself. "Oh, I'm just a cog in the great machine, doing my part to serve my captain and country."

"You're a hostage," Ggorgos rumbled at him. They were all in the galley, where crew members without immediate duties tended to congregate during the "interminable waiting" phase of any operation.

"And here I thought I was a spy." Voyou turned around in his chair. "Tib Pelta, didn't you say I was a spy?"

"You can be both," Tib said from a corner, where she was ostentatiously cleaning a gun.

"Then Calred, back on the *Grim Countenance*, is he a hostage, or a spy, or both?"

"I prefer to think of it as a cultural exchange program," Felix said. "Gaining a greater appreciation of one another's worldviews. We're all learning, and also, we're all having fun."

Voyou smiled. "*I* certainly am."

The decision to exchange Voyou and Calred was the only solution they'd found to the problem of forming an alliance with someone you found basically untrustworthy. Severyne and Felix had agreed they should take up positions on either side of the wormhole, to double their chances of capturing Terrak and Azad – if the fugitives slipped past one, the other could catch them. They'd argued back and forth over who should wait on *which* side of the wormhole, though, and finally they'd literally used a random number generator to decide who went where. Felix rolled an odd number, so he was here, the first line of defense. He didn't much like this position, but he wouldn't have totally liked the alternative, either. If he was on the Mentak Coalition side of the wormhole, he'd be able to respond at a moment's notice if a cry for help went up from Entelegyne. But on this side, he could monitor traffic heading into the wormhole, allowing him to leap on any ship that seemed like it might contain their quarry.

Obviously Severyne couldn't be left on the other side of the wormhole unattended, where she might snatch Terrak *and* Azad and fly off into the darkness. Severyne couldn't abide leaving Felix unmonitored on *his* side, for the same reason, even though Felix was basically an honorable guy, within the boundaries of his duties. Their solution was the exchange: Severyne got Calred, and Felix got Voyou, bridge officer for bridge officer. Felix thought Severyne had the better end of the deal. Calred was *much* better to play cards with.

"We're receiving a transmission." Tib was looking at the small screen on her wrist. She swiped her fingers across the gauntlet and put the transmission up on a larger wall screen.

A tired-looking Hacan said, "Greetings."

Felix whistled. "Terrak is reaching out to *us*?"

"Not us specifically," Tib said. "This message is going out wide, transmitted from… let me see… Chelicera Station."

"Let's get to the station then!" Felix leapt to his feet.

"No, strike that, it's being *relayed* through the comms system at Chelicera Station. Terrak is broadcasting remotely, let me see if I can find–"

"Perhaps we should listen to what he's *saying*?" Voyou offered, not very loudly, but very pointedly.

They all turned their attention to the Hacan's speech.

"…is Terrak," he said. "I am – or rather, I was, before dark forces conspired to destroy my reputation – a special trade ambassador for the Emirates of Hacan. I have a long and distinguished career, spanning decades, and while I have made my fair share of enemies over the years, as anyone does in business and politics, not even my most vociferous detractors would call me a *killer*." He shook his head dolefully, mane swaying. Felix thought he looked very convincing; he had a lot of gravitas.

Terrak said, "But killer is what they call me now, throughout the inhabited galaxy. The authorities claim I murdered one of my oldest friends, and when asked why I would commit such a terrible crime, they make vague comments about 'personal disagreements'. There were no disagreements. I loved Qqurant like a sibling. No, my friends, I have been falsely accused in an attempt to silence me, because I have uncovered a terrible truth. A truth that threatens us all. A truth I will reveal to you now."

"There's a stencil on the wall over his left shoulder," Tib said. "Part of a ship ID number I think, hold on…"

Terrak kept talking, growing more impassioned and lively as he did. "I attended a summit on Shilsaad Station and noticed my dear friend Qqurant was acting strangely. I approached him and found him confused and disoriented. He walked away, and avoided me, so I asked friends if they'd heard anything to explain this strangeness – had the poor fellow suffered some tragedy, was he distracted, had I offended him in some way? No one had an explanation, but the question was out there in the world, and people were wondering. That night, when I returned to my rooms, I was *attacked*."

Terrak described being assaulted by an unknown Yssaril, who tried to spray him with a mysterious canister. "After I fought off the craven assailant, and they fled, I received a call from Qqurant himself, asking me to come to his room. When I went to meet him, I found him dead, slain with my own ceremonial spear, stolen from my closet. Security rushed in just moments after I arrived, tipped off, I'm sure, by the real murderer. Since their gambit with the canister failed, they chose instead to ruin my reputation… and worse. They took me into custody, and I would have died in an 'accident' the next day, if not for the intervention of a human operative investigating the very conspiracy I had unwittingly stumbled into."

Well, that fit with what Felix had gathered from the Facilitator. If there was a conspiracy afoot, Terrak was lobbing a bomb at them by talking about it publicly. There was sure to be a reaction… and that reaction might *reveal* the conspiracy. Either way, Felix had to get to Terrak. He was either a deranged fugitive or a whistleblower whose life was in danger, and Felix wanted him locked up safely in the brig while he figured out which.

Terrak took a deep breath. "What I have to tell you is deeply troubling. A leading chemist analyzed the contents of that canister – the one these villains tried to use on *me* – and discovered it contains fungal spores stolen from the Arborec and weaponized to sap the will of victims. Those who breathe the spores are made puppets of the as-yet-unknown conspirators. We have been investigating the conspiracy and have discovered that highly placed members of the military and governments of several major polities have been compromised. Their minds are not their own, and they are acting against their own interests, and the interests they are sworn to serve. My poor friend Qqurant was one of their pawns, and we believe his strange behavior was caused by the spores – the effects of mind control seem to cause those very minds to deteriorate. The analytical data the chemist gathered can be downloaded here–"

"The *Vermilion*!" Tib shouted. "That's where he's transmitting from! It's a trading vessel, recently sold to a dummy corporation, and it departed Chelicera Station an hour ago. I got some security footage from the docks, showing the crew board, and they were wearing hoods, but it's clearly a Hacan and a human woman."

"Set an intercept course for this *Vermilion*," Felix said.

Ggorgos, who'd been silent up until this point, nodded in agreement. "Yes." She cocked her head and looked at Felix. "What is all this nonsense about *spores*? I knew Terrak was a murderer. I did not realize he suffered paranoid delusions."

"The Hacan is talking about you, now, Felix," Voyou said.

Felix snapped his attention back to the screen. "…and his crew of Mentak Coalition clandestine operatives have pursued us relentlessly. We have created a possible cure for those affected by the spores and had planned to test it on a victim we've identified… but the wormhole we need to pass through has been blockaded by the *Temerarious*. Is this Duval compromised by the spores, in league with the conspirators, or just an unwitting dupe? In any case, we fear we'll be captured, and have chosen to release what we know before we can be silenced. We only want you to consider: has someone close to *you* changed recently? Begun to behave in ways that are wildly out of character? Furthermore, ask yourself, who's *really* behind the formation of the Greater Coalition, and the opposing force created by the Barony of Letnev, the Legion? Call your representatives. Ask them to investigate–"

"Aren't you supposed to be a covert operative, Captain Duval?" Voyou said. "But there's your name, broadcast all over the system. Probably beyond, if anyone finds this interesting enough to pass along, and someone certainly will. Everyone loves a juicy conspiracy."

Felix groaned. Jhuri wasn't going to like this. Felix didn't like it much either. They needed to capture Terrak and wrap this up *fast*. "Just… catch that ship. I need to make a call."

"I do, too," Voyou said. "Supraluminal, to the other side of the wormhole. I'm sure my captain would love to know about all this."

THE FAITHFUL XI

<Disaster!> the guides cried in Immental's mind. She clutched her head, waves of nausea pulsing through her. She was only glad she was alone in her quarters, and not in a conference or appearing before the Baron.

She collapsed, curling into a ball, and then forced herself to speak through the pain. "This… Terrak's transmission… it can be contained, guides. All is not lost. We will capture the fugitives. Duval is en route to intercept their ship and stop the broadcast. We will discredit Terrak or bring them into your communion and make them recant."

<The summits on Arc Prime and Moll Primus must go forward as planned! The great work must proceed!>

A burning sensation washed over her, like ants biting every bit of her exposed skin. "Guides!" she cried. "I… cannot… serve you… if… I feel such… pain…"

<Fix this, or this pain will feel like nothing at all.>

The agony did not cease immediately, but it tapered off. Sadly, it was not replaced by a corresponding intensity of bliss, just a neutrality. Her sense of obedience felt suddenly less like a pleasure and more like a shackle. Immental was no longer being tormented, but she realized she would not be rewarded unless she did something worthy of reward.

CHAPTER 26
TERRAK

"It would be nice if that transmission alone could make a difference," I said. We were sitting in the cramped cockpit of the *Nine-Tenths of the Law*, watching the bomb I'd just dropped on the galaxy.

"Ha," Azad said. "The idea that just releasing some horrible truth to the public automatically leads to meaningful change is a fairy tale. Little kids and the occasional university student are the only ones who believe it. Most people will just think you've gone insane, and the really clever ones will think you're *pretending* to be insane to try and prove diminished capacity and save your own ass in a murder trial. Fortunately, we're up against secretive, paranoid forces who are terrified of having their plans brought to light. Who knows? Maybe the message *will* freak out a few people in high places, make them nervous, and jam up the works a bit. I'd welcome that. But what matters is, the puppetmasters are terrified of the mere possibility of exposure. Look at how they reacted when you asked some friends at a cocktail party a few questions. And now, you just – put it all out there! The conspirators will drop everything they're doing to chase down the *Vermilion*."

That was the hope, anyway. It wasn't much of a plan, but it was something. Azad was a great believer in the power of sowing confusion. "I hope they don't just destroy the vessel," I said. "Those people you hired to fly the *Vermilion* may not be innocent, exactly, but they don't deserve to die."

"I think the bad guys would rather capture us and fill our brains with spores at this point. They'll want you to recant this transmission, and say you made it all up, and they'll want me to tell them who's funding me, so they can figure out who else they need to co-opt or silence."

"If they do manage to capture us, they can force us to do whatever they like," I said.

"Best we don't get caught, then. I don't want to be backed into that particular corner. I've never been a big fan of those hollow teeth full of poison. Frothing and twitching is not the way I want to go out."

"Better than living with a brain full of fungus," I said.

"No argument there." She flicked switches and toggles on the control board. "Let's see if we can slip past Felix and company in the chaos."

CHAPTER 27
FELIX

"We're in pursuit of the *Vermilion*," Felix said. "They're fast, but we're faster. We should be able to overtake them in a couple of hours." He was beginning to have his doubts – could it really be this easy? What if this was some sort of ruse created by Terrak and Azad? He tried to tell himself Terrak was a lazy diplomat and Azad was a blunt instrument who favored violence, not subterfuge… but diplomats had to be clever, and while Azad was crass, that didn't mean she was simple. Still, he had to assume they were on board. If they let the *Vermilion* go, and the fugitives *were* on board…

"I want this finished, Felix," Jhuri said. "It's dragged on too long. Let me know as soon as Terrak is in custody."

"Of course."

Jhuri started to turn away from the screen, and Felix said, "Wait! Where are you going?"

The Hylar flushed colors of annoyance. "I'm rather busy here, Felix. I have to go brief the Xxcha on your current status, even though Ggorgos has probably already told them everything you told me. I swear, information flow only goes one way around here–"

"Boss. The *video*. Terrak was talking about the conspiracy! The… the whole thing I've been secretly investigating!" Not that Felix had gotten very far in said investigation. In fact, he'd gotten nowhere at all. But still. "If that video isn't total confirmation of your theory, it's at least a strong suggestion that you're on the right track."

Jhuri sighed. "Felix, forget about all that. The conspiracy idea is nonsense. I don't know what I was thinking."

Felix stared at the screen. "Jhuri… What's with the sudden shift?"

"I thought it was possible there might be a small cabal of people opposed to the Greater Union, maybe drugging people or trying to discredit rivals," Jhuri said. "That's the kind of political idiocy that happens from time to time. But these claims Terrak made? That people in all the major factions are being mind-controlled by *space mushrooms*? It's absurd. Put it out of your mind. Just apprehend Terrak and bring him to justice." Jhuri switched off the transmission.

Felix put his head in his hands. *They got to Jhuri.*

CHAPTER 28
SEVERYNE

"Join the pursuit!" Immental shouted from the screen. "Transit the wormhole and go after this *Vermilion*!"

"I will do so if that is your order," Severyne said calmly. "I would, however, advise against such an action."

"Capturing Terrak is your only priority! What *else* should you be doing?"

"Waiting for Amina Azad to show up on this side of the wormhole, admiral."

Immental frowned. "What do you mean?"

"I know Azad. She would not reveal her position this way. Appeals to the good will and good sense of the public are not in her nature."

"But the Hacan – Azad can't necessarily control him. He could have done it on his own. Maybe he even left Azad behind when he got this new ship."

"I acknowledge the possibility," Severyne said. "Which is why I am happy to let Duval rush off in pursuit of the vessel. I do not, personally, believe Azad and Terrak are even on the *Vermilion*. Perhaps I am wrong, and Duval will capture them – if so, Voyou will see to it that our interests are secured, and nothing will be lost. But if I am right… if this transmission is part of a scheme, and a distraction… we should not leave the wormhole unguarded. I think Terrak and Azad are still on their way. They know about Duval's forces – Azad spoke to them from Huntsman's Moon. They don't know the Barony is involved, though. They will never expect us to be waiting here, ready to pounce when they appear."

"That… may be so," Immental said. "And I suppose by the time you caught up with the *Vermilion*, everything would be over anyway. Assuming Duval can even intercept the ship."

"I believe his competence will extend that far, admiral. His ship is quite swift; I've used it myself. I will remain here, with your permission, and report if we detect any sign of the fugitives."

"Very well." Immental started to turn away, then looked back at the screen. "Captain Dampierre… Severyne… you haven't asked me about the contents of that video. The Hacan spy's outlandish claims."

"It seems self-evident to me that Terrak is either suffering from paranoid delusions or making up an outrageous story to distract from his own guilt. Is there reason to think otherwise?"

"No," Immental said. "That is our assessment as well."

"At least he didn't tell the *actual* truth – that he's secretly a Barony agent. That would have been embarrassing for us. As it stands, Terrak has only embarrassed himself."

"Yes," the admiral said. "Indeed. Well said."

Severyne affected a slightly confused look. "I am curious, though – do we know why Terrak and Azad *actually* want to visit this Coalition colony world? If there is no conspiracy, no cure to administer, what business could they possibly have with Fleet Captain Harlow?"

Immental said, "I… should think it's obvious. Terrak committed a murder at a summit, doubtless intended to disrupt the Coalition. Now, he plans to attack Harlow, an architect of the Union, to further throw the proceedings into chaos."

"Ah. Yes. That *does* make sense. But admiral… if their aim is to weaken the Greater Union… why are we trying to *stop* them?"

For just a moment, Immental's expression was disturbingly blank. Then she narrowed her eyes and said, "Terrak is a rogue Barony asset, and your mission is to capture him, not to speculate about his plans, or the infinitely more complex and subtle plans of your superiors."

"Of course, admiral. My apologies."

"Get Terrak. I'll await your report."

The screen flickered off.

Severyne swiveled back and forth in her chair. Such nervous habits were unseemly in an officer of her rank and distinction, but there was no one here to see it, so she indulged. She was surprised to discover she missed Voyou. They'd gone through a lot together, including surviving a deathtrap created by an ancient alien tyrant, and as a result, he was one of the few people in the galaxy she felt comfortable talking with. Having someone to share ideas with was helpful in developing new and better ideas. She had so much to think about now. Like the fact that the admiral seemed to be–

Someone knocked at her door. Actually knocked, instead of calling ahead. She frowned, slid open a drawer, and wrapped her fingers around the grip of a pistol. "Come," she called.

The door slid open, and Calred stepped in, ducking his head so he wouldn't hit it on the way through. Severyne found the presence of a Hacan in her ready room as incongruous as seeing a toad on a dinner plate. The two of them had shared a ship before, when he was her prisoner, and she'd liked him better when he wasn't allowed to wander about. Sadly, locking him up now would only strain her partnership with Duval, so Calred retained his irritating liberty. "What do you want?" she said.

"Just to talk over recent events." He sat down in a chair without asking permission. The top button of his uniform jacket was undone. The Mentak were so *slovenly*. "I heard about the *Vermilion*. You think it's a trick, right? Amina Azad doesn't leave a trail that wide and easy to follow."

Slovenly, yes, but quicker on the uptake than Admiral Immental, which was the problem. Immental was reckoned the finest tactical and strategic mind in the Barony. That was the reason her support of the Legion initiative was so successful, even though such an alliance went against basic Letnev principles of superiority and self-reliance. A ruse like Azad's shouldn't have taken the admiral in. She'd lost a step. The question was, why? The pressures of the upcoming summit on Arc Prime? Or something more sinister? She was increasingly concerned that the admiral was compromised, and if that were true, it meant a great many *other* things were probably true, too.

Severyne didn't say any of that. She said, "The beads woven into your mane look very stupid."

Calred chuckled. "I'm eager to take fashion advice from the Letnev. I understand the bold new look on Arc Prime this season is a splash of dark gray to accent all the black. So. We're going to stay parked right here and wait for Azad to wander into our clutches, I assume?"

"That is my intention. Will you tell your captain that he's almost certainly off on a pointless adventure?"

The Hacan crossed one leg over the other, getting even more comfortable in a chair that was designed to make comfort as difficult to achieve as possible in the absence of literal spikes. "Nah, I don't think so. Someone has to check the *Vermilion* anyway, just on the off chance Terrak and Azad *are* on board, and if I told Felix I thought it was a fool's errand, I'd just sap his enthusiasm. Felix does better work when he's fully committed."

"I can't tell if you're being loyal or disloyal to your captain," Severyne mused.

"I'm being practical, which is usually better than either of those. How about all this mind-control-spore stuff Terrak spouted? What do you think about it?"

"I think it's irrelevant to my mission."

Calred snorted. "You can do the obedient-little-Letnev routine with me if you like, I don't mind, but we're in here alone, Severyne, and I've seen you try to murder people with a *stick*. You can talk freely with me."

Severyne allowed herself to smile. "Our shared history as enemies creates a degree of closeness between us, then? In some ways, we are closer than friends? I have heard that position espoused before. I think believing it is a good way to get knifed in the back. But I will assume you speak in good faith, and offer my answer in greater detail: I have no reason to believe that a secret conspiracy is using weaponized Arborec spores to mind-control people in order to manipulate galactic politics. It is the sort of extraordinary claim that I will not credit until I see real evidence." She left unspoken her determination to *discover* that evidence, if it existed.

"Sensible Sev," Calred said. "How long do you think before Azad pops through the wormhole?"

"If I were her, I wouldn't wait long. I'd begin the journey as soon as the bait was released and your captain went racing after it. She's probably on her way now."

"We need our guy alive," Calred said. "So, no blasting them out of the sky, right?"

"I also wish to recover my target intact."

"Right. What was I thinking? You wouldn't kill Azad from a distance anyway. You'd want to do that up close, right?" He showed his teeth. "Though you'd probably have a hard time deciding whether to kill her or kiss her, if the way you two looked at each other last time is any–"

"You are dismissed, Calred. I will let you know if your services are needed further."

He gave her a lazy Mentak-style salute and sauntered out.

Severyne went back to swiveling in her chair. A conversation with Calred wasn't as good as talking to Voyou, but it was better than talking to herself, and had, indeed, clarified certain factors in her mind. She had a mission to fulfill … but she also had a *responsibility*, to serve the best interests of the Letnev people, and, of course, to look after her own future prospects. It would be a delicate balance, but Severyne thrived in dynamic situations.

CHAPTER 29
TERRAK

Azad piloted the *Nine-Tenths of the Law* to the wormhole, paid the toll, then let the automated systems handle the actual transit. We emerged on the other side, near a space station that was larger and rather less scruffy than Chelicera, equipped to handle the vast freighters the Mentak Coalition sent to the local colony worlds. The automated traffic control system scanned us, but we were legally owned (by another fake corporation) and didn't send up any red flags, so the system waved us through without requiring a manual inspection.

"It's a pretty short trip from here to Entelegyne," Azad said.

"Assuming this ship doesn't fall to pieces before we get there." I was in the co-pilot's seat, though I wasn't doing any co-piloting. There just weren't any other seats, only a couple of tiny bunks that were really just slots in the bulkheads.

"Hey, I looked the ship over pretty well. My best estimate is that it'll fall apart slightly *after* we reach our destination, so that's fine." She consulted the scanners. "This planet we're going to is really just… wow. There's basically nobody there. It's all automated farms, and even the supervisors use telepresence bots, with only occasional visits in person. The fleet captain has a pretty sweet little bungalow on the southern continent, with a staff of just two people. Talk about getting away from it all. It's possible she's got some extra personnel hidden on the grounds, since the puppetmasters suspect we're coming, but my guess is they don't want to let anybody they don't control near Harlow. She's supposed to be an honored guest at the summit on Moll Primus, but I'd be willing to bet she's barely able to string a coherent sentence together now, if she's been under the influence as long as we think."

"Is she really the best candidate for the cure, then?"

"What, because she might be a vegetable with a brain full of vegetables? She might be the best candidate. If the cure works on her, then it *really works*, you know?"

I grunted. "What if it doesn't work? If we go to all this trouble, and the cure simply fails, or kills her?" The idea of going to all this effort, making these hairsbreadth escapes, expending such ingenuity, only to *fail*, was troubling. We were being hunted, and we wouldn't escape our pursuers forever. We needed to make progress.

Azad was less concerned. "If it doesn't work, I'll tell my bosses what happened – seizures, frothing, death, nothing at all – and take some blood and tissue samples, and we find another scientist to do some analysis, and my bosses send a tweaked recipe, and we try again. Nobody ever said science was easy or pretty. That said… the people I work for are smart, and they'd already done a lot of work on finding ways to disrupt Arborec communication. I'm hopeful that what we've got here will do the trick."

We sailed through the star-speckled void, and eventually an orb appeared in the distance, growing in size in the screens until it became a green and cloud-streaked planet. "Entelegyne. Looks pretty from up here. You just know it's all bugs and allergens and mud when you get to the surface though. Ugh."

I frowned, gazing at the screen. "Azad… something just occluded one of the stars to the left of the planet."

"What are you talking about?"

"There was a star, visible *there*, and then, it went dark."

"Are you sure?" Azad pulled up an overlay of the local star chart on the screen, and all the matching stars turned green. One dot stayed stubbornly red, with no corresponding light source in reality. "Huh. You're right. Could be an asteroid, or space junk. Anything, really."

"It could be a ship. It could be the *Temerarious*."

"No way. They're off after the *Vermilion*, I'm sure of it. Duval is a dog – you throw a stick, and he's going to chase it. He might worry he's being tricked, but he's not going to let it go, or delegate it, either. He's got personal feelings about me, and they are negative." She manipulated a few switches and buttons, then sighed. "Damn. I wish the sensors on this ship were better. We'll have to get a lot closer before I can see what we're dealing with."

"There." I pointed at the screen. "The star is back. Whatever that object is, it's *moving*, and I think it's most sensible to assume it's a vessel that's looking for us."

Azad made a little growl in her throat. "Maybe the Mentak Coalition sent another ship out here, just to cover the contingencies. I really thought the puppetmasters would try to keep the circle small, to contain things… but maybe we changed their math when we spilled the truth all over the spacewaves. They could dispatch uninfected people to capture us now without worrying we'd give something away, since we *already* gave it away, I just didn't think they'd have time to mobilize crews. Maybe there was a ship in the vicinity already… Well, whatever, we deal with what's in front of us. We're on the right trajectory to reach the planet, so I can cut our power and we'll just keep sailing along. If they notice us at all, they'll think we're just a passing asteroid–"

The control console buzzed. "Incoming call," I said. "Heavily encrypted, too. They don't want anyone overhearing."

Azad sighed. "I guess it would be rude not to answer."

CHAPTER 30
SEVERYNE

Calred pounded on the door this time, and Severyne opened it with a scowl ready and waiting on her face. "I am not *Felix*," she said. "You don't bang on my door and demand my attention."

"I'm not allowed to use the onboard comms, Severyne. The rest of the crew literally ignores me when I talk to them. This is the only way I can get your attention."

"You're a *hostage*, Calred, only here in order to compel Duval's cooperation. None of us want or need to talk to you. Now if you'll excuse me, I'm required in the hangar bay."

Calred tried to loom over her. He could do so physically, but she was not intimidated. If he even breathed on her more heavily than she liked, she would have his knees removed. She'd agreed to return him to Felix alive, not unharmed. "That's why I'm here!" he shouted. "I heard someone mention a landing party. Why are you landing? Correction – why are *we* landing? You agreed I'd be included in this operation, remember?"

"I was about to send for you," Severyne lied. "We're landing because a ship is approaching the planet, and I believe Terrak and Azad are on board."

"So, capture them!"

"What a clever idea," she said flatly. "We ran simulations. Attempting to take them in space is too dangerous. If we try to disable their ship, we might inadvertently destroy it, and boarding parties are also chancy. Azad is a great fan of traps and ambushes, and there's no need to send my crew into harm's way. Fire could be exchanged, and their ship is frankly a flying piece of trash, so accidental decompression could result as well. We know where Azad and Terrak are going. We'll simply land and capture them on the ground."

"Do you think the fleet captain will take kindly to a group of Letnev soldiers appearing on her doorstep?"

"I do not. Which is why we will land quietly and proceed carefully. And, if we do make contact, why, we'll have *you* there to smooth things over, won't we? An officer in good standing in the Mentak Coalition Navy." She patted Calred on his immense bicep. "Come along."

"I'll need a weapon. I will not face Amina Azad without a gun in my hand. I don't even like being around *you* when I'm unarmed."

"Of course, Calred. You're one of the team, and my team *always* comes prepared."

Severyne, Calred, and four Barony marines in black armor and blank face masks boarded a shuttle and dropped from the *Grim Countenance* to the planet. Their vessel bounced through the atmosphere, plummeted to within a few hundred meters of the surface, then skimmed over a wide, grassy plain toward the fleet captain's estate.

The shuttle settled down in the shadow of a rock formation, and the group disembarked. Two marines went first to make sure the area was clear, then Severyne followed with Calred at her side, followed by the other marines. There were no dangerous fauna on this continent, so there was no fence or other real barricades around the estate – just ornamental stone walls, low enough to step over.

Severyne squinted at the sky. She envied her troops their light-filtering masks as they marched around her with their guns at the ready. "Sunshine. Appalling. I've never seen the point of it. I know, everyone says it helps the plants grow, but we grow things just fine in the dark back home."

"I'm just happy I can finally see," Calred said, rifle resting over his shoulder. "It's so dark on your ship I keep banging into things."

"That is because you are a gargantuan oaf."

"Could a gargantuan oaf do this?" Calred brought his rifle down and discharged an energy burst into a pile of rocks, scorching the stone and making Severyne turn and stare at him. All her troopers trained their guns on him, just awaiting her order to turn him into charred meat.

Calred held his rifle pointed at the sky, held his free hand up, and smiled a wide smile. Hacan could smile very widely indeed. "Please, be calm. I just wanted to make sure the weapon worked. I used the lowest setting, and it hardly even made a noise. I just had this silly idea you might give me a rifle with no charge and wanted to ease my mind."

"Giving you an inoperative weapon would violate the terms of our partnership."

"You're the one who said I was just a hostage."

"That's because you were annoying me. I trust you're satisfied now?"

"Very."

"Good. Don't fire that weapon again without my explicit orders, Calred, or I'll have my marines shoot your feet off and leave you and your cauterized stumps in the bushes. We want our quarry alive. The guns are for purposes of intimidation or unexpected resistance."

"Yes, ma'am." He offered another lazy salute. That was probably the only kind a Mentak Coalition soldier knew how to give. It was astonishing to her that such a rabble had risen to become a galactic power.

They continued moving slowly and carefully across the grounds of the fleet captain's estate. It was so… so… *pointless*. There were little arched wooden bridges over trickles of water already narrow enough to step across. Severyne spied tiny stone buildings nestled among bright flowers. They paused near an octagonal structure with a peaked roof and sides that were open, apart from railings. "What is *that*?"

"It's a gazebo." Calred sounded amused.

"Why would you want a structure like that? It's completely indefensible."

"That's true. I can't think of a single time in history a gazebo withstood a siege."

"And this is aquaculture, I suppose?" Severyne went to the rocky edge of a large fishpond, connected to other ponds on the grounds by narrow channels spanned by more tiny bridges. "I can see the appeal of fresh seafood, but really, it's needlessly ornamental."

"Nobody eats these fish, Severyne. They're just here to be pretty and make you feel peaceful. They're bred to be decorative. See, their scales are silver, orange, ooh, there's one that's all white."

"And I suppose that… damp structure… isn't meant for irrigation?"

"It's a fountain. You must have seen fountains before."

Severyne clucked her tongue. "The Mentak Coalition is decadent. You sicken me."

"The feeling is mutual. The sickening, I mean. Not the decadence. Nobody would accuse you of having any fun."

"Decadence doesn't mean *fun*–"

"Hey, Sev," a voice called. It seemed to emerge from behind a pile of mossy boulders, doubtless arranged with great precision for no particular purpose. Severyne stiffened her spine, and she found herself, improbably, wondering if her collar was straight or her hair was mussed. "And Calred! Wow, what a big happy fancy fun reunion."

"Azad," Calred growled, and swung his rifle down.

THE FAITHFUL XII

Jhuri ended the call with Felix. "That … didn't feel right," he said.

Kote Strom – someone Jhuri had considered an annoying incompetent, before the gift of the sacrament revealed them to be partners in the great work – scowled from her seat, just out of view of Jhuri's screen. "What didn't feel right? You don't think Duval believed you?"

"I don't know," Jhuri said. "I tried to be as convincing as possible, but the guides insisted I be firm and direct and scornful, to mock the whole idea of a conspiracy. Given that I recently told Felix to *investigate* a conspiracy, I worry that wasn't an effective approach."

Strom was chilly now: "You question the wisdom of the guides?"

The idea sent a shudder of visceral horror through Jhuri's entire nervous system. "Of course not! That's not what I meant. It felt … wrong to lie to Felix, instead of bringing him into the fold. We have a member of the faithful on board the *Temerarious* already, so it would be easy enough to offer Felix the sacrament–"

"The guides say no. The guides say it is important to have agents who are unaware of their existence."

"But why?" Jhuri said.

"They did not say." Kote Strom looked briefly stricken. "But I think it's because – because we *decline*, we lose our ability to–" Her eyes rolled back in her head and she fell off the stool.

<Because not all are worthy to partake in our glory,> the guides whispered into Jhuri's ear.

"Oh," Jhuri said. "Yes. That makes sense."

Kote sat up, touching the side of her head and wincing.

<You will both attend the summit on Moll Primus,> the guides whispered. *<To help ensure all goes smoothly. Arrangements have already been made.>*

"To make sure what goes smoothly, guides?" Jhuri asked. He didn't *want* to question the guides, but he was head of Coalition covert operations; being nosy was basically part of his DNA, and the question just came out of him by reflex.

<All will be revealed in time,> the guides said, and for some reason, Jhuri found that answer perfectly satisfying.

CHAPTER 31
TERRAK

When the mysterious ship hailed us, Azad pushed a button on the ship's console, and a Letnev woman's face appeared on a screen. I recognized her immediately as the same person from Azad's much-folded photograph.

"Sev!" Azad said. "What in the hell are you… oh. Oh, no. You haven't gone green on me, have you, Sev?"

"I have been dispatched to capture your associate, Azad," the woman said, face completely expressionless. "I am told that he is a Barony intelligence asset, now attempting to defect to the Federation of Sol."

I snorted. "Ridiculous. There's no point in cooperating with the Barony. They're even stingy when it comes to bribes."

"No, no, it all makes perfect sense," Azad said. "Terrak is, what, a triple agent, and I'm exfiltrating him after a botched operation. Wait. Why am I exfiltrating him to a Mentak Coalition colony world? I forget. I'm sure there's a good reason."

"I am merely reporting the substance of my orders," the Letnev woman said.

"Did you see our blistering expose, Sev? Either you've already got spores on the brain, or you're at least a little bit suspicious that your superiors might."

"Your allegations are outlandish. I would require real proof in order to take them seriously."

"We're a little short of proof at the moment," Azad said. "That's kind of why we're in this system."

Sev sighed. "Yes, Azad. I know. So, let's go down to the planet and *get* the proof, all right?"

Azad cackled. "You mean it? Really? The old gang is getting back together again?"

Still no mirth from the Letnev. Did Azad just enjoy needling her? Did the *Letnev* woman enjoy it, and just didn't show it? If they'd ever been a couple, it was hard to imagine an odder one.

Sev said, "If you're lying, or mistaken, you will be taken into custody and handed over to my superiors. If you are telling the truth… that would interest me. I would have to reconsider my options."

"I'll meet you on the ground, then. My bosses sent me a sketch of the captain's estate. There's a bit on the western side, away from the main house, with a pile of boulders and a fountain and a gazebo and a fishpond – really, this place is a *lot*. I'll meet you by the fountain, all right?"

"Gazebo. Fountain. Hmm. As you say. I will organize a landing party. Be advised – Calred, from the *Temerarious*, is with me. He will not be informed of our arrangement. He is likely to be hostile when he encounters you."

"That is… some strange bedfellows you've got going on there, Sev. How'd that happen?"

"I am cooperating with Duval to capture you both. He took one of my bridge officers, and I took one of his, to ensure that both parties obey the terms of our partnership."

Azad grunted. "The Barony and the Mentak Coalition working together on an operation? Does that seem like something that would happen naturally, or something that might, say, be organized by a malign fungal intelligence–"

"We will find out one way or another soon, Azad. I will see you at the rendezvous point." Her image vanished.

"I gather that was an old friend of yours?" I asked.

Azad leaned back in her chair, shaking her head and smiling. She seemed genuinely wonderstruck. "That was Captain Severyne Joelle Dampierre of the Barony warship *Grim Countenance*. She's… an ex. Ex-ally, ex-enemy, ex-lover, ex lots of things."

"It sounds like your relationship has gone through many permutations." Azad had made a suggestive comment about a Letnev when we first met. I assumed this Sev was she. I could see how the woman would make a strong impression.

She chuckled. "It sounds that way, but to be really accurate, Severyne was ally, enemy, and lover all at the same time. The puppetmasters probably sent her after me because we have history. She's the closest thing the Barony has to an expert on Amina Azad. Lucky for us she has a wild disobedient streak, huh? Any other Letnev soldier would have just bagged us and tossed us in a cell as instructed."

"You trust her, then?" I asked.

"Oh, I absolutely trust Sev. I trust her to do what's best for her. Being the pawn of a vast conspiracy is not what's best for her. Once we show her we're telling the truth… she'll help us out, and come up with a way to cover herself in glory in the process."

"I very much hope the cure works, then."

"What with our lives depending on it, you mean? Yeah. We should be careful, though. Sev probably hasn't gone green – I don't think she'd bother with this level of subterfuge if she was working for the bad guys, especially since she could take our little ship with her big one easily enough. But she'll be traveling with a Hacan who likes shooting stuff, and her personal guards too, and who knows whether any of them have been compromised?"

"I will continue with my policy of trusting no one," I assured her.

"It'll be good to see Sev again," Amina said. "If me and her start to make out or something, just avert your eyes until we're finished."

The humans sometimes said "opposites attract", but that only made sense to me when talking about magnets. "You baffle me, Azad. I have seen evidence of your competence, but you don't seem to take *anything* seriously."

"I'm always serious, big guy." She leaned back, looking pleased with herself. "In my line of work, every day could be my last – sometimes every second. But that means I'm also serious about enjoying myself as much as humanly possible. And humans are *good* at enjoying themselves."

CHAPTER 32
SEVERYNE

"Don't point that thing at people, Calred." Severyne pushed the barrel of his rifle down until it was aimed at the ground. He scowled but didn't resist. "Azad, Terrak, come out where I can see you."

Azad strolled out from behind the pile of rocks and stood on the far side of a small wooden bridge from Severyne. Her hair was mussed, her grin wide, and her clothes rumpled. She remained one of the most arresting things Severyne had ever seen. She opened her arms wide. "Are we hugging? We're hugging, right? I was never a hugger before I met you, Sev, but something about your warmth and openness, it fundamentally *changed* me."

"We are not hugging," Severyne said. "We are here to settle a question."

"Hugging after, then?"

Severyne only sighed.

Calred looked from Severyne to Azad and back again, and finally growled, "Someone had better tell me what's going on."

"Hello, cousin." A Hacan stepped out to stand behind Azad. He was older than Calred, with gray in his mane, wearing a plain gray robe.

"I'm not your cousin. I've got plenty of cousins, and none of them are murderers."

Terrak tilted his head. "Really? I was speaking figuratively, but among my cousins, there are at least, hmm, three murderers, though two were ruled self-defense–"

"Shut up!" Calred said. "We're here to take you into custody for your crimes against the Mentak Coalition and the Greater Union and the Kingdom of Xxcha!" He swung his head around to Severyne. "*Aren't* we?"

The Hacan was behaving intemperately, but that was no surprise. As long as he didn't try to actually shoot anyone, she could tolerate his irritation. "Sounds like a bit of a jurisdictional tangle," Severyne said. "I can't see why I'd do anything for any of the factions you mentioned. But, yes, we were sent to apprehend you and your partner. First, though, let's settle the outstanding question of this conspiracy."

"You're not…" Calred groaned. "You said their mushroom mind-control story was ridiculous!"

"You have such a lazy mind." Severyne shook her head. "What I *said* was, I would require real evidence in order to believe such a thing. They propose to offer such evidence."

"Sure do," Azad said cheerfully. "One of you hold the old woman down, and I'll give her the cure, and we'll see what happens."

Calred shook his head, beaded mane swaying. "You can't inject an unknown chemical into a Mentak Coalition fleet captain! She might *die!*"

"I regret to inform you that the Barony of Letnev is not overly concerned about the well-being of Mentak Coalition military officers. Even retired ones."

Calred whipped his gun up and squeezed the trigger repeatedly as he swept the barrel across Terrak, Azad, and Severyne in a single rapid maneuver.

That was clearly the idea, anyway. Since the rifle didn't fire, it was an ineffective approach. Severyne's troopers pointed their weapons at Calred and took the gun away from him while he stood looking baffled.

Severyne held up her hand, revealing a small black fob with a single button in the center. "This is a remote safety. We use them sometimes in training. I was afraid you might… react badly to this turn of events. The question is, did you fire on us because you were outraged by my plan as a Mentak Coalition officer, or because you were terrified as a puppet of the conspirators?"

"You won't get away with this," Calred said.

"I will refrain from shooting your feet off, in case you *are* uncompromised," Severyne said. "But we'll have to bind you and leave you here under guard."

Calred closed his eyes for a moment, and shivered, and then whimpered. He said, "I'm sorry," and then another word – "gods", perhaps? – before launching himself at Severyne, claws out.

CHAPTER 33
FELIX

The *Temerarious* caught up to the *Vermilion* and ordered it to halt and prepare to be boarded. The ship complied right away, which caused a sinking feeling in the depths of Felix's gut. There was no way Amina Azad would just surrender like that.

Felix and Ggorgos boarded, and they found the ship's occupants on their knees in the cargo area, hands behind their heads, as ordered. They still had their hoods up. Ggorgos pointed her weapon at them – an energy rifle equipped with a grenade launcher under the barrel and a bayonet above – while Felix approached. He pushed back the woman's hood, already knowing what he'd see. She had dark hair, and she was human, but that was as far as her resemblance to Amina Azad went. He pushed back the Hacan's hood, and he was older than Terrak, with a big scar down his muzzle. Their scans had turned up no additional life signs, so Azad wasn't hiding in the crawlspace with a pistol in each fist. These two were all they'd get.

Felix sighed. "Why did you broadcast that message?"

"What message?" The woman seemed genuinely bewildered.

"What is your relationship to the fugitives Terrak and Amina Azad?" Ggorgos said.

"Who?" the Hacan said. "Is one of those the woman who hired us?"

Felix pulled up images of the fugitives on his tablet, though he was just going through the motions. Azad had tricked them. He knew it. He accepted it. He took some small comfort from the fact that she probably hadn't expected to encounter Severyne on the other side of the wormhole, so maybe *she'd* gotten a nasty surprise, too. "Was it her?"

The woman nodded. "Yeah, she hired us to transport… something. We don't know about any broadcast."

"Transport what?" Ggorgos snapped.

"Can I?" The woman gestured, and Ggorgos gave assent. She went to a locker, opened it, and removed a small box wrapped with a purple ribbon. She brought it over and handed it to Felix.

"Scanning," Ggorgos said. "The package does not contain explosives. I detect no devices at all. It seems to be empty."

"I thought it seemed kind of light," the woman said.

Felix tore off the ribbon and opened the box.

It wasn't entirely empty. There was a napkin, the sort Felix had seen a million times underneath his drinks at bars. Someone had scribbled a drawing on the paper: a caricature of a human (probably meant to be Felix, what with the mustache) who had curving devil horns on his head. "Happy hunting!" was scrawled across the bottom, and then, "Your friend, AA." She was the *worst*. He hated her, only slightly more than he hated himself. Azad had set out some tempting bait, but he'd been the one to chase right after it. Except, what *else* could he have done?

Felix showed the drawing to Ggorgos. To his surprise, the Xxcha ground out a laugh. "This Azad is an audacious character, isn't she?"

"I thought you'd shout and blow things up." Felix put the napkin in his pocket. "I didn't expect you to appreciate her wit."

Ggorgos said, "There was always a chance this was a ruse. It had to be checked out anyway." That reassured Felix, mildly. "No matter. The *Grim Countenance* is watching the other side of the wormhole. We will call them from the ship and ask if they've seen our quarry." Ggorgos stowed her rifle on a magnetic rack that jutted out of one of the facets on the back of her shell. She turned to the crew. "We apologize for the intrusion. Check your comms – you'll find you've been broadcasting a… rather strange message on a loop."

"Ah… thank you?" The woman looked at her Hacan partner. "We get to keep the ship?"

"I don't see why not," Felix said. "It was lawfully purchased, and you were hired to fly it. Just, in the future… refrain from making deals in bars with shady characters?"

"Yes, sir," the woman said, and didn't even bother to sound sincere about it.

As they headed back to their ship, Voyou started shouting into their comms: "They're on the *planet*! We have to go back!"

"How do you know where they are?" Felix asked suspiciously. He knew he was seeing conspiracies everywhere, but in his defense, there probably *were* conspiracies everywhere.

"It… just stands to reason." Voyou's tone was sulky. That was new; his emotional range had previously seemed limited to "supercilious" and "bored." "If Azad and Terrak aren't here, then they must be on Entelegyne."

"A reasonable supposition," Ggorgos said. "We will proceed with all due haste. With luck, the Letnev ship has intercepted them, or will soon."

"Surely they would have mentioned it," Felix said, suddenly with new things to worry about. "Sev might pretend she forgot to call, but Cal would tell us." He hailed Calred on his crew's personal channel – Duval's Devils only, no Ggorgos allowed – and received no answer. He called Tib instead. "Hail the *Grim Countenance* for me and ask for a situation report."

"Will do."

Felix and Ggorgos returned to the bridge and began making their way back to the wormhole. By the time the *Temerarious* had left the *Vermilion* well behind, Tib said, "The communications officer on the *Grim Countenance* says Captain Dampierre is in a meeting, and Calred is unavailable for comment."

That sounded like a cover story, though a cover story for *what*? Felix looked at Ggorgos, who was, as usual, totally expressionless, and then realized she hadn't heard any of that exchange. "Tib can't reach Calred or Severyne." Frustration bubbled up inside him. "What are they *doing* over there?"

"I am unsure," Ggorgos said. "But I now believe we should proceed with *excessive* haste."

CHAPTER 34
TERRAK

Calred launched himself at Captain Dampierre, clearly intending to deliver a killing blow. I was too far away, across the creek, to do anything about it. I didn't know either of them, but in a group like this, with so many divided loyalties, violence had a way of multiplying and spreading out, so I prepared myself to flee or fight as needed.

Severyne seemed to expect the attack, however, stepping deftly aside as two of her guards moved forward in tandem, almost as though they'd rehearsed the move. The soldiers hit Calred from either side with shock-sticks, and he went down, spasming and groaning. They stood over him, clearly awaiting further instructions. Severyne said, "Hmm."

"Safe to say the big guy has fungus on the brain, wouldn't you agree?" Azad stepped across the creek, ignoring the ornamental bridge, and threw her arms wide again, as though to embrace the woman. Severyne stepped deftly aside from *that*, too, keeping her hands clasped behind her back and appearing to not even notice the overture. She was the sort of woman who could look down her nose at someone a meter taller than her. You almost had to admire it.

"Calred seems to be compromised, yes," Severyne agreed. "That was as good as an admission."

"We could test the cure on him," I said.

Azad grinned at me. "What, no mercy for this Hacan? Is it because he's not down on his luck like the last guy?"

I sighed. "I objected to infecting an innocent person with mysterious spores, Azad. This poor man is already sick. If we can help him, we should."

Calred rolled over, moaning. "No." He tried to rise up on his elbows, but another jab in the shoulder with a shock-stick put him down again. "Please... don't... the guides... they won't let you take me, we have orders, and without them, nothing means anything, everything is gray, please."

"I quite like gray," Severyne said. "Proceed with the cure. Guards, hold him if he struggles."

Azad knelt beside the Hacan, humming to herself and plucking things from the pouches on her vest: a syringe, a vial, a small silver flask. She unscrewed the latter, took a swig, then splashed some of the alcohol on the crook of Calred's elbow. The Hacan tried to rise again, but a pair of guards held him down. Azad peered at Calred's arm, found a vein, slipped in the syringe, and depressed the plunger. She removed the needle, capped it, and put it with her supplies. Then she looked down at her… patient? Calred was muttering, "No, no, no", and "I'm sorry", and the like. It was pitiful and horrible and all I could think about was the fact that I'd nearly been like him, infected and compromised and lost to myself.

"How quickly can we expect a reaction?" Severyne sounded impatient, though I was beginning to gather that was how she always sounded.

Azad looked up at her. "Should be pretty fast, according to the lab notes. My bosses think the spores activate various happy-chemical receptors in the brains, so first off, the cure will mess with those. Keep the chemicals from binding or make them bind better or whatever will cause the effects to diminish. I'm not a neuroscientist. Then the antifungals will start to take effect, killing off whatever's growing in there. The neural regeneration stuff will take a lot longer, could be hours or days before the victim returns to full functionality–"

Calred rolled over on his side and threw up a thin stream of mostly bile, then coughed pitifully.

"I half-expected to see little mushroom caps floating in his vomit," I said, trying to make light of a situation that was anything but. No one was amused. Everyone stared at Calred, desperate to see what he'd do: die in convulsions, try to kill us, scream in defiance–

Calred began to weep. He covered his face with his hands, and Severyne's guards moved to shock him again, I suppose just on general principles, but she stilled them with a gesture. "Wait." She didn't look sympathetic, but she no longer looked murderous, either.

"He's… not dead," Azad said. "That's a good sign." She elbowed me. "See, we could have injected the old guy after all, he would have been fine."

I growled at her. She didn't seem particularly intimidated.

"I'm sorry, I'm sorry, it was… I was in a fog." Calred's voice was muffled. "I feel so empty now, but… but the guides, I don't hear their voices anymore. I'm sorry–"

"Save your apologies for later," Severyne snapped. "We need information now. Who are these guides? Your handlers in the conspiracy?"

Calred struggled to sit up, and managed, just about, though his posture was slumped. There were tears shining in the corners of his eyes. "It's not like that. The guides are more like… mentors. They want what's best for us. They want to create a better world, and when you take their sacrament, they show you how you can help. It feels *good* to help."

"Great, but who actually are they?" This from Azad, who positively vibrated at the prospect of obtaining hard information from one of the compromised.

"I don't know, and I never thought to ask." Calred wiped his mouth on the back of his hand. "Stars, there are really spores in my *brain*–"

"Focus!" Severyne snapped her fingers in front of his face. "Surely you have some information we can actually use?"

"I…" His eyes widened. "Oh. One thing. They know you're here."

"Who does?" I asked. "The fleet captain?" I looked around, but there were plants and ornamental bits of stone everywhere, enough to hide a dozen of the infected. I felt horribly exposed.

Calred shook his head. "I get the impression the fleet captain is pretty far gone, but she has employees – two of the faithful." He winced. "That's what the guides call us. Faithful. I sort of… connected up with Harlow and her staff when we landed. I can't feel them anymore… They must think I'm dead. Or cured. Not being connected to the other faithful, or to the guides, it's like having my head sealed in an iron box–"

Azad knelt down and looked into Calred's face. "What do you mean, you connected with them? Like, telepathy?"

"Not exactly. I can't read their minds, but I can – I could – sense the presence of other faithful, and tell how close they are, and whether they're awake or asleep or in pain, things like that. It's only the guides who speak in my mind with actual words, but we can share information through them – if I tell them something, they can inform the other faithful."

"You were in constant contact with these guides?" Severyne asked.

"No, not really. We always have our standing orders, and the sacrament keeps us blissed out, but in terms of actively communicating, the voices of the guides get weaker and stronger and sometimes fade entirely. Here, though, I could hear the guides clearly – there must be a node in the house, like the one on the ship."

"*What* ship?" Severyne snarled, just as Azad said, "What's a node?"

"Your ship," Calred said to Severyne. "Though there's one on mine, too." He looked to Azad. "A node is… it doesn't look like much. The faithful who recruited me gave me one, when I was on a rest and relaxation trip, right after they sprayed me with spores. The node was barely even a seed then – it looked like a speck of green. I put it in a little water and gave it a little blood and it grew into a sort of mushroom, with a red flower on top. The guides said the node would help me communicate with them and connect with the other faithful, and I was supposed to harvest the spores and grow nodes and hide them everywhere I went, to extend the network."

Azad grunted. "That node sounds like a miniature version of a Letani. The whole point of those is to allow the Arborec to communicate when they're away from their home planet – every Letani generates a local spore cloud that lets the creatures with them communicate. It's like they carry their own communications network with them."

"You put one of these nodes on my ship?" Severyne's eyes widened in outrage, like someone had insulted her dignity, or maybe beat up her best friend.

It was the most emotion I'd seen her display so far. Some captains are like that with their ships.

Calred shook his head. "No. But only because I didn't need to. There was already one on board."

Severyne went completely still. "Who on my crew is compromised?" The guards started glancing at each other and taking careful steps back, giving themselves room. My claws slid out of their pads without me consciously intending them to.

"Voyou," Calred said. "We thought it was funny, the way you had us swap ships, when we both shared the same true loyalty."

Severyne swore. It was quite a good curse, in an Emirate dialect. She must have liked Voyou, to react so strongly. "Where did you learn to say *that*?" I asked.

"She's met Sagasa," Azad said. "That's one of his favorites."

"We should move," Calred said. "The fleet captain's caretakers will come looking for us. They'll be able to find the spot where I … went offline. If we stand around, they'll shoot us from cover."

"Yes, fine," Severyne snapped. "We'll proceed with caution and take a round-about route to the house." She gestured, and the guards formed up, a couple still staying within striking range of Calred. I didn't think he was faking his recovery, but we couldn't really be sure. We couldn't be sure of much of *anything*, could we?

While we walked, Severyne called her ship. "Get in touch with the *Temerarious* and tell them that Voyou is compromised." A pause. "What do you *mean* you can't reach them?"

CHAPTER 35
FELIX

"What do you mean the comms are down?" Felix said.

"There's a fault in central processing," Tib said. "No idea what's going on. I'll go down and take a look. Calred is the engineer, though, so if it's more complicated than a loose cable, I don't know what I can do about it."

"Your efforts are appreciated." After she was gone, Felix sat in the captain's chair on the bridge and considered the trajectory details on the screen. Even at top speed, it would be almost two hours before they reached the wormhole, and then they had to transit and get to the planet, and who knew what they'd find once they got there? In space, everything took forever except the things that happened very fast.

Ggorgos came onto the bridge and walked over to the tactical board, though there was nothing for her to shoot at just then. She was very good at being expressionless, but Felix detected a hint of frustration or impatience on her beaky face.

"This is going to be a very tedious few hours, isn't it?" Felix said. "I hate waiting. Is there anything worse than being bored, when you know there's action happening somewhere else?"

The Xxcha merely grunted.

Then Tib spoke over a private channel into his ear: "Captain, I'm down in central processing, and it's not a loose cable. The communications system has been sabotaged."

I guess that's worse, Felix thought.

THE FAITHFUL XIII

TX138 was eating some kind of still-wriggling small crustacean, crunching through the tiny creature's exoskeleton, but without apparent pleasure. It was like watching a miniature crushing machine at work. The L1Z1X liaison swallowed, then turned her red eyes toward Captain Tournasault, twenty-year veteran of the Barony fleet and relatively new member of the faithful. TX138 said, "Would you like some?" She pushed a bowl across the table. The things in the bowl were trying to escape.

"I am quite all right, thank you," Tournasault said. "Why did you summon me to your quarters? You were ordered to induct your superior into the faith, but you and I are the only faithful I can sense on the ship." And, to be honest, TX138 seemed a little... *faint*, compared to the other faithful Tournasault had met. The L1Z1X had definitely taken the sacrament, but the connection was fuzzy.

"I will do as ordered, I think," TX138 said. The L1Z1X were deeply distressing creatures, horrible amalgamations of the biological and the mechanical, their red eyes glowing with devastating zeal. They were odd, and secretive, and their relationship with reality seemed tenuous at best. For one thing, they thought they were the rightful rulers of the empire, when in reality they were twisted perversions of the once-mighty race who'd *lost* an empire. Tournasault hated being around them, as a rule, and even with TX138 felt only a shadow of the usual connection he felt in the presence of other faithful.

"You think? You must! The summit is only days away. Soon we'll reach Arc Prime, and your leader hasn't even committed to signing the treaty yet."

"There are some points that do not yet satisfy us," TX138 said. "Certain crucial details remain unclear. When, precisely, will the other members of the Legion pledge fealty to the undying empire of the L1Z1X?"

Tournasault groaned. "Never. That isn't what's happening. As we keep *telling* you."

"How very strange. You continue to deny objective reality. That is unacceptable."

"Listen." Perhaps Tournasault could make a connection, faithful-to-faithful, despite the profound strangeness of this creature. "The guides have explained their plan to you, haven't they?"

"Unity," TX138 said. "They strive to create a better future... but any better future is, by definition, the dominion of the L1Z1X Mindnet. The future belongs to us. We are attempting to reconcile these discrepancies." TX138's red eyes flashed, and she shuddered. "Mmm. More positive reinforcement. How pleasant."

<*They are… resistant to our efforts,*> the guides whispered in Tournasault's mind. <*These creatures are so cybernetically altered that our sacrament is not as effective in them as usual. They have extensive voluntary control of their own endocrine systems… You must convince her to serve, faithful. You must.*>

Tournasault thought furiously. Thinking deeply and coming up with tactics and stratagems had once come so easily to him, but more and more it seemed a struggle. Finally, he said, "TX138, your superior – LV286, isn't it – is he very wise?"

"He speaks for Ibna Vel Syd, the greatest ruler in the galaxy, heir to all the stars, yes. LV286 is great and good."

"Then… wouldn't it make sense… to give LV286 the sacrament? Surely his wisdom would enable him to reconcile these… troubling details… you're struggling with?"

TX138 sat perfectly still, her face – if you could call it a face, with so many tubes going in and out, and all that metal – perfectly blank. Then she smiled. It was horrible, but welcome, nonetheless. "That is an excellent suggestion."

Tournasault sat back, and the guides rewarded him with an incremental increase in bliss.

CHAPTER 36
AZAD

"The guides probably told Voyou to take out the communications system when I went offline, knowing I might be compromised," Calred said, limping along behind Azad. "The guides have been really worried about this cure. They think you're a threat to the great work."

"Oh, there's a great work," Azad said. "Maybe you should tell us about that." She was annoyed. She'd had this idea that once she managed to cure one of the mushroom zombies, she'd actually get answers, and be able to tell her employer those answers, and get paid – well, paid more. But so far, the only new thing they'd learned was existence of those nodes, little vegetative communications satellites hidden on ships and stations all over the galaxy.

Calred sighed. "All I know is there *is* a plan, and I was a small part of it. I was supposed to keep an eye on my boss, Jhuri, and neutralize him if he got suspicious about the conspiracy. Then I got sent on *this* mission, to capture Terrak, and my main job then was updating the guides on our progress. And…" He swallowed. "Killing or compromising you and Terrak, before you had a chance to tell anyone what you'd found out."

"It would have been funny to see you try," Azad said. "You don't know anything about the bigger picture?"

"Just that the guides are eager for the Greater Union to succeed. They didn't want anything to disrupt the treaty process. Maybe the guides really *do* mean well, and they just want to promote peace and harmony in the…" He trailed off. "No. I suppose not."

"Seems unlikely," Severyne said absently. "Wait." She held up her fist to halt the group, then peered through tiny gaps in a stand of tall reed-like plants that formed a natural barrier. "I can see the house. So many windows, how can anyone stand it? Useful for surveillance, though… I don't see movement. Where were the faithful when you could still sense them, Calred?"

"All three of them were in the house, but when I got disconnected, I'm sure they freaked out. The fleet captain might still be inside – I don't think she's very mobile. She just gave off a vague impression of blissed-out confusion. The other two were sharp, though."

"Still, there are only two of them. We can handle that," Severyne said.

"Only two that we know of," Azad said. "There could be uninfected mercenaries or something, and they'll shoot us just as dead as the faithful would."

"The guides didn't mention anything about outside contractors," Calred said. "I think they wanted to keep the fleet captain's condition a secret. An architect of the Greater Union descending into rapid dementia would be bad for the project, probably. The guides thought between Severyne and Felix, the situation was pretty well covered."

"Then let's take the house." Severyne nodded to her troops, who fanned out and disappeared from view around both sides of the reed wall. Severyne took a small cylinder from her belt, twisted her wrist, and snapped the cylinder out into a pole nearly two meters long. She looked at Azad and Terrak. "I know *she's* armed. Are you?"

"Only with my natural attributes." Terrak showed his fangs.

"Can you shoot?"

Terrak shrugged. "I have been known to, at a firing range."

Severyne tossed a sidearm, and the Hacan caught it, almost fumbling the weapon. Azad rolled her eyes. Amateurs. "Try not to let anyone take that away and use it on you," Severyne said.

"I love this take-charge thing you're doing, Sev," Azad said. She hadn't expected to ever see her again, and it was making an enjoyable mission even better. Everything was always more fun with her, and sure, Sev was looking her most strait-laced right now, but she inevitably loosened up and got more impulsive after they spent a little time together. This time they were even on the same *side*. "Maybe when this mission is over, you and me could find a little private time to do a thorough debrief. Not that I'm actually *wearing* any briefs–"

"Please focus on the task at hand." Severyne cocked her head, listening to something on her comms. "My troops have made entry through a back and side door. They've located the fleet captain's quarters and have the area secured. They've seen no sign of the caretakers as yet. Perhaps they're out wandering in the garden, but just in case they're hidden elsewhere in the house... I'll take the side entrance there. You and the honorable ambassador can go through the front." She walked away without waiting to see if Azad and Terrak agreed.

"Don't you love a woman who knows what she wants?" Azad said, watching the Letnev disappear around the side of the house. "What she wants other people to do, I mean. I wonder how she'd react to a little saucy insubordination?"

"I have resisted this question, but... what exactly is the nature of your relationship with Captain Dampierre?" Terrak asked.

"What, now you're curious, when I don't have time to share salacious details?" Azad said. "Let's just say 'complicated'. That's the best kind of relationship, don't you think?"

"It's certainly the word I'd use to describe ours," Terrak said.

"We're differently complicated." Azad led him around the reed wall, toward the front entrance of the house. Viewed from above, the house was shaped like a star mashed together with a pentagon, but seen from the ground, the structure was low and rambling, made of thick timbers and expanses of glass, with rooms jutting out at unusual angles. The front doors were dark wood, elaborately carved with images of vines and spaceships, which Azad thought was pretty muddled, conceptually and aesthetically, but she was hardly an art critic. There were glass panels on either side of the doors, not even foggy or tinted, giving her a clear view of the vestibule beyond. There was a round table in the middle of the foyer, with a crystal vase full of drooping flowers on top, and a coat rack on one side of the door, with several pairs of shoes lined up neatly in a row beneath it.

"I don't see any machine gun nests or land mines or caltrops, so in we go." Azad tugged on the door handle, expecting resistance, but it opened smoothly. "I guess when you're the only people on the planet you don't worry too much about burglars." She slipped in, scanning the space beyond the vestibule–

Someone landed on her head and shoulders, driving her to the ground. Azad tried to get up, but a limb clamped around her throat, pulled tight, and cut off her air. She rolled onto her side and twisted violently around, but couldn't dislodge the attacker. She caught a glimpse of the rafters above – the caretakers must have been hiding up there, waiting to pounce.

It was definitely caretakers plural – the other one was busy trying to kill Terrak, and *that* one, a human man with wispy gray hair, was armed with a large carving knife. Terrak should have died right away, despite the size differential, because corrupt old trade ambassadors weren't famed for their ability to fend off ambush knife attacks. And yet… the Hacan had somehow avoided getting stabbed in the neck in the initial assault and was even now easily dodging the man's wild swipes. Terrak dropped and spun and swept the assailant's legs out from under him. Terrak aimed his sidearm while rising and fired a pulse into the man's chest, as casually as if he did it every day. The fallen man went still.

Azad watched, her vision beginning to fill with black spots, as Terrak picked up the knife, squinted, and threw it at her head. She couldn't even squawk in terror because she had no breath–

And then the weight on her screamed and vanished, and Azad rolled over, gasping. Terrak fired his pistol again, past Azad this time. She turned her head and saw her own assailant fall – a woman, equally gray-haired, with a knife buried in her shoulder, eyes rolled back in her head.

"Sorry for the knife-play," Terrak said. "My pistol was on the stun setting, and the charge will transfer to anyone the target is touching, so I thought it best to get her off you first–"

"You're not a trade ambassador," Azad gasped. "Not with moves like that. What are you *really*?"

CHAPTER 37
TERRAK

I helped Azad to her feet and tried to brush off her question. My entire career, my entire *life*, is based on keeping certain secrets. She wasn't willing to let it go, though. "You've had training in combat," she insisted, "and there's *nothing* in your background about that. It's not the sort of thing you'd hide – you'd act all faux-humble about it but make sure everyone knew – so tell me the truth."

The truth. Ah, well.

"I do work for my government," I said. "Just… not in the capacity you assumed."

I have not been entirely honest in this account, and this part can never be released. Any truly honest memoirs I recorded could never be published, even posthumously.

I *am* a trade ambassador. Every bit of documentation in my life attests to that fact. The rumor mill says I am also a favor trader, and just corrupt enough to be useful to a wide range of people, without being so corrupt that I bring unwanted attention or unforeseen difficulties. That is, functionally, an accurate description of myself and my work.

Both those identities, however, are covers.

I was recruited into the Emirates of Hacan clandestine services right out of the Collegium. I showed certain attributes that were useful in a potential field agent: mainly charisma, a gift for manipulation, the capacity to put matters of conscience aside when necessary, and a certain adeptness at swift acts of violence. (As I've gotten older, I try to minimize the need for the latter. There are usually better ways.) I spent my early career working for various trading houses engaged in inter-system commerce, making valuable connections and passing on intelligence to my government whenever possible. Eventually, it became plausible to endow me with diplomatic credentials, which meant less time skulking in alleys and breaking into embassies. Instead, I was invited to parties at the same embassies, which made stealing documents so much easier.

So, yes, I'm a spy, if not exactly like Azad, then at least not radically dissimilar. I've had a long and varied career, but this was, by far, the strangest assignment I'd had, and not just because of my unlikely partner.

Azad groaned. "Don't tell me you were you investigating the conspiracy too?"

I shrugged, then offered a hand to help her up. "My superiors had some suspicions, though they didn't go nearly as far as yours did. We'd received reports of a few people acting strangely, and one of them was an old colleague of mine, Qqurant, so I was dispatched to investigate. I did not anticipate such a… swift and aggressive response to my preliminary questioning. I was trying to figure out how to get word to my handlers, to avoid being murdered in custody, when you appeared. And since you seemed to have better leads than I did, when you proposed our collaboration…"

"You *got* me!" Azad crowed. I'd expected her to be furious, but she seemed delighted. "Do you know how long it's been since somebody *got* me? I thought I was using you, and all this time you were using me. Respect, Terrak. If that's even your real name."

"I prefer to think we have been engaged in a partnership."

"Ha, sure, right." She prodded one of the fallen caretakers with her toe. "Guess we oughta jam them full of the cure. But first. Severyne!" she shouted. "Sev, come here, we got them!"

I winced. "I would prefer it if you didn't share the truth of my–"

Azad waved away my concerns. "Don't worry, Sev and I don't whisper secrets in one another's ears. You and me can be covertly covert *together*."

"It's not unheard of for the Emirates and the Federation of Sol to take part in joint actions occasionally," I said.

"Right, see? We're practically sanctioned."

Severyne appeared, with a guard at her shoulder. She looked over the bodies and nodded. "Come along. The fleet captain is here. She is insensible. Perhaps your drugs will help." She turned and walked away.

Azad sighed and grabbed one of the caretakers by the ankles. "Can you get the other one?" she asked. "Who knows how long spore-zombies stay down when they're stunned?"

CHAPTER 38
SEVERYNE

Severyne sat by Fleet Captain Harlow's bedside, glancing up only briefly when Azad and Terrak entered, dragging the unconscious caretakers with them. Calred was sitting on the other side of the bed, his chin on his chest, lightly snoring. Being flooded with anti-fungals and neural regrowth serum was apparently tiring. "Bind the captives," Severyne said to her guards, then beckoned Azad over. "Look at this woman's eyes. They're green."

"Some humans have green eyes, Sev… oh." Azad leaned close. "There are green specks in the *veins* in her eyes. That is bizarre."

"You think she was an early convert to this conspiracy, yes?" Severyne said. "If so, the long-term effects are debilitating. She has mumbled a few things, about guides and faith and the sacrament, but she is largely unresponsive to stimuli." She poked the woman in the cheek, hard, eliciting no reaction.

"The chromium woman of the raider fleets," Terrak said.

Severyne frowned at him. "What?"

He inclined his head toward the woman in the bed. "Her name came up occasionally in meetings once the Greater Union idea took hold. She was a powerful force in the Mentak Coalition, guiding the agenda of their raider fleets for years. She chose her targets not just opportunistically, but in order to support long-term strategic goals of the Mentak military *and* trading interests. Her attacks helped the Coalition secure monopolies on certain commodities and allowed them to apply pressure when it came to negotiating treaties in disputed border areas. She was brilliant, and by all accounts retired only because she felt it was time for her handpicked protégés to shine. To see her like this…" He shook his head.

"Let's see if we can snap her out of it." Azad took out her syringes and vials. The fleet captain was already hooked up to an intravenous line – presumably because she was so far gone that she couldn't drink or eat on her own – so introducing the cure into her veins was easy. Severyne watched with interest. The cure had worked on Calred, but Harlow was much further gone.

The fleet captain stirred and moaned shortly after the cure was injected but didn't wake. Azad said, "The lab notes say that for subjects who've been under the influence of the spores longer, the process might take extra time. Terrak, do you think you can shoot her maid and butler full of juice? The dosages for humans are written on the printout there."

"What will you be doing?"

"I need to make a call."

Terrak agreed, and Azad left the room. While he was busying himself with the drugs, Severyne said, "Is Azad contacting her handlers?"

"I assume she's letting them know the cure actually works," Terrak said.

"Hmm. She's working for the Federation of Sol?"

"I assume so. Do you have reason to think otherwise?"

Severyne shook her head. "I have simply learned to take nothing for granted when it comes to her."

"Probably a good policy." The Hacan finished administering the cure, then said, "What will *you* do now? Report the conspiracy to your superiors?"

"I have not yet determined my next course of action," Severyne said. "I was sent to capture a Barony operative attempting to defect to the Federation. I was deceived. The question is whether the people giving me the orders were also merely deceived… or if they were compromised."

"Maybe when Harlow wakes up, she can tell us something," Terrak said.

"How wonderful," Severyne said. "I'm putting my future prospects into the trembling hands of an unconscious, drooling human."

CHAPTER 39
FELIX

Felix held a gun on Ggorgos. "Take off your shell."

Voyou and Tib Pelta were hanging back. Tib had a gun, too; Voyou just had a smug look on his face.

Ggorgos seemed untroubled. "You are making a mistake, Duval. I did not sabotage your communications equipment. Why assume I am responsible, and not the Letnev?"

Felix shook his head. "Voyou hasn't been on the ship long enough to account for all the things that made me suspicious. I know everything, Ggorgos. I know you were sent to my ship as an agent of the conspiracy."

"What *are* you talking about?" Voyou said.

"Everything Terrak said in that broadcast is true," Felix said. "Jhuri told me to investigate, but then he told me to *stop*, and I think it's because he's been compromised, too. This ends now."

"Have you been sleeping enough, Duval?" Ggorgos said. "Perhaps you are dehydrated. Here–" She took a step forward, and Felix took a step back.

"Take off your shell and get in the cell, Ggorgos."

"I am not a conspirator, Duval. I am here to catch a killer. Terrak's paranoia has infected you."

Felix ground his teeth. "If you are compromised, it's not your fault, and you can probably be cured. There's an experimental medication. I just need to contain you until we can confirm the cure works, and then we'll administer it, all right? But I can't have you running around my ship with that arsenal on your back."

"You will regret this, Duval." Ggorgos pressed a few spots on her shell, in a deliberate sequence, and the armor hissed and separated into two halves. Each half extended telescoping legs that allowed them to stand upright by themselves. Ggorgos stepped out of the divided shell, and it was all Felix could do not to avert his eyes. He'd seldom seen any Xxcha without an exocarapace before, and she seemed weirdly vulnerable. Ggorgos walked into the cell with great dignity, and Felix slammed the button that powered on the forcefield barrier.

"We're going to fix you up, Ggorgos, don't worry." Felix beckoned Voyou and Tib, and they all returned to the bridge. "Tib, get us through that wormhole."

They had prior authorization to transit at will, so their inability to communicate with the wormhole station wouldn't get them blown to bits, at least.

"Could I do anything to help, captain?" Voyou said. "Since you're down *two* crew members now."

"Sitting down and shutting up would be wonderful."

"Those are duties at which I excel, as it happens."

The *Temerarious* passed through the wormhole uneventfully. Felix was trying to imagine what kind of report he could send to his possibly-mind-controlled superior. *Having dead comms is a benefit in some respects*, he thought. *That makes explaining myself a problem for future Felix.* "Let's get to the planet as fast as we can, Tib."

"I wasn't planning to dawdle, captain." She entered the course. "So, this conspiracy thing…"

"It's true, Tib." Felix tapped the screen on the arm of his chair. "There. I gave you access to my notes. Read them, and you'll know as much as I do. I'm sure you'll reach the same conclusion I did. Ggorgos has been passing information to her *real* employers. They've known every step we've taken. Ggorgos must have sabotaged the comms to keep us from finding out what's happening with the fugitives and the *Grim Countenance* and the fleet captain. I just wish I knew *why*."

Tib scanned through the data. Felix watched their trajectory slowly unfurl on the screen until he couldn't stand being still anymore, then rose and paced up and down on the bridge. Voyou sat quietly but looked smug about it. The Letnev were always happy to revel in the misery of humans, even when they were on the same side.

"That's… interesting stuff, captain." Tib raised her eyes from her console. "I'm not sure what to make of it all, but yeah, locking up Ggorgos was probably a good call. Better safe, and everything. We're approaching the planet. Without comms we can't tell the fleet captain we're coming, or contact the *Grim Countenance*, which is still lurking around here somewhere, so…"

"I'll take the shuttle down to the estate," Felix said.

"You'll take me with you, I trust?" Voyou said. "You *did* promise Captain Dampierre that I would be included in all mission-critical activities–"

Felix rubbed his face. When had he last shaved? "Yes, fine, you can come, just do as you're told and keep working on that sitting quietly thing we talked about."

The shuttle comms were dead, too, of course, the wires yanked out from beneath the console and left dangling, but the other systems were intact. Felix set a course for the fleet captain's estate. The journey was remarkably swift, as planetary travel always was, compared to the relatively slow passage through the vastness of interstellar space.

They glided over a low plain… and soon saw another shuttle parked on the ground, this one of Barony design. "Severyne must be down here already," Felix muttered. "But why?" He'd *finally* gotten a handle on things to his satisfaction, and now there were new unknowns to baffle him.

"Something is wrong here," Voyou said.

Felix looked over. The Letnev's superciliousness had vanished – he was chewing his lip, brow furrowed, eyes darting back and forth as though searching for something in the long grass. "What do you mean?"

"I… I don't know. It's a feeling."

"I didn't realize the Letnev believed in intuition."

"My instincts are finely honed, captain." The boast seemed unusually hollow.

Felix settled his shuttle down near the Letnev one, then disembarked, Voyou at his side. Felix checked the other shuttle, but it was empty. He and Voyou moved slowly onto the grounds of the estate, on the lookout for hostiles – or friendlies, or the ambiguous – and saw no one. "It's all too *quiet*," the Letnev said, almost moaning.

Had Voyou never been in a combat situation? Trust Severyne to send him a useless officer. "Shh. I prefer quiet to small arms fire or explosions," Felix said. They reached the front doors of the estate, which were standing wide open. Felix pointed at dark smears on the floor just inside the foyer. "Blood. Be careful."

"Felix!" a voice boomed. Calred appeared in a hallway, pointing at Voyou. "Grab him!"

Felix had been through fire with Calred, and didn't hesitate, immediately seizing Voyou and wrenching the man's arms behind him in a submission hold. Severyne appeared behind Calred – along with Amina Azad and Terrak. The latter was holding something in his hand – something like a squashed mushroom, with a drooping red flower on top.

"Having trouble talking to your guides, Voyou?" Severyne said. "We found and destroyed the local node."

Voyou struggled in Felix's arms, so he wrenched the man's arm up harder. "Would someone please explain to me what's going on?" Felix demanded. "I'm ready to start shooting things I don't understand."

Azad stepped forward, holding a syringe. "We're going to fix up Voyou real quick, and then we're going to talk to the fleet captain. She just woke all the way up. You've got pretty good timing for once."

"What… what do you mean, fix me up?" Voyou's voice was high and panicky.

"We will eradicate these spores in your system," Severyne said. "You will be cured–"

Voyou snapped his head back, even though doing so meant dislocating his shoulders, and slammed his skull into Felix's face. Felix stumbled back, his nose a concentrated burst of pain, and Voyou raced out the door.

"Don't let him reach a shuttle!" Calred shouted. Through eyes blurred with pain-tears, Felix watched Severyne race off in pursuit.

CHAPTER 40
SEVERYNE

Voyou didn't get to a shuttle. He was crouched beside a fishpond, shouting, in a vicious argument with himself. "I know my orders, but I… I can still be useful, I can still *fight*, they won't turn me, my devotion, it's… it's… I can't… I *must*."

With a final cry of anguish, he lay down on the bank and plunged his head into the fishpond. As she ran toward him, he began to thrash, but didn't remove his face from the water. He was still by the time she was close enough to drag him out. She attempted resuscitation, but to no effect. He'd drowned himself.

No, that wasn't right. These "guides" had driven him to the act. They'd ordered him to die rather than be turned – rather than allow Severyne and her allies to save him. The guides had put the mental equivalent of a secret agent's hidden cyanide pill into her undercommandant's mind. The guides had murdered Voyou, not out of anger or cruelty, but in a cold calculation to deny Severyne's alliance another asset.

Severyne sat beside his body for a moment. Voyou had been with her during the annexation of Darit. He'd remained loyal and steadfast throughout the Xing affair. They'd survived the World of Light together. He was perhaps the closest thing she had to a friend in all the galaxy.

Severyne did not cry, but another part of her already stony heart hardened.

Then she rose, and went back inside, to see what would come next.

THE FAITHFUL XIV

Jes'Gald was a G'hom, a member of the elite Tekklar unit, the most fearsome and ferocious warriors of the Sardakk N'orr. He had been chosen to accompany the Envoy and select members of the Veiled Brood to the Legion summit on Arc Prime. Jes'Gald was fearsome even by the standards of his order, and accustomed to seeing humanoids cower in his presence. There was no better feeling than scuttling forward with his brothers to war for the glory of Sardakk, the Queen Mother, and grinding lesser beings beneath his scything forelimbs and spiked legs.

The Letnev in his quarters stood perfectly at ease, though, and why not? They were both numbered among the faithful, a bond that transcended petty concerns like species. Captain Palesque had inducted Jes'Gald into the faith shortly after their first meeting, when Jes'Gald had been assigned to make sure the "honored guest" didn't wander off or get into any trouble. Now they were on board the finest ship in the N'orr fleet, making their final preparations for the summit.

Or that was the idea. At the moment, Palesque was trying to explain why the mere sight of a N'orr made so many species scream and flee. "It's because you look like bugs, you see." Palesque gestured with a glass. He was sitting on a mound of resin on the floor of Jes'Gald's curved, cavelike quarters. "A lot of species have a basic fear of insects. They're small, they infiltrate, they infest, they can appear when you aren't looking, they have too many eyes, too many limbs, their presence suggests squalor and disease… I'm not saying that perception is *fair*, mind you, and I'm sure there are Letnev and humans and so forth who adore bugs, but generally… humanoids, especially, find bugs worrying. And you're *immense* bugs. What are you, four meters long?"

"Your system of measurement is barbaric," Jes'Gald said.

"It works well enough for us. Anyway, that's why so many species have a negative visceral reaction to your lot. You're giant versions of something we find disturbing even when it's small. I don't suppose you have any particular instinctive feelings about bipedal primates?"

"Such creatures never evolved on our world," Jes'Gald said. "It is a shame. They would have been a valuable form of protein. Thank you for your insights. Should we discuss the next steps?"

"Hmm? Oh, yes, of course. Sorry. It's easy to get distracted, when the voices of the guides are this faint."

"Their voices become *stronger*?" Jes'Gald was astonished at the idea. The whisper of the guides had already convinced him that loyalty to the Queen Mother and her envoys was of secondary importance and should be set aside in favor of devotion to the great work. If that voice grew stronger…

"Oh, yes. You can't imagine." Palesque smiled. "Won't it be wonderful to share the sacrament with your envoy?"

The N'orr were a collective race, though not in the way many other species assumed. Their strength came from their unity of purpose and a capacity for cooperation that other races could only dream of. Some fools thought they were a hive mind – that the soldiers of N'orr were mindless drones – but they were wrong. The N'orr were individuals, bound together by common goals and values, and were all the stronger for it. "I want to share this joyous purpose with *all* my people," Jes'Gald said.

"To the Legion, and the guides, and our glorious future, then," Palesque said, raising his glass.

CHAPTER 41
FELIX

Felix used the communications system in the admiral's house to call up to the *Temerarious* and told Tib to set Ggorgos free. "It seems Cal was the leak all along. He's OK now, though. Their cure works."

Tib swore at length. Felix let her finish, then said, "I couldn't have said it better myself. I feel like an idiot *and* a bad friend *and* a bad officer. He just… seemed like Cal to me."

"It's fine that he fooled you," Tib said. "I'm furious that he fooled *me*."

Felix almost smiled. "As for Ggorgos… she's exactly what she seems to be. I don't know if she'll ever forgive me, but I'll settle for her not stomping me into a puddle of goo."

"Here's hoping," Tib said.

"I know we hate to leave the ship unattended, but I think you and Ggorgos should both get down here."

Once he was finished, he returned to the fleet captain's room. Harlow was awake now, though not speaking much. She was mostly sipping clear broth from a cup and glaring at everyone around her. Her newly cured caretakers were fussing over her, fluffing pillows and checking her vital signs.

"Don't beat yourself up for not figuring me out, Felix," Calred said. "I was extremely convincing. I didn't have instructions to do anything I wouldn't normally do, except… report on all our comings and goings to the voices in my head." He groaned. "Am I going to be court martialed? I'm not fully versed in all the nuances of our military code, but I seem to recall that treason is bad."

"You're a great actor," Felix said. "I can believe I'm a dolt, but Tib didn't notice either, and she's professionally suspicious."

"As for treason, I'll put in a word on your behalf," Fleet Captain Harlow said, her voice a croak. "Unless I'm up before the tribunal right beside you." She shooed her caretakers away and sat up in bed, wincing. She gazed at the group gathered around her bed and laughed, a sharp bark of a sound. "So, this is the salvation of the galaxy – two Coalition operatives, a Federation of Sol assassin, a fugitive trade ambassador, a Barony warship captain, and her shock-troops?"

"There's also an Xxcha who's unusually gifted at violence on the way, and my

Yssaril first officer, too," Felix said. "But… yes. I think that's about it. I can't speak for Severyne, but I'm pretty sure my boss is compromised."

"Jhuri?" Harlow clucked her tongue. "I hadn't heard. If so, he's a recent convert. In the Barony, though, yes – Admiral Immental was one of the last recruits I heard about before things got… hazy for me." She ran her hands through her hair, frowning. "I must look a mess. How long have I been out? When is the summit on Arc Prime?"

"It's scheduled to begin in four days, fleet captain," one of the caretakers said.

Harlow jolted like she'd been slapped. "Four *days*? Then we're about four and a half days from all-out interstellar war."

They all looked at one another, wide-eyed. When Felix had contemplated worst-case scenarios for the conspiracy's plans, he hadn't even considered something that bad or that rapid.

"Explain what you mean," Severyne said to Harlow.

"Before you explain anything else," Azad said, "would you just tell us who is *behind* all this? Or are you just as clueless as every other puppet we've talked to today?"

"Oh, no," Harlow said. "I know who organized the conspiracy. I helped them *plan* the conspiracy." She smiled at Calred. "So, as you can see, your little treason is nothing compared to mine."

CHAPTER 42
TERRAK

I listened to Harlow's story just like the rest of them: with mounting dread. Here's what she told us, as best I can remember. I will omit Duval's moans of dismay, and Severyne's hisses, and Azad's admiring whistles, to focus on the essentials.

"Last year, I received a visitor," Harlow explained. "An old bridge officer of mine named Grisham, who was serving in the diplomatic corps. They'd upset someone in a position of power, so Grisham got assigned to deal with the Arborec. Nobody likes being the liaison for that faction – negotiations can be frustrating, because we don't share a lot of fundamental assumptions with the Arborec. Even if we manage to make substantive progress, you're stuck negotiating with dead-eyed, blank-faced corpses, puppeted around by vegetable intellects. I'm Mentak Coalition through and through. I grew up surrounded by all sorts of species and am as comfortable as anyone in the company of aliens... but even I find dealing with the Arborec off-putting. Anyway, this associate of mine was sent on a mission, and they met with a Letani – you know about those?"

"Ambassadors of the Arborec," I said. "Each one carries a sort of copy of the central consciousness."

"Oh, an individual Letani isn't capable of carrying a whole *copy* of the hive-mind," Harlow said. "Each Letani is at best a portion of the Symphony, specialized for a given task – some are focused on trade negotiations, others on information gathering, others warfare. They're individual enough that they actually have names of their own, though mostly for the sake of communicating with creatures like us. My protégé met with one of the Letani, called Ohseroh, in a neutral area, to discuss matters of a... sensitive nature. Specifically, the exchange of certain weapons."

"We trade weapons with the Arborec?" Felix said.

"Not officially. While they were talking to the Letani's Dirzuga mouthpiece, one of the other... lifeforms on the Arborec ship, a sort of ambulatory assemblage of slime molds, swarmed around Grisham's ankles and pinned them in place. Then the Dirzuga coughed in Grisham's face, and... that poor soul became the first of the faithful."

"The *Arborec* are behind the conspiracy?" Azad seemed genuinely shocked.

"But… they don't do stuff like that. They don't just abstain from playing the great game, they don't even seem to know there's a game going on! I've never heard of them trying to turn a double agent or anything."

"If you let me continue, the situation will become clearer," Harlow said sternly. "Grisham was their first experimental subject. The Letani, Ohseroh… worked on them for a while, until my friend was under their complete control, but could still function, and pass for a person with free will. Ohseroh did a lot of damage as they perfected their process, though, and not long after Grisham came to see me – to *recruit* me – they died. Something very bad happened to their brain. Grisham suffered an imbalance profound enough to disrupt their autonomic systems. It was very sad, but at the time, I *wasn't* sad, because I just saw them dying for the cause of the guides, and that was the only cause that mattered." She shook her head. "I was a fool. I had no choice, but that doesn't make me feel much better."

"Why were you chosen as the second recruit?" I asked. "Just because you were the most influential person their patient zero could plausibly visit?"

"Yes, but… my influence might be larger than you realized. I was a good choice. Here, help me out of this bed." Her caretakers assisted her in getting to her feet, and then she shuffled over to a chair by the window and sat in a shaft of sunlight through the window. "I suppose there's no harm in telling you this, since we've now formed a conspiracy of our very own – a counter-conspiracy, if you will. I wasn't just a fleet captain. I was also the longtime head of special projects. I used to be your boss's boss, Felix."

Azad cackled. "You ran Mentak Coalition covert operations? Oh, that's beautiful. No wonder the puppetmasters wanted you."

"I was quite a catch," Harlow said. "The Letani who flooded my brain with chemical devotion didn't just want me for my political connections, or for the secrets I knew. Grisham told it about my real position, and after that, the Letani wanted my *advice*. Ohseroh had figured out how to do one thing very well: take control of people's minds and coerce their loyalty. What the Letani didn't know how to do was use that ability to achieve its goals. For that, it needed expert counsel – someone who understood the way all these baffling creatures made of meat actually think, and the ins and outs of our social and political systems. I was a perfect candidate. Ohseroh and I spent countless hours discussing possibilities, refining the details, and running scenarios. I betrayed my nation, and I was ecstatic to do it, because nothing felt as good as obedience. Even now, everything feels… muted, dim. You all look like you're behind dirty glass…" Her attention started to drift, and she visibly forced herself to focus. "At any rate. The guides – Ohseroh, that is, who tends to talk about itself in the plural, probably out of old habits – and I came up with the great work together."

"What great work?" Felix asked.

"The plan to achieve total war," Harlow said.

There was a moment of profound silence at that, as you might expect, with the requisite groans, hisses, and whistles. I contributed a moan of dismay myself. I suppose if you have a vast conspiracy in your control, it doesn't pay to think small.

Harlow continued, "As close to total war as we could engineer, anyway. I explained to my new god that the really impressive wars were never limited to just two nations facing off against one another. The biggest ones involved *multiple* nations, bound together by mutual interests, and usually also by treaties. 'Imagine,' I said, 'if we could get several of the most powerful factions in the galaxy to form an alliance, opposed to another, equally powerful alliance. If we could engineer a conflict between even a couple of major players in those respective treaty organizations, the chains of obligation would drag *all* the factions into a conflagration. Many of the lesser states would inevitably become entangled and forced to choose sides, spreading the devastation further.'"

"The Greater Union versus the Legion, with a side of everybody else," Felix said.

"Yes, obviously," Severyne said. "Do try to keep up."

"OK, but for what possible purpose?" Felix said. "How does all-out interstellar war help the Arborec?"

"Confusion to your enemies," Azad said. "It's never a bad plan."

"A war like that would clear the field," Severyne added. "If the Arborec can goad the Legion and the Greater Union into attacking one another, that would plunge the galaxy into open chaos. Untold billions would die. The devastation is incalculable. And from the ashes… the Arborec would rise, unified and triumphant."

"Ashes make good fertilizer," Azad said. "Plus, with spore-zombies in all branches of the military services and in the government, they'd get plenty of good intel they could use to keep the war going. They could make sure nobody makes peace or gains a decisive advantage. But like I said, the Arborec don't *do* stuff like this. I don't get it."

"It's *not* the Arborec," Harlow said. "It's just Ohseroh, acting alone. One Letani, budded off from the Symphony of the hivemind. Specifically created to ponder the problem of conflict with we strange biological creatures and determine whether trading weapons with us was sensible or not. We wanted to trade with the Arborec, for their technology, which is impressive and strange, entirely at right angles to the sort of tech other factions develop. Not even the deepest, darkest Hylar labs have bioweapons like the Arborec can make with ease. But what did we want those weapons *for*? What was the point of it all? The Arborec understand competition for resources, because they dealt with that problem before they completely took over their home world, but when our conflicts go beyond such simple terms – into ideology, and revenge, and honor, and all those other bizarre alien concepts – the Arborec lose the thread. They just don't comprehend any of it. So they made Ohseroh, a Letani stranger than most, more individual than most, and told it to talk to those of us who desired weapons of war and come up with a plan for how to deal with us, and to protect the interests of the Arborec."

"The Arborec wanted this Letani to figure out how to prevent war," I said. "And instead, it determined the best course of action was a very *large* war?" I was unprepared to deal with an enemy like this. I could understand those motivated by avarice and lust for power, but the Arborec were *different*.

Harlow nodded. "Ohseroh sent word to the hivemind back home. It explained how the Arzuga fungus could be altered to allow the Arborec to take over living bodies of many species – the Embers of Muaat are immune, and of course the Creuss, and some others – and proposed an ambitious plan to infiltrate and destroy. The Arborec refused. Not out of compassion, or any great regard they have for the other species, but just because the plan was too risky. If anyone realized what the Arborec was doing, all the peoples of the galaxy would band together to destroy their homeworld and silence the Symphony forever. Even if the plan worked, the galaxy would be a nightmare for generations, torn apart, impossible to govern, and difficult to put back together. The possible rewards didn't merit the risks."

"So… what?" I asked. "The Letani took initiative? They aren't supposed to do that. They're just extensions of the will of the Arborec."

"Yes," the fleet captain said. "But this Letani was created for an unusual purpose, as I said, and there must have been… flaws in its cultivation. Ohseroh went rogue. It became convinced its plan was worthwhile and refused to rejoin the Symphony and be subsumed into the overmind. Instead, Ohseroh stole a ship, and set out to enact its plan. Ohseroh believes that, if it succeeds – when it succeeds – the overmind will welcome it back, and hail it as a hero. Even though the Arborec don't really *do* heroes."

"It's a bad plan, and I don't like it," Azad said. "A little chaos is tasty, but I like living in a galaxy that's not completely on fire."

Ggorgos and Tib walked in just then. "We are up to date," the Xxcha rumbled. "Felix kept us patched in on the house comms system."

Felix cleared his throat. "Ggorgos, I'd like to apologize–"

The Xxcha held up a hand. "You did what you thought best with the information in your possession. We will speak of it no more." She addressed the fleet captain. "I concur with the human criminal. It is a bad plan. How do we stop it?"

Harlow said, "I don't know if we can. The summit on Moll Primus is in *four days*? Then the Legion meeting – that's scheduled for roughly the same time, yes? I know there was more back-and-forth there."

"Our new allies like to squabble," Severyne said. "But, yes, it was decided that to hold the summit *after* the Greater Union's would make it appear that we were reacting out of fear of that organization, so our meeting is scheduled to begin one hour earlier."

"That is so petty," Azad said. "I love it."

"I've been lost in the fog for a while," Harlow said. "But this next part was the linchpin of the plan, so I doubt it's changed." She took a breath. "There will be coordinated attacks on both summits. A crew of the faithful, in a Mentak Coalition warship, will attack the meeting on Arc Prime. At the same time, a crew on a Barony warship will assault Moll Primus."

That was an astonishingly audacious plan, the sort of terrorist attacks that would live in infamy for generations, but—

Felix spoke up with my objection before I could. "A single ship won't do much damage, especially on such heavily protected worlds."

"We – *they* – have compromised people in key positions to let the attacking vessels get closer than you'd expect," Harlow said. "But the point isn't really the damage they can wreak. Ohseroh isn't interested in assassinating the Baron or the Table of Captains or the Headmaster or any of the other leaders. They just want to make a brazen *attempt* on the lives of those leaders and position the opposing alliances as existential threats to one another. With their leaders personally attacked, the people will be outraged, and support war between the Union and the Legion. Plus, getting all the leaders together in a Moll Primus bunker or an Arc Prime vault is a good opportunity to infect the ones who remain unconverted, which will make this whole elaborate puppet theater of a war even easier to orchestrate."

"We must stop those ships before they attack," Ggorgos said.

"Sure," Azad said. "But we also have to stop the Letani."

"I concur," I said. "Kill the puppetmaster, and you needn't waste time cutting strings one by one."

"We must achieve all three of those objectives, while acting in direct opposition to the orders from our compromised leaders," Severyne said. "If we fail…"

"If we fail, we've got bigger problems than court martials," Azad said. "And if we *win*, think what that could do for your career, Sev?"

The scythe-like curve of a smile appeared on Severyne's face. "I have been thinking about just that."

Felix cracked his knuckles. "OK, then. Let's go save the galaxy."

CHAPTER 43
FELIX

"Our plan has *three* prongs," Azad said gleefully. She was sitting across the room from Felix, talking to Terrak, but, of course, she was very loud. "That's so many prongs! I can't decide who has the best prong. Maybe us? But also, the other ones sound pretty fun. Do you think we'll get to destroy a spaceship? I'll be upset if we don't get to destroy even *one* spaceship."

Felix was glad his prong didn't overlap with Azad's. This was going to be hard enough without contending with her unpredictable exuberance. He was standing with Calred, Tib, and Ggorgos. They were going to take the *Temerarious* and burn hard toward Arc Prime and try to intercept this Coalition warship. The trip was going to be a little tricky, since Felix was fairly sure they were going to be declared rogue and hunted down as fugitives themselves… and the Letnev wouldn't be happy about a Coalition ship zipping around space they controlled… but what was the alternative? Sending the *Grim Countenance*? Having a Barony ship shoot down a Coalition ship was just asking for an international incident, while sending a Coalition ship to do so could still be incredibly messy, but less likely to end in just the kind of war they were trying to prevent.

At the same time, Severyne would take her hideous ship toward Moll Primus – the very idea was horrific to Felix; that was the homeworld of his people – and intercept the Barony vessel.

Meanwhile, Terrak and Azad would take the fleet captain's personal ship and track down this rogue Letani, following a lead the fleet captain had provided. They would, ideally, eradicate *that* part of the threat.

If even one of us fails, everything fails, Felix thought. If either one of the Legion or Greater Union summits were attacked, it could still spark a war. If Ohseroh wasn't neutralized, the Letani would just continue its conspiracy, infecting new people, and probably taking better precautions against being discovered. The stakes were *so high*. It was terrifying and exhilarating and he was doing something that *mattered*.

"We should get moving," Felix said. "We're going to be cutting it close, and that's assuming the planned flight paths of the attack vessels haven't changed during the fleet captain's, ah… time offline."

"I will not be going with you," Ggorgos said. "I will accompany the Letnev woman instead."

That was unexpected. "Why would you do that?"

"She has lost her most trusted lieutenant," Ggorgos replied. "I believe she could use the support. She is also tasked with protecting the summit where the leaders of my kingdom will be in attendance. My greatest loyalty is to protect my people. I will do so."

"I don't think that's the best–" Felix began, but Ggorgos was already stomping across the room toward Severyne, who was standing with her shock troops, making sharp slicing gestures with her hands as she spoke to them.

He looked at Tib. "That's because I made her take her shell off and locked her in the brig, isn't it?"

"It is a thousand percent because of that, yes," Tib said. "I can't say I'll miss her, exactly, though."

"She was growing on me," Felix said. "After I figured out she wasn't part of an evil conspiracy, especially."

"I could tell you were suspicious of her." Calred was monotone, washed-out, and low energy. Azad said the condition should improve in time as the cure worked to repair the damage done to his neural tissue, but that he was going to be chemically depleted in the meantime, and prone to anxiety, anhedonia, and depression. "I… seeing you look at her that way made me happy, because it meant you weren't suspicious of *me*, and my directive from the guides was to go unnoticed."

"You're OK now." Felix clapped him on the shoulder. "And, hey, we're back to the original Duval's Devils, together again."

"Except our handler probably has a brain full of spores," Tib said. "Once Cal gets the comms working again, we're likely going to have some very unhappy messages from Jhuri."

"Maybe don't make fixing the comms a priority," Felix said.

CHAPTER 44
SEVERYNE

Severyne heard the stomping behind her and turned to watch the Xxcha's approach. Ggorgos was an alarming sight, with her armored shell and glowing eyepiece, but Severyne made a point of never letting alarm show. "May I help you?" she asked instead, in a tone that suggested she hoped not.

"I will accompany you to destroy the Coalition ship."

Severyne arched an eyebrow. "Oh, will you? I do not require oversight from–"

"I am not offering oversight, but assistance. I am very capable."

"I can believe that," Severyne said. "But the Xxcha hate the Letnev. There was that... unfortunate business... with your planet being destroyed."

Ggorgos grunted. "Current problems concern me more than ancient crimes. The enemy of my enemy is my temporary and contingent ally."

Severyne didn't laugh, but she did let a smile through her barricades. "Even so, I assure you, I am more than capable of completing this part of the mission myself. Go back to your fellows."

The Xxcha looked around the room, then took a step closer to Severyne, lowering her head to speak quietly into the Letnev's ear. "You have to get me away from Felix Duval before I finally lose my patience and punch him through a bulkhead."

Now Severyne did laugh, a brief burst of delight that made Azad look over at her curiously. (She was always aware of where Azad was looking.) "Very well," she said. "I think we can find common cause. Welcome to the crew of the *Grim Countenance*. Shall we begin?"

THE FAITHFUL XV

Jhuri and Kote Strom perambulated through the grounds of the Mentak Coalition capitol on Moll Primus, watching workers erect stages and set up chairs as harried organizers of various species rushed around shouting into earpieces. "This looks like the sort of chaos that eventually resolves into something impressive," Jhuri observed. "I still can't believe all the parties are on board. I really thought we'd lose the Kingdom of Xxcha."

"The guides managed to reach the right people there," Kote said. "The Greater Union will go forward, and glory will follow."

"I don't suppose you know the goal of the great work?"

"The guides have not seen fit to share the wholeness of their vision with me. Only that the formation of the Greater Union is key to the plan."

"Mmm, yes. They told me the same thing. Have the guides seemed… troubled to you, lately?"

"Perhaps a bit preoccupied," Kote allowed.

"I hope it doesn't have anything to do with Felix and the hunt for the fugitives. My operatives haven't reported in for a while, and the guides refuse to discuss the subject with me."

"I doubt it's anything as mundane as *that*," Kote said. "The guides have more on their minds than your small operation. Preparing for our glorious future takes a lot of attention."

"You seem a bit preoccupied, too."

Kote winced. "Is it apparent? I have been given an assignment. I have to select some volunteers, and… well… Jhuri, in your official capacity, you have access to explosives, don't you?"

"When it comes to armament, I can lay my pseudopods on just about anything short of a dreadnought at a moment's notice."

"I'll let you know what I need. The guides say everything is going well, but that it's important to have backup plans."

Immental emerged from the meeting with her cousin, the Baron. She had a splitting headache that the guides, in their wisdom, had opted not to soothe. She usually enjoyed the company of the Baron, who appreciated someone who could match wits with him, but he'd just declared her "dull company" and said, "I hope you return to your usual self after all this tedious business with the summit is done." She'd been looking for an opportunity to give him the sacrament, but there were guards and advisers and toadies and other cousins all over the reception room, and there was never a chance.

The Baron *would* sign the treaty – he was already being hailed as a visionary, ready to take the Letnev into the future they deserved. That was all thanks to the efforts of the state propaganda machine, guided by a few of the faithful in the right positions. But Immental was the one organizing the summit itself, and there were so many moving parts! The N'orr envoy was not among the faithful, and now she had reports that the L1Z1X were giving the captains assigned to them trouble, and of course the Gashlai couldn't be inducted into the faith at *all*, but had to be brought along with ordinary inducements, like preferential trading terms and the promise of violent death to their enemies.

The Baron was putting the entire burden of the summit's success on her, since she'd been the one who convinced him of the Legion's importance, and while she could delegate, it wasn't as if anyone else were *competent–*

The guides spoke to her. She stopped in the hallway, glanced around to make sure she was unobserved, and then said, "*Bombs?* Why do we need bombs, wise ones?"

CHAPTER 45
TERRAK

Azad and I had to wait a little while for the fleet captain's personal ship to be made ready, and for a few other preparations to be completed. Harlow's vessel, the *Darkest Mercy*, was no warship, sadly, and I didn't like the idea of going up against the leader of a vast conspiracy with nothing but our wits. Harlow did have a collection of personal armaments she'd collected, stolen in raids, and won in battle, though, and offered us our pick. Azad was having a merry time sorting through the vault, exclaiming over bits of deadly kit, while I contented myself with borrowing a variable-output energy pistol and a Muaat fire knife (with a modified handle so creatures who *weren't* fireproof could hold it).

"Whoa, this is a Creuss rifle!" Azad held up a device that looked more like a bit of curving silver abstract art than a weapon. "They call it a ghost gun – I've heard they can shoot through walls without putting a hole through them, fire around corners, and do all kinds of other weird stuff that shouldn't work, unless we have some fundamental misunderstandings about the laws of physics." She sighed. "No charge though." She tossed it aside and turned back to the wall of weapons in the captain's vault. "Hylar repeating rifle, no, they're too fussy and over-engineered, prone to breaking... good old Federation of Sol issue pulse rifle, super boring, I practically grew up with one in my hand... Yssaril shame-knife, those are nasty, but I don't think an evil plant is going to be bothered by a scar that won't heal... Sardakk bracers, I kinda don't think they'd fit on my wrists and I doubt they'd work right if I strapped them to my thighs... Ooh, hello. You'll do." She picked up a machine gun that bristled with attachments. "This is some classic Mentak Coalition ridiculousness right here – a bunch of mostly stolen technology cobbled together into a whole that somehow more or less works." She fiddled with some switches near the grip. "I can swap between kinetic and plasma loads, there's an inbuilt grenade launcher, and if you overload this here you can do a one-time electricity discharge that's lethal... ha, there's even a tiny little localized EMP, and get this: a no-fuel flamethrower!"

I frowned. "How do you make a flamethrower with no fuel?"

"It's not a totally accurate name – there is fuel, it's just a small quantity of water instead of a large quantity of something more flammable. It uses hydrolysis to split the water molecules into hydrogen and oxygen, then uses *those* as the accelerant."

"That actually works?"

"So I'm told. Until you run out of water, and it's heavy to haul around too much of that. But it does mean you don't have to carry a tank of accelerant around and risk turning yourself into an incendiary grenade if you catch a stray round. This is the gun for me. I'm going to name her Sev."

"Why?"

Azad posed with the gun at a jaunty angle. "Because she's versatile, and deadly, and more fun than she looks."

"You really want to tell me the story of your relationship with the Letnev captain, don't you?"

"I mean, we're going to be on this ship for a few days, and we have to talk about *something*." She took a last glance around the vault and nodded to herself. "Let's go see if the cook and the butler have our supplies ready yet. We should get hunting."

CHAPTER 46
FELIX

"Calred showed me where the Letani node was hidden," Tib reported. "Behind a panel on the lower deck. I sent in a maintenance robot to bag and incinerate it and kicked up the air filters to their highest setting to clear out any remaining spores. Cal says the spores produced by the node don't actually infect people, it's just biological communications gear, but why take chances?"

"Good work," Felix said. "How are we doing on the cure?"

"The chemjet printers in the infirmary are creating as much as we've got reagents for. Should be enough for eight or twelve doses, depending on whether we're sticking it into humans or Hacan or Yssaril or what."

"The people on board the *Sly Mongoose* aren't criminals or terrorists or conspirators. They're victims, and, if at all possible, I want to cure them rather than kill them."

"It would be nice if we could just put the cure in gas grenades instead of injecting it into people one at a time," Tib said. "I'd rather douse everyone at once."

"I gather the dosage is important," Felix said. "I have a whole chart with species and weight ranges that Azad gave us. If we just gassed everyone, they'd probably mostly die."

"That would be somewhat counterproductive," Tib admitted.

Calred's voice spoke from the PA system. He was still pretty low-energy. There were combat and focus drugs that led to that kind of mood crash, but they *did* pass, eventually. Felix hoped this would, too. "Comms are back online, captain. Voyou made a big mess with the wiring, but the damage wasn't that deep. And... yeah, lots of messages in the queue from Jhuri."

"I should go deal with that." Felix trudged back to his quarters. There were thirty-seven messages waiting from Jhuri. His superior had never been one to micromanage – Felix checked in more often than Jhuri liked, honestly – which only bolstered Felix's certainty that the Hylar had been compromised. The messages were all variations on "what the hell is going on?" and "where the hell are you?" Felix composed a brief message, text only, and sent it via an encryption protocol that would bounce across half a dozen systems before landing in Jhuri's inbox:

Comms damaged in fight. Calred lost. Terrak and Azad escaped. Headed toward the Jorun asteroid field. In pursuit. Updates to follow.

Jhuri wouldn't know where they really were and wouldn't know where they were really going… but, hopefully, he wouldn't send anyone to apprehend them. Claiming Calred had died would explain why he was out of contact with his fungal superiors and might allay Jhuri's suspicions to a degree. As far as any of them knew, the rogue Letani didn't know what, exactly, happened on Entelegyne, and couldn't necessarily distinguish a cured servant from a dead one. But Ohseroh's puppets would probably all be on high alert.

Two days passed in travel. They transited a wormhole controlled by an independent trading conglomerate, using false documents and a faked transponder signal. As covert operatives, they were good at staying hidden – even from their own government, as it turned out. In another day they would pass into Barony-controlled space, and then, they'd have to hide even better.

The Letnev home planet, Arc Prime, was an anomaly: a planet without a star to call its own, sailing on a strange course through the void, surrounded by a constantly shifting cloud of ships and stations. Felix sat with Tib and Calred in the galley of the *Temerarious* and watched Barony-controlled propaganda broadcasts about the upcoming summit. There were images of the Baron, or one of his body doubles, dressed in a military uniform that dripped with medals and sashes and chains, waving from behind a forcefield. Admiral Immental, who Severyne said was a spore-zombie, did most of the actual talking, appearing behind a podium and using very un-Letnev-sounding phrases like "a new era of cooperation" and "in unity, there is strength" and "working together to forge a better tomorrow". There was a lot of footage of the meeting space, too, which Felix watched with morbid interest. It was entirely too easy to imagine it being blown to bits by the *Sly Mongoose*.

The Legion summit wouldn't actually be held on Arc Prime, where all the cities were subterranean – apparently the Embers of Muaat had balked at the idea of being trapped underground with their new friends. The going theory was, the Embers were the only people involved in either of these alliances who *weren't* being controlled, to some degree, by Ohseroh – the energy-based physiology of the Gashlai made them immune to the spores. They'd agreed to join the Legion because they hated the Hylar and liked the idea of ganging up against them. The conspiracy had to make allowances to accommodate an uninfected species, and Felix hoped they were having a terrible time with it.

Since Arc Prime wasn't an acceptable location, the summit was being held on the prototype of the Barony's new Dark Star weapons system – the Barony's answer to the infamous Muaat War Suns, only even bigger. The Dark Star was basically a city in space, a mobile weapons platform that, according to Letnev propaganda, would "forever secure the supremacy of the Letnev, and their allies in the Legion, across the whole of the galaxy". Even accounting for Barony exaggeration, the idea of such a weapon in their hands was sobering.

"That sounds bad," Calred said.

"I've seen some of our intelligence reports about that prototype," Tib said. She had lots of friends elsewhere in the clandestine services. "Everyone says the Dark Star looks impressive – bristling with cannons, the usual ornamental spikes, enough engines to move a moon – but it's pretty much a hollow shell. The Letnev engineers are having a horrible time with the electrical systems. They're having trouble dealing with their waste heat, they need multiple gravity generators for something so big and calibrating them to work together is tricky... we reckon the Letnev are years from having a Dark Star that actually works. Using it as a prop for the summit is probably the most use they'll get out of it for a while."

"They'll get even less use out of it if the *Sly Mongoose* manages to blow it up," Calred said.

"I think the idea is just to fire on the Dark Star, and make some noise, and then die as glorious martyrs to the vegetable cause," Felix said. "They wouldn't want to actually kill any of the highly placed puppet people. But even firing on the summit is enough to start a war, so let's make sure it doesn't come to that. When do we rendezvous with the zombie ship?"

"Not long, if Harlow was right," Tib said. "The *Sly Mongoose* was chosen because they were able to turn its whole crew into the faithful, and because it was out on a long-range secret reconnaissance mission on the edge of Barony space anyway, and nobody would notice if it shifted course a little. But Harlow's brain was basically soup for a while there, and plans might have changed. We just don't know. If the ship is on the course she predicted, we should intersect in about twelve hours."

"I'll just be sitting here staring at the clock until then, I suppose," Felix said.

Fourteen hours later, there was still no sign of the *Sly Mongoose*. The Legion summit was scheduled to begin in roughly eight hours, and the Greater Union summit in nine. All the dignitaries were already present or would be soon. Maybe the *Sly Mongoose* was already deeper than expected into Barony space, where the *Temerarious* couldn't hope to follow without being noticed, since there were no puppets clearing a path for them. Maybe they were too late. They had to face the possibility.

"Total war." Felix sat on the bridge with Tib and Calred. He felt as despondent as Cal looked. "How will it start, do you think?"

"From the edges, moving in," Tib said. "The Legion will hit Greater Union colony worlds near its own holdings first. We'll do the same to the Legion colonies."

"We could send the Letnev a warning," Calred said. "Tell them an attack is coming."

Felix shook his head. "They wouldn't take a message from a Coalition ship seriously. They'd think we were just trying to disrupt or delay their event." He sighed. "I sent an anonymous warning anyway, though. Didn't get a response. They treated it like a hoax bomb threat, I'm sure."

"Harlow said the conspiracy has good information control," Tib said. "Ohse-roh is super paranoid about people learning its plans, as demonstrated by their whole framing-Terrak-for-murder thing. I'm sure they're monitoring communications, especially after that tell-all broadcast."

"I did a little searching about the speech, hoping it might have changed things," Felix said. "The consensus on the networks is that Terrak is trying to set up an insanity defense, making it seem like he's suffering from paranoia and delusions of grandeur."

"This is one of those cases where the truth is indistinguishable from paranoia," Calred said. "We–"

The main screen lit up, revealing a tiny blob of heat in the cold of space. Their sensors would never have detected that signature if they hadn't been looking for it and looking hard; recon ships were stealthy. Felix shot to his feet. "Is that the *Sly Mongoose*?"

"Looks like it." Tib slid the controls on a console. "They're on the expected trajectory, just a little behind schedule."

"What kept them?" Felix said. "I can't imagine Ohseroh likes tardiness."

Tib shrugged. "Could have been anything – engine trouble, avoiding a Barony patrol, who knows? But they're here now, and I don't think they've noticed us yet."

"All right," Felix said. "Let's make our pirate ancestors proud and take that ship."

They didn't dare risk a disabling shot – in theory, they could damage the *Sly Mongoose*'s engines and leave the ship drifting and otherwise unharmed, but there was always a risk of breaching the reactor and causing an explosion. Felix wasn't about to let this conspiracy claim any more Mentak Coalition lives. Instead, they launched boarding pods at maximum range.

The *Temerarious* was equipped with six pods, and they sent all of them, three managed remotely by Tib from her pod (she was exceptionally good at multitasking), while Felix and Calred piloted the other two. The breaching vessels were tiny, barely bigger than escape pods, just big enough for a couple of crew, but their exteriors bristled with equipment. The pods were draped in every bit of stealth tech the Mentak Coalition navy had developed or stolen, and since they were much smaller than a cruiser, that tech was more effective – the pods didn't produce much in the way of heat, radiation, or other energy signatures compared to a full-sized vessel.

The pods approached the smooth bulk of the *Sly Mongoose* – the cruiser was actually the same model as the *Temerarious*, but newer – and matched velocity. Felix nudged the controls in his pod and gently attached himself to the larger ship's hull with magnetic clamps. The other pods settled in at different points on the ship, like leeches on a swimmer. Duval's Devils didn't risk talking to each other now – using comms this close to the ship would risk detection – but they knew what to do.

One of the uncrewed pods, stuck to the side of the *Sly Mongoose* halfway down its length, extended an array of manipulator arms, tipped with torches, saws, and grasping claws, and began to very noisily and obviously tear into the skin of the ship. The other two empty pods were doing the same thing, at different locations.

While the unoccupied pods were making as much noise as possible, Felix's pod very quietly sliced away at the hull beneath it, cutting a small circle from the skin of the ship and moving it aside. The bottom of the pod irised open, allowing Felix to clamber into the hole. He wore an environment suit specially designed for boarding hostile vessels, so it was more limber than most, but at the expense of a limited air supply and decreased thickness; basically, if he snagged on a sharp piece of metal, he'd probably die.

Felix crawled into the hole, just beneath the outer layer of the hull, and waited in claustrophobic darkness. The space was barely big enough for him to kneel in, but he only had to wait long enough for the boarding pod to replace the cut-away portion of the hull and seal it back in place above him. Once he was no longer exposed to vacuum, Felix used a portable cutting torch to slice through a much thinner inner surface, and then dropped into a narrow maintenance tunnel. Now he was actually *on* the ship, instead of just being stuck in its skin like a splinter.

Felix had chosen his position carefully; knowing the basic layout as well as his own helped. Now he was in the pressurized atmosphere of the ship, but he left his tight-fitting helmet on anyway. This was a ship full of spore-zombies, so breathing around them seemed inadvisable.

There were klaxons wailing, which suggested a certain amount of chaos. Felix checked his pistol, confirmed it held a full load. They weren't sure how many people were on board. Harlow had estimated six crew, but there might be more. They'd brought enough darts to take down twice that many.

Felix peered through a vent, into a corridor, and watched the legs of a human crew member rush by. Once the way was clear, he opened the access hatch and stepped into the corridor. The running crewperson disappeared around a corner, and Felix loped after her, selecting the appropriate load on his pistol as he ran. Just like with the cure, the dose of tranquilizer you needed to take down a human was different from that needed for a Hacan or an Xxcha or an Yssaril.

Felix lifted the pistol and fired a dart into the woman's back, right between her shoulder blades. She stopped and began clawing at her, but she couldn't reach the dart. The part of your back you couldn't reach to scratch by yourself, Felix remembered, was called the "acnestis". Funny, the things that went through one's mind in the heat of combat. Well, not combat, exactly…

The woman spun toward Felix. She had short, blonde hair and wide, staring eyes. She rushed toward him, stumbling but clearly determined. He waited for her to fall… but instead, she said, "Guides, give me strength," and then jolted upright, as if a surge of electricity had passed through her.

Felix knew the Letani sacrament worked by hacking a victim's brain chemistry and flooding them with chemicals that created a sense of love, devotion, and bliss. But there was no reason it couldn't *also* flood them with adrenaline and cortisol, perhaps even enough to overcome the strength of a sedative in the system.

The woman launched herself at Felix, and since she wasn't wearing a spacesuit, she was a lot faster and more agile than he was. She plowed into him, knocking him down, and pinned his body with her own. She tried to tear his helmet off, snarling at him, and he struck her in the face with his pistol once, twice, three times. She didn't appear to feel pain, though. She was beyond all that. She was in the throes of devotion.

Calred lifted the woman off Felix, stuck a stun gun in the side of her neck, and triggered the jolt. He dropped her, twitching, to the floor of the corridor. "Hello, captain," he said on their suit comms. "I find my former colleagues in the great spore religion very annoying."

Felix took the hand Calred offered and got to his feet. "Did you secure the rest of the ship already?"

The Hacan shook his head. "We took out two other crew members. There are at least two more barricaded on the bridge."

"Nice of them to gather together for our convenience. Let's get down there."

Calred picked up the woman and slung her over his shoulder. They walked down the ship's corridors, and just as they reached the secure door to the bridge, the alarms and klaxons stopped. The door slid open, revealing Tib on the other side. Her boarding pod had attached itself near the command deck, and as an Yssaril, she was adept at moving invisibly. There were two unconscious crew members, a Hylar lieutenant and a Hacan wearing captain's insignia, on the floor behind her. "The *Sly Mongoose* is ours, captain."

Calred found and destroyed the *Sly Mongoose*'s node, jettisoning it from an airlock, while Tib and Felix oversaw things in the infirmary. They administered the cure to all five members of the crew – including a second human and an Yssaril – and waited for them to come up out of their sedation. Felix was surprised it all went so smoothly… but, then again, people mind-controlled by the guides didn't become tactical geniuses or unstoppable fighting machines. If anything, they were slower to improvise and react and more easily distracted. The strength of the conspiracy was in its numbers, and its reach into the halls of power, not the prowess of its individual puppets. Now that they knew how to cut the strings, Felix and his allies had a chance.

The captain, a Hacan named Karlon, was the first to blink his way to consciousness. He covered his face with his hands and wailed. "No, no, what have we *done*!"

"You failed," Tib said. "You're welcome."

"We were going to attack *Arc Prime*!" he said. "Because… for the future… to make the galaxy better, but…" Tears welled from his eyes. "None of it makes any sense."

"It's OK." Felix put a hand on his shoulder. He didn't know how it felt to unwillingly betray his people, but he knew how it felt to know you'd failed your crew, and he sympathized. "You're OK. We're going to take you home."

"I…" He looked beseechingly into Felix's face. "What will happen to us there?"

"Well," Felix said, "I figure either we'll be celebrated as heroes, or we'll be executed for treason. It's all a bit of a coin flip, really. Depends on how things go in other places. But at least you'll live and die as your own person, and not a puppet for someone else."

"Living would be preferable," the captain said.

Felix walked to the far side of the room to stand by Tib. "Well, we saved the Baron of Letnev from the indignity of an attack. Hurray. I wonder how Severyne and Ggorgos are doing with *their* part of the mission?"

CHAPTER 47
SEVERYNE

Severyne told the crew of the *Grim Countenance* that they were going dark, cutting off all communications, and fulfilling a secret mission on behalf of the Baron. She told them she would not be taking any questions, especially not regarding the identity of the peculiar Xxcha who had accompanied her up from the planet; the nature of Ggorgos's involvement was deeply classified. Her people were sufficiently loyal, overawed, or terrified of her that they complied without complaint. Only Voyou would have dared to ask any questions, and… well. There was no time for sentimentality now. There was too much at stake.

To her surprise, Severyne discovered that she quite liked Ggorgos. She'd always thought of the Xxcha as weaklings, devoted to diplomacy even when it was clearly a losing proposition, but Ggorgos was different. Severyne almost said, "You are Xxcha with the soul of a Letnev," but refrained, afraid it wouldn't be taken as the compliment it was intended to be.

The two of them discussed strategy, briefly, on the first night of their journey, but that didn't take long; the two of them were remarkably in accord when it came to finding the best way forward.

For the following days, as they moved to intercept the rogue Barony cruiser *The Soldier of the City* before it could penetrate the heart of Mentak Coalition space and launch an attack on the Greater Union summit, Ggorgos and Severyne just… talked. Sometimes they talked while playing the traditional Letnev game Spiralstone, or a somewhat similar strategy game the Xxcha played called The Hidden Shell, and sometimes they talked while sipping small cups of Barony liquor (fermented from the finest lichens), and sometimes they simply sat in Severyne's ready room and gazed out the windows at the stars and discussed the places they'd been and the things they'd seen and the people they'd killed there. She missed having Voyou to talk to, and carefully avoided looking into the empty space his absence opened inside her but having Ggorgos for company made that space less of an abyss.

They also complained about Felix Duval. At least they didn't have to talk *to* him at all; the three teams of the counter-conspiracy were siloed off to make sure Ohseroh couldn't intercept any information about their plans. Their mission could only succeed if their strikes were unforeseen and simultaneous.

Roughly ten hours before the summit was scheduled to begin on Moll Primus, they caught *The Soldier of the City* emerging from an asteroid field. The *Grim Countenance* sat, patient as a spider, and waited for the prey to pass within range.

"Would you like to do the honors, Ggorgos?" Sev asked, standing beside the Xxcha on the bridge, watching the dot on the viewscreen that represented the rogue Barony ship.

"That's unusually magnanimous of you," the Xxcha asked.

"Oh, no. It's just that I won't derive any satisfaction from sparing the Mentak Coalition from an attack, and I thought you might."

"I will."

"Ggorgos has tactical command!" Severyne snapped at the bridge crew.

"Target locked," the soldier at the tactical board said.

"Destroy that ship," Ggorgos said.

The *Grim Countenance* rumbled, faintly, as it launched multiple fusillades of torpedoes.

After a moment, the glowing dot on the screen ceased to exist, its fragments joining the debris in the asteroid field.

"Target destroyed," the soldier said.

"Well done," Severyne said, to Ggorgos and to the bridge crew in general. A compliment from her was only slightly less rare than sunshine on Arc Prime.

Ggorgos said, "How much do you want to bet that Duval pointlessly made his part of the mission more complicated than ours?"

Severyne chuckled. "As long as he gets the job done, his inevitable lapses in judgment are tolerable." She nodded to one of her bridge officers. "Take us back to Barony space, helmsman."

"I hope Azad and Terrak have as easy a time as we did," Ggorgos said.

"Mmm, not that easy," Severyne said. "Azad will be disappointed if things aren't at least a little bit nightmarish."

THE FAITHFUL XVI

<We have lost contact with the Sly Mongoose,> the guide whispered to Immental. *<You must engage the failsafe protocol.>*

Immental closed her eyes. She was in a meeting room on the Dark Star with the L1Z1X ambassador, and this was *not* a good time to get the worst possible news.

The L1Z1X leader, Ibna Vel Syd, had not come to the summit, the only explanation being that his "current form is temporarily incompatible with standards modes of travel". Instead, the Barony welcomed his proxy, LV286, a red-eyed maniac with metal sticking out of his face from beneath his mysteriously stained robes. LV286 was not one of the faithful… or at least, not completely so. The guides said that the L1Z1X were "resistant to the sacrament", though not fully immune like the Gashlai were. The L1Z1X had taken so much cybernetic control over their biological systems that the guides couldn't control them as easily as other species. (It was odd that Immental could understand *how* she was being manipulated, without that knowledge conferring even the slightest bit of resistance to the manipulation. It really served to show how perfect and powerful the guides were, didn't it?)

"You are distracted," LV286 said.

"I am merely frustrated, ambassador," she said as smoothly as possible. "The summit is mere hours from now, and you have yet to commit to joining our Legion."

"You have yet to agree to take on a subservient role to the Mindnet."

"The whole point of the Legion is that we are a partnership of equals."

The red eyes twinkled. "But we are not equal. We are the rightful rulers of the galaxy, and you are the descendants of rebellious scum." This was said with no apparent rancor, or even awareness that it was insulting. "We are generously offering to take you under our protection, yet again. Ibna Vel Syd is baffled by your refusal to embrace his largesse. The guides also refuse to direct their power toward the restoration of our rule. We would empty your skins and fill them with wonders, yet you rebuff us."

"Your offer is… very kind, and as I've said, I will be sure to tell the Baron, but again, the nature of this particular alliance is one of–"

A bolt of pain shot through her head, like a spike driven through her temples. *<Prepare the backup plan!>* the guides shrieked.

"Ambassador, forgive me, I must… I have an urgent matter I must attend to."

"The guides are calling?" The monster tittered. "Too many masters to serve, admiral, too many, better to serve only the L1Z1X." She rose from the table, and LV286 looked at her with those intent, glittering eyes. "Wonders," he said. "Think on them, and tremble, with ecstasy and dread."

"I certainly will." She turned and left the conference room, ignoring the beeps in her comms – everyone had an emergency today, and everyone wanted *her* to solve them, but her first allegiance was to the guides, as they'd just … strenuously reminded her.

If the *Sly Mongoose* wasn't coming to fire on the summit and start a war, that meant Immental had to distribute her stash of high explosives to members of the faithful. Several had been chosen to pretend they were Greater Union double agents, sent to sabotage the meeting. Just as the dignitaries prepared to sign the treaty, those faithful would declare their allegiance to the Union, detonate their bombs, and destroy large, nonessential portions of the Dark Star – along with themselves. One of the faithful would have a malfunctioning bomb, so she could be taken into custody and interrogated, allowing her to repeat her cover story as often and loudly as necessary to convince everyone that the Greater Union was an immediate threat.

When it came to starting a war, a coordinated suicide bombing was nowhere near as good as a Mentak Coalition warship opening fire on the station – acts by individuals could too easily be written off as the work of radical terrorists, not official actors – but then, if it had been a *better* idea, it wouldn't have been the backup plan.

Immental wondered if she would be called upon to detonate one of the bombs herself. If so, she would die secure in the knowledge that her life had served the great work: ushering in a single galactic community, overseen by the wisdom and beneficence of the guides. But she vastly preferred the idea of living to see that future personally.

CHAPTER 48
TERRAK

I was reclining in one of the plush armchairs on Fleet Captain Harlow's personal vessel, the *Darkest Mercy*, when the call came in. The ship was a pleasure craft built by one of the shipyards in the Federation of Sol, either bought by the Mentak or captured by their raider fleet. It was the second-nicest ship I'd ever traveled on: there was a chandelier in the galley, a palatial shower (spacious even by my standards), plush carpets, actual beds, and every other conceivable comfort of home and beyond. The ship was also incredibly fast and quiet. It was possible to forget you were on board a spacefaring vessel at all, at least until you looked out a window and saw stars instead of trees or the sea.

The comms chimed pleasantly with an incoming priority call, and I answered from a console in the chair's arm. "I have the details you requested on the *Crystal Stair*," the message from Catriona said. "I'll charge it to your account."

An encrypted data packet downloaded, then unspooled itself across the screen. I pushed the information to Azad's tablet, highlighting the coordinates of our target ship's last known location. (Azad was in the library, where there were actual paper books, looking for anything that had dirty pictures in it, probably. On our first day of travel, she told me about her affair and rivalry and partnership with Severyne Dampierre, and now there were dirty pictures etched in *my* mind. Since I don't find hairless primates particularly attractive, those were most unwelcome. That's what I get for finally giving in to my curiosity.)

Harlow had a high degree of certainty that our rogue Letani was on board the *Crystal Stair*, a two-generations-old Mentak Coalition cruiser that was supposedly decommissioned and sold off. "Ohseroh couldn't remain on board its original ship, not after going rogue," Harlow told us. "The Letani managed to keep its crew – an array of the various lifeforms that live on the Arborec home world, all bound together by fungal symbiosis – under its control, but the ship itself was too easy to track by the Arborec. With the help of some loyal puppets I helped Ohseroh recruit, the Letani faked an accident and destroyed the original vessel in a bid to convince the hivemind back home that Ohseroh was dead. We rerouted the *Crystal Stair* away from its destination in the scrapyard, made sure the relevant paperwork was destroyed, and loaded Ohseroh and its helpers on board. There are a couple of faithful on board, too, a Letnev and a human, in case they ever need faces to present to local authorities. The ship has been cruising around ever since, under independent trader colors, with its movements disguised as much as possible by our confederates, erasing logs and so on. Ohseroh travels back and forth between Mentak Coalition and Barony space, where it has the highest concentration of loyalists and nodes. As it goes, it seeds additional nodes in moons and ships and planets and stations wherever possible. That increases Ohseroh's range and ability to directly communicate with its adherents. Think of the *Crystal Stair* as the Letani's mobile command center."

"I know you were the key to infiltrating the Coalition, but how did Ohseroh make such progress in the Barony?" I'd asked.

Harlow explained, "I had a double agent among the Letnev back when I ran covert operations, and I was able to set up a meeting so Ohseroh could infect them. From there, the faithful worked their way up through the Barony, almost to the very top."

Azad wasn't thrilled with the information. "'Somewhere in Barony or Coalition space' isn't much help when it comes to tracking down a ship, Harlow."

"I believe I can narrow it down," I assured her, and so I had. A ship that travels so much needs to be regularly restocked with fuel and supplies, even if most of the crew does consist of plant-creatures, and no one can cover their tracks perfectly. I reached out to Catriona, my data analyst par excellence, who wasn't at all concerned about my status as a wanted fugitive. She pored over data from the known locations Harlow could provide for the *Crystal Stair*, and then worked her usual magic. She'd just come through with coordinates: a ship matching the description of the *Crystal Stair*, with a registered name that proved to be false when Catriona investigated, had been seen yesterday departing the Nicodemidae system. That was in Barony space, not a terribly long journey from Arc Prime itself.

Azad strolled into the lounge and dropped into the chair across from mine. "Looks like Ohseroh is planning to oversee the Legion summit from close range, huh?"

"It makes sense," I said. "Harlow says the Gashlai are immune to the spores, and the L1Z1X are resistant, so the Legion meeting is more likely to hit snags that need smoothing over."

"They have no idea what kind of snags they're in store for," Azad said. "I'm going to set a course. You start sharpening your claws."

"I prefer to prevail with sharp wits, as a rule."

Azad snorted. "Good luck using your charm on an insane mushroom bent on galactic domination."

"I do love a challenge." I paused, before deciding to broach something that had been worrying me. "Do you think Harlow's theory is right? That stopping Ohseroh will free those in its thrall? If not… what happens to a bunch of mind-controlled puppets when there's no one to pull their strings?"

Azad shrugged. "I'm not an expert or anything, but I remember hearing once that the largest single living organism on Jord is a big mushroom colony. It looks like thousands of individual growths, but underground, it's all connected by a single mycelium. The Arborec homeworld is bigger than *that*, and even so, it's a single symbiotic organism. It's possible that Ohseroh is connected to all the puppets, and if we kill it, we cut the strings. Otherwise…" She sighed. "We'll have to inject a *lot* of spore-zombies with the cure. While they're being driven insane with grief for their dead god. So. Let's hope… not that."

CHAPTER 49
AZAD

Azad was terrible at waiting, which was a bad quality in a covert operative, but since she was excellent at every *other* part of the job, she generally managed. She spent the journey to the Nicodemidae system disassembling and reassembling her new gun, exercising, starting arguments with Terrak, fantasizing about past debaucheries, enjoying the contents of the fleet captain's exceptionally well stocked liquor cabinet, enduring Terrak's culinary experiments with her equally well stocked spice rack, and reading. (Everyone was always surprised when they found out she liked to read. She loved reading. Reading was how you learned everything you couldn't learn by doing.)

They finally reached the *Crystal Stair*'s last known location, and then picked the most logical route to reach Arc Prime. Azad figured the Letani wouldn't get too close to the actual summit, just near enough to monitor the situation, and since it had such a high concentration of spores in Barony space, it wouldn't have to get all *that* close. There was a promising asteroid field where you could easily hide a ship of the *Crystal Stair*'s size, and keep an eye on the proceedings through conventional means as well as fungal tech.

The *Darkest Mercy* approached the asteroid field, and Azad made final preparations. While Azad bustled around, Terrak sat watching the live broadcasts about the Greater Union summit – the footage from the Legion summit preparations on Arc Prime was all state propaganda anyway, and a lot more boring. The capital city of Moll Primus was all polished and shiny, hung with banners, the streets and stadiums filled with cheering people. It felt less like a diplomatic meeting than a festival, with various games and contests and musical exhibitions held all over the city, featuring the most skilled and talented people from all the invited systems. "Ohseroh didn't plan for all *this*," she said, leaning over Terrak's shoulder to watch. "It can't possibly give a crap about cultural exchange."

"No, but there are plenty of people involved in the planning who haven't been mind-controlled, and this … is just what people do."

"Any excuse for a party." Azad toggled the main viewscreen to show the approaching cloud of rocks before them. The asteroid field was many thousands of kilometers across, dense and deep, perfect to conceal a vessel. "The *Crystal Stair* is hiding in there somewhere. I'm sure of it."

"How do you intend to find it?"

"Easy." She opened a short-range communication band, the sort used for ship-to-ship communications. The transmission was strictly local and wouldn't be picked up by anyone outside of the immediate area. She turned on the camera and grinned into the lens. "Hello, Ohseroh," she said. "It's Azad and Terrak. We need to talk to you." Time to see if the Letani was capable of curiosity.

The sensors lit up, and there was the ship, barely a thousand kilometers away, hidden in the thick of the asteroids… except it wasn't trying to hide anymore.

The image flickered. A Letnev man appeared on their screen. His eyes were glazed, and there was some kind of moss hanging from his chin. The air around him was visibly full of floating particulates. "We should kill you." The voice was monotone.

"Why?" Azad said. She'd only given it fifty-fifty odds the Letani's puppet would answer at all, so she was feeling good about things. "We've seen the error of our ways. You're clearly going to win this war – you're smarter than *we* are. We've met some of your faithful, and they're all happy and fulfilled and sing your praises all day long. We can't possibly defeat you, and everyone says we'd be fools to even try. So, we've come to beg forgiveness. Let us join your fellowship."

"This is a trick. This is subterfuge."

"No, it's not. I would never. You want us to recant all that stuff Terrak said on his broadcast, right? We'd be happy to–"

"That is no longer necessary. Our plan is on the cusp of success."

"Really? Because–"

The *Crystal Stair* fired on the *Darkest Mercy*. Despite being decommissioned, Ohseroh's ship still had weapons, courtesy of its various fungal loyalists. The fleet captain's unarmed pleasure vessel was an easy target.

"That was rude," Azad said, after turning off the comms. But not unexpected, of course.

She and Terrak had sent their message from a shuttle, far enough away from the *Crystal Stair* to avoid the debris field, but close enough to relay their comms through the larger ship, to make it seem like that's where the message originated. "So much for throwing ourselves on the mercy of the spore-lord."

"Ohseroh won't see us coming now, at least," Terrak said. "Your plan worked."

"I've benefited greatly over the years from people thinking I was dead."

The shuttle moved slowly through the asteroid field, careful to keep itself obscured from the *Crystal Stair*, though the ship didn't appear to be on particularly high alert – there was no sign of the vessel using active sensors. They'd settled back into a position of concealment over caution. "Is it really so easy to trick Ohseroh?" Terrak murmured.

"Don't forget, the evil mushroom needed Harlow to come up with an actual plan," Azad said. "Ohseroh is really good at a couple of things, and not so good at others. That's the downside of specialization, and why I prefer to be a generalist."

They settled in behind a large asteroid within visual range of the *Crystal Stair*, then suited up. "Remember, helmets stay on, even when we board," Azad said. "There's no telling what kind of stuff is floating around in there." She strapped her huge gun onto her back. This mission had involved a lot of annoying sitting around and going to-and-fro, but this was the fun part. She was glad to have the Hacan along for company too. Sure, she was a covert operator, but that didn't mean she didn't appreciate an audience. "Ready?"

"No," Terrak said. "But off we go anyway."

CHAPTER 50
TERRAK

I hate extravehicular activities. My greatest strength is talking to people, and that isn't nearly as much use when tumbling around in the black. We had personal propulsion devices, so we were unlikely to go flying off hopelessly into the void, but it's still disorienting to float in the vacuum, even more so when there are rocks all around. The smallest asteroids were as big as houses, and the largest as big as ships. I grew up on a planet, and I find it fundamentally surreal to see pitted stones just hovering around me.

Azad launched herself toward the dark bulk of the *Crystal Stair*, maneuvering with air jets, and I did the same. She was better at checking her speed with counteracting bursts of air; I just bumped into small rocks, certain I'd rip a hole in my suit and die. We did reach the airlock of the enemy ship eventually, though I thumped against the side of the *Crystal Stair* so hard I was sure someone would hear the bang and come to investigate.

No one did. Azad pried open a panel beside the airlock with a flat-edged tool, then hooked up a small device to the wires inside. Harlow had given us override codes for this generation of ship, and our boarding plan hinged on those still being functional. I hated this plan, but at least it was better than the alternative, which involved breaching charges, and would be a lot noisier and attention-getting. It had been a long time since I'd been on an infiltrate-and-execute operation, and I really hoped the moves would come back to me.

I'd asked why we couldn't just blow up the entire ship and then go for a drink, but Azad said we didn't have enough firepower to be sure we'd kill Ohseroh, and also we had to confirm the Letani was actually on board, and also also, wouldn't infiltration be more *fun*? "I like to look my enemies in the face before I destroy them," she said.

I told her, "Letani don't *have* faces. They just have a sort of red flower on top–"

"Then I want to look her right in the bee-hole," Azad said.

The airlock door popped open, and Azad grinned at me through her helmet's faceplate.

Her grin turned into astonishment when vinelike tentacles whipped out of the opening and yanked her inside the airlock.

CHAPTER 51
AZAD

Azad had never really dealt with the Arborec before. She knew they were a conglomeration of various ambulatory plants, but that hadn't mentally prepared her for being attacked by a sort of vine-octopus stuck to the wall inside the airlock. She'd had the vague idea that the plant things would need air to survive, but apparently not this one – it was anaerobic, maybe, or had its own dedicated air sacs, or who knew what? She wasn't a xeno-botanist. She wished she was. They would know how to kill a thing like this.

Azad struggled as the vines drew her toward something that looked disturbingly like a mouth at the center of the growth. The maw wasn't big enough to swallow her whole, but that wasn't reassuring, really; it meant the thing would have to swallow her in pieces instead. What a way to go. Ugh. Only one way out now, and maybe she wouldn't get paid if she went that way, but at least her enemy would lose too, which was a comfort. She reached behind her for the discreet button on the bottom of the hilt of her gun, the *real* reason she'd chosen that weapon–

Then Terrak was there, too, also wrapped in a vine and getting yanked in, but *he* had a knife, and when he hit a discreet button on the hilt, the dull gray blade glowed with white fire. Terrak slashed at the vines holding them, severing them and causing spurts of dark gray fluid that floated in gross little globules.

Azad reached out for the pistol on Terrak's hip, tugging it loose from the holster and toggling it to plasma ammo. She shot a few rounds of superheated goo at the vine-monster until sufficient portions of its body were blackened and glowing, and then it stopped waving its tentacles around. The recoil slammed her into a wall, but that was OK. She could handle getting a little bruised, and she'd taken the best of the combat drugs Lonrah had made for her before they left the shuttle, so pain was currently a problem for Future Amina.

Azad handed Terrak back his gun and gave him a little salute, then pulled the outer airlock closed. Getting through the inner door was easier – you just hit a button and waited for the pressures to equalize. The gravity generator kicked in, too, making the globs of fluid fall and splash on them. Even more gross. She pushed the door open when the light went green and ducked her head as she stepped into the corridor.

The interior of the ship looked like a rotten fruit. The walls, floor, and ceiling were covered in greenish-gray molds and lichens. There was another vine-monster stuck to the ceiling off to the right, but no other visible life forms. Or maybe there were. Maybe the blanket of moss was a whole *person*. If so, it didn't seem to care she was walking on it, so never mind.

She wondered if the vine-monsters sensed vibrations or body heat or something to find their prey. Probably not worth trying to sneak by. These creatures were all psychically linked, and since they'd killed one, the others would know they were coming. She slung her rifle around to ready position, turned on the flamethrower function, and sprayed a line of fire at the vine-monster. It charred, smoked, and blackened, vines waving wildly as alarms began to blare. Spaceships really hated fire. Suppression foam sprayed from the ceiling, but not very well, because everything was covered in moss and mold up there. Fortunately, the blanket of slime was too damp to burn well, though it smoked abominably, and Azad was glad she had her own air source. Sometimes she really did have the *weirdest* job, but she wouldn't have it any other way.

She beckoned to her partner, then sprinted down the corridor, Terrak at her heels. Harlow said Ohseroh was in a large cargo area near the engine room, so that's where they were headed. They passed closed doors, gummed up with slime molds, and she wondered if the lifts would even work. If not, there were always ladders–

Terrak screamed, and when she turned, there was a *thing* on him. It looked like a compost heap with roots for legs, and it was engulfing him, and also tearing off his helmet in the process.

CHAPTER 52
TERRAK

I thought the thing that attacked me was just a heap of vegetable matter on the floor, until it rose and sent me stumbling, and then tried to consume me. I slashed out with the burning blade, and that helped, until it extended thick tendrils and pinned my arms. Then it got my helmet off, the reek of rotting leaves in my nose, and I knew, I just *knew*, that it was going to jam its foul body into my mouth and down my throat.

Azad came back for me, jamming her rifle's barrel into the bulk of the thing and pulling the trigger. The heap shuddered apart, falling to fragments around me. "Sonic pulse," Azad said. She gave me my helmet and I put it back on after brushing some goo off the faceplate. "Do you feel mind-controlled?" she asked.

"I do not." We'd both taken shots of the cure before boarding – Azad said her bosses were "pretty sure" it would have a prophylactic effect and keep them from getting compromised. "Like, eighty percent sure."

I had not been reassured by that number, but either the mind-control spores weren't airborne here, or the cure did its job.

Azad looked at him with narrowed eyes. "You'd say that even if you were compromised, though. How about you walk ahead of me?"

I couldn't argue with her logic, so I took the lead, making my way more carefully now, though I sensed her impatience. We reached the elevator, and amazingly, it still worked – I'd assumed it would be jammed with vines, but upon reflection, I realized this wasn't wild growth. Everything that grew here was cultivated and deliberate under the care of Ohseroh, and it wouldn't impair the ship's vital functions.

I didn't need Azad to tell me to stand to one side before the lift doors opened, so neither of us was caught in the gunfire that sprayed out when they did. Azad tossed a flash-bang inside the elevator car, and after the noise and the burst of light, she dodged in and dragged out the Letnev man we'd seen on the screen earlier. He fought wildly, biting and scratching and clawing at her suit, until she finally banged his head against the wall hard enough to make him stop… which was, unfortunately, also hard enough to break his skull. A spray of spores shot out of the crack like it was under pressure, and she shuddered and dropped his body to the floor.

We descended silently to the engineering floor. The other known puppet on board the *Crystal Stair*, a human woman, opened fire as soon as the doors opened, but we were lying flat on the floor against such an eventuality. Azad shot the woman's legs out from under her.

Overall, our mission was going well, and I hated that "going well" in this case involved so much blood and death. "I wish we could have saved them," I said, after checking the woman's vitals and failing to find any.

"Can't save everybody," Azad said.

"We can try. The whole point of the work we do should be to save lives and minimize suffering, Azad."

"You must have *way* different kinds of handlers than I do." She gestured for me to take the lead, and we made our way to the engineering storage bay, where replacement parts and supplies were stored... usually.

When the doors opened for us, we saw the space had been cleared to make way for something else.

In its basic shape, the Letani was just like the little nodes we'd rooted out. They were something like a mushroom, crossed with a carnivorous plant, crossed with a squid, topped with a red flower, and this was the same... only Ohseroh was immense, filling the bay, bobbing flower towering above us. Its root-tendrils extended all over the cargo area, many stuck to the walls and ceilings, others free to move and curling toward us. The immense flower lowered down toward us, almost like a head looking at us, though I knew that was entirely the wrong paradigm.

A figure shambled forward, connected to the Letani by a series of vines that terminated in the back of its head. It was a human, or had been – now it was a corpse, flesh gray, features slack. A Dirzuga, in the tatters of a Mentak Coalition uniform. I wondered if it was Grisham, the protégé Harlow had mentioned, possessed so long by the Letani that their body had given out, and been repurposed for this. Such a waste, and such a horror. Treating people like objects or tools was the greatest crime I could imagine, and it was even worse, because I'd done it myself, often enough.

At least we could stop Ohseroh from doing it anymore.

"Terrak," the Dirzuga said. "Azad. You have come. You have come to make my new Symphony into cacophony instead. But you are too late. You have stopped my ships, but I had other plans, always other plans–"

Azad shot the Dirzuga in the face, making its head explode in a cloud of blood, brain matter, and spores. Then she launched three grenades straight into the middle of Ohseroh's flower, projectiles disappearing into the cup of the blossom. She spun and ran from the hangar, and I followed, booms filling the air behind us and making the deck vibrate.

"I gave it a frag and a couple of incendiaries!" she shouted.

"You just *killed it*?" I shouted. I'd somehow imagined a longer stand-off, perhaps an exchange of banter, or the Letani pleading with us to join its cause – Azad seemed to thrive on such drama, after all.

"I said I wanted to look it in the bee-hole!" Azad yelled. "Not that I wanted to talk to it! What would I talk to an insane *plant* about?"

She grabbed my arm and dragged me toward the engine room itself. "We can't be sure it's dead, though. Who knows how hardy these things are, or if they can regenerate from a twig or something, you know?"

"We could burn the entire cargo area," I said. "Turn it all to ashes. Or vent the remains into space. Or–"

"Or just blow up the whole ship."

"You said we didn't have enough explosives."

"We didn't have enough explosives to blow up the ship from the *outside*. From the inside, though…" She took her rifle off its strap and looked around the control room. "This will do." She held up the gun and grinned at me. "When I enumerated the features of this rifle, I left one important function out. This all-purpose may-hem machine is sometimes called a 'scuttle-gun'. The Mentak Coalition raiders use them when they need to… well, scuttle something. You can set a timer, here." She twisted a dial. "Then you press this button, here." She depressed a spot under the hilt. "Then you put the rifle as close to the magnetic bottle housing the fusion reac-tor as you can. When the timer runs out, the gun sets off a burst designed to breach containment, and then… you get a brief uncontrolled fusion reaction. And, subse-quently, no more ship." She leaned the rifle against the engineering console.

I took an instinctive step away, which was foolish. It was like backing up a little to avoid being hit by a nuclear explosion. *Exactly* like that, in fact. "That seems extreme."

"We can't leave any of those mind-control spores laying around for someone else to pick up," she said. "That's one of my fundamental mission parameters. Gotta burn it all. Cleansing fire scenario. I'm just glad I found the scuttle-gun. It would have been tricky to rig the ship to blow remotely otherwise. This way, we have time to get back to the shuttle and out of the blast radius, and I don't have to convince you to stay behind to make the ultimate sacrifice."

"You are not that convincing," I said.

"That timer isn't *infinite*, so let's move."

We moved, back to the airlock, past the dead we'd left behind, and into space again. We reached the shuttle, boarded, and made our way as rapidly as possible out of the asteroid field.

Not long after we cleared the area, a bright light filled our screens as the *Crys-tal Stair* became a cloud of dust and spores. I have never seen such a beautiful and welcome moment of destruction.

"We did it," Azad said. "Look at us. Saviors of the galaxy over here. Who would have thought, a couple of old spies like us, doing something pretty much totally unambiguously on the side of good for once?"

"It's an unusual feeling," I agreed. "I am a bit troubled by Ohseroh saying we were too late, and that there were other plans in place…"

"Maybe we ruined those other plans by blowing everything up. That's the assumption I'm going with. Makes me a lot happier."

"In the absence of verification, I suppose we might as well be hopeful," I said. "But… what do we do now? Both the available ships have been destroyed. We won't make it far in this shuttle."

"I'll call and get us a ride."

"What, send a distress signal? The *Barony* will pick us up. That would be bad. We don't even know if the puppets have been stopped. Even if they have been neutralized, I'm sure it will take time for the truth of what happened here to be understood by the powers that be."

"You act like this is my first time destroying things in a hostile system," Azad said. "My bosses have an exfiltration team on standby. Don't worry. We'll give you a ride to a nice neutral moon where you can wait until this all gets sorted out."

"Where I can wait? Where will *you* be?"

"To make my final report, and collect my bonus," Azad said.

THE FAITHFUL XVII

Immental stood beneath the viewing dome at the top of the ship, the dark orb of her homeworld beneath her, and another dark orb, etched with fiery lines of red, floating above her. She had envisioned a Gashlai War Sun above Arc Prime before, of course, but only in her nightmares. Now, its presence was a symbol of her imminent triumph. There were N'orr ships there, too, like the nests of those foul insects on a vaster scale, and a L1Z1X flagship, an old imperial design embellished with grotesque technological extrusions – not unlike the L1Z1X themselves. The guides had finally exerted sufficient chemical pressure to bring those monsters into alignment with their plans. These were the members of her Legion. The galaxy would burn, the guides said, under her command, and from the devastation, a better future would blossom.

They just had to get through today.

<Are the bombers in place?> the guides asked. There was a sense of urgency in the chorus of voices that Immental had never heard from them before.

"Yes, wise ones. Just after the last signatory ratifies the treaty, a coordinated attack–"

<No. No no no.>

"No, guides? A change in plans?" Immental hoped so. Setting off bombs on board the Dark Star was a dangerous proposition. It wasn't like bombing the surface of Moll Primus, where there was air to breathe; if the destruction was greater than intended here, they'd all be vented into space.

<No. Proceed. There are… distractions. Our focus. Is split. The plan. The plan must not fail. I must return to the Symphony. I must prove that I am right, and I am good. No, no, my voice, they took my voice.>

"Guides? I don't understand what…" Immental swayed, and then fell to her knees, a great burst of pain going off behind her eyes. What… why… what was *happening*, where were the guides, where were her–?

"No." Oh, no, by the dark, what had she done, what had she been doing? Her head spun like she'd downed too much mushroom liquor, and she fell from her knees onto her side. Something was trickling out of her nose, and her ears, and the corners of her *eyes*… she touched her face, and her hand came away bloody, but the blood was flecked with tiny green specks. The sacrament. Purging itself from her body. She was relieved and disgusted and horrified and enraged.

The guides were gone, and … and they were never *guides* at all, they were enemies, controlling her mind, pushing her toward abominable acts. And now… what had stopped them? She wondered if Severyne had something to do with this. The woman had dropped all contact, and Voyou had gone dark, so maybe she'd discovered the conspiracy, and somehow, impossibly, moved against it.

Such speculations suddenly seemed irrelevant as a black pit of despair opened inside Immental. She knew what the guides were now, that they'd controlled her, and used her, but still, their absence was a howling void within her. She had to fill that void somehow.

The only thing she could think to fill it with was duty.

Immental struggled upright. If this was happening to her, it was happening to all the faithful. N'orr, and L1Z1X, and Letnev, falling and frothing and bleeding – she activated her comms. "Get the Baron off the station!" she shouted. "Now, now, now!"

What would the L1Z1X and the N'orr do when they realized they'd been compromised this way? Who would they blame? Would they think it was a Barony plot?

She began making more calls, frantically spinning a cover story: "We are under biological attack, our enemies are attempting to disrupt the Legion, get everyone to safety, send the dignitaries back to their ships, now, now, *NOW!*"

Immental staggered into a wall, her balance failing her. It was hard to hold herself up, but she *had* to. She had to fix this. Immental looked up, through the dome, her vision tinged with red from her bloody tears, and watched the War Sun fire its engines and depart the skies of Arc Prime.

When Jhuri opened his eyes and struggled up from the puddle of disgusting goo surrounding his body, he realized pretty quickly what was going on. The bombers assembled in the capitol basement were starting to moan and get up too, their faces covered in blood flecked with specks of green. *I see*, he thought.

Jhuri looked over at Kote Strom, who was openly weeping in the corner, and said, "Pull yourself together. Get those bomb vests deactivated. Do something *useful*, you little toad." It was probably irrational for Jhuri to be furious at Kote for spraying him in the face with spores – Kote had been a victim of the guides, too – but Jhuri wasn't at his most rational. He wanted to crawl into a hole and pull the hole after him and sleep for a year.

Instead, he activated his comms. "Put me through to the Table of Captains immediately," he barked at his least favorite executive secretary. "Yes, I know people are falling over and bleeding from their eye sockets – I'd like the opportunity to tell our leadership why."

While Jhuri waited to be connected, he thought, *I wonder if Felix had something to do with this.* If so, the man was going to be even more smug than usual. But, if Felix had… by the seas… really just *saved the galaxy*, well, he deserved to feel a little smug, didn't he?

CHAPTER 53
TERRAK

Thus ends my chronicle. I went to my superiors and told them I didn't want any accolades or rewards… except one. I wished to retire from covert operations, and from my ambassadorship. "This is the high point of my career," I told them. "I will never again save the entire galaxy. I'd like *that* to be the note I end on, not some squalid backroom deal. Let me go out on top."

My superiors don't like letting people like me retire, but they'd already seen me make one transmission spreading secrets throughout the galaxy, and I think they were afraid, if they refused, that I'd do the same with some of *theirs*.

I bought a vineyard on a pleasant Emirates colony world. For the remainder of my days, I will sit on my villa's porch, and I will sip, and I will look at the stars.

My boss asked me: "Do you really think you can stand to be idle, Terrak? Do you really think you can *retire*?"

I told him I absolutely could, and I meant it.

Of course, on occasion, some friends might visit me.

Maybe, sometimes, I'll arrange for a favor, or two. Make an introduction. Help someone out when they need it.

I'm only retired, after all. I'm not dead.

CHAPTER 54
FELIX

Jhuri was waiting in the anteroom of the reception hall on Moll Primus when the crew arrived. Felix sauntered over to him while Tib and Calred ordered drinks from a floating servitor. "Hey there, boss," Felix said. "All done puking up green goo?"

"I wish I had expelled that foulness by vomiting." The Hylar shuddered. "It oozed out of me in far more unpleasant ways."

Felix winced. "Never mind. Sorry I asked. How are you feeling? I hear some people take the comedown pretty hard."

"I have never been more depressed and anxious in my life, thank you, but I am on medication to take the edge off, and I am assured my brain will return to something resembling its usual operations in time." He gestured with a tentacle. "I'm proud of you, Felix. You've earned this."

"Medals of commendation all around, and a promotion to admiral for me?" He couldn't help but puff out his chest. "Well, it's a start. I never thought I'd be a flag officer, that's for sure. I sort of figured myself as terminal at captain."

Jhuri chuckled. "Don't worry, they won't actually put you in charge of a fleet. You're still part of the Special Projects division. You'll just get more money and more respect on those rare occasions when you mingle with your fellow officers. But you'll mostly keep flying around in the dark, fighting off the monsters. There are *lots* of monsters, and we're facing them alone, as usual."

"The Greater Union is done, huh?" He hadn't been terribly invested in the idea, but it was still a shame. Uniting even a *chunk* of the galaxy in a peaceful fashion was a lovely dream.

"When many of the invited guests at a summit start to ooze green-flecked blood from every orifice in their heads, it tends to diminish enthusiasm for the whole process," Jhuri said. "We're just lucky our brief allies didn't fully turn on one another. The fact that people from every faction demonstrably suffered was helpful. Our cover story is that we suffered a biological attack from terrorists and are pausing plans for the Greater Union while we sort out the security situation. Those who were infected know the truth, of course, and the leadership in all the factions have been informed as well. They're all understandably furious with the Arborec, but Fleet Captain Harlow's testimony made it clear the Arborec aren't even *truly* to blame, any more than our government is responsible for every fringe group or bomb-throwing radical who happens to have Mentak Coalition citizenship. We are getting some very juicy Arborec technology in the way of apology… although, unfortunately, so is every other faction involved, including those in the Legion."

"Have you heard anything from Ggorgos? I know she succeeded in her mission, since Moll Primus wasn't attacked, but I haven't heard anything from her." They hadn't exactly parted on the best terms, what with him locking her in the brig and all, but he'd hoped she would forgive him. It had been a confusing time. Of course, it was possible she wasn't thinking about him at all.

"I received a report on her report," Jhuri said. "Ggorgos and Captain Dampierre engaged and destroyed the *Soldier of the City*."

Felix winced. "They just blew it up? They didn't try to cure the crew?"

"Are you surprised?"

He sighed. "I guess not. Disappointed, of course. We saved *ours*. They made it home safe, though?"

"Dampierre dropped off Ggorgos in a shuttle near a Coalition station and then, presumably, returned to the Barony to get her own medal, or else get imprisoned for embarrassing her superiors by being more competent than they are – you never know how the Letnev are going to react to things like this."

"We can hope for imprisonment, anyway," Felix said. "Any word on Terrak and Azad?"

"Terrak was picked up drinking Hacan firewine on a neutral moon and being modest about his very small role in saving the universe. As for Azad? Gone. No idea where. We made inquiries with the Federation of Sol, who claim she wasn't even working for them, and hasn't been on their payroll since she left the navy. We know *that's* a lie – she was definitely a deniable asset for Federation covert operations for some time after her discharge – but we don't know if she still is. The Federation seemed as shocked and horrified to learn about the conspiracy as the rest of us, which suggests they didn't know about it any earlier… but then, humans are good liars."

"Well, we try," Felix said. "It all turned out well, honestly, don't you think?" There was no use dwelling on the horrible parts. They'd get to him in his dreams, and he didn't want to give them any more waking attention than necessary. Moving forward was the best way to get past something.

Jhuri rolled one eye toward him. "Apart from revealing the horrifying flaws in our security, exposing our vulnerabilities to exploitation, and bringing the entire galaxy to the brink of war? Yes, I'd say, other than that, everything is marvelous."

"That's the spirit," Felix said, and then it was time to go accept his accolades. All's well that ends well, after all. If you didn't think about all the people who'd been killed along the way, at least.

CHAPTER 55
SEVERYNE

Severyne had never been in the Baron's presence before. Few Letnev ever were, as he preferred to govern from a distance, but now she was in the palace, deep beneath the surface of Arc Prime, marching to the throne room between a pair of towering guards in full regalia, complete with ceremonial pikes. She was wearing a freshly tailored uniform, with her new rank insignia on the shoulders, and boots so shiny they could have been black mirrors. She was, she supposed, happy. The sensation was strange but not unpleasant.

The Baron sat in a chair made of stone and metal, his own uniform dripping with medals and braid, with a sash across his chest. His face was noble and composed. "Severyne Joelle Dampierre. Welcome to the presence."

She gave a small bow. "Your lordship. You honor me."

"The honor, this time, is ours." The Baron leaned forward. "You singlehandedly uncovered a conspiracy in the highest echelons of our society, organized a resistance, manipulated our ancient rivals into serving our cause, and saved our society from ruin."

Severyne had, in her report, slightly exaggerated the importance of her own role. And why not? There was no one in the Barony who could plausibly contradict her. "I did what any loyal Letnev would, your lordship."

"Loyal. Yes. You sent a query through the viscount, asking after Admiral Immental. Why this concern?"

"She was my superior officer, your lordship, and so sorely afflicted by the foul attack on our sovereignty. I hope she has recovered."

"Your concern does you credit. My cousin is … recovering. She has, of course, been relieved from duty. Can anyone, once compromised, truly be trusted?"

"Your wisdom is great, my baron," Severyne said. She'd heard the old man couldn't quite get his head around the fact that the spores couldn't really be resisted – that succumbing to them was inevitable, not the result of poor willpower or lack of true Letnev fiber. But Severyne didn't really mind. She could use the Baron's prejudice to her own advantage, after all.

"I have decided to grant you a boon, Severyne."

She thrilled as much at the familiar form of address as she did at the substance of the comment – which she'd been expecting, thanks to the viscount's hints, but was still delighted to hear confirmed. "You are too kind, your lordship."

"Any posting, any command, any crew you wish – you have proven that you will serve the Barony above all, and you may choose in what capacity you fulfill that service. I will say, this offer includes the opportunity to take Immental's place as an admiral and become my close advisor."

"That is very tempting, your lordship." Interminable meetings with the Baron and his cousins, all of them looking down on her from their lofty seats of ancient privilege? No, that wouldn't do. "But, if I consider my qualifications with a clear eye… I think I could best serve you as head of the clandestine services."

The Baron leaned back, which Severyne interpreted as surprise. "Really? Retire my cousin Dieudonne? I suppose he has been in the post for a long time, but why?"

"With all due respect to his long service and many accomplishments, Baron… a vast conspiracy infiltrated our society, and Dieudonne was wholly unaware. I would never suggest that he has become complacent, but I feel I would bring a certain level of… youthful zeal and attention to the post."

"I am inclined to grant your desire, Severyne. But you *do* know, to take on a role like this, such a lofty position, so early in your career… you will be subject to great scrutiny. Some may resent you. There will be all sorts of challenges you cannot foresee. And failure… failure will not be tolerated."

"Nor should it be, your lordship." Severyne was secure in the knowledge that she'd never yet met a failure she couldn't turn into a success… at least for herself.

"Your formal appointment will be made in two weeks," the Baron said. "There are certain matters that must be attended to first." Like firing that doddering fool Dieudonne. "In the meantime, we have taken the liberty of securing you a suite on one of our finest pleasure planets, in the famous crystal caves. Enjoy yourself, Severyne. You have the gratitude of your Baron, and of your nation."

"I live to serve," she said.

Severyne slept for most of the trip to the crystal caves. She was fresh and rested when she arrived. She shooed off the various handlers and assistants who escorted her to the resort's lobby, sending them back to the ship. There was no reason for any of *them* to enjoy all this luxury. They hadn't saved the Barony from disaster.

When Severyne entered her gorgeous, lavish, palatial suite, she was surprised to find someone waiting for her there.

CHAPTER 56
AZAD

After a long journey with some extremely boring people, Amina Azad was finally ready to receive her reward.

She'd left Terrak behind and set out on a battered old trading vessel, but two ship transfers later and she was deposited onto a ship made of forcefields and linked crystalline structures. Her hosts assured her the name of the vessel could not be accurately translated for human understanding but might be simplified as the *Lineaments of Gratified Desire*. Azad annoyed the crew by consistently referring to the ship as "Lenny."

Azad was escorted down the boarding ramp by a pair of male Naalu. They were, in essence, humanoid from the waist up, and serpents from the waist down, though Azad was sure a xenobiologist would have pointed out all the reasons why that was a hopelessly inaccurate way to describe them. Her escorts led her down and out and into a glittering square on the Naalu homeworld of Druaa, which she'd heard described as "a paradise of crystal spires". She looked around. Fair enough. Lots of shiny buildings, certainly. She was warm enough. The air had a faint, dry sort of scent that made her think of deserts for some reason. She wouldn't want to live here, but she could see why it appealed to people who liked this sort of thing.

Her escorts hadn't brought her to some remote outpost or back alley, as she'd expected – this was a city center. There were random Naalu slithering around, down streets and up ramps, but none of them gave her a second glance, and very few bothered with a first one. The place was oddly quiet. She was used to a certain amount of background noise in a city, but then, the Naalu didn't talk much, not where the average person could hear.

Her escorts took her to a building that might have been carved from a single large emerald. A door shimmered open when they approached, and inside was a grand anteroom, with a polished opalescent floor and ramps spiraling up into the heights. "I guess you don't do stairs," she said. "They'd probably be tough on the old soft underbelly, huh?"

"S'zakith will see you now." One of the escorts gestured toward a corridor. Azad gave a jaunty wave and strolled where he'd indicated. She wasn't afraid, exactly, but she was keenly aware that if her bosses wanted to make her disappear instead of paying her, they could do that. She'd taken precautions, of course, but precautions against the Naalu were tricky. It was hard to outsmart people who could manipulate your mind and erase your memory.

Azad hadn't known a lot about her bosses before they contacted her. She knew they were isolationists, and thought they were better than everyone else; that they had native telepathic abilities, augmented with technology to the point where they could be weaponized; and that people who looked into Naalu affairs too closely had a tendency to vanish, or worse. She'd worked with a guy, back before she left the Federation of Sol's service, who was sent to do some recon in Naalu space, and when he finally returned, he didn't remember her name, and even had to be reminded of his own every couple of hours.

So, when the Naalu asked her to investigate the conspiracy, she'd laughed. "I thought controlling the minds of lesser races was a *Naalu* thing."

It is, S'zakith had whispered into her mind. *That's why we are so unhappy to learn someone else is doing it, and in such a clumsy way.*

"Why hire a mercenary like me?" she'd asked. "Don't you have little spies with whispers in their brains embedded here and there who can do this for you?"

Independent freelancers are best for this sort of work, S'zakith said. *Those who are under our influence for too long develop a sort of… learned helplessness. They become so accustomed to serving our will that they start to lack personal initiative. We need someone who can think quickly and react to changing circumstances without waiting for our guidance.*

"That's me, all right," Azad had said. They'd agreed to her price so readily she wished she'd doubled it.

S'zakith was waiting in a dim room hung with glowing purple crystals. She was coiled behind a table with a single glass and a decanter resting on it. When Azad entered, the Naalu poured a measure of golden liquid and handed the glass to Azad.

For a job well done, she said.

Azad toasted her, sniffed, and took a sip. It wasn't her preferred form of whiskey – she doubted they grew much corn here – but it was something in the same family, a hint of sweet and a hint of burn and a lot of fruit and wood. "Thank you."

I have told you, you need not speak aloud. You can simply direct your thoughts toward me.

Azad shrugged. "Then we're both staring at each other in total silence, and I know that's an ordinary Saturday night for your people, but it would make me start to giggle, or else think we were about to kiss." She looked around for something to sit on – there was nothing, of course – and settled for leaning against a fluted pillar. "Why did you bring me all the way here? I know you were shadowing me for most of the mission – your telepathy doesn't have infinite range, but you were always there, whenever I mentally reached out to give a report. You must have been distracting minds and wiping memories the whole way to cover your tracks. I figured you'd just transfer me to your ship for the final debrief."

I did, for the most part, stay close, she acknowledged. *Though not as close as you imagine. The range of our telepathy might surprise you, especially with technological augmentation. I wanted to be available in case you needed resources, but you were remarkably independent.*

"I'm famous for that. Still, you could have used your amazing brain powers to smooth the way for me here and there. Make a guard look the other way, hide me from sight, stuff like that."

Azad detected a strong sense of amusement. *Are you so sure I didn't?*

"Ha, all right, you've got me there. Maybe my luck isn't as good as I thought. Still – why am I here?"

Very few humans are permitted to visit Druaa. I thought you might enjoy the experience.

"I'm always happy to see new places, though it's less exciting when I can't tell anyone I've been here. But come on, really, why?"

Because the rest of the galaxy is filthy and vile, and I wanted to come home, S'zakith said.

"Now that, I believe. So. The debrief–"

I have read your mind. Thoroughly. The debrief is done.

Azad grinned. "You're making me wish my old commanding officer had telepathy. She would grill me for hours about every little detail. So. Do I get paid now, or is this a 'murder the help' type situation? Because if it's the latter, you should know, I took precautions–"

In the event of your untimely death, documents will be released revealing that we hired you, and that we knew about the conspiracy, and that it interfered with our own conspiracy, and so forth, S'zakith said. *Yes, I know. I told you, I read your mind. Your plan would not be effective in the end, but it is also unnecessary.* She placed a small black bag on the table.

Azad picked up the bag and looked inside. There were glittery things, worth a lot and negotiable in many places. There were data sticks, and the information on those was worth a lot more. The Naalu had an excellent intelligence network, and they were happy to offer Azad information on other factions that she could sell to the top bidder. It was possible everything in the bag was fake, but if they were going to cheat her, they wouldn't have done it at the payment stage. The Naalu were plenty rich. "Excellent. And… that bonus we talked about, if I wrapped up this whole affair before the Greater Union and the Legion signed their treaties?"

You did meet the terms of the agreement, S'zakith said. *It pleases us to have the rest of the galaxy fragmented and at odds with one another. You said you wanted our help to get you into a place someone like you could not normally enter?*

"I did. My original plan was to use your mind-games to clear a path so I could stroll right into the Federation of Sol central reserve and do some untraceable embezzling from an all-access terminal. Set myself up for life and screw over my former employers at the same time, you know?"

We know. We are only asking as a courtesy. Again, I can read–

"Yeah, yeah." Azad waved her hand, downed the rest of the whiskey, and put the glass down. "I changed my mind. Now, for my bonus, I want you to smuggle me in someplace else…"

CHAPTER 57
SEVERYNE

"You can't be here," Severyne said.

Azad smiled at her, that self-confident, self-satisfied, self-indulgent smile that always made Severyne forget everything else. "Here, under your sheet? Here, in your bed? Here, in your rooms? Here, at your exclusive fancy Letnev resort?"

"*All* of those!"

"This isn't even all that impressive. I had a plan to sneak into your quarters at the Baron's actual palace, but when I heard you were coming for a week of rest and relaxation, well, I thought, what better way to relax than with me? You can forget about getting any rest, though."

"This… Azad… *Amina*…" Severyne sat on the edge of the bed. It was clear that Azad was naked under the sheet, and that made it hard to think about anything else. "Is this some operation? Some secret plan? Are you trying to make me into a double agent for the Federation, or something?"

"These are fair questions." Azad reached over and put a hand on Severyne's thigh. "I'm pretty sick of conspiracies and secret agendas and treachery and all that, though, Sev. I was hoping for something a little simpler right now. You and me, we can't be together. Not really. We wouldn't even halfway work. But I figured, sometimes, occasionally… maybe we could *get* together." She sat up and murmured in Severyne's ear, "I hear the Baron promoted you. That you got everything you ever wanted." That hand on Severyne's thigh moved. "How about now you get everything *else* you ever wanted?"

The right thing to do would be to summon guards and have Azad hauled away – she *was* still wanted in Letnev space – and interrogated and imprisoned. But then, obeying Immental's orders without question would have been the right thing to do as well. Severyne hadn't gotten where she was by doing the right thing, but by doing the right thing for *her*.

"Oh, all right," Severyne said. "Your human depravity intrigues me."

"You know what you are?" Azad said into Severyne's ear, some time later. "You're my *bonus*."

EPILOGUE
THE INFORMATION BROKER

On a remote station in the orbit of an icy planetoid, the mysterious information broker known to some as the Nomad sat in a small room before a screen. A call came in, a call they'd been waiting for. The Nomad turned on the screen, which revealed the features of a Naalu female with mesmerizing green eyes. (Many would be mesmerized; the Nomad was not.)

"Yes?" The Nomad's voice was heavily filtered, and their features and form were obscured in an elaborate environment suit. The Naalu were desperate to know their true identity and purpose, but then, so was everyone else who'd ever heard of the Nomad.

"It is done," the Naalu said. "The conspiracy is broken. A rogue Letani was behind it all, and the creature has been eradicated."

"Good."

The Naalu said, "There will be some… inevitable disorder among the affected factions, of course. But we have averted the widespread war and chaos you warned us about."

"I'm glad," the Nomad said. "If the conspiracy had been allowed to continue… Let's just say I didn't like where it was going. You wouldn't have, either."

"How did you *know* about the conspiracy?" the Naalu said, clearly frustrated at having to ask the question, instead of just forcing the Nomad to tell, or plucking the knowledge from their mind. "You told us someone was using a new form of mind control practically as soon as the conspiracy began."

The Nomad said, "Information is my business. I pick up bits and pieces, here and there."

"We have our own plans in place, Nomad," the Naalu warned. "More subtle and elegant than the plot we just thwarted, to be sure, but still… just because we cooperated with you against this threat does not mean we will tolerate you meddling in *our* stratagems. Be careful about using any 'bits and pieces' you pick up regarding our Collective."

"Threat received," the Nomad said calmly, and ended the call.

The Nomad stood and walked to a window, lookingw out at the sparkling lights in the immense darkness. As always, they thought about the future.

About all the things they had yet to do, in order to make sure there would still *be* a future to think about.

ACKNOWLEDGMENTS

Thanks as always to the whole Aconyte team, especially Lottie Llewelyn-Wells, who deftly edited this volume in addition to all the other things she does. I'm grateful to the *Twilight Imperium* creative team for letting me play in their world. Line up this book next to the earlier two, and you can see the full triptych of artwork by cover illustrator Scott Schomburg! I've never had a triptych before. It's a delight.

Thanks to my agent Ginger Clark and her associate Nicole Eisenbraun for handling the business things so I can focus on words.

My wife Heather Shaw and our kid River are endlessly supportive of my weird job and its strange hours. Thanks to my nearest and dearest, Ais, Amanda, Emily, Katrina, and Sarah, for making life brighter and less lonely.

Thanks to all my supportive writer friends. I wish I could see you in real life again, but hey, at least we have the DMs. My gratitude to my boss Liza and my co-workers at *Locus* magazine, the best day job a writer can have.

My greatest thanks go to you, the readers, who've come on this journey with me. I hope you enjoy the conclusion of the trilogy. As Shakespeare basically said, "Journeys end in lovers meeting and titanic space battles".

ABOUT THE AUTHOR

TIM PRATT is a Hugo Award-winning SF and fantasy author, and finalist for the World Fantasy, Sturgeon, Stoker, Mythopoeic, and Nebula Awards, among others. He is the author of over twenty novels, and scores of short stories. Since 2001 he has worked for *Locus*, the magazine of the science fiction and fantasy field, where he currently serves as senior editor.

timpratt.org // bsky.app/profile/timpratt.org

TWILIGHT IMPERIUM

WELCOME TO A GALAXY OF ETERNAL CONFLICT. EXPLORE AN EPIC SPACE OPERA WHILE PROVING YOUR SUPERIORITY OVER THOSE WHO WOULD DISPUTE YOUR CLAIM TO THE THRONE. USE YOUR MILITARY MIGHT, CLEVER DIPLOMACY, AND ECONOMIC BARGAINING TO CONTROL THE GALAXY.

Explore an incredible universe
with Fantasy Flight Games.
fantasyflightgames.com

TWILIGHT IMPERIUM™

VENTURE DEEPER INTO THE VAST TWILIGHT IMPERIUM UNIVERSE IN THESE BRILLIANT NEW SPACE OPERA NOVELS

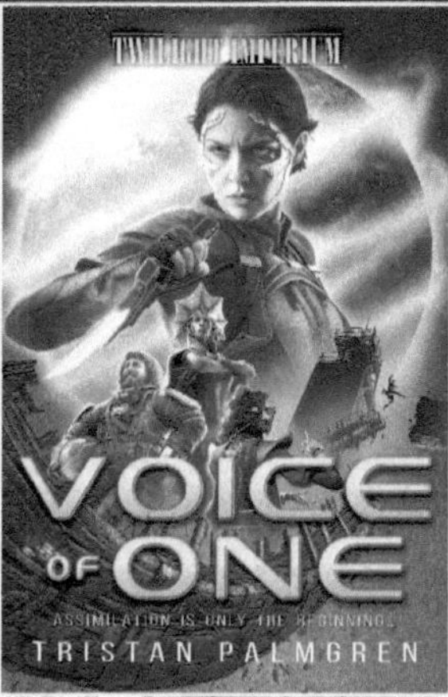

ASSIMILATION IS ONLY THE BEGINNING

Deep space action from the epic game world of Twilight Imperium. When a member of the L1Z1X Mindnet is torn away from the collective by mutated Arborec, freedom becomes something worth fighting for.

The Twilight Wars have begun, and the race for galactic dominion will shatter the rival factions.

Explore the war-torn galaxy in this stunning anthology.

ACONYTEBOOKS.COM

WORLD EXPANDING FICTION

ACONYTEBOOKS.COM   **@ACONYTEBOOKS**